ELIZABETH

CW01426031

The Book of Roses, Volume One

Kelly River

CONTENTS

PROLOGUE

Elizabeth realised far too late that the horse was stolen. She was old enough to work it out by herself, but not wise enough to have seen it coming. The lean palfrey they'd been keeping in the meadow was Sir Luke's. He had to be. He was far too large and well-kept to belong to anyone but a knight. At least, he had been well-kept, before his mane grew ratty and his coat rough from a summer out of stable. Elizabeth felt sorry for the poor thing. He was as obedient as a huntsman's hound and as nimble as a fox, yet here he was, dishevelled and hungry, the grass around his hooves cropped all the way down to the earth.

Sam shoved the sack of oats into her arms. The weight of it made her shoulders sag as she shifted her grip to avoid touching the patch of mud on the bottom.

"You do it," Elizabeth complained. "It's too heavy for me."

"You're only going a few steps with it. Go on, he likes you more."

Elizabeth wrinkled her nose at her half-brother and shuffled forward. The horse tugged against the rope tethering him to a low oak branch, his muzzle dipping inquisitively toward the sack.

"Don't give him all of it," Sam said. "We need those oats to last."

Liz pulled the sack away and scooped out a handful of oats. Even though she was annoyed with Sam, the tickle of the horse's tongue on her palm made her smile.

"Where did you get a whole sack?" she asked.

"Never you mind. If I bring it back to the house, will you put it somewhere Mother won't notice?"

Elizabeth nodded. She'd taken over most of the housekeeping after Sam left home, not that they had much of a house to keep. Mother was always busy working with the castle servants or spending time at the public house across the street. She wouldn't notice an extra sack.

Elizabeth scooped out another handful of oats. "Can we ride him today?"

"Not today. It'll be too late by the time I get back." Sam reached up to check the horse's tether. He was about five years older than Elizabeth, either seventeen or eighteen—neither of them could remember exactly which—and much taller than her. Folk rarely took them for siblings, for Elizabeth's blonde colouring and youthfully pudgy face echoed nothing of Sam's sharp adolescent features and messy brown hair.

She finished feeding the horse and tied up the sack. It made her sad to push the animal's head down when he tried to nibble at the string. They couldn't keep him here forever.

"Sir Luke's in the village today," she told her brother.

Sam frowned. "In Rosepath?"

"This is his horse, isn't it? What'll he do if he finds out you took it?"

"Whip me to death, I suppose."

Elizabeth swallowed uncomfortably. She'd seen thieves get whipped in public. Last winter, Count Leo had old Steve Pedlar flogged for stealing from the castle. He'd left a trail of blood all the way across the marketplace when he staggered home. Three days later, when someone finally went to check on him, they'd found him dead in his cot.

"You have to take him back to the stable."

"I can't." Sam bent down to take the sack. He slung it easily over his shoulder and put his arm around her. "Someone'll notice. And you won't be able to ride him anymore."

"I don't want you to get in trouble."

"You'll never get a chance like this again, Liz. Folk like us don't get to ride fine horses."

"I will one day. I'll work hard and save all my money."

Sam smirked and shook his head. "We're poor as dirt. Most serfs have it better. At least they've got their lords taking care of them. Come on, why are you dawdling?"

Elizabeth pulled free of his arm and hung back at the edge of the meadow. "Can I stay with the horse for a bit?"

Sam shrugged. "Go on then. I'll leave the sack behind the woodpile. Make sure you hide it properly when you get home, alright?"

Elizabeth nodded. She waited until Sam disappeared into the woods, then hurried back to the oak. She felt stupid. She'd been learning to ride on this horse all summer long, and only now had she put it together that it was stolen. Stupid, silly Sam always pretended he knew what he was doing. He made everything sound fine right until it grew teeth and bit him in the rear. If he'd been able to stay out of trouble, Mother wouldn't have sent him away to be a stable boy for Sir Luke in the first place.

She hopped into the air and grabbed the low oak branch. The horse bumped her with his head, perhaps expecting more oats. Realising that she wouldn't be able to untie the knot while she was dangling like this, Elizabeth swung her leg up onto the branch. The sound of splitting fabric sent a jolt of panic up her spine as the hem of her dress tore. She spat a curse like the ones Count Leo's men used. Mother would be furious. She'd have to borrow some thread from Gilly Tailor and mend it herself that afternoon.

Climbing along the branch, she reached the knotted rope and tried to tug it loose. It was a thick one, the sort they used on boats, Sam said. Elizabeth had never been on a boat, and she had no idea why they needed ropes on them, but she'd taken him at his word.

"Stupid Sam," she grumbled, trying in vain to pick the imposing knot apart with her fingernails. The rope had grown stiff and unyielding over the summer, sinking into the branch like twine around dough. "You've got to go, Horse, or Sir Luke's going to find you. Or outlaws. Or it'll get cold, and you'll freeze." As sorry as she felt for the animal, it was her brother she was most concerned for. She couldn't tell Mother about this. She couldn't tell anyone. All she could do was set the horse free and hope he found his way home to Sir Luke.

By the time she'd picked a few fibres loose, her fingernails were hurting. At this pace, she'd be here all afternoon. She kept at it a while longer, pursuing her task with the single-minded determination of a child, not stopping to consider that she might have more luck with the knot around the horse's neck instead. What she really needed was a knife. That would make short work of the rope. It would mean another trip to the village and back, but she could make it before dark if she hurried. Mother was never home before sunset.

She climbed back down, this time taking care not to worsen the rip in her dress. It wasn't a terribly long walk from the meadow to Rosepath village, but it was inconvenient. No roads or hunting trails came this way, and the dense woodland meant there were no farms nearby. That was why Sam had picked this spot to hide the horse. Holly pricked Elizabeth's ankles as she walked, twigs scratching her hair and mud sucking at her boots. She couldn't wait until summer hardened up the ground properly again.

The shadows were starting to lengthen by the time she reached the meadows on the northern edge of Rosepath. Her nose tickled with the scent of freshly mown hay. A pair of farmhands were resting against the fence with their scythes, but they paid her no mind as she hurried past. Up ahead, the smooth white walls of Rosepath Castle stood like a mountain peak atop the green hill. That was the home of Count Leo, lord of their estate. If it hadn't been for the castle, most travellers would never have guessed there was a village nestled between the trees at the foot of the hill.

Elizabeth followed the edge of the meadows nearest the forest as she made her way home. There was only one proper street running through Rosepath, but it was a long one, stretching all the way from the castle to the road that cut through the forest on its eastern side. Beyond that, fields and farm buildings populated a stretch of open land in the otherwise densely wooded area. Elizabeth picked her way between yards and woodpiles until she reached her mother's house. Like all the houses on this part of the street, it was a plain, single-roomed dwelling they rented from Count Leo. It wasn't much, but it did have a proper hearth and a solid beaten-earth floor that didn't get soggy when it rained. That was more than could be said of the last house they'd lived in.

Elizabeth found the sack of oats behind the woodpile. She hesitated for a moment, wondering whether they still needed it. They wouldn't have to feed the horse anymore if she set him free. But oats were oats, and a whole sack was too valuable to throw away, even if they were only fit for horses. She could mix them into the pottage to make it go a little further. No one would notice.

She dragged the sack around to the front of the house and untied the piece of rope they used to hold the door shut. She looked up at the castle as she swung the door open, wondering what it would be like to live in a house made of stone. They had doors that locked with keys up at the castle along with wooden staircases and big windows that filled every room with light.

Remembering that she needed to hurry, she dragged the sack into the gloomy hovel and shoved it behind the bed.

11

The fire had almost gone out in her absence, so she stuffed another couple of logs into the hearth, stirred the lukewarm cauldron of pottage, and took their good, sharp knife down from its hiding place atop one of the roof beams.

A shadow darkened the room as someone stepped into the doorway. Elizabeth flinched away instinctively. Taller than the lintel, his shoulders filling the entire frame, stood Sir Luke of Green Grange. He was a good ten years older than Sam, muscular and well-dressed, with oil in his neat beard and a scowl on his face. The only part of him that looked like it belonged in Elizabeth's house was the mud spattered up his fine leather boots.

"Is this where Sam lives?" he barked at her. His voice was so loud in the quiet house that Elizabeth flinched again.

"No."

"Well, everyone else on the street says he does, so either they're lying to me or you are."

"I'm not. He doesn't live here," Elizabeth said stiffly. "He lives in your stable house over in Green Grange."

"I'm not in the mood for brats with smart mouths. Who are you? His sister? Where is he?"

Elizabeth gave him a surly look. Mother told her not to get on the wrong side of lords, but she didn't like Sir Luke one bit. He was rude, and she wasn't going to be bullied into getting Sam in trouble.

"I don't know."

"Oh, I think you do." Sir Luke stepped inside and made a grab for her. She darted out of his reach behind the hearth. When he tried to follow, she bolted for the open door, but the knight was faster. His fingers dug into her arm and he shook her fiercely. With a yelp, she tried to swat at him, only to stop herself at the last moment when she realised she still had the knife in her hand. Sir Luke's face twisted with anger when he saw the blade. He grabbed her wrist and bent it back until she dropped the knife with a cry of pain.

"Little thieves and thugs in this village," Sir Luke spat.

"Get outside. I'll have you birched and your brother flogged."
He shoved her through the doorway into the street.

Elizabeth's stomach shrivelled with fear. Sir Luke's grip
was impossibly tight, and he wasn't letting go. She hadn't
done anything wrong, had she? She hadn't meant to swing the
knife at him. It wasn't her who'd stolen the horse. But none
of that seemed to matter. Sir Luke was angry, and when lords
got angry, someone paid for it. That was how Sam said it
always happened. Elizabeth tried to pull away, but it was no
use. Sir Luke yanked her down the street, threatening to trip
her if she didn't keep up. Elizabeth saw Gilly Tailor carrying a
bale of cloth into her house. She caught the woman's eye and
gave her a pleading look.

"Why've you got your hands on that girl?" Gilly called
over. Sir Luke's grip loosened. Elizabeth's hope sparked back
to life for a fleeting moment before Gilly saw who she was
addressing and dipped her head. "Apologies, milord," she
mumbled apologetically before shouldering her door open
and disappearing inside. Elizabeth's heart sank.

"Come on," Sir Luke said, scanning the street as they
walked toward the castle. "Where's your brother hiding?"

"I don't know!"

"If you tell me, I'll let you go and we'll say no more about
this. How does that sound?"

Elizabeth didn't trust him, but if she didn't say anything
he would drag her to the castle and tell Count Leo she'd
attacked him with a knife. Then she'd be whipped in the
marketplace and bleed to death like Steve Pedlar.

"Maybe down by the old gallows," Elizabeth sniffled.
"We go there sometimes."

"Is that where I saw the village children earlier?"

Elizabeth shrugged. She and the other youngsters often
went to the gallows. They were at the edge of the woods in a
secluded spot on the south side of Rosepath. No one had
been hanged there in years. The only time the gallows saw use
these days was as a stage for performances during festivities.

Sir Luke turned off the street and tugged Elizabeth between the yards until they reached a worn foot trail leading into the forest. This was one of those semi-secretive spots where youngsters could congregate away from the eyes of their elders, distant enough to be inconspicuous, yet not so hidden as to invite suspicion that they were up to no good. As Sir Luke strode forward, Elizabeth heard the sound of laughter. A circle of boys and girls, all between Elizabeth and Sam's age, stood at the far end of the gallows. She thought there were a dozen of them, but she couldn't be sure, for she didn't know exactly how many a dozen meant, only that it was a bit more than ten, which was the number of fingers on her hands.

To her dismay, Sam was with them. He must've stayed behind to gossip with his old friends before running back to Green Grange. As one of the older boys in the group–a grown man, by all standards–he was currently the centre of attention. He leant against the gallows with an easy smile, his eyes on one of the castle servant girls who had pretty freckles and a big chest.

"Sam!" Sir Luke shouted. Once again his bark provoked a flinch from Elizabeth. His fingers were crushing her flesh into the bone, promising a bad bruise tomorrow.

Sam straightened up and made as if to bolt before the sight of Elizabeth made him hesitate. The others immediately fell silent. Whether they recognised Sir Luke or not, it was plain from his tone and bearing that Sam was in trouble. There was a subtle stir of movement as the circle shifted away from him.

Erring on the side of innocence, Sam smiled and made a bow. "Milord."

"Where's my horse, Sam?"

"In the stable with the others."

"My *old* horse. The good one. The one that went missing. I've heard from three different witnesses this morning that you turned up here at the start of summer on a fine horse you had no business riding." He raised his free hand, punctuating each statement with a vicious jab of his finger. "I woke up this morning and heard you'd disappeared again with a sack of oats from the cellar. So don't try and lie to me, you little bastard. Where's my damned horse?"

"Excuse me, sir, but I do not think–" a girl's voice tried to pipe up from the sidelines, but Sir Luke continued talking over her. The girl wore a fine green dress and her hair was tied up in ribbons. It was Lady Kaylein, Count Leo's daughter. She was out of place amongst the village children, but perhaps she'd come down with the castle servants that day. Despite being the same age as Elizabeth, they'd never spoken. Nobles did not idly mingle with commoners, and Kaylein's father was a frightening man.

Kaylein looked flustered and uncertain when Sir Luke spoke over her. She wasn't used to being ignored. Elizabeth tried to catch her eye.

"Milady," she hissed, hoping Sir Luke would ignore her as well. "Milady!"

Kaylein's eyes flashed in her direction.

"Please, fetch your mother, please!" Elizabeth begged. "He's going to whip me!"

Sir Luke shook her by the arm.

"Leave her alone," Sam said, taking a step forward.

"Come to the castle with me and I will."

Sam hesitated. He'd been summoned to Count Leo's court before, and it had never ended well for him. Elizabeth wished he would just run, but Sam was an idiot. With this many people watching, especially a girl he liked, he was going to do something stupid. If only they would all leave, then he'd have the good sense to run away before something terrible happened.

"Come on then," Sir Luke said, flexing his free arm. "We'll get this settled one way or another." He carried no weapon, but he was a big man, and knights knew how to fight better than anyone. He would kill Sam if they came to blows.

In desperation, Elizabeth looked to Lady Kaylein once more, but the noblewoman's eyes were fixed on Sir Luke. Everyone expected a fight.

Elizabeth began to scream. She didn't care if she looked like a wailing child. Sam was going to get hurt, and it was better to be humiliated than to get a beating. Sir Luke shook her again, but she only cried harder. She swallowed her snot, trying to make herself sick, and when Sir Luke grabbed her by both shoulders she retched up a mouthful of vomit on his surcoat. He let go of her, recoiling in disgust. Through her tears, Elizabeth saw Lady Kaylein and her maidservant hurrying away. The other youngsters followed like flies scattering from a cowpat. Elizabeth's screaming was going to draw the attention of half the village, then everyone would be in trouble. She wondered whether she was making things worse for herself, but it was too late to worry about that now. She fell to her knees, spat on the grass, and gave her brother an imploring look.

"Run away, Sam!"

This time he didn't hesitate. With his friends gone, his pride deserted him and he darted into the woods. Sir Luke gave chase, but Elizabeth threw her arms around his leg and made him stumble. The back of his heel struck her mouth. She tasted blood. By the time he shook her loose, Sam was gone.

Sir Luke rounded on Elizabeth. His fist balled up a handful of her dress, popping the seams beneath her arms as he dragged her to her feet.

"He'll hang for this," he yelled into her face. "Don't you understand the law, you stupid girl? You've made an outlaw of him. He'll never set foot in this village again!"

Elizabeth stared at the ground, sucking her cut lip as she wiped her face with the back of a trembling sleeve. She'd never felt more wretched and terrified. Sir Luke was going to have her whipped. She stood there helplessly, thinking she would be an outlaw too if she tried to run away. Sir Luke paced back and forth, wiping his coat with a handful of grass. People started arriving from the village to investigate the commotion. Elizabeth didn't look at them, enduring her shame in silence. Only when a clear, well-spoken voice cut through the hubbub did she jolt upright, shocked out of her misery by the presence of a woman she'd been taught to respect.

"Sir Luke? What is all this?"

Countess Eleanor, tall and dark-haired, approached the gallows with her daughter Kaylein scurrying behind. Her heavy gown tumbled over the grass in her wake, as thick and opulent as a velvet blanket. Elizabeth sniffed back her tears. Again she tried to catch Kaylein's eye, but the other girl was trying to look anywhere else, her cheeks flushed with embarrassment.

"My lady." Sir Luke bowed. "I wouldn't distress you with this unsavoury business. If the count could be found–"

"My husband is occupied this afternoon. Tell me what is going on."

To Elizabeth, Lady Eleanor looked like one of the saints they had carvings of on church walls. She carried herself with the confidence of a woman who knew the answer to every question in the world. Sir Luke, tall and frightening mere moments ago, suddenly looked young and awkward in her presence.

"Of course," he said stiffly. "Well, my horse was stolen, you see, by this girl's brother. And when I confronted her about it, she tried to attack me with a knife."

"No I didn't!" Elizabeth protested. She didn't know if speaking up would help her situation, but she was desperate. If anyone could save her, it was Lady Eleanor. "I just had the knife to cut a rope when he came in and grabbed me. I never attacked him!"

The countess stared at her. The intensity of her gaze made Elizabeth want to look away, but that was something a guilty person would do.

"Your mother washes linens for me, doesn't she?"

"Yes, milady."

"When she isn't bothering men at the public houses."

This time Elizabeth did look away, her cheeks flushing like Kaylein's. She knew what else her mother did for money besides washing. There was a reason she and Sam had never known their fathers.

"It's to be expected," Sir Luke said. Now that he'd been cowed by Lady Eleanor, his tone was more subdued, but there was still an imperious quality to it that made Elizabeth feel ashamed. "Loose morals tend to run in families. I'll go to the sheriff about my horse, but I still think this girl deserves to be punished."

"Quite right," Lady Eleanor said.

Elizabeth's throat tightened with fear. She was going to be whipped.

"I never attacked him! I didn't do anything wrong!"

A flitter of something that might have been compassion crossed Lady Eleanor's face, vanishing as quickly as it had appeared.

"Don't dispute me, girl. You made a mess of Sir Luke's fine coat. If you can make a mess, you can clean one up. You'll come to the castle first thing tomorrow and scrub every step in the south tower." Sir Luke looked like he was about to object, but before he could say anything the countess cut him off. "And Count Leo will certainly do all he can to assist the sheriff in tracking down the boy who took your horse, Sir Luke."

Elizabeth might have been young and uneducated, but she had a sharp wit when it came to deciphering how the world worked. While letters and numbers confused her, she recognised an elegant solution to a messy situation when she saw one. It was as clever as the rhyme of a riddle. Lady Eleanor had agreed to punish Elizabeth, but it was no real punishment at all, and Sir Luke would appear ungrateful if he protested. She'd drawn a line under the situation while showing herself to be both merciful and just in front of her subjects.

"Thank you, my lady." Sir Luke's forehead dipped in a small bow. "Might I trouble your servants for a clean cloth and some warm water?"

With the spectacle over, the villagers returned to their work. They would all be talking about Sam for the next few days. Elizabeth was glad she'd be busy washing the tower steps so no one could bother her about it. Mother would be angry, and poor Sam would never be able to come home again, but he hadn't been whipped or hanged, and for that, at least, she was grateful. Elizabeth knew to take her blessings where she could get them.

Before the sun went down, she ran back to the meadow with the knife, hoping she still had time to cut Sir Luke's horse free. When she arrived, she found the meadow empty. The rope dangled loose from the oak branch, a trail of soft hoofprints leading away into the forest. Sam must have taken the horse and run.

Elizabeth walked home. The next day, she got up early and went straight to the castle. By noon, the steps of the south tower were spotless. She sat in the doorway looking out into the bailey, eating a crust of bread given to her by a kindly man-at-arms named Emrick. When Lady Eleanor saw her sitting there, she came over from the stables.

"Thank you for yesterday, milady," Elizabeth said, hastily swallowing her mouthful.

"You're an impetuous girl, Elizabeth."

"Sorry, milady."

Eleanor smiled. "That's a quality I rather admire in noblewomen, less so in the daughters of my servants." She looked in through the tower door. "Have you finished already?"

Elizabeth nodded.

"You're a hard worker. I don't suppose you have anything

to occupy yourself with besides keeping your mother's house, do you?"

Elizabeth shook her head.

"Perhaps we can find work for you here at the castle–if you can learn to mind your tongue." Eleanor crouched down so that their eyes were level. "Spirit is a fine thing to have, but you must be careful about how you express it." She pointed to Elizabeth's heart. "Keep it in there," then she made a pinching motion at her lips, "not here."

"I will, milady."

"Good. Off home with you now."

Elizabeth gathered up her torn dress and hurried back down the hill. Even though she was sad about her brother, the prospect of working at the castle excited her. Perhaps one day soon she would get to see what it was like to live in a house where the walls were stone, the rooms had windows, and the floor never got wet when it rained.

CHAPTER 1

It was the twenty-first year of King Ralf's reign, Elizabeth was just shy of eighteen, and today she was going to buy her house. While the villagers were organising the marketplace for the first spring fair, Elizabeth took a candle and a trowel into the cellar of the south tower and began digging. She knew the spot. It was right beneath the stairs she'd scrubbed for Lady Eleanor four and a half years ago; the stairs that had led to her getting her job as a maid two years later.

Not being a family of means, Elizabeth and her mother had never had a safe place to store money. Most people buried it beneath their houses. Elizabeth's mother had gone one step further and buried hers beneath the castle, in this old, damp cellar that had never been finished and nobody used. It was a good hiding spot. Elizabeth's fingers found the rotting leather bag and dragged it out of the soil beneath a loose floor stone. The silver coins inside had lost their lustre, but their weight was an easy match for the pennies Elizabeth had saved in her money belt. She could barely contain her swell of excitement as she poured the contents into her belt and buckled it up. It would be awkward carrying the money around all day, but nobody was going to rob her here in the castle. She would go straight to Count Leo's steward the moment Lady Eleanor dismissed her that evening and buy her house. This time tomorrow, it would be all hers. It was a tiny, almost insignificant holding to the nobles, but to Elizabeth, it was everything. Her mother had lived her whole life in the shadow of fickle landlords, and it had driven her into an early grave at the age of thirty-eight—just a few weeks before Elizabeth got her job at the castle. She was sad her mother hadn't lived to see her make something of herself. Then again, had it not been for her death, Lady Eleanor might never have remembered the teenage girl in the torn dress who'd once done such a fine job scrubbing the tower steps.

Elizabeth was determined not to go the same way as her mother. Her small house wasn't much, but it would be a start. She was cleverer than most people took her for, and she reckoned that without the need to pay rent to Count Leo, her current wages would make her a well-off woman by the time she was twenty. That day still seemed a long way off, but the thought of being able to buy a riding horse, a pen full of livestock, or a plot of land in one of the neighbouring dales filled her with hope. If she had to keep paying rent, she would be little richer than a serf all her life, but that would begin to change once she had a house of her own. She was lucky to have found such gainful employment. Lady Eleanor was a fair, even generous mistress, and she ran her household with a lighter touch than her husband. According to Emrick Marshal, old knights like Count Leo grew irritable in times of peace. Elizabeth did her best to stay out of his way.

It was cold down in the tower cellar, but Elizabeth had brought a padded vest to wear over her simple linen dress so she could stay warm. Securing her money belt beneath her clothing, she laced up the garment and climbed back upstairs. She'd made a mess of herself digging in the dirt. Once she'd brushed off the worst of the mud and scoured her hands with sand from a cleaning bucket, she opened the tower door and went outside. A smile filled her lips as the bright spring sunlight fell upon her. She'd grown into a fair-featured girl with a head of hair the colour of dappled straw. Worn loose, it was long enough to fall halfway to her waist, but she preferred to keep it tied back in a rough knot when she was working. Lady Eleanor told her she would make a fine wife for a merchant or a tradesman someday—which was really just her way of reminding a servant girl not to make eyes at either of her sons. Scandal had already threatened to grip the household a year ago when Hugh, the eldest of the Rosepath heirs, told one of the kitchen girls he intended to marry her. Count Leo had put a swift stop to that, and the girl had been dismissed from the castle shortly thereafter.

Rosepath Castle held a quaintly decorative courtyard green within its walls, built by lords who had prized the aesthetics of a beautiful castle over the practical implications of its construction. Elizabeth passed by the stables, giving old Roy the stable master a wave as she went. At the north end of the bailey stood the ageing keep. A thin moat surrounded it, spanned by a drawbridge that had long since ceased to function. Flowered vines grew up its rusty chains and reeds sprouted from the earth that had been heaped up to support the underside when the wood started cracking. Everyone knew Count Leo hated the impractical moat. According to the histories written by the village monks, it had taken years to build. The water had drained itself away into the hillside a hundred times before the builders found a way to seal it in. It precluded any cellars from being built beneath the keep, and all the outbuildings had to be far away at the other end of the bailey. Count Leo often talked about having it filled in now that the castle had modern walls and gatehouses to defend it, but Lady Eleanor appreciated the moat for its ornamental value if not its military usefulness, and so it remained.

Emrick the castle marshal nodded to Elizabeth on her way into the keep, letting her through without troubling the man-at-arms stationed in the guardroom. Everyone who worked at the castle knew her well by now. It was a source of constant pride to Elizabeth that she could walk straight through the gates as if she belonged there. Even if she was only keeping the chambers clean and the latrines fresh, it was still an honour to be part of such a prestigious household. Her mother would have been proud.

The keep was where Count Leo and his family lived along with a handful of servants and senior officials. Everyone else quartered in the buildings around the bailey or down in the village. Elizabeth sometimes slept on the floor of the castle hall during winter, or when Lady Eleanor kept her working late and she didn't want to walk home in the dark. It was certainly cheaper and more convenient than living by herself, but Elizabeth struggled to give up the memories of Sam and her mother by leaving the last home they'd shared. It was her dream to have her own house, not live in someone else's.

In the fashion of many old buildings, the keep was compact and tightly ordered, with a great hall, storeroom, garrison, latrines, and kitchen space on the ground floor, while the living chambers were upstairs. A short walk through the guardroom—which more often served as an informal parlour and work area for the servants—brought Elizabeth into the boisterous clamour of the great hall. Today it was packed with prominent citizens from the surrounding villages attending Count Leo's court. Elizabeth stayed respectfully out of the way, remaining as inconspicuous as a servant should. She skirted the edge of the hall, avoiding stepping on fur-lined cloaks and expensive leather boots until she caught Lady Eleanor's eye. The countess was standing at the head of the room to the side of her husband's high table, watching and listening without making herself a direct part of the proceedings. While she seldom challenged Count Leo on matters of county governance, she was fiercely protective of life in Rosepath village, as she had demonstrated when she intervened with Sir Luke four years ago. Elizabeth had always admired her for that.

Eleanor did not smile when she saw Elizabeth approach, but women like her rarely did. Without the preamble of a greeting, she beckoned her over and said: "You're to take my daughter riding today."

"Yes, milady." It was the day of the week Elizabeth looked forward to most. "Is she ready to go?"

"I've not seen her. The girl's probably still in bed. Rouse her if she is, would you?"

Elizabeth shot a quick glance at Count Leo through the crowd. The greying, near-bald nobleman looked every bit as fearsome as the day she'd met him. "And the count still has no objections to me teaching her, milady?"

"He can't object to what he doesn't know. Roy can barely ride half a mile before his joints give out these days. You handle a horse more than well enough to teach my daughter."

And you aren't a man. Elizabeth knew that was the unspoken reason Eleanor allowed a maid to instruct Kaylein instead of a trained equestrian. Roy was getting too old, his clumsy apprentice handled horses better than he rode them, and the stable boys were all young, spirited, and unmarried. After what had happened with Hugh, Eleanor wouldn't risk any more of her children inviting scandal into their household. Elizabeth wondered, with a tickle of amusement, whether the countess had possessed a wild streak of her own in her youth. Perhaps that was why she was so cautious with her children. Eleanor's eyes narrowed slightly, and Elizabeth flushed with embarrassment. She always had a way of seeing through her. With a hasty curtsey, Elizabeth excused herself and hurried upstairs.

Lady Kaylein's bedroom was tucked away up a second short flight of steps at the back end of the keep. Elizabeth breathed a sigh of relief when she saw the door standing ajar. That meant Kaylein was up and she wouldn't have to suffer through the awkwardness of rousing the young noblewoman from her bed. She liked Kaylein, but there had always been a natural divide between them despite their closeness in age.

Elizabeth was a commoner by birth, while Kaylein was the count's daughter. In some ways, Elizabeth felt gravely inferior to her, especially when Kaylein spoke of heady topics like religion and history and matters of state. But at other times, the noble girl seemed shockingly naïve. The concept of paying rent and setting aside money for the winter baffled Kaylein. She abhorred physical work, and despite having taken riding lessons for several months, she still refused to touch a saddle or climb atop her mare without a servant's assistance. Perhaps that was just the way it was when you were a noble.

Elizabeth knocked gingerly on the door and pushed it open. Kaylein was standing at the window brushing the tangles out of her chestnut-coloured hair. She'd chosen to wear a beautiful green gown with yellow trimming that day, every part of it flawlessly tailored to her figure without any bagginess or loose stitching. She looked like a princess from a minstrel's poem, Elizabeth thought with a twinge of envy. She was as beautiful as her mother, and her room, with its lavish tapestries and shelves of books, housed more wealth than Elizabeth would see in her lifetime.

Kaylein turned with a smile and set her brush down before shuttering the window.

"Come along, Liz, you're late! I want to ride all the way to the dales today, then I'll need you to wash this dress so that it's fresh for tomorrow."

"Of course, milady." They would never have time to reach the dales on the safe route Lady Eleanor allowed them to ride, but Kaylein didn't know that. Travel was another concept that seemed woefully beyond the noblewoman's grasp. Elizabeth had barely seen the edge of their home county, yet she still understood roughly how far a mile was and how wide an acre stretched.

"Are you alright riding in that dress?" Elizabeth asked. "Wouldn't you prefer something more suitable?"

"No, no, this dress is perfect for the weather today. Have

you seen how green the forest looks?" Kaylein sighed wistfully. "They say there are places in Siraba where the lords build castles made from bricks of green jade. Can you imagine, Liz, not having to live in a keep made from such dreary grey stone? Not having to cover it all up with plaster and horrible flaky paint?"

"I can't imagine it at all, milady." Elizabeth didn't know what jade was, nor did the idea of living in a castle seem at all dreary to her, regardless of its colour.

They made their way downstairs and exited the keep, crossing the courtyard to the stables where Roy's apprentice had two fine mares waiting for them. Elizabeth's was slightly bigger, for the stable master knew she could handle a larger beast, while Kaylein's was sleek, black, and every bit as beautiful as her. They mounted up and left the castle via the west gate, avoiding the village of Rosepath on the hill's eastern side. Progress was always a little slow as Lady Kaylein fussed over her saddle at the beginning, but soon she settled down and they sped up to a gentle trot. It would be some time before they managed anything faster than that. Kaylein had made steady yet slow progress over the past few months, and she could ride a horse with the daintiness of a noblewoman if not the speed and control Elizabeth was capable of.

"Liz, it has always perplexed me," Kaylein said once they were on the forest path. "You are of humble birth, are you not? As was your mother? And your father?"

"I never knew my father, but yes, milady. Serving you is the most noble thing I've ever done."

"Well, you ride a horse like a knight! How ever did you learn? You can't have afforded a steed of your own, surely."

Embarrassment warmed Elizabeth's cheeks for the second time that day as she paused to consider her answer. Her money belt jingled beneath her clothing, her horse nickering as the spring sunlight painted dappled shadows over her mane.

"It was from my half-brother, Sam."

Kaylein frowned. She looked a lot like her mother when she did that. "Oh, yes. I remember him."

"He taught me one summer when I was thirteen. I didn't get the chance to ride again till your mother found out I could handle a horse, but I suppose I picked it up quickly." She decided not to remind Kaylein of the incident with Sir Luke, lest she infer exactly whose horse Sam had taught her to ride on.

"I wouldn't have thought your brother a man of means. I'd have seen him at court by now if he was, wouldn't I?"

"He left some years ago, as you might recall. We've not seen each other since." Elizabeth tried not to think about the fact that Sam had probably been hanged or killed by outlaws by now. He'd always been a troublemaker, but he was one of the few close friends she'd ever had. It didn't seem right, what had happened to him.

"Has he not come home at all?"

"No, milady. It was just me and my mother. Then just me."

A quiet moment passed before Kaylein said: "I find you to be quite an admirable woman, Elizabeth. It must be very difficult with no husband or family to support you." Her voice held the polite stiffness of a noblewoman who didn't truly understand the hardships she spoke of, but Elizabeth appreciated that she was trying to be kind.

"Thank you, milady. Hopefully after today I'll not have to worry so much."

"Oh?" Kaylein raised her eyebrows anxiously. "You're not leaving us, are you? Are you getting married?"

"No, no." Elizabeth laughed. "I've been saving up to buy my house, remember? Well, today's the day I buy it."

"Oh, congratulations!" Kaylein looked slightly disappointed, as if she'd been expecting something grander. "You know, you've been with us for quite some time. I could ask Mother to find proper lodgings at the castle if you don't like sleeping in the hall. Then you wouldn't have to walk up from the village every day."

Elizabeth smiled graciously. It was a generous offer, and it would make her feel very important to have a bed of her own in the servants' dormitory. Had Kaylein made it a year ago, she would have accepted without hesitation, but she had the chance to do something else with her life now. Not many people could say that, least of all women. Most obeyed their parents, married when they were of age, and fell into the family line of work. As the orphaned daughter of a mother with no trade, Elizabeth's future was not written in stone. Living at the castle would be an implicit commitment to a lifetime of servitude. As much as she would have been content with that, she dreamt of being the lady of her own house someday. Not a castle or a manor, but perhaps one of the nice stone buildings owned by the merchants near the marketplace. A little something to call her own. Maybe she would run an inn, or pursue a trade, or marry one of those wealthy merchants Lady Eleanor talked about. Regardless of where she ended up, buying her wooden hovel was the first step down the path of independence.

They rode out of the woods and across a stretch of quiet meadows before turning back at noon. Elizabeth gave Kaylein sparing pointers on how to handle her mare whenever the animal grew irritable or began jostling her. She had learned from experience that it was best to advise the noblewoman only when necessary. Kaylein struggled with instructions sometimes, for she was not used to being told what to do by servants. Elizabeth didn't mind. At least she wasn't like her brothers, who were both aggressive, war-hungry men, already eager for the day their father would let them ride south to the border where they might join a marquess's army and fight foreign heathens. Count Leo's conquests had been legendary in his youth, but more than twenty years of peace had made it difficult for young knights to make names for themselves without seeking danger

29

abroad. Elizabeth didn't understand their appetite for fighting any better than she understood Kaylein's lust for jade-bricked castles.

The journey back to Rosepath was as uneventful as always. No other villages lay on the path they took, and Count Leo prided himself on keeping the nearby forests free of outlaws. He attributed this to his harsh treatment of criminals, but Elizabeth suspected it had more to do with Lady Eleanor's patronage of the village monastery, which prided itself on helping the destitute get back on their feet.

"People who have food in their bellies and a place to rest their heads have no incentive to turn to thievery," Eleanor had told her husband one day at court. Leo had countered by pointing out that it was irresponsible to waste money on people who were incapable of providing for themselves, to which his wife rebutted that they could afford to waste money in times of peace. Not wanting to be seen as a greedy miser, Leo conceded the point, though it continued to come up in arguments at the high table. Elizabeth thought her mistress very wise in her ability to match wits with her husband so deftly.

When they came back in through the west gate, Elizabeth pulled her horse up short. An unusual sight greeted them in the middle of the courtyard. A dozen men occupied the green, most of them wearing swords and mail shirts, their horses plodding and stumbling as if they'd galloped for miles.

"What in the world are those men doing?" Kaylein said, indignant at the mess the horses were making of the grass. Steeds were supposed to be brought to the stables, not led across the well-kept green.

"They must be here to see your father, milady. Perhaps it's best we go inside."

"Certainly. He'll be very angry at this."

Elizabeth's unease pursued her as she led her mare to the stables. The courtyard was quiet, and the guard stationed outside the keep was clutching the hilt of his sword. The

30

visitors must have been important, or else they would have been denied entry at the gate, but no one seemed willing to approach them. Elizabeth averted her eyes as one of the men leered at her on her way back to the keep. It was a relief when they reached the drawbridge and Emrick Marshal ushered them inside.

"In you come, ladies. Best not be wandering about today."

"Why not, Emrick?" Kaylein asked. "Who are those men?"

"Count Francis of Cairnford and his knights." He pointed to the heraldry worn by several of the horsemen: a yellow hawk embroidered upon red backing. "But no one sent word he was on his way."

"Oh, yes, I recall him now. Well then, he and his men should be welcomed inside."

"They will be, just as soon as your father says so. You never know his temper when it comes to Count Francis. Might be he invites him in for a feast, might be he challenges him to a duel on the green. I've lost track of whether they're friends or foes this year."

"Francis!" Count Leo's voice bellowed from behind Emrick. He strode across the drawbridge with his arms wide. A middle-aged man with sandy hair stepped forward from the group of horsemen, spreading his arms to return the count's embrace. He was strikingly handsome, but the smile he wore looked stiff and forced.

Elizabeth heard Emrick breathe a sigh of relief.

"A feast it is, then." He took his hand off his sword, and Elizabeth finally began to relax. Emrick was a shrewd man. She felt safe trusting his judgement.

Elizabeth wanted to stay and listen to the gruff exchange between the two counts, but she didn't get the chance to catch more than a few words before Kaylein led her inside. They were probably here for an important reason if they'd been unable to send word ahead of time. They'd come dressed for battle. Perhaps there was a war happening? She tried not to worry, for such things were the business of nobles, not servants like her. Wars were fought far away, not here in the heart of the kingdom.

When she came back downstairs with Kaylein's dress she found Count Francis and his men making themselves at home in the great hall. The bustle of townspeople from earlier had given way to the bawdy merrymaking of soldiers. It looked like half of Leo's men-at-arms had joined them, eager to swap stories with knights from the neighbouring county. The man who had leered at Elizabeth earlier gave her a wink as she walked by. Up close, she could see that he was a fresh-faced, friendly-looking boy with dark hair and even darker eyes.

"Is your mistress going to keep you busy all day?" he asked.

"I hope not," Elizabeth said, thinking of the money in her belt. "I'm a busy enough woman as it is."

The man laughed. "Don't stay busy too long. I might not be here when you get back."

Elizabeth flushed. She knew her way around stable boys and farmer's sons well enough, but not men of nobility. Affecting indifference, she carried on walking and left the great hall, heading out of the castle to take Kaylein's dress down to the laundry house by the river. On her way, she saw Roy Stabler fretting over the holes Count Francis's horses had torn in the grass with their heavy iron shoes. No doubt he'd get the blame for that tomorrow.

The sun was beginning to set by the time she climbed back up the hill with Kaylein's freshly washed dress. The chill of the evening wind caught the sweat on her brow and made her shiver. It was a good thing she'd put on her padded vest that morning. In the distance, she could see fireflies beginning to trail their sparks along the edge of the forest. The public houses in the village would be filling up with farmers and tradesmen filtering in from work. The sound of someone chopping at a tree trunk echoed off the castle walls.

Elizabeth began to wonder who could possibly be felling lumber this late, but the thought fled her mind when she remembered that she still had to see the castle steward before he retired for the evening.

She threw Kaylein's sodden dress over her shoulder and picked up her pace. She didn't want to miss her chance and have to wait till tomorrow. It would make her nervous to walk home with so much money in her belt. Rosepath was not a dangerous place, but she'd had drunken men threaten her after dark, and sometimes she noticed signs that other people had been in her house when she returned home from work. Fortunately for her, she kept nothing worth stealing.

The revelry in the keep was in full swing when she returned. The wine was flowing freely, and Count Leo seemed rather drunker than everyone else. Elizabeth wondered whether the young knight from earlier might catch her eye again, but he was engaged in a quiet conversation with Count Francis in a corner. Lady Eleanor beckoned Elizabeth to the high table.

"I'll need you to stay and help keep these men fed tonight, then clean up after them when they retire," she added the latter instruction with a touch of exasperation. "There'll be a silver penny in it for you. You can ask Daisy to bring a mattress down."

Elizabeth's heart sank. Normally she would have been thrilled at the prospect of earning an extra silver penny; few mistresses rewarded their servants for taking on additional duties. But if Lady Eleanor kept her working all night, she wouldn't have time to see the steward.

The countess seemed to read her thoughts as always. "I can't offer you two silver pennies, Elizabeth. Don't worry, they probably won't stay up all night. You can have supper in the kitchen after they're done."

"It's not that, milady, it's just that I was hoping to see the steward before he retires. I've been saving up to buy my house, you see, and I have all this money ready." She trailed off in the face of her mistress's piercing stare, feeling foolish for having leapt into her story unprompted. She looked down at the floor sheepishly, then heard Eleanor chuckle.

"Go and buy your house, you silly girl. You can come back and tell me all about it. I daresay it'll be more interesting than listening to my husband reminisce about the war all evening."

Elizabeth was so happy she could have hugged Eleanor, but that would have been a step too far. Bursting with excitement, she held out Kaylein's dress with a broad grin on her face. The countess took it and motioned for her to shoo.

Elizabeth all but skipped across the drawbridge, hitching up her dress as she hurried toward the chapel on the eastern wall of the courtyard. The steward always spent the twilight hours of the day in there, preferring to make use of the chaplain's parchment and writing desk in lieu of organising an office in the noisy castle. Elizabeth hurried up the steps, her boots echoing off the stone as she crossed the chapel into its narrow sacristy. The chaplain and the steward were conversing over their desk when Elizabeth came in.

"Is it too late for me to buy my deed?" she said breathlessly.

The steward smiled and motioned her over. "I can write it now if we light a few more candles. Father, do you mind?"

The chaplain, Father Gregory, went over to a chest and produced a handful of candles, setting them in a row along the top of the desk as he touched a glowing taper to their wicks one by one.

"Elizabeth, Elizabeth," the steward muttered, smoothing down a fresh sheet of parchment and trimming his quill. "No family name, was there?"

She shook her head.

"Elizabeth of Rosepath, then." He paused before his quill touched the parchment. "You have the payment, of course? I think we agreed on thirty silver shillings."

Elizabeth nodded and reached beneath her dress to

unbuckle her money belt. The chaplain averted his eyes, looking flustered.

"There's more than thirty in there, I think," Elizabeth said, feeling a touch foolish for not knowing the exact number. The other servants had taught her how to count well enough to fetch a dozen cups or a score of eggs, but larger numbers remained a mystery to her. That was something she'd have to get better at if she wanted to own anything more than a wooden hovel. Still, she was certain she had silver and copper pennies totalling up to more than thirty silver shillings when combined with her mother's savings.

Father Gregory shook his head as the steward counted out the money. "Thirty silver shillings is a charlatan's price for one of those flimsy wooden houses."

"She isn't buying a wooden house," the steward replied. "She's buying a plot of land in Rosepath. The count would charge more for that land if it was bare." Satisfied that the money was all there, he scooped a handful of pennies back into Elizabeth's belt and returned it to her. "Now, your deed. Have Lady Eleanor lock it up with the rest of the village documents as soon as it's done. The count will need to look it over and add his seal, but he won't object as long as the payment ends up in his coffers."

Elizabeth peered over the top of the writing desk, watching as the steward scribed what she could only assume was her name in neat black strokes upon the parchment. Completing the full deed took a long time, for there were many lines of lettering and decorative flourishes that needed to be added. Kaylein would know what all those letters meant. The process of writing was fascinating to Elizabeth, but she doubted she would ever need to learn it herself.

The candles had started to dribble by the time the deed was finished. Elizabeth thanked the steward profusely as she waited for the ink to dry. Father Gregory seemed to disapprove of her familiarity, but the sheer exuberance written on Elizabeth's face stifled any scolding she might have received. With the parchment rolled up tight and secured with a loop of twine, Elizabeth tucked it beneath her arm and hurried back across the courtyard. Night had fallen upon the best day of her life. Even the deep shadows around the keep appeared soft and gentle that evening.

She was too happy to notice the body of the night watchman floating amidst the reeds, or the smear of blood on the drawbridge where he'd fallen.

CHAPTER 2

No one ever shut the keep this early. The main gates closed after dark, but a night watchman kept a small door open till the household was abed. Elizabeth rapped on the wood with her knuckles and called out, but no one answered.

Taking care not to crease the parchment too much, she tucked her deed into her money belt and gave the door a firm push, hoping it had just swung shut by accident. The wood rattled. She pushed again, harder, and heard a thump on the other side. The door swung inward with a scraping sound. Elizabeth frowned. The locking bar had fallen out of the brackets when she pushed. Everyone knew those brackets were too narrow at the bottom. They were like a set of springy jaws you had to jam the bar into, otherwise it would pop out. Whoever had tried to lock the door must have done so in a hurry.

For the first time since leaving the chapel, Elizabeth's excitement faltered. She stepped over the threshold cautiously, squinting into the gloom. A single candle burned on the night watchman's table, but otherwise the room was dark. Why wasn't the watchman here, and why had someone tried to bar the door? The voices in the great hall had fallen silent as well. There was a muffled noise overhead as someone moved upstairs, then the sound of voices buzzing like distant bees. A loud thump followed. Despite the strangeness of the situation, Elizabeth couldn't bring herself to believe anything was truly wrong. The day had been going so wonderfully, after all, and her happiness warmed her with optimism like a cup of strong wine. Lady Eleanor would know what was going on.

Smiling again, Elizabeth hummed to herself as she made her way across the guardroom to the great hall. The door was shut, but there were no bars on this one. She slipped in quietly, and her heart froze in her chest.

Madge the kitchener lay in a pool of blood at her feet. The bodies of Count Leo's men-at-arms and servants littered the room. Some were still in their seats, others slumped halfway off the benches, but most had spilt their blood across the stone floor directly in front of her. A cold, bitter smell like rotten metal filled the room. Elizabeth closed her eyes in shock, not believing what she was seeing. She wanted to vomit. There was so much blood on the floor. If she blinked hard enough, it would go away. But once her eyes were shut, the thought of opening them again terrified her.

Somewhere upstairs, a woman screamed.

The stillness of the keep shattered as Elizabeth opened her eyes and took in the hellish carnage around her. Footsteps thudded overhead as people ran about on the second floor. A man's yell joined the woman's scream, and the sound of clashing metal rang sharply from one of the parlours behind her. Elizabeth pushed the door shut in a panic and backed into the great hall, her eyes darting to the two other doorways at the far end. Some of the bodies around her were moaning. Her boot slipped in the blood, and a whimper left her lips as she almost fell on top of a man whose face had been split in half by a sword. His name was Walter Dale. He'd given her a cup of warm mead when she was shivering in the laundry house one morning last winter.

Averting her eyes from the terrible sight, Elizabeth stumbled down the length of the hall.

What should she do? Where should she go? It sounded like someone was fighting their way back into the guardroom behind her. There was no way out of the keep but through there. She wanted to scream for help, but the fear of who might answer stopped her.

Count Francis and his men must have done this. They'd come into the keep armed and armoured while Count Leo and his men got drunk. Elizabeth remembered thinking it strange that some of Francis's men hadn't taken off their mail shirts when they sat down.

With a pang of dread, she forced herself to look at the bodies lying around the count's table. Leo was slumped against the wall, his eyes open and blank, one hand on the hilt of a sword he'd failed to unsheathe before someone stabbed him through the underside of the jaw. Dark blood covered his chest like a wine stain. Elizabeth's knees shook as she saw the body of Lady Eleanor lying face-down beside him. She had one hand on her husband's leg.

The urge to run seized Elizabeth so sharply she could think of nothing else. She made for the door, trying not to look at the bodies as she hurried past. But as her foot touched Eleanor's dress, the countess moaned. The voice of her mistress yanked her back, tripping up the panic that had been poised to blot everything else from her mind. No matter how scared she was, she couldn't leave Lady Eleanor to die. Swallowing the nausea in her throat, she crouched beside the noblewoman, getting blood on her hands as she tried to lift her upright. Eleanor cried out in pain and grabbed Elizabeth's wrist, squeezing her with a grip that grew weaker by the second.

"Kaylein," she groaned. Her voice sounded wrong, choked and wet. Elizabeth's eyes blurred with tears. She stopped trying to lift Eleanor and cradled her in her arms.

"Milady." She could think of nothing else to say.

"Elizabeth." Eleanor's grip momentarily firmed. "Find Kaylein and run. Please, find my girl–" A painful wheeze cut her off, and her hand fell limp to the floor.

"I don't think I can carry you."

"Don't. Just Kaylein. Take her away."

"I don't know where she is!"

"Her room." With great effort, Eleanor looked up at her. The countess's skin was pale, her expression hazy with pain, but she fixed Elizabeth with a pleading look. It wasn't the look of a mistress to a servant, it was that of a mother desperate to save her child. "Hurry."

She didn't want to. The thought of leaving Eleanor to die on the cold stone floor was horrible. But she had to. She could hear the sounds of fighting outside the great hall again, sounds that would bring death the moment they entered the room.

"I'm sorry, milady," Elizabeth wept, kissing her mistress's forehead and setting her back down.

Why was this happening? All she wanted to do was run, yet she couldn't betray Eleanor's dying wish. If Count Francis's men hadn't found Kaylein yet, they would soon. The distance between the great hall and her bedroom seemed terrifyingly far.

Elizabeth stood up and forced herself to walk to the door beside the high table. She hesitated as she stepped over Count Leo's body, her eyes catching the glint of his silver scabbard. Reaching for the sword, she tugged it free of his stiffening fingers. The ornamental scabbard made it feel impossibly heavy. This was the sword Leo kept on the wall behind his table, intended for show rather than use. The smooth silver decorations on the hilt made it difficult to grip with blood on her hands. She struggled to drag the blade free, hooking her forefinger beneath the crossguard and giving it a sharp yank until it came loose with a rattle. She stared at the length of steel as it flashed in the candlelight. It was the first time she'd ever held a sword. Trying to take confidence from the weapon's newfound lightness, she tiptoed to the doorway. Every room might hold the bodies of more people she knew; every blind corner might conceal one of Count Francis's men. When Elizabeth stopped to listen for footsteps, she was startled by a metallic tapping sound on the floor next to her. When she looked down, she realised it was the tip of the sword hitting the stones as her hand shook.

Blinking her eyes clear, she lifted the blade in front of her and stepped into the small room housing the stairwell. There was no one in front of her, no one behind. She took another deep breath and climbed the stairs. Each footfall brought with it an agonising creak. The landing area at the top of the stairs was empty, but shadows leapt across the wall from the doorway to Lady Eleanor's chamber. Elizabeth could hear men fighting inside, yelling and grunting as weapons banged and furniture fell. The same woman from before screamed again, so close that Elizabeth jumped and lifted Leo's sword, backing into a shadowy corner until the scream stopped. Her fear was tightening into a kind of numb focus, urging her to move quickly. It wasn't far to Kaylein's bedroom, just to the end of the landing and up another flight of stairs. Count Francis's men might not have checked it yet.

The far end of the landing was dark, but a fallen candle burned on the steps leading to Kaylein's room. Dread filled Elizabeth as she looked up and saw a man in chain mail slamming his shoulder into the door. He held a bloodied sword in his left hand. Again she wanted to run, but the thought of what the knight would do to Kaylein when he broke down the door stopped her. Elizabeth mounted the first step, holding the tip of her weapon as far out in front of her as she could.

What am I doing? she thought. *I will die. He will hear me and kill me.*

But the knight hadn't noticed her yet. His attention was still focused on the door, and Elizabeth's boots were quiet on the steps. Would a sword go through chain mail? She thought it might, but she would have to thrust hard. Perhaps if she stabbed him in the leg he would fall down, then she could slash his neck and kill him. The thought of killing a man disturbed Elizabeth, but it was a distant concern after what she'd witnessed in the great hall.

You will not die, she told herself halfway up the steps. *It will be quick. He won't see you.*

She'd almost convinced herself to believe it when the knight turned and saw her.

For an instant, she could only stare back, shocked by the deep shadows cast over his face by the guttering candle. Like a startled animal, Elizabeth leapt up the next two steps in one bound and thrust Count Leo's sword forward.

The knight turned her blade aside like it was nothing. His guard was reflexive, the motion of a man who had trained with a sword all his life. In a panic, Elizabeth tried to stab him again. This time he laughed and stepped forward with his guard, trapping her blade between his arm and the wall. She had no room to move. The man was inches away from her, and he'd put himself in a position to follow through with a swipe of his sword while her arms were outstretched. She threw herself back to get out of his reach, letting go of Leo's sword and hearing it ring against the stone as it fell. Her feet slipped out from under her, but instead of stone she fell against solid flesh. The smell of a man's sweat filled her nostrils as a thick arm gripped her about the waist. Elizabeth tried to squirm free, but the man turned and pushed her out of the way behind him, advancing to meet the knight at the top of the stairs.

It was Emrick. The marshal was breathing hard, but his exhaustion didn't slow him down. Count Francis's knight backed up the steps and lifted his blade, readying himself to parry another upward thrust. It made sense to stab rather than swing in the narrow stairwell, but Emrick took him off guard by making a shallow swipe at his feet instead. The knight cried out in pain and fell backwards as his opponent's sword bit into his ankle. He managed to get his weapon up in time to block Emrick's follow-up thrust, taking the stab in his hand instead of his groin as the sword skittered down his blade and pierced his glove. The knight dropped his weapon. Emrick leapt on top of him, gripped his sword like he was driving a stake into the ground, and plunged it through the man's chest.

Elizabeth had barely picked herself up before the fight was over. Her heart pounded in her ears, her knees throbbing where they'd struck the stone steps.

"Get Lady Kaylein," Emrick panted, pulling his sword out of the dying man and stepping aside so she could pass. Elizabeth squeezed by him, having to step on the fallen knight as she went. She was too shocked to feel relieved. Emrick moved to block the stairwell behind her, protecting the doorway from anyone else who might come up.

"Lady Kaylein!" Elizabeth called, hammering on the door. "It's me, Liz!"

She heard the sound of a bar dropping to the floor, and the door swung open to reveal a terrified-looking Kaylein.

"What's happening?" she said in a thin voice. "Who was that man?"

"One of Count Francis's knights." Now that she had someone more frightened than herself to take care of, Elizabeth found she could think more clearly. "We have to leave with Emrick. There's still fighting in the keep."

Kaylein screamed. Elizabeth spun around to see Emrick facing another knight on the stairs.

"Push him back! Get his feet!" someone shouted from the landing.

"Out the window!" Emrick yelled, backing into the doorway as his attacker swung at him.

Elizabeth looked across the bedroom. The window was shuttered. She called for Kaylein to help her open it, but the noblewoman was frozen in place, staring in horror at the men pressing their way up the stairwell toward Emrick. They only

43

had moments before the knights burst in. Elizabeth threw one of the shutters open, ran to Kaylein's side, and pulled her to the window. The noblewoman struggled, but she was as thin as a twig, and Elizabeth's stocky body held the strength of a hard worker.

"No, Liz, stop!" Kaylein cried as Elizabeth tried to push her over the sill. Elizabeth grabbed her legs and heaved with all her might. She toppled head over heels, disappearing into the darkness outside. A splash followed as she hit the moat.

Elizabeth turned to see if Emrick was coming, but the man-at-arms was down on one knee. The young knight who'd winked at her earlier stood over him. The realisation that Emrick was giving his life so they could escape struck Elizabeth harder than any of the horrors she'd witnessed that night. She couldn't squander the time he'd bought them. Hitching up her dress, she swung her leg over the window sill and tumbled out.

At the last moment, she remembered how narrow the moat was and arrested her momentum by clinging on to the stonework with her fingertips. She fell straight down instead of outwards, hitting the water a second later. It was freezing cold, engulfing her body and swallowing her head beneath the surface. She felt the bottom beneath her feet and kicked back up. Her dress dragged and billowed in the water, tangling around her legs as she tried to swim toward the sound of Kaylein's splashing. The knights could jump after them, though they might hesitate if they didn't know what they were about to land on.

Elizabeth found one of Kaylein's thrashing arms and gripped it, not bothering to try and calm her down. The water was deep, but the bank wasn't far. She felt grass beneath her fingers and dragged Kaylein over until her hands were on the edge. The pair hauled themselves out, water pouring from their sodden clothing.

"Liz," Kaylein whimpered. "Liz!"

Not knowing what to say, Elizabeth pulled the terrified

girl into her arms, struggling to think past her own fear. For a brief moment, she'd expected Emrick to take charge, but now they were on their own again. They had to leave the castle. Perhaps they could hide in the village until it was safe to come back. From the top of the south tower, she heard the boom of the castle bell sounding the alarm. Count Leo had many more fighting men in his garrison. Francis's handful of knights couldn't possibly defeat them all. Perhaps they'd be able to hold the keep, but then what?

Elizabeth began doubting herself again, wishing she knew why any of this was happening. Her confrontation with the man in the stairwell had taught her how woefully little she knew about fighting. A group of knights didn't attack without a plan, and if their plan was going well, she wanted to be as far away from it as possible. Perhaps the village wasn't safe enough. If they went to the stables, they could get horses and ride to Tannersfield, but Kaylein would be slow, and Elizabeth didn't think she could handle a horse big enough to carry them both. Count Francis's knights might already be waiting for them in the courtyard. There was nowhere for them to hide behind the keep, only a thin strip of grass separating the moat from the bailey wall.

"Milady," Elizabeth said quickly. "Do you have a key to the postern gate? We can slip out through there and hide in the forest till it's safe to come back."

"I don't have any keys! Where's my father?"

"I don't know. Come on, maybe the gate's unlocked." It would do no good to tell Kaylein the truth at a time like this. Elizabeth was trying not to think about it herself. Now that her eyes weren't dulled by the bright candlelight of Kaylein's chamber, she could see well enough to grope her way along the wall. She took Kaylein's hand and pulled her forward until they reached the postern, a small iron gate tucked out of sight behind the keep. It hadn't seen use in years. From the outside, it was all but invisible, sandwiched between two overgrown mounds that blocked it from view. The hill beyond sloped down sharply into an empty meadow.

Elizabeth gripped the bars and pulled. Metal ground against stone, but the gate didn't move.

"Oh, please," she groaned, giving the gate another hard yank. Flakes of rust came away beneath her fingers. "Milady, help me pull!"

"What good will that do?" Kaylein sniffed, her voice shaking from the cold.

"The metal's rusted. It might break if we pull hard enough."

To Elizabeth's relief, Kaylein came to help. On the count of three, they yanked as hard as they could. This time something gave, and a shower of mortar dust pattered into the grass at their feet. Another pull weakened the gate further. On the third, it swung open. Elizabeth wondered whether it had been locked at all, or just rusted shut.

"Where are we going, Liz? My clothes are all wet." Kaylein sounded desperately miserable. She didn't know what was going on or how much danger they were in, only that armed men had burst into her room to attack her. She was right about their clothes, though. Elizabeth was shivering, and the wind outside the castle walls would only make them colder. They might freeze to death if they didn't change into something dry.

Telling herself that Count Francis's men would probably stay in the castle, Elizabeth resolved to head into the meadow and follow the hill around to the village. They would go straight to her house. She could put on her other set of linens and give Kaylein her cloak, and then–

The plan dropped out of her mind as she stared across the meadow at a swarm of dark figures emerging from the forest. Staff-length torches carried by horsemen revealed the glint of metal spear tips and round helmets. It looked like there were a hundred of them, an entire army coming out of the woods north of Rosepath. Count Leo had no such army mustered on his doorstep. They had to be Count Francis's men. Had they been hiding in the woods all evening, waiting for the sound of the castle bell to signal their attack?

Kaylein gasped when she saw them. Elizabeth pulled her down, hiding in the shadows at the base of the wall. Several horsemen broke off from the army's flank, their silhouettes racing across the meadow until they disappeared into the darkness at the edge of the village. The others headed in the opposite direction, snaking up the path from the meadow to the castle's western gate. Though they moved without a word, Elizabeth could hear their boots crunching on the gravel less than a hundred yards away.

"We have to leave the village," she whispered, her chest tightening with a flutter of fear. Count Leo didn't have enough men to fight off an army. Nowhere in Rosepath would be safe now. By dawn, the village would be in the hands of Count Francis.

"No, we should go back into the castle!" Kaylein protested, tugging at her arm. "My father's men will protect us. They have to close the gates, and—"

"Your father's dead, milady. I think everyone in the keep is."

Kaylein stared at her in shock. Elizabeth wished she didn't have to tell her like this, but it was better than letting her go back inside. The army had left the meadow, dividing themselves between the village and the west gate. There was an opening in the middle now, but it was still a straight run across open ground, and the moon was bright that night. It would be better to wait until the west path was clear, then they could follow it down to the river where the woods abutted the castle. Against all her instincts, Elizabeth forced herself to stay still. She heard screams from the direction of the village. She didn't want to look, fearing she would see flames licking across the roof of her little house.

"I think most of them have gone into the castle now," she said at last, trying to keep her teeth from chattering. "We'll go to the bottom of the hill, then across the river and into the woods."

Kaylein didn't say anything, but she followed numbly when Elizabeth tugged on her hand. They would have to cross the path the soldiers had taken on their approach. Some of them might still be nearby. As they rounded the base of the hill, Elizabeth looked up and saw the castle gates standing wide open. Francis and his men must have opened them from the inside.

Elizabeth's wet dress flopped clumsily around her ankles as she ran, threatening to trip her up with each step. She was breathing hard by the time they reached the bridge at the edge of the forest. Her boots thudded loudly against the wood, the water inside them squelching beneath her heels.

"Who's that?" a voice shouted behind them.

Elizabeth looked over her shoulder. A group of five men had come out from behind the laundry house, one of them carrying a long torch. They were so close she could make out the yellow hawks embroidered on their surcoats.

"Keep running, milady," she panted, feeling Kaylein's weight tugging on her arm as the noblewoman fell behind. The trees were close, but the men were closer. She prayed they wouldn't give chase. Her lungs burning, she staggered into the shadows of the forest and glanced back. The men were coming after them, but slowly, as if they were reluctant to enter the darkness beneath the trees. Kaylein whimpered as Elizabeth yanked her off the path, thorns tearing at their ankles and thin branches whipping their arms. They were making so much noise it seemed impossible their pursuers wouldn't find them, but getting lost in the forest was their only hope. Elizabeth tripped into a ditch and scrambled up the other side, trying not to lose her grip on Kaylein's hand. A voice called out behind them and a sudden burst of torchlight flickered through the trees, half-obscured by the dense undergrowth. They went deeper, tramping through mud and crawling through bushes, navigating by touch and sound until the darkness swallowed them and the torchlight vanished. Kaylein let go of her hand and fell over. Elizabeth dropped to her knees, wrapped her arms around the wheezing noblewoman, and waited.

The bushes rustled and cracked around them. Every noise sounded like a footstep, but Elizabeth was too exhausted to get up and run again. Her heavy breathing sounded like the roar of a smith's furnace in her ears. The soldiers must have turned back by now. No sane person would go searching this deep in the woods after dark. Her thoughts returned to the blood-soaked great hall. She'd thought no sane person would do something like that, either. She remembered the pleading look on Lady Eleanor's face and squeezed Kaylein tight.

Eventually, Elizabeth grew so cold that she had to get up. The forest was sheltering them from the worst of the wind, but it was still a chilly spring night. People who slept outside in winter sometimes had their toes rot off. Elizabeth wiggled her toes vigorously, afraid they were already going numb.

"We'll find our way back to the path and keep walking," she told Kaylein. "It's the only way we'll stay warm." Kaylein said nothing. She hadn't spoken a word since learning of her father's death. "If we take the path north, it'll join up with the road to Tannersfield eventually."

Then what will we do? Elizabeth thought with growing despondence. Tannersfield was the largest town in the county. It took half a day to get there on foot, and they would have to stumble through the forest in the dark. They'd be walking all night. Perhaps Kaylein had friends or relatives in Tannersfield who might take them in. Elizabeth was starting to feel hollow with hunger. She'd been so excited to buy her deed that she hadn't stopped for supper that evening.

Reaching into her money belt, she realised she hadn't buckled it up properly when she came back from the chapel. It must have come open at some point during their panicked escape. Both the deed she'd spent years working for and her last few pennies were gone.

CHAPTER 3

It was late into the night by the time all the bodies were brought into the great hall. Sir Edward of Tannersfield searched the keep until he found a surviving servant hiding in a linen trunk upstairs. On Count Francis's orders, he dragged her into the hall, held his sword to her throat, and ordered her to identify the bodies one at a time. Earlier in the day, he might have balked at the thought of intimidating a woman at sword point, but the battle had filled him with such energy that he felt like he could do anything. It was a shame this servant girl wasn't the wide-hipped one with the straw-coloured hair he'd flirted with earlier. He wouldn't have minded getting his hands on her before the night's end.

"And this one?" Count Francis said, gesturing to the corpse of a young man.

"Hugh, the count's son," the girl replied in a blank voice.

"Good."

They moved on to the next body.

The battle had been over before it really began. Only the men in the keep had put up a fight, and half of them had been blind drunk by that point. Edward and three others had slipped across the courtyard and taken both gatehouses once the keep was secure. After that, they'd rung the bell to signal the men hiding in the forest. By the time the rest of Leo's garrison realised what was happening, they had an army pouring through the west gate.

There had been some fighting in the village, but Edward hadn't heard much about that yet. Likely it was just ransacking and plunder. Francis had told his men to leave the village alone, but the older knights said such orders were rarely listened to. The fury of battle was not easily quenched by reason. Edward understood that now. When the fighting began, he'd gone for Count Leo's men-at-arms at first, letting the others kill the women and servants, but when a kitchen boy picked up a jug and cracked it over the back of Sir Cary's head Edward feared one of the others might do the same thing to him. He'd been less discriminating in who he swung his sword at after that. When the people upstairs tried to run or beg for their lives, he imagined them creeping up behind him once his back was turned. Then he'd been able to kill them. Count Francis was brutally meticulous. He'd ordered Leo and all his relatives dead by the night's end. That meant killing everyone in the keep, just to make sure.

Francis looked unhappy when they identified the final corpse. Edward didn't know why. He'd taken Rosepath in one fell swoop, and if luck was on their side, the rest of the county would soon follow. Edward felt fiercely proud of his part in it. All his fights up until now had been with outlaws and drunken troublemakers in Tannersfield, but this was a proper battle, the kind the older knights talked about. After tonight, he'd be able to join in when they shared tales of past glories around the hearth.

"None of these is the daughter," Francis said, jerking Edward out of his self-congratulatory musings. "Search the whole castle and the village. Offer fifty silver shillings for the girl in case anyone feels like hiding her." He took a step toward the frightened servant. "Which room is the lady Kaylein's?"

"At the back of the keep, up the stairs outside Lady Eleanor's. It's got the tapestries."

"I was up there," Edward said. "It's where I killed that tough old bastard who finished Paul and Owain."

"Did you see the girl?"

Edward shook his head. "Just a servant. I think she went out the window when she saw us coming."

"Go and check the back of the keep. If she climbed out the window, Leo's daughter might've gone the same way."

Edward nodded and let go of the servant girl, letting her drop to her knees alongside the bodies. "Cheer up," he said, tapping her side with the flat of his sword. "You've had a better night than the rest of them."

The girl looked up at him with a hateful scowl that caught him off guard. He'd genuinely been trying to lighten her mood. Stung by her scorn, he gave her a sharp kick in the leg. The way she shied away from the blow made Edward feel a little better. She had no right to look at him that way, making him feel like a common thug. It wasn't as if he'd wanted to hurt the servants.

The look stuck in his mind as he left the keep, distracting him from his search. As he groped through the shadows behind the keep, he took out his frustrations on the men helping him.

"Didn't either of you bring a damned lantern?" he snapped. Near the end of the wall, they found a rusty postern gate that had been left half open. Edward saw the metal glistening in the moonlight and took off one of his mailed gloves to feel it. It was slightly wet. They checked outside the castle and made a circuit of the wall, but could find no further evidence of Lady Kaylein's escape. Without a light, it was hard to tell one shadow from another. The news put Francis in an even fouler mood when they returned to the keep.

"It could've been worse." Edward shrugged. "Could've been one of the sons who got away."

"A daughter can be just as dangerous as a son if she

marries the wrong man. As long as she's alive, I'll always be looking over my shoulder for the next upstart knight who fancies staking his claim to Tannersfield County. Deposed noblewomen make attractive brides for ambitious men."

"Can't the church deal with her?"

Francis shook his head. "They'll make sure I'm not punished for this once their heir's on the throne, but they can't stop Kaylein from trying to take back her birthright afterwards." He sighed. "I don't want another war."

It's a bit late for that, Edward thought, but he knew better than to say it out loud. "Maybe she'll never get married. Or she'll wed some rich merchant who can buy her another castle."

Francis just glared at him. Despite being strikingly handsome for a man over forty, he had a steely coldness to his eyes that never failed to unnerve Edward.

"I want you to take some men and search the road to Tannersfield. If Lady Kaylein left the village, that's the most likely place she'll go. You did well tonight, Edward. Do well for me again and find the girl." He clapped him on the arm, but there was little warmth in the gesture.

"Do you want her brought back here?"

"I want her dead."

Edward bowed. He didn't relish the thought of another night on the road after several days of forced march to Rosepath, but the lingering excitement of the battle staved off his weariness. If the straw-haired servant girl had gone with Lady Kaylein, he might see her again too.

Unlike most of the other knights, Edward didn't have the money to hire his own company of men-at-arms, so he asked for volunteers. Three men stepped forward. He didn't know any of them by name, but he recognised them as followers of Sir Halfdan, a loyal and trustworthy servant of the count. It rankled Edward that he wasn't noble-born or wealthy like the others. At fifteen he'd been a large boy for his age, and the sheriff of Tannersfield had hired him on as part of the town watch. Two years later, he'd made enough of an impression for the sheriff to become his patron and pay for his knighthood. At the time, he'd thought it strange that he'd been sent to serve Count Francis rather than staying in Tannersfield, but with the aid of cleverer people than himself he'd eventually worked it out. The sheriff was a cunning man, the sort who would rather have a loyal friend in every court in the kingdom than a strong garrison at home. He wanted Edward to be his ally in Count Francis's household. Edward was happy to play the part if it meant he could keep wearing expensive armour and riding a big warhorse. He liked the way it made people stop and stare when he rode through town. Still, he didn't plan on remaining in the sheriff's patronage forever. Count Francis was a more powerful man than the sheriff of Tannersfield, and if Edward impressed him enough, he would eventually be given land of his own. The rent from an estate would allow him to pay for horses, hire men-at-arms, and live in a comfortable manor house. He wouldn't need the old sheriff anymore.

He rode down to the village with the others at his back, surveying the aftermath of the battle. It didn't look too bad. Nothing had burned, and the worst of the fighting seemed to have been confined to the castle. The bodies of a few of Count Leo's men were laid out near one of the stone houses, suggesting that they'd tried to mount a brief but futile resistance. Most buildings were shut save for the public houses, which had been forcibly opened so Francis's men could spend the night enjoying themselves. A few frightened shouts reached Edward's ears as he went by, but that was to be expected. Francis's army would be moving on to the capital soon, and the men wanted to drink, plunder, and find some women while they had the chance.

It was a unique set of circumstances that had brought the count's army to Rosepath. A week ago, word had arrived via one of Francis's confidants that King Ralf was on his deathbed. Francis had begun calling on his knights and barons that very day, gathering as large a force as he could muster before setting out for the capital. A question hung over the matter of succession, and power vacuums were breeding grounds for ambition. It had presented Francis with the perfect opportunity to settle an old score with Count Leo.

On the journey to Rosepath, Edward had learned that there were two contenders for the throne: King Ralf's son, Fendrel, and his steward, Nicolas. Propriety dictated that young Fendrel should inherit the crown, but he was barely a teenager, and there was a good chance the steward would seize power instead. The church supported Fendrel, but many of Ralf's nobles were wary of putting an unproven lad on the throne. Since Count Francis had powerful allies in the church, he was on the side of the royalists. Francis didn't expect a war over the matter of succession, but such things could never be taken for granted. He wanted to be the first noble to arrive at the capital with an army, presenting a show of force that would quell Nicolas's ambitions before they had a chance to escalate. In exchange for his support, the church cardinals would arrange for Francis to be pardoned for Count Leo's murder.

Despite his loyalty to his lord, Edward didn't like the way powerful men made such deals. It seemed conniving and dishonourable to him. But that was the way of politics, and he was in no position to object.

They reached the edge of the village and turned north down the road, heading into the forest that stretched all the way from Rosepath to Tannersfield. Edward wished he could bring one of the long torches with him so he could see better, but fire often frightened horses, and he struggled to get his courser to obey him at the best of times. It would be faster this way. The quicker they went, the better their chances of finding Lady Kaylein. Edward hoped he would be the one to catch her. More men would be searching all over the area, but he'd been tasked with checking the most likely route. If he could do this, he was sure to secure his reputation as one of

Francis's most promising young knights.

Speckles of rain began to rattle the tree canopy overhead. Edward's men slowed behind him, but he urged his horse on through the bad weather, yelling for them to keep up. Before long, the rainclouds had smothered out the moonlight. Edward couldn't see much, but he had good night eyes. He'd know if they passed anyone on the road. There was little chance of the girl avoiding them if she'd come this way. As he rode, Edward thought about what he would have to do when he caught her. His excitement dimmed, giving way to doubt. What if she looked at him the way the servant had in the hall, with fear and loathing in her eyes? It had been one thing to kill women in the heat of battle, but running one down in the dark when she was alone and defenceless felt different. He grimaced and tried to put the thought out of his mind, thinking about how pleased Count Francis would be to learn of Lady Kaylein's death.

As long as he was carrying out his lord's orders, he couldn't be held to blame.

* * *

Kaylein's silence weighed heavily on Elizabeth as they trudged through the forest. It made her reflect on the loved ones she'd lost and the hope for her future that had died alongside Kaylein's family. The pair of them had nothing now, not even a penny to their names. More than once she tried to ask Kaylein whether she had friends or relatives they could go to, but the noblewoman either said nothing or simply shook her head.

Elizabeth wondered whether talking about her own mother's death would help. Then maybe Kaylein would be able to weep and grieve. It might still be too soon, though. She didn't want to make this night any harder than it had to be. Kaylein's loss had been far more abrupt and shocking than anything Elizabeth had experienced. She found herself wondering what was worse: to watch a loved one slowly diminish and pass away, or to have them snatched from you in an instant.

The worst loss had been her half-brother, Sam. For years she'd expected him to come riding home one afternoon filled with stories about how he'd outwitted the sheriff's men, roved across the county, worked a dozen jobs, and wooed a hundred pretty girls. That would have been just like Sam. She smiled at the memory of her naïve hope despite the sadness it brought, trying to think of happy things that would keep her numb feet moving forward.

But Sam had never come back, and Elizabeth couldn't keep her spirits up no matter how hard she tried. The shock of what had happened in the keep clung to her like the damp fabric of her dress, sticking to her skin and chafing her soul. All her money was gone. Her comfortable life in Rosepath. Kaylein's family. Lady Eleanor. For Elizabeth, the harshness of life had been a slow and steady grindstone against her spirit ever since she was a child, but for Kaylein it had hit all at once. Perhaps she would never come out of this stupor. It wasn't unheard of for people to be struck dumb when terrible things happened to them. Elizabeth wished there was a priest to offer Kaylein some words of comfort. She was a faithful girl. The books of religious scripture on her shelves had been as numerous as the academic ones.

They kept following the narrow path through the darkness. Their legs got sore when they walked, but the breeze chilled them to the bone when they rested. Soreness and exhaustion were better than freezing, so they walked more than they rested. It was a slow, frightening trek full of phantom noises and treacherous brambles. The forest was oppressively dark at night. Sometimes they couldn't see the path in front of them and only the absence of trees told them they were going in the right direction. Elizabeth's stomach rumbled intermittently, forcing her to focus on the pain in her feet so she could ignore it. After a while, she realised

Kaylein hadn't been wearing any boots when they jumped out the window, so she took hers off and slid them onto the noblewoman's feet.

The forest trek made Elizabeth regret the softness of her life in Rosepath. She could have walked these forest paths barefoot all day long as a child, but years of working in the castle had dissolved her callouses and made her feet tender. Stones poked and cut her in the darkness. Twigs scraped her ankles. Mud squished between her toes. The only upside to the numbness was that she couldn't feel most of it.

After what felt like half the night, Elizabeth worried that the forest path wasn't as she remembered. What if they'd missed the road to Tannersfield? They must have been walking for miles, yet the path remained narrow. She couldn't tell whether it curved east the way it was supposed to, or twisted deeper into the forest. The thought of turning back filled her with hopelessness, so she kept leading Kaylein on, praying they would arrive somewhere eventually.

It was a desperate relief when they stepped onto a broad, flat patch of worn earth. The tree canopy opened up above them, providing just enough light to reveal the road running north.

"We're here, milady," Elizabeth said, trying to sound optimistic. "Remember this road? It'll take us all the way to town, then we can find somewhere to rest."

But where? With what money? Try as she might, Elizabeth couldn't answer those questions. The monastery in Rosepath would've taken them in, but only because of Lady Eleanor's influence. People said that under King Ralf's rule, many churches had become greedy, neglecting the poor and growing fat off the crown's taxes. Elizabeth didn't know whether that was true, but homelessness was said to be rampant in Tannersfield. They would be two beggars amongst many. She shuddered at the thought, not wanting to imagine the hardship such a life would entail.

A pattering of rain began to fall, drowning out the noise

of the forest around them. Elizabeth was grateful for the familiar sound stifling the eerie nighttime ambience. Despite their attempts to stay sheltered at the side of the road, they were soon soaked. Elizabeth stubbed her toe on a tree root and decided she might as well walk in the rain where the footing was easier. Before long her teeth were chattering. Dawn still hadn't broken, and she had no idea how far they were from Tannersfield.

The spring faire will probably be ruined by this rain, she thought, before remembering that the weather was probably the least of Rosepath's concerns right now.

Up ahead, a tiny light illuminated a small stone building. There were several such houses along this road, though most had fallen into disuse. They were verderer's cottages, manned by the officials who oversaw the king's forests. As they drew nearer, Elizabeth saw a figure standing outside. He was yelling loudly and hammering his fist against the door. Elizabeth put out a hand to stop Kaylein.

"Best we wait a bit, milady."

She strained her ears to make out what the man was saying over the pattering rain. He seemed to want to come in, but whoever was inside wasn't responding. The traveller had probably been caught in the downpour just like them, and the verderer—or the squatters—didn't want to open their door to a stranger after dark. Elizabeth edged closer and saw the traveller was dressed in a heavy hooded cloak. He didn't seem to be armed, but he sounded angry and unpleasant. Decent folk had no business travelling after nightfall.

"We'll go past on the other side of the road," she whispered to Kaylein. "He won't notice us in the rain."

The traveller continued yelling into the cottage door, apparently unwilling to move on until the occupants opened up or he shouted himself out of breath. As they were going past, Elizabeth heard a whinny and saw the traveller's horse tethered to a tree next to them. The animal had bulging bags slung across its back and a travelling bundle in place of a saddle. It looked like a merchant's packhorse. Elizabeth's stomach rumbled again. Those saddlebags probably contained food and money. The thought of stealing pained her, but she didn't fancy her chances courting the ill-tempered traveller's charity. All they needed was a few pennies. That would be enough to buy them food and a place to rest until they could work out what to do.

Casting a fearful glance in the direction of the cottage, Elizabeth told Kaylein to wait in the trees and crept over to the horse. She was about to break the king's law, but that didn't seem to matter very much right now. She'd already seen a hundred laws broken this night.

Moving slowly so as not to startle the horse, she reached for the nearest saddlebag and unbuckled it. There was something hard and wooden inside, along with a leather satchel and a bag of what might have been nails. The satchel clattered slightly when she hefted it, so she put it back. She was looking for food.

The merchant swore behind her. He'd moved away from the door and was peering in through the thick wooden shutters.

Elizabeth moved around to the other saddlebag. When she reached for it, the horse snorted and stepped away, squashing the contents against a tree. Not wanting to waste time, Elizabeth checked the bundle strapped to the animal's back instead. For the first time since leaving the castle, she felt blessed with good luck. The bundle contained three or four heavy cloaks wrapped in an oiled blanket. Working at the knot holding them in place, Elizabeth glanced back at the merchant. He was still preoccupied trying to look through the window.

The knot came undone with a pop. Elizabeth unwrapped the blanket and pulled out the topmost cloak. It was big, meant for a man rather than a woman, but it warmed her shoulders the moment she threw it on. She was still pulling out a second cloak for Kaylein when her heart jolted at the sound of the merchant's footsteps splashing across the road behind her. The cloaks would keep them warm, but they still needed food and money. She reached into the saddlebag and grabbed the first thing her hand closed on—the rattling leather satchel. Perhaps she could sell whatever was in it for a few pennies. Clutching the bundle to her chest, she ducked beneath the horse's legs and ran into the forest. Once she was out of sight, she chanced a look back, holding her breath as she waited. The merchant didn't seem to have noticed her. Throwing one last curse in the cottage's direction, he untied the bridle and led his horse away.

Elizabeth shivered with relief. She crept back to where Kaylein was hiding and put the other cloak over her shoulders. With the hoods up, they would be far less conspicuous. Two soaked young women—one without shoes and the other in a noblewoman's dress—would attract a lot of attention in Tannersfield. Elizabeth didn't think attention was something they wanted right now.

They set off north down the road again, heading in the opposite direction to the merchant. Elizabeth reached into the satchel and began exploring the contents with her fingertips. The first object she touched was long and wooden, with a smooth handle and a large square block at the end. A mallet. She groped for the next item and something sharp pricked her. She yanked her hand out, sucking at the tiny nick. On her next attempt, she was more cautious, probing gently until she found the sharp metal object again. It felt like a thick, narrow, edgeless knife with a strange round handle. Withdrawing it slowly, she squinted at the object in the darkness. It was a wood chisel. She'd stolen a bag of carpenter's tools.

Tucking the chisel into her belt, she rummaged through the rest of the contents and found a half-eaten wheel of cheese and some bread wrapped in cloth. There was also a hand saw, a roll of measuring string, and a heavy rectangular tool she'd seen carpenters use to dress wood. She didn't know the name of that one. She split the cheese in half and gave some to Kaylein, but she wouldn't eat.

"Please, milady, we have to keep our strength up. I don't know about you, but I can barely hold my eyes open. A bit of food should help with that." She offered the cheese again, but Kaylein ignored it. "Your mother told me to take care of you. She'd be angry if I let you starve."

Kaylein turned to stare at her. She accepted the cheese and took a small bite.

Elizabeth squeezed her shoulder. "It'll be alright, milady. I promise it will. We've got cloaks and food now, and once we reach Tannersfield I'll find us a place to rest." It didn't seem like much, but it was all Elizabeth could offer. Kaylein nodded distractedly and took another bite of cheese. Elizabeth put her arm around her, lending her companion a little extra warmth as they ambled down the road toward Tannersfield.

They had just finished eating when the sound of hooves came splashing up the road behind them.

CHAPTER 4

Edward almost rode over the two travellers when they appeared out of the darkness in front of him. They leapt aside, shrinking back toward the edge of the forest as he reined in his horse and turned it around. He couldn't see their faces, but they had the stature of women. Judging by the silence on the road behind him, his companions hadn't caught up yet. He'd left two of them to search a locked cottage while the other dealt with an uppity merchant who'd accused them of theft when they stopped to question him.

"Hold!" he shouted as the pair edged toward the trees. "Who are you two? What are you doing out here in the middle of the night?"

"Just going to Tannersfield, milord," one of them said. Her voice sounded familiar.

He beckoned them over. "Take down those hoods and come here."

The woman froze, then whispered: "Run, milady!"

They made for the trees. Edward's heart leapt with excitement. It was Lady Kaylein. It had to be! The first girl was quick, but the other one didn't move fast enough. Edward kicked his horse forward and grabbed at her, seizing the hood of her cloak and a fistful of hair along with it. She screamed as he dragged her down the road until he lost his grip and she fell into the mud.

He pulled up his horse and dismounted quickly, reaching for his sword. A parting in the clouds illuminated the road in silvery moonlight. He recognised the straw-haired servant girl running to help her fallen mistress.

"Leave her there!" Edward yelled, pointing with his sword. "She's the only one I'm after!"

The servant ignored him, pleading with Kaylein to run as she tugged the dazed noblewoman to her feet. The stupidity of the girl annoyed him. Didn't she understand he was giving her a chance to live? His frustration only lasted a second when he realised Lady Kaylein wasn't as stunned as she'd appeared. She found her feet quickly and turned to run. Edward gave chase. The women went into the trees, vanishing the second the shadows covered them. Visible or not, they couldn't stop themselves from making a racket as they loped through the dense undergrowth. Edward followed the noise of crashing shrubs as he went after them. Spry branches whipped back in their wake, slapping against Edward's chest and shoulders, but he barely felt the sting through his mail shirt.

Moonlight spilt through the trees once more, revealing the servant girl's bouncing hair as she pushed her mistress ahead of her. Edward lunged forward and seized her by the shoulder. She was stronger than he expected, forcing him to hold tight so she didn't writhe free. He yanked the girl back and tried to shove her aside so he could get at Kaylein. Realising what he was doing, she threw all her weight against his chest. Had Edward been a smaller man, she might have knocked him over.

"Stop it!" he yelled, lifting his sword in anger. He didn't want to kill her, but he would if she kept getting in his way. The girl's struggles ceased. Edward lowered his blade, thinking she was giving up. Then her hand flashed up from her waist, something long and sharp glinting in the moonlight. Edward recoiled in fear, throwing out his gloved hand to protect himself. Pain shot up his arm as the blade went between his knuckles. He stumbled away, a flash of colour blinding him as the back of his head hit a tree. Pain exploded through his injured hand when he tried to clench it. She'd stabbed him through the soft leather where there was no mail. Anger took hold of him, so intense that he let out a roar and swung at the woman. His sword rattled off tree branches, catching nothing but bark and air. Edward blinked hard and staggered forward. He could barely see anything. The clouds had covered the moon again, leaving only the rustle of disturbed foliage in the girl's wake. He forced himself to stop and listen for the sound of his quarry. They were running again, and this time they had a head start. With a curse, Edward braced his injured hand against his chest and gave chase. The wound felt like it might be a bad one, but he couldn't worry about that now.

This time he advanced more cautiously. The servant girl was armed and might wound him again if he wasn't careful. He wouldn't hold back this time. Any flirtatious feelings he'd harboured toward her evaporated, replaced with bitter humiliation that only worsened as the throbbing in his hand intensified. He couldn't tell Count Francis about this. He'd pretend he'd been wounded in the battle if anyone asked. The idea that he'd faced down a garrison of soldiers earlier that night only to be injured by a pair of girls made his ears burn and his stomach twist.

The sounds were getting farther away. Kaylein and the servant were running for their lives, while he had slowed down in his caution. He broke into a sprint, dodging past the shapes of trees and shouldering through bushes until a thick bramble caught his feet and tripped him. The shadows spun in a dizzying whirl. When his head cleared, the sounds of the two women had blurred into the persistent patter of the rain.

Edward tried to pick up their trail one more time. He'd

lost his sense of direction when he tripped. They might be ahead or behind him. With mounting desperation, he took a few steps forward, then back. Still he heard nothing. When he realised he didn't even know which direction the road lay in anymore, he gave up. He groped his way back through the forest until he found the patch of brambles, then tried to retrace his steps. Eventually he saw moonlight shining on the road. He was relieved to be out of the woods, but his hand hurt worse than ever.

The other men were waiting with his horse when he stepped out of the forest.

"Find her?" one of them asked.

"Almost. They ran into the trees before I could get them." He tried to hide the fact that he was wounded, pressing his left hand to his hip to stop it from trembling. The inside of his glove was sticky with blood.

"Well, we can't search the forest in the dark. Should we go back?"

"No," Edward said. "We ride on to Tannersfield."

"Then what?"

"We'll watch the roads. The town only has three gates. They'll have to come in by one of them."

"How long are we going to wait?" The man sounded weary. Edward realised they wouldn't be able to keep watch all day. Francis would be moving on with his army soon, and they needed time to rest before they set out. The pain in his hand was making him dizzy.

"Until midday," he decided. "Then we'll go back to the castle."

The men didn't seem very happy with the plan, but they fell in behind him when he mounted up.

"What does Lady Kaylein look like?" one of them asked.

"I don't know," Edward admitted. He hadn't been able to get a good look at her in the dark. The servant girl had drawn his eye instead. "But she's with one of her maids. She's got long hair like hay."

"Two young women travelling alone shouldn't be hard to spot."

Edward hoped he was right.

They rode on through the night, reaching the edge of the forest a few hours before dawn. By then the weather had cleared and the moon was back, shining bright on the rooftops ahead of them. Tannersfield town looked bigger than Edward remembered, its houses having crept past the old stone walls to butt up against a rough palisade that fringed the edge of the river. Open fields covered the hills to the north and east, while the road west dove into another dense forest.

"You two go to the east and west gates, and you stay here on the other side of the road from me," Edward instructed his men. He rode back into the forest and tied his horse up out of sight, then sat down to wait. He squatted in the bushes, blinking hard to keep his eyelids from drooping. He didn't want to doze off before the sun came up. Puddles glistened on the road in front of him, rippling faintly in the breeze. At least the rain had stopped.

Edward wiggled off his glove so he could examine his left hand. He had to bite his lip as the leather tugged against the open wound. It seemed much worse with the glove off. Sticky blood covered his palm, oozing from an ugly hole that went deep between his two lower knuckles. He tried to move his little finger, but it barely twitched.

At least it wasn't my sword hand, he thought bitterly. Whatever the girl stuck him with had been wider than a knife. She had a strong arm on her. He wouldn't let his guard down around a woman again. They could be as vicious as cats when they were cornered. An ember of anger still burned in his chest, but it was dimming beneath the weight of pain and exhaustion. The euphoria of battle had completely left him, and he was beginning to feel fed up. Only the thought of catching his quarry kept his eyes open.

Dawn crept into the horizon with agonizing slowness.

Edward watched the sky brighten until he could make out the silhouette of the sheriff's castle rising above the town. He wished he was there now, having a priest tend his wound while the servants brought him a hot breakfast. He kicked the ground, wallowing in self-pity until the noise of hoofbeats on the road perked his attention. A man passed by on horseback, riding hard for the town gates. He looked like a messenger, probably sent by Count Francis to inform the sheriff of the situation in Rosepath. Francis always said it was better to spread word of your misdeeds before your enemies had a chance. That way you could set the tone of the narrative. The sheriff wouldn't challenge Francis directly, of course; county sheriffs didn't have the manpower to stop roving armies. What mattered was to make sure the sheriff's herald told everyone that Count Leo had been deposed to ensure the succession of the next rightful king, not butchered with his family in an unprovoked attack.

A few more riders came after the messenger, followed by an enormous knot of foot traffic halfway through the morning. Edward rose to his feet, staggering as a wave of pain and weariness hit him. The crowd looked like a sorry bunch, mostly peasants carrying bags of food and bundles of clothing. A dirty girl clutched a chicken in her arms while her father wrestled with a cord tether around the neck of a braying mule. Two young men helped along a third who had a black eye and a ripped shirt. A ripple of conversation spread through the group as Tannersfield hove into view. Some called out prayers of thanks while others spoke words of encouragement to their weary families. The sound of a child crying made Edward's head ache. They must be refugees fleeing Rosepath. Edward scanned the faces in the crowd anxiously. There were a lot of them, maybe thirty or forty, and most were wearing hooded cloaks. He couldn't tell if Lady Kaylein was with them.

"You people!" he called as he stumbled out of the bushes. No one heard him over the noise. He drew his sword and yelled again, louder. An old man at the edge of the crowd saw him and cried out in alarm.

"Wait!" Edward shouted, but the man's cry had already set the fox among the chickens. Seeing an armed soldier with mud splashed on his mail and blood dripping from his hand, the peasants ran for the town gates. They probably thought he was one of the soldiers who'd terrorised them the night before, or an outlaw springing a trap. "Will none of you idiots wait?!" Edward bellowed after them. A few heads turned in his direction, but nobody wanted to be the one who stayed behind.

Edward tried to catch sight of the straw-haired girl as the crowd fled, but the bobbing heads blurred together in his vision. He swayed on the spot, almost dropping his sword. It wasn't just the lack of sleep; the pain in his hand was getting worse. He'd been bleeding a lot.

Edward's companion ran over from the other side of the road and gripped his arm.

"Are you alright, Sir Edward?"

"I'm fine!" He pushed the man away irritably, wishing he'd put his glove back on. He stared after the peasants and felt the dragging weight of defeat. If Kaylein was with them, she would disappear into the streets of Tannersfield before he could catch her. There was no way four tired men could search the whole town before Count Francis's army moved on. Tannersfield was an enormous place, and it was built like a warren. How had the triumph of last night devolved into this?

"We're going back to Rosepath," Edward said dejectedly.

"Didn't you want to wait a bit longer? The girl might not have been with that lot."

"We're going back!" Edward snapped. "This has been nothing but a waste of time!"

"Alright. I'll fetch the others. The count won't be happy."

No, he won't, Edward thought. He just hoped Francis hadn't forgotten about his heroism last night.

69

They made the journey back to Rosepath in silence. Edward drove his horse ahead despite the beast's tiredness and irritability. A few more peasants scattered out of his way on the road, but he didn't see anyone who could have been Kaylein.

The sun was warming the morning sky by the time they reached the village. Edward wanted nothing more than to lie down on a mattress and sleep. Perhaps he'd be able to move his fingers again when he woke up. Most of Count Francis's army had gone to the castle, leaving the streets of Rosepath eerily quiet in the light of day. A few people were trying to set up the marketplace for what looked like a sorry attempt at some kind of spring faire, but most of the houses still had their doors barred and their windows shuttered. Rosepath was one of those comfortable little villages that was unused to strife, peacefully divorced from the bustling chaos of a trade centre like Tannersfield. The farmers here kept their land just beyond the treeline, which allowed the countryside within view of the village to appear rich and unspoilt. It was little wonder Count Leo had decided to make his home here. Rosepath was situated prominently within the centre of the county without lying on any of the main travelling routes, making it a perfect place for a lord to enjoy all the fruits of his domain while keeping its hardships out of sight.

Edward rode up to the castle and left his horse with the stablers, picking his way through a makeshift camp the soldiers had set up in the courtyard. He'd begun to hope Francis would be in bed after the long night, but when he went into the keep he found the count standing in the great hall conversing intently with a group of knights and townspeople.

Rubbing his eyes and straightening himself up, Edward waited to catch the count's attention. The bodies had been removed, but there were still bloodstains everywhere. The servant who'd given him the dirty look the night before was on her knees scrubbing at one of them with a pail of water. He stared at her while he waited, daring her to glance up at him, but she kept her eyes on the floor.

"Edward," Francis called, beckoning him forward as he dismissed two other men. "Do you have good news for me?" The count's warning tone made Edward think he should be coy with his report. It might not go over well with the locals if they spoke openly of their plan to murder Lady Kaylein.

"I found what you were looking for on the road to Tannersfield."

Francis nodded. "Just as I thought."

"But I'm afraid we couldn't stay to see the job finished. I didn't have enough men to search the forest in the dark."

It was difficult to tell whether Francis was angry or not. He had a stiff, contemplative look about him, and he remained silent for several moments until a monk with a flushed face and furiously narrowed eyebrows spoke up.

"You're hunting Lady Kaylein, aren't you?"

"She'll mean trouble for everyone here if she goes free," Francis replied sharply. He wasn't fond of other people dictating the tone of his meetings, but the truth was out there now. If he couldn't get away with being coy, he would be brutally honest.

"It's a wicked man who wets his sword with the blood of innocent women."

"We'll see if you still think that way when she comes back with an army of her own to sack this village. I can't imagine it'll be any more pleasant than what happened here last night."

The monk's brow furrowed even further, but he folded his arms and fell silent.

Francis turned back to Edward. "So, you found her, but she got away?"

"Yes," Edward admitted. He felt foolish standing there without anything more to say for himself, but what *could* he say? That he'd been stabbed by a servant, hit his head on a

71

tree, and tripped over a bramble like an idiot in a farce?

"I expect she'll go to the sheriff," Francis continued. "If we're going to deal with her then it has to be now–before Ralf's successor is crowned. It will be very awkward for the church to arrange a second pardon afterwards."

The monk huffed indignantly.

"The sheriff is my patron," Edward said, feeling a glimmer of hope. "I might be able to convince him to help us find her."

"Exactly my thoughts," said Francis. "But we can't dally here in Rosepath. I'm leaving for the capital tomorrow. It won't matter whether Lady Kaylein is alive or dead if the church don't get their boy king on the throne."

Edward rubbed a thumb against his injured palm. Things were starting to get messy. The whole point of taking Rosepath swiftly and brutally had been to avoid a drawn-out struggle over the county like this.

"I want you to stay here in Rosepath, Edward," Francis said. "You'll have thirty men to keep the castle defended and enough money to pay their upkeep for two months. Make yourself useful and find Lady Kaylein during that time."

"Two months!" Edward exclaimed. "I'm to wait here for that long?"

Francis glared at him. "I mean to return within a few weeks, but if war breaks out, I can't say what will happen. I may have to be absent for far longer."

"I thought you said war wasn't likely?"

"It isn't. But it's better to prepare for the worst than to let it catch you unawares."

Edward grimaced in frustration. The thought of being left behind aggravated him. Even though his lord was trusting him with stewardship of a castle, it felt more like a punishment than a reward. Francis's other knights would be accompanying him to the capital, either to witness a coronation or to strike the first blow in a great war. Meanwhile, Edward would be stuck searching Tannersfield for a lost noblewoman. Such tasks didn't win men land and titles.

"Edward." Francis fixed him with his steely eyes. "I hope you appreciate the faith I'm putting in you to see this done."

"Of course, my lord."

He really didn't. Francis wanted him here because he had a close relationship with the sheriff of Tannersfield. There were older, more experienced knights who would have been a better fit to take stewardship of Rosepath Castle, but none who could be relied upon to secure the sheriff's help in finding Lady Kaylein.

"Are you sure about this lad, Count Francis?" one of the unfamiliar men said. The scepticism in his voice rankled Edward. His clothes were rich with expensive red dye, but he was too plump and foppishly dressed to be a knight. "He's young to take charge of a castle."

"I'm a man of nineteen!" Edward protested. To his ire, the rich man looked like he was stifling a laugh. Despite his size and strength, Edward still had a round, boyish face that made people talk down to him. He hated it.

"If there's one thing Sir Edward understands, it's how to follow orders," Francis said. "He'll remain here at the castle and do as he's told."

It was settled, then. He was getting left behind while the rest of the army moved on to greater things. He stomped out of the hall when Francis dismissed him and went looking for somewhere to sleep. Perhaps he'd feel better when he woke up. He considered having someone look at his hand, but it wasn't bleeding anymore, and the pain had settled to a dull throb. He just wanted to close his eyes and forget everything that had happened after the battle. He'd had his first taste of glory last night, but then it had been snatched away. For a few stirring hours, he'd been a knight standing shoulder to shoulder with his lord, sword in hand, brothers in arms at his back.

Edward found himself a bed upstairs in the senior

servants' dormitory. He threw off his sword belt and mail and slumped down on a cot. His shoulders ached from carrying the weight of the heavy armour all night, and within moments he was asleep.

At first he dreamt of the battle, the thrill of anticipation, the triumph of striking down Count Leo's men-at-arms. Then his dreams filled with the faces of the servants who'd begged for their lives. He remembered how Lady Eleanor had tried to protect her dying husband before taking Count Francis's sword through her stomach. Then there was the servant girl who'd looked at him like he was dirt, and the straw-haired maid who'd stabbed him in the forest. He awoke sweating in the dark, reaching for his sword in desperation. The darkness frightened him. He could still smell blood in the air. When he remembered where he was, he slumped down with a shaky sigh, cradling his wounded hand to his chest.

He didn't dream again. The next time he woke, the sun was up and the keep was bustling with activity. The men were preparing to leave. Edward was morose all morning, wishing he was going with them. He had a monk wash his hand and bind it up to ease the discomfort. He could move his ring finger a bit more now, but the little one still barely twitched.

He climbed the south tower to watch Count Francis lead his army out of the village, gazing despondently after the red banner until it disappeared into the trees. He didn't know what to do with himself when he sat down in the lord's chair that afternoon. The chaplain had already been sent to start hiring new servants, and the rest of the castle staff seemed to be settling back into their routines without the need of his oversight. Had it not been for the lingering bloodstains, no one would have guessed what happened in the keep two days ago.

Edward was bored without the other knights to talk to. He didn't know any of the soldiers Count Francis had left him with. He'd have to go to Tannersfield and see the sheriff soon, but his enthusiasm for finding Lady Kaylein had dimmed. Perhaps he'd go tomorrow.

Later that afternoon, he called in some of the men to drink in the great hall. Enjoying Count Leo's wine and cold meats distracted him for a while, yet his restlessness persisted. Time and again his mind wandered to Francis and the others, wondering what adventures awaited them in the capital. Edward had always been a man of action. Wine, food and women were good for a while, but if he spent all day indulging he always felt sluggish and dissatisfied afterwards. He'd had to work every day when he was a boy. For better or worse, his upbringing had taught him that leisure was something to be earned and savoured, not slipped on and off like a comfortable cloak.

After the men had drunk most of Count Leo's wine, Edward resolved to see the sheriff first thing in the morning. Enthusiastic or not, he needed to keep himself busy. He was about to catch an early night when one of the men came in with a message that someone was outside asking to see him. Edward wondered if it was one of the townspeople Francis had been speaking to yesterday. He didn't like the idea of having to deal with the rich merchant or the angry monk again. To his relief, it was someone else: a broad-shouldered man with blonde hair and a thick beard who looked about a dozen years Edward's senior. Unlike most of the villagers, his posture betrayed no nervousness when he stood before him.

"What do you want?" Edward asked.

"Building materials for the village, milord. Plenty of doors got broken in by your men the other night. There's a bit of old stonework that got damaged outside the monastery, and a farmer's house was pulled down near the road."

"What do you want me to do about it?"

The man's face twitched. "Count Leo always helped when the village needed repairs after a storm or an accident. There's a stockpile of timber and stone in his storehouse. More than enough to fix the damage."

"Doesn't the village have its own stores?"

"Some of us do," the man said slowly, "but does our new lord not want to see his village rebuilt?"

Edward felt a tickle of satisfaction at being called a lord. When Count Francis left him here, he'd assumed his power would be very limited; he was more a glorified watchman than an actual steward. But this builder had come to him in a position of subservience, addressing him as if he were the lord of the manor. These people regarded him as their new master.

"Suppose I give you some of Leo's wood and stone," Edward said. "What do I get in return?"

"You get your village repaired, and the people are happy."

"What about this castle?"

The builder looked around. "If there's work that needs doing, I can do it."

"I want the drawbridge replaced and the postern gate in the back wall blocked off."

"I can do the gate by myself, but I'd need to hire some men for the drawbridge. That's a big job."

Edward took a moment to think. Overseeing the work would give him something to do, and it would be a pleasant surprise for Count Francis to find the castle's defences repaired when he returned.

"If you replace the drawbridge and block the postern, I'll give you whatever you need for the village."

"Alright. What about our pay?"

"Isn't my wood and stone good enough?"

"I can't hire builders without money, milord. Men have families to feed."

Edward tapped his foot irritably. It seemed unfair for the man to ask for money on top of free building materials, but he did have a point. "What if I feed you while you're working? That seems more than fair."

The builder was starting to look exasperated, as if Edward didn't know what he was talking about. "That still doesn't provide for our wives and children."

"Then I'll give each man a loaf of bread and a jug of ale to take home in the evening. You can't ask for more than that."

"Skilled builders usually get a silver penny a day for this kind of work."

Edward rose to his feet. His patience with the man's belligerent attitude was wearing thin. "Do you want me to open the castle stores or not?"

The builder shrugged. Was he giving Edward an ultimatum? Backing down now would be humiliating, and Edward would be damned if he let this man walk all over him. Count Francis would never have tolerated this kind of behaviour from his subjects.

Edward backhanded the builder across the face. The man flinched away in shock, touching his face as a trickle of blood ran from his nose.

"You're going to fix my drawbridge and my gate," Edward told him, "and if you need to hire more workers, you'll pay them out of your own pocket."

The builder struggled to meet his gaze. His confidence was gone, replaced with a look of fear. Edward suppressed a grin. That had wiped the cocky look off his face.

"I'll see what I can do, milord," the man said in a flat tone.

Edward knew his type. They were confident and composed when things were going their way, but they didn't have the courage to stand up to a real show of strength. Put a sword in their face, and they'd back down in a second. Edward had dealt with dozens of men like him when he worked for the sheriff. It was usually the well-off ones, merchants or tradesmen, the ones who had property and families to worry about. Men lost a lot of their bite once they started leading comfortable lives like that.

"You'd better," Edward said, "or I'll have you building a new set of gallows next."

He watched the builder trudge out of the great hall. The nerve of the man, talking to him like he was an idiot after he'd tried to be generous. You didn't come to a lord's house begging for scraps only to demand a place at his table when he opened the door.

Lord, Edward thought to himself, pacing the hall with his hands behind his back. He liked being called that. He might not be a true lord like Francis, and he didn't have the money to do much with his newfound authority just yet, but there might be other ways for him to leave his mark on this village.

Ideas began to percolate in Edward's mind as he made a tour of the castle, inspecting its stores and pantry to determine exactly what Count Leo had stockpiled. He wasn't going to sit idle while the sheriff searched for Lady Kaylein. By the time Count Francis returned, he intended to have proven himself a worthy steward of Rosepath Castle.

CHAPTER 5

It took a long time for Elizabeth's fingers to loosen around the chisel. Another awful, stumbling slog through the forest followed their escape from the knight. They couldn't risk the road again now that Count Francis's men were searching for them. The sun was cresting the hills by the time they broke the treeline east of Tannersfield. They were at the edge of a farm that looked to be about an hour's walk from town. A young boy wandered sleepily between the rows of seedlings, waggling a stick back and forth to scare off the birds. Elizabeth had been finding it harder and harder to keep Kaylein moving since they left the road. They wouldn't make it to Tannersfield before her legs gave out. Retreating a short distance into the forest, she found a dry spot between the roots of a tree and let Kaylein rest her head on her shoulder.

"Close your eyes for a bit, milady. Once you're feeling ready, we can head into town."

Kaylein fell asleep in moments, too exhausted even for her grief to keep her awake. Elizabeth tried to hold her eyes open, still afraid the knight might come bursting through the undergrowth, but eventually she slipped into a doze.

When she woke, the sun was in her eyes. It had grown

pleasantly warm while she slept, and the breeze had taken some of the dampness out of her clothes. She dug through her stolen satchel and ate a few mouthfuls from the loaf of bread.

"Is everyone really dead, Liz?" Kaylein's voice whispered.

Elizabeth took her hand. "I think so, milady. I saw your mother and father myself. Those men didn't even spare the servants."

"But Hugh and Barnard? No one's better with a sword than Hugh. Do you think they might have slipped away like us?"

"I don't know. Maybe." Elizabeth didn't want to give her false hope, but perhaps false hope was better than nothing. She doubted either of Kaylein's brothers had survived. Hugh and Barnard were fierce men like their father. They'd have fought to the death before running.

"Why did they do this?" Kaylein said tearfully. "They shouldn't have. It's against the king's law! King Ralf will come here with an army and he'll kill Francis and I'll take back Rosepath Castle!"

"Don't worry about that for now, milady," Elizabeth soothed her as she began to hiccup. "Your mother told me to take care of you, so that's what I'm going to do. We should head into town soon and find somewhere to stay."

"Yes," Kaylein said, wiping her eyes and swallowing a few times. "Yes, the sheriff will take us in when he hears about what's happened."

Elizabeth didn't like how uncertain she sounded. She wanted to believe Kaylein was right and they would find safety in the sheriff's castle until King Ralf's men arrived to punish Francis, but what if that didn't happen? The main thing Elizabeth knew about law and governance was that it was often more complicated than it seemed. If King Ralf was going to hang Francis for what he'd done, why had Francis done it in the first place? Powerful lords weren't stupid. What if the sheriff didn't help them at all? What if Count Francis had bribed or threatened him?

"Do you really think that'll be the way of it, milady?"

Kaylein was silent for a moment, her puffy red eyes staring into the distance. "What else can happen?"

"Things don't always go the way you plan."

"But they have to! I don't have anywhere else to go. I don't know what else I can do!"

"We could keep our heads down and find work in town. I lived here for a couple of years when I was younger."

Kaylein shook her head. "I don't know how, Liz! I don't even know how you and the others keep our castle running!"

Elizabeth's brow creased with worry. Kaylein was right; she would struggle. The noblewoman knew a lot about history, religion, far-off countries, and matters of court, but she had next to no practical skills that would help her find work in a town like Tannersfield. She couldn't even ride a horse properly.

"Well, I can work," Elizabeth said. "There's bound to be someone looking for a housemaid. It's not hard to pick up. Maybe you can do it, too."

Kaylein sniffed and looked down at the earth. "Can't we just go to the sheriff?"

"I think we should wait first, at least until we know what's happening. Count Francis might send more men looking for you. The sheriff's castle is the first place they'd go. Maybe if we wait a while he'll take his army away and we can go home."

Kaylein didn't say anything to that.

"We should keep our hoods up in town," Elizabeth continued. "And I probably shouldn't call you milady anymore. What if I just call you Kay instead?"

"Alright."

"And if anyone asks, we'll say we come from Granary down the road east. That's the village where I was born."

Kaylein looked at Elizabeth with fresh tears in her eyes, then squeezed her hand and embraced her. "I'd be dead if it weren't for you, Liz."

Elizabeth stroked Kaylein's hair as she held her, but could think of nothing to say. It was strange hugging a woman she'd spent years serving. Now she was the one in the position of authority, duty-bound to shelter her mistress the same way Lady Eleanor had once sheltered her. Perhaps Kaylein wasn't her superior anymore. They wouldn't be entering Tannersfield as mistress and servant, but as two penniless women searching for work.

They finished the rest of the bread and Elizabeth found a clear puddle to drink some water from. Kaylein asked why they couldn't drink from the river, then blanched when Elizabeth told her what a river was full of by the time it left a town as big as Tannersfield. They skirted the edge of the farm and found a cart track that took them to the town's east gate. It was just starting to get busy with travellers when they arrived.

Every time Elizabeth visited Tannersfield, it always seemed to have grown larger. These days it dwarfed the surrounding countryside. Old farmland had been swallowed up by peasant dwellings, pushing the fields farther and farther up the northern hills. The sheriff's castle, which had once overlooked acres of open ground, now loomed over the town like a dark stone mitre, its walls blackened with soot and grime from the surrounding buildings.

Elizabeth didn't have fond memories of Tannersfield. It seemed even less welcoming now than it had ten years ago. The noise around the east gate was constant, the narrow bridge jammed up with so many people that a watchman was making them form lines so their carts didn't run anyone over. Kaylein put up her hood as they approached and Elizabeth gripped the carpenter's chisel tight beneath her cloak. The tip was still dirty with the knight's blood. Thieves had stolen from her a couple of times in Rosepath, but it was nothing compared to the number of robberies she'd witnessed in Tannersfield.

To her relief, there was no toll to enter town. It wasn't uncommon for the sheriff to ask a penny for entry when a bridge needed repairing or a new wall had to be built. The line eventually shifted forward until they crossed the bridge into the town proper. Immediately the noise increased tenfold. Pigs squealed and chickens clucked in the yards, street pedlars yelled to passers-by, workmen's hammers thudded, carts rattled, and everyone else raised their voices to shout over the din. Kaylein whispered something anxious into Elizabeth's ear, but she couldn't hear her. They had to push their way through the heaving crowd with their heads down, Elizabeth holding on to Kaylein with one hand while she clutched her chisel with the other. People kept stepping on her bare toes, making the cuts and bruises from the forest walk flare with fresh pain.

The crowd thinned out once they passed beyond the stone wall that marked the old town boundary. Elizabeth led them off the main road and down a street that curved around the inner edge of the wall. Tannersfield was lopsided in shape, meandering and chaotic on the north and eastern sides that abutted the river, while the south and west streets were arranged more tidily. There was a lot of dung in the road, Elizabeth noticed. With this many people coming and going, the town watch probably struggled to keep the streets clean of animal refuse, not to mention the lavatory buckets lazy people emptied outside instead of going to the river like they were supposed to. The ripe smell assaulted each breath until she wanted to gag.

The calls of the marketplace traders hummed like a beehive in the distance. Tannersfield had an enormous market in the centre of town, one of the biggest in the kingdom, so people said. Most of Elizabeth's recent visits had been at the behest of Lady Eleanor when she needed something that couldn't be bought in Rosepath. The market was the obvious place to go if she wanted to sell her stolen carpenter's tools, but that was another likely place Count

Francis's men might go looking for them. There would be a carpenter's street somewhere that might be a safer bet. She asked an old woman tending a yard of pigs where she could find Carpenter's Street, and was directed all the way to the other side of town.

Seeing Elizabeth's disappointment, the woman added: "You can find a few more on this side if you aren't picky. There's a workshop three streets over full of boys who don't get on with the guildsmen."

It didn't take long for them to find it. Along with carpenters, there were all sorts of tradesmen manning workshops on this street, presumably those who lacked the prestige to work alongside their more established counterparts. The sounds of wood being sawed, metal beaten, stone chipped, and cloth fulled drowned out the dissonant chatter of the town. The industrious atmosphere soothed Elizabeth after the noisy crowds. She liked being around people who made things for a living.

"I'm going to find someone who'll buy these tools," she told Kaylein. "You can rest your feet for a bit."

"Don't leave me alone!" Kaylein cried when Elizabeth moved away.

She took the noblewoman's arm and led her to where a handful of children were watching some men assemble a cart in the carpenters' work yard.

"You'll be fine here. No one's going to bother us on a street like this."

"I'll say not," one of the carpenters called over. "Only an idiot makes trouble for folks who keep houses full of saws and hammers."

Some of the children giggled. The carpenter, a grizzled man with a thick black beard and a gap in his front teeth, set down the side of the cart he'd been holding and gave Kaylein a smile. "Don't fret, miss. Let your friend here go about her business. We'll keep an eye on you."

Kaylein sat down hesitantly on the yard wall behind the

children.

Taking advantage of the carpenter's friendliness, Elizabeth approached him and asked: "Do you buy tools here?"

"One moment, girl. Let me finish here and I'll have time for you." He spoke briefly with the cartwright who was overseeing the operation, whistled sharply for an apprentice to take over from him, then turned back to Elizabeth. "Yes. I'll buy tools if they're good."

Elizabeth smiled with relief. "I don't suppose there's anywhere I can buy lodgings here, too?"

The carpenter shook his head. "In this part of town? Not unless you've got a few gold crowns tucked away in your purse, which I'll guess you don't." He looked at her bare feet pointedly.

"Where else might we go?"

"Up to the north side, across the main road past the monastery. It's not a good place to live, but it's cheap."

Elizabeth remembered the north side of town. If it was the same as it had been ten years ago, she didn't relish the thought of going back. But until they could afford somewhere better, she and Kaylein might have no choice.

Leaving the others to finish the cart, the carpenter led Elizabeth across the yard into his workshop. It was a long, rectangular hall full of workbenches, tool racks, and half-finished woodworking projects. Large iron-barred windows let in light and drew a breeze that struggled to disperse the overpowering smell of sawdust. Elizabeth took out her satchel and showed the bearded carpenter what was inside. The chisel she tucked into her money belt; that was a tool she meant to keep.

"Hmm. Would be better if it was a full set," the carpenter said. "When people use a mallet they often want a chisel, too."

"I don't mind if you want to pay less."

He looked over the tools one by one, examining their quality and testing them on a well-worn block of wood at the

85

end of his bench. Elizabeth suspected he was also checking for marks that might indicate whether the tools belonged to someone he knew. Craftsmen often engraved their tools with initials to prevent them being stolen. She'd checked these ones beforehand, and they were all blank.

"These belong to your father?" the carpenter asked conversationally. "Uncle, maybe?"

"My brother," Elizabeth said. "He wanted to be a carpenter, but he gave it up." It was only half a lie. Sam had tried his hand at several trades as a young man, including a short stint as a carpenter's apprentice, but it hadn't lasted long enough for him to get his own tools.

The carpenter shaved a few curls of wood with the heavy rectangular tool Elizabeth didn't know the name of, then set it down and nodded with satisfaction.

"They're decent. I'll give you two silver shillings for them."

"Two?" Elizabeth had been hoping for four or five. Good craftsmen's tools could be worth a lot of money.

"I'll make it three if you throw in the chisel."

She thought about it for a moment, but shook her head. Two shillings was a fair price. The carpenter didn't know where these tools came from, and he would want to make a decent profit if he sold them on. She doubted she would find a better offer elsewhere.

"I'll take two shillings, then."

"Good girl. Wait there, I'll be back in a moment." The carpenter left her at the bench and went outside, returning a moment later with a purse of copper and silver pennies.

"Thank you." She buckled the money into her belt, making sure it was fastened tight this time. The carpenter looked concerned when he saw the damp dress beneath her cloak, but he didn't say anything. Elizabeth went back outside with the satisfying weight of the money resting against her hips. She was relieved not to be completely destitute anymore. Two silver shillings could buy them food and lodgings for a few weeks if they weren't picky. That would be enough time for her to get a job and find out what was happening in Rosepath. Being able to sell the tools to the first carpenter she'd approached had been a stroke of luck.

She told Kaylein about looking for lodgings on the north side of town, and they left the tradesman's street to find the main road. The noise from the marketplace was growing louder as the day wore on. Small towns only held market once a week, but there was no end to the commerce in Tannersfield. They had to weave their way between a procession of horses and carts as they crossed the road. Kaylein looked mortified when a burly woman yelled at them, so for her benefit Elizabeth swore back at the woman until she turned away in indignation.

"Most folk are more bark than bite," she told Kaylein, repeating what her mother had told her when they lived in Tannersfield. "You've just got to scare them worse than they scare you."

"What if she'd been a man?" Kaylein asked quietly.

"Depends on the man." Elizabeth touched the handle of the chisel in her belt. "We got away from one last night, didn't we?"

She knew it wasn't quite so simple. They couldn't hide in the forest if they met trouble in Tannersfield. It was unnerving being back here after so many years, but Elizabeth didn't feel as intimidated by the town as she'd been before. Perhaps it was because she was older, or perhaps after seeing Count Leo's hall strewn with bodies it took a lot more to frighten her. She tried not to dwell on that. Thinking about Rosepath made her feel awful.

A pair of men passed by wearing thick gambeson jackets and clubs at their belts. They were members of the town watch, men who handled public services like firefighting, guard duty, refuse disposal, and law enforcement. There was no shortage of demand for the latter in Tannersfield. Elizabeth recalled that the marketplace gallows usually saw use at least once a month, and the town jail was often full. Just like Count Leo, the sheriff dealt with lawbreakers harshly. In such a busy town, he was rarely short of work.

Nothing much of note lay on the northeastern side of town besides the church and adjoining monastery, which formed part of a large stone compound with barred windows and heavy doors. Elizabeth didn't know how monks found the peace of mind to meditate in such a noisy town, but monks were a mystery to her in general. When she'd been young she remembered giggling over the news that a separate nunnery had been built on the opposite side of town after fornication became a problem in the compound. Why weren't monks and nuns allowed to marry if they still wanted to get up to the same mischief as everybody else?

After skirting around the monks' compound, they passed beneath the shadow of the sheriff's castle and moved into the streets housing Tannersfield's poorest. Kaylein coughed as the smell of refuse soured the air. Most of the people living here were probably labouring in the fields at this time of day, leaving the streets oddly quiet. It would only get noisy after sunset, by which time Elizabeth hoped to have a door between her and the people drinking away their day's pay in the alehouses. She started out by looking for large buildings that might be owned by wealthy individuals with sleeping space in their halls. Her search led to a sorry-looking street near the old town wall full of small wooden dwellings patched up with wattle and daub. At the far end of the street, two sizeable public houses stood opposite one another. Some of the women washing clothes outside the furthest house had painted faces and rouged cheeks, suggesting that it was a brothel. Elizabeth tried the other building first.

Inside they met a middle-aged woman named Emma with dirty hair and a perpetual scowl, who told them they could rent one of her hovels in the street for a copper penny a day. The previous occupant, overdue on his rent, would need turning out, so they'd have to wait until tomorrow before moving in. Elizabeth wondered whether staying here was a good idea, but Kaylein was starting to look exhausted again, and she'd barely spoken a word since they left the carpenter's yard.

They bought some bread and weak beer to drink before leaving, reassured that at least tomorrow they would have somewhere to stay. They inquired with four other landlords, but none were charging less than Emma, and the only one who had lodgings available that day asked for a whole copper shilling up front. Rather than dragging the miserable-looking Kaylein down any more unpleasant streets, Elizabeth resigned herself to staying at Emma's public house that night. The scowling landlady, sensing their desperation, insisted on taking a silver penny for the use of her best room when they returned. Not wanting to scupper her chances of getting the house tomorrow, Elizabeth agreed, even though she could see there was plenty of space for them to sleep in the hall.

Once they'd paid and eaten a sparse supper, Emma showed them to a room behind the kitchen with a table and a straw-stuffed mattress. Kaylein curled up on the bedding and immediately fell asleep. Elizabeth felt safer now that they had four walls around them. She hadn't seen any of Count Francis's men in town that day. Perhaps it would be safe for them to go to the sheriff after all. Surely some considerate noble would take Kaylein into their household once news of the massacre spread.

Elizabeth closed her eyes, listening to the sounds of the whores trying to attract customers across the road. The noise helped her forget about everything they'd lost in Rosepath. The sounds coming from the brothel held a soothing familiarity. Her mother had worked in a similar place the last time they lived here. Priests and god-fearing folk called them houses of sin, but Elizabeth had seen just as many sinners in churches and manor halls. Sinner or not, her mother had been a good person. She'd never spoken to Elizabeth and Sam about their fathers, which meant they'd probably been conceived in a house like the one across the road. Elizabeth felt ashamed when she thought about that, then angry, for what shame was there in having a mother who'd done all she could to raise two children on her own? Other girls had always mocked her for it. Despite their bullying, Elizabeth secretly envied them, for as cruel as they were, at least their parents were alive and married. But she didn't know the truth of her parentage for sure, so whenever people like Kaylein asked she could honestly answer that she didn't know, sparing her that shame.

Perhaps that was why her mother had never told her.

The next day, Emma took them halfway down the street to the house they would be renting. It was a single room just big enough to live in with a beaten earth floor and a shallow fire pit in the middle. There was no furniture. All in all, it wasn't much different from Elizabeth's house in Rosepath, though she'd had a proper hearth and a raised platform for a bed back there. Emma scattered some fresh straw on the floor and went back up the street, calling over her shoulder that she'd need another penny from them tomorrow.

"Where are we supposed to sleep?" Kaylein asked.

"On the straw," Elizabeth said.

"Oh." The noblewoman stood in the doorway staring bleakly into the dark room. Her face was dirty, her once-pretty hair tangled and lank beneath her hood. Elizabeth's biggest worry was not for herself, but for what she was going to do with Kaylein. She looked like she wanted to lie down in a corner and never get up. "When are we going to see the sheriff?"

"Once we know it's safe. We should wait a few days till word gets around about what's happened. I didn't see any of Count Francis's men yesterday, but that doesn't mean they won't come looking."

"What am I to do in the meantime?"

"You can stay here today if you want. I need to look for

work. If it turns out we can't go back to Rosepath, we can't afford to sit idle. That money from the tools won't last forever."

"You're leaving me alone?"

Elizabeth didn't want to, but if Francis's men were searching for Kaylein it would be best if she stayed out of sight. Besides which, Elizabeth knew she would get around town faster on her own. If they kept sharing one pair of boots between them, someone's feet would start to fester.

"It'll be alright. Keep the door barred if you're worried. It's not as if we have anything to steal."

"Very well."

Elizabeth pressed her lips together in concern as Kaylein sat down by the fire pit and wrapped her cloak around her. She didn't seem frightened anymore, just weary and sad. Elizabeth decided to sit with her for a while and try to get her to talk, but it did little good. The only thing that roused Kaylein's interest was the idea of going to the sheriff.

Rather than making use of Emma's foul privy, Elizabeth went out through a collapsed part of the old town wall to relieve herself in the nearby river, then she went looking for work. She wasn't going to find anything in this part of town. Maids who worked in brothels often ended up doing more than housekeeping, and she'd already inquired at all the public houses she visited yesterday. She went south across the main road and began her search on the street where she'd sold the carpenter's tools. She asked at several different workshops, but no one had any need of a maidservant or housekeeper. Elizabeth was disappointed. It would have been nice to work alongside the friendly tradesmen.

After that she went from house to house on the south side of town, telling every wealthy family she could find that she had experience working for the count and countess. None of them seemed to believe that the dirty teenager standing in the street had ever worked for nobility, and again her search proved fruitless. She wished she'd had more time

91

to rest her feet yesterday evening. They were still bruised and stinging, and by noon she was walking with a limp. She considered going back to the house, but decided against it. Having money to pay rent was more important than aching feet.

She tried the smaller houses next. Some of the housekeepers she spoke to were sympathetic to her plight, some indifferent, but none were willing to offer her a job. It seemed like there was an abundance of labour in Tannersfield. Judging by the number of beggars she saw on the main road, getting work was difficult for everyone. On her way through the marketplace, she considered using her money to buy a pair of boots for Kaylein so they could walk to another town. They could stop at villages along the way, perhaps finding free shelter and food at charitable convents. There was no guarantee it would be easier to find work anywhere else, though, and the roads leading out of Tannersfield were not as safe as the countryside around Rosepath.

After more fruitless inquiries, Elizabeth decided to search on the eastern side of town tomorrow. Perhaps finding employment as a servant again was simply too much to hope for. But what else could she do? She didn't have the strength for farm work like the girls who'd grown up helping their parents in the fields, nor was she skilled, educated, or male enough to consider a trade. She would have leapt at the opportunity to become an apprentice in one of the female-dominated trades like weaving or brewing, but apprentices were paid no wage, and Elizabeth needed money if she was going to support Kaylein.

She returned to the north side of town at sunset, stopping to buy bread and beer from Emma along the way. She paid the next day's rent in advance and received a lavatory bucket in exchange, which had thankfully been cleaned since the last tenant used it.

Back at the house, she found Kaylein in much the same

state as she'd left her. She asked about the sheriff again after they'd eaten. Elizabeth promised she would go to the castle tomorrow. When they slept that night, she heard Kaylein crying and rolled over to put her arms around her. The way Kaylein clung to her reminded Elizabeth of the way she'd gripped a little rag doll she had when she was young. It was terribly unjust, what had happened to her. It wasn't her fault an ambitious lord had decided to depose her father. It wasn't her fault she'd never been taught how to cope with poverty. She hoped Kaylein would eventually come through this ordeal strengthened by it, the same way Elizabeth had been forced to toughen up when her mother fell ill.

The next morning, Elizabeth began her search again. The wooden soles of her boots made her bruised feet ache, but the cuts she'd received in the forest were starting to heal. On her way through the marketplace, she remembered her promise about going to see the sheriff, so she turned and took the road north up the short slope leading to the castle. She felt nervous as she approached, realising that the other people going this way were men and women of status. They wore expensive gowns dyed red and yellow and blue, their shoulders draped with heavy cloaks trimmed in fur. She saw a knight with a filigreed scabbard escorting a merchant with a hat made from a fox's pelt. There was a priest dressed in brilliant white robes flanked by two novices holding up the hem to spare it from the mud. None of them gave Elizabeth a second glance as she crept by.

How did someone go about meeting with the sheriff, anyway? Did he hold court like a lord? By the time she reached the castle gates, she realised she had no idea how she was going to fulfil her promise to Kaylein. She'd grown accustomed to coming and going at Rosepath Castle, but this wasn't Rosepath. Here she was just a dirty commoner with no name and no one to speak for her.

The look she got from the men-at-arms outside the gate told her she wasn't getting inside. Perhaps if she'd thought to come up with an excuse for her business she could have talked her way past them, but instead she just turned away awkwardly. Feeling defeated, she slumped against the wall of a nearby house and gazed up at the castle in frustration. News about Rosepath would surely have reached town by now. Perhaps if she could catch a servant leaving the castle they'd be able to tell her what the sheriff's intentions were.

The sound of clattering hooves drew her eye. A group of mounted men exited the castle gates, and her heart leapt when she recognised one of them as the sheriff. He'd visited Rosepath Castle several times when Elizabeth worked there, and with each visit his hair had grown a little longer and his back a little more hunched. Now he stooped over his horse like a greying crow, wincing every time the beast bounced him. This was her chance to ask him about Rosepath. She hoped he wouldn't take offence to a girl accosting him in the street.

She got two steps forward before freezing in her tracks. Dark-haired and dark-eyed, the young knight she'd stabbed in the forest rode into view alongside the sheriff, smiling and laughing as if they were old friends.

Elizabeth turned away and lifted her hood, scarcely daring to breathe as the horses rode by. Several men in the sheriff's entourage wore the red and yellow colours of Count Francis's household. A tense lump rose in Elizabeth's throat. It didn't bode well if the sheriff was holding friendly talks with them.

A stablehand had come out to watch the riders go. Elizabeth took her chance to speak with him before he went back inside.

"Who was that knight?" she asked.

"With the sheriff? That's Sir Edward of Tannersfield." The young man grinned. "Or maybe he's Lord of Rosepath now. You hear old Count Leo's dead?"

"Yes. What about Count Francis? I heard he had an army in Rosepath."

"Don't know about that. I think Sir Edward's the one in

charge there now. Makes you proud, doesn't it? He used to be just like the rest of us, and now he's sitting in the count's castle."

"No, it doesn't make me feel proud." How was it fair that a murderous knight could be rewarded for what he'd done? Elizabeth had been afraid something like this might happen, but the confirmation still came as a dismal blow to her spirits. The sheriff was supposed to bring lawbreakers to justice, not welcome them into his castle. Why had her brother been forced to run away from home for stealing a horse while men who murdered innocent people received land and titles? She felt a flash of anger at the unfairness of it all, but it shrivelled into something bitter and indignant in her chest, resigning itself to the cold reality of her situation.

She wouldn't be going home with Kaylein. The sheriff wasn't going to help them. They would have to try and survive in Tannersfield now, and pray that Sir Edward didn't come looking for them again.

CHAPTER 6

Elizabeth's search for work suffered in the wake of the bad
news. She found herself slowing down as she fretted over
what she and Kaylein would do next. When she spoke to
potential employers, she couldn't shake the feeling that she
was putting across a feeble and absent-minded impression of
herself. She only got as far as the nunnery that afternoon
before deciding to stop and sit down. The pain in her feet
was getting worse. She perched on a low hitching post and
rubbed her sore ankles, wishing she had a horse to carry her
back across town. The nunnery looked a lot like the
monastery, but it was newer and cleaner. A rectangular
compound housing the cloisters stood at the front
surrounded by several smaller buildings and a large chapel at
the back. Elizabeth didn't know why, but she always imagined
convents as cold and empty places. She'd heard that nuns
slept on stone floors, drinking only boiled water and eating
dry oats, praying all day and meditating all night. The truth
was probably less cut and dry, for convents often produced
food, wine, books, candles, and other valuable goods. The
nunnery was probably like a little village behind those walls,
isolated but industrious.

She went back to Kaylein earlier than usual, hoping that a few hours of rest would have her feet feeling better in the morning. Her mood worsened when Emma charged her two copper pennies instead of one for her food that day.

"Ask my baker," the landlady said when Elizabeth asked why the price had gone up. "He couldn't make as many loaves today, so I've got to charge more for less."

"Isn't that his fault? Why do I have to pay more?"

"I told you, ask him."

"But you're the one setting the price!"

Emma just glared and folded her arms. Elizabeth left in a temper, wishing she had the power to do anything beyond bowing her head and shouldering on through every hardship Tannersfield threw at her. If Emma kept charging extra, they'd run out of money much sooner than she'd anticipated. It might be a good idea to send Kaylein out to buy food somewhere cheaper. Not only would it allow them to survive a little longer on the money from the carpenter's tools, but it would give Kaylein something to do. Having a new plan elevated Elizabeth's mood slightly, but she was still feeling worn down. She didn't want to tell Kaylein about Sir Edward and the sheriff, but she knew it was all the noblewoman would ask about, so she got it over with as soon as she returned home.

"How can the king allow this to happen?" Kaylein said in disbelief. "He is supposed to protect his subjects and uphold justice! Unless there is war–" She trailed off, covering her mouth with a hand. "Do you think King Ralf might be dead?"

"I don't know. Is that when wars happen? When a king dies?"

"Yes. Every civil war in our kingdom has followed a monarch's passing. If a successor cannot be agreed upon, the aspirants to the throne rally their allies and try to take the crown by force. My father always said King Ralf's passing would be contentious."

"Does that mean Count Francis wants the throne?"

"No, he has no claim, but perhaps he plans to fight for one of its heirs. I don't know, Liz! He's a vile man. I wish he were dead." Kaylein drew in a pained breath and rubbed her brow. "What are we going to do? I can't live here. The ground keeps me awake all night, the air makes me want to vomit, and now that horrible knight is living in my father's castle!"

"We *can* live here," Elizabeth insisted. "We have to. Maybe when we've got some money we can find somewhere else, but that won't be for a while."

Kaylein shook her head in frustration. "I wish I were a boy. Then I would find a sword and go to Rosepath and kill that man and take my castle back."

Elizabeth saw her face colour with anger, but it faded in moments. Kaylein was not a violent woman at heart. Like her mother, she was prim, academic, and thoughtful. She would never have been able to muster the bloodlust to take an army to war. Her shoulders drooped, her whole body seeming to crumple inwards as she stared down at the floor.

"Maybe it's best we forget about Rosepath," Elizabeth said gently. "Think about what we can make of ourselves here instead."

"I can't forget about it. It's my whole life."

"It was mine, too, but it's not anymore. We have to start afresh."

Kaylein sniffed and swallowed. When she spoke again, she tried to sound hopeful, but there was a note of misery in her voice that suggested she didn't believe what she was saying. "I will go to the capital someday and speak with the king. I will persuade him to make Francis give back my father's land."

Elizabeth gave her a comforting smile.

She talked about the town while they waited for dusk to fall, hoping something might spark Kaylein's enthusiasm to get back on her feet. She described the convents and the marketplace, the castle, the workshops, and all the rich

98

houses she'd seen over the past two days. It held Kaylein's attention for a while, but she said little in response.

The next morning, Elizabeth gave her a penny and said she could go looking for somewhere to buy cheap food if she wanted. Kaylein seemed frightened by the idea and asked if she could have the chisel. Reluctantly, Elizabeth had to say no. If Kaylein got robbed, she would only lose a penny. Elizabeth was carrying all their money in her belt. If they lost that, they'd be out on the streets and starving.

Coming home early the previous day had been a good idea. She felt better rested that morning, and her feet didn't hurt as much. A fierce determination to do right by Kaylein drove her out the door. She resolved that by the end of the day, she would have found herself a job. She couldn't let men like Count Francis and Sir Edward break their spirits.

That afternoon she happened on a street near the market full of large stone storehouses, presumably used by merchants who needed somewhere to keep their goods. Most of them would want to hire strong young men as porters, not girls who could tidy up, but Elizabeth checked every building regardless. Her hopes began to rise when she went into one of the bigger storehouses near the end of the street. It had two huge doorways for bringing in carts, one at street level, the other leading down a ramp to a wet undercroft.

Unlike the other storehouses, nobody seemed to be using this one. When Elizabeth went inside, she understood why. She'd gone no more than two paces before a rat scurried over her feet. Refuse littered the floor: frayed rope, rotten leather, dry mud, and straw that looked like it hadn't been changed in months. She walked down the centre of the building past the thick wooden columns holding up the vaulted roof. At the far end, she found a stack of boxes closed with shackle locks. Even though they probably contained goods worth enough money to feed Elizabeth for a year, the absence of any other storage made the pile look meagre and pathetic. There wasn't even anyone keeping an eye on it.

"Hello?" Elizabeth called. Her only response was a scuttling sound in one of the corners. Any thief could have walked in and broken the locks off those boxes. She went outside and tried the undercroft. There were a few more boxes and barrels heaped up beneath the stone vaults, but if anything the partially submerged cellar was even filthier than the floor above. Puddles of water had accumulated where the floor dipped, and the smell of rat dung had a sour tinge to it.

"Hello?" Elizabeth called again. The undercroft was dark, but she could see a candle glowing at the far end. Someone grunted and picked it up. A portly man with cataracts in his eyes stepped out of the gloom, wrinkling his face as he leaned down to get a better look at her. Perhaps his poor vision was the reason the place was in such a state, though Elizabeth had no idea how he could stand the smell. Perhaps his nose was as bad as his eyes.

"Hello," the man said. "What do you want?"

"A job. This place is a mess. It's no wonder you don't have anyone renting it."

"If you want a tidy storehouse, there's plenty of others on this street. I make enough money doing what I do."

"But you could make a lot more," Elizabeth said quickly, changing her tact now that she'd snagged the man's attention. "All this place needs is a clean. The rats might take a while to get rid of, but I could deal with those, too. I've worked in houses with vermin before. You just need a couple of big cats to scare them off."

"I don't mind the rats," the storehouse owner grumbled. "Why should I get rid of them?"

"No one's going to store food in a place like this. The rats would ruin it in a day. They probably chew up clothes and leather, too. And they make the place stink."

"It's too much work."

"But I'd be doing the work for you! I'd only ask a couple of pennies a day. In a month, you'll be making so much money you won't even notice the expense."

"I know my own business better than some girl. Get on out. I don't want you here."

Elizabeth couldn't believe his obtuseness. "I'll work for one penny a day, then, and if you're not seeing better profits in a month, I can leave."

"I'd rather pay you nothing and have you leave now."

"Don't you understand why no one's renting this place?" Elizabeth's tone grew heated. Why was the man being so stupid? Anyone could see he was running his livelihood into the ground. It would cost almost nothing to fix it, and she was offering to take on all the dirty work. Yet he only seemed to get more annoyed the harder she tried to explain it to him.

"I've heard enough from you," the storehouse owner said, grabbing her by the arm and pulling her toward the door.

"Why?" Elizabeth pleaded. "What if I start working for nothing, then you pay me after you turn a profit!" Her words fell on deaf ears. The man shoved her into the street and swung the heavy doors shut behind her. She was speechless. Lady Eleanor had warned her to rein in her tongue when she had ideas above her station, but she'd always been willing to hear her out when it came to work matters. Elizabeth felt a pang of grief for the loss of her mistress. She knew she'd been lucky to work in a place like Rosepath Castle, but she hadn't truly appreciated her fortune until now. Lady Eleanor had run her household intelligently, efficiently, and in collaboration with her servants rather than competition. People like the storehouse owner didn't even know how to keep their floors clean.

Once again, Elizabeth felt helpless. Even the people who needed her help didn't want it. With a heavy heart, she rubbed her aching feet and began searching again.

A dozen more refusals followed as the afternoon wore on. She felt stupid standing there in silence as prospective employers appraised her, but she was afraid of sounding impertinent if she spoke up about her skills again. She was beginning to understand why her mother had settled for work in a brothel. It might be easier and better paying than this fruitless search.

Would I be good at it? she thought wearily. She'd had sex three times with a farmhand who brought her berries from the forest on Sundays, so she knew what to expect. There had been a couple of other boys she'd let kiss and touch her, and the experience always made her feel warm and giggly. But taking money for it would be different, and Kaylein would be mortified by the idea.

Elizabeth ignored the pain in her feet and kept walking as the sun went down, telling herself over and over that she needed to find a job before the day's end. She wasn't sure what part of town she was in as she traipsed exhaustedly from door to door, repeating the same words she'd said a hundred times, anticipating each rejection before it came. She knocked, asked for work, and was turned away. Perhaps it really was hopeless. In small villages, people regarded strangers with suspicion and only hired folk they knew. Elizabeth thought it would be different in a busy place like Tannersfield, but perhaps that was wishful thinking.

Blinking hard, she turned into another street she could've sworn she'd visited already. Something sandy crunched beneath her boots as she crossed a large yard. She went to the open door of a long building and called inside. A tall man with a thick black beard and a gap in his teeth got up from a bench and came over. It was the carpenter she'd sold the tools to. Her circuit of town had led her all the way back to his workshop.

"Sorry," she mumbled. "I was just looking for work. I didn't realise where I was."

The carpenter looked sympathetic, but his answer was the same as before. "I'm sorry too, girl. My wife isn't looking for an apprentice, and there's not much else I need doing here."

Elizabeth's head slumped in a nod. She was about to turn away when she thought better of it and asked: "That chisel I didn't sell you the other day—would you swap it for a knife?"

He nodded. "I could. What sort of knife?"

"A long, sharp one."

The carpenter sighed. "I probably have something." He went into his workshop and returned with a long, keen blade with a polished wooden handle and a narrow point. "Will this do for you?"

"If someone tries to rob me, it'll be better than a chisel." She reached for the knife, but the carpenter held it back.

"I've seen you walk past here three times since you sold me those tools. You and that friend of yours are struggling, aren't you?"

"That money you gave us is all we have."

"If you need work, you should try Brewster's Street. The alewives hire girls."

"I already did. I feel like I've tried every street in Tannersfield."

The carpenter tapped the knife against his palm, then handed it over in exchange for the chisel. "Try not to use that for anything but cutting cheese, alright?"

Elizabeth forced a smile. "I'll try." She turned and walked away, feeling the sawdust and wood shavings crunch beneath her boots. At least she'd ended the day with something to show for it.

The carpenter muttered something behind her, then called: "I'll give you a penny a day to come in and clean the workshop."

Elizabeth stopped. After so many rejections, she didn't want to get her hopes up. She tried to control her upwelling of relief, but when she turned around she felt tears beading in the corners of her eyes.

"That's just after we've finished work," the carpenter said gruffly, raising a finger as if to temper her expectations. "I don't expect my wife'll be too happy about it, but it's starting to hurt her back doing all the sweeping by herself. That's all I can offer, take it or leave it."

Elizabeth didn't need any further convincing. She wanted

to throw her arms around the carpenter and hug him.

"Thank you."

A penny a day wasn't enough to keep Elizabeth and Kaylein going indefinitely, but it pushed the spectre of poverty into a comfortably distant future. The black-bearded carpenter, whose name was Joseph, insisted he only needed help after work, but that didn't stop Elizabeth from finding plenty of chores to do during the day. She was keen to make herself useful, not only because she feared dismissal, but because she liked Joseph and wanted to impress him. Working at Rosepath Castle had taught her how to get things done without bothering the noble family, so she made sure not to get in anyone's way. If Joseph and the other carpenters were busy indoors, she swept the yard. If they were in the yard, she tidied the workshop. If they were using both, she ran errands along the street.

Joseph's workshop wasn't like the others Elizabeth had visited. Most people worked from their homes. If a town was large enough to have multiple tradespeople sharing the same craft, they inevitably began living on the same street to better share customers and resources. Joseph had bucked this tradition by building a workshop outside his house that was large enough for several carpenters to share. He owned a substantial collection of specialised tools, a shed for storing dried and dressed timber, and his yard was big enough for ambitious jobs that would usually need to be done off-site. As a result, he had a dozen carpenters willing to pay a nominal rent to use his workspace rather than trying their luck on the competitive carpenters' street across town. Joseph's unconventional way of doing things had earned him the ire of the local guild, which governed the rules and standards of professional carpentry in Tannersfield, but as a respected master in his own right he held enough sway to stand up for himself.

As the days went by, Elizabeth often found herself

watching the carpenters as they worked. Some of them asked, only half-joking, whether she was trying to steal their secrets, for knowledge of a trade craft was treasured by its practitioners and coveted by the unskilled. She answered truthfully that she was just trying to learn how the workshop was organised. The answer, it turned out, was not very well at all. Soon she wasn't just sweeping up sawdust, but making sure the tools were always returned to the same wall pegs, taking unused wood back to the storage shed, returning each carpenter's work to the same bench each evening, and setting out food and drink when it was time for the midday meal. By the end of the first week, Elizabeth wasn't just the cleaning girl, she was a full-time servant. And if there was one thing Elizabeth knew how to do well, it was to serve.

Even Joseph's wife, a stout woman named Rose who had glared at her all day when she arrived, couldn't object to how quickly she'd transformed the place. Tradesmen didn't typically employ maidservants, but for a penny a day it seemed like Joseph had gained a service well worth his money. Elizabeth's help was a luxury that took the rough edges off the carpenters' daily routine. Rose didn't need to worry about cleaning before sundown, time was saved thanks to her organisational efforts, and no one had to wait for their midday meal.

"You talk a bit like a noblewoman," Joseph told her when she came into the workshop one morning. "But there's more commoner in you than noble, isn't there?"

"I've spent a lot of time around nobles," Elizabeth said offhandedly. "I should hope I've picked up some good habits."

Joseph laughed, looking up from the sketch he was making with a stick of charcoal. "It's no wonder no one else would hire you. A less patient man might take that attitude of yours for uppitiness. Word of advice from me: the next time Rose is looking for her tools, don't tell her where they are. She doesn't like it when you act like you know the place better than her. She wanted to give you a slap last night."

"But I knew where they were."

"It's not about that, girl, it's the way you told her. Makes the poor woman think you're making a mockery of her with that formal tone you use."

Elizabeth was bemused. "I'm just trying to be polite. That's how my lady always taught me to address her."

"Well, Rose isn't a lady, and her temper's as short as her little toe. Let her find things on her own when she's in one of her moods."

"Alright. I'll keep out of her way."

"Good girl. Maybe she'll carve you a nice spoon if you stay on her good side."

Joseph and his carpenters did most of the heavy work that came in–dressing timber, making fence posts, helping cartwrights replace broken axles–but Rose was an expert at delicate carving. She was the one who made Joseph's projects elegant after he'd made them functional. Everyday jobs like knife handles and tool hafts comprised most of her work, but even those had a form and functionality to them that impressed Elizabeth, especially when she decorated them with pretty designs for the richer customers. Being around such talented craftspeople fascinated her.

During her second week, Elizabeth sought out more jobs she could do for Joseph. If she wanted to keep providing for herself and Kaylein, she needed to prove she was worth more than a copper penny a day. She'd noticed that the carpenters were always running across the street to get nails, hinges, and other iron parts from the blacksmith, which frequently interrupted their work. Elizabeth proposed that she should find out which projects the carpenters were working on each morning, check the supply shed to see if they had what they needed, then go and buy anything that was missing. That way, work could continue uninterrupted all day long. Joseph wholeheartedly approved of the idea.

"How do you think to do all this, Liz?" an apprentice

called Fred asked her one morning as she was about to head over to the blacksmith with a handful of Joseph's copper shillings in her belt.

Elizabeth shrugged. "It just makes sense to me, I suppose. My old mistress always had me do things this way. Find the cracks, then fill them in. I remember her shouting at me a lot till I learned."

"Sounds like a real noble bitch."

Elizabeth frowned at him. "No. She was a fine woman."

By the end of the second week, Elizabeth was earning two copper pennies a day. It was just enough for her and Kaylein to break even, but they still couldn't afford firewood or new clothes, and there was nothing to set aside for the future. Besides which, Kaylein was getting worse. She went out to buy food once in a while, but for the most part all she did was sit in the house sleeping or staring into the empty fire pit until the sun went down. She was starting to look thin and pale, and Elizabeth feared she might be dying of grief.

In an effort to drag Kaylein out of her stupor, Elizabeth began looking for jobs again, taking some time each morning to ask around town before heading to Joseph's. The only employer she found was a laundress looking for an assistant. She took Kaylein to see her the next day, but the laundress immediately dismissed her when she saw how skinny and dainty she was. There was little enough work for the able-bodied in Tannersfield, less still for frail girls who'd spent their lives having others do things for them.

Kaylein started going out even less after that, complaining that people were staring at her. It was probably because of her dress. If anyone caught a glimpse of it beneath her cloak, they would recognise the richly coloured cloth as something only a woman of means could afford. The next day, Elizabeth sold Kaylein's dress to a tailor and got a simple linen one from the market to replace it. She wasn't optimistic about getting a good price for the ruined garment; it was filthy, stained, and torn in several places from the journey through the forest. The material was of a high quality, however, and she was shocked when the tailor offered her six silver shillings for the parts he could reuse. She hadn't realised nobles paid so much for their clothing.

With more than six silver shillings in her belt, Elizabeth started feeling nervous about her money again. She was carrying around a substantial sum now, and every time the coins jingled she imagined the eyes of a dozen thieves swivelling in her direction. She asked Joseph one evening whether she could leave her money with him instead. He agreed, offering to put it in a big iron-banded chest in his house.

Joseph's home was a comfortable stone building behind the workshop. There were two rooms inside, the first of which held a trestle table and chairs alongside a hearth with smoke holes in the mortar behind it. Elizabeth liked well-ventilated fires. It was always nice to stay warm without having to put your head in a cloud of smoke every time you stood up. She'd come to miss the comfort of a fire. It was getting warmer in the evenings, but the nights could still be bitterly cold in the hovel.

After work, Elizabeth emptied out her money on Joseph's table and began counting it. It was going to get mixed up with the rest of Joseph's coins, so she needed to know exactly how much was going in. When she struggled with the large numbers, the carpenter came to her rescue.

"Just break all the numbers down till they're nice and simple. There's twelve pennies to a shilling. Copper for copper, silver for silver."

"But I want to know how many silver shillings all these copper pennies are worth."

"Right," Joseph said with a patient nod. "Five copper pennies are worth one silver penny, so that means there's five copper shillings in one silver shilling."

Elizabeth's brow furrowed as she tried to follow the carpenter's path of reasoning. He explained it to her again, then told her how that translated into sixty copper pennies totalling one silver shilling. The prospect of counting so high was daunting. Sixty was a very large number, and Elizabeth was only used to counting to twelve most of the time. Pennies to shillings was easy to understand–you just had to count to twelve–but converting copper to silver was much more complicated. She tried to do what Joseph had suggested, adding up twelve copper pennies into one copper shilling, then five copper shillings into one silver shilling. She hit another snag when she ran out of copper pennies to count and started having to combine them with silver ones to reach her total. Joseph helped her along, sliding one silver penny to the side of the table and arranging five copper pennies in a row above it. That way, he said, she could visualise a silver penny for what it was worth in copper, pretending she was adding five copper pennies to the pile each time she added a silver one. The visual aid made things a lot easier for Elizabeth, and she managed to work through the rest of the counting without too many stumbles. Joseph seemed proud of her. It warmed her to think she might have impressed him. Being acknowledged by a self-made man made her feel like she might follow in his footsteps someday. She liked to imagine her father could have been a carpenter.

"You're a sharper girl than I took you for, Liz," he said as he locked up her coins in the money chest. "Your noble mistress taught you a lot, hm?"

"She didn't teach me proper counting," Elizabeth admitted, "though I've always wanted to learn."

"A carpenter needs to know his numbers. Measuring, geometry." He tapped the side of his nose. "But those are a master's secrets. Tell you the truth, it's counting out the money that gives me the biggest headache. Every time I hire the others for a big project I need to count their wages, budget for materials, buy new tools–then there's the rent each week. You can help me work it out if you'd like. You'll pick up your numbers fast doing that."

"My own wages won't be very hard to work out." She smiled sheepishly.

"You know I'd like to pay you more, but you're getting by, aren't you? Maybe we can persuade Rose to take you on as an apprentice someday, then you won't need to worry about money."

"I know. Thank you, Joseph. You've been very kind to me." She hadn't meant to make him think she was ungrateful. Even though Joseph could charge a master craftsman's wage for his work, most of it went back into the workshop's upkeep, his daily living expenses, and fees to the carpenters' guild. The guild was a weak institution, Joseph said, more concerned with infighting over petty politics than upholding the integrity of the trade, and some of its less scrupulous members were always eager to squeeze him for more than his fair share of silver. Joseph still made a good living, but he wasn't so rich that a bad year couldn't eat up his savings. Elizabeth was keenly aware that her own wages were one of the first expenses he'd have to cut if money became tight.

"Who was your old mistress, anyway?" Joseph asked.

"She was–" Elizabeth began, then hesitated, thinking about Count Francis and his knights. "A noblewoman."

"I know that, girl. What was her name?"

She said nothing. Joseph looked down at the floor and folded his arms. When he spoke again it was with the same slow, patient tone he'd used when he was explaining counting to her.

"Those tools you sold me didn't come from your brother, did they?"

Elizabeth shook her head.

Joseph sighed. "Alright, girl. I'm not going to try and guess whether you robbed those tools from your mistress, or your father wanted you to marry some man you didn't like, or whatever else it was that left you desperate enough to come to Tannersfield on your own. I think you're a decent young lady, so I won't ask. But whatever trouble it was that brought

110

you here, I don't want it turning up at my workshop. Understand?"

"It won't," Elizabeth said firmly. An image flashed through her mind of Sir Edward marching into the yard with a band of knights, overturning the benches and stabbing Joseph and his carpenters. "I promise it won't."

Joseph nodded with a grunt of satisfaction. "Alright. Then we'll say no more about it. Rose and I never had children, so the boys are our family. It may not be the richest business, but what we have here is important to us. I won't put it at risk."

"I hope I can tell you the truth someday, but right now I don't think I can."

Joseph grunted again and gestured toward the door. "Go and hurry home now. It'll be dark soon. Don't want you crossing town after sunset."

Elizabeth curtseyed and took her leave. Joseph was a good man. After the uncertainty of leaving Rosepath, he'd given her something she'd been afraid she might lose: hope for the future. The thought brought a lump to her throat as she walked home. She liked her new work. She liked Joseph and the carpenters. She would probably end up liking Rose, too. But she could take no joy in it while Kaylein was suffering. During the daytime, she could almost forget about what they'd been through, but at night she still had to hold the noblewoman and tell her, in words that had begun to sound increasingly hollow, how everything was going to be alright. Kaylein had no relatives she could go to—not within travelling distance, at any rate—and the noble families who might have taken her in could not be trusted if Count Francis now held sway in Tannersfield County.

They needed to find work for Kaylein. There had to be something that would motivate her to leave the house and regain her grip on life.

CHAPTER 7

The past weeks had been a tyranny of highs and lows upon Edward's spirit. Styling himself as lord of Rosepath was a privilege he indulged to its fullest, yet his attempts to find Lady Kaylein had borne no fruit. A ray of sunshine cut through his growing moroseness when he received letters from the capital informing him that Count Francis's allies had come out on top in the struggle for the crown. Ralf's pious son Fendrel would succeed him, leaving the clergy poised to exert their influence over the lad. That meant more taxes for the church, more autonomy for their abbeys, and seats for the clergy on governing bodies. It had been a contentious decision. Some nobles saw it as a challenge to their authority as lords of the land. Fortunately, the disagreements had been confined to court so far. No one seemed willing to stoke the fires of war over the dispute, only to posture and argue. Francis wrote that his army had been instrumental in dissuading the other nobles from challenging Fendrel's claim to the throne. He was employing a balance of bargaining and intimidation to quell the naysayers, but it was taking time. He expected not to return from the capital for several more weeks.

Edward idly wondered, as a newly-appointed page read him Francis's letters, just what sort of boy Prince Fendrel was and why he was willing to let the church walk all over him. He'd probably hear all about it once the count returned. He dismissed the page and sat down to supper with a few of his men in the great hall. The new servants he'd hired all seemed to be doing their jobs adequately, but he couldn't shake the feeling that they were a sloppier bunch than those who staffed Count Francis's castle in Cairnford. It wasn't good enough. The count was making great strides in the capital while he was here kicking his heels. He sliced an apple with his knife irritably, thinking back to his disappointing meeting with the sheriff the day after Francis left. His patron hadn't been enthusiastic about searching for Lady Kaylein. He said that if she had any sense she would have fled the county already. Edward tried to convince him otherwise, impressing upon him the danger she might pose if she was allowed to roam free, but for all his faults, the sheriff was still an enforcer of the king's law. He had no stake in Francis's scheme to take over Tannersfield County, and he would not go out of his way to hunt down an innocent woman. Yet he was a shrewd enough man to understand that a fractious relationship with his new count would come back to haunt him in the future. While he would not go looking for Kaylein himself, he was willing to turn a blind eye to whatever Count Francis's men did during their time here.

So Edward had sent soldiers to search the streets of Tannersfield and the surrounding villages. Day after day, they reported back with nothing. It was as if Kaylein had fallen into a hole and vanished.

With the hunt for the noblewoman at a dead end, Edward refocused his efforts on impressing Count Francis with something else: money. Nobles valued knights who grew their estates and delivered ever-swelling streams of silver to their coffers. Edward knew nothing about finance, so he went to the sheriff again for advice. His patron recommended he use Count Leo's stockpile to build houses in Rosepath, which would attract more tenants and more rent. Tannersfield was dealing with a baffling problem, one that many people feared but few ever witnessed: overpopulation. The town had been growing and growing, and as it grew it attracted itinerants from all over the county. Most moved on when they realised there was little work to be had and a dwindling amount of arable land to cultivate, but a few dregs always stayed behind. Those dregs built up like dirt between the floorboards, cluttering the streets with beggars until they overflowed into the countryside. Outlawry around Tannersfield was on the rise, and if the vagrants didn't find somewhere to settle it was only going to get worse. With no end to the problem in sight, the sheriff was making plans to grow the town watch, place new tolls on the gates, expand the jail, and build a new courthouse. The intention was to provide more jobs and keep the vagrants out while simultaneously giving him the power to deal with the growing number of lawbreakers.

Edward was nervous about investing in a project he didn't understand, so he called a court meeting in Rosepath to discuss the idea with some of the leading citizens. To his distaste, the loudest voice in the hall belonged to the wealthy merchant who'd laughed at him when he reported his failure to Count Francis. At first Edward wanted to have the man thrown out, but the merchant turned out to be a toadying sort, full of compliments and praise now that the balance of power had shifted. Edward agreed to take supper with him afterwards, recognising that he could use a merchant's help if he wanted to make money. They talked, and when the subject of building new houses came up the merchant, who people called Harald Redcloak, agreed with the sheriff's proposal. If Edward spread word that there was work to be had in Rosepath, people would flood in from Tannersfield and start renting his new houses. The idea seemed devilishly clever to Edward. He was glad he'd resisted the urge to have Harald thrown out. The man's simpering attitude could be abrasive, but his expertise was invaluable. No doubt he'd try to ply Edward for some favour later on, but a merchant couldn't make a knight do anything he didn't want to.

Within a few days of sending a herald to Tannersfield, Edward had filled all the empty positions in the castle. Count Leo's chaplain, steward, stabler, and a few others from the old guard remained, but most of the staff were brand new. The only servant Edward recognised from the original household was the girl he'd made identify the bodies in the great hall, the one who'd given him the dirty look. She kept her eyes on the floor now, where they belonged.

One evening after supper, Edward sent a herald to the village to summon Harald Redcloak. The merchant arrived swiftly, red-faced and perspiring from his hike up the hill.

"No horse today, Harald?" Edward asked with a hint of mockery. The merchant was a portly man and rarely went anywhere without his steed. He bowed and took off his feathered cap as he entered the great hall, sitting down on the other side of the table when a servant drew back a chair for him.

"I never want to keep you waiting, my lord. It's not much of a walk."

"It's no walk at all. Anyway, I need your advice. When do I start seeing money from my new tenants?"

"It's a long-term investment."

"Well, I need money now. Count Francis is finishing up his business in the capital, and I want a chest full of silver for him when he returns."

Harald stroked his chin in contemplation. "There are many ways to make money, my lord. Did you have anything particular in mind?"

"Hiring cheaper servants, selling the rest of Leo's stockpile, building more houses, something like that. Come on, you were full of ideas the last time we talked. How do I make this place rich in a few weeks?"

"If it's fast money you need then I'd advise against building any more houses or investing in trade. Those things take a while to pay off."

"Hm." Edward drummed his fingers on the table. "Count Leo made his money somehow, didn't he? Shouldn't I be receiving a tithe from his serfs? Rent from the farms?"

"That's a little more complicated. Most of that money belongs to the count of Tannersfield, and right now there is no count. It'll probably be collected by the sheriff until this trouble with the crown is settled."

Edward stood up and began to pace. There was little chance of him convincing the sheriff to hand over the money before Count Francis was formally named as Leo's successor. The problem was, he had no official authority as lord of Rosepath. The locals living in the street hovels were willing to hand over a few pennies when he told them he needed rent, but he might get in trouble if he started taking tithes he had no right to. The only reliable subjects he had were his soldiers.

"What kind of work is there for fighting men around these parts?" he asked.

Harald grinned and touched a finger to his lips. "Not much in Rosepath, but Tannersfield might be a different story. You've heard the talk, haven't you? There's a new saying going around: the blood clots in Tannersfield."

"Outlaws." Edward returned Harald's grin. "Of course. People say the forest's teeming with them." And he would be the hero who brought those thieves and murderers to justice. He didn't need all thirty of Count Francis's men to keep the castle safe; a few could be put to work doing what they did best.

"There's a coalition of my fellow merchants in the Tannersfield guild petitioning the sheriff to clean up the roads. He's paying a silver shilling to anyone who brings him a known outlaw, though I've heard he'll settle for their heads."

"We can do better than that. We'll have him hire us to search the forest and break up any outlaw camps we find." Edward was getting excited. This was exactly the kind of work he was good at, and it would please Francis to learn that his new county had been made safe while he was away.

"Again, you prove yourself as wise and prudent a lord as I knew you would be."

"Watch your sly tongue," Edward said. He startled Harald by leaping over the table and throwing an arm around him. He shook the merchant in the kind of rough embrace he would have shared with one of his soldiers. Harald didn't seem to enjoy it. "I'd take you with me if I didn't think you'd piss yourself at the sight of a sword."

"I endeavour to keep all my piss inside me in your company, Sir Edward."

Edward laughed. "Well, at least you know your place. Stay and have some wine with me. I'm getting a taste for the stuff."

They sat down again and Edward called for one of the servants. The girl from the night of the battle came in, looking sullen as always.

Edward scowled at her. "What's your name, anyway?"

"Daisy, milord."

"Get us some wine, and start looking a bit more like your namesake for once. I want you bright as a flower." He laughed at his joke and looked at Harald, who smiled politely. Edward carried on laughing as Daisy left, slamming his fist on the table. A shock of pain raced up his arm. He snatched his arm back with a curse, rubbing his fingers until the discomfort subsided. The wound Lady Kaylein's servant had given him was mostly healed, but it still bothered him with the occasional twinge. Though the throbbing had subsided, the numbness remained. He knew older men who'd lost sensation and movement in parts of their bodies after taking particularly deep wounds, and it dismayed him to think that

117

he might have suffered a similarly debilitating injury at such a young age. Still, it was only one finger, and it wasn't on his sword hand.

As he settled down to drink with Harald Redcloak, he fantasised about finding Lady Kaylein's straw-haired servant somewhere in the woods. He imagined her falling to her knees and begging for mercy as he grabbed a handful of her hair and pressed his sword to her throat. That would serve her right for attacking a knight. He probably wouldn't kill her, he decided, but drag her back to Rosepath and have her locked up. Perhaps she'd even tell him where Lady Kaylein was. The fantasy warmed Edward almost as much as the wine, and soon he was laughing again at Harald's obsequious jokes.

Three days later, Edward was in the forest with four reliable men-at-arms. They were a short distance south of Tannersfield, dressed in thick gambeson jackets and simple open-fronted helmets with tight chin straps. Mail was too heavy and noisy for this kind of work. Edward had hired a few woodsman's boys in town for a penny each and told them to bring him news of any vagrant camps. One had seemed reluctant about it, saying he didn't think the people living in the woods were outlaws, just poor folk who'd been forced to leave town. Edward didn't believe him. People didn't live in the woods unless they were desperate, and desperate people invariably turned to lawbreaking. He knew that shame all too keenly.

They'd been hiking for an hour before they found the first camp the boys had described. Edward froze and held up a hand to halt the others. A man's voice spoke a few unintelligible words beyond a screen of bushes, then an axe began striking wood at rhythmic intervals. Someone was taking lumber from the count's forest. That alone was reason enough to challenge them.

"Alderic, Stephen," Edward whispered. "Go around the

sides. Yell if they see you and we'll all run in."

His men moved off to do as he'd said. There wasn't much need for military planning, but Edward wanted to minimise the chances of the outlaws getting away. His heart beat faster as he crept forward, his fingers tightening around the hilt of his sword. This would be the first time he got to swing it since the night of the battle. He hoped some of the outlaws would put up a good fight.

Once he'd given Alderic and Stephen enough time to get into place, he shouldered through the bushes into the outlaw camp. Two scruffy men stood to his left, one holding a heavy woodsman's axe, the other a cup of water, while a woman and a third man sat by a fire. The woman's eyes moved to his sword, and she gasped in fear. The man with the axe took a step forward. Edward yelled for his men to attack.

Five swords fell upon the outlaws in an instant, killing one of the men in the blink of an eye. The armed one came at Edward, swinging his axe as if he was trying to cut down a tree. Edward sidestepped the blow easily, bringing up his sword and driving the point through the man's gut. He withdrew before the weight of the falling body could wrench the weapon from his hand. The couple who'd been sitting by the fire ran for the trees. Edward leapt over the fire pit and gave chase, feeling far more agile in his light clothing than he'd done when he chased Lady Kaylein. The couple broke apart, the man going left while the woman went right. Edward glanced around and saw Stephen catching up to the man, so he went after the woman. She was quick, but her dirty dress tangled around her legs as she ran, and when she inevitably tripped Edward caught up and grabbed her by the arm. To his relief, she didn't struggle or beg.

"Are there more of you nearby?" he demanded. "Tell me, and I'll take you to the sheriff alive."

The woman looked frightened. Edward lowered his sword slightly, then he remembered the wound between his fingers. The woman was holding something in her right hand. He saw

119

the glint of sunlight on a knife blade. Edward's muscles tensed reflexively. Before she had a chance to stab him, he raised his sword and plunged it through her chest. She went pale, eyes widening in shock as blood soaked through the front of her dress. She tried to say something before she died, but the sound became a wet cough in her throat. The woman fell to the ground choking on her own blood, twisting like a fish out of water.

Edward was breathing heavily. She'd almost taken him off guard, but he hadn't made the same mistake twice. There was no guilt this time, and that made him feel good. These people had been outlaws, and this one had been getting ready to stab him when he offered mercy. He'd acted appropriately.

Edward wiped his sword on the woman's body as her writhing slowly subsided. Stephen and the others came back dragging the body of the final man behind them.

"Good work, boys," Edward said. "Hopefully the next bunch give us more of a challenge, eh?"

Alderic gestured back to the camp with his sword. "What shall we do with the others? Take their heads for the sheriff?"

Edward wrinkled his nose at the thought. Yes, he supposed they'd have to. He wished they could have brought a cart into the forest to take the bodies back. The idea of carrying a bundle of severed heads around unsettled him. He'd make one of the others do it.

"Leave them here for now, but throw some more wood on that fire so we can find it again later. We'll take the heads on our way back."

Enthused by their early victory, they pressed on with the search. The other vagrant camps they'd heard about were all within half a morning's walk of Tannersfield, but Edward and his men were unfamiliar with the area, and it was hard to know where to find the right trails when so much of the forest looked the same. Stephen was the only man with hunting experience, so he took the lead.

By the early afternoon, they'd found a stream. Stephen

said it would lead them to one of the camps the woodsman's boys had described. He pointed to a patch of mud beside the water. It didn't take a hunter's eye to see that it had recently been churned up by several pairs of feet. They drew their swords and moved away from the stream, treading softly as Stephen led them up a steep earthen bank. Excitement tingled in Edward's stomach, but it was tinged with fear this time. The tracks looked like they belonged to at least half a dozen people. It was easy to feel confident when you outnumbered your enemy, less so when they held the upper hand. He noticed his wounded hand trembling and clutched it tight against his chest. He wasn't scared of outlaws.

The smell of smoke gave away the camp before they saw it. A light breeze rattled the branches, carrying the scent of burning wood and roasting meat. This time Edward kept his men in one group. If the outlaws outnumbered them, he didn't want to get separated. They stood just far enough apart to swing their swords and followed the smell of smoke until they spied a fire between the trees. It was bigger than the last one, set in the middle of a leafy clearing with half a dozen makeshift shelters surrounding it. Edward eyed the dwellings nervously. By the look of the dried conifer branches draped over the wooden scaffolds, the camp had been here for a while. These outlaws might stand and fight if they considered this place their home. Five people sat around the fire, but their backs were turned to Edward and the others. That was a stroke of luck, for there were no bushes to conceal their approach this time.

They reached the edge of the clearing and stopped. Edward was reluctant to advance further. That would mean putting two of the shelters at his back, and there might be more outlaws hiding inside. A young man with messy brown hair and a pointed chin looked up and noticed them.

"What do you want?" he yelled, jumping to his feet.

Edward hesitated, his mind racing. Should he try to arrest them? Perhaps he could take these ones back alive. Two more men came out of the shelters. One carried a rusty sword and looked like he was ready for a fight.

Edward charged. As soon as he'd committed himself to the attack, his nervousness deserted him. This was what he'd set out to do. The outlaws scattered, two running for the shelters while the others grabbed weapons. Within moments Edward and his men were among them, fighting in a half-circle as five outlaws matched them man to man. Only one had a sword, but two were wielding axes, and the others had sticks thick enough to knock a man senseless. Edward faced down one of the axemen. He backed off, holding himself just out of reach while he waited for an opening. This one was smarter than the last outlaw he'd fought. He held back as well, daring Edward to make the first move. Someone screamed to their right, but Edward didn't let himself get distracted. He edged back and forth, flicking the air with his sword to try and bait his opponent forward. Stephen stumbled against Edward's shoulder, and the outlaw lunged. He swung the axe like a soldier, measuring the blow so he didn't overextend. Edward struck out with a clumsy parry that took most of the impact on the edge of his sword. The shock of the heavy axe haft reverberated from his wrist to his shoulder. If he blocked another blow like that, his sword might break. The outlaw yanked his weapon free and swung again. Edward dodged past him, taking advantage of the man's short weapon to be more aggressive. He swung. The outlaw dodged. Sweat dripped from Edward's brow, but he was grinning. This was a real battle, without doubt or uncertainty.

Now that he'd turned around, Edward could see what was happening behind him. His men were all still on their feet. Two outlaws had fallen, but more were coming out of the shelters with clubs. They needed to put down their enemies quickly to even the odds. He lunged in and stabbed at his opponent's chest. The man tried to back off, but he wasn't fast enough this time. The tip of Edward's sword pierced his shirt and slipped between the ribs. The wound might not have been fatal, but it was enough to take the man out of the fight. Edward withdrew his blade and spun around. Before he knew it, he was fighting two men at once, one wielding a sword, the other a club. Edward had never fought two people simultaneously. A fleeting fear gripped him, but the rhythms of combat swept it aside. Steel rang as he swatted away a wild stab. He stumbled as the club knocked him in the arm, leaving his guard wide open. To his surprise, the swordsman backed off rather than going in for the kill.

They were afraid of him. Even without his mail and horse, they could tell they were facing a knight. The thought emboldened Edward. He threw a vicious cut at the outlaw with the club. The blow was so fierce it cleaved through the wood and chopped the whittled branch in half, carrying through and gashing the outlaw's arm. He fell back with a cry. Edward rounded on his remaining opponent. The battle was almost over. Half a dozen bleeding outlaws lay on the ground, and the fight was going out of the others fast.

With a roar of aggression, Edward leapt forward and swung at the swordsman, clashing against his blade once, twice, then throwing a thrust beneath his guard when he stumbled. The outlaw keeled over with a scream of pain. Edward swung at his hand and disarmed him, taking the man's sword away along with some of his fingers. He wanted to relish the sight of his victory, but the look on the man's pain-stricken face sickened him. He stepped on the outlaw's stomach and finished him with a stab through the chest.

"Check the shelters!" Edward yelled as the last of the outlaws fell. Excitement burned through his body like hot wine. He'd not felt this powerful since the battle in the keep. Blood pounded in his ears and perspiration ran from his face, but he felt like he could've run a hundred miles. Besides a rising bruise on Stephen's cheek, none of his men looked like they'd been hurt. They ran into the shelters and rounded up the remaining outlaws, dragging out two women and the brown-haired man who'd spotted them.

"Bring them here," Edward called, panting as he wiped off his blade. One of the women was young, perhaps fifteen. The other had grey hair and looked like she might have been her grandmother. The brown-haired man glanced between the women and Edward with terror in his eyes.

"There are more of you out here," Edward said, pointing at the man with his sword. "Where are they?"

He swallowed fearfully, but the old woman spoke first.

"What will you do to them?" She was trying to sound brave, but her voice wavered.

Edward moved his sword to point at her. "I'm going to deliver the sheriff's justice."

"We've broken no law!"

"Then why do you have swords and clubs?"

"We need to protect ourselves!"

"From what? Deer and squirrels?"

The old woman's lip trembled. This time there was hatred in her voice. "From men like you."

"Me?" Edward laughed. "I'm a servant of the king!"

"You're a beast and a devil."

She was looking at him the same way Daisy had the night of the battle. There was such malice in the woman's expression, such loathing and disgust, that the shock of it broke through Edward's exuberance. She truly believed he was a villain.

Indignation stung Edward like salt water on an open wound. How dare she, an outlaw, make him feel that way! He wanted to plunge his sword through her chest then and there, but something else took hold of him. It was a feeling deeper than anger, and it writhed inside him like a snake. The tip of his sword moved to point at the girl instead.

"Alderic. Put her head in the fire."

The girl started screaming, but it wasn't her screams Edward was interested in. The look of horror on the old woman's face fed the hungry serpent inside him. His heart beat faster, pounding hot and hard in his ears. He wanted to squeeze the defiance out of her. She was the wicked one. The devil. The witch. He could do anything he wanted out here in the woods, and right now he wanted to make this old woman regret the look she'd given him.

"Don't!" she wailed, crawling forward to grip Edward's leg as Alderic dragged the terrified girl toward the flames. "I'll tell you what you want to know!"

"I know you will," Edward said, his left hand burning with pain as he clenched it tight. "Or your head's going in that fire next."

CHAPTER 8

Tannersfield was abuzz with the news that a new king had been crowned. Elizabeth missed the marketplace announcement from the royal herald, but when she went to pay Emma her rent that evening it was all anyone was talking about. She got the full story from Joseph the next day. King Ralf was dead, and his fourteen-year-old son Fendrel was on the throne. Everyone had expected Ralf's steward Nicolas to take his place. Though Fendrel was Ralf's direct successor, it was unwritten law that no man or woman should take the throne before their twentieth birthday. The natural solution should have been for Fendrel to remain Crown Prince while Nicolas ruled until he was older. No one seemed to know why tradition had been bucked this time. There were rumblings that great armies had massed at the capital, which meant the peace of the kingdom might have hinged on the outcome. The threat of war disturbed Elizabeth, but it seemed like everything had been settled by the time the king's herald arrived. For now, she was content to forget about matters of succession and get on with her work. Joseph shared her mindset.

"Royals can make the laws, we'll make the furniture," he

told her. "I know what I'd rather be doing."

Elizabeth liked Joseph's way of looking at things. It seemed a common perspective among master craftsmen. The world was a big place, and once you started worrying about kings and dynasties you started feeling like an ant in a storm, where one stray raindrop might wash you away. People who dedicated their lives to the intricacies of a craft didn't have time for worries like that. They had too many other important thoughts to fill their heads with.

It continually amazed Elizabeth just how clever Joseph was. Even though he didn't care for matters of politics, he still seemed knowledgeable about the world. She guessed he'd been educated in a schoolhouse, for he could read and write along with having a strong grasp of history and mathematics. His knowledge of numbers didn't stop at being able to add up money, either; he could use numbers to make cuts in timber that would bring precise angles out of the wood, ensuring joints fit snugly and frames didn't break. Elizabeth could watch him sketch for hours using his square and straight edge to make those miraculous calculations. Every time he ran out of writing charcoal, it gave her a happy little lift to bring him a new piece.

Elizabeth hadn't been counting the days since she left Rosepath, but she guessed it had been close to a month now. She hadn't seen Sir Edward in Tannersfield again. There had been talk of soldiers in town a few weeks ago, but they seemed to have moved on as well. Count Leo's death was still a popular topic of conversation in the public houses, and most people seemed to think Kaylein had either fled the county or been killed alongside her brothers. Sitting and listening to such conversations made Elizabeth's stomach flutter uncomfortably, especially when people made up their own gruesome accounts of what had happened. Sir Edward's name came up often, and it dismayed Elizabeth whenever she heard people speak of him in a positive light. Some townsfolk seemed to regard him as a local hero, while others decried him as a traitor who'd turned against the lord of his home county. The latter sort were usually drunk, for it was unwise to speak ill of knights in public. Still, there were rumours that a curse had fallen over Rosepath since Edward's arrival. People said grisly things had been happening in the forest, describing packs of wild animals, outlaws, and vicious devil-worshipping swordsmen who butchered anyone who stayed out after dark.

Elizabeth shared the gossip with Kaylein every evening along with news from the workshop. Kaylein smiled when Elizabeth spoke excitedly about how she could count copper pennies into silver shillings now, but there was always a strained, weary look in her eyes, as though she was fondly recalling something from another lifetime that she could see, but no longer touch. Elizabeth hoped the smiles were a good sign. She'd tried several times to find work for Kaylein, but jobs only seemed to be getting scarcer in Tannersfield. The small exodus from Rosepath had left even more beggars on the streets. A week ago, Elizabeth had threatened a young man with her knife when he tried to grab a loaf of bread from her, only to realise a moment later that he was Gilly Tailor's son. She'd torn off a third of the loaf and given him two copper pennies.

Besides the lack of work, no further ill fortunes befell Elizabeth and Kaylein. They always made sure to keep their door barred after dark. Thieves wanted easy prey, so they took care to make themselves difficult pickings. Elizabeth wore her money belt open over her dress whenever she was at Emma's house, showing off that it held nothing besides a long, sharp knife. As long as they were careful and alert, they could survive on the north side of town.

That was why, when Elizabeth returned home later than usual one evening, she was shocked to find their door half-open. Kaylein rarely went out by herself, and never this late. Hurrying over, she put down her bread and beer and took her knife out. She pushed the door inward with a tense arm. The hovel was empty.

"Kay?" Elizabeth called, glancing anxiously up and down the street. The shadows had already lengthened across the road. Elizabeth put her food and drink inside and tucked her knife into her belt, but she kept her fingers on the handle. Her first thought was that Kaylein must have gone to Emma's, but she'd just come from there. She went down the street and stopped at some of the open doors, asking her neighbours whether they'd seen Kaylein. Some of them weren't even aware she'd been living with another person.

By the time she got to the end of the street, her anxiety was gnawing a hole in her stomach. The light was fading by the minute. She thought for a terrible moment that she might never see Kaylein again, and she began running. The idea of Kaylein disappearing without a word frightened her more than the thought of Sir Edward.

After a hurried search of another street, Elizabeth forced herself to stop and think. She was breathing hard, and if she kept running without direction she'd exhaust herself. What if Kaylein had just gone to empty their lavatory bucket in the river? Elizabeth usually did that herself in the mornings, but sometimes she forgot. Perhaps the noblewoman was finally taking to the dirty jobs she'd used to leave to her servants. Yes, that was much more likely. There was no reason to work herself up into a panic.

Retracing her steps, she made her way to the collapsed part of the old town wall and headed out past the dwellings at the river's edge. Elizabeth and Kaylein usually went upstream to a small wooden footbridge to do their washing. Some of the town women gathered there to bathe on Saturdays. Kaylein had reluctantly come along the last two times, but she'd been deeply uncomfortable and had refused to take her dress off despite everyone else being naked. Elizabeth tried to tease her good-naturedly about it, but Kaylein wasn't very amused. The memory brought on another pang of anguish. Elizabeth hurried faster toward the bridge. In the dim light, she could see a figure sitting near the middle, their legs dangling over the edge where the water was deepest.

Elizabeth slowed as she drew nearer, letting out a sigh of relief as she recognised her friend's chestnut hair.

"Kay?" she said, hearing the little bridge creak as she stepped forward.

Kaylein turned her head slightly, but she kept her eyes on the water racing past beneath her toes. Elizabeth worried she might be swept away if she fell in this close to the middle. She didn't think Kaylein could swim.

"I was worried sick about you," Elizabeth said. "We should go home before it gets dark. I left our bread and beer in there with no one to watch it. The rats'll have supper for us if we don't hurry."

"Did you hear the news?" Kaylein said in a quiet voice.

"About the king?"

Kaylein shook her head. "Some men from the town watch were talking about it at Emma's earlier. King Fendrel has made Count Francis the duke of Cairnford and Tannersfield." She paused, letting the words hang in the air for a moment. When she spoke again, her voice cracked. "They're not even going to punish him. He's being rewarded for what he did."

Elizabeth sat down and tried to put an arm around her shoulders.

"Don't tell me it'll be alright!" Kaylein said, recoiling from her touch. "It won't! I know it won't. I'm not a stupid child anymore."

"It could be, if we forget about Rosepath and try to move on."

Tears fell upon Kaylein's hands. "That isn't alright. Nothing will ever be the same as it was before."

"It'll be different."

"I know." Kaylein drew in a shaky breath. "But I can't live with it. I can't stay here, Liz. It'll kill me."

"You just need to find work, that's all. We've got a house

and money, and with a bit of luck we can move somewhere nicer soon. The tradesmen on Joseph's street give me a penny here and there to run errands. I reckon we could afford to rent one of their rooms in a few months."

"A few months." There was a bleak note in Kaylein's voice. "I'll have dropped myself into this river by then."

A chill pricked Elizabeth's skin. She gripped Kaylein's arm tight. "You don't mean that."

"I sit here every day and think about it. You're always at work, so you don't know." She paused again. "But you're right. I know I can't. Mother wouldn't want me to. Father would be ashamed."

Elizabeth wished she knew what to say to make her friend feel better. She'd thought the passage of time was helping Kaylein, but maybe she'd only been seeing what she wanted to see. Things had been getting better for her ever since she started working for Joseph, and that had blinded her to the truth that Kaylein was slowly drowning in her despair. She tried to imagine what it must have been like, sitting alone in their house for weeks on end with nothing but the memories of her dead family for company. A lump rose in her throat.

"I think I'm going to give myself to the convent," Kaylein said.

Elizabeth blinked in shock. "You can't be a nun! You're a noblewoman."

"No, I'm not. I'm nothing now. My father's estate belongs to Francis."

"Still, some nobleman might want to marry you. Maybe if you had a powerful husband the king would change his mind?" Elizabeth's heart ached with a feeling of desperation.

"I don't want that. I've thought about it a lot. I'd probably be fighting all my life for something I might never achieve. Even if I got Rosepath back, Francis would never let me forget about it. Hugh and Barnard always made fights between lords sound so magnificent and heroic, but they're not. They're bloody and horrible."

Elizabeth felt hope slipping away from her. Why did she feel like this? The convent was probably the best place for Kaylein. It would provide work and shelter, and educated women often flourished in the church.

"Maybe I could talk to Joseph and get him to hire you on?"

"You said he barely agreed to hire you."

"But–" Elizabeth pleaded. "Don't go, milady."

Kaylein turned and touched her cheek. She looked very much like her mother in that moment, calm and acceptant beneath the weight of the world. "I will lose my mind in that house, Liz. You've done so much for me, and I shan't ever forget it, but I don't think it's enough. I have to look to God now."

Elizabeth's heart sank. Deep down, she knew Kaylein was right. The broken and destitute often found meaning in service to God when all else failed them. The nuns would feed and clothe her, and she would be safe from the dangers of the town and Count Francis's knights. It was so obvious she should've suggested it herself.

But she didn't want to lose her friend.

"You were going to buy your house the day we left Rosepath, weren't you?" Kaylein said. "I want you to be able to do that here instead. I know you like working with the carpenters. It isn't fair for you to waste all your money supporting me when you should be saving for the future."

"It's no trouble, milady."

Kaylein shook her head. "You don't have to call me that anymore."

For weeks Elizabeth had been the one mothering Kaylein. Now their positions were reversed. She felt like a child who couldn't let go, while Kaylein was making the hard, sensible decision that was best for both of them. All Elizabeth could think about was how empty the house would feel with Kaylein gone.

She sniffed and wiped her nose. "Do you think they'll let

me visit you at the convent?"

"I don't know. I hope so."

Elizabeth pulled her into a tight hug. Her eyes felt hot and painful. She wished they were back in Rosepath, with Lady Eleanor running the house and Kaylein reading her books and Count Leo shouting at everyone. Somehow, she'd believed they would eventually return to something resembling that life. Maybe not in a castle, but a nice stone house in the countryside, where Kaylein would marry a kind, handsome nobleman and Elizabeth would be their housekeeper.

But that wasn't to be. Kaylein was going to become a nun, and the church would be her new family. Elizabeth wondered whether she should go with her. She wouldn't need to worry about money as a nun. Perhaps she'd even find new purpose serving God? But Elizabeth had never been an exceptionally pious girl. She said her prayers and went to church, but she couldn't conceive of forsaking a normal life in service to the Lord. It was people like Joseph and Lady Eleanor who inspired her, not priors and bishops.

When she broke the embrace, she realised Kaylein had been squeezing her back just as hard. She stood up and helped her to her feet.

"In a few years, you'll probably be an abbot," she said, trying to smile.

"Abbess," Kaylein corrected her.

"See, you already know everything about it."

Despite the fading light, they took a slow walk back to the house. Elizabeth tried to keep thinking about how good the nunnery would be for Kaylein. The Rosepath monks had always been reading books. They recited verse and practised all sorts of intricate rituals in church. Kaylein would be good at those things. Maybe she'd teach other girls to read and write in a schoolhouse. Yet no matter how hard she tried, Elizabeth couldn't shake the feeling that she was losing her last little piece of Rosepath. She lay awake that night feeling the same way she'd felt after her mother died; the same way she'd felt when she realised Sam was never coming home. It wasn't fair. Why did things have to be this way? It felt like Count Francis and Sir Edward had returned one last time to take Kaylein away from her. Did men like them even understand the hurt they inflicted on the world?

She caught a few fitful hours of rest before dawn, dreaming that she was running down the road from Rosepath again. Sir Edward was chasing her as she pulled a flagging Kaylein along, but the road was muddy and it kept sucking her down. No matter how hard she ran, the town always seemed just out of reach.

She woke feeling stiff and weary.

That morning, Kaylein left for the convent. She promised she would visit the workshop if she could, but she didn't know whether novices were allowed to come and go freely. Nuns were supposed to live secluded lives behind convent walls. Elizabeth's fatigue made their parting a painful one. She clung to Kaylein in the road and begged her to reconsider once more. Kaylein looked like her mother again as she told her that her mind was set. They each had their own paths to follow now.

Elizabeth stared after her long after she'd disappeared into the marketplace crowd.

She tried not to think about the empty house that would be waiting for her that evening. When she arrived at the workshop, Joseph seemed to sense her sullen mood. He let her be for a while, then spoke with her when they were alone in the yard.

"That's the glummest face I've seen on you since the night you turned up here."

"Sorry. I'm sure I'll be feeling better tomorrow."

"What is it?" He frowned. "Woman's time?"

"What?"

"It's just that Rose always gets a bit–Ah, never mind. It

doesn't put her in any better of a mood when I try to talk to her about it, either."

"Oh, no, it isn't that." She didn't feel much like talking, but Joseph's concern warmed her. "My friend I've been living with left to become a nun today."

"God bless her, then. Hope she's one of the lucky ones. Even the convents are turning folk away these days."

"They won't turn her away. She can read and write like a scholar, and she probably knows the holy books better than they do."

Joseph looked curious, but he didn't press her for further details. He knew that Elizabeth's mysterious companion was one of the things she didn't like talking about.

"At least you'll have a bit more money for yourself," he said. "Speaking of which, Colin Brewer on Market Street needs half a dozen barrels made."

"You don't make barrels, do you?"

"No, but he thinks every man who works with wood does the same job. Doesn't know the trade as well as his mother yet. There's a cooper by the name of William two streets over. Go and let him know, would you? He'll thank us for putting the business his way. Might even give you a penny for the trouble."

Elizabeth headed off to pass the message along. She appreciated Joseph's efforts to keep her busy. There wasn't a lot to do at the workshop that day, and errands were a welcome distraction. After she came back, Joseph sent her across town with another message for a senior member of the carpenters' guild. Joseph didn't like guild business—it was too much like dealing with lords and lawmakers to him—but he had a responsibility to his fellow craftsmen to uphold the integrity of the trade in Tannersfield. The guild planned to bring a petition before the sheriff next week, and Joseph was obliged to join them if he wanted to remain in their good graces.

On her way across town, Elizabeth passed by the

nunnery. Kaylein would be in there now, locked away behind those cold grey walls. She hoped the nuns would treat her kindly.

That evening she stayed at the workshop until the sun went down and Joseph shooed her out to lock up. On the way home, she fantasised about living in a big stone house like his, where she could light a warm fire every night and lie down on a mattress stuffed with soft wool. The daydream kept her going until she arrived back at her gloomy hovel. She left the door open a crack so she could watch the light fade while she ate her bread and drank her beer. She'd bought enough food for two people without thinking. If the rats didn't get at it, she'd take the leftover bread to the workshop and share it with the apprentices tomorrow.

Eventually the street grew dark and Elizabeth barred the door. This would be the first time she'd slept here alone. Back in Rosepath, she'd gone to sleep embracing her mother's old cloak when she felt this way. After her mother died, she'd come to think of the people at the castle as her family. She put her arms around herself and lay down, trying to find a comfortable spot on the straw. She usually slept with her back against Kaylein, and without her friend there she kept rolling over uncomfortably.

Perhaps Joseph and the carpenters would become her new family. She wanted to hope so, but the thought made her feel afraid and foolish. They'd only known her a month. There was every chance things wouldn't work out and she'd have to find herself another job elsewhere. It was silly to start thinking of people she barely knew as family. Yet without Kaylein, she felt desperately lonely.

Silly or not, the only thing that helped her sleep that night was the thought of going back to the workshop tomorrow.

CHAPTER 9

Kaylein lied for the first time in her life the day she came to the convent. She'd told little white lies before, of course, but this was different. It was a true lie, a lie told in a house of God, and the instant she spoke it, she knew she had crossed a threshold the old Kaylein never would have. She'd changed in the month since her family died.

The sisters at the nunnery showed little interest when she knocked on the gates, but they allowed her inside and made her wait in the cloisters with two other female visitors. Kaylein wondered whether they were hoping to be admitted as novices as well, but she didn't feel confident enough to ask. For what felt like hours she stood staring at a statue in the small open courtyard. It resembled the carvings she'd seen of Saint Caridwen, a woman who had purportedly carried the ashes of a benevolent cardinal hundreds of miles so he could be returned to the place of his birth. She was depicted with bare feet and a hooded cloak, with the cardinal's urn held up in both hands toward heaven. Kaylein recalled her own shoeless journey through the forest and felt a surge of empathy for the saint—or perhaps she was more like the dead cardinal in her story? She'd felt half dead as

Elizabeth all but carried her here, fighting off knights and giving up her own boots so that she might reach safety.

Kaylein had never been able to express it properly, but she was deeply fond of Liz. Even before they left Rosepath, she'd always looked forward to their rides in the forest. Despite being of low birth, Liz was bright and attentive in a way Kaylein admired. One day she would find a way to repay her for all she'd done.

A nun startled her by placing a hand on her shoulder. She'd become lost in her thoughts staring at the statue of Saint Caridwen. Unlike the other sisters, who dressed in plain black robes, this woman was clad in white.

"The mother superior will see you now," she said.

Kaylein followed the older woman to the back end of the cloistered walk and into the chapel beyond. The nun's boots echoed confidently in the quiet space, but Kaylein's steps were a silent tiptoe. Beyond the altar, there was a small hall with three doors leading in different directions. The one directly opposite the chapel appeared to be the prioress's room. The nun knocked on the door and waited for a response.

Kaylein had never been in a convent before. She'd glimpsed parts of Rosepath's small monastery when she went to church, but women were not allowed inside unless they had important business with the prior. From her readings, she'd gleaned that they were supposed to be plain and humble places, but, as she was quickly learning, many things in the world were not as neat and tidy as books made them seem. The voice of the prioress called for them to enter, and Kaylein was ushered inside.

"Sit down," the prioress said, gesturing to a chair near the door. The room was simply furnished, but not as devoid of character as Kaylein had expected. The prioress, middle-aged and softly featured with curly blonde hair beneath her hood, sat at a writing desk beside the bed. She was clad in the same white robes as the other nun, a mark of her seniority. A tall cabinet stood against the wall displaying a collection of magnificently decorated book covers through its open doors.

"What has brought you here, my child?" the prioress asked.

"I would like to join the convent."

"Sadly, the convent is full. My novice mistress is already complaining about her workload, and we are running out of space in our dormitories. There are many smaller priories nearby that would welcome you. That being said, I would be willing to consider accepting a woman of exceptional talent." She gave Kaylein an uncomfortably knowing look. "Would you be a woman of exceptional talent?"

Kaylein answered quickly, for the thought of wandering the roads in search of another convent terrified her. "I am familiar with all seven of the prime scriptures. I am numerate and versed in the history of the church, and I know a little about medicine as well."

"I assume that means you can read and write, also?"

"Yes, Mother."

"What is your name?"

"Kaylein." She said it without thinking and immediately corrected herself: "Kay."

"You will use your given name before God. Where did you come from, Kaylein?"

This time she knew she had to lie. Elizabeth could do it easily, but when Kaylein tried her mind went blank. She hadn't thought to make up a story about who she was. The decision to give herself to the convent had been so monumental it had overshadowed all other concerns. Just as the silence became uncomfortable, she remembered the name of the village where Elizabeth had been born.

"Granary."

"Is that so? And why did you feel the need to leave that little village and come all the way here? Green Grange Abbey is much closer."

Kaylein's face began to burn. The mother superior could

see right through her. Was God watching, too? Judging her for the lies she was telling to earn a place in His house?

"My mother died," she said, trying desperately hard not to think about Rosepath. "She was very sickly and she passed on. I have no money and nowhere to live." The words began tumbling out of her mouth as lies gave way to truth. "I don't think anyone else will take me in. I'm nothing but a burden, and I don't know where else to turn. If I try to go home I fear something terrible may happen, but if I do nothing I will—" She had to stop and swallow. The prioress held up a hand to forestall any further explanation. Her expression had softened slightly.

"I know you did not come from Granary, Lady Kaylein. You are Count Leo's daughter. I recognised you the moment you walked in."

Kaylein didn't know what to say. She felt her chest tightening and her throat closing up.

"I'm sorry I lied," she said weakly.

"You will do penance for it. I understand why you came here. It must have been a heavy decision for a woman of your birth."

"Please don't tell anyone who I am."

The prioress shook her head. "God demands the precept of truth. If you are to stay here, it must be as Kaylein, once daughter of Leo, now daughter of God."

"But men have tried to kill me because of my name."

"As I said, you will be Count Leo's daughter no longer. If what I have heard is correct, I understand that a very powerful man deposed your family. That man is a known ally of the church and our new king. He will not touch you so long as you live within these walls." The prioress stood and approached her, then held out the back of her hand. Kaylein was familiar with church rituals. The ceremonial act of kissing the prioress's hand marked a solemn commitment. The thought of such a subservient gesture rankled the proud young noble Kaylein had once been, but the desperate woman she'd become could have wept with relief. She would throw aside her noble airs in an instant to feel safe again.

"Are you certain you will be able to protect me from him?"

"God's protection is worth more than a thousand soldiers."

Falling to her knees, Kaylein leant forward and kissed the back of the prioress's hand.

Convent life was hard at first. Kaylein had to sleep on a stone slab in a bare room with no door and a narrow window that let in a draft. She was cloistered with a dozen other novices in one of the nunnery's western buildings. Most of the others had cots in a proper dormitory, but the lack of space meant Kaylein had to sleep in a cell normally reserved for meditation. A thin blanket and her new black robes were all she had to cushion her bony body. In the mornings, she went to prayer in the chapel with the other nuns, then she ate, washed, and prayed again. There was a great deal of prayer. It surrounded every aspect of convent life. Kaylein found it difficult to concentrate at first, but eventually the verses became a soothing mantra. When she'd been living with Elizabeth, her worst enemy had been her own thoughts. Prayer acted as a shield against the darkness in her mind.

After breakfast and prayer, she went to the convent's schoolhouse with the other novices, but the novice mistress quickly realised that Kaylein was gaining nothing from the classes. She was already more literate than any of the others and probably had a better grasp of theology than the sister teaching them. Kaylein was excused from schooling and given time to meditate instead. She didn't like meditation. It was too much like being alone in the house again. During those moments, she questioned whether she had made the right decision. Kaylein was faithful, but she was unsure whether her faith was strong enough to support a lifetime of devotion to God. Some of the other sisters seemed possessed of almost otherworldly zeal, be it for prayer, meditation, washing, spinning, brewing, weaving, or debating one another in chapter. They worked as tirelessly as farmers, and by the time the sun went down Kaylein was always exhausted from her meagre efforts to keep up. She wasn't used to the afternoon chores that kept the convent running. Laundry hurt her arms and made her sweat. After working with the hot water for too long, her hands became raw and started to bleed. The other nuns didn't seem to have the same problem. If she dared complain, they told her she was soft and lazy. She often went to sleep upset after a day in the laundry room, angry and hurt that the others thought so little of her. In the past, people like them would have held their tongues and curtseyed in her presence. Now they scoffed at her.

After a few days, she accepted that feeling sorry for herself wouldn't make the work any easier.

She stopped complaining, even when her hands bled and she grew faint from the heat. The others still thought she was lazy, but they were less vocal about it from then on. No matter how hard she tried, she never managed to work as fast as everyone else. There was always more washing to do. Along with their own garments, the nuns washed clothes for some of the locals in exchange for a modest fee. It was considered holy to have your clothes washed by nuns or monks, for whom the precept of cleanliness was one of the highest virtues.

Along with washing, Kaylein had to help with brewing and baking in the kitchen block, which she struggled with even more. Try as she might, she couldn't wrap her head around the precise steps and timings involved in the preparation of victuals. It gave her a newfound sense of respect for the cooks who'd served her father's household. For the most part, the nuns only ate plain vegetables, fruit, bread, cheese, and small portions of salted meat. That was already more than enough for Kaylein to cope with. She could only imagine the effort that must have gone into roasting, seasoning, stuffing, glazing, and presenting the dishes she'd eaten at her father's table.

She tried to do exactly what the other sisters told her when she worked in the kitchen block, for her attempts to figure things out on her own had led to half a dozen burnt loaves and a ruined barrel of ale. It made her feel like a child needing to be led around by the hand. She could tell the others would have preferred it if she wasn't there at all. The only saving grace was that the sisters working in the kitchen were older and kinder than the laundresses, so she didn't have to suffer additional mockery on top of her scoldings.

The one thing Kaylein did excel at, however, was writing. After the prioress realised she was gaining nothing from the schoolhouse and struggling with manual chores, she asked Kaylein whether she would like to try her hand in the writing room instead. She leapt at the opportunity. It had been a childhood dream of hers to pen books. Her mother had owned all sorts of books, collections of poems and plays, accounts of far-off countries, medical treatises, annals of the kingdom, philosophies, folktales, and more. She'd liked the books with long poems the best, for they always seemed to capture something romantic and whimsical that the drier texts did not. The religious canon had been part of her schooling as well, and she was endlessly fascinated by the way the philosopher monks of old had debated, analysed, and reinterpreted the word of God to pen the seven prime scriptures that canonised every precept of virtue and sin.

The next day, she was allowed into the writing room, a bright and pleasant chamber on the second floor of the chapter house next to the chapel at the northwest corner of the nunnery. It had to be high up, for rooms on the ground floor did not let in enough light for writing, enclosed as they were by the convent's outer wall. Through the big windows, Kaylein could hear townspeople passing by in the street below, but if she was ever caught gazing down the sub-prioress slapped her hand with a willow switch. She had to make do with listening. The convent could feel very insular at times, and being able to hear the bustle of people coming and going reminded Kaylein there was still a world outside.

After hearing of Kaylein's talents from the sub-prioress, the mother superior herself came to the writing room to examine her work. She asked her to pen a simple verse on a piece of parchment, then had her repeat the exercise in uniform lettering. Kaylein's hand was perfect, her lines straight and her inking clean.

From that day on, she was assigned to the writing room regularly, spending her afternoons copying books with the other scribes. The convent subsisted on a regular income from the farms it owned, its washing services, and the taxes every priory was entitled to under the king's law, but it was the books it sold that truly allowed it to grow wealthy. They cost as much as twenty silver shillings apiece, and a set of half a dozen easily fetched a gold crown. Kaylein had never thought about how much money her father paid for her books when she was younger, but living with Elizabeth had given her a startling appreciation for just how wealthy they'd been. If most people earned just a few copper pennies a day, the value of a single book represented at least a year's wages for a common labourer.

Every other afternoon, Kaylein would sit with a finished book weighted open on a stand above her desk and a sheaf of unbound pages in front of her. She replicated the text from the open book in painstaking detail between ruled lines on the blank parchment, using a sharp knife in her left hand to trim her quill and smooth out any mistakes she made in the lettering. The rhythms of the process absorbed her for hours. Sometimes the sub-prioress hovered nearby with her willow switch, but Kaylein rarely made mistakes, and when she did they were small enough that a careful scrape of her knife could usually correct them. The other scribes worked faster than her, but Kaylein's work was elegant and consistent, and she knew that with practice she would be just as fast as them.

Her efforts received little praise, for pride was a precept the nuns discouraged, but the lack of admonition told her she was doing well.

Kaylein's laborious chores in between writing days became more bearable once she had something to look forward to. Over time, the manual work began to lose its exhausting edge. Her hands developed callouses and stopped bleeding when she did laundry. Even kitchen work ceased to intimidate her once she stopped feeling like a burden. There were certain rhythms to it, just like writing. It would probably be years before she could be trusted to make food on her own, but at least she wasn't spilling water and burning herself anymore.

Three weeks after her arrival, the prioress spoke to her about her progress during a walk around the cloisters.

"It is always the way with novices that they take to some tasks more readily than others. A well-run convent is like a well-run castle—every servant has their place."

"Will I be able to fully commit myself to scribing soon, Mother Jane?" Kaylein asked.

"After you have taken your vows. Remember, you must cultivate patience. The tasks you dislike now will temper you into a better woman once you have grown to appreciate their importance."

"And when will I be allowed to go outside the convent?"

The prioress gave her a stern look. "You should not be so eager to leave. It is hard, I know, to give up the life you had outside these walls, but clinging to it will only make the separation harder. If you find the isolation too taxing, it may be a sign that God has no place for you here."

"I don't! I mean, He does. I believe He does," Kaylein stammered. She wanted to see Elizabeth again, but she also wanted to prove she could dedicate herself to life in the nunnery. It wasn't just faith that inspired her—though she hoped that would come in time—but the structure the convent had given to her shapeless existence. When she was absorbed in writing or exhausting herself with chores, the raw wounds of Rosepath lost their sting. She didn't know if they would ever heal completely, but it no longer felt like they were slowly killing her. Like a cut that had scabbed over, she could move without it hurting. In time, the scab might fade to a scar. The pain had been with her for so long now that she struggled to remember life without it. Part of her didn't want to. It seemed like a betrayal, somehow, to allow the burden of her family's death to be forgotten. It would be like admitting she no longer cared for them.

"You are a unique girl, Kaylein," the prioress said. She was a demanding but sympathetic woman, and Kaylein respected the pragmatic way she ran the convent. "Most of the desperate women we accept are your opposites. They know how to wash clothes and cook meals, but they've never set foot in a schoolhouse or picked up a quill. The few educated novices we receive often have aspirations of rising to greatness in the church, yet I don't see any such ambition in you."

Kaylein paused to think about it. The mother superior was always encouraging her to be thoughtful. She looked up at the statue of Saint Caridwen.

"I just want to be left alone. I don't want anyone to notice me."

"Why is that?"

Again Kaylein tried to peer inwards. Mother Jane was patient, allowing her to think as they paced around the cloisters. Kaylein shivered and wrapped her arms around herself as if trying to hide within the black folds of her robe.

"If I'm noticed, someone might come looking for me."

"And you fear they would do to you what they did to your father?"

Kaylein nodded.

"Have faith, Sister Kaylein. God would not have spared you your family's fate if he did not see some greater purpose in your future. You must take courage from that."

"Will God punish the men who killed my family?"

"If they are deserving of it, yes. Their spirits will suffer all the torments they visited upon you when they are judged in hell."

The thought soothed Kaylein in a morbid way. Hell was the place a bad person's soul went after they died, and there it remained until they grew to understand the wickedness of all of the wrongdoings they'd committed in life. Then, cleansed, their soul returned to the world and was reborn. Kaylein wondered why so many people were born evil if every soul was supposed to atone before it could return. Perhaps Mother Jane would explain it to her one day. She hoped she would go to heaven when she died, where her spirit would be able to relive all the goodness she had spread in life rather than suffering penance for her wrongdoings. She wanted to spread good. She imagined people reading the books she scribed and experiencing the same joy she'd felt when she read in her room at Rosepath Castle. A warm feeling spread through her chest.

Mother Jane stopped and smiled at her.

"I'm sorry, Mother," Kaylein said. "I have taken too much of your time."

"No, it isn't that. I saw a look of great peace come over you just now."

"Oh." Kaylein felt a little sheepish. "I was just thinking of heaven."

"I told you your father's enemies would suffer in hell, and you began thinking of heaven." She took Kaylein gently by the shoulders. "That is a pure thought for a nun to have. Hold on to those thoughts, Kaylein. You are a bright young woman, and your future in the church will be just as bright if you apply yourself. It may well be that the tragedy you suffered was in God's plan. It is often His way to inflict great hardship upon us so that we may better empathise with the suffering of others. Just remember that it is not our place to defeat all the evil in this world, only to ease its burden as much as we are able."

A warm sensation caressed Kaylein's heart again. Was this what priests meant when they spoke about being touched by God's light? It was the first pure feeling she'd experienced since leaving Rosepath. She resolved to reflect upon it in her meditations.

"Thank you, Mother," she said. "I think God did the right thing by bringing me here."

"God may have been your guide, but you were the one who stepped through the door. Have faith in yourself, and faith in Him will follow."

Kaylein averted her eyes. The mother superior had an uncanny knack of peering into her soul.

"I am not–" she faltered, unsure of how to phrase it. She'd been afraid of voicing this thought aloud, but after the conversation they'd just had, she felt like Mother Jane would understand. "I am not sure I'm as faithful as some of the other sisters. I came here because it seemed practical, not because I wished to devote my life to God."

Mother Jane smiled. "Service to God *is* practical. The prayers we say and the rituals we perform are not just acts of faith, but ways of reminding ourselves of our chosen purpose. A nun's purpose is to do God's work here in the world, whether we feel His presence strongly or not. A bailiff does not have to love his lord to serve him loyally, does he? If I turned away every faithless woman who came here, I would never have met many of my dearest sisters. It is natural that you need time to find your faith, Kaylein. For some, it never comes at all, yet that does not stop them from being good women who make this world a brighter place. As long as you remain dedicated to your duties here, I will not question the strength of your faith."

The warmth in Kaylein's chest continued to spread. The tethers binding her to the weight of her past felt looser. She really could be a new woman here: Kaylein, daughter of God.

She wouldn't have to worry about any of the things that had troubled her before. Marriage, politics, Count Francis—they didn't exist in the convent.

"Thank you, Mother Superior."

Mother Jane gave her a simple nod. She had probably meant for it to look formal, but a shimmer of joy radiated through her expression, and for a moment she looked as young and vibrant as an angel.

She has God's light, Kaylein thought.

When she retired to her cell, there was a stillness to her thoughts that lulled her to sleep despite the hard stone against her back and the draft blowing in through the window. It wasn't happiness—that was something she didn't think she would feel again for a long time—but it was one step closer. It was quiet, and it was pure. If she could keep holding on to that feeling, if she could reflect on it in her meditations and allow it to grow, then one day she might feel the same joy she'd glimpsed in Mother Jane.

Kaylein slept without dreaming, and when she woke she went to prayer with an open mind. She prayed for the spirits of her mother and father, her brothers, her servants, and for Elizabeth.

As she knelt in the chapel, the light from the arched windows fell upon her face and the warmth grew stronger in her heart.

CHAPTER 10

Francis returned to Rosepath two months to the day after his departure. Edward wondered whether he'd done it on purpose. The count–no, Edward had to keep reminding himself he was the duke now–had a talent for timing, never arriving too early if he could strike an impression by threatening to be late. He'd used that to his advantage the night they killed Count Leo, delaying the attack until his own men were just drunk enough to give them courage while Leo's were already raucous and sloppy.

The delay had been making Edward anxious. The help from Harald Redcloak combined with the sheriff's pay for putting down outlaws had kept Rosepath's coffers relatively full, but Edward didn't know whether he could keep paying his men indefinitely. He needed a proper estate for that, something he hoped Francis would reward him with upon his return.

Surely then the nightmares about the girl he'd burned in the forest would go away.

He ordered ten of his men to line up at the castle gates to welcome Francis back. He dressed himself in a fine silk cloak he'd found in the keep, kneeling in deference as the duke rode up with a company of men-at-arms behind him.

"Welcome back, my lord duke," he said with a smile, rising to his feet as Francis approached.

"Sir Edward," Francis replied curtly. A deep weariness etched the corners of his eyes, the look of a man who'd grown accustomed to sleepless nights. The tumult at the capital must have taken its toll on him. Edward noticed for the first time that there were hints of grey in his lord's sandy hair.

"Take the duke's horse to the stable," Edward said, waving over Roy the stable master. He'd probably have to replace the doddering old man soon, but that would be getting ahead of himself. Francis hadn't given him permanent stewardship of Rosepath Castle yet.

The horsemen dismounted and Edward took them to the keep, making sure to point out the new drawbridge on the way in.

"You should've got rid of it," Francis said. "A keep doesn't need a moat. Put it outside the castle walls, then it might be useful."

The duke's dismissal hurt Edward. He thought he'd been very resourceful in getting the drawbridge replaced without spending any money. He tried not to let his disappointment show, reminding himself that he had plenty of other accomplishments to impress his lord with. They sat down to eat in the great hall, where the servants had set out a supper of the finest preserved meats, wines, and cheeses left over from Count Leo's stores. Once his appetite was satiated, Francis turned straight to business.

"You didn't deal with Leo's daughter."

"I went to the sheriff straight away, my lord," Edward explained. "If he couldn't find her, no one can."

Francis stared at him across the table, thumbing the side of his goblet deliberately. "Really. When was the last time you spoke with the sheriff?"

"Just a week ago. There's been trouble with outlaws in the

forest, but I've made sure–"

"Then why didn't he tell you that Lady Kaylein has been living at the convent?"

Edward's mouth dropped open stupidly. He hadn't thought about Count Leo's daughter in weeks. It had seemed like a lost cause. Some of the men began to chuckle at his expression, and he shut his mouth quickly, feeling his ears burn with embarrassment.

"He should've told me about that," Edward muttered.

"It seems like neither of you have been keeping a very close eye on my county." Francis paused to take a bite of his meat, chewing it with agonising slowness. The ghostly pain lingering in Edward's left hand returned as he gripped the edge of his chair. Francis took a long drink from his goblet before continuing. "I suppose it's all worked out rather well for us, hasn't it?"

Edward's brow tightened in confusion.

"I'd have preferred her dead," Francis elaborated, "but this is the next best thing. Nuns divest themselves of worldly property. She isn't going to lay claim to her father's estate, and she won't be marrying anyone, either. I shouldn't think I'll have to worry about Tannersfield for the time being."

"You won't, my lord," Edward said, seeing his chance to steer the conversation in a more favourable direction. "The town's full of beggars and vagrants these days. We were worried the roads might be getting dangerous, but I've taken care of that. We've seen more than thirty outlaws dead or sent to the sheriff since you left."

"Thirty." Francis looked impressed. "How many of my men-at-arms did that cost you?"

"Not one, my lord." It was mostly true. A man had been killed in the forest last week by a poacher who was a deadly shot with a bow, but Edward had replaced him by hiring another soldier in Tannersfield. Francis wasn't likely to notice, and if he did he wouldn't care.

"My my. You've impressed me, Edward."

152

"That isn't all," Edward continued, emboldened by his lord's approval. "I blocked off that postern gate in the back wall, hired new servants for half the wage of the old ones, and built new houses in the village."

Francis swirled a mouthful of wine around his teeth before replying. "Start paying the servants a proper wage. It's no good to keep them unhappy. Sooner or later they'll leave to find better work elsewhere."

"But there's no work in Tannersfield."

"Do it anyway. This is my county now, and I won't have people pining for the days when Leo was their lord." Francis scowled, a look of hatred flashing across his face. "I'm glad I got to kill that man myself."

Edward bowed his head. "I'll see to it." Francis had always nursed an insatiable hatred for Count Leo despite the amicable show they put on in public. All Edward knew was that they'd been brothers-in-arms as young men, both earning themselves counties through loyal service to King Ralf during the last great war. Part of Edward was disappointed that war hadn't broken out over this new succession, for then he might have fought his own path to glory the same way Francis had.

"These outlaws," Francis said, "did you bring them all to stand trial?"

"Yes, all the ones who didn't try to kill us." That was a partial lie as well. Some of the outlaws who surrendered had gone to Tannersfield or been locked up at Rosepath Castle, but in the heat of the moment most ended up on the wrong end of a sword.

"I can't imagine many outlaws finding the courage to fight a company of armed men," Francis said.

"They can be aggressive when they're defending their homes."

"Homes?" Francis's eyes narrowed. "You know not everyone living in the forest is an outlaw, Edward."

"These ones were! I swear, my lord, half of them would've

153

killed us if we hadn't killed them first."

"Were all these people known lawbreakers?"

Edward almost choked on the food he'd just swallowed. "I have to assume so."

"Even as my vassal, you're still bound by the king's law. If you killed innocent people, you could stand trial for it."

A tickle of fear ran up Edward's back. That couldn't be true, could it? No, the people in the forest had all been guilty. He had nothing to fear. Besides, even if he'd made a mistake, who was going to challenge him over it? He could hardly be blamed for the occasional slip, not when the woods were so rife with footpads.

"The sheriff wouldn't allow it," Edward said. "Anyway, I've done nothing wrong."

"I hope so," Francis said. "The church made sure I was pardoned, but I might have been in trouble if Nicolas took the throne. I took a measured risk in killing Leo. Don't run yourself into an early grave by getting excited about butchering peasants. You might be able to get away with it when the kingdom's eyes are elsewhere, but not now that things have settled down."

Edward swallowed, his throat tightening even further. He thought again about what he'd done to the teenage girl in the forest and the horrendous sounds she'd made when her face began to burn. He'd stabbed her with his sword before the fire could kill her just to make her stop. Then he'd cut off her grandmother's head when she kept screaming. The remaining young man had been deathly silent the whole time. Edward's taste for violence had soured afterwards, so he'd taken him back to the castle and locked him up in a room at the base of the south tower. He was probably still there, assuming someone was remembering to feed him. Edward had tried his best to forget the whole thing. The anger he'd felt that day had made him do something terrible. He was a righteous man, he knew it in his soul, but not everyone would understand that. Francis and the sheriff could never find out about what he'd done to those outlaws.

"We made some good money from it, anyway," Edward said in a dry voice. The others had started giving him strange looks. He cleared his throat and took a gulp of wine.

"If I want money, I'll get it from my new land," Francis said. "Let the sheriff deal with the outlaw problem. It's his job, not yours."

"If that's what you want, my lord."

"It is." Francis gave him a stern look and went back to his food. Edward's shoulders loosened in relief. He'd been afraid Francis would be furious with him, but he only seemed mildly annoyed. This was all Harald Redcloak's fault. He was the one who'd given him the idea of hunting outlaws in the first place.

Edward tried to carry on with the meal as if he was enjoying it, but he'd begun worrying about the man locked up in the tower. His left hand started throbbing, something that rarely happened these days unless he strained it. He must have been squeezing the edge of his chair harder than he'd thought.

"So, you're a duke now," he said when Francis's silence began to bother him.

"I said as much in my last letter."

"And we have the king's favour? And that of the church?"

"Mainly the church." Francis wiped his mouth with a cloth and tossed it down on the table. "King Fendrel is a boy who doesn't know friend from foe, but he does love God, and the cardinals are leading him in the right direction."

"What about Ralf's steward and his old supporters?"

"They're not willing to risk war, though they argued up a storm over the past month. Most of them are too comfortable where they are to risk being branded traitors to the crown. I heard Marquess Larmond started causing trouble not long before I left, but by then everything was already settled. It seems he's mustered the nerve sack a few towns in the marches. It's nothing to worry about. As soon as his knights run out of money and abandon him, he'll hang."

Another nervous thought occurred to Edward. "If Lady Kaylein's with the church, couldn't they make the king give her back her birthright?"

Duke Francis laughed. "Then they'd be risking a war with me, and right now I'm their favourite noble. All the church wants is to keep getting its share of the king's taxes." He smiled ruefully. "Marquess Larmond always hated having to share his wealth with God. But I'll give up a few gold crowns to the church every month if it means keeping my dukedom. Most of the other nobles feel the same way. Here's to King Fendrel's long life, and another generation of peace." Francis raised his goblet. The other men followed suit with a chorus of agreement. Edward drank last.

"Will you be going back to Cairnford then, my lord?"

"Yes. I'm giving my son the castle here at Rosepath. A little wedding gift for him."

Edward's goblet hit the table with a bang. He couldn't believe it. All the work he'd done here, and the duke hadn't even considered letting him stay on as steward.

Francis shot him a bemused look. "You didn't think you were going to be here forever, did you, Edward?"

Edward tried to laugh it off, but his stomach was tying itself in knots. "Of course not! I just didn't know your son was getting married."

"Yes, that was another little concession I had to make during my time in the capital. Marquess Alistair of Henmarch was firmly in Larmond's rebel camp for a while. He needed some convincing to give Fendrel his support, so I offered to bring his daughter into my family. I hear she's quite the beauty. No doubt Isaac will be glad to settle down with an estate of his own and a castle he can fill with my grandchildren."

Edward forced a smile as his gut shrivelled into a sickly lump against his spine. Francis's son Isaac didn't know a thing about running a castle. He wasn't even a knight! Just some

156

gallivanter who'd spent half his youth travelling the world with his father's gold. Edward had been the one who'd taken care of Rosepath while his lord was away. He'd kept the coffers full and the forests safe. He deserved the castle more than Isaac.

The rest of the food he ate that evening stuck in his throat. He had to drink a lot of wine to force it down, and soon he was drunk. Despite his attempts to take an interest in the tales Francis and his men were telling about the capital, he couldn't focus. He must have displeased the duke somehow. Why else would he have denied him the castle? Had his men told him the truth about what they'd been doing in the forest? Surely they wouldn't. They'd been complicit too, after all. But what about the man locked up in the south tower? He might say anything.

Edward told himself he was being foolish. Francis had barely left his sight since he arrived. He couldn't know about the prisoner.

Duke Francis retired to bed early that evening, but most of the other men stayed up to drink and share stories. They sent a servant into town to find them some whores, which stirred Edward's interest for a moment, but even a nice fat-bottomed girl wasn't likely to improve his mood that evening. He left the hall not long after Francis and headed upstairs to his room. The lord's bedchamber had remained unoccupied since Leo's death. Edward hadn't been bold enough to claim it for himself, but he preferred the smaller room at the back end of the keep anyway. It was the chamber Lady Kaylein had escaped from, presumably her old bedroom, judging by the clothes and furnishings. Edward had considered getting rid of some of the girlish accoutrements, but they were probably worth a lot of money, so he'd stuffed them away in a large trunk at the foot of the bed.

That evening he paced up and down the room in frustration, opening the shutters, closing them, staring at the tapestries, picking up his sword belt, throwing it away again, and working himself into a growing temper. He stared at a shelf of books beside the bed. They'd been gathering dust in the two months he'd been here. Just like the dresses, dolls, and tapestries, they were probably worth a king's ransom, but to Edward they might as well have been kindling. He grabbed one and threw it across the room in anger, hearing the pages flap as half a dozen thin wooden bookmarks scattered across the rug. He should have sold everything in this room if he wanted money, but no, he'd had to listen to Harald Redcloak and his stupid schemes.

Going back to the window again, Edward opened the shutters and leaned out, breathing deep of the night air to try and calm himself. His head was still swimming from the wine. He needed to deal with the prisoner in the tower, but he was too inebriated to trust himself with a sword right now. The outlaw might slip past him when he opened the door, or knock the sword from his hand and turn it against him. Edward shuddered as he remembered what he'd done to the man's friends. He probably hated him with all his heart. For a fleeting moment, Edward thought about begging his forgiveness, as if that would somehow make things better. Then he felt indignant for entertaining the thought of grovelling to an outlaw. People like that didn't deserve pity. He'd grown up poor just like everyone else on the north side of Tannersfield, and the only reason he'd resorted to thievery was because his father forced him. It would have been easy for Edward to take to a life of lawlessness, but no, he'd become a knight, first serving the sheriff and now the duke! For the past two months, he'd slept in a room with tapestries and a feather bed, and he wasn't going to give it up without a fight.

Perhaps Francis would let him stay and serve his son instead. Some lords barely knew how to take care of themselves. They needed men like Edward to handle business for them. Isaac was always off riding horses and hunting with his dogs. He was exactly that kind of lord.

Edward took a few more deep breaths and drank some water from a jug he kept by the bed. It tasted old and musty. He spat it out the window and heard it splash into the moat. He didn't think he was going to sleep that night. He was too tightly wound, too caught up in the snare of his own worries. Perhaps he would go out to the tower and deal with the prisoner after all. All that awaited him in bed was more nightmares.

Buckling on his sword belt, he opened the door and listened. He couldn't hear the men talking downstairs anymore. They'd probably taken the whores to their bunks by now. Edward took off his silken cloak and tucked a knife into his belt, then crept down to the landing. The light sound of snoring reached his ears from behind one of the bedroom doors, but otherwise all was quiet. He carried on downstairs to the great hall. A few servants were still cleaning up the mess, but they paid him little heed.

I could always go to the village, Edward thought, feeling nervous again about confronting the prisoner while he was still drunk. There was bound to be some woman he could buy for a penny or two. He might end up enjoying it. Sometimes when he spent the night with whores they put their arms around him after he was finished and let him sleep with his head on their breasts. That was always nice. It made him forget about the things that usually troubled him when he went to sleep.

His feet strayed in the direction of the castle gates as he crossed the courtyard, and he started thinking about Lady Kaylein's straw-haired servant girl. He'd rather have her around than sour-faced Daisy. Maybe he could have gone to sleep with his head on her breast, touching the soft curves of her body and savouring the taste of her lips against his. Then he remembered how she'd stabbed him in the forest, and his desire turned to anger. He'd never touch a woman like her, not even out of spite. He clenched his jaw and looked toward the tower again. He'd need to get the key from the gatehouse

159

before he went in.

The gatehouse door was open. It had two rooms: one where the watchman could keep an eye on the gate through a pair of arrow slits on either side, and another with a hearth that kept the guards warm during winter.

The night watchman was fast asleep in his chair against the far wall. Treading softly, Edward crept into the second room. The smell of smoke from a recently burnt-out candle hung in the air. It was pitch black inside save for a few slivers of light coming through the arrow slits facing the courtyard. Edward went back into the other room and lifted an oil lamp from the watchman's table. He was starting to feel nervous again, wondering what the watchman would tell Francis if he woke up. After their earlier conversation, he doubted the duke would approve of him killing an unarmed prisoner in the dead of night. Francis might want to speak with the man, then he'd find out what had happened in the forest.

The fear of being outed spurred Edward on. He lifted the lamp and went back into the dark room. On the wall by the door, he found several pegs holding rings of heavy iron keys. He hesitated, wondering which was the right one. He couldn't very well rouse the guard and ask him. He would just have to take them all. Looping the metal rings over his wrist carefully so they didn't rattle, he crept back outside and crossed the courtyard to the tower door. He set down his lamp and tried the keys one by one, exhaling with relief when the lock opened after just four attempts.

Edward hurried inside and held up the light, taking care not to slip down the stairs that led into the dank cellar beneath the tower. The outlaw was locked up in a secure room against the right wall. He thought he heard a noise coming from inside, but it could have been a rodent scurrying in the darkness. Edward was sweating. What was he going to do with the body afterwards? He could put it in the cellar. There were some old barrels down there large enough to fit a body. Tomorrow he could have Stephen and Alderic roll it

160

out and dump it in the woods. Yes, that would work. The important thing was to make sure Francis didn't get the chance to speak with the man.

Edward lifted the lamp to a small barred window in the door and tried to look in, but it was difficult to make out anything on the other side. He only had a narrow view into one end of the semicircular chamber. Setting the lamp down between his feet, he tried the same key he'd used to unlock the outer door. It didn't work. He tried another one. The iron rattled loudly against the keyhole, setting Edward's nerves on edge. None of the keys seemed to fit. He heard a shuffling sound from the other side and hissed in through the window: "You'd better stay where I can see you, or I'll gut you the moment I open this door!"

Edward had to go through two whole rings before he found the right key. He grabbed the handle of his knife and drew it silently. The door creaked open with a nudge of his shoulder. He pushed the lamp in with his boot. The outlaw was wrapped in his cloak against the far wall, hunched up as if he was sick or dying. Edward allowed himself a smile. It was going to be easy after all. Without hesitation, he crossed the room, knelt, and thrust his knife into the man's back. The blade went straight through, crumpling the cloak as if there was nothing there. Edward drew back in surprise, intensely confused by the lack of resistance. There was no body inside the cloak. It was bundled up around a pile of straw. In his half-drunk state, he'd fallen for a cheap trick.

He whirled around, leaping for the door even before he saw the outlaw's shadow coming out from behind it. Edward's hand closed on the back of the man's shirt. He pulled hard and the linen ripped. The outlaw stumbled, shadows flashing across the tower walls in a surreal dance as both men staggered out of the chamber. Miraculously, neither of them kicked over the lamp. Edward thought he had the upper hand, but his opponent spun around and threw a knee into his chest before he could right himself. Edward toppled back with a gasp, his balance listing. His foot slipped off the edge of the stairwell. Panicking, he tried to lurch his body aside before he fell into the cellar. He managed to avoid falling down the stairs, but he lost what remained of his balance in the process, dropping his knife as he put out his hands to stop his chin smashing into the stone floor. He rolled over, snatching for his sword. It was half drawn before the outlaw kicked him in the chest, pain shooting through his ribs as the breath left his lungs in a gasping cough.

Edward tried to throw a punch, but the man straddled him and pinned his arm against his chest. His free hand clasped Edward's wrist, preventing him from drawing his sword the rest of the way. Suddenly Edward was helpless. He struggled violently, trying to throw his attacker off, but the outlaw leaned down until the bony tip of his elbow pressed against Edward's throat. The unwashed stink of the man's hair made Edward gag.

"I don't want to kill you."

Edward struggled harder.

"Stop!" the outlaw spat. "Stop it, you bastard, or I'll crush your throat!"

A flood of fear superseded Edward's panic as he realised how helpless he was. The pressure of the man's elbow was making it hard to breathe. He stopped struggling.

"Good," the outlaw said. He glanced at his cell door. The key was still in the lock. "I'm going to lock you in there and take your sword. Let go of it."

Edward did not. The outlaw dug his elbow in harder. Edward's fear became terror as he started to choke. He didn't want to die like this, not in the dark with the stench of this man's hair in his throat. He had no choice but to release his grip. The pressure on his neck eased. Taking care not to let Edward get hold of the handle again, the outlaw drew his sword free of the scabbard and rested it against his chest. He leaned in close.

"Tell me something before I put you in there. Do you

know what happened to a girl called Elizabeth? She used to work here."

Edward tried to speak, but he could only make a rough coughing sound. The outlaw lifted his elbow a little.

"I don't know," Edward croaked out.

"She'd be–" The outlaw paused, shaking his head in confusion. "About sixteen or eighteen. That sort of age. She's got straw-coloured hair. She liked to wear it long."

Edward didn't have time to be surprised by the familiar description. He was too focused on tensing his free hand so that he could make a grab for the blade of his sword. He knew the metal was blunt near the hilt. If he could get a grip on it, he might be able to lever the point upward into his attacker's face.

"I think she's–" Edward began, then he made his move. It caught the outlaw by surprise. He'd eased his grip to let Edward talk, and now that he had one hand on the sword he couldn't hold him down so easily. Edward grabbed the blade and twisted his body to the side as hard as he could, throwing all his weight into the motion. The outlaw fumbled, letting go of him to try and grip the sword with both hands. With a desperate surge of energy, Edward levered the tip of the blade toward the man's face. He was sure he was about to cut him, but the outlaw rolled off at the last second and yanked the sword out of his hand. Edward let go before the sharp edge could slide over his fingers. He was free to move now. With a snarl, he leapt to his feet and shoved the outlaw in the chest. The man tripped and almost fell down the cellar stairs, shooting his arms out to catch himself on either side of the rectangular opening. A metallic ring echoed through the tower as Edward's sword hit the floor and vanished into the shadows.

He wasn't going to let the outlaw overpower him again. Panting for breath, he threw himself into the gloom beside the stairs, scrabbling through the darkness until his fingers were rewarded with the nick of sharp steel. He found the hilt of his sword and whirled around, lifting the blade to strike. He was a second too late. Moonlight spilled into the tower as the outlaw threw open the door and fled into the courtyard.

Coward, Edward thought, hurrying to give chase, but the outlaw had a head start on him. The man was as quick as he was wily. Edward's throat still hurt, and he was wheezing before he got halfway across the courtyard. The outlaw was already at the western gate. It was shut, but the left side had a small door that was only locked by a simple bar on the inside. The outlaw yanked the bar out and went through. A few moments later, Edward saw the shadow of a night watchman come out of the gatehouse. He'd probably been dozing like the other one.

Before the night watchman could see him, Edward stepped back into the shadows at the base of the wall. He was breathing hard from the fight, shaken by his brush with death. His chance to catch the outlaw had slipped through his fingers. The second the man crossed the river, he'd disappear into the forest. All Edward could do now was cover his tracks.

He hurried back to the tower and gathered up the lamp, keys, and his knife. He blew out the flame before sneaking back to the eastern gatehouse. The watchman was still dozing in his chair. His counterpart hadn't raised the alarm. Once the keys were safely back on their pegs, Edward made his way around the edge of the courtyard until he reached the chapel. If anyone questioned him, he'd pretend he'd gone out to pray.

Once he was inside the chapel, he started calming down. The hammering pace of his heart slowed, and he began to breathe more easily. He didn't think he'd been seen. There were no sounds of commotion from the western gatehouse. Perhaps the watchman had recognised the outlaw and didn't want to be blamed for his escape?

Edward closed his eyes and allowed himself a moment of relief, thumping a fist against his chest to try and dislodge the lingering ache in his throat. Perhaps this was for the best.

Now he wouldn't need to worry about disposing of the outlaw's body. The man would disappear back where he'd come from. The problem was gone, and Duke Francis would never know the truth about what had happened.

Yet as Edward walked back to the keep, a finger of doubt plucked at his heart. Even if the people he'd killed in the forest didn't come back to haunt him in the waking world, he knew they'd still be there in his dreams.

CHAPTER 11

Four months after she began working for Joseph, Elizabeth plucked up the courage to ask if she could live at the workshop. She'd grown to hate her lonely hovel on the north side of town. Every week her street became more crowded, whether it was families piling into the small houses or beggars lining the muddy road. She spared a morsel of bread for the nice ones whenever she could, but not all of them were nice. Sometimes she had insults thrown at her, other times handfuls of dirt. Every so often the town watch came through to chase the vagrants out, but they always came back again the next day. Tannersfield was so full it felt like the town was bursting at the seams. Even the sheriff's increasing tolls on the gates hadn't been enough to stem the tide. The truth was, Tannersfield was an easy place to sneak into, and the growing talk of danger in the forest had driven people to seek refuge behind the town walls. Some said Sir Edward himself was responsible for the troubles. A few tales had surfaced–of the sort that usually came from a nephew's-wife's-friend–about how the knight was terrorising the countryside, making no distinction between outlaws and vagrants as he dispensed his own version of the sheriff's bloody justice.

The gradually increasing population combined with the natural touch of rowdiness summer seemed to inflict on people meant that the north side of town had become a much more dangerous place to live. In the past month Elizabeth had been robbed twice, first by a man who'd threatened her with a knife, second by a group who'd followed her calling out crass invitations on the way home. She'd grown frightened when they started to catch up, so she scattered a handful of pennies in the road and ran away when they stopped to collect them. She'd only lost a couple of copper shillings all told, but that was still a lot when she was struggling to save every penny.

Joseph's expression darkened when Elizabeth told him about the men who'd followed her. When she asked whether she could sleep in the workshop, he agreed. The smell of sawdust kept her awake the first night, and the wooden floor was even harder than the earth of her hovel, but being close to Joseph and the carpenters made her feel safe. She offered to pay Joseph the same copper penny she'd given Emma each day by way of rent, but he wouldn't hear of it.

"We'll see if we can get you a mattress," he said. "Though we might have to stuff it with sawdust. Don't like the thought of you sleeping out there on the floor. You can have an old cloak to wrap up in if you need it."

Elizabeth accepted the offer gratefully. The workshop might have been safe, but it wasn't built for sleeping. The broad windows were meant to let in light, which meant they also let in the cold, and the thin linen sheets and iron bars covering them did precious little to keep out the draft. Thankfully most nights were mild and balmy for now, but the place would become bitterly cold in winter. She hoped Joseph or one of the others might let her sleep in their house when the weather turned.

With each passing week, she grew fonder of the carpenters. Joseph was a wonderfully kind man beneath his

167

gruff and straightforward exterior, and his wife Rose was the sort of woman who was dear to her friends and fearsome to her enemies. Elizabeth thought people like Rose possessed something worth aspiring to. She'd known many women who shared her perpetually cynical demeanour, but few balanced it out with a loving heart. It reminded her of Lady Eleanor. Sometimes when Joseph was teaching her about mathematics—they had moved on from adding and were now tackling something fiendishly difficult called multiplication—Rose would scoff at Elizabeth's struggles, but she would always bring them bowls of tasty stew and rest a warm hand on Elizabeth's shoulder when she said goodnight afterwards. Joseph and his wife were honest, hard-working people, and Elizabeth felt a kinship with them she'd never shared with the nobles of Rosepath. It helped her not to miss Kaylein so much.

There was something homely about living with the carpenters, a feeling that had become painfully conspicuous in its absence. Her heart craved a comfortable nook it could settle into. She wanted to belong. In her daydreams, Elizabeth no longer imagined herself owning land out in the dales, but a house on this very street. She could rent her yard to craftsmen and build a workshop like Joseph's. Perhaps she'd understand a few things about woodworking by then, and she could whittle and carve her own projects like Rose. The money she was saving up in Joseph's chest would buy her a house like that someday. Something made of stone that would last for years and years. Then, even if she died young like her mother, her children would still have something strong and permanent to shelter them. A husband and children were an inevitability if she wanted to settle down. A settled woman needed a husband, that was what everybody always said. Elizabeth didn't mind the idea of becoming a mother, but she wouldn't marry a man she hated just to have money. She'd sooner go to work at Emma's brothel. Perhaps her mother had felt the same way. No, Elizabeth decided; she would secure herself financially before thinking about marriage and children. She wouldn't make eyes at any boys, and she certainly wouldn't let any of them take her to bed.

Elizabeth began work as soon as she got up, rising early to make sure all the tools and benches were prepared before the carpenters arrived. She got into the habit of remembering what each carpenter had been doing the night before and made sure the tools he needed were set out on his bench when he arrived.

As the days passed, Elizabeth began to notice little things here and there that were hampering the workshop's efficiency. One apprentice was sent to do the work of two. Two were sent to do the work of one. People borrowed each other's tools and benches without asking. Too much wood was dressed one day and too little the next, bottlenecking the men's work.

Elizabeth kept her observations to herself at first, not wanting to appear rude or presumptuous by questioning men who undoubtedly knew their trade better than her. If she was going to speak up, she needed to do it tactfully, with a pragmatic solution that Joseph would appreciate. Elizabeth respected the master carpenter too much to blurt out her half-baked thoughts before they were ready.

She carried on paying careful attention to the way the workshop ran, and after a few weeks she was confident she could devise a smoother way of organising the carpenters' work. The major problem, as she saw it, was that several different craftsmen all worked in Joseph's yard with little coordination between them. It wasn't like a building site where a foreman would delegate different jobs to different masters. Only the apprentices followed instructions, while the journeymen made their own decisions on which jobs they took, what they needed, where they worked, and how much time they spent. The bumbling chaos might have worked well enough, Elizabeth thought, were it not for the larger jobs the carpenters took on as a group. When a house had to be built, a roof repaired, a bridge constructed, or an urgent order of timber dressed, Joseph needed a team of men he could rely on to start work at a moment's notice. These projects were always the most lucrative, and if Joseph didn't snap them up they would go to the guildsmen on Carpenter's Street. When a wealthy customer came to the yard with such a commission, one of two things happened. Either Joseph had too few carpenters available and the job was lost, or one or two men ended up dropping their current projects to pitch in. The latter resulted in long delays and exasperated customers. It wasn't just inefficient, it was damaging to the workshop's reputation.

Things needed to be run more like a building site, Elizabeth decided. She'd listened in on many conversations between Count Leo and his master builder when they discussed construction projects in Rosepath. If an overseer could be appointed to manage all the jobs and properly distribute the workload, it would cause far less disruption when the big jobs arrived. The customers would be happier and the carpenters would get more work done.

Elizabeth presented her idea to Joseph one morning over breakfast. He had moved the trestle table out of his house into a little square yard behind the workshop so that he could enjoy his morning bread in the open air. Elizabeth usually joined him.

"The workshop's a bit messy at times, I'll grant you," he said. "But that's just the way of things in a place like ours. The boys don't work under me, and I wouldn't expect them to. They're their own men. It's important they take responsibility for their work, especially those who want to be masters someday."

"But you handle the organisation and wages when you take on group work, and they all pay to use your workshop."

"Aye, but that's only for the big projects. I know we get under each other's feet sometimes, but the boys never hold a grudge. Truth be told, I've had the same thoughts myself, Liz,

170

but it's already enough work handling things the way they are. I've got no time to be looking over each man's shoulder. I'm a carpenter at heart, not a foreman."

Elizabeth took a deep breath. "What if I was your foreman?"

He paused, a piece of bread halfway to his mouth as if he couldn't tell whether she was joking.

"I already keep an eye on everyone's work," Elizabeth explained in a hurry. "I get the tools and materials ready at the start of each day. I keep the shed supplied when we're running low on things. I know who's nearly finished a job and who needs more time. And I've learned enough about the boys to know who's good at what."

Joseph grunted and popped the bread into his mouth. "So what's your idea, girl?"

"I'll keep an eye on everything, just like a foreman does. Even the small jobs. I'll delegate the work based on who can get it done best and fastest. I'll make sure no one takes on too much or too little, so you don't have half your people free and half busy every time a big job comes in."

"*Delegate.*" Joseph grinned. "There you go, sounding like a noblewoman again. I don't know, Liz, that sounds like a guild within a guild, telling craftsmen what jobs they can and can't take. Not all the boys would like that, especially not coming from a woman."

"You could still be the one telling them what they're doing," Elizabeth persisted. "I'd just help you organise it all. We could keep a record of all the jobs, like how a cellarer keeps a ledger of what's in his stores."

"That'd be easier if you could write."

Elizabeth's spirits sank for the first time since coming up with her idea. She hadn't thought about that. It was true, this was the sort of work people usually did with ledgers and tablets, otherwise they started forgetting things and making mistakes.

"I've got a good memory, though," she said, trying to

sound confident. "And there aren't *that* many carpenters working here." She was worried Joseph might dismiss the idea, but he still had half his bread left to eat, and he was usually willing to indulge her thoughts until work started.

"There's still the problem of taking away the boys' freedom," he said. "You think Thin Robin would like it if I started telling him he couldn't work on doors anymore? Man's in love with his doors."

Thin Robin was one of the more abrasive craftsmen at Joseph's workshop. In truth, he was part of the reason Elizabeth had noticed problems with their productivity in the first place. Joseph was right; he got snippy and irritable when anyone else was commissioned to make a door, neglecting his own work to hover over their shoulder and offer unsolicited advice.

"Then why don't we have Robin make all the doors?" she said. "He's good at it, isn't he? But he always falls behind on his work when someone else gets a job he wants. Then he starts rushing and makes mistakes. That farmer wouldn't pay for his fence posts last week because Robin cut them too short."

Joseph paused between bites. Elizabeth twisted her fingers together in excitement. For the first time since they began speaking, he seemed to be seriously considering the idea.

"That's true enough," he said after a while. "Some men like Robin work better under a master. He wouldn't like the idea at first, but he might be happier for it in the long run."

"And he'd do better work. Before I came here my mistress always put the servants wherever she thought they'd do best. If they needed help, she hired more people. If they were doing a bad job, she tried them out in different positions till she found something they were good at. The boys all share the same workshop, but they act like they're working on their own. I think this place needs to be organised more like a big household."

Joseph nodded slowly. "Well, there's at least one idea in there I like: making sure people get the jobs they're good at. Might make things run a bit smoother, and we'd put out more quality work at the end of it."

"Which would mean happier customers and more jobs coming our way. I've seen it on the street; the busiest workshops are always the ones with the best reputations."

"Our reputation isn't bad," Joseph said defensively.

"No, but we still lose people to Carpenter's Street, don't we?"

Joseph rubbed his chin, disappearing into thought as he finished his bread. Like the sun creeping over the horizon, a smile spread across his grizzled face.

"I suppose if I let you do this you'll be wanting better pay."

Elizabeth flushed with embarrassment. "I just want the workshop to do well. Maybe I could get an extra penny here and there if you think I deserve it."

"Well, if we start seeing more money from this it'll be yours to pocket. If not," he shrugged, "I'm happy to keep you running errands. I just hope you can manage it. You're a sharp girl, but I've never seen someone your age herd a workshop of carpenters."

"So you'll let me do it?"

"I think I might let you try. You've had some good ideas before, haven't you? Besides, we could always use more work." Joseph dusted off his hands and stood up. "Talk to me about it again tonight. If we can persuade the boys it's a good idea, we'll see what we can do."

Elizabeth grinned from ear to ear. She wanted to hug the carpenter, but she knew physical affection made Joseph uncomfortable. "Thank you. I'll do everything I can to make it work."

He nodded and made a shooing motion toward the workshop. "Go on now, there's a day's work waiting to be done."

The changes in organisation did not go as smoothly as Elizabeth had hoped. Not only were the carpenters resistant to the idea, but so were the customers. Elizabeth tried to handle most of the work herself, taking the details of any new jobs that came in to Joseph at the end of the day so that he could decide who to assign them to. But customers did not want to pass the details of their commissions to an eighteen-year-old girl, they wanted to speak with a master carpenter. Half the people who stepped into the yard walked straight past her and went to one of the men instead. If Elizabeth tried to intervene she risked annoying both parties, especially if she was dealing with Thin Robin.

The actual organisation of the workshop was not the difficult part. If someone wanted a door made, they gave it to Robin, furniture went to Adam and Luther, specialised dressing was Peter's speciality, and so on. If one of them was busy, they gave the job to whoever else was free. No one's backlog kept them tied up for more than a few days at a time, which should have meant that everybody was always available to start bigger jobs at short notice. The system made sense to Elizabeth. The troublesome part was the people.

"The sheriff's carpenter's my cousin," Adam grumbled as they discussed the day's jobs in the workshop one morning. "He came to me because he knew I could do those beams for the new courthouse. If someone else turns up on the building site, he won't like it."

"You've got plenty of work to be getting on with here," Joseph replied. "And if your cousin's got a lick of sense he'll be glad to have a man as handy as Peter working for him. We've sent plenty of our boys his way before, haven't we?"

"I just don't see why we have to do everything like we're monks counting our verses."

"You'll be more of a help here at the workshop," Joseph said. "Now that harvest season's started we'll be helping the cartwrights fix broken carts all the way through till winter, and no one knows their way around wheels and axles better than you."

"Work for the sheriff's more important than that."

"You know Peter will get those beams made just as good as you."

The disagreement continued to swing back and forth. As Elizabeth listened, she couldn't help but feel like she was the one responsible. Lady Eleanor had made organising a castle seem as simple as riding a horse, but she'd been a countess, someone with complete authority over her subjects and decades of experience handling them. Elizabeth had dived into her idea headlong, and now she was struggling to stay afloat. The plan should have been working. The reasoning behind it was sound. Yet, as she was fast coming to learn, sound ideas were often thwarted by the fickleness of human hearts.

A few days later, after another disagreement between Adam and Thin Robin, she shared her concerns with Joseph over supper at his house.

"Maybe it isn't working," she said. "Everyone's got a short temper these days. Perhaps we'd be better off keeping things the way they were."

"We've only been at it a couple of weeks," Joseph replied, not looking up from the sketch he was finishing in a cross-legged position by the fire. Rose nudged him in the side with her foot, a reminder for him to finish his bowl of stew before it got cold.

"Where's your spirit, girl?" the carpenter's wife said. "I thought you were made of sterner stuff than that. You survived on your own in that hovel for how long? And now you're worried about a few carpenters huffing and puffing?" She clicked her tongue reproachfully. "Some of those boys could use a firmer hand. Joseph's too soft on them, I've always told him."

"Thought you liked me being soft." Joseph smiled.

"Shut up and eat that stew." She dug her toes into his side

again.

Joseph swallowed a spoonful of broth, then said: "You know, we've taken more work this week than we did last. It's early to tell still, but squeezing in some of those extra jobs might have helped."

"See?" Rose gave Elizabeth a nudge this time. "Don't give it up till you've let things sit for a while."

"I just didn't expect it would be like this."

"Not much in life's how you expect it, girl. You just stick at it and do the best with what you've got, don't you?"

Elizabeth allowed herself a smile. "If I could yell at them the way you do they probably wouldn't complain so much."

"Then yell at them."

"I can't do that. You're Joseph's wife. I'm just the girl who sweeps up."

Rose scoffed at her. "And that's all you'll be if you don't show them otherwise. If they give you any trouble, stop fetching their nails in the mornings. Leave some of that sawdust heaped up on their benches. Then you'll see them change their tone. They've gotten cosy with the way you keep things for them. Like lords in their own castle."

"Rose has a point," Joseph said. "You do talk to the boys like they're lords sometimes. Makes them think of you as a servant."

"That's just how I got used to talking."

Rose made an irritated sound around her mouthful of stew. "I've heard you yell at those beggars who come by eyeing our tools. You've got a mean tongue on you when the mood strikes."

"Don't let her push you into starting arguments, now," Joseph said firmly. "But stick with this, and if anyone causes a fuss don't be afraid to stand up for yourself. Show some confidence, even if you don't feel it." He tapped the side of his nose with his sketching charcoal. "That's half of what it takes to be a master."

Elizabeth wasn't sure whether he was joking, but the

carpenter's faith buoyed up her faltering enthusiasm. "I just wish it was that simple with the customers. Half of them ignore me and go straight to the men."

"True. We'll have to do something about that." Joseph took another mouthful of his stew. "Might help if you didn't look like you'd walked halfway across the kingdom in that dress."

Elizabeth looked down at herself. Her dress was creased and stained, the hem ragged with a hundred different tears. "I suppose I could buy new clothes."

"Go to Martha Tailor," Rose said. "Two streets over from market road, on the west side. She's not usually cheap, but she will be if you tell her we sent you. Saved her business when Joseph mended her roof for free five years ago."

Elizabeth would rather have waited till more of the stitching fell out of her old dress, but on Rose's advice she decided to head across town in search of Martha Tailor the next day. It was on the west side of the marketplace, so she would be able to stop at the nunnery and ask after Kaylein again. It had become a routine of hers to try every few days. She suspected the nuns were getting annoyed with her by now, but maybe if they got annoyed enough they would relent.

Most days Elizabeth preferred to circumvent the busy marketplace, but it was a slow day at the workshop, so she decided to wander through the stalls instead. People bustled and bobbed like herds of sheep in the enormous square, farmers and tradesmen coming in with their produce and leaving with purses full of silver. Weights clattered upon scales as merchants haggled, poultry squawked in cages made of sticks, and heralds bellowed their news from the top of the gallows. There had been at least one hanging a week recently, but the gallows were only seeing use as a speaking platform that day. Elizabeth hadn't attended a hanging in years. As a child, they'd been exciting public events, but ever since Sam left she'd been afraid she might see her brother's body

177

swinging from the noose one day.

She left the marketplace and went to the nunnery first, hoping to get her disappointment out of the way early. It would be better to go home thinking about a clean new dress rather than worrying over how Kaylein fared at the convent. Stopping at the entrance, she lifted the heavy iron ring on one of the doors and let it bang a few times. A black-robed nun lifted the bar and let her in. Elizabeth was ushered into a small room that separated the road from the inner cloisters. She'd been in here often enough to know that the door on the right led to a chamber for the sister who minded the gates, while the door on the left opened into a parlour where deliveries could be made and meetings held without allowing visitors into the convent proper.

"You're not here for the mother superior, are you?" the nun asked, giving Elizabeth a sceptical look.

"I am if she'll see me."

"I was told to expect distinguished guests."

Elizabeth glanced toward the parlour. "Is the mother superior in there now?"

"Yes, but I don't think–"

"I'll only be a moment!" Elizabeth insisted. "And I'll leave right away if your guests arrive."

The nun pressed her lips together. She cracked the door open to peer across the road, then gave Elizabeth a nod. "Generosity was the precept of this morning's sermon. Be quick."

"Thank you, Sister."

Elizabeth didn't wait for the nun to usher her through. She'd never had a chance to speak with the prioress before. Opening the parlour door, she slipped in and saw a white-robed woman reading at a table in the corner. She wasn't as old as Elizabeth had expected, with a gentle face that might have been pretty had it not creased with a sudden glare.

"Who are you?" the prioress demanded. She sounded tense, as though the interruption had thrown her off balance.

178

"My name's Elizabeth, Mother." She curtseyed. "I'm a friend of Kaylein's. I was wondering if I might ask after her?"

The prioress settled back into her chair, but her brow remained furrowed. "I see. Forgive my rudeness. I am expecting an important meeting soon, so you will have to be brief."

"Is Kaylein well?" Elizabeth asked.

"She is, yes. Certainly better than when she arrived."

The knot of worry Elizabeth had been fretting over loosened a little. "And is she happy?"

The prioress paused, then lowered her voice. "Are you aware of who Kaylein is?"

The knot tightened back up.

"I've known her for years," Elizabeth answered cautiously.

"Then you know what became of her family. Given the circumstances, I would hesitate to call Kaylein's existence a happy one. But she has found focus and purpose in service to God. In time, I believe she may find happiness as well."

"When do you think I might be able to see her?"

The prioress closed her book and folded her hands atop it. "That will depend on when she takes her first vows. Perhaps in a few months, at the earliest, though a novice is permitted up to a year to consider."

Elizabeth tried not to feel too disappointed. A year was a long time, but if Kaylein was eager to join the church perhaps she would take her vows sooner.

"Will she be a proper nun then?"

"No. A novice must take three sets of vows before being sworn into God's service. The first is a pledge of commitment in which Kaylein will swear to uphold the virtuous precepts of our order. She will then be allowed to leave the convent when her duties require it. Her second vows will see her confirmed as a sister of our priory, while her third and final vows will pledge her spirit to God's service for the rest of her life."

179

"How long will all that take?"

"It varies with each sister, though a novice typically takes all three sets of vows within five years."

"Five years!" Elizabeth was dismayed. She'd thought once Kaylein swore her vows they could be friends again. Perhaps they could have continued their riding lessons together, and in return Kaylein might have taught her how to read and write. But five years was an eternity.

The prioress's tone softened. "If she takes her first vows early perhaps the two of you may attend the service of winter solstice together. You must understand, it is not a nun's place to come and go as she pleases. It is important that Kaylein become accustomed to monastic life before she exposes herself to the temptations of the outside world again."

The sound of a door opening and a murmur of voices filtered in from outside. The prioress rose to her feet. Elizabeth's time was up.

"Thank you, Mother. Please tell Kaylein that she is in my thoughts and prayers."

The prioress gave her a stiff nod. Elizabeth curtseyed once more and took her leave.

Her fingers had barely brushed the ringed handle before the door swung open. Elizabeth stumbled back. A tall man stood before her, the fur trim of his cloak shockingly white against the dark crimson of his tunic. Elizabeth's heart skipped a beat.

Duke Francis stared down at her.

CHAPTER 12

"Excuse me, my lady."

Francis spoke with the patient courtesy of a lord humouring a favoured servant. Elizabeth had heard that tone before, the day he embraced Count Leo. Was there murder behind the duke's handsome smile today, too? Her feet remained frozen to the stone floor as she reeled from his sudden appearance. She might have stood there indefinitely had he not raised a hand to usher her aside, causing her to flinch back in shock. Francis ignored her reaction, not seeming to have recognised her. Sir Edward followed him into the room. Tall and broad-shouldered, he was wearing a cloak of white silk that had belonged to Kaylein's brother Hugh. He turned his dark eyes toward Elizabeth, stared for a moment, then lunged forward and snatched her forearm.

Elizabeth fought back the urge to scream. She twisted against his grasp, but he was fearsomely strong. Between his white knuckles, she saw a mottled red line marking the spot she had stabbed him. Her free hand shot to her knife, fingers tightening around the handle.

"Sir Edward!" Duke Francis barked. "What in heaven's name are you doing?"

"This is the one who stabbed me in the forest, my lord."

"Stabbed you? When?"

Sir Edward's face flushed a deep red. The look frightened Elizabeth. There was a petulant fury beneath his shame. It was the sort of look an angry boy might wear moments before flying into an uncontrollable rage.

"Well?" Francis demanded.

"The night we took Rosepath."

Francis studied Elizabeth with curiosity, then turned his gaze back on Edward. "Unhand her. You're in a convent."

"But she's a criminal!"

The prioress banged her book on the table. "The king's law may rule outside these walls, but in my convent we obey the rule of God. I will not stand for violence."

Edward let go. Elizabeth resisted the urge to bolt for the door in an undignified scramble, trying to slow the pounding of her heart with deep breaths.

"I'll see you in the pillory for what you did," the knight hissed as she brushed past him on her way out. Elizabeth tried not to let her fear show. Had he caught her anywhere else, she doubted she would have been so lucky.

The unbearable weight of Sir Edward's eyes on her back lifted as the door banged shut behind her. She let out a shuddering breath, putting out a hand to steady herself against the wall.

"You look like you've seen a ghost," the nun minding the gates said, then frowned and made a sign of penance. Nuns were probably not supposed to speak of ghosts. Elizabeth saw that she was holding a sword belt, probably Sir Edward's, and a terrifying thought occurred to her.

"Why is Duke Francis here?"

"He has business with the mother superior."

"Is it about one of your nuns?"

"It might be."

Muffled though it was, Elizabeth could still hear the duke's voice through the parlour door. Kaylein's name stood

182

out amidst the murmur as clearly as if he had yelled it into her ear.

She bit her lip, glancing between the two doors, one that would lead her to safety, the other back into a wolf's den. She thought about what a relief it would be to return to the workshop, to the warm company of Joseph and Rose. Then she thought of Kaylein, and Lady Eleanor's dying wish. She could no longer remember the words Eleanor had spoken that night, only the look in her eyes as she implored her to protect her daughter. The same fear Elizabeth had felt when she picked up Count Leo's sword gripped her again, but she knew that if she ran away she would never forgive herself.

With her heart in her mouth, she turned around and pushed the parlour door open. Duke Francis was still speaking when Elizabeth ran past him and Sir Edward, falling to her knees before the prioress.

"You mustn't let them see Kaylein!" she begged. "If you know what happened to her family, you can't!"

"How dare you interrupt us!" the prioress exclaimed. She spoke with a preacher's fervour, her voice full of hellish fire. There was no trace of the kindly woman Elizabeth had spoken to before. "You bring this chaos into my convent, and you expect me to stand here and indulge it?!"

Elizabeth trembled, convinced she had made a terrible mistake, but when she looked up the prioress's gaze was fixed on Duke Francis.

"You should be ashamed, all of you! An innocent girl has suffered for the wickedness and ambition of the power-hungry. She has given herself to God in search of refuge, and you pile up at my door seeking to drag her back out like a pack of rabid dogs!"

"Calm down, woman." Duke Francis spoke bluntly now, courtesy forgotten. "It is beneath you to indulge this girl's hysteria."

"Leave my convent. You will not see Kaylein–any of you–while she is under my care."

Duke Francis didn't move. Edward shifted from foot to foot uncomfortably.

"Have you composed yourself now, Prioress?" Francis said after a moment of pointed silence. "I am a man of God. My sins have been absolved, and I have no desire to burden my spirit with any more. You have my word that I have no intention of harming Lady Kaylein."

"Then why have you come here?" The prioress still sounded angry, but Elizabeth could see the motion of her hands being wrung behind her back. Francis's refusal to leave had been a firm reminder that he was the most powerful man in the county.

"I had hoped to tell Lady Kaylein of my intentions in person—before you and this girl chose to assume the worst of me. Perhaps the bishop will need to be informed that the precept of forgiveness is sadly lacking in this convent." Francis took a step forward. "Rather than making any more a fool of yourself, I suggest you deliver this message to Lady Kaylein. I will spare her my wrath. So long as she remains here, in service to God, I see no reason why the matter of her bloodline should come between us again. From now on, the peace and prosperity of this county are my foremost concern. If Kaylein does nothing to challenge that, she has nothing to fear from me."

"What about her?" Edward said, pointing at Elizabeth.

"I think it would be wise for this girl not to repeat any of her accusations in this town again." Francis's words were heavy with an unspoken threat. Once again Elizabeth feared she would have received far worse than a verbal rebuke had she not been in a house of God.

"I will give Kaylein your message," the prioress said. "Now please leave, all of you. I hope never to trouble my convent with this business again."

"We are alike in that hope, Mother."

Francis and Edward exited the room.

Elizabeth remained kneeling on the floor. Once she was

sure the two men had gone she whispered: "Is there another door I might leave by, Mother?"

The prioress bent down and helped Elizabeth to her feet. "Are you afraid of those men?"

"That knight, Sir Edward, he chased Kaylein and I the night we fled Rosepath."

"He said you stabbed him. Was it self defence?"

"Yes. Francis sent him to kill Kaylein like her brothers. I'm sure of it."

The prioress sighed. "Then by the king's law, you have done no wrong. It is no crime to defend oneself, even against a knight."

"I don't think Sir Edward sees it that way."

"No. And the duke cares only for the law when it suits his needs. Come with me. I will take you to the side gate."

Elizabeth hurried after the prioress as she led her into the cloisters at a brisk walk. She still couldn't believe she'd left the parlour unscathed. When she'd been kneeling there on the floor she'd imagined being flogged or thrown in the sheriff's jail for her impudence. The realisation of how reckless she'd been brought a tremor to her legs. She hoped Duke Francis meant what he said about leaving Kaylein alone.

On their way through the cloisters Elizabeth tried to peer beneath the hoods of some of the passing nuns, hoping to catch a glimpse of Kaylein, but none of the faces were familiar to her. The prioress took her down a narrow walk between two of the convent buildings, then unlocked a heavy door at the end and let her out. She emerged on a quiet street that ran along the western wall of the convent. The door closed behind her.

Elizabeth lowered her hood and drew her cloak close to her body. Duke Francis had seemed willing to overlook her, but Edward clearly hadn't forgotten what she'd done. He was a young and prideful knight, and those were always the worst kinds. When Elizabeth had bickered with the town boys as a child most would insult her back and forget about it the next

185

day. Then there had been the ones who would wait for weeks before pushing her down in the mud or pulling her hair in church. She suspected Edward was the latter type, cruel and resentful, nurturing his grudges like a swineherd raising sows for the slaughter. He was probably waiting for her outside the convent gates right now.

Well, I hope he waits there all day, she thought, taking courage from the realisation that she'd escaped him once again. It helped to still her trembling legs, and by the time she'd walked to the end of the street she was feeling a little better. She didn't go past the front of the convent, but took the road north instead, walking all the way around the sheriff's castle before cutting back across the marketplace.

Trying to take her mind off what had happened, she perused the market stalls for a while and bought herself some ripe apples and a hardtack bisket she could eat in the night if she got hungry. The penny she paid for them didn't go as far as it would've had she bought bread and ale, but after the shock of coming face to face with Sir Edward she wanted something nice to calm her nerves. It had been a while since she'd had fresh fruit, and the tart sweetness of the apples was delicious. It was always worth enjoying fruit while it was in season. By the time she'd finished eating, she felt confident enough to leave the marketplace and head over to Martha Tailor's house.

Martha was a widow, nervous and apologetic in her demeanour, and she seemed upset that the only thing she had to offer Elizabeth was a patchwork garment repaired using material from older dresses. That didn't bother Elizabeth at all. If she could pay for something now, she would take it. Some people might have considered the rustic brown dress Martha offered her common and ugly, but Elizabeth thought it looked very practical for a carpenter's assistant. There was a lighter strip of material running up the front that had been patched in. Martha seemed to think it ruined the garment, but Elizabeth liked it. Nobles often matched different colours to

186

make themselves look elegant, and the neat off-white strip lent the dress a sense of distinction. Elizabeth thanked the woman profusely and paid three copper shillings to take the dress home with her.

During her walk back to the workshop, she found herself daydreaming about a house once again. She wanted somewhere with a proper bed and big chests she could store things in. It would have a fire, too. Not just a stone-lined pit in the floor, but a large wall hearth with a chimney to carry the smoke out. She would warm stones next to it so that she could put them in her bath and slip them into her pockets in winter. Whenever she'd been ill as a child her mother had wrapped hot stones in leather and put them on her mattress to make it warm, then she'd covered her up in a big soft cloak and told her stories about brave princesses and plucky minstrels while she cuddled her rag doll.

Elizabeth smiled fondly at the memory, but her daydreams were tinged with an undercurrent of unease this time. She felt like she was trying too hard to forget about what had happened in the nunnery. Tannersfield was a large town, but Edward was only half a day's ride down the road. What if he came looking for her again? He might lie to the sheriff and say she'd attacked him. She wouldn't be believed if she tried to argue otherwise. But surely Edward would go home to Cairnford soon? According to the heralds, a man called Lord Isaac was set to marry an heiress named Lady Emilia and become the new lord of Rosepath. Their wedding was supposed to happen on the winter solstice. Many people would be walking to Rosepath to witness the event, but Elizabeth thought that was a stupid idea. The road would probably be frozen by then, and it was a bitter trek from Tannersfield to Rosepath in the cold. Why go all that way just for a glimpse of some noble couple when you could be getting a solid day's work done back home?

For the time being she contented herself with the knowledge that Sir Edward would probably be gone once

Lord Isaac arrived. She'd never see him again, and he would eventually forget about her. She managed to return to the workshop with a smile on her face, thinking about how nice she would look when she greeted Joseph's customers in her new dress tomorrow. She resolved to be more assertive with them, making sure everyone knew they were to deal with her and not the tradesmen.

"That took you a while," Joseph said when she came back into the yard. He was busy dressing a length of timber with his moulding planes, small, precise tools made for shaping wood. By running them along the edge of a piece Joseph could carve off thin strips at accurate angles, creating soft curves or decorative grooves.

"I went to the nunnery on my way and stopped by the market for a bit," Elizabeth said. "I got a dress, though!"

Joseph grunted, remaining focused on his work. "Good girl. You can put the old one with Rose's things. I doubt she'll mind."

Elizabeth grinned. "She will."

"Aye, but, you know, in her good way."

"I know." Elizabeth rested a hand on the carpenter's shoulder as she went by, silently thanking him for his generosity. Despite never having raised a child, she thought Joseph was the sort of man who would be very good at it. He had a way with her that encouraged her to be her own woman. He offered support and guidance when she floundered. He knew when to put his foot down, but he was never strict. She wanted to make him proud of her.

Now that she was back at the workshop, her worries about Sir Edward faded. Instead, she decided to worry about the far more practical concern of getting the carpenters to agree with her new plan of organisation.

Now there was a problem worth losing sleep over.

The next morning, a tall monk arrived at the workshop. He ignored Elizabeth and headed toward the carpenters in the yard. Elizabeth stepped squarely in front of him. Standing up to dismissive customers seemed trivial after braving the ire of Duke Francis.

"You'll have to deal with me, Brother," she said. "The carpenters are busy working right now."

The monk gave her a stern look, but Elizabeth's expression was sterner. She'd decided to take Rose's advice to heart, not just with the carpenters, but the customers as well. True, she might incense some of them, but if they never learned to respect her nothing would change.

"I usually speak with Joseph Carpenter."

"I'm Elizabeth Carpenter, his assistant." Even though it was a little improper, it gave Elizabeth a surge of confidence to call herself Carpenter. She was a carpenter's assistant, after all, so why shouldn't she?

"I haven't seen you here before," the monk protested, but he was starting to sound unsure of himself.

"If you tell me what you're looking for I'll make sure the message gets to him." She heard a snigger from one of the apprentices in the yard. She wasn't sure whether they were laughing at her or the monk, but she chose to ignore them.

"Very well," the monk said, reaching inside his satchel and producing a roll of parchment. It was crinkled and worn, and there were greasy tallow stains where a candle had dripped on the corner. A sketch depicted a statue of one of the saints–Elizabeth couldn't remember which one–along with some lines and letters she couldn't read.

"The monastery needs half a dozen of these made for the feast of Saint Anden," the monk explained. "Would your master be able to do that?"

A twinge of unease threatened to shake Elizabeth's confidence. The lines and letters referred to the statue's dimensions, she understood that much from the sketches Joseph had shown her, but whether it was supposed to fit in the palm of her hand or tower over her head was a mystery. She stared at the letters, struggling to remember whether she'd seen anything in Joseph's sketches that resembled them, but it was a fruitless effort.

"Well?" the monk asked. "Can you do it?"

"Wait here a moment," Elizabeth said. The monk sighed as she hurried into the workshop.

Joseph looked up from his work and glanced over the sketch when she showed him. "They're only eleven inches tall. Rose can do half a dozen of these. They're not very detailed, so it shouldn't take her more than a couple of days. Tell him to come back on Friday and we'll have his statues done."

Elizabeth went back to the monk and passed along the information. She kept up her confident facade, but internally she was disappointed in herself. She would have been able to answer the monk right away if only she'd known what the letters on the parchment meant. When work stopped for the midday meal Joseph noticed her uneven mood.

"You need to learn how to read," he said.

"I know. I thought I could make do without, but I didn't expect people to start showing me plans."

"Most don't, but a few have sketches of things they've had made before. I did that one of the statue myself a few years back."

"Can you teach me?" Elizabeth asked.

"Bloody hell, girl, I'm already teaching you numbers." Joseph rubbed a hand through his beard. He didn't often get exasperated with her, but she could tell he was weighing up just how much time he was willing to invest in his new assistant. "I don't know. Maybe someday, but I'm not sure when. I suppose we could teach you to read numbers easily enough. Letters and words are a bit harder."

"Is reading numbers more important than knowing words?"

"Numbers were what you couldn't read on that sketch. There wasn't anything else written on it besides the name of Saint Anden."

"Maybe she should go to school with the nuns," one of the apprentices said from the bench behind them. "Liz is dumb as a mallet."

Joseph cuffed him across the back of the head. "She's got a sharper mind than you, boy. It's not her fault she hasn't been taught how to use it."

"I'm just saying," the young man grumbled. "She's lucky she's got that big arse for us to look at."

Elizabeth turned around. "Why don't you show us your arse, Fred? Got as many spots on it as your face?"

A peal of laughter erupted from the other carpenters. Fred narrowed his eyes and wiggled his nose at her. She returned the expression. The best way to get along with the boys, she'd learned, was to play them at their own game.

"I don't care how nice your arses look, you keep them covered up while you're working," Joseph said. A smile twitched the corner of his mouth. "Wouldn't want Saint Anden feeling offended." A few more chuckles stirred the air as the carpenters went back to their food.

Elizabeth kept thinking about how she might learn to read. It would be important if she wanted people to trust her as Joseph's assistant. Learning to read numbers might do for now, but she wanted to be able to understand plans and discuss them with the same certainty Joseph did. Schoolhouses were very expensive, and there was only one of them in Tannersfield that she knew of. The monks and nuns taught literacy as well, but only to novices of their order or wealthy individuals who could afford to pay more than the schoolhouse charged. Joseph would probably never find time for it himself. The only reason their mathematics lessons had become a routine was because they counted out the workshop's finances together once a week. Joseph liked to go to a public house most other evenings, or else he'd take Rose to bed early and Elizabeth would giggle about the noises she'd heard them making with the apprentices the next day.

191

Joseph worked hard, and she didn't want him sacrificing his free time for her sake. She hated feeling like a burden. For now, she would content herself with learning her numbers. Maybe one day, if the opportunity presented itself, she'd be able to start on letters.

Elizabeth found herself handling the routine jobs with greater ease once she accepted her limitations. When someone came by with written plans or technical details in mind, she directed them to Joseph. Everyone else she handled in person. Word slowly got around that she was the one to speak to at Joseph's workshop. Even the other carpenters began pointing people in her direction. Some did it begrudgingly, others with enthusiasm, but most of the boys enjoyed the way Joseph was distributing jobs now. Only those whose pride spoke louder than their good sense still insisted on doing things the old way.

The only downside to Elizabeth's newfound authority was that she struggled to find time for her chores around the workshop. After dwelling on it for a few days, she decided it was a problem she could solve with a bit of clever thinking. It was just a matter of organisation, after all, and organisation was something she was beginning to realise she had a talent for. Lady Eleanor had shuffled servants around all the time when they got in each other's way, so Elizabeth would just have to do the same thing with her work schedule. Rather than continuously flitting between different tasks, she broke her day down into different blocks of chores. In the mornings she would get up early and prepare the workshop for the carpenters, then head out and buy any supplies they needed for the day. Work would have started by the time she got back, but customers didn't tend to arrive until later on. That meant she usually had a little while to run errands for Joseph. After that, she would spend midday and the afternoon in the yard cleaning up after the others. That way she would always be on hand to deal with any customers who came by. At the end of the day, after she'd swept and tidied the workshop, she would sit down to have supper with Joseph and Rose and go over the work schedule for tomorrow.

One week at a time, the scaffolding of Elizabeth's plan solidified into a tight and consistent routine. There was still griping from some of the carpenters, but even Thin Robin had started to settle down now that he was spending most of his time making the doors he so loved. It was heartening to see the chaotic workshop pull itself together. By the end of the month, it was clear to everyone that they were getting through more work at a faster pace and at a higher level of quality than before. The carpenters rarely found themselves idle or overworked, and by spreading the workload they could transition into large jobs quickly and efficiently.

It was Elizabeth's attitude as much as her planning that had helped. She'd finally become accustomed to the fact that she was no longer working in a noble household, but a workshop of hardy craftsmen. They responded to practical, self-assured women like Rose, not polite and obsequious servants. As difficult as it was to break the habits of the past years, Elizabeth started to behave more like the person she'd been outside Rosepath Castle and less like Lady Eleanor's maidservant. The confidence she expressed in her exchanges with the carpenters was backed up by her organisational skills, with one feeding into the other until the men no longer saw her as the girl who swept the floors, but as one of their own.

Elizabeth did not see Sir Edward again all autumn. By the time the weather began to turn, Joseph reported that they were taking in more money than they usually did at this time of year. Even more promisingly, he had one of the kingdom's cardinals looking to hire him to work on a house in the springtime. It was a big and expensive project that would put him in charge of a full team of carpenters on a building site half a morning's walk from Tannersfield.

"I don't want you getting a big head, Liz," he told her over a trencher of vegetables and pork one evening, "but I might not have got that job without you. Whoever recommended us to the cardinal must've been someone important. It's like you said: fine folk are turning an eye to our little workshop now that we've got the boys focused on what they're best at." He snorted in amusement. "I never thought it would pay to get so meticulous with our work. When I was a lad my father was my master and we were the only carpenters in the village. Never have to worry about your reputation when you've no one else to compete with. Tannersfield's different, though. It pays to stand out from the crowd here."

"You'll be a rich man if you keep this up," Elizabeth said. "The more time you spend on building sites the more money you'll be making. You'll get a reputation as the master builder all the nobles hire! You could even rent the workshop out to other carpenters while you're away."

"You never run out of ideas, do you? I suppose you'll be wanting to run the place yourself while I'm gone."

Elizabeth didn't feel ashamed about asking for more this time. "I could, you know. I can count well enough to handle rent and wages by myself, and the boys are used to listening to me."

"What did he say about getting a big head?" Rose gave Elizabeth a swat on the arm. "You've not yet been here a year and you're already talking like you know the craft back to front."

"Well, who else is going to keep things running while you're away?"

Joseph shook his head with a wry smile. "She's got us there, Rose. How are we going to keep this all up while we're gone?"

"We put Luther in charge like we always do."

"We've been leaving him in charge long enough to know he's at his best with a chisel in his hand. Man's a master of

194

wood, not business."

Rose folded her arms and gave Elizabeth a hard look. "And what if the girl snatches up the month's takings and runs off with some boy as soon as the wind changes?" She was half-joking, but there was enough weight behind her words to make Joseph take them seriously. Despite having warmed to Elizabeth quickly, it was still true that they'd known her less than a year.

"We're not leaving you in charge, Liz, but I'll think about letting you share the responsibility with Luther. You can organise, but he'll have the final word, same as with us. That's not something to worry about now, though. We've got a whole winter before the job starts."

"I'm not planning on going anywhere."

"Ah, you say that now, but you're still young. Might be some handsome fellow catches your eye like Rose says, or maybe you'll get fed up herding carpenters and try your hand at something else."

"This is the only place I want to be. I've moved around so much I'm sick of it. All I want is someplace to settle down."

Joseph seemed to believe her, but Rose still looked sceptical.

"Let's talk about it again after winter," Joseph said, making it clear from his tone that the subject was closed for now. "Speaking of which." He put his purse on the table and fished out a pair of silver shillings. "I think you've about earned these with all the extra work you've been doing."

Elizabeth's eyes widened. She held out her hand eagerly, but Joseph kept the coins between his fingers.

"Now, say I was to rent out my front room to a girl who'd catch her death sleeping in the workshop outside. How much d'you reckon that might cost her for the winter, Rose?"

"I'd say about two silver shillings, especially if she's getting a warm fire and free meals out of it."

Elizabeth closed her palm, a broad smile spreading across her face. They were inviting her to stay.

195

"I'll put these back in my purse then, shall I?" Joseph said.

Elizabeth nodded. She could think of nothing better to spend her money on. Joseph's house would be the nicest, warmest place she'd ever spent the winter.

She was certain of it now: this was where she would build a life for herself. For as long as Joseph wanted her, she would continue working for him. No handsome young men were going to turn her head. No worries about Kaylein, no doubts about the future, not even the threat of Sir Edward. She was going to do everything she could to make Joseph's workshop her home.

This was the nook her heart could settle into.

CHAPTER 13

It was November, and the writing room was starting to get cold. Kaylein shivered in her chair, hearing the old wood creak beneath her knees as she squinted through the mist of her breath. Her back ached from bending forward all afternoon. If it got much colder she wouldn't be able to keep her hands from trembling as she wrote. The oncoming winter seemed like it was going to be a bitter one. What would she do with herself if she couldn't pass the time writing? Mother Jane had hinted that she might take her first vows and start seeing to chores outside the convent, but Kaylein wasn't sure if she was ready for that. Besides Liz, everyone and everything outside the convent frightened her. The news that Duke Francis had visited a few months ago had kept her awake for a week straight despite the mother superior's assurance that he meant her no harm. Apparently his son was getting married in Rosepath a month from now. A few of the nuns would be visiting the church to assist with the preparations. Kaylein dreaded hearing their stories about it when they returned. She would gladly have forgotten Rosepath existed. The idea of some new lord living in the castle she'd grown up in brought a queasy feeling to her stomach and tears to her eyes.

She pressed her chapped lips together and frowned, focusing on her work. Dwelling on Rosepath did her no good. It was God who needed her devotion now, not the phantoms of the past. Taking a moment to concentrate, she ignored the worrisome feelings within her and delved deeper, seeking the warm core that gave her strength when she prayed. Calm, pure, and soothing, it reminded her that no matter what happened, no matter how bleak things seemed, there would always be a divine force watching over her. God's light was her refuge from the darkness.

Kaylein kept working until the cold became unbearable, then she closed the book she was copying from and left her page to dry. All the other sisters had already left the writing room. It would be nice to have a fire up here, she thought, but the open windows would just let the heat out. Perhaps they could light candles and write in the chapter house downstairs.

Kaylein closed the shutters and tidied her writing desk, then picked up the pages she'd completed and tucked the copying book beneath her arm. It was the second volume of the seven prime scriptures that comprised the church's religious canon. Most priests and laypeople only referred to the first volume in their daily lives, for it outlined the major precepts of sin and virtue along with detailing the nature of heaven, hell, and the world between. Kaylein had read all seven of the prime scriptures in her youth, but she'd come to know them much more intimately during her time at the nunnery. They had all been written by different saints, with the later volumes exploring more philosophical interpretations of the precepts set out in the first scripture. Kaylein found the first scripture to be somewhat dry and impersonal, with rules that seemed too simplistic to properly articulate God's will. If thievery was a sin, did that mean she and Elizabeth were going to hell for stealing from the merchant on the road from Rosepath? They never would've survived the streets of Tannersfield without the contents of that merchant's satchel. Killing was also a sin, yet kings went to war all the time, and no king came to power without God's blessing. Kaylein preferred the later volumes of the seven prime scriptures, for they seemed to have been written by men who shared her moral conundrums. They challenged, reinterpreted, and sometimes outright refuted the sacred doctrine of their forebears. There was vigour and passion in their words. While God commanded obedience, he also commanded honesty, and from her readings Kaylein honestly believed that no just god would want his people shackled by the simplistic moral code of the first prime scripture.

This line of thinking had gotten her in trouble with some of the other nuns, so she tried to reserve her opinions for conversations with the more academic sisters, those who saw religious debate as a way of broadening their understanding rather than proving their superiority. Mother Jane was one such woman, and Kaylein always looked forward to their walks through the cloisters together.

Before she left the writing room, she slipped her finished pages between two thin sheets of wood and secured them together with a loop of twine. The sheets acted like a book cover that would keep the pages safe until they could be bound into a full volume. With the binder under one arm and the copying book under the other, she headed downstairs into the chapter house. The long room was empty save for the rectangle of benches at the far end where the nuns sat to discuss the convent's daily business. Housed beneath the stairs was the convent's sacristy, where valuables and holy relics were kept. Mother Jane did not believe in hoarding gaudy ornaments encrusted with gold and jewels like her counterparts in the monastery, but she did find great value in books. The sacristy was packed with shelved cabinets containing volumes upon volumes of religious scripture, both canon and speculative, along with books on medicine, history, and the sciences.

Kaylein knocked lightly at the door and the sacrist, Sister Helen, let her in. Helen unlocked the nearest cabinet and motioned for Kaylein to deposit her work inside. There was a shelf for books and a shelf for unfinished pages ready to be beautified by the illuminator, who would use gold leaf and coloured inks to illustrate Kaylein's work in a manner that captured God's radiance. Kaylein put everything where it belonged and left Sister Helen to lock up behind her, thinking proudly of how her work might one day sit on the shelf of a cardinal or a king.

As she headed into the cloisters she tugged her robe tight about her body, feeling the wintry chill more keenly as she passed Saint Caridwen's statue. The cloisters were eerily quiet. Even the distant bustle of Tannersfield sounded subdued that day. The whole world slowed down when winter arrived. It wasn't yet late enough for her to retire to the dormitory or head to the refectory for supper, so she would be expected to assist the other nuns with their afternoon chores. She didn't particularly want to do that. Scribing was the only activity that made her feel useful, yet idleness was a precept of sin. Begrudgingly, she resolved to go looking for someone who needed her help. Today was a busy laundry day, which meant most of the sisters would be helping in the washroom where the convent's water channel ran in from the river.

Rather than going to help with the washing—still Kaylein's least favourite chore—she scoured the other corners of the convent for work. Perhaps she could sweep up the warm refectory, or help old Sister Trea take inventory in the comforting mustiness of the cellar. Her walk took her into the eastern dormitory. The fully initiated sisters slept here, separate from the novices who bunked on the west side of the convent. Kaylein and the other youngsters were often tasked with keeping this dormitory clean for their senior sisters. She didn't mind tidying, for it was a reminder of the relative comfort she could look forward to in a few years' time. The dormitory comprised three long rooms furnished with wooden beds and proper hearths to keep the place warm. It was strange to think that she now relished the prospect of sleeping on a wooden cot with a straw mattress. A year ago she would've turned up her nose at anything less than a feather bed.

The dormitory walls muffled the distant noise of the town, lending an almost holy silence to the empty rooms. Kaylein closed her eyes to savour it. She might have stood there for a long time had a sudden snort of laughter from one of the adjacent chambers not startled her out of her reverie. She poked her head into the room, expecting to find another novice sweeping up, but the dormitory was dark and all the shutters were closed. Somebody had lit a candle at the far end and set it on a table beside the beds. It was wasteful to burn candles while it was still light. By its soft glow, Kaylein could make out two figures sitting on the edge of the nearest bed. Both had their hoods down—yet another impropriety during the hours of the day—and from the fiery red hair of one and the slight build of the other Kaylein recognised them as sisters Grace and Isabel. Neither of them noticed her looking in, for they were too engrossed in the kiss they were sharing. Kaylein smiled. It was sweet to see nuns exchange kisses of friendship. Her smile turned into a frown as the kiss lingered. A nervous feeling took root in her stomach. She heard Sister Grace make a strange noise, and then, to Kaylein's horror, she reached up to caress Sister Isabel's cheek and pushed her tongue into her mouth. This was not a kiss between friends.

Hardly daring to breathe, Kaylein pulled herself out of the room and pressed her back against the wall. An intense feeling of confusion twisted up her thoughts. She'd never considered that two women *could* kiss each other that way, let alone sisters who had sworn themselves to the precept of chastity. The realisation that she had just witnessed a serious sin gripped Kaylein like an iron glove. She had to take this to the mother superior at once.

Being careful not to let her footsteps sound on the stone

floor, she hurried back through the dormitory into the cloisters. At first she could think of nothing besides finding Mother Jane and reporting the two nuns for their disobedience, but once the initial panic had faded her pace faltered and the confusion returned. She liked Sister Grace, and Sister Isabel had never done anything to make her think poorly of her. Grace often helped in the kitchen. She'd always overlooked Kaylein's mistakes and tried to help her rather than laying on admonishments and swats of the willow switch. She was a warm-hearted woman, relaxed and compassionate, and Kaylein struggled to believe she was a sinner worthy of punishment.

The conflict weighed heavily upon her, so much so that she stopped in front of the statue of Saint Caridwen and clasped her hands together in prayer. What did God want her to do? Perhaps she should keep the matter to herself and trust Grace and Isabel to confess on their own. Perhaps she should confront them directly rather than going to Mother Jane behind their backs. But Mother Jane was wise, and if anyone knew how to deal with a confusing situation like this, it was her.

Kaylein tried to find the inner warmth of God's light, but she was too flustered to centre herself. Why would two women do something like that? Kaylein had never kissed anyone before, so she didn't understand why it was so special. She'd always thought she would find out when she got married, but that was no longer a possibility. Her only exposure to romance and sexuality had been a handful of conversations with other noble girls about their future husbands, usually at feasts or faires in Tannersfield. The topic made her awkward and flustered, just like when she saw women selling themselves outside a brothel. That was exactly how she felt right now.

Eventually, she gave up on prayer and tried to remember the guidance of the prime scriptures. The doctrine on chastity was very clear in the first scripture: sex outside marriage was a

202

sin, and the breaking of a vow of chastity a greater sin still. Yet kissing was not sex, was it? Kaylein didn't think two women *could* have sex, nor two men, for that matter. That was why they kept monasteries and nunneries separate, to make sure it never happened. Her ignorance on the subject frustrated her. How were nuns supposed to understand these things if they were forbidden from partaking in them? Even speaking of carnal matters often earned a novice penance from her senior sisters.

She wished Liz were there. She understood all the things servants gossiped about behind closed doors. A sense of isolation stole over Kaylein, drawing the last of the warmth from the air. The ground felt hard and uncomfortable beneath her feet. There was no one like Liz at the convent. Kaylein liked Mother Jane and some of the older nuns, but since she rarely shared chores or schooling hours with the other novices she'd struggled to make friends. Part of her understood why Grace and Isabel had slipped away to the dormitory, even if she didn't understand why they'd been kissing. Even with God at her side, life in the convent could be very lonely.

"This isn't the place for prayer, Sister Kaylein."

She looked up and saw Sub-Prioress Joan looking down at her. The older woman had grey in her hair and a fearsome manner with the novices, but she was cordial to those who studied hard. As an educated woman with knowledge of the scriptures, Kaylein hadn't fallen afoul of her wrath too many times thus far.

"I am–" Kaylein began, but her throat was stiff and the words came out awkwardly. She coughed into the back of her hand and tried again. It helped to imagine she was speaking to her father or mother, otherwise she had a habit of offending the senior nuns by sounding haughty with them. "I find the statue of the saint peaceful. She helps me focus."

"Just like us, Saint Caridwen was a servant of God, and God demands obedience. If you need to pray you should do it in the chapel, lest God think you are praying to Saint Caridwen instead of him."

God knows who I am praying to, Kaylein thought, but she didn't dare disagree with the sub-prioress. She turned away from the statue and made a humble bow. "I will try and take my prayers to the chapel from now on."

"You will do more than try. Be firm in your convictions. We must strive to be more than mortal women in our service to God, thusly we set an example that others might follow. Back to work now. There is plenty of room for you to help with the laundry."

Reluctantly, Kaylein resigned herself to scrubbing dresses and undergarments for the rest of the afternoon. Her mind kept returning to what she'd seen in the dormitory. When everyone sat down for supper she found it difficult to make eye contact with Sister Grace, who seemed to be smiling a lot and speaking louder than usual. Sister Joan had to tell her to lower her voice twice. The sub-prioress could not abide boisterousness.

Kaylein had never kept a secret like this before, and the conundrum of what to do with it kept her on edge the entire meal. When Sister Grace asked her whether she was feeling well she almost choked on her daily half-cup of warm wine. She swallowed the rest without savouring it and excused herself. The impulse to go to the mother superior scratched at her like an itch, stirring a secondary conflict within Kaylein that stewed about her thoughts as she crossed the darkening cloisters to the novices' dormitory.

What would God want?

That was the question she kept returning to. At the beginning of the year, Kaylein had been a confident, self-assured woman, believing that everything in the world was exactly as she understood and precisely as she expected. If she had a problem, a servant would take care of it for her. If there was trouble, her father would make it go away. The night Count Francis attacked, all of those assumptions had been shattered, and now she felt like a child again. There was a pressing need within her, a desperation, even, to let someone else take charge. At first, that person had been Elizabeth. Now, it was the convent, and, by extension, God. Yet Kaylein was starting to realise that she could not be a passive subject all her life. It was a cowardly and feeble way to live, and it would have made her father ashamed of her. In recent weeks she'd grown confident enough to start saying things that stirred controversy among the other nuns, such as her interpretations of the scriptures. She'd lived too much of her life as a noble to completely abandon the ego that had been bred into her since birth. As much as she wanted to defer to God's will, some questions could not be answered through scripture and prayer.

This decision was one she would have to make for herself. It was frightening, but she couldn't spend the rest of her life hiding from difficult choices. The guilt of failing to live up to her parents' expectations would eat away at her if she did. She might never be a woman of status again, but she didn't want to be a coward.

Sleep was a long time in coming that evening. If only Grace and Isabel had committed some simple sin, like hoarding money or speaking ill of the Lord. Those were things Kaylein could understand. When she dwelt on the memory of their kiss, she felt like she was sitting too close to a fire in an itchy wool gown. After a restless night, she resolved to speak with the mother superior. She didn't intend to tell her what she'd seen, not yet at least, but she needed guidance, or else she would end up writhing around in her itchy thoughts all day.

Mother Jane usually made herself available for private counsel after morning prayer, so Kaylein sat near the front of the chapel and hurried past the altar as soon as service ended.

"Less haste, Sister," Mother Jane reprimanded her. "You'll knock someone over dashing around like that."

"I am sorry, Mother. Could I speak with you for a

moment?"

Mother Jane gestured into her room. "My door is open."

Once they were both seated Kaylein tried to begin, but she didn't know where to start. The subject embarrassed her. Mother Jane sat behind her writing desk patiently, seeming content to let her lesson on hastiness sink in a while longer.

"I have a... theoretical question, Mother, about something I do not understand."

"Yours has ever proven to be a keen mind when it comes to religious theory, Sister Kaylein."

"It is about the precept of chastity."

Mother Jane took a deep breath, allowing her back to straighten as her lungs filled. She always did this when steeling herself for a difficult subject. "Young novices often bring up that precept at least once."

"It isn't for my own sake, Mother," Kaylein stammered, feeling her face flush red. "I don't want to break the precept. I don't even understand such things."

"Yet you have a theoretical question, hm?" Mother Jane did not sound convinced. Kaylein dreaded the thought of vaguely alluding to what she'd seen, only for the prioress to suspect that *she'd* been one of the sisters involved. She tried to swallow her discomfort and press on. It was too late to back out now.

"It shouldn't be possible to break a vow of chastity here in the convent, should it?"

"What makes you say that?"

"Well, there are no men."

Mother Jane gave her a thin-lipped look. "That is true, and therein lies the difficulty with the precept of chastity. Have the other sisters been speaking to you about this?"

"No. Why, has something happened?" She felt momentarily hopeful that Grace and Isabel might have confessed their sin already.

Mother Jane shook her head. "Never mind. If you have doubts then you should err on the side of strictness. Resist the temptation to do anything God might consider unchaste."

"What if a nun did do something unchaste," Kaylein's face burned, "with one of the other sisters?"

"Then that would be a violation of her vows, and she would be punished for it."

"But what makes an act unchaste? What if it was just a kiss?"

Mother Jane considered her response before answering. "Sometimes you are a very difficult novice, Sister Kaylein. A woman without your knowledge of the scriptures would take the simplest interpretation of chastity and leave it at that."

It almost sounded like a compliment, but Kaylein wasn't sure. "I know it's been discussed at length in the more modern scriptures. Do you know of any particular verses I might be able to study?"

"The problem with your question, Sister Kaylein, is that there is–" the mother superior pursed her lips, "–debate on the subject of chastity among nuns. For monks it is very clear: any act of penetration is wholly carnal, and carnal acts are forbidden under our vows."

Hearing the prioress speak of these things so candidly seemed almost sinful in itself, yet her crisp and academic tone made her sound more like a physician explaining something sensitive than a gossip talking about sex. Kaylein had read about how babies were made in a book of medicine once, and it hadn't seemed so awkward to her when it was laid out in clear and practical terms.

"With nuns, there is no act of... penetration," she said with some difficulty.

"Indeed, and therein lies the debate. Is it even possible for two women to violate a vow of chastity if they are incapable of sex as the scriptures define it? The first prime scripture was written by Saint Anden, a monk, and presumably one with little knowledge of the sins unique to women."

"If monks and nuns are bound by vows of chastity then how can any of us understand carnal sins in the first place?"

"Not all of us are born into chastity. Among your sisters are former mothers and former whores, and you will find any number of penitent adulterers within a convent. Besides, one need not partake in sin to observe its effects from afar. Those who revel in carnal pleasures with many partners are often stricken ill, and men who ravish women are abhorred for good reason. It is because these extremes are so impure that we must logically assume absolute chastity reflects a contrasting purity."

"Love is not sinful though, is it?"

"I did not think we were speaking of love, my child."

Again the pangs of indecision wracked Kaylein. The question of love was another thing that confused her. What if Grace and Isabel loved each other? Could a woman love a woman? Kaylein had loved her mother, but that was different.

"I can tell you are troubled by this, Sister," the prioress said.

"Only because it does not seem as if there is a good answer. God wants nuns to be chaste, but there is no definitive scripture on what that means. God wants us to love, but he does not want us to love lightly. Where is the line drawn?"

"You have the soul of a philosopher. For women like you and I, these questions are always on our minds. They test our faith and challenge our convictions, which is why so many in our church choose to dismiss them in favour of the simple answers found within the first prime scripture."

Kaylein's shoulders slumped in disappointment. "Then there is no answer?"

"There is always an answer, we simply have yet to find it. Only God knows with absolute certainty."

"You would have to make a decision if you caught two sisters doing something that might violate their vow of chastity, though, wouldn't you?"

"If this question were more than theoretical, then yes, I

would. I would have to think on it deeply, consider the nature of the sin, and set an appropriate penance."

Kaylein felt defeated. She'd been sure the mother superior's advice would crystallise her foggy thoughts, yet the problem seemed more obtuse than ever.

"That's exactly what I have been trying to do," she said dejectedly. "Think and pray. And it's led me nowhere."

"Did you see two sisters breaking their vow of chastity?"

Kaylein couldn't lie now that she'd been asked directly. That would only make her complicit in the sin. Her line of questioning had probably made it obvious, anyway, so she nodded her head in admission. Mother Jane remained silent for a long time until Kaylein looked up at her. When the prioress spoke, it was not with the tone of disapproval Kaylein had been expecting.

"Most sisters would have come to me immediately with this."

"I am sorry, Mother. I will do penance if I must."

"Make it part of your evening prayers." The mother superior's lenience shocked Kaylein. Offering a prayer was barely penance at all. "Tell me who you saw and what they were doing."

Kaylein did, but she kept the details as minimal as possible. One weight lifted from her chest, only for another to settle in its place. It was guilt. Had she done the right thing?

"Thank you," Mother Jane said. "I will meditate on this and assign sisters Grace and Isabel their due penance." She still didn't sound angry. Something else seemed to be on her mind, something that had crept up on her while they talked. The prioress was studying Kaylein curiously, as though she was the real problem that needed to be solved, the matter with Grace and Isabel merely an afterthought.

"If that is all, you may go back to your morning duties," Mother Jane said. "Perhaps you should think more on this in your meditations."

"Will you tell me your answer once you settle on it, Mother?"

The prioress smiled. "If I did that, how would you ever come up with an answer of your own?"

Kaylein left the room feeling bemused. This was by far the strangest thing that had happened to her since joining the convent. The matter was in the mother superior's hands now, yet her own part still felt unresolved. Perhaps it would be easier if she simply took the precepts at their face value. It wasn't the place of a novice to agonise over religious philosophy. Yet the stubborn noblewoman within her refused to let it go. Try as she might, she was no passive follower. She wanted to rationalise her own interpretations of God's will, and if the scriptures failed to provide the answers she needed she felt duty-bound to decipher them herself.

Kaylein knew that another sleepless night awaited her that evening. The questions of chastity, purity, and right and wrong needled at her incessantly. Even her writing could not distract her that day. She found herself longing to commit her inner thoughts to the page instead of the verses she was transcribing. If she could make them tangible, if she could stare at them and mull them over and share them with insightful women like Mother Jane, then perhaps she could settle upon an answer. The prioress had told her she had the heart of a philosopher, but novices did not pen original scripture. That was the purview of priors and bishops, figures of status within the church whose ideas were respected. If she ever wanted to express her thoughts the way the great philosophers did, she would need to prove herself a woman worth listening to.

Two weeks later, Kaylein took her first vows.

CHAPTER 14

Frost dusted the road from Cairnford, speckling the ridges of frozen hoofprints like a crust of sugar. Isaac had first tasted sugar in his travels to the south. They'd baked delicious breads and pastries with that sweet-tasting powder, glazed fruits with it, and even mixed it into oats to make a treat of bland porridge. There was nothing like that here. Here the road was glossy with mud and ice, making Blackberry nicker anxiously whenever they crossed a treacherous patch. He stroked his poor horse's mane, wishing he had time to stop and make a fire. Unlike most horses, Blackberry loved a nice fire. She was an elegant chestnut-coated palfrey, and she was Isaac's best friend.

"I'd marry you if only you'd been born with a couple more arms and a couple less legs." He sighed. Blackberry snorted and tossed her mane. She didn't understand him, of course, but she had a way of sensing the sentiment behind his words.

Isaac was dreading his upcoming marriage to Lady Emilia. It was only a few days away now, due to take place on the morning of the winter solstice. He'd put it off for as long as he could. For months it had seemed like a distant worry, a problem for a future Isaac to deal with, an older, wiser Isaac who was ready to settle down and be lord of his own castle. Yet the months had slipped by, and Isaac had not become that man. When Father's letter arrived summoning him to Rosepath, his wedding day had ceased to be a distant worry. Now it was very real–and terribly imminent.

He rubbed Blackberry's mane again, reminding himself that he'd always have her. He never felt nervous travelling the roads without an escort. Blackberry was as swift as the wind, and she could spirit him away from danger in the blink of an eye. Life didn't seem worth living if a man couldn't ride the roads without fear. Besides, when he travelled with Father's men he had a miserable time of it. They were loud and drank too much ale, and they were always asking him questions he didn't want to answer, like which women he preferred and how many castles he planned on building when he was duke. People thought Isaac peculiar, and he supposed they were right. He'd inherited Duke Francis's sandy hair and good looks, but his disposition was closer to his mother's. She had declined to attend the wedding. Isaac could hardly blame her; he didn't want to be there either. In the past her refusal might have sent Father into a rage, but these days he tended to overlook Mother's eccentricities. She preferred to remain at Cairnford Castle, and Father was so busy being a duke that he rarely had time to argue with her anymore.

Trying his best not to think about the wedding, Isaac slackened his grip on the reins and guided Blackberry around another patch of ice with a subtle nudge of his knees. She was clever enough to avoid it on her own, but Isaac's guidance made her move more confidently. Even though she didn't mind being tugged about by the reins, Isaac knew she was quicker without them sometimes. Reins made Blackberry reluctant to move without his say-so, despite the fact that she knew her own hooves better than him. The pair of them were swiftest when they worked in tandem, each an equal partner in their travels.

If it weren't for the ice they would've reached Rosepath by

now. A shred of anxiety lingered in Isaac's stomach when he thought about the possibility of night falling before he got there, but he tried not to worry about it. He tried not to worry about most things.

That was why they always snuck up on him.

To his relief, the road broadened and flattened out once it twisted north. He was deep into Tannersfield county by now. Judging by the thick forest encroaching upon the road, Rosepath should be just a few hours away. He'd never been there before, but he knew it was somewhere in the forest south of Tannersfield town. He always had a way of finding where he was going in the end. Sooner or later every road led to a village, and every village had someone you could ask for directions.

Midway through the afternoon he started catching up with a family that were headed the same way as him. Despite his distaste for journeying with his father's men, Isaac didn't mind joining up with travellers on the road. None of them knew who he was, which meant they didn't ask uncomfortable questions.

The father of the travelling family looked behind him when he heard Blackberry's hooves crunching over the frosty mud. He stepped toward the trees and motioned his children aside. There were three of them, all gaunt-looking things, and their mother was clutching a baby to her chest. A tense moment followed as Isaac approached, but the father relaxed when he saw that the well-dressed man on horseback was unarmed. Isaac understood why people got nervous around knights and men-at-arms, but weapons had never bothered him personally. Men had always worn swords in Father's castle.

"Milord." The father inclined his head politely as Isaac rode up.

"Hello, friend," Isaac replied. "Might I ask where you're headed?"

"Rosepath. For the wedding."

Isaac resisted the urge to grimace. For a blessed moment, he'd been able to forget about the wedding. "I suppose I am, too. Do you know the way there?"

The man glanced up and down the road uncomfortably before one of his children said: "He doesn't."

"Neither do I." Isaac smiled. "Do you think we might find the way together?"

The father cleared his throat. "I suppose it wouldn't hurt."

To Isaac's relief, no one called him "milord" again. They probably took him for a well-spoken journeyman, or perhaps an unusually affluent minstrel. He wasn't travelling with weapons or an escort, and even though he wore fine leather boots and well-made clothes there was nothing gaudy about his appearance.

The family turned out to be heading to Rosepath in the hopes of receiving alms from the church, which was apparently known for its charity, though the father insisted they were doing their duty as subjects of the new duke by paying respects at his son's wedding. They seemed to be pleasant people, though they had clearly fallen upon hard times. Isaac pretended some of his apples were going stale so that he could share them with the children, for the father was embarrassed by his poverty and reluctant to admit they needed help. Blackberry started nudging one of the young girls along when she started to tire, and Isaac let her ride in front of him in the saddle so she could rest her legs. Eventually, they came to a fork in the road, one branch continuing north while the other peeled away to the west. The group slowed to a halt. No one knew which turning led to Rosepath.

Blackberry started to snort, sniffed the dirt a few times, then took the northern path.

"Blackberry thinks it's this way," Isaac said.

The father gave him a sceptical look. "A horse can't know that."

"I don't think she knows we're going to Rosepath, but she

smells that other horses have been this way. Where else would a lot of horses be headed?"

The man seemed a little bemused, but he didn't argue. A lot of people started thinking Isaac was a queer sort when they found out he treated his horse more like a person than a pet.

The light was beginning to fade when they smelled smoke coming through the trees on their left. Once the undergrowth thinned, they saw a long village sprawling out between frosty meadows to the north and thick forest to the south. A pale and elegant castle perched atop a hill at its crown.

My new home, Isaac thought with a sinking heart. It wasn't that he disliked the look of the place–it seemed far more homely than windswept Cairnford–but Isaac had never felt freer than when he'd left his father's castle to go travelling five years ago. Now whenever he looked at castles, he saw stuffy stone prisons that kept their lords shackled to the spot.

At least he would be shackled somewhere nice.

He bade the family farewell and rode ahead into the village. A lot of people had arrived for the wedding. The public houses had crowds outside despite the cold weather, and half a dozen rough peasant dwellings seemed to have been recently thrown together in the meadow. Isaac didn't turn any heads on his way to the castle, for there were plenty of horse riders clattering to and from the paved marketplace. He savoured the anonymity while it lasted. In a few days' time, everyone in the village would know his face.

A pair of men-at-arms stopped him at the castle gates, but he was quickly ushered inside when they recognised him. An old stable master approached and offered to take Blackberry. Isaac declined politely. He liked to make sure she was properly settled whenever she spent the night in a new stable. Once she was comfortable with the other horses he crossed the courtyard, marvelling at its well-kept green. It was unusual for small baileys to have grass inside, for hooves and feet usually stamped it into mud, but the former lord of Rosepath seemed to have taken great care in maintaining dedicated footpaths around the greenery.

In the time he'd spent at the stable someone had evidently announced his arrival, for a group of men and a surly-looking servant girl came out to greet him. A young knight with dark hair and an expensive-looking silk cloak stepped forward. It was Sir Edward, one of his father's thugs. He didn't seem particularly happy to see Isaac, but when he spoke it was with the practised formality of a subject addressing his lord.

"My lord Isaac. Your father and Marquess Alistair await you in the great hall."

The butterflies in Isaac's stomach returned. Marquess Alistair was the father of his bride-to-be, Lady Emilia. They'd only met once before, fifteen years ago, when Isaac was seven. He recalled Alistair as a brash and argumentative man that Father had been loathe to offer lodgings at Cairnford Castle. Emilia, two years Isaac's senior, had sat with him and the other noble children at dinner. One of Isaac's favourite dogs had died from an infection that morning, and Emilia had made him cry when she said it would go to hell because dogs were filthy and all they knew was sin. Isaac's sister, Cristiana, had started an argument with her, and that had made him feel even worse, because needing a girl to stand up for you was almost as bad as being made to cry by one.

But that had been a long time ago. He was a man now, and Emilia would be a completely different person. Her father might have softened with age. It couldn't possibly be as bad as he feared.

Despite his assurances, the feeling of nausea only grew worse as he crossed the courtyard. By the time Sir Edward led them over the supple planks of the drawbridge he'd begun to sweat.

"Is Lady Emilia staying at the keep, too?" he asked nervously, hoping conversation might help settle his writhing stomach.

"She's upstairs with your sister," Sir Edward said.

That calmed Isaac's nerves just a touch. At least Cristiana was here. They weren't the closest of siblings, but she understood him in a way others seldom did. His sister was one of the few people he'd missed during his travels. Perhaps he'd be able to excuse himself quickly and spend the rest of the evening talking to her.

Rosepath's great hall wasn't as big as the one at Cairnford Castle. The air was stuffy and smoky from poor ventilation, and there were dark stains on the floor that the servants had tried to cover with rush mats. Isaac suspected the keep was probably older than the smart walls surrounding it, but his ponderous thoughts vanished when he saw his father standing beside the high table. A cluster of guests surrounded him, all dressed in trimmed cloaks, thick winter tunics, fine gowns and decorated girdles. Marquess Alistair was among them, a little thinner and greyer than Isaac remembered him, but still sporting the same fearsomely full moustache. Father looked deathly weary with their conversation, but his face lit up when Isaac entered the room.

"There we are, a groom for our bride at last!" he called. "The marquess feared he might have to send his knights out to hunt you down."

"I wouldn't want that, Father," Isaac said, sneaking a sidelong glance at Alistair as Duke Francis embraced him. It was a stiff hug, for Father was not a warm man, and Isaac suspected it was more for the benefit of the guests than himself. Marquess Alistair eyed him with an appraisive air. For a fleeting instant, Isaac wondered whether the man might call off his daughter's engagement if he found her betrothed to be lacking in some way, and his heart leapt at the possibility. Yet the hope died a moment later as Alistair's lips broadened into a smile.

"Young master Isaac. Not so young any more are we, eh?"

"I told you he'd grown into a handsome man," Francis said. "Suitable for your daughter, I trust."

217

"Oh yes. She'll be very pleased."

"You're most kind, my lord marquess," Isaac said. His stomach lurched as he bent to give Alistair a bow. Everyone in the room seemed to be speaking very loudly. The smoky air tasted thick and cloying. He needed to find a reason to excuse himself. "Is there any chance I might see Lady Emilia? I've been dying to meet her before the wedding."

Alistair chuckled. "I don't see why not. What do you say, Francis? We can leave the children to get to know each other while you finish telling me about how you took this place from Leo. How did you get the soldiers so close without anyone noticing?"

Francis pressed his lips together, looking as drawn and pale as Isaac felt. "If you insist." Alistair led them toward the stairs, but Francis hung back and whispered: "The sooner we're rid of this insufferable man the better."

Isaac could only nod, thankful to be getting away from the noise of the great hall. He wished he was outside taking care of Blackberry. As earthy as stables could be, he liked the smell of them better than smoky old keeps.

They climbed a flight of stairs and crossed a narrow landing to a bedroom. There was a thick rug on the floor, a warm fire, and a bed large enough for two people. Isaac's sister was sitting on the corner next to a woman who could only have been Lady Emilia. Isaac's lips parted slightly as a wholly different discomfort took hold of him. She was beautiful. Dark-haired and fair-skinned, she wore an embroidered yellow gown that contrasted with the shadows playing over her face to throw her features into delicate relief. Isaac couldn't help but think about how he would soon have the chance to kiss those subtly plump lips and run his hands over the curves beneath her dress. Emilia rose to her feet, smiling at him. She was even prettier when she smiled, and he felt a stirring of desire in his loins.

"Lady Emilia," Duke Francis said, stepping past Isaac with an air of formality. "It's about time you met my son."

218

"Yes," Emilia said. Even her voice had an attractive quality to it, like a warm breeze. "Cristiana has been telling me all about him. I'm honoured to meet you, Fiancée."

"And you." Isaac cleared his throat. "I'm pleased to meet you, of course."

"Enjoy your last few days of this," Alistair said. "Once you're wed you'll be the lord and lady of this village. No more gallivanting around like youngsters."

"Of course, Father," Emilia said.

Alistair grunted and slapped Francis on the arm, much to the duke's obvious annoyance. "Back to that story then, Francis?" The pair exited the room and shut the door behind them. Isaac listened to the sound of their footsteps receding down the stairs, standing in silence while Emilia stared at him.

"Say something, then," Cristiana said. She had a teasing look on her face, as was her way. People said she was attractive like Isaac, though she had more of their father's severe look about her, something she accentuated by wearing her hair up in a crown of coiled braids rather than letting it fall freely.

"I, um," Isaac began. He tried to smile, which made Emilia laugh. He was probably making a fool of himself. "I like this village very much."

"What about *her*?" Cristiana whispered with no attempt at subtlety. Emilia began giggling even harder.

"You're very pretty, Lady Emilia."

"Oh, Isaac," she said once she'd finished laughing. "You've not changed a bit. How long has it been since I last saw you?"

"Fifteen years. You told me my dog was going to hell."

Cristiana gave him an incredulous look. He wasn't good at talking to women.

Emilia just giggled again. She seemed the giggling sort. "I hope you're not still angry at me for that."

"No, but I did like that dog."

219

"Well, I'm sure it went to heaven. Perhaps we can ask the priest at our ceremony."

"In front of half of Rosepath." Cristiana rolled her eyes. "Father might call off the wedding then and there."

"He's very firm, isn't he?" Emilia said. "I'm glad you're not like that, Isaac."

"How do you know I'm not?"

"I said your sister's been telling me everything about you."

Isaac's brow perked hopefully. "Did she tell you about Blackberry?"

"Blackberries?"

"No, she's—oh, never mind."

"Emilia doesn't much care for animals," Cristiana said.

"Not even horses?"

Emilia shrugged. "I'll ride one if I have to."

Isaac's initial wave of desire began to dim. What would their lives be like as lord and lady of this castle? He'd always wanted to keep lots of dogs like Father, not just for hunting, but because he enjoyed having them around the castle. As his wife Emilia would have to obey him and abide by his wishes, but he didn't want her to be miserable. Mother had always been miserable when Father ignored what she wanted.

"How do you feel about dogs?" he asked.

"I think you found that out when we were children."

He forced a difficult smile. "I don't have to keep dogs if you don't like them. Maybe I can find a hound master in the village. There must be good hunting nearby, with all these forests."

Emilia didn't look very interested. "I suppose so. Sir Edward would know. He's been the lord here for a while now."

"I should ask him. He must be a reliable man for Father to trust him with all this."

"Or a bloodthirsty one." Cristiana frowned. "I don't like him, Isaac. I heard people saying things about him in Tannersfield."

220

"Well, if he proves troublesome you can always have the sheriff hang him," Emilia said matter-of-factly.

Isaac frowned. "I wouldn't do that."

"Why not? Your father killed the last lord who lived here, and he was a count. A little knight shouldn't be any trouble."

Isaac exchanged a look with his sister. He wasn't growing any more comfortable with the conversation, and the talk of what had happened to Count Leo only made it worse. Father rarely spoke of it, and when he did it was with the vicious sort of hatred he only usually expressed when talking about the war. Count Leo had wronged him back then in some way, Isaac knew that much, but nobles weren't supposed to kill other nobles during peacetime.

"You look weary, Brother," Cristiana said, finally taking pity on him. "It must have been a long ride."

"It was, yes. I'd like to take off my boots and get something to eat." He wondered whether he should take his fiancée's hand and kiss her farewell, but he couldn't muster the enthusiasm. Instead, he gave her a stiff bow. "I'm glad to see you again, Emilia."

She covered her lips, looking prettier than ever as she tittered and wiggled her fingertips in a wave.

Cristiana took Isaac by the hand and led him into an adjoining bedroom. This one was a close reflection of the first, but it had a more masculine look to it, with animal pelts and hunting trophies adorning the walls. Isaac thought he would prefer to sleep in here. He swallowed and rubbed his neck, wondering what it would feel like to lie in the big bed with Emilia beside him.

"Is it because she doesn't like horses?" Cristiana asked.

"What?"

"Well, there's something that's putting you off about her." His sister's voice was hushed so that no one outside might hear, yet she spoke with the same demanding tone she always used when her heart was set on something.

"I don't know," he whispered back. "I've felt awful ever

since I arrived. I think I just need to recover from the journey."

Cristiana didn't look convinced. She put her hands on her hips and glared down at him as he sat to take off his boots. "She's as beautiful a woman as any man could want! She's the sort who'll laugh at your jokes even when you sound like a fool, and she has plenty of experience running a household."

"But I don't love her, Cristie."

His sister looked like she might laugh. "Even you couldn't have thought we'd get to marry for love. Love's for peasants and minstrels. I'm sure you'll get to like her well enough in a few months."

"That's easy for you to say," Isaac threw his boots into a corner and fell back on the bed, "you're not the one getting married."

"You can say the same thing back to me on my wedding day if it'll make you feel any better."

"It won't."

Cristiana sighed, her expression softening. She took her hands off her hips and came to sit beside him. "I know you'd rather be off exploring foreign countries or... heaven knows, running some stable or dog kennel in the countryside, but you'll have a whole castle of your own here in Rosepath. Father says he's going to petition the king to make you count of Tannersfield next year, then when he dies you'll inherit Cairnford as well. You'll be a duke!"

Isaac shook his head. "You'd make a better duke than me."

"Well I'm a girl, so unless I kill you that isn't going to happen."

That coaxed a smile out of him. "Do you think you'd want to come and live here in Rosepath once I'm married? I'll need someone to teach me how to be a lord."

"I don't know if I can. Father wants me to find a husband as well, probably a lord in another county. Ever since he became duke he's been trying to settle all his unfinished business. I think he's ready to hang up his sword and start counting taxes."

Isaac nodded, staring blankly at the wall. The world at home had stayed still during his years of travel, but now everything was changing. He was lord of Rosepath. Father was a duke. Cristiana would probably marry a count or marquess. Theirs was fast becoming one of the most powerful families in the kingdom, yet Isaac had never felt more helpless.

"You're like a kicked puppy when you're miserable," Cristiana said. "I can never bear it."

"I don't need you to stand up for me anymore."

"I know. Speak to Father, will you? Perhaps he can put off the wedding for a while, at least until you're ready."

Isaac shook his head. "He isn't going to do that."

"Well, what else are you going to do? Run away and be an outlaw?"

"Don't be stupid."

"Then speak to him."

"Alright, alright. You're right. You always are about these things."

"Good." Cristiana smiled and pulled her legs up onto the bed. "Now tell me some fun stories about your journey. I'm worn out taking care of your fiancée."

At long last, Isaac felt his nervousness subsiding. He might not have known much about being a lord, but he could go on a good adventure and tell an even better story about it afterwards. Cristiana always enjoyed his stories. She'd laugh when she heard how Blackberry had shown them the way to Rosepath.

"The first night after I left I had to persuade a priest to give me lodgings, and he spent all night trying to convince me he wasn't sleeping with his housekeeper."

Soon the story was in full swing, and even the thought of Emilia's pretty face couldn't distract Isaac from his tale.

CHAPTER 15

The world seemed far away from the top of Rosepath Castle's south tower, the villagers a colony of ants marching down the long street to swirl in the marketplace and trickle off into the meadow. The makeshift dwellings out there would probably blow over before the winter's end, but for now they were turning the meadow into a second village, bustling with peasants and pedlars who could find no lodgings elsewhere.

At least the merchants will do well out of it, Isaac thought in an effort to lighten his mood. The wedding had made Rosepath market so busy he could hear people hawking their wares all the way from the top of the tower.

Sir Edward cleared his throat behind him. As the man most familiar with Rosepath Castle, he'd been tasked with attending Isaac. Isaac often lost himself in ponderous thought, while Edward was the sort of person who could never sit still long enough to take in the world around him.

"I just want to watch the village a while longer," Isaac said.

"You don't want to freeze up here, my lord," Edward replied tersely. "The duke won't be happy if you're unwell on your wedding day."

"Do I look like a stiff breeze could knock me over?" Isaac shot Edward a smile. The knight didn't return it. Isaac was a tall, lean man, but he wasn't as burly as a knight or a farmer. He knew from experience that it was best to try and make a joke of it, even though it sometimes made him uncomfortable. The alternative was suffering the mockery of his father's men when he struggled to carry as much firewood or down as much ale as them.

But Sir Edward was right. The winter wind was bitterly cold up here, and Isaac was already shivering. He felt sorry for the people lodging in the meadow. The idea of so many guests braving the frosty roads for his sake didn't sit well with him. They'd gain more from attending the market than from watching him lead Emilia down the aisle tomorrow. He knew that was why some of them were here, but many more seemed genuinely enthralled by the prospect of witnessing a noble wedding. It was supposed to be a grand, romantic spectacle. He supposed he would have to put on a good show so they weren't disappointed. He would smile and wave and pretend to be delighted with his new bride like a prince in a poem. That would make the people happy, even if he was feeling sick to his stomach the whole time.

Despite having spent more time with Emilia, he still hadn't warmed to her. She was good-humoured and laughed easily, but the pair of them had nothing in common. While he liked thinking about what lay beyond the horizon, she seemed uninterested in anything that wasn't directly in front of her. Isaac thought most common folk were more companionable than nobles, but Emilia considered them beneath her interest. She didn't care about how a succulent cut of venison found its way to her plate or how a stable master raised a good riding horse. To her, the real world did not consist of roads, mountains, and meadows, but of regal halls, fine banquets, and melodic minstrels.

Perhaps once he got used to her moods he would find his time with her more enjoyable. He could go out hunting in the forest while she took care of the castle, then they'd be able to make love in the evenings, which enticed him more than anything else. Isaac had yet to lie with a woman. He wanted to, but whenever the opportunity had presented itself he'd shied away from it. The way his father's men talked about whores made visiting a brothel seem unappealing, as if it would spoil the experience for him somehow. In his mind, it was an act he wanted to savour and enjoy, like a tailor taking his time with soft thread and fine fabric. There had been a sweet, dark-skinned girl he'd met in his travels, a spice merchant's daughter named Adela, who he'd planned on taking to bed one evening. Before they could slip away into the stables her father had caught them kissing in the shadows behind his house, and he'd forbade Isaac from coming near her again.

It never would have worked with Adela, anyway. At the time he'd been heartbroken, but his father's men would have dragged him home if he'd tried to stay, and it would have been cruel to take her away from her family. They'd barely known enough words in each other's language to communicate, and Isaac's homeland would have proven as strange to her as hers was to him. Adela hadn't been as pretty as Emilia, yet whenever Isaac thought about her he experienced a far stronger surge of desire. Perhaps there really was something wrong with him.

He descended the tower steps and returned to the keep, where the servants were beginning to set out a light midday meal. Marquess Alistair had gone out hawking with Cristiana and some of the other noble guests. Isaac sat next to Emilia opposite his father, who watched the pair of them closely throughout the meal. They talked about the Rosepath market and how it might be a great boon to the village if it could draw some of the trade away from Tannersfield. Talk of business and finance bored Isaac, but he did his best to engage with it. As a lord, he would need to understand these things.

According to his father, Tannersfield was in a tumultuous state these days, with outlaws in the forest and thieves in the streets. Some merchants were eager to find new places to do business, and while Rosepath was tucked away off the main trading route, it was still one of the closest major settlements. Isaac mentioned that it would be a shame to spoil the peacefulness of the place by expanding the market and putting up more houses, but Emilia and his father thought he was being foolish.

After the meal, he excused himself and asked for a moment alone with Father. The pair of them went upstairs. Isaac would have preferred to talk in one of the warm bedrooms, but Father had his own taste for fresh air that afternoon, and he led them up a sturdy wooden ladder to the keep roof. They paced around the battlements, admiring the view until they'd made a full circuit, then stopped to look down into the courtyard.

"Father," Isaac began, "I don't know if I'm ready for this."

"You're ready. You can ride a horse, handle a sword, travel the kingdom; you're ready to be lord of Rosepath."

"I don't just mean being a lord." He swallowed uncomfortably. "I mean being married. How am I to be a good husband to Emilia?"

"Take her to bed every night and make sure she has enough money to keep the household running."

"Is that it?"

Francis turned toward him. "You'll have more important things to worry about than keeping your wife happy, Isaac. I mean to make you count of Tannersfield someday. Prove to me that you're a son worthy of that responsibility."

"How can I?" Isaac knew he was tempting Father's anger, but this was his one chance to postpone the wedding. "I know how to take care of horses, not counties! You said it yourself when we were eating: Tannersfield is facing troubled times. A lord is supposed to deal with things like that, isn't he? What am I to do?"

Duke Francis placed a firm hand on his shoulder. "You will learn. Don't worry about Tannersfield. I'll have Sir Edward stay with you to ease things along. He's not the sharpest man, but he's loyal, and the sheriff here is his patron. A sheriff and a count who work together can be a formidable force."

Isaac took a deep breath. Father had planned everything out ahead of time, just like he always did. "What about Emilia, then?"

Duke Francis seemed annoyed by the question. "What about her?"

"I don't know if she'll be happy with me. I barely know her."

"She'll be a countess soon. She'll be happy enough."

His father's dismissal incensed him. "Mother wasn't."

The duke's steely gaze flashed with anger, but that wasn't the part that wounded Isaac. It was the look of disappointment that followed, the frustration with a son who had never grown into the man he was supposed to be. It cut Isaac deeply, bringing all his doubts into stark focus.

He looked away, blinking into the wind in case it drew a tear from his eye. He knew he would remember his father's look when he took his wedding vows tomorrow. It would stay with him, a lingering reminder of everything he was not. How long would it take before he lived up to Duke Francis's expectations? A year? Ten years? Or was his father's respect something that would forever elude him, following him to his grave like another man's shadow? He started feeling warm despite the chill wind, and he had to lean forward and grip the battlements as a wave of nausea swept over him.

"Do your duty," Francis muttered. "That's all I ask of you."

"Yes, Father."

"It's normal for a woman to be nervous before her wedding day, but not a man. Emilia will obey you, both by

God's law and the king's, as will your subjects. Now, I don't want to hear any more about this."

Isaac nodded.

He didn't think he could go through with it. He'd rather live as a peasant than stay with a woman he didn't care for in a castle that felt like a cage. If his father didn't believe in him, how was he supposed to believe in himself? It didn't occur to him how foolish he was being. All he could think about was taking Blackberry and riding her down the road until he forgot about Rosepath.

A nervous energy quickened his step as he descended the stairs. There was a desperation to it, the urgency of a man hurrying to outrun a storm darkening the clouds behind him. He just wanted to leave. If he could get away from Father and Emilia and the castle then perhaps his thoughts would clear. He'd come back once his mood had settled. The rooms seemed horribly small as he hurried through the keep, squeezing in on him from all sides. His breath caught in his throat as he turned to avoid bumping shoulders with a passing servant.

He crossed the courtyard and went into the stables, pausing to stroke Blackberry's mane and touch his forehead to her muzzle. She pawed the ground and snorted at him, eager to ride again after her time in confinement.

"We'll just go out for a bit," he whispered. "You'd like that, wouldn't you?"

She nickered affectionately.

Isaac smiled and rubbed her neck. "Me too."

A groom offered to help saddle her, but Isaac was used to doing it himself. His saddlebags were still there from when he'd arrived, so he threw those on too. Blackberry might want some oats if they stayed out for a long time. Just as he was preparing to mount up, Marquess Alistair's party returned through the western gate. Cristiana saw him and dismounted, leading her palfrey over before passing it to the groom.

"Where are you going?" she asked.

Isaac didn't know how to answer her, so he just said: "Away."

She took his arm and led him around the side of the stable. Blackberry followed, affording them a measure of privacy by blocking the path behind them.

"You're going to do something stupid, aren't you?" Cristiana said.

"I really don't know."

She didn't attempt to persuade him otherwise. "Are you going to be an outlaw, then?"

"I'm not sure."

"You're an absolute idiot, Isaac."

He shrugged. "Yes."

Cristiana bit her lip, her brow creasing with anguish. "You really can't bear the thought of marrying her, can you?"

"It's not just that, it's everything Father wants of me. He knows I'm not that sort of man."

"Did he say that?"

"He didn't have to. You know what he's like."

Cristiana looked at the ground and nodded. "He's going to make you go through with it no matter how you feel."

"Tell me what to do, Cristie."

"No. If you won't listen to Father then you won't listen to me. It's not in your heart to be anyone else's servant." She stepped forward and hugged him. Isaac squeezed her tight, stricken with the realisation that they hadn't embraced like this since they were children. "To hell with him," Cristiana said under her breath. "He always gets what he wants. Go and cause him some trouble for once."

Isaac kissed her cheek. Cristie always had a way of understanding him. People said she was the wilful one, yet she'd never disobeyed their father. Perhaps part of her had always wanted to, and now, through Isaac, she was finally getting her chance.

"I'm not sure when I'll be coming back," he said, truly not knowing. He might return before nightfall and marry Emilia

230

tomorrow, or he might keep on riding until he reached Tannersfield, then the next town, and the next.

"You never know anything. Just take care of yourself. The world isn't as safe as you think."

"I'll be alright with Blackberry."

She drew away from him with a frown. "I hope so."

Isaac mounted up and rode Blackberry across the courtyard, letting her prance back and forth to stretch her legs before nudging her toward the gate. On the final turn, he looked back at his sister and gave her a smile. She returned it, but did not wave. Was this even a goodbye?

"Where are you off to, milord?" one of the men-at-arms asked as he headed through the eastern gate.

"Just for a ride," he replied. "I'll be back soon."

"Can't keep that pretty fiancée of yours waiting."

Isaac tried not to dwell too much on Emilia as he rode down the hill to the marketplace. She'd be terribly disappointed if he didn't return. Would she think it was her fault? He hoped not. Marquess Alistair would probably be furious, and Isaac couldn't help but grin as he imagined Father desperately trying to explain why he had no groom tomorrow. Cristiana was right. It was about time Father faced some comeuppance. He urged Blackberry on faster. If he went far enough, he might not have time to make it back even if he changed his mind.

The merchants coming into the village had to make way in a hurry as Isaac trotted through the crowd. He guided Blackberry around their carts and sped up to a gallop when they reached the open road. There wasn't as much ice as there had been a few days ago. Taking it as a good omen, he let Blackberry go as fast as she wanted once they were away from the village.

Isaac was already starting to feel better. Just being away from Rosepath had him feeling more like himself. He knew he might still change his mind and turn around before nightfall, but the taste of freedom was like a slit in a blanket that had been smothering him. He felt like he could breathe again. What an adventure it would be, to forget about his family and ride across the kingdom on his own. It would be like his travelling years again, except this time he wouldn't have Father's men breathing down his neck. If he fell in love with a girl, he could stay and marry her, and no one would be able to tell him otherwise. A smile lit Isaac's face. Maybe he'd spend years on the road. He could beg lodgings at monasteries, eat wild fruit from the forest, and catch fish in the rivers. He could probably spend his whole life exploring the wilderness and still have half the kingdom left to discover.

A group of travellers called something out to him as he rode by, but he didn't hear them. He was too swept up in the romance of the adventure. As long as he kept on riding, anything seemed possible.

Blackberry was starting to tire from the gallop when Isaac saw something glistening in the road ahead. He was fortunate his horse had sharp eyes, for he barely had time to press his weight down in the saddle before she slowed of her own accord. He leaned forward, squinting at the obstacle. A slick of ice spanned the road from one side to the other. Roads commonly flooded at this time of year, especially well-trod ones that sat low in the land, but this didn't seem like common flooding. Not only was all the ice in one spot, but it hadn't rained in days. It looked more like someone had poured water into a natural furrow in the earth. Perhaps it was a spill from some carting accident?

Isaac dismounted and led Blackberry forward by the reins, searching for a spot that looked safe to cross. The slick wasn't more than a few yards wide, but it was thick enough to slip on. Some of the ice had been broken up by the wheels of passing carts, so Isaac decided to tread in the furrows of their tracks.

"Watch your step now," he said to Blackberry, making sure to put his boots in the places where they could grip the exposed earth. His horse began to whinny, nudging at his arm. The poor thing knew the ice was dangerous.

"I know, I know," he murmured. "Almost there."

They were nearly across the ice when a figure burst from the bushes on Isaac's left. He only caught the movement in the corner of his eye, at first taking it for a bolting animal, not reacting fast enough to stop the man before he threw himself bodily into his side. Isaac went down with a yell of surprise, letting go of Blackberry's reins as he hit the ground hard. Pain shot through his hip as it struck the ice. He reached out his hands to try and brace himself, but they slipped and skidded. Rough ice abraded his palms, forcing him to tuck them in before he skinned them raw. With no way to arrest his momentum, he slid halfway across the road before coming to a stop.

"What the hell are you doing?!" he yelled. His assailant, a dirty young man with tousled brown hair, had managed to keep his footing on the cart tracks. He was wrestling with Blackberry's reins as the mare squealed and reared, frightened by the ice and the man's aggressive behaviour.

"Let her be!" Isaac shouted, struggling to his feet. He began to panic as the ice slipped out from under his boots, afraid that Blackberry would trip too. He stumbled again, scrabbling forward on his hands and knees in a desperate attempt to get off the ice.

"Shh, sh-sh-sh," the outlaw soothed, his voice loud and breathy. To Isaac's dismay, Blackberry began to calm down. Isaac reached for his knife—then remembered that he'd left it on the table after he ate. He hadn't been planning on leaving at the time, and in his haste he'd not thought to pick it up on his way down from the roof.

"Let go of her!" he yelled again. His heart jolted in his chest as he realised he might not get there in time. The outlaw had succeeded in leading Blackberry off the ice and was positioning himself to mount up.

Isaac finally managed to scrabble his way to the edge of the slick. He leapt upright and broke into a run. Pain shot up his bruised right leg as it slammed into the frozen ground, but he didn't care. The outlaw was in the saddle now. Blackberry whinnied in anguish, desperately confused. She tried to pull in Isaac's direction, but the outlaw yanked her away with the bridle and kicked her flank, spurring her into a frightened trot.

Throw him off, Isaac thought desperately. He got close enough to reach out and touch Blackberry's tail before she pulled away. The outlaw kept urging her on, expanding the gap between them as Isaac gave chase. He couldn't believe what was happening. Surely Blackberry would rear and turn around. If he ran fast enough he would catch them. But the outlaw sped her into a gallop, putting more and more distance between them by the second. Blackberry's chestnut outline grew steadily smaller, the sound of her hooves receding until it was almost inaudible and she was a thumb-sized spot of brown on the road before him.

Only then did Isaac realise that his lungs were burning from running so hard. He slowed, stumbled, and fell to his knees heaving shrill breaths. His leg throbbed like the devil. What had just happened? How had it happened? A moment ago he'd been riding with the wind in his hair and a smile on his face. Now he felt like he'd been kicked in the stomach. With painful slowness, the realisation crept up on him that Blackberry was gone. He clenched his fist and shook his head in anger. She couldn't be gone. She'd turn around and come back. Things like this didn't happen. In all his years of roaming, he'd not once crossed paths with an outlaw. Other people got robbed by forest thieves, not him.

Isaac felt like he was trapped in a terrible mirage, as if he'd taken a misstep somewhere on the road and slipped into a world that no longer cared about him—a world where the evils that preyed on others now had a taste for the sons of dukes. He shivered from the cold. The skeletal branches of bare trees rattled overhead. Legs shaking, he picked himself up and raised the hood of his cloak. This wasn't a daze. It was real. The anguish of Blackberry's loss made him want to double over and weep. He couldn't bear the thought of the outlaw riding her carelessly across the county, driving her too hard until she was exhausted and then selling her off to some disreputable merchant. He raked a hand through his hair and closed his eyes, staggering forward as he struggled to get a grip on himself. Was this his punishment for running away? He didn't have much choice but to turn around and go back to Rosepath. Maybe Father's men could hunt down the thief and bring Blackberry back. She'd already been galloping for a while, so she wouldn't be able to go far if the outlaw kept riding her so hard. He'd probably be forced to stop in Tannersfield for the night.

That realisation reined in Isaac's despair for a moment. He must be most of the way to Tannersfield by now. If he went back to Rosepath, his father's men probably wouldn't be able to do anything until morning, but if he kept on going he might be able to catch the thief before sundown. Yes, that was what he'd do. It would be better than running home like a fool. He'd spend all night searching Tannersfield if he had to. He was still deeply shaken, but with a plan in mind he no longer felt like a wounded animal. The determination to save Blackberry forced his legs to begin moving. A dull pain throbbed in his hip as he walked, but he grit his teeth through it. It was probably just a bruise from the fall. It wasn't going to stop him getting his horse back.

A shadow of unease followed Isaac as he walked through the afternoon. Would other outlaws attack him on the road to Tannersfield? Now that it had happened once, it felt like it could happen again. He wished he had his knife with him. There wasn't even a spare penny in the pouch on his belt. All his travelling supplies had been in his saddlebags. When the ache in his leg grew worse he found a fallen branch to use as a walking stick. It would probably serve as a decent club if anyone else accosted him, though he wasn't confident in his ability to fight off another outlaw. The branch was heavy and cumbersome, nothing like the light swords he'd trained with as a youth. His instructors had always said his martial technique was good, but he'd never been able to put his heart into fighting. That was why he usually let the other boys beat him; they wanted to win, while he just wanted to get the lessons over with so he could go out riding or hunting with his dogs.

As the day wore on, growing greyer and colder, he again questioned his decision to leave. It really had been stupid. Most people would have killed for the chance to live their life as a lord with a beautiful wife and loyal subjects, never having to worry about food or money or how they would get through the next winter. He should have turned back, yet he didn't. It was too late now, anyway. Twilight would fall soon. He was going to miss the wedding tomorrow. Emilia would be distraught, Marquess Alistair would be furious, and Father would be shamed. But Cristiana would be smiling.

Isaac tried to put his problems to the back of his mind the way he always did when he was travelling. It proved harder than usual, for his fear of the open road returned whenever he heard a twig snap or a bush rustle. He didn't encounter any travellers heading his way, so the journey proved a lonely one. He focused on Blackberry, reminding himself that he still had a chance to catch up with the thief before tomorrow.

Exhausting though it was, his brisk pace brought him to the edge of Tannersfield town before sunset. The place was bigger than Cairnford, though not as large as some settlements Isaac had seen. It was dense and compact, which would make finding Blackberry difficult. Dense towns were warrens of irregular streets and cluttered marketplaces. Someone might lead Blackberry past him in the crowd without him even noticing. He couldn't worry about that. If he did, it would mean accepting the possibility that he'd never see his horse again.

There seemed to be some sort of guard post at the gate

holding up a cart and a handful of travellers. When Isaac tried to walk through a man-at-arms stopped him and demanded a penny for entrance. He asked why, frustrated at not being allowed in. The man-at-arms told him it was the sheriff's toll, and if he didn't like it he would have to stay outside.

Isaac stepped away, bemused. He'd never gone anywhere without a pouch of silver at his belt. What did people do when they arrived without any money?

One of the men waiting behind the cart caught his eye and flashed him a smile, beckoning him over. He was older than Isaac and heavyset, with the look of a labourer about him.

"No pennies?" the man inquired.

"Not one."

"That's a shame. Those are nice clothes you've got on. A man like you should have a few copper to spare."

"Well, I don't. I was robbed in the forest."

The man nodded sympathetically, then gave him another smile. "I can give you a penny."

"What for?"

The man glanced after the cart as it began to move through the gate. "Same thing I'd pay a whore for. You're a good-looking lad. It'll be a quick earn, I promise."

Isaac stared at him for a moment, then shook his head. The man chuckled, shrugged, and turned away. The request itself hadn't disturbed Isaac so much as the fact that, for a brief moment, he'd considered it. He needed a penny to get into town, and he needed to find Blackberry quickly. Nothing else seemed important when he was desperate. A shiver of empathy touched him as he thought of all the women who'd offered him similar services outside town gates in the past, back when he'd been the one with excess pennies to spare. Desperate situations led to desperate ends.

Trying to put the encounter out of his mind, he followed the wall around the edge of town, looking for another gate that might not be charging a toll. It was sometimes the case that lords only made people pay to come in via the larger roads that merchants needed to use for transporting goods. He could see lots of farms around Tannersfield, which meant there were probably plenty of labourers living in town. They'd have some way of coming and going without paying a penny each day.

Isaac had circled halfway around Tannersfield before he found something. All the gates had men-at-arms guarding them, even the ones that were too small for carts. They all demanded pennies Isaac did not have. His luck changed on the northern side of town when he came across a group of boys hopping back and forth across the frozen river. At first he thought to warn them against what they were doing, for the icy water would be deadly at this time of year. The river was far too wide to leap across in one bound, but there was a narrow point where a section of the palisade wall had sunk into the mud on the far side, listing outwards over the river like a half-raised drawbridge. In a death-defying bound, one of the boys jumped from the bank, kicked off a partially-submerged rock, and grabbed one of the jutting stakes of the palisade. The boy wrapped his legs around the stake and shimmied down to the base, where a girl reached out to pull him through the gap. A large older boy jumped next, and when the leaning stake did not budge Isaac decided it was probably sturdy enough to take a grown man's weight.

"Hey," he called out to the children. They turned sheepish gazes on him, clearly expecting a reprimand. "Let me go next." The nervous looks gave way to laughter, and the boys made way for him. He took a short run-up and leapt over the river, hopping off the rock as the first boy had done, and threw his arms around the leaning stake. The wood held firm as he clamped on and threw a leg over, hauling himself around so that he wasn't dangling over the ice. He shimmied down and felt the hands of several children pulling on the back of his cloak. Once they'd tugged him through the gap, he nodded his thanks and hurried off.

238

The light was beginning to fade fast. The part of town he'd found himself in was ripe with a scent that even the winter cold couldn't freeze out. He hurried down the street in search of a public house. In a town this big, it was a waste to search blindly. He needed to find someone who could tell him where people kept and sold horses.

His search took him around the back of the castle and past a walled convent building. He saw a pair of horses tied to a hitching post on the side of the road, but neither of them was Blackberry. Shortly afterwards he found a busy public house near the marketplace with a tall brazier burning outside. Isaac went in and negotiated his way through the patrons, dodging loud merchants and a very drunk minstrel until he found the owner. Thankfully the man did not ask Isaac to buy any ale before parting with his knowledge of the local horse trade. Apparently there were several stables in town attached to public houses, but only two that were owned by horse coursers—the merchants who specialised in the buying and selling of horses. Isaac thanked the owner and took his leave. It was dark outside by the time he left, which made following the directions he'd been given all the more difficult. He pulled his cloak about him, feeling the warmth of his breath tingle against his lips. His face had begun to sting from the cold, and his bruised leg longed for a rest.

After what felt like an hour, he eventually found the first stable in the southwestern quadrant of the town, but it was locked up for the night. The door to the long barn that housed the stalls was shut, as was the door to the attached house where the owner must have lived. Horses nickered behind the barred windows. Isaac called Blackberry's name a few times, but the only response he received was a curious snort from one of the animals. Trying not to let himself get discouraged, he went around to the house and banged on the door until it opened. The merchant standing before him had dribbles of greasy stew clinging to his beard. He must have been eating his supper, and while he was none too pleased at the interruption he indulged Isaac long enough to tell him that he hadn't bought any horses that day, nor had anyone come by with a chestnut-coloured palfrey.

Isaac left with a sinking heart and made his way back to the marketplace. The silhouette of the gallows loomed over him, adding a hostile edge to the evening chill. A drunkard grabbed at his cloak as he passed another public house. Isaac flinched away, the shock of the encounter with the outlaw coming back to him, but the man stumbled and fell over harmlessly. Isaac rubbed his eyes with cold hands, trying to fight back the weariness that was steadily creeping up on him. He couldn't rest yet. He had to find Blackberry, even if it meant searching every stable in town. She'd been his friend ever since he fed her bowls of mashed beetroot as a yearling. When his friends were away, when he was avoiding one of his martial lessons, or when Cristiana was in a bad mood, he'd always been able to find solace with Blackberry. She'd been with him on all of his travels. Through mountain passes and across barren deserts, halfway across the known world, they'd been inseparable. He couldn't lose her now, not to some outlaw in a squalid town like Tannersfield.

Isaac steeled himself for a long night. As tense as he was, he realised he'd accomplished at least one thing when he set out from Rosepath; he hadn't thought about Emilia or the wedding in hours.

CHAPTER 16

Tannersfield's second horse courser had a larger stable than the first. Despite being old and weathered, the L-shaped stable building backed out onto a gated yard that would have been the envy of many an equestrian, large enough to gallop a horse from one end to the other with room to spare. Despite the size of the place, Isaac almost walked past without seeing it. This late at night it was difficult to tell one shadow from another. Had it not been for the conspicuously large yard, he might have been searching till dawn.

When he knocked at the front door a young woman answered. She was a similar age to Isaac, with auburn curls and a pretty face, and she held a wooden lantern that cast dim candlelight through its rawhide panels. Before she could say anything, an older man pulled her back and stepped into the doorway.

"What did I say about opening the door this late?" he snapped, snatching the lantern from the woman–presumably his daughter–and turning to Isaac. "What do you want?" He lifted the light and leaned forward, squinting through a fringe of long hair.

"I'm sorry to bother you so late," Isaac said. "Has anyone

sold you a horse today? She's a mare, a chestnut-coloured palfrey."

The man's nervous hesitation indicated that he knew something.

"Please," Isaac implored him. "I'd do anything to find that horse."

The merchant nodded slowly. "Yes, I bought a horse like that. I'd say she's worth at least seventy silver shillings if you're looking to buy."

Isaac was so relieved he had to put a hand against the doorway to steady himself. He wanted to slump down and laugh. But he wasn't reunited with Blackberry yet.

"That horse was stolen from me."

The merchant didn't look convinced. "I'm sorry to hear it. It's the sheriff you'll be wanting to speak to if it's justice you're after."

"I just want my horse."

"Seventy silver shillings, then."

Isaac shook his head. "I've no money."

"Sorry lad, but I can't just give away the mare on your word. Then I'd be the one getting robbed."

Isaac was sceptical of the man's plight. Horse coursers made excellent money, and he'd probably paid the thief far less than seventy silver shillings. He began to despair again. His only recourse was to go back to Rosepath tomorrow and beg the money from his father. By then he'd already be late for the wedding. Father would be furious, and Isaac would be forced to go through with the ceremony before he could slip away again. There had to be another way.

"Can I at least see her?"

The merchant's daughter butted in. "Oh, let him take a look. The horse might not even be his."

The man sighed, looked Isaac up and down, then motioned for him to step inside.

"Thank you," Isaac said. They crossed the living area and went through a door into the stables. The daughter lit another lantern and took the rawhide off so they could see better. Despite not having been cleaned very thoroughly, the stable was warm and well-stocked with hay. At least Blackberry had been left somewhere comfortable. The horses snorted and nickered as Isaac walked down the row of stalls, some of them shying away from the candlelight. One, however, drew closer. Isaac felt like his heart would burst with relief as he hurried forward and threw his arm around Blackberry's mane, letting her sniff and nuzzle him to her heart's content.

"I thought you'd gotten away from me, you silly girl. Why did you let that man ride you, hm?"

Her warm breath huffed against his face, dulling the numbness of the cold. She gave him a nudge that was slightly harder than usual as if scolding him for leaving her alone. He was overjoyed. For a few terrible hours, he'd feared the worst, but now everything would be alright.

The horse courser looked perplexed as he set his lantern down on a nearby mounting block, but his demeanour softened when he spoke. "I see the mare knows you. I suppose you did get robbed after all."

"Of course he did," the daughter said. "Why else would he come here in the middle of the night?"

Isaac tore his attention away from Blackberry, though he wished he could have taken her for a ride around the yard to get a feel for her mood. He was worried she might be anxious, and it was always easier to judge her temperament when they were riding.

"I'll get the money to pay for her," he said. "I just need time."

"Alright," the merchant said, "but if it's longer than a week, I can't promise anything. That stable space isn't free."

"I'll pay for her upkeep if I have to," Isaac added. He didn't know how he was going to afford it, but that was something he could worry about later.

After a pause, the daughter said: "Let him. We don't do much business through winter, anyway."

"Fine, fine." It sounded like the merchant was accustomed to being brow-beaten by his daughter. "If you pay the upkeep, I'll keep her around as long as I can. But the sooner you get the money for me the better."

"Did you recognise the man who sold her to you?" Isaac asked. He wasn't often prone to anger, but now that he knew Blackberry was safe his thoughts turned toward the thief. He wanted that ill-gotten silver back, and he was prepared to fight for it.

"No. I never saw him before."

"He had scruffy brown hair." Isaac paused, trying to think back to what had happened. He'd been focused on Blackberry during the scuffle, and it had all been over so fast. The only clear thing he remembered was the sight of the man's back as he rode away, his dirty cloak flapping behind him and his brown hair bouncing in the wind.

"That sounds like the one," the merchant said. "Filthy look about him, though that's true of a lot of folk coming through here these days."

"Have you any idea where he went? Did he talk about leaving town, or did he mean to stay?"

The merchant shrugged. "I don't know."

"I do," his daughter said. "Cheeky bastard asked if I wanted to come to Elias Brewer's house with him after I was done getting the horse settled. I told him he'd better take a bath first."

"Where is that?" Isaac asked, his previous weariness forgotten.

"Next to the monastery. The door should still be open. Some of those monks are in there all night, and Elias doesn't worry much about troublemakers with a house of holy men on his doorstep."

"I'd go to the sheriff if I were you, lad," the merchant said. "Better to let him deal with this. If it's your word against the thief's then I'll speak up on your behalf. I can tell the horse is more yours than his."

"I'll keep it in mind. Thank you, friend."

Isaac said goodbye to Blackberry and let the merchant's daughter show him out. He had no intention of going to the sheriff. The risk of being recognised aside, the sheriff's castle was the first place his father's men would come looking for him.

He'd made his decision; he could not go back to Rosepath. Changing his mind at this point would mean the worst of both worlds. He would be shamed for trying to leave and forced to marry Emilia anyway. No, he was on his own now. His problems were his to solve, and he would succeed or fail on his own merits. Despite his dire situation, the thought was a strangely liberating one.

All he had to do now was track down the thief and get back the money the merchant had paid for Blackberry.

As he strode up the main road the ache in his leg reminded him of the anguish his attacker had put him through, and his fists clenched in anger. He'd remained blissfully isolated from the harshness of thievery and destitution all his life. He'd never been in a serious fight before. Recalling how the labourer outside the gates had propositioned him, and the moment in which he'd considered it, he realised he'd taken a great many things for granted. It was as if he'd been floating on a cloud all his life, and today he had been dropped unceremoniously to earth. Losing a horse could ruin a person. Thieves shouldn't be allowed to get away with things like that. It was no wonder highway robbery was a hanging offence.

Elias Brewer's house did not prove difficult to find. The monastery was next to the church, which was so large Isaac could see its silhouette against the sky from halfway across town. There was a sizeable house next door with firelight flickering behind the linen-covered holes in the window shutters. The door opened when Isaac tried it, and he stepped into a smoky room half-full of men sitting at benches with

245

their ale. The murmur of conversation was heavy, but not loud. Isaac saw no women in the hall, presumably because there were monks present. That might be one of the concessions of running a public house next to a monastery; no feminine distractions for the brothers. The thief would have been disappointed if he'd tried to bring the horse courser's daughter here.

Isaac closed the door behind him before the wind could blow in. A man rose from the nearest bench and motioned him over with a wave.

"Are you Elias Brewer?" Isaac asked, keeping his voice low. He was scanning the room for any sign of the brown-haired outlaw, but it didn't look like he was here.

"That's me, sir. I've good beds available if you're looking for lodgings, or else there's plenty of ale and a bench for you here in the hall."

"Did a man come in earlier with a lot of money? He would have had scruffy brown hair and a bad smell about him."

Elias immediately adopted the same uncertain look Isaac had seen on the horse courser's face. "People like that often have angry men come looking for them."

"It'll be the sheriff's men next if I don't find out where he is."

"I can't be doing with that kind of trouble."

"Then we should keep this between ourselves."

Elias put his hands on his hips and gave Isaac a hard look. "You're a knight, aren't you? Or a squire. You speak like you come from the manor."

Isaac realised the man was getting worried despite his show of bravado. He tried to hide his own nervousness as he leaned in and lowered his voice. "The quicker we deal with this, the less trouble there'll be. Just tell me where he is and I'll be on my way."

The brewer inclined his head toward a curtain hanging over a doorway at the back of the room. "He's back there. In the last bed before the end. I don't want the sheriff's men in here."

"The sheriff, Elias?" an elderly monk said from a nearby bench, leaning forward and cupping a hand behind his ear. "What's happening with the sheriff?"

"Nothing for you to worry about, Brother. More ale?" Elias turned away from Isaac and went to attend his patron.

"Mm, yes," the monk slurred. "Our temperance must be tested, on winter nights especially, with—yes." He gave Elias a firm nod and drained his cup of ale, abandoning whatever philosophical excuse he'd been trying to make.

Taking advantage of the brewer's distraction, Isaac slipped behind the curtain and found himself in a long room with five curtained alcoves on the left side and a single door on the right. The alcoves probably housed the beds Elias rented out. Good beds indeed. Privacy was a rare consideration in most public houses. A row of candles burned along a stone shelf to Isaac's right. This was an expensive, well-built house, and Elias was surely charging a lot of money to his guests if he could afford to leave candles burning all night long. No wonder the thief had come here looking for comfortable lodgings.

Isaac checked the door briefly but found that it was locked. He made his way down the room until he was one curtain from the end, then leaned in and listened. Someone was breathing slowly on the other side. When he tried to look underneath, he saw nothing but blackness. Now that he was here, his anxiety rose again. What was he going to do? Threaten the man? He didn't even have a knife on him. Perhaps if he surprised the thief while he was sleeping he'd be so startled that he'd hand over the money without a fight.

Isaac paced up and down the room for a moment, then went to get one of the candles. It was no use waiting. He'd only make himself more nervous. The sooner this was over and done with, the sooner he'd get Blackberry back.

It didn't sound like anyone else was sleeping in the other

247

alcoves, so he returned to the curtain and eased it aside. He lifted the candle, its light flickering as his hand trembled. The small sleeping space contained a stool, a barrel, a bucket, and a bed. The smell of an unwashed body told him he'd found his thief. Isaac's heart beat faster as he took a step toward the dark shape lying on the mattress. The man appeared to be sleeping soundly. He let the curtain fall behind him and set the candle down on top of the barrel, keeping his gaze on the outlaw the entire time.

A board creaked beneath his boot, startling him. The outlaw might have twitched in his sleep, or perhaps it was just the candlelight dancing, but it spurred Isaac into action. Leaping onto the bed, he straddled the man and reached for his arms—but he was sleeping in a strange position, and Isaac found himself clutching handfuls of his cloak instead. The outlaw awoke with a snuffling start, squirming between Isaac's legs. Isaac clawed frantically at the cloak, trying to get it out of the way, before realising that it was wrapping the man up like a cocoon. He'd trussed himself in his own blanket. Isaac put his knees on the edges of the cloak to pin it against the mattress. The outlaw struggled, but he couldn't move. Isaac grabbed his shoulders and held him down.

"Where's the money you got for my horse?" he hissed.

The outlaw's lips twitched as he gazed up at him. Darkness made the man's expression difficult to discern, but he didn't seem afraid. What if he had a knife hidden somewhere under his cloak? Isaac gripped the man's shoulders more firmly and repeated his question.

"I haven't got it," the outlaw said.

"Then who does?"

"Spent it all."

"You're a liar! You can't spend dozens of silver shillings in one evening."

"I swear on God's name."

"Tell me where it is, or I'll drag you straight to the sheriff!"

248

The outlaw's confidence faltered. He squirmed again, realised he was going nowhere, and relented. "It's in a purse under the cloak."

"Which side?" Isaac didn't want to give the man a chance to break free. He was surprisingly strong, and even with the aid of the cloak it was taking all of Isaac's weight to keep him pinned.

"On the left side of my belt."

Isaac shifted position so that he had one knee up on the man's shoulder, freeing his right hand to search for the purse. His hands were still shaking, and it took several attempts to get the cloak out of the way. The outlaw's clothes were filthy with dried mud and grime, and the sour scent rising from his body was cloying. He'd clearly been living rough for some time. At last Isaac's fingers closed around a bulging purse. He breathed a sigh of relief. He wasn't going to untie it, so he yanked hard and was rewarded with the pop of the cord breaking.

"Are you going to take me to the sheriff?" the outlaw asked. Despite his predicament, he sounded more bitter than afraid. Perhaps this wasn't the first time he'd been threatened with the law.

"Why shouldn't I? You've stolen my horse and probably done worse to others."

The man shook his head. "I've never done worse than what the sheriff's done to folk like me."

"I don't believe you."

"I never killed anyone."

Isaac glared down at the man, trying to remember the anger he'd felt on the road, the fear and desperation of losing Blackberry. But the outlaw sounded so wretched that he couldn't bring himself to hate him. The sheriff of Tannersfield had a fearsome reputation. A man who stole horses would face the gallows, or a mutilation that would probably end up killing him anyway. Isaac didn't want something like that on his conscience.

"If I get off, will you stay put?" he asked. The outlaw nodded. Isaac felt along the man's belt again until he found his only weapon, a crudely whittled club. He yanked it loose and hefted it in his right hand. "I'll hit you with this if you try anything." Holding himself ready, he eased his knees up one at a time and climbed off the bed. To his relief, the outlaw didn't move. "I'm going to leave. If you've any sense of decency, you won't steal again."

"Leave me a penny and I won't. I swear on God's name."

The man had cheek, just like the horse courser's daughter had said, but his desperation elicited a twinge of compassion from Isaac. He'd suffered his own taste of destitution earlier that day. People did desperate things when they felt like they had no other choice.

Cristiana would have called him an idiot for what he was about to do. This outlaw had wronged him, yet Isaac could see he'd go straight back to thievery if he left him penniless. Setting the purse down on the barrel, he felt inside and took out a coin.

"If I give you this, what'll you do with it?"

"Buy food." The outlaw eased himself up off the bed. Isaac raised the club, but the man held out his hands in a gesture of submission. "I'm not going to do anything. I never hurt anyone for my bread."

"You shoved me down on the ice earlier."

The outlaw shrugged. "Didn't hurt you though, did it?"

It did, Isaac thought, but he was being petty. A shove was hardly life-threatening. A curious question occurred to him as he thought back on the encounter. "How do you know how to handle a horse?" It wasn't a skill he would've expected from the average outlaw. The man must have worked for someone rich enough to own horses in the past.

"Stable boy for a knight. I did it for a year, but it wasn't for me. Knights are all bastards."

"And outlaws aren't?"

The man just shrugged again. His gaze returned to the

250

pouch. "Are you a knight?"

"No," Isaac said quickly. "I'm a traveller."

"A rich one with a nice horse."

"Not anymore, thanks to you. How much did the merchant pay you for her?"

"Forty silver shillings. There's a bit less in there now." He nodded to the pouch.

Isaac winced. "I need seventy to buy her back."

Yet again the man shrugged. Then, surprisingly, he said: "Sorry."

"Why in the heavens did you do it if you're sorry?"

"I can't survive the winter out there on my own. Not without a gang."

"Is that what you were going to do with the money from my horse? Hire a new gang?"

The outlaw chuckled. "If you're not a knight, you're some noble boy for sure."

"I'm not!"

"Yes you are. You've never been outside a castle in your life, have you?"

"Actually, I've been all over the world," Isaac said hotly. His arm was getting tired from holding up the club. He didn't know why he was lingering here.

Perhaps it was because he had no idea what he was going to do next.

"And the bishop sups wine from a whore's washbucket," the outlaw said. "You don't know a thing about living rough."

"So what *were* you going to do with all my money, then?" Isaac asked. The outlaw didn't seem dangerous, but he had a provocative manner that made Isaac feel like he was out of his depth.

"Buy as many cheap draught horses as I could get and rent them out to farmers. Then I'd get digging work in the fields till spring." Another shrug. "I might've made some good money doing all that."

Isaac had to admit, it was a surprisingly sound plan,

probably better than any money-making scheme he could have come up with. On a whim, he asked: "Where can you buy cheap draught horses?"

The outlaw hesitated. "You're not going to take me to the sheriff?"

Isaac finally lowered the club "Truth be told, I don't particularly want to see him either."

The outlaw grinned, and in an instant his demeanour changed. He leaned forward, rubbing his hands together conspiratorially. "Farm work's good if you want to stay out from under the sheriff's nose. No one rubs farmers the wrong way worse than the sheriff's bailiffs, taxing them poor just for the land they live on. They'd sooner hire outlaws than report them to the sheriff."

"I'm not an outlaw."

"Why don't you want the sheriff to find you, then? Come on, I bet it's good. Did you have it off with some other lord's wife?"

"I haven't done anything!" Isaac insisted. "I'd just rather not see the sheriff." He regretted having mentioned it.

The outlaw leaned back and folded his arms. Now that he no longer seemed distrustful of Isaac he'd adopted a cocky, overly familiar air, the way a man might behave when he was trying to impress his friends or woo a woman. Isaac thought it made him look foolish, yet he had to admire the man's gumption.

"Noble or not," the outlaw said, "I reckon you're alright. I'm sorry I stole the horse from you. Really. And I won't swear it on God's name this time. God never did any good by me." He offered Isaac his hand.

"Will you tell me how to make money with draught horses?"

"Oh yes. If you want farm work we'll be going the same way, won't we? Maybe we'll be friends."

Isaac forced a dry smile. He didn't relish the idea of spending more time with this man, but he did need a way of earning enough money to buy Blackberry back. Extending his arm gingerly, he took the proffered hand. His fingers tightened around the club as they shook, but the outlaw gave him no reason to use it.

"They call me Sam of Nowhere."

"Isaac."

"I'll show you where to get some cheap horses tomorrow," Sam winked, "if you slip me a few more pennies."

Isaac ignored the man's presumption. "And where to rent them out?"

"Of course. We've got to stick together, boys like us."

Isaac hadn't realised it at first, probably due to the darkness and the grime on Sam's face, but they appeared to be of a similar age. Beneath the dirt and messy hair he had large, soft eyes that lent a touch of humanity to his otherwise harsh appearance. Gaunt though he was, he wore his smile with ease.

"Come out to the front with me," Isaac said. "Let's talk about these horses."

"I'd rather sleep."

"Well I'm hungry, and I don't want you snatching this purse from me while we're alone back here. I'll get us some food and ale."

Sam's expression brightened. "Alright. Lead on, milord."

"Don't call me that."

Sam made a pinching motion against his lips. If Isaac was an idiot, then this Sam of Nowhere was twice the idiot. He seemed reasonable enough, but given what had happened earlier Isaac wasn't about to let his guard down. With a bit of luck, he'd be able to leave Sam here and see about buying the draught horses on his own. He wasn't sure how much money he'd be able to make renting them out, nor how long it would take to earn enough to buy Blackberry back, but it was the only idea he had at the moment. If it would get him out of town, it was probably a better plan than staying put. His father's men were sure to come looking for him tomorrow.

Elias Brewer looked surprised when he saw Isaac and Sam emerge from the back of the house together. He brought them some good ale and fresh pies and left them alone to talk.

Of all Isaac's days of travelling, this might well have been the most memorable one. He'd woken up thinking he was going to marry Lady Emilia, run away from his wedding, been robbed on the road, and now he was sharing ale with his attacker. He still wasn't sure what to make of it. The experience had exhausted him, yet he didn't feel like sleeping. Perhaps this was a fevered dream and in a few hours he'd awake back at Rosepath Castle with his responsibilities still looming over him.

At first he talked to Sam about the draught horses, but the practical side of their conversation slipped away when it became apparent that they shared a common passion for animals. Hunting, travelling, and horses were all pastimes Sam enjoyed. He'd been all over Tannersfield and Cairnford, sometimes working, sometimes stealing, sometimes living wild in the forest. The more he talked, the more Isaac realised that this man had lived the life of adventure he'd always dreamed about, yet it was not all dashing tales of scrapes with the law and romps with farm girls. Their meeting on the road attested to the desperation such a life could lead to. Sam described how the forest had become a dangerous place in recent months, with outlaws raiding each other's camps and sometimes killing each other for food. He'd been with a sizeable gang earlier that year, but they'd been murdered by a knight called Sir Edward. Isaac was surprised to hear a name he recognised, and he shuddered when Sam described the grisly way Edward had pushed a young girl's head into a fire before executing her grandmother. He couldn't believe men like that served his father, nor that they could commit such acts of cruelty under the pretence of upholding the king's law. It made him sympathise even more with the desperation that had driven Sam to rob him. Being on your own wasn't easy, especially in winter. Perhaps Isaac needed a savvy companion like Sam if he was going to survive without his father's protection.

The ale loosened their tongues well into the early hours of the morning, though Isaac remained careful not to reveal anything about who he really was. Sam's tales fascinated him, and his fascinated Sam. While Sam knew a lot about Tannersfield and Cairnford, he'd never travelled the world at large, and the vividness with which Isaac described the dark-haired girls of Siraba and the rugged steppes of Khoketan left his eyes wide and his jaw hanging open.

As the night grew long, Isaac learned how Sam had tried his hand at a dozen different crafts as a young man before stealing a horse from the knight he served when he was seventeen. The only thing he regretted in life was having to abandon his sister Elizabeth when the law caught up with him. He described her as a sensible, hard-working girl who would probably end up doing far better for herself than he ever would. Isaac supposed they were alike in that regard as well; he too had a sensible, determined sister he regretted leaving behind.

Whenever he saw her again, Isaac thought, he would have a tale to tell like no other.

CHAPTER 17

Elizabeth tried to ignore the gossip circulating town in the weeks following the winter solstice. The disappearance of Lady Emilia's groom was all anyone talked about, and it quickly grew tiresome. Most of it was rumour, for she'd heard a dozen different stories about what had happened to Lord Isaac by now and none of them were consistent. Some people said he'd been killed by outlaws. Others said he'd *become* an outlaw. A handful thought he'd run off to marry a peasant girl, while a few more were convinced that he'd gone to raise a rebellion against the boy king Fendrel. All anyone knew for certain was that the wedding had not happened and Marquess Alistair had left Rosepath in outrage a few days later. The only part of the affair that mattered to Elizabeth was that Sir Edward remained de-facto lord of Rosepath as a result. It was worrisome to know that he was still around, yet even that couldn't dampen her spirits entirely, for the new year was a bright one. Joseph's big building project had begun, and she'd been allowed to see Kaylein again.

It was April now. Spring was just beginning to breathe colour back into the countryside after a slow, grey winter, and Elizabeth walked side by side with Kaylein down the road leading east from Tannersfield. The hem of Elizabeth's brown work dress brushed the dirt alongside Kaylein's dark robe. Brother Daniel followed at a distance with his quarterstaff. The quiet monk had been their chaperone several times over the past few weeks. It was no secret that the roads around Tannersfield had grown dangerous lately, but convents did not employ men-at-arms, so when nuns travelled they often did so in the company of monks. Brother Daniel was well-suited to the task. The young man was as burly as an ox and towered several inches over everyone else in town. If Elizabeth had to guess based on the measuring numbers Joseph had taught her, she would have put him at close to six and a half feet tall. True to his vows, Brother Daniel also seemed to possess no interest in women, and Mother Jane was fond of requesting his services as a result. Not all monks were so reliably chaste.

Regardless of Daniel's size, travelling with a nun and a monk was protection enough for Elizabeth. Only the truly desperate or the truly wicked would dare attack someone wearing the vestments of the church, for everyone knew such a grave sin would condemn them straight to hell. Kaylein talked a lot about heaven and hell these days. A year had passed since they fled Rosepath, and Elizabeth was pleased to see her friend putting the past behind her. She was very different, humbler in many ways, yet she hadn't lost her passion. The enthusiasm she'd harboured for her noble pastimes had found new outlets in monastic life. Books and reading absorbed her these days, so much so that Elizabeth sometimes worried Kaylein was still hiding from the world within her pages. But even if she was, it seemed to be doing her good. There were times when she appeared happy and exuberant again, and those moments were a joy to witness. Elizabeth didn't understand most of the religious ideas her friend talked about, but they seemed interesting, and Kaylein discussed them with such fervour that Elizabeth rarely found herself bored. In a strange way, their relationship had settled

257

back into something resembling their time at Rosepath. Kaylein was the sheltered, academic one with far-flung ideas that went over Elizabeth's head, while Elizabeth's life consisted of practical day-to-day work that seemed equally foreign to Kaylein.

Yet despite their differences, the ordeal they'd shared had forged a bond between them that Elizabeth suspected would last the rest of their lives. There were things they could say to each other that no one else understood. Elizabeth always looked forward to their walks. At first they'd only attended church together, but with a little encouragement from Elizabeth–and she suspected a lot more from Mother Jane–Kaylein had begun volunteering for chores that got her out of the nunnery on a weekly basis.

Today they were heading to Joseph's building site beyond the farms. Work had started a few weeks ago, and it just so happened that both the carpenters and the church shared a vested interest in the project. The house Joseph was working on was intended for the son of a cardinal, one of the wealthiest and most influential clerics in the kingdom. It was to have multiple rooms, two floors, a courtyard, a partial undercroft at the back, stables, and its own separate chapel where travelling pilgrims could stop and worship. The entire project would keep Joseph and several of his carpenters employed for the rest of the year, and as a master craftsman he was being paid good money to oversee all of the woodwork on site. Alongside the construction, Elizabeth had found out via Kaylein that the cardinal's mistress–the mother of the son who would be living in the new house–wanted a nun to conduct daily blessings at the building site. Kaylein was not that nun, for such a responsibility could not be entrusted to a novice, but it was necessary to stay in contact with the sister who'd been given the job. Once a week, Kaylein volunteered to bring news from the nunnery along with a week's supply of wine, bread, cheese, salt fish, and anything else the sister needed.

258

Elizabeth made her weekly visits to keep Joseph appraised of business at the workshop. She would ask him questions about work, discuss rent and wages, and make any necessary preparations to have supplies delivered from Tannersfield. Joseph returned to town occasionally to attend guild meetings and check on the workshop, but the building site was a quarter day's walk down the road and he had never learned to ride a horse, so it was impractical to make the journey with any regularity. Rather than wasting time travelling, he and Rose lived on the building site in a rough wooden house alongside the other builders. The eldest master carpenter still at the workshop, Luther, was now running things in Joseph's absence, and Elizabeth was his assistant. Luther handled the carpentry while Elizabeth dealt with wages and organisation. Both of them understood their responsibilities well, and it was an easy arrangement. Elizabeth still felt out of her depth when she ran into customers who refused to deal with a woman, but she had grown steadily more confident over the past few months. She was good at what she did. Organising people was like solving a pattern, not so different from counting out wages. There was something intensely satisfying about being presented with a problem—be it mathematical or social—and worrying away at it until she found a solution.

The only thing that continued to hold her back was her illiteracy.

"Do you ever think you could teach me to read, Kay?" she asked as they walked down the road. It was the warmest day of the year so far, and a pleasant breeze was blowing in from the northern fields. New leaves rustled at the edge of the forest to the south, while birds flitted over from their perch on a dry stone wall to peck at muddy husks of grain that had fallen off the back of a cart.

"I'm not sure how I could," Kaylein said. "What would we use?"

"A piece of charcoal and a bit of bark?"

"Oh, you can't learn to read like that, Liz. You need a

proper book."

"I learned numbers that way."

Kaylein frowned as if the idea perplexed her. "Perhaps it would work for learning letters one at a time, but you need to see them in full sentences to grasp reading properly. It's so much easier when you have a book."

Elizabeth conceded that she was probably right. Like most educated people, Joseph had learned literacy by reading from the first prime scripture in a monks' schoolhouse. The other carpenters who'd picked up the skill second-hand took a long time to read anything, and they often had to sound the letters out one by one when they got stuck. Elizabeth wanted to be able to read the way Joseph and Kaylein did, without even having to move her lips. It seemed almost magical to her, the way they could stare at a page of cluttered symbols and comprehend their meaning as smoothly as if the words had been spoken aloud.

"It'll be a long time before I can afford a book." Elizabeth sighed. She thought of the heaps of silver pennies in Joseph's money chest and reprimanded herself for wondering how many books they would buy. She'd been entrusted to keep watch over that money, collecting the rent and taking only a little to pay her own wages.

"I wish you could come into the convent," Kaylein said. "We have so many books, and I'm transcribing new ones all the time." She paused, gazing at the road in thought. The thud of Brother Daniel's staff followed them at a distance. "What if I wrote one for you?"

"You can't do that." Elizabeth knew how expensive ink and parchment were. It would be tantamount to stealing from the nunnery.

"Not all at once, but I think there might be a way. Sometimes we have to dispose of spoilt pages, usually when someone makes a bad mistake or the parchment tears. That can happen sometimes when you're scraping with a knife. We can't put those pages into finished books, so the novices use them for writing practice. I don't think anyone would mind if I took a few spoilt pages here and there."

"You could bring me a book a page at a time!"

Kaylein smiled. "You may end up with a lot of unfinished verses, but I could add something of my own as well." A wistful look crossed her face. "I've been dreaming of putting my thoughts to parchment ever since I joined the convent, Liz. I don't suppose it makes any sense to you, but God's will can be very confusing to understand at times. That is why we need books, so that we can turn our thoughts into something firm that will never slip away from us."

"What would you write about?"

"I'm not sure. I have so many ideas. I'm a little afraid they might be silly, or," she put a hand to her throat, lowering her voice, "blasphemous."

"You could ask the mother superior about them."

"I'm not sure that would help. She is always encouraging me to meditate on my own thoughts rather than repeating what the scriptures say."

Elizabeth raised her eyebrows. "That doesn't sound very much like a prioress."

"I know. She's been very strange with me ever since–" Kaylein flushed and bit back whatever she was about to say. "Well, the point is that she's strict with the others, but I don't think she feels strictness is necessary with me."

"You're too good a nun, that's why. I told you you'd be an abbess before you knew it."

Kaylein shot an anxious glance back in the direction of town. "Do you think that's it? Do you think she's grooming me for a senior role?"

"You'd be perfect for it. You're used to giving people orders and you know all the scriptures. It doesn't sound like you cause any trouble for her. Why shouldn't she want you to make something of yourself?"

Kaylein bit her lip and looked down. "I'm not sure I would want that. I haven't really thought about it."

"Are you sure you still want to be a nun?"

Kaylein nodded without hesitation. "God was there for me when I needed Him. He gave me back something I thought I had lost. I can't think of anywhere else I'd rather be."

Elizabeth touched her arm companionably. "That's how I feel about the workshop."

Kaylein smiled. "Anyway, I shan't need to think about that until I've taken my final vows. And I'm definitely going to write something for you the next time I get my hands on some scrap parchment, though I suspect my verse will be just awful."

"I won't be able to tell either way," Elizabeth laughed.

They carried on talking about the things Kaylein might write about until they crossed a bridge over a small river and turned north toward the building site. A beaten path had been trod through the undergrowth and the bushes had been cut back to allow carts to pass. The land was mostly open on this side of the road, but enough vegetation remained to shelter a few hiding spots. A mason had been robbed out here when he left the building site to relieve himself one evening, and the nun in attendance was still treating the head wound he'd suffered in the ensuing fight.

Brother Daniel took the lead to watch for any danger. Elizabeth knew it was probably safe, but Kaylein grew quiet and drew close to her. She took her friend's arm in reassurance. Between Brother Daniel's staff and the knife at her belt, she suspected they could handle an outlaw or two.

The path wound up an incline for half a mile before it reached the building site. It was a nice spot for a manor house: verdant, but not overgrown. The river they'd crossed earlier trickled past on the western side. When the house was finished a person would be able to stand on the roof and see the land for miles around. To Elizabeth, it seemed almost absurd to call such a large building a house. It was practically a palace. Areas were pegged out with rope to designate where the chapel and stables would go, and trenches had already been dug for the manor wall. Dozens of workers were labouring to make sure it all came together. If you included the families that had come to live with them, the total workforce came close to a hundred people. Some were still digging foundations for the pegged-out areas, but construction on the main house was already well underway.

"I should go and find Sister Grace," Kaylein said.

Elizabeth bid her farewell and asked Brother Daniel whether he would like her to bring him something to eat. He accepted gratefully. Though he was a man of few words, Elizabeth could tell he took pride in his duties, and it made him happy when someone offered him a reward.

There were three temporary structures surrounding the building site: a long work shed that also served as a dormitory for the craftsmen, an open-fronted kitchen with benches and cooking pits, and a house near the river where Sister Grace stayed with the young children she'd been tasked with minding during the work day. Elizabeth went to the kitchen first and bought a hearty helping of bread and pork for a penny. It amazed her how cheap food was on the building site. The cardinal had persuaded Duke Francis to give his labourers hunting rights in the surrounding countryside, so meat was plentiful. Children trapped rabbits and squirrels while the adults hunted deer and boar. Elizabeth had been impressed the first time she saw the builders' wives practising with bows. It turned out they did a lot of the providing while their men worked. Then, when winter came and the builders were paid in full, the women would be able to live comfortably on their husbands' wages until spring arrived. It was a good system, and Elizabeth admired the shrewd cardinal's foresight in securing hunting rights for his workers. Not only would it keep them happy and productive, but he was probably getting away with paying them slightly less as a result. Some business decisions, Elizabeth had learned, often came at the expense of workers, but this one struck a mutually beneficial compromise. She resolved to remember it in case she ever had to manage a workforce in the future.

After she had brought Brother Daniel his food she went to find Joseph. He was busy dressing wood with the other carpenters, shaping the beams that would eventually hold up the house's second floor. They talked while he worked, going over business at the workshop and discussing how many bundles of nails and iron spikes Elizabeth would need to deliver next week. It always seemed like carpenters were running out of nails. Some of the other builders thought Joseph was wasteful in relying on them so heavily, but he insisted they made projects quicker to finish and stronger in the long run. That opinion had earned him the ire of a few other builders on the site who thought they should limit their costs and drag the job out until next year. More days' work meant more pay, but Joseph would have none of it. Not only did he want to impress the cardinal with the speed and efficacy of his work, but he had no desire to risk leaving the job unfinished when winter inevitably slowed work to a crawl.

Elizabeth liked to linger in Joseph and Rose's company, but they were both busy that day, so she left them to get on with their work and went to find Kaylein instead. On her way around the building site she saw Brother Daniel demonstrating to a group of children how he might fight off an outlaw with his quarterstaff. He looked very proud of himself, and the youngsters were watching the enormous man in open-mouthed awe. She suspected a few of them might go back to their parents wanting to become monks that evening.

Kaylein was fetching water from the river when Elizabeth found her. She had her hood down and a few locks of chestnut hair had escaped the tie at the nape of her neck. Kaylein had become very strict with her appearance since becoming a nun. The loose hair and downed hood suggested something had flustered her.

"Sister Grace wants me to stay with her overnight," she

264

admitted when Elizabeth asked her about it. "The builders have been coming down with fever. It's quite mild so far, but she's exhausted tending to everyone by herself."

"I'm sure Daniel can come back for you tomorrow."

Kaylein pressed her lips together tightly. It was an expression she seemed to have picked up from Mother Jane, one she always adopted when something uncomfortable was bothering her.

When no answer came forth Elizabeth asked: "Don't you like Sister Grace?"

"Oh no, it isn't that at all!" Kaylein insisted. "I like her very much."

Elizabeth folded her arms and raised her eyebrows the way a mother might regard a guilty child. It struck her that she would never have dared look at Kaylein this way when they were mistress and servant.

Kaylein set down her pail of water and tried to avoid Elizabeth's gaze, but eventually she relented. "Sister Grace is *unusual.*"

Elizabeth wasn't sure whether to be shocked or amused by the story Kaylein recounted thereafter. She kept the details vague, but with a little pressing she revealed that she'd caught Sister Grace kissing another nun several months prior. That was the reason Grace had been sent away to tend the spiritual needs of the builders—so that she and her partner would not be tempted while they served out their penance.

"Stop laughing!" Kaylein said indignantly when she saw the look on Elizabeth's face. Her cheeks turned bright red. "It's a serious sin!"

"I'm sorry," Elizabeth replied, trying to compose herself. "It's just that I couldn't imagine you being tempted by another nun like that."

"I don't know what the temptation of sin feels like! I've always slept in a separate dormitory from Sister Grace."

"What are you afraid she's going to do?"

Kaylein looked away, her face glowing. "She wouldn't do

anything. I wish I hadn't told you now."

"It's quite a good story."

"You mustn't tell anyone!" Kaylein insisted. "I mean it, Liz. You can't gossip about this like a servant."

"I won't, I promise."

"Do you swear?"

"I swear." Elizabeth put a hand on Kaylein's arm. In truth, she would have loved to share the story with Fred and the other apprentices. The boys would have been giddy to hear a tale about two chaste nuns kissing, but for her friend's sake, she would keep it to herself.

Kaylein relaxed slightly. "It was one of the incidents that made me want to write. The scriptures feel so incomplete in certain areas. Nuns like Sister Grace believe they're allowed to do these things because there is no definitive rule against it in the holy canon. I know it's wrong for men to be with men, but is it the same for women?"

"I don't think there's anything wrong with it. Some people are just like that."

Kaylein looked aghast. "Nobles aren't!"

"Well, maybe not nobles, but common folk. My mother said there was a good-looking man at one of her brothels who earned just as much money as any of the girls, and it wasn't women who kept coming in to see him."

"Your mother did—" Kaylein stammered, "*that?*"

A shameful heat rose to Elizabeth's face. She'd forgotten she hadn't mentioned it to Kaylein before. Now her friend was regarding her with a look somewhere between bemusement and disgust.

"It's just a job," she said quietly.

"It's sinful."

The warmth of Elizabeth's shame took on an angry colour. "I'm sorry she didn't get to live in a convent and only sin when it suited her."

"I just never thought—"

"Am I a sinner because I stabbed that knight when he

came after us?" Elizabeth said heatedly. "I'd have killed that man outside your bedroom if only I knew how to use a sword! God might protect nuns, but the rest of us have to protect ourselves."

"That isn't true. God protects us all."

"Not from men like Duke Francis."

Kaylein looked away, her flush of embarrassment paling. Elizabeth felt a tug of remorse for opening up old wounds, but her lingering anger prevented her from apologising. How could Kaylein be so petty, after all they'd been through? It was just like the way some of Joseph's customers looked at her.

She waited stubbornly for a response, but Kaylein said nothing.

"I'll tell Daniel to come back for you tomorrow," Elizabeth said coldly, then turned on her heel and walked away.

It was one thing for strangers to look down on her, but having a friend act the same way was deeply hurtful. Kaylein was still caught up in ideas about the world that were so far above Elizabeth's understanding they might as well be clouds in the sky. Hot tears pressed at her eyes as she hurried back to the building site. She had tried so hard to salvage the wreckage of her life after Duke Francis's attack, yet some things never changed. She was still the illiterate daughter of a whore, a woman trying to do a man's job. Perhaps she was foolish for thinking she would ever be someone like Kaylein's equal.

She walked past Brother Daniel without explaining what was going on. He hesitated awkwardly at the edge of the building site before hurrying after her.

"Where is Sister Kaylein?"

"She's staying till tomorrow," Elizabeth said. She didn't bother looking back to check whether the monk was following her.

Lady Eleanor had known all about her mother, yet she'd

been able to look past it. Why couldn't Kaylein be more like her? Elizabeth allowed her anger to fester as she followed the path back to the road, letting buried thoughts rise to the surface to simmer and seethe.

She'd been striding down the road to Tannersfield for a long time before she realised that Brother Daniel was panting behind her. Just how fast had she been going to run the burly monk out of breath? Her legs throbbed with exhaustion. Pressing a hand to her chest, she felt her heart racing. As she slowed down, her temper began to cool, leaving behind an ache of regret. Why had Kaylein reacted that way, and why had she been so cold in response? She hoped they hadn't ruined their friendship.

Brother Daniel caught up, but he was too polite to say anything, which only made Elizabeth feel worse.

"I'm sorry," she said. "Kaylein's staying overnight to help Sister Grace. We had a disagreement."

Daniel only nodded and cleared his throat. They carried on in silence, heading past the farms as the houses of Tannersfield hove into view over a rise in the road.

Perhaps it would be better if Elizabeth forgot about where she'd come from and focused on where she was going. Thinking about the future gave her a sense of purpose, while the past held little more than fear and regret. Her mother was dead. She would never see Sam again. Rosepath was best left forgotten. Whether she liked it or not, she was a lowborn commoner. She could feel ashamed about that, or she could accept her place in the world.

The thought was a sobering one, but it seemed better than wallowing in self-pity. If she made the mistake of thinking too highly of herself she might invite the ire of her betters, and that was something Elizabeth wanted to avoid. She already lived with the lingering fear that Sir Edward might come looking for her one day. All she wanted was to be left alone with her work, make an honest living, and build a little corner of the world she could settle in. Was there any point in making that more difficult for herself by getting upset when people judged her for being as common as common could be? Pride was for men and nobles. She had no business getting angry at Kaylein for the way she'd reacted.

That was what Elizabeth told herself. It helped to soften her temper, but it felt like she was putting out a fire with a handful of mud. It left behind a murky feeling, as though she'd given up on something pure, and it put her in a sour mood. She wanted to rile against it. She was still feeling hurt, and her legs ached from the brisk walk.

Perhaps it was because of her irritability that she stopped to listen when she saw a farmer arguing with another man on a path leading into the fields. Their exchange sounded indignant, and the curt tone of the second man reminded Elizabeth of Kaylein. He was sandy-haired and wore good clothes, but Elizabeth didn't think he was a noble, for his outfit was stained with mud and the hem of his coat had become threadbare. More likely he was a penny-pinching merchant who wanted to act like a nobleman without spending the money to complete the look. She allowed the thought to percolate, stirring it into the murk of her bad mood. Needing an outlet, she turned down the path and approached the two men from behind. She didn't know the farmer's name, but she'd seen him when she came this way before. He'd given Brother Daniel some cider one evening and seemed like a decent sort. His burly, bearded look reminded her of Joseph, and in her present mood that was more than enough to convince her to weigh in on his side.

"What are you bothering him about?" she snapped at the sandy-haired man's back. He turned around with a look of indignation. There was something vaguely familiar about his well-formed features that set Elizabeth on edge.

"I don't see why it's your business."

"You're making a fool of yourself by the road," the farmer said. "That makes it the business of everyone walking by."

"There's nothing foolish about asking for an explanation!"

269

The handsome man gave Elizabeth an imploring look. "You'll agree with me, won't you? This man's renting my horses, and one of them keeps throwing shoes that inexplicably go missing afterwards. This is the third one he's 'lost' in the past two weeks."

"Horses lose shoes when they're doing farm work," Elizabeth said.

"Yes, and that would be fine if he'd just pick them up so that I can have the smith put them back on. I can't believe they keep vanishing into thin air."

"They're your horses," the farmer said. "Your responsibility. That's what we agreed on."

"I've been paying almost as much for new shoes as I'm making from you in rent."

"You're lucky I'm paying you at all. It's taken weeks to get this year's ploughing done with those lazy horses of yours."

"And I suppose when you sell all those 'missing' horseshoes that'll make up for it?"

The farmer folded his arms stubbornly.

"You look like you can afford to lose a bit of money," Elizabeth said. It perplexed her that this livery owner was making trouble for the farmer after seemingly having rented him useless horses. Most swindlers didn't usually have the nerve when someone beat them at their own game.

"Do I? Is that how I look?" The man turned back to Elizabeth. "I need this money! I'd be happy to lower the rent if he's unhappy, but not if I have to keep paying for new horseshoes on top of it."

"You should've thought about that before you took my money for a pack of lame mules," the farmer said. "I'll be done with them by the week's end, anyhow." He grinned. "If I find any of your horseshoes by then, I promise I'll give them back."

The sandy-haired man's posture deflated. He gave Elizabeth one last hopeful look, but she'd made it clear that she was on the farmer's side.

"Why don't you go to the sheriff if you want to accuse him of stealing horseshoes?" she asked. He paled slightly and turned away. Elizabeth couldn't resist giving him a smug look. That was the response she'd expected. This man tried to talk and dress like a person of importance, but he probably had more to fear from the sheriff than the farmer did. Swindlers rarely managed to stay ahead of their reputations for long.

"Please, just don't lose any more horseshoes," the man grumbled before trudging back to the road.

"Thank you, lass," the farmer said, giving Elizabeth a nod. "He's a stubborn one. Don't think he knows much about dealing with folk like you and I."

"I didn't like the look of him anyway." She was starting to feel better now. It felt good to have helped win a small victory against someone with more money than sense. The sandy-haired man had been a convenient target for her ire, allowing her to redirect it away from Kaylein.

When Elizabeth returned to the road she realised he was going the same way as her. She refused to timidly slow down behind him, so they ended up matching pace on opposite sides of the road. Every now and again she stole a glance in his direction, trying to work out why he looked familiar to her. Perhaps he'd come to the workshop at some point, or maybe she'd seen him at market. After a while, he turned off the road and disappeared down a hunting trail that led into the forest. It seemed strange for a man like him to venture into the forest alone, but Elizabeth was glad he was gone. Her thoughts returned to Kaylein. Now that her anger had burnt itself out, she regretted what had happened. Kaylein shouldn't have reacted the way she did, but Elizabeth shouldn't have stormed off either. She'd made things bitter between them, and that was never a good note to leave an argument on. One of them was going to have to apologise. Her first thought was that it should be Kaylein, but perhaps that was just her temper talking. She reminded herself that she didn't have any business feeling prideful about things. Nuns, just like nobles, were due the respect of the common folk, and Elizabeth would never have dreamt of asking Kaylein to apologise to her when they were mistress and servant.

With a heavy heart, Elizabeth headed back to Tannersfield, daydreaming about what it might be like to be a nun or a noblewoman or a respected master like Joseph, someone whose status was a given. It would be nice, one day, not to have to fight tooth and nail for something others took for granted.

CHAPTER 18

Sir Edward could not have been happier with the way things had turned out. At the beginning of winter, he'd been dejectedly awaiting his departure from Rosepath, only to be disappointed again when Duke Francis announced that he would be staying behind to serve Lord Isaac. At the time, he'd felt like he'd dug his own grave. All of the work he'd put into smoothing things over with the sheriff, all his efforts to keep the forest safe, not to mention his stalwart dedication to running the castle, only to be passed off like a lapdog to the duke's unworthy son!

But none of that had happened, he thought with a grin, putting his boots up on the bedroom table. He was feeling particularly good about himself that day, for it was a bright April morning on what the calendars would record as the second year of King Fendrel's reign. He sat back in one of Count Leo's old chairs, idly swiping through the pages of a book that had belonged to Lady Kaylein. He couldn't read any of the words, but there were illustrations of men performing surgery and priests draining bad humours that were depicted as malevolent demons. The grisly images intrigued Edward, and holding a book made him feel like a lord. He still wasn't a true lord, not yet, but surely it was only a matter of time. Duke Francis had left him in charge again after his son went missing, and months had passed since. It seemed no one else in Francis's inner circle wanted stewardship of Rosepath. Only his daughter, Lady Cristiana, had expressed an interest, but she was an unmarried woman, so that was out of the question. With no other suitable candidates, Edward was the only logical choice.

There had been superstitious talk of Rosepath harbouring a curse ever since Isaac's disappearance. A friar had been caught ranting about it in the village market earlier that year, for which Edward had had him flogged, but the fool's words still seemed to have struck a chord with the general populace. Over the past few months, there had been a notable increase in the number of skilled workers leaving Rosepath to seek greener pastures. When workers left, local businesses had to scale back and the market shrank. That meant less money coming into the village and less rent for Edward. It made no sense, for according to Harald Redcloak, workers should have been flocking to Rosepath in droves seeking relief from the poverty in Tannersfield. Had the village's reputation really been so soured that folk would rather try their luck elsewhere?

Harald told him not to worry, for he had plans to meet with the guildsmen of Tannersfield and hatch a scheme to bring more workers to Rosepath by the end of the year. Harald annoyed Edward sometimes, but he seemed to understand money well enough, and his schemes succeeded more often than they failed. He decided not to worry about the state of Rosepath, nor the stupid rumours that had been circulating about him ever since that business with the outlaws last year, and instead focused on everything that was going well for him.

Though he was not a particularly pious man, a part of Edward did wonder whether God had rewarded him for his years of loyal service. Loyalty and obedience were great virtues, and it was nothing short of a miracle that Isaac had disappeared as abruptly as he did. Edward was sleeping better these days, too, having almost completely forgotten about what he'd done to Count Leo's servants and the outlaws. Now that his dreams were no longer troubled by those unpleasant memories, he was convinced he'd done nothing wrong. Wicked men were not rewarded with this kind of good fortune. Even the prisoner who'd escaped from the tower last year had vanished into thin air, never to trouble him again.

Edward flipped another page and turned his book toward the light, admiring a sketch of a naked woman with words written upon various outlined parts of her body. The sketch would have been a lot better without those words, he thought. A knock at the door startled him. He shut the book quickly and tossed it down on the table.

"Come," he called, rising to his feet.

The servant girl Daisy came in and bowed to him. "Duke Francis has arrived, milord."

"Excellent. Prepare the hall for him, and have Gwayne get some fresh horses ready for this afternoon. I want to take the duke and his daughter hunting." He'd gotten rid of Roy, the previous stable master, during the winter. The old man had been slow and useless, and after having dawdled with a horse one time too many Edward had turned him and his wife out of the castle. Roy's replacement, Gwayne, was a backwards sort, having come from a remote village called Kinedwyn somewhere up in the hills, but the man ran his stable with a strict efficiency that Edward admired. The more things Edward changed about Rosepath, the more he felt like its rightful lord.

Edward straightened his surcoat before heading down to greet Duke Francis, admiring the fine red garment with the yellow hawk of Cairnford emblazoned upon the breast. He clasped his favourite white silk cloak around his neck and dampened his face with a bowl of water to make sure he looked presentable, then opened the door and went downstairs. Francis was already taking refreshment in the great hall. Accompanying him was his daughter, Cristiana, along with a dozen servants and men-at-arms.

The duke was looking even more strained than Edward remembered. Isaac's disappearance had been a great blow to his honour, for it reflected poorly upon the entire family. Francis had been quick to contradict any rumours that his son had run away, but many people—Marquess Alistair included—had not believed him. He'd been left looking like a fool on the day of the wedding. With each passing month it seemed like the handsome lines of his face were becoming sharper, the strands of white in his hair more prominent.

For his duke's sake, Edward tried to conceal his good mood, greeting him sombrely and respectfully. He gave Cristiana a bow before taking his seat at the high table. He quite liked Cristiana, though the two of them had rarely spoken at length. During the three years he'd served her father he'd noticed she possessed an aggressive wit that lent her a natural sense of authority over others. She was also quite attractive, which always improved a woman in Edward's eyes.

"Will you be gracing us with your presence for long, my lord duke?" he asked after Francis had drunk some wine and nibbled a few plums.

"Just a few days. I have business with the sheriff, then I'll be heading back to Cairnford."

Edward nodded, allowed for a momentary lull, then broached the question that was really on his mind: "You said in your letter that you wanted to discuss the future of Rosepath."

Francis made a dismissive gesture. "Later. Let me enjoy my wine first."

"Of course," Edward said quickly. "I've had fresh horses prepared if you'd like to go hunting this afternoon."

"A little late for a full hunt, isn't it?" Cristiana said. "I'm sure Father would rather take out the hawks."

"You're not used to the hunting around Rosepath, milady." Edward grinned, and was slightly disappointed when Cristiana didn't smile back. "I've got people in the forest watching the trails every day. My man Stephen can lead me to half a dozen deer any time I ask him."

"Better deer than outlaws," Francis said. "What of that, anyway? Is the sheriff dealing with the lawlessness in the forest?"

Edward's grin faded. That was the sheriff's problem, not his, but he still felt marginally responsible for having to report the news. "He claims he is."

"I take it you think he is not."

"Far be it from me to speak ill of my patron, my lord." Edward allowed himself an internal smile this time as Francis nodded. He'd handled that one like a nobleman, shifting the blame to someone else without openly accusing them. It made him look good and the sheriff look bad. He'd have to thank Harald for teaching him that trick with a cup of wine later.

Edward secretly hoped the outlaw problem would become so bad that the sheriff would appeal to him and his men for help again. That would leave his patron indebted to him, and Francis could hardly accuse him of terrorising the countryside if it became necessary to maintain order. He was itching to see some action again.

"I could pass an afternoon with some hunting," Francis said, "if it's as good as you claim."

"The best in the county, my lord."

Francis nodded. "We'll take the bows. I feel like something light after a morning's riding."

Edward called for his servants to make the appropriate preparations, wondering whether it was another symptom of Francis's age that he had opted for a less strenuous type of hunt. The bow was not as prestigious as the spear or sword when it came to testing oneself against wild animals. Some

277

nobles shunned it entirely, believing it to be the sport of peasants. Proper hunting was like a battle, and Edward enjoyed making it as challenging as possible. A boar or a stag could be every bit as deadly as an armed soldier when they were cornered, and it took some of the thrill out of it to finish the job with a bow.

Once the duke and his party were rested they set out with some of Francis's retainers and Edward's huntsmen. Cristiana joined them, taking a bow of her own and a quiver of arrows so that she could ride alongside her father. With a pack of hounds in the lead, they exited the castle through the western gate, clattered over the bridge at the bottom of the hill, and set out down the forest trail. Dense woodland paths were not suited to light hunting with horse and bow, so Edward led them toward the dales. Before long they met up with one of the huntsmen who'd been scouting ahead. He took the lead on a fresh horse, guiding them to open grassland where they could catch deer out in the open.

It proved to be a simple and untaxing hunt once they broke into groups and ran the deer down with the help of the hounds. Edward wasn't very good with a bow, so he held his shots and allowed Francis and Cristiana to take most of them. They managed to bring down two fawns and a buck before the light began to fade. No grand result, but perfectly reasonable for an impromptu half-day's hunt. If nothing else, it seemed to put Francis in better spirits. On the way back he rode alongside Edward and broached the real reason for his visit.

"I've barely been able to sit easy all year, Edward. If it isn't one thing, it's another. That fool Alistair is set to cause trouble for us if the king doesn't put him in his place."

"Is he our enemy now?" Edward asked eagerly.

Francis grimaced. "Perhaps. You'll recall he took some persuading to side with the church over the matter of King Fendrel's accession. Marrying his daughter to my son was part of the bargain we struck."

"And there's still been no word of Isaac?"

Francis shook his head. "The stupid boy seems to have fled the county. Cristiana thinks—" He caught himself as his face began to colour with anger and took a deep breath. "Anyway, I can't give Lady Emilia a groom without him, and Alistair has no interest in wedding one of his sons to Cristiana. The marquess chooses to believe that he has been spurned and our promise broken."

Edward waited for the duke to continue, sensing that there was more to this than a simple slighting of honour.

"Alistair has joined forces with Marquess Larmond of Saintsmarch. You'll recall that Larmond tried his hand at raising a little rebellion when King Fendrel was crowned last year."

Edward did, but he wasn't sure what significance that implied. "I thought you said Larmond was sure to run himself out of money before winter?"

"Yes," Francis said dourly, "but it seems our rogue marquess has been a little more resourceful than we thought. With Alistair on his side, he could become a danger. Do you know where their home counties, Henmarch and Saintsmarch, are?"

Edward shook his head.

"They're adjacent lands on our southern border. One county in disarray might be a nuisance, but two is a serious concern. Larmond and Alistair could open up the kingdom to our enemies if they set their hearts on deposing King Fendrel."

"It's war, then!" Edward said, unable to keep the excitement out of his voice.

Francis gave him a withering look. "It's no more war than it was when King Ralf died. But I'll admit, the scent of it is in the air again. If Larmond and Alistair try to raise a rebellion then the king will call upon his vassals to stamp it out."

"What would you have me do, my lord?"

"I need reliable men here if Alistair chooses to raid

279

Tannersfield in revenge for what happened. Larmond hasn't met anyone in open battle yet, but he's been raiding villages up and down the border. The pair of them together may push north at some point." Francis fixed Edward with a steely look. "Until this matter is resolved, you will maintain a strong garrison here at Rosepath and you will be prepared to march whenever I call on you."

Edward could have laughed out loud in delight. "Permanently, my lord?"

"Indefinitely. Matters may change. Larmond and Alistair's uprising might burn itself out within a month, or my son may reappear." An angry look clouded the duke's face again when he mentioned Isaac. "I'd rather persuade Alistair to switch sides with a marriage than a battle."

"He can't be that fickle."

"The impulsive swine does whatever takes his fancy. He's as fickle as they come."

"But until the trouble is dealt with, I am to remain lord of Rosepath?"

"You are. For all your faults, Edward, you have proven very loyal. I need loyal men right now. I'm granting you the lands of Rosepath village and the neighbouring dales to support your garrison. You can't live on the sheriff's charity forever."

Despite his best efforts, Edward could not conceal the stupid smile that spread across his face. It was everything he'd ever wanted: land, a castle, and subjects of his own. There might soon be a war, and then he'd have the chance to truly prove himself. The giddy thought occurred to him that he could even be made sheriff one day. The current sheriff was getting old, and King Fendrel would need a man with knowledge of the county to replace him. A good word from Francis and his allies could make Edward that man, especially if he acquitted himself well fighting for the crown.

He drew himself up tall in the saddle, allowing his chest to swell with pride. He looked over at Cristiana, who gave him a polite smile of congratulation. A more timid man might have seen coldness in that smile, but Edward knew she was impressed. She had to be, for who wouldn't admire a knight earning such honours from his lord? He would share wine with her later. Harald Redcloak could wait.

Edward felt like he was floating on a cloud all the way back to Rosepath. He flexed his left hand, wondering whether maybe, just maybe, this might be the day the feeling returned to his little finger. He rubbed his knuckles thoughtfully, wondering what had ever become of the girl who'd stabbed him. He hadn't seen her again since the nunnery, but she remained in his thoughts. He'd learned her name from the nun at the door—Elizabeth. An unfortunately common name, and not one he'd had any success in tracking down. Despite a few attempts at searching Tannersfield, he'd always come up short. Harald Redcloak seemed to think she must be living somewhere nearby, for if the nuns knew her by name she was probably still in contact with Lady Kaylein. If she wasn't in town she must be in one of the nearby villages. Edward still had a chance at getting his revenge. When he toured the dales to collect his rent he'd be sure to keep an eye out for her. Someone had to know where the uppity little wench was hiding.

Dusk was falling by the time the hunting party rumbled back into the castle on a wave of hoofbeats. Gwayne and his stablehands tended to the horses with the strict efficiency Edward had come to expect of them. Everyone was in the mood for food and drink, so the servants broke open the stores and set out extra tables for Francis's retainers. Edward was happy to throw a feast. The kitchener had been roasting a hog all day in preparation for the duke's arrival, and there was enough bread, butter, fish, cheese, seasoned eggs, thick pottage, and strong ale to make sure everyone was well catered for. Edward was in such a good mood that he told the kitchener to take any leftovers into the village for the beggars tomorrow. Acts of charity were not in Edward's character, but for once he felt like sharing his wealth. The people needed to know their new lord could be merciful. It was a difficult balance, managing his image in the eyes of his subjects. It would be helpful if he had a wife to take care of such things for him. Count Leo had cultivated a fearsome reputation, but Countess Eleanor's generosity had endeared her to the locals. Edward didn't particularly care about winning his subjects' hearts–he wanted their respect and deference, not their love–but a lord's wife could afford to have a softer touch. He appreciated the idea of people being afraid of him while liking his wife well enough for that fear never to sour into resentment.

As he mused on thoughts of marriage, his attention strayed to Cristiana again. She'd shown an interest in becoming the lady of Rosepath, had she not? And for that, she needed a lord. Edward was the lord. He'd never entertained such an ambitious idea before, for Cristiana was a noble and him a mere commoner raised up to the status of knight, yet over the past year Edward had begun to think of himself as more than that. As of today, he was no longer a boy surviving on the patronage of the sheriff but a man with land of his own. Some of Francis's other knights had married lesser noblewomen in the past–no one quite as important as Cristiana, of course, but Edward felt sure he could do better than them. He was only twenty and already he was in a position many older men would have envied. Who knew where he would be in ten years' time?

A full stomach and several cups of ale elevated his mood, filling him with the kind of confidence that made lofty ideas feel attainable. He laughed with Francis's men, bragged about the success of the hunt, and received no reprimand when he presumptuously clapped the duke on the shoulder the way he would a common drinking companion. Francis was in good spirits that night, and Edward made sure to call for more drink whenever the duke's cup threatened to run dry.

Cristiana sat across the table from them with one of her

maidservants, drinking little but eating and laughing with the others. Every now and again she leaned over to whisper something in her servant's ear, and the pair of them would grin over their shared secret. Edward wondered whether they were talking about him. He felt a half-drunken twinge of desire as he stared at the neckline of Cristiana's purple dress, wishing he could feast his eyes on more than her bare collarbone. She wasn't as big-breasted or wide-hipped as the sort of women he usually went for, but she possessed a kind of lofty, unobtainable beauty that was desirable in a different way.

When the cheer began to die down and the feast settled into a dozen pockets of soft conversation, Edward decided to make his move. This had been one of the best days of his life, and the drink had given him the confidence to believe that it might get better still. Striding calmly around the table, he bowed to the duke's daughter and offered her his arm.

"Would you join me for a drink, milady? A quick walk might help the food settle."

"Well, what's it to be, a drink or a walk? You're looking a little unsteady to manage both." Cristiana and her maidservant shared a chuckle, but Edward didn't allow himself to be put off. Women didn't appreciate timidness.

"A walk first, then a drink," he said firmly. "You don't want to stay in this loud hall all evening."

"Actually, I've been enjoying it," Cristiana replied, taking a deliberate sip from her cup as she gazed around the room. "Though I would like to see more of this keep. The kitchens, perhaps, where they prepared this lovely feast for us."

"Of course, milady. And there are some wonderful tapestries upstairs that might catch your eye." He was thinking of the ones in his bedroom.

"Very well, Sir Edward," she said with a sigh. "Show me your keep. I explored precious little of it last time I was here."

He grinned, puffing out his chest as she rested her hand upon his proffered arm. They exited the great hall and

Edward took her on a circuit of the ground floor, showing her the guard room, kitchen, and pantry.

"You don't have your kitchen outside," Cristiana observed.

"It used to be near the stables, but it burned down. Daisy says it's been in here ever since."

"Let us pray it does not burn down again."

Edward hurried her on. He didn't know why she was interested in the servant areas. They were still bustling with activity, and he wanted to get her somewhere private where they could talk. If he tried to impress her in front of Francis's other men they might try to outdo him with boasts of their own, and that would make him look bad.

"I helped your father take this keep, you know," he remarked as they made their way upstairs. "That was my first real battle. I knew how to fight, obviously, but not against knights and lords." He didn't think there had actually been any knights amongst Leo's men, but Cristiana wouldn't know that.

"I'm sure you distinguished yourself admirably."

Edward nodded, glad to hear her agree. "One of them was a tough old brute, strong as an ox, and about as big, too! He killed a couple of us single-handed before I finished him off. It was right up here, at the top of these stairs." He gestured toward his chamber and led her on. "That's a good way for a man to fight—in a doorway. He can hold off a whole army if he's skilled enough. They can only come at him one at a time, you see, so as long as he's got strength in his sword arm he can keep cutting them down. That didn't save the one here, though. Not against a knight like me."

"Very impressive," Cristiana said distractedly, taking her hand off his arm as he ushered her into his room. A servant had lit candles, and she took one of them so that she could admire the tapestries on the walls, making a lazy circle of the chamber as she pretended to ignore Edward. He folded his arms and sauntered after her, indulging her little game. He didn't mind if she wanted to play coy.

"This depicts the great mountain of Siraba, doesn't it?" Cristiana remarked as she examined a landscape emblazoned in contrasting yellow and brown upon one of the drapes.

Edward shrugged. "I don't see much point in recognising places I've never been."

"No, you wouldn't." Cristiana moved on, leaving Edward bemused. He decided to fill two cups with mead from a small cask he'd been keeping under his bed and sat down at the table, waiting for her to join him.

"It's no wonder your father decided to give me lands and lordship here," he said. "I've been doing fine work in Rosepath. The village is going to see a lot of new trade soon." He paused, waiting for her to ask him more about it, but she didn't seem to have heard. More loudly, he continued: "I had to build a new drawbridge when I saw the state this place was in. Old Count Leo couldn't have been as tough as people said, with a run-down keep like that!" Cristiana made another circle of the room, examining some of the books on the shelves, then made as if to leave. Dismayed, Edward rose to his feet and brought the cup of mead to her. "Your drink, milady."

Her hesitation made him nervous. She should have been impressed by all the things he'd been saying to her. Why was she acting as if she'd barely heard him? Was she feeling unwell?

After a pause, she reached out to grip the cup and their fingers brushed for a tantalising moment.

"I did agree to a drink, didn't I?"

"Yes, you did." Edward smiled, inviting her to sit again. This time she joined him at the table. "You are very beautiful, Lady Cristiana." He leaned toward the candle between them, looking at her intently so that she knew he was being sincere. "It takes a noble man to appreciate the beauty of a strong woman."

She clasped a hand to her breast, eyes widening as her

mouth opened in amazement. "It does? Why, only someone so refined as yourself could make such an astute observation, Sir Edward."

"You humble me, milady." He allowed his hand to edge toward hers, oblivious to everything but his desire. It rose within him with the same candescent allure as the candle's flame, hungry to burn brighter. "I'm going to be a very important man soon. A baron, perhaps, or maybe even the next sheriff. If Marquess Alistair comes here, I'll slay the villain myself." He took her hand and clasped it between his. "When I do that, it should be with a beautiful wife at my side."

Lady Cristiana leaned forward, staring into his eyes. He squeezed her fingers tighter, feeling a surge of longing for the woman. This was it. She was falling in love with him. In a moment he would lean forward, kiss her, and she would be his.

"Sir Edward," she said softly, "you are no better at wooing women than you are at shooting a bow. I'd stick to ladies you can buy for a penny." With a playful curl of her lips, she puffed out the candle between them. Edward coughed on the wisp of smoke that rose from the wick, stunned by what had just happened. Was she making a joke? How could she, during a tender moment like this?

Then he heard her laugh. It was a playful, mocking sound, a sound he would have enjoyed had it been directed at anyone else but him. He slammed his cup down, driving his chair back with an ugly scraping sound. Cristiana was already on her feet and turning to leave.

A familiar fury took hold of him, writhing like a serpent in his blood. Was he not good enough for her? He was better than any man in this castle! How could she reject him so callously after he'd put his heart and soul into winning her over? Instinctively, he reached out and snatched her arm, yanking her back to face him.

A cold look stole over Cristiana's face, freezing him to the spot as he realised what he'd just done. She was staring at him with her father's metal-sharp eyes, pinprick lights of the candles dancing in her icy glare.

"Take your hand off me."

Edward stood there staring at her, a tempest of anger and fear boiling beneath his skin.

"I warn you, Sir Edward, I can have your new land taken away as swiftly as it was given."

That shocked him into letting go. His hand felt like it had been locked in place, and it tingled stiffly when he relaxed his grip. He took a step back and bumped into his chair. He felt like he should say something, but when he opened his mouth no words came to mind, so he just gawped at her.

Cristiana's expression shifted back toward placid neutrality.

"I would make a fine husband for you!" Edward called as she turned away.

She'd stepped out of the candlelight, but he could still see the scorn in her smile as she glanced over her shoulder. It made him want to grab his chair and hurl it across the room.

"Even if you would, that is hardly for you to decide. I will marry a man of my father's choosing."

Then I will make him choose me. Edward thought as Cristiana walked out. He shoved his chair over, stalking the length of the room in a rage. The tapestry of the Siraban mountain reminded him of the indignity he'd just suffered, and with a snarl he tore it from its fastenings and bundled it into a chest at the foot of his bed. How could she toy with him like that? He'd never known a woman to be so wicked!

The indignation was maddening. For a moment he thought to stride back into the great hall and demand that Francis let him marry her. Then she would be the one feeling like a fool! Yet before Edward reached the door he turned around again and stamped back to the window, realising how reckless he was being. The weight of Cristiana's threat still hung in the air, stinging his ears like a brand.

He opened the shutters and stared out over the castle walls, his arms shaking as he gripped the window sill. She was right; he did have a lot to lose now, and Francis and Cristiana were among the few people with the power to take it all away from him. He couldn't lose his new lands. The fear had a sobering effect on him, clearing his mind enough for him to realise how stupid he'd been to lay his hands on the duke's daughter. What if she told her father what had happened?

Edward slammed the shutters and went downstairs, almost tripping in his drunken haste. His fear grew as he imagined the scene he might walk in on; Cristiana pointing to the doorway indignantly, Duke Francis rising to his feet in anger, half a dozen men-at-arms glowering as they prepared to drag Edward away to be flogged for his insolence. The pounding of his heart grew louder, his panic rising to a crescendo as he turned through the door into the great hall.

But the room was exactly as he had left it. Duke Francis was conversing mildly with Harald Redcloak, the servants were clearing away the food and pouring more ale, and Cristiana was back with her maidservant as if nothing had happened. Edward blinked in confusion, stunned by the power of his own imagined fear. He wanted to go back upstairs and be alone, but it would look strange if he left again now. He forced himself to return to his seat and drink more ale, but it did nothing to assuage his nervous anger.

Cristiana barely spared him another glance the whole night.

CHAPTER 19

Kaylein knew she had to apologise to Elizabeth for what had happened. An entire month had passed, and the guilt was beginning to gnaw at her. She'd been so flustered following their disagreement that she'd forgotten to feel nervous about staying overnight with Sister Grace—not that she'd had any real reason to worry about that. Sister Grace was not going to pounce on her and kiss her in her sleep. She hadn't volunteered to go to the building site again, fearful that Liz would still be angry and she would have to endure a day in the company of someone who hated her.

In the end, it was not guilt but loneliness that persuaded Kaylein to visit Joseph's workshop. She missed having someone she could talk to. Sub-Prioress Joan sent her to buy extra candles from the market, so she set out with a leather satchel over her shoulder and two shillings in her pouch, steeling herself for the busy town. Handling money still felt strange to her. It was something she'd rarely done as a noblewoman, and hoarding personal wealth was forbidden by a nun's vows. Many novices struggled with the precept of poverty, especially those from poorer backgrounds who had learned from an early age to covet every penny they earned.

Kaylein had expected to struggle with it, having become accustomed to dresses and books and jewellery as a young woman. But she had been lucky in that regard, albeit in a horribly morbid fashion, for after the mouths of trauma she'd struggled through last spring a vow of poverty seemed like the least of her worries. It had become routine to her, and by the time her veil of grief lifted she was used to it.

The nunnery still had money and possessions, of course, but those belonged to God, not any one sister. They were used for the good of the convent and the advancement of its holy purpose, though Kaylein had observed that some nuns interpreted that purpose differently than others. A few of the senior sisters liked to cause a fuss for the mother superior over things like the warmth of their dormitories, the strength of their wine, the hours they worked, and the privileges they were afforded. Some attempted to justify themselves with loose citations of the scriptures that were difficult to argue with, making such topics a frequent waste of time in chapter.

Kaylein had become much more savvy to the hierarchies of the convent since taking her first vows. It dismayed her to realise how vindictive and self-interested some of her fellow sisters could be. There was a subsect of women within the church whose loyalties clearly lay with self-advancement first and the worship of God second. It was not as bad as it was within monasteries, Mother Jane said, for the highest position a woman could hope to attain was that of prioress or abbess, whereas men could rival the power of noble lords if they rose to become bishops or cardinals. Still, it was often easier for a woman to make a name for herself within the church than outside it, and that allure was tempting to many who sought authority over others.

When Kaylein saw her fellow sisters bickering and vying for influence it made her all the more determined to challenge the contrived interpretations of the scriptures that allowed them to behave that way. She found herself mentally constructing rebuttals to their arguments in chapter, realising that her own knowledge of the scriptures often outstripped theirs. She never dared say anything, for she had no desire to make enemies while she was still a novice, but her mind was alight with ideas.

Eventually, a few of her thoughts had worked their way onto pieces of scrap parchment that had been left in the writing room. She fretted about carrying the parchments around in her robe all day, wondering whether she was breaking her vow of poverty by keeping them to herself, but they were not for her, they were for Elizabeth. A sacrist did not feel guilty about looking after a convent's holy objects, so she should not feel guilty about holding a gift intended for another. What she did feel guilty about was sneaking a pot of ink and a quill out of the writing room so that she could write in her dormitory. She made sure to do it only when she stayed late and was able to return the borrowed implements early the next morning, for she was terribly afraid of being caught. Mother Jane might understand, but others wouldn't, and if she was caught then her punishment would be discussed in chapter before the whole convent.

Yet she had done it for Elizabeth, and the desire to give her friend something to read by way of an apology had helped push her into leaving the nunnery again. She'd finished three half-pages now, and they rustled beneath her robes as she walked, pinched tight against her hip by her waist tie.

That morning she'd prayed for Elizabeth to accept her apology, even though she knew it was selfish. Some nuns thought God guided their actions precisely in accordance with His will, but Kaylein did not believe that. That was an excuse people used to avoid accountability. God was not a dictator, only a guide. His light could help a person choose the right words at the right time, or lend their voice the conviction it needed to touch another's heart. There was a reason particularly devout priests were often such good orators. Kaylein hoped God would grant her confidence today, for she would be devastated if Elizabeth spurned her again.

Kaylein had only visited Joseph's workshop a few times before. Elizabeth told her they'd been there the first day they came to Tannersfield, but she couldn't remember that. Large swathes of her memory seemed to be missing from those first few months following her flight from Rosepath. The journey through the forest that night felt like it had happened years ago, fragmented images and fears swallowing up its clarity. Perhaps it was God's light helping her move on by taking away the bad memories.

The workshop looked busy when she arrived. Joseph and many of his friends were away at the building site, but other carpenters were making use of the yard in the meantime, most of them travelling journeymen who couldn't find work on Carpenter's Street. Elizabeth was presently engaged in an argument with one of them in the yard. The man stood a full head taller than her, but she glared up at him indignantly with one hand on her hip and the other jabbing firmly toward the ground. Liz had always had a kind of rough practicality about her that Kaylein admired, and it was showing itself off resplendently in that moment. Her straw-blonde hair was folded into a knot at the back of her head and her cheeks had flushed with anger. Her stance was that of a woman who would sooner throw a punch than back down.

"Your rent pays for you to use those tools from dawn till dusk," she was saying, "in *this* workshop and this workshop alone. If you want to take them home, you'll have to buy them."

"Who's going to use them overnight?" the man countered. "It'll help me do my work quicker if I borrow them. Besides, it's a waste to buy them just for myself."

"Then what am I to tell Joseph if they go missing, hm? Just because he's away it doesn't mean his rules followed him out the door. You'd better believe that if any of those planes disappear you'll be the one paying for them, Peter

Carpenter!"

Peter Carpenter blew out an exasperated breath and stepped back. "Saints above, woman. Are you sure you're not Rose's daughter?"

The carpenter probably didn't catch it, but Kaylein noticed a glimmer of satisfaction in Elizabeth's expression as she folded her arms and sent him back to work. The comparison had flattered her. Taking advantage of her friend's good mood, Kaylein walked into the yard and waved to catch her attention.

"Kay!" Liz smiled, rushing forward to take her by the hands. Relief washed over Kaylein. She wasn't angry. "Where have you been? It's been weeks! I've missed you on my walks."

"I'm so sorry. I was terribly worried you might hate me."

"Of course I don't hate you." Elizabeth raised her eyebrows reproachfully. "Though you were very rude."

Kaylein flushed. "I hope you can forgive me. I didn't mean to... Well, it isn't as if I can blame you for the way your mother lived. That isn't God's way." Elizabeth looked a little perplexed by her answer, so she quickly added: "And we have many good women at the convent who once followed your mother's profession." Kaylein sensed she hadn't done a very good job of apologising, but Elizabeth seemed willing to let it go.

"Let's not talk about that," she said. "I want to know what you've been doing all this time. Come on in. I can leave the boys to their work for a while." Elizabeth tugged her toward the workshop, but Kaylein hesitated.

"I can't stay long. Sister Joan will be expecting me back soon. I was sent to buy candles from the market."

"Didn't you get some on the way here?"

"No," she confessed. She'd been so busy worrying about her friend's reaction that it had slipped her mind.

"I can sell you some of mine if you like."

"They need to be big."

"I only ever get big ones. They last longer, and there's more tallow to reuse afterwards."

"That would be very kind of you." In truth, the convent preferred to burn wax candles over tallow. Despite the extra expense, the clean, pleasant smell was thought to be more appropriate for a house of God, and wax left fewer marks on the walls and ceilings when it burned. But Elizabeth wouldn't know that, and Kaylein was hesitant to call attention to her friend's common way of living so soon after their last falling out. She still felt like she was treading on eggshells.

Elizabeth led her to a stone house behind the workshop and took a heavy iron key from her belt to unlock the door.

"Are you living here?" Kaylein asked.

"Only sleeping." Elizabeth gestured to a crumpled mattress near the hearth. "I'd never touch anything in the back. I'm keeping it all perfect for Joseph and Rose."

"This is lovely, Liz." A touch of homesickness stirred in Kaylein as she gazed around the stone house. It was very much like some of the rooms in Rosepath Castle: warm and compact, with an oily, musty smell that spoke of warm fires and close living. "You're doing so well for yourself."

Elizabeth turned to face her with a sheepish expression. "I'm hoping Joseph will let me stay when he comes back, at least until I can afford a house of my own. He and Rose have been like family this past winter."

Kaylein smiled. "You deserve it."

Elizabeth flushed and turned away, inviting her to take a seat at the table. There weren't any windows in the house, so she left the door open for light. "What about you? How's life in the convent?"

Settling herself down, Kaylein told her about everything of note that had happened since their last meeting. Mother Jane had been sick with the fever for a week–the same fever that had stricken the builders and half of Tannersfield–but God had lent her the fortitude to fight it off, much to the relief of the novices who had suffered a week of hardships under Sub-Prioress Joan in the interim. Kaylein had helped some of the younger nuns with their schooling. A toad had made Sister Isabel scream bloody murder when it jumped out of the water channel at her. There had been a night of tense prayer when a fire broke out two streets away from the convent. She saved the news of her writing till last, producing the three sheets of parchment and laying them out on the table for Elizabeth to admire. To Kaylein's delight, her friend was ecstatic.

"This one is just the alphabet," she explained, pointing to the letters she'd penned beneath a half-page of unfinished verse that had been interrupted by an ugly rip in the side of the parchment. "You should start with learning these before you try to read words."

Elizabeth nodded enthusiastically. "Joseph's helped me with some letters before. That one's E, for Elizabeth." She pointed at the letter F with a look of triumph.

"Not quite," Kaylein said. "E has three horizontal lines stemming from the vertical one, but you were close. To help memories the whole set, you can repeat them in order."

"Like counting."

"Exactly!"

"I can count to a hundred now," Elizabeth said. "There are a lot less than a hundred letters here."

"Only twenty-six. Our language is quite simple to write with. The Siraban alphabet has over a hundred characters."

Elizabeth raised an eyebrow as if sceptical that any language could be so complicated. "Well, I'm not going to learn Siraban."

"I doubt you'll ever need to, not unless you want to run a workshop in another country."

They discussed the alphabet for a while, Kaylein pointing out a few specific letters to Elizabeth when she asked, then they moved on to the other parchments.

"It might be some time before you can read these," Kaylein said. "But I wanted to give you something with real sentences."

"What did you write about?" Liz gazed at the sheets in a futile effort to decipher their meaning.

"Oh, nothing all that interesting. Just thoughts I wish some of the other sisters would bear in mind when they discuss the scriptures."

"Can you explain them to me?"

Kaylein leaned forward, taking one of the pages and tracing a finger along the lines she'd written. "I laid out the starting point that I think all religious arguments should base themselves upon. We can't assert that we know the will of God better than the saints–that is blasphemous. So everything we interpret must be derived from the seven prime scriptures. The first scripture is thought to be the purest record of God's will, because the author, Saint Anden, was visited by God in person. Every saint who penned one of the prime scriptures thereafter was touched by God in their own way, but their interpretations of His word are thought to be diluted. They are revisions of what was written by Saint Anden, not replacements." She looked up to check that Elizabeth was still following her. "As far back as the second prime scripture, the author brings legitimacy to his claims by referencing and reinterpreting the work of Saint Anden. The further back you go in the scriptures, the more authority your words hold. I think that for anyone in the church to take your arguments seriously, you must root them in the context of the first scripture. That's what I wrote about on these two pages for you."

Elizabeth looked like she'd lost the thread in the end, but she nodded all the same. "You're so clever, Kay. Maybe God wanted you to write books for Him."

"I don't know." Kaylein sat back, trying not to let her friend's words make her feel too good about herself, for pride was a precept of sin. "I won't be able to write anything properly until I finish my novitiate. Then I shall need to convince Mother Jane that I have something worth writing. I don't suppose many people in the church will take notice of me, though. Only men write great works of theology."

"That's stupid," Elizabeth said. "Why don't you just pretend you're a monk, then?"

The idea was so simple it shocked Kaylein. For a moment it sounded ludicrous, but when she thought about it, it made sense. She couldn't very well pretend she was a man to someone's face, but if her writing was copied and sent to other convents, who would know? All she had to do was change the name of the author from Sister Kaylein to Brother John or Father Simon and her words would immediately carry weight. She wondered whether people would be able to tell the difference. Would something about her tone convey that she was a woman? It might be a sin to lie about something like that. She would have to dwell on it in her meditations.

"That's a good idea, Liz. I don't think we'll have to worry about it for a while, though. I won't be a proper nun for a few years yet."

"How soon can you take your next vows?"

"Mother Jane says it's proper to wait at least a year, and I have two more sets of vows to complete. It would be a couple of years at the earliest before I could start writing."

"That's so long," Elizabeth groaned. "Will you keep on writing things for me in the meantime?"

"Of course! For as long as you want to keep reading."

"I'll probably be learning for a lot more than two years. I wish you could give me lessons."

"I do, too." Kaylein sat up suddenly, realising she'd spent far longer at the workshop than she meant to. All the talk of reading, writing, and the scriptures had distracted her. Sister Joan would be furious.

Seeing the mortified look on her face, Elizabeth gave her a guilty smile and went to open a chest by the wall. "I'll fetch you those candles. Don't let anyone steal them on the way back."

"I doubt anyone will bother robbing a nun for candles," Kaylein said. She wished Elizabeth hadn't reminded her how dangerous Tannersfield was these days. She knew she was safer than most by virtue of the robes she wore, but it still made her nervous to walk the streets without an escort. Father would never have let things get this bad. No, not Father—Mother. Father had ruled lawbreakers with an iron fist, but Mother was the one who encouraged Rosepath Monastery to send vagrants on their way with enough food to reach Cairnford or Rambirch. She'd made a habit of keeping abreast of which settlements might need workers in the coming seasons, and she passed that information to the monastery so that the destitute did not become beggars or outlaws. Awful Sir Edward had probably never considered anything like that. What made the situation in Tannersfield especially upsetting was that the church received ample money from the new king's taxes to help the needy.

Yet that money was being spent on things like houses for the love children of cardinals.

Kaylein offered up a silent prayer as Liz pulled an armful of long candles out of the chest. Perhaps the people of Tannersfield had sinned and this was their punishment: cruel lords and a wicked duke. She still couldn't believe Francis was considered a friend of the church. God did not want to be celebrated through acts of violence and political opportunism. There were dark times ahead for Tannersfield County, and it was the duty of people like her to be a candle shining in the night until dawn broke once more. She hoped she would have the strength to keep burning.

Despite her troubled thoughts, Kaylein left the workshop feeling relieved, for she'd successfully made amends with Elizabeth. She hurried back across town, hoping she could deliver the candles before Sister Joan realised how long she'd been gone. As she skirted the marketplace, her thoughts returned to the future of Tannersfield. A man had been hanged that morning, and his body still dangled from the

298

gallows as a ghastly warning to others. Kaylein doubted it would prove very effective. The hangings had only become more frequent over the past year. No threat was great enough to deter people when they were desperate.

If only she was still a noblewoman. For as much as she tried not to dwell on the past, the sight of the dangling body filled her with indignation. A year ago, she could have done something about this. She was still the rightful heir to Tannersfield county. That was why Duke Francis had wanted her dead. A painful flush coloured her cheeks as she thought of her father. He would have urged her to find a powerful husband, raise an army, depose Francis, and demand back the rights to her family's land. Legally, Tannersfield belonged to Francis now, but people said the barons were not fond of their new duke, and Kaylein knew that kings preferred lords who could command the loyalty of their subjects. Yet she knew nothing of warfare, nor of marriage. Violence was anathema to Kaylein, and she hated the thought of doing to others what Francis had done to her. Such an attack might even spark a civil war. She didn't want to drag the kingdom into turmoil just so that she could take back her birthright. Besides, she had pledged her life to God now. She could never marry anyone so long as she remained in service to the church.

She tried to tell herself that her guilt was pointless, yet it remained with her all the way back to the convent. Seeing no sign of Sister Joan, she deposited the candles in the chapel and went to the dormitory to meditate. She could not combat Duke Francis's tyranny by force, but what if she could do something else? Any effort to undermine him would be a victory. The church was his greatest ally, and she was part of the church now. She would never wield a cardinal's power, but over the course of her lifetime she might garner some small measure of influence within the holy order. That, at least, was something.

Kaylein stared at the blank stone wall in consternation,

wringing her thoughts like a damp rag hoping some droplet of wisdom might seep out. Elizabeth's idea about writing a book under a monk's name kept returning to her. What if she penned scripture that condemned the relationship between the church and violent lords like Francis? It was a lofty idea, far more uncertain than abandoning her vows and marrying a man who could muster an army, but perhaps it was more pure in its purpose. Such an undertaking might prove the work of a lifetime. Francis was likely to die of old age before she stood any chance of stirring reform in the church, yet the idea still appealed to her. A student of God did not live exclusively for herself, but for all the lives that followed. Even if she could do nothing against Francis himself, she might inspire others to take a stand against men like him in the future. Perhaps one day, a hundred years from now, a bishop might read her work, whisper in a count's ear, and a second tragedy like hers would be averted.

That thought strengthened Kaylein's resolve. In condemning Francis through her writing, she would serve God's will while honouring the memory of her family. It would be years before she could begin in earnest, yet none of that time would be wasted. She would practice on pieces of scrap parchment for Elizabeth, refine her thoughts during her meditations, and continue learning from Mother Jane until she was ready to take her final vows.

God's light filled her once again during evening prayer. This time it flickered with vengeful passion. First He had given her peace, now He had given her purpose. She had a goal set before her—a goal she could dedicate her life to pursuing. However many years it took, she would work to challenge the authority of nobles like Francis from afar. Armies could win wars, but ideas could change kingdoms, too. All Kaylein needed was the right idea.

CHAPTER 20

That summer, Sam persuaded Isaac to break the king's law. Like so many of Sam's schemes, Isaac doubted it would miraculously alleviate all their woes, but it would at the very least earn them a few shillings. And right now he needed a few shillings. David, the horse courser in Tannersfield, had made it clear that he wouldn't keep Blackberry stabled much longer. He allowed Isaac to spend time with his horse and ride her around the yard when he came by to pay for her upkeep, but he was a hard businessman, and after half a year he was growing tired of holding on to a mare for a man who kept promising he'd have the money soon. After Isaac's last visit, David had thrown down an ultimatum: get the money by the end of the month, or he'd sell the horse to someone else.

Sam's scheme with the draught horses hadn't been the reliable investment he'd made it out to be. From the moment Isaac met the seller in a discreet paddock outside Tannersfield he'd suspected the animals were stolen. Every farmer Isaac rented the draught horses to had been disappointed with their performance. Some paid their rent begrudgingly, others, like the one who'd kept losing horseshoes, had devised ways of costing Isaac as much money as he charged them. After David's ultimatum, Isaac took the horses into town and sold them wherever he could. He got a fair price for each, but it was still a few shillings short of what he needed to buy Blackberry. There was no hope of making up the rest of the money through honest work. Labouring on farms and a building site near Tannersfield had provided for his living expenses that year, but it was basic work for basic pay.

That was when he turned to Sam. They'd stayed together throughout the winter and spring, finding work on the farms and sharing the burden of building a rough wattle-and-daub hut together. Despite their companionship, Isaac had never grown to fully trust the man. He slipped away from him as often as he could to bury his money in the forest, still half-expecting to wake up one morning with his purse strings cut. But whether he trusted him or not, Isaac liked Sam, and he sensed the feeling was mutual. They were cut from the same cloth; adventurers who lived life from one day to the next. Commitments and responsibilities were worries for the future, even if that meant travelling from farm to farm never knowing where their next meal was coming from. It was an existence fringed with excitement and a hint of danger. Sometimes, when the nights were cold and the bread stale, Isaac thought about going home to Cairnford, but the memories of his father and Lady Emilia stilled that temptation. For once in his life, he was truly free, and that was worth more than all the warm hearths and fresh bread in the world. The only worry worth dwelling on right now was his separation from Blackberry.

Two days after Isaac sold the draught horses, Sam came out of their hut with a surreptitious smile on his face. Isaac knew to be wary of that smile, for it usually preceded some underhanded scheme.

"We can have your money by the end of the week," Sam announced.

Isaac eyed him sceptically from his seat in the grass,

tossing an apple core to a mangy old dog that had taken to sharing their fire in the mornings. Sam called the hound Chomp, for he seemed to eat anything they threw at him.

"I'm not stealing from anyone around here," Isaac said. They were living in a small cluster of worker dwellings on the edge of one of the farms. It couldn't exactly be called a village, but the folk there all looked out for one another, and most of them seemed decent enough.

"Of course you're not," Sam replied. "You don't steal from your own, not that this bunch would have anything worth stealing. How about a farmer instead?"

"That won't end well for us." Farmers guarded their land viciously, and since most were serfs indentured to local lords they were well-protected by the law. Nobles didn't take kindly to outlaws interfering with their income.

"Well, we're not stupid, are we, Isaac?" Sam grinned when he saw the look on his companion's face. "Alright–I'm no wise man and you're a spoilt noble boy, but I've dodged the hangman's noose enough times to know what I'm good at. And you're sharp. Why do you think I stuck with you this long?"

Isaac shrugged. "Guilt?"

"Don't be daft. You're a good thinker. You tracked me down, didn't you? Most folk I've known wouldn't have had the sense for that."

"Whatever this is, you can't do it without my help, can you?"

"And you can't get your fair lady back without mine." He was talking about Blackberry. One of Sam's favourite pastimes was joking that Isaac was madly in love with his horse. "You know Henry Shearer's flock?"

Isaac did. Henry Shearer was a bad-tempered sheep farmer who lived near the building site they were working on. He didn't have much land, but he was a free man who was fiercely proud of his small holding. A sizeable pack of farm dogs guarded his sheep, which were said to produce some of

303

the highest quality wool in the area.

Sam continued: "If there's any farmer worth stealing from, it's him. Those dogs of his like you. I reckon you could slip us by without them raising a fuss."

"He's trained his dogs to listen to the people who feed them. That's how a lot of folk do it. I just give them some scraps when I'm heading by that way and they leave me be." Isaac gestured to Chomp, who was gazing at him expectantly in the hopes of being thrown another apple core. "Chomp might've been one of his when he was younger."

"You can get any animal to be friendly with you," Sam said. "If you didn't speak like a nobleman I'd reckon you'd been raised on a farm, the way you handle them."

Isaac sensed he knew where this was going. "Are we going to steal one of his sheep?"

Sam shook his head. "That's a hassle, and we'd probably get caught. Have you seen the way old Henry's dogs act around them?"

"They bark at anyone who comes close."

"Right, but only when the sheep are out to pasture. He hasn't taught them to stand guard when the flock's safe in its pen."

"Oh, he has," Isaac said. "The second the gate starts rattling those dogs go wild. That farmhand who worked for him last summer said he couldn't bear it. He always thought they were going to tear his throat out whenever he had to open the gate."

"Right—so that's why we won't touch the gate. We're not stealing any sheep. We're going to take their fleeces."

Isaac raised an eyebrow. The idea seemed far-fetched. Henry Shearer's flock had full coats ready for the summer shearing, but he couldn't imagine being able to sneak in and cut the wool off their backs in the middle of the night. Then again, Henry's wool was worth a lot of money, as his comfortable farmhouse attested to. It certainly wouldn't ruin the man to lose a few shillings on his haul of fleeces this summer. Isaac didn't like the idea of stealing, but if the victim was someone as unpleasant as Henry Shearer he fancied he could stomach it. Besides, if he didn't raise the money to buy Blackberry soon he might lose her forever.

"Henry Shearer has a couple of sons," Isaac said. "If they get their hands on us, we'll be in trouble."

"We can run faster than them."

"But not the dogs."

"So make friends with the dogs. Give them some food. As long as they leave us alone, we'll be fine."

It still sounded risky to Isaac, but the plan seemed workable. The last few times he'd been on Henry Shearer's land the dogs hadn't bothered him. They weren't naturally bloodthirsty beasts, but they could be aggressive with their master's encouragement. Isaac knew the difference between a dog that would bite and one that would only bark, and most of Henry Shearer's pack seemed to be the latter. A farmer didn't want his guards too vicious, after all, lest they turn on his own flock.

Isaac's good sense told him this was probably a bad idea, but his fear of losing Blackberry was stronger. Father would be furious if he knew what he was doing.

"Alright," he said, "when should we go?" A ripple of excitement ran through him. It would be dangerous, yes, but if it worked he might be riding Blackberry away from Tannersfield before the end of the week.

"Tomorrow," Sam said. "I feel good about tomorrow."

"Why not tonight? The sky looks like it'll be clear, and the moon's about full. We won't be able to shear sheep if we can't see anything."

Sam rubbed his chin. "I suppose that's clever. That's why you're a good boy to have around, Isaac. I need your ideas."

That was probably true. Sam handled everyday living well enough–he was quite adept at talking people into giving him work and a bed for the night–but Isaac had had to dissuade him from embarking upon several foolhardy schemes over the past few months. First, he'd wanted to steal another horse using the same ice patch he'd ambushed Isaac with. Isaac had explained that horse thievery hadn't worked out well for him the first time. It was incredibly risky, and any horses he stole might be tired or uncooperative. Furthermore, David the horse courser knew Sam's face now, and he'd warned the other livestock merchants in town not to buy from him. The shady man who'd sold them the draught horses had since moved on, likely with the sheriff's men behind him. More recently, Sam had thought to steal construction materials from the building site by having one of them throw wood into the river at night while the other collected it downstream in the forest. Isaac had pointed out that it might be a bad idea to rob their employers. Even if they managed to find the timber in the dark, they would face the unenviable task of dragging it back to town.

Isaac expected there were probably similar arguments to be made against stealing wool from Henry Shearer, but none of them were compelling enough to dissuade him this time. Unlike Isaac, Sam had no reservations when it came to thievery. Anyone richer than him was fair game in his mind, and given that he lived in near-perpetual poverty that accounted for almost everyone. His companion's predisposition toward lawlessness baffled Isaac sometimes. Sam was a strong young man, which made him one of the lucky few who could always find work. Despite being uneducated and impulsive, he was not witless. He could have easily held down a job as a labourer or an apprentice if he set his mind to it.

"Why do you keep wanting to do things like this?" Isaac asked, wondering whether he'd earned enough of Sam's trust to get an honest answer out of him.

"You need the money, don't you?"

"I do, but you don't. You must've saved up a few pennies these past months. What were you going to do with all that silver you got for Blackberry, anyway?"

306

Sam shrugged. "Like I said, buy those draught horses and make more."

"And then what? If we get these fleeces, what'll you do with your share?"

Another shrug. "What'll you do after you get Blackberry?"

"Ride somewhere else, I suppose."

"Then maybe I'll come with you."

Isaac shook his head, none the wiser. "Not many people steal just for the fun of it."

"Do you want to get these fleeces or not?"

Isaac relented, realising he was not going to get an answer that day. Perhaps Sam didn't have an answer to give. Some people believed what they believed and did what they felt like doing, never questioning where those impulses came from or where they might lead.

"We should go at dusk," Isaac said. "It won't take long to get there. What are we going to use to cut the wool?"

"I'll take care of that. Just get us a nice big sack with a tie."

They agreed to meet on the road by a bridge that crossed the river near the building site. Thinking about the dogs, Isaac decided to get some scraps from the builders who'd been out hunting, and he managed to fill his satchel with bits of blood-scented bone and animal hide for a penny. He hoped Henry Shearer's hounds would be placated by the offerings, otherwise the smell of meat might have them barking up a storm of excitement.

Sunset was painting a thread of orange across the northern hilltops when Sam arrived. He came from the direction of the farms, panting hard with a pair of shearing scissors in one hand. Isaac decided not to ask where they'd come from. No one else was within eyeshot of the bridge, but he still felt ill at ease. He wasn't sure what worried him more: the thought of being caught and thrown in the sheriff's jail, or being dragged back to Cairnford to answer to his father.

"We'll wait just a bit longer," Sam said. "Want to make

sure everyone's asleep before we arrive."

Just as Isaac had anticipated, the night was set to be a clear one. They whiled away their time skipping stones down the river as the sun went down. There was a peacefulness to the nighttime that Isaac had always enjoyed, but he found it difficult to savour the evening's whimsy knowing what he was about to do. Once it was dark, they set out for Henry Shearer's farm. It was less than half an hour's walk from the bridge, marked off by a dry stone wall with a shallow ditch on the outer side. Neither obstacle proved a problem for Sam and Isaac, who were both tall and limber. They hauled themselves up using the gaps in the stones as footholds and peered over the top. The farmhouse stared back at them from the far side of the walled yard. No lights burned behind the shutters, which meant everyone was probably in bed. A broad cart track ran the length of the yard, the sheep pen abutting the house on one side while a handful of rough wooden dog houses occupied the other. Were the shadowy shapes outside them sleeping hounds, or just mounds of dung in the grass?

Isaac gave a low whistle. One of the shadows twitched and pricked up a pair of ears. He passed Sam the empty sack he'd been carrying and reached into his satchel. His fingers closed on the nub of a meaty bone that was still flecked with scraps of venison. He tossed it in the direction of the shadow. It sprang to its feet with a growl.

"Don't get them too excited," Sam whispered.

"Better they get excited while we're still on this side of the wall," Isaac said. Two more dogs emerged from the shadows and padded toward the bone, the motion of their paws creating an eerie blur of movement beneath their silhouettes. They sniffed at the first hound, then turned away in disappointment as their companion lay down to crunch contentedly on his treat. Again Isaac whistled. Bone in mouth, the hound stood up and walked toward him. Isaac swung a leg over the wall and dropped down on the other side. The dog dropped the bone to sniff and nuzzle him, intrigued by his familiar scent. It was a scent that often came in the company of food, which meant it was friendly.

Sensing no aggression from the dog, Isaac reached out his hand. A moment later it was covered in slobber. He scratched the dog behind the neck and whispered for Sam to join him. Sam pulled himself over the wall. The dog approached him and began to growl when he flinched away.

"Don't make him nervous," Isaac whispered.

"I could snip his neck with these shears. They're sharp as a razor."

"No!" Isaac hissed, reaching out hurriedly when he saw Sam's arm rise. Killing a friendly dog horrified him as much as the thought of killing a person. "Give me those." He twisted the shears out of Sam's grasp.

"I suppose we couldn't snip them all."

His friend's lackadaisical attitude toward killing dogs unnerved Isaac, but it was a sadly common sentiment among most people. Some farmers never spent enough time around their animals to get a sense of their moods and dispositions. To a lot of people, tending animals was just a job, but Isaac had grown up around masters of horse and hound who loved their animals like their own children. With their instruction, Isaac had learned to appreciate all the ways in which animals could be delightfully similar to people. No farmer, butcher, tanner, or preacher had ever convinced him that they were soulless tools to be used and discarded. He wished he had time to explain that to Sam.

"If you hurt any of them, the others will get upset."

"I won't hurt them if they don't hurt me," Sam replied nervously.

They crept toward the farmhouse and sheep pen. The dog beside them picked up his bone and followed, tail wagging. As they moved forward half a dozen more shadows emerged from the dog houses. Isaac tossed more scraps from his satchel to some of them. When a pair began growling over the same bone, he made sure to throw another one, ending the dispute before it erupted into a bout of barking. Sweat prickled his skin. The growling and snuffling of the dogs sounded painfully conspicuous to Isaac, but was it loud enough to carry through the farmhouse's stone walls?

"We're doing well," Sam whispered.

Another hound bounded toward them. Sam flinched away, but Isaac held his ground. The dog butted his leg, growling aggressively. Isaac reached beneath his chin and tickled him. A moment later he was rolling on his back, demanding more attention. Isaac gave him a few more scratches and was rewarded with a warbling growl of pleasure.

"Damn me to hell if you've not got a blessed touch with these things," Sam whispered. They were close enough to the house that Isaac didn't dare respond. He pressed a finger to his lips, hoping Sam could see him in the darkness, and gave the dog a scrap of hide to chew on.

They'd accumulated a small congregation of hounds by the time they reached the sheep pen. None had barked, but their growls and yips kept Isaac on edge. There was no noise coming from the farmhouse, so he passed Sam the shears and swung himself into the sheep pen. The woven fence creaked and made a cracking sound as it wobbled beneath him. Isaac almost kicked a sheep when he landed on the other side, but he saw the animal's woolly coat at the last moment and parted his legs so that he landed astride it instead. The ewe bleated and thrashed about fearfully.

"Shh, shh," Isaac whispered in a panic, expecting the farmhouse door to slam open at any moment. The animal scampered out from between his legs and joined the rest of her flock as they withdrew into a bleating huddle on the far side of the pen. The woven fence creaked and swayed again as Sam hauled himself over. Isaac reached for his companion's arm and gripped it tight, urging him to stay still.

In the shadow of the farmhouse wall, Isaac heard the

310

sound of a shutter creaking open. He didn't breathe. His heartbeat throbbed in his ears. They were crouching in the shadow of the fence, but it was impossible to tell how much of them was visible in the clear moonlight. He prayed that whoever was looking out had bad eyes. After an unbearably long wait, he heard another dull creak followed by the thump of the shutter closing. Still Isaac held his breath.

No more noises came from the farmhouse. Sam shifted, and Isaac leant over to whisper as quietly as he could: "Wait. Let the sheep calm down."

The flock were still huddling nervously on the far side of the pen, but they'd stopped bleating. Those that had been asleep were awake now. Isaac wished he knew what sheep enjoyed as feed besides grass. He resolved to find out if he left Henry Shearer's farm in one piece.

Wetting his dry lips with a swipe of his tongue, he moved toward the closest ewe. Sam followed. The animal bleated, but when Isaac reached out to put his hands around her she relented to his grasp.

"That's a pretty girl," he whispered, scratching her the way he would a dog.

Sam tugged open the neck of the sack and set it down next to the sheep. With Isaac holding her still, he got to work with the shears. The rhythmic *snick, snick* sounded almost as loud as the pounding of Isaac's heart. The ewe in his arms remained mercifully quiet for a while, but when Sam yanked on her fleece to dislodge a clump of wool she threw her head back and gave a startled yelp of discomfort.

"Be gentle with her!" Isaac hissed. Beads of hot sweat rolled down his back. They didn't have the shadow of the fence to hide them anymore. If anyone looked out from the farmhouse, there would be no mistaking what was happening in the pen.

"You do it," Sam whispered, pressing the shears into Isaac's hand. "I'm going to snip her by accident."

Fearing he might be right, Isaac accepted the shears and

311

they swapped positions. He'd never sheared a sheep before, nor used scissors for anything besides trimming cord, but he'd seen other people work them plenty of times. When he ran his hand through the sheep's fleece he got a feel for its thickness. Skilled shearers could trim all the way down to the skin, but Isaac wasn't that confident. He worked slowly and methodically, trying to soothe the animal whenever he could. At first he tried not to cut too much of the fleece away, but he realised that the fibres of wool matted together thickly at the surface while growing finer further down. Praying he would not nick the sheep with the razor-sharp shears, he began cutting closer to the skin. Soon thick handfuls of the fleece were falling away with ease. Sam helped scoop them aside so that they tumbled down into the open sack.

"We can fit a lot in here," Sam whispered. "At least a few shillings' worth."

"If it's enough for me to buy Blackberry, I'll pay you back your share later," Isaac said.

Sam chuckled. "Wouldn't want to keep you from your lady."

Isaac wished he could share his friend's humour. Working the shearing scissors was hard, and his palm was already beginning to ache. He hadn't realised how much effort it took to trim a single fleece, let alone a whole flock's worth. The shears were large and heavy, two sharp triangles of metal connected by a loop at the base that was designed to spring back against the hand. Isaac had to squeeze hard to make the blades close all the way, then ease off the pressure gently so that the handles didn't leap out of his grasp. It became even more difficult once he'd finished trimming all the wool off the sheep's back. He couldn't see anything in the shadow of his own body, which made cutting the fleece on the sheep's sides a dangerously clumsy affair. He didn't want to risk nicking the animal.

"Let's get another one," Sam whispered when he saw Isaac having trouble. "Just trim the backs. That's the easy part."

Isaac nodded and they let the sheep go. Bundling up the sack of wool, they moved on to another docile-looking animal and began the process anew. It felt like it took an hour, even though Isaac was growing more confident with his cuts. His hand ached with the strain of pumping the shears, but he didn't want to pass them off to Sam. If his friend manhandled the sheep again, they might have worse things to worry about than a few aches.

"How much more do you think we can fit in the sack?" he whispered, his voice breathy with exertion as he finished up the second sheep.

"A lot," Sam said. He sounded confident, but Isaac checked for himself. They'd built up a sizeable heap of wool already, and it didn't look like they'd have room for more than one or two more half-fleeces. But the wool was deceptively voluminous, and when they squashed it down it fit easily into a compact bale. Sam began bundling it up more tightly as Isaac moved on to the next sheep.

After that, the process became rhythmic. The desire to take what they had and run grew stronger by the moment, but it always seemed like there was more room in the sack, so they kept on shearing. The last thing Isaac wanted was to sell the wool and find he was still a few shillings short. He cut fleeces until his hand was numb, then switched to the other hand and kept going. The dogs snuffled around inquisitively outside the pen. They could smell the strangers inside, but since no one had rattled the gate there was no need to sound the alarm.

Just as Isaac's left hand was starting to burn from the strain, the farmhouse door banged open. He froze mid-cut, feeling the springy resistance of the shears fighting against his grasp. As slowly as he could, he relaxed his fingers and let go of the sheep. He didn't dare say a word to Sam. Whoever had come outside was standing mere yards away from them, but the door was on the western side of the house, while the sheep pen abutted the south.

Turning toward Sam, Isaac jabbed his finger insistently at the sack. Sam was already securing the cord tight. They could hide in the shadows near the fence, but the farmer would see the gaggle of half-sheared sheep and know something was wrong if he looked over.

"What are you all doing over here?" a gruff voice sounded. "Where'd you get this?" There followed the sound of a growling tug-of-war as one of the dogs tried to hang on to the meaty bone Isaac had given him.

Sam finished tying the sack and motioned for Isaac to move. The moonlight was spilling into the pen from the direction of the farmer's voice. To hide in the shadows, they would have to move toward him. The thought terrified Isaac, but they didn't have any other choice. He realised he was gripping the shears painfully tight. He prayed he wouldn't have to use them on the farmer. He'd come here to pilfer a few fleeces, not hurt anyone. His skin crawled with guilt. Thievery was never as simple as Sam made it sound. Things would go wrong. People would catch them. And if they couldn't slip away, they would have to fight. With a fresh twinge of fear, he wondered whether the farmer had a weapon. It wasn't uncommon for landowners to own spears or swords for self-defence, to say nothing of the collection of wicked farming tools the Shearers doubtless had.

Half-crouching, half-standing, Isaac crept after Sam, breathing shallowly and rolling his feet so that his boots didn't slap in the mud.

They were a pace short of the shadows when the farmer turned and saw them.

A deafening rally of barks went up from the dogs as the man yelled in alarm: "Get out here!" He struck the side of the pen so hard the whole fence rattled. It looked like he had a club or axe in his hand. "Get out here!"

Isaac realised the man wasn't just shouting at them, but whoever was in the farmhouse. In a few moments, the whole

314

family would be after them. With his heart in his mouth, he darted for the other end of the pen, but the farmer followed him, striking the fence and yelling as he went. The air dinned with the cries of excited animals. Sam's hands were full with the sack, so Isaac ran past him and tried to push open the pen gate. The farmer caught up and swung his weapon over the fence. An angry rush of air touched Isaac's face as he jerked back just in time to avoid the blade of a heavy lumber axe. Fear galvanised him into moving without thinking. He clambered to his feet again and ran for the opposite side of the pen. The farmer meant to kill them, and he would be well within his rights to do so. Outlaws had no protection from the law. Isaac would have cursed his stupidity for allowing Sam to talk him into this were he not running for his life.

The farmer had to go around the pen to reach the other side, which allowed Isaac and Sam time to get ahead of him, but his voice hounded their footsteps all the way, bellowing louder than ever.

"Get out here, all of you! Get out!"

Another figure appeared from the shadows behind the house. Isaac tried to haul himself over the fence, but the man darted forward and swung a sledgehammer at his hands. The blow missed, cracking a dent in the top of the fence instead.

His desperation rising by the heartbeat, Isaac spun away and looked toward the other side of the pen. Sheep butted into his legs, threatening to trip him as they blundered around in a panic. Fighting his way through the flock, he made for the gate again. Sam followed, tripped over a sheep, pulled himself up, and ran on. The first farmer had moved away from the gate and was guarding the southern fence. Isaac heard the farmhouse door bang open once more. They'd be trapped if Henry Shearer and both his sons came to guard a side of the pen each.

Doing the only thing he could think of, Isaac ran for the gate and threw his body against it as hard as he could. The wood cracked against his shoulder, sagging outward as it dragged the surrounding parts of the woven fence along with it. Sam crashed into the gate beside him, adding his weight to the push. The post holding the flimsy structure upright broke with a snap. The entire western side of the pen sagged to the ground like a piece of folding ribbon. Barking dogs scrabbled over the edge as frightened sheep leapt for freedom. The man who'd been shouting started to curse as his animals spilt into the yard.

Grabbing Sam by the arm, Isaac got to his feet and stumbled through the chaos. A growling dog clamped its teeth down on the hem of his coat, refusing to let go even as its paws skidded over the earth. There was no time to try and throw the hound off. Isaac ran with a limping gait, staggering every other step as he dragged the dog after him. Miraculously, the farmers had not caught up with them yet. There were too many animals getting in their way. The yard was in shambles.

A scrap of Isaac's coat finally came loose with a ripping sound. Free from the dog, he made a desperate dash for the wall. Sam was already there, throwing the sack ahead of him before scrambling up the dry stones.

More dogs barked at Isaac's heels. Now they sounded vicious. Whether he believed they were the type to bite or not, they sounded like they were ready to savage him. With his heart pounding against his ribs, hands still aching from the shears, he reached the wall and threw himself upward. His left hand opened to grasp the stones, and the shears flew out of his grip to land somewhere in the grass on the far side. He hauled his legs up, slipped as a stone came loose, and cried out in fear as he fell back within reach of the dogs. Isaac thanked God that no teeth sank into his ankles as he scrabbled back up again. He swung one leg over the top, rolled, and dropped down into the ditch on the far side.

It was as if he'd been drowning and the fresh air on the far side of the wall was the first breath he'd taken in hours. He stumbled against the side of the ditch, dizzy with relief.

316

Somehow, they'd made it out.

Sam already had the shears in one hand and the sack of wool in the other. He tossed the sack to Isaac and clambered out of the ditch. "Let's get running—out through the fields!"

Isaac nodded breathlessly. They wouldn't be going back to their hut via the king's road that night.

But they'd done it. Isaac's relief was so intense he couldn't even feel angry at Sam for having talked him into something so reckless. It had worked, and now they had a thick bundle of wool to sell.

Over the wall behind them, Henry Shearer's voice roared in fury: "I know who you are! I know who you are, you wretched bastards! I'll have you flogged to death and feed your skin to my dogs! I know the sheriff! I know who you are, you bastards!" He screamed again and again, calling them every foul name under the sun. They fled to the tree line at the end of the Shearers' pasture then followed the undergrowth north. From there they could cross the western fields until they got back to their hut. There was no sign of anyone following them from the farmhouse. Henry and his sons probably had their hands full dealing with the loose sheep.

"Should've been a crier, with lungs on him like that," Sam panted. Isaac could hear the grin in his voice.

"He couldn't really know who we are, could he?"

"No chance. He would've said our names if he did."

"What if he only recognised our faces?"

Sam didn't say anything for a moment, then he shrugged. "Not in the dark. He won't find us. You can ride off on Blackberry and never have to worry about him again."

Yet Isaac did worry. He worried all the way back to the hut, fearing that Henry Shearer's dire warnings would come back to haunt them.

He would just have to hope the farmer proved as toothless as his dogs.

317

CHAPTER 21

For a short while, it seemed like everything was going to be alright. Sam's plan appeared to have paid off wonderfully. Once the initial rush of elation had subsided, Isaac spent a morning preparing to scold his friend for the risk they'd taken, but when Sam returned from town with a purse full of money his mood changed. There were enough shillings in there to buy back Blackberry. Isaac put his misgivings aside; he could scold Sam later.

That afternoon he dug up his money bag from the forest and went to pay David the horse courser. Blackberry was as happy to see him as always, nickering affectionately when he rubbed her mane and prancing around the yard as she stretched her legs, but it wasn't until they rode out through the gate that she realised her time in the stable was finally over. The pair of them were free again.

Isaac's first thought was to ride off straight away. Nothing appealed to him more than the idea of taking to the open road with his horse. He could put Tannersfield and Rosepath behind him forever, free from all the obligations and fears that had bound him to this place. Half a year ago, he would have done it. Now, as he trotted Blackberry down the path beside the stable house, he reined in that urge. What would he do for money? How would he keep Blackberry safe from more outlaws? Was he going to abandon Sam now that he had what he wanted? For all of his faults, Sam was his friend, and it had been a long time since Isaac had a friend. His only close companion growing up had been a boy called Thomas, the son of one of his father's knights who had joined the church to become a priest. They'd lost touch after Isaac went travelling, and in the years that followed he'd never stayed in the same place long enough to establish close ties with anyone else.

He couldn't abandon Sam, and he needed to prepare himself properly before he took to the road again. For perhaps the first time in his life, Isaac realised he needed to start planning for the future. Reuniting with Blackberry had been his sole focus for so long that he was at something of a loss now that he had her back. He couldn't take her to the farm settlement. There were no stables there, and he didn't want her getting unwell from living in a squalid animal pen or beneath the eaves of a barn where anyone might walk up and steal her. She would have to stay in town for now, which would cost him more money. He could afford it with his wages from the building site, but just barely. There would be little chance of him saving up enough money to ride off across the kingdom before the end of the year.

Perhaps he could go stealing with Sam again. But no—he'd told himself he wasn't going to do that. He would die a happy man if he could live the rest of his life without having another angry farmer chase him with an axe. There was also the question of what he would do the next time his money ran out. He couldn't travel the kingdom stealing from people every time his finances looked dire, nor did he want to spend the rest of his life doing hard labour for pennies.

A reflective sense of melancholy took hold of him as he stopped on the road outside David's house. He realised, not for the first time in recent months, just how readily he'd taken his father's money for granted. Again he was struck by the temptation to return home, and again he dismissed it. That kind of security came at a cost. Things might be difficult for him right now, but in time, surely, he would find some way of living comfortably while keeping hold of his freedom. That path was a long and daunting one, and thinking about it made Isaac uneasy. For now, he would focus on making enough money to leave Tannersfield. He could worry about what came next later.

David recommended a good stable to him near the old wall on the eastern side of Tannersfield, but Isaac wanted to go out riding first. He took Blackberry as far down the road as he could before nightfall, savouring the company of the one true friend who had been with him since he was a lad. She reminded him fondly of all the little quirks she exhibited when they were riding together, quirks he had unconsciously grown to miss in their six months apart. The rhythm of her gait told him whether she was tired or full of energy, the flicking of her ears indicated when something caught her attention, and the gentle resistance she gave against his knees showed him which way she wanted to go next. Riding the draught horses had been like bumping down the road on a cart that kept getting stuck. Blackberry made him feel like a swan skating across open water.

The sun went down far too quickly for Isaac's liking, dimming his spirits when he remembered that it would be a long time before he could go riding like this whenever he wanted. He'd missed a day of work on the building site in his eagerness to be reunited with his horse, and the master mason would doubtless be angry with him.

He walked back to the farms in the dark after getting Blackberry stabled. He stayed away from the side of the road that touched the forest, keeping his eyes and ears open in case anyone accosted him. But he made it home unscathed, and the following morning the master mason allowed him to keep working after docking him an extra day's pay for his disappearance. Fortune still seemed to be on Isaac's side. Had he been a man of faith, he might have offered God a prayer of gratitude for his recent series of lucky escapes.

Henry Shearer's dire threats had drifted from his mind until, like a distant drumming of rain, the hoofbeats of half a dozen horses came pounding up the path. The builders often took a break midway through the afternoon at this time of year, for the long summer days meant that labour carried on well into the evenings. Most of the workers were sitting around talking and drinking from a barrel of fresh water when they heard the horses arrive.

"Probably the cardinal's son come to see his new house," one of the masons said when Isaac set down an uncut stone for the chapel next to him. He'd kept on working, hoping to make up for his absence the previous day. He wiped his brow and looked up. He'd never met the cardinal's son before, and he was curious to see what the man looked like. Half the other workers had risen to their feet as well. Some of them moved toward the centre of the building site, forming a loose semicircle between the unfinished buildings as the horsemen rode up the path.

Isaac did not recognise the lead rider at first, then he saw the white silk cloak, the red surcoat of Cairnford, and the glinting mail shirt beneath. Sir Edward rode into the building site with five men-at-arms behind him, yanking on his courser's reins as the pale stallion snorted and whinnied angrily. The animal did not seem particularly well trained, for Edward had to handle it roughly to bring it to a halt, and the workers shrank back anxiously as its heavy hooves punched dents in the earth near their feet. Isaac took advantage of the ripple of unease spreading through the crowd to step behind the half-built wall of the chapel. He didn't want any of his father's men recognising him.

Edward rode his horse in a circle around the building site, showing no regard for the crowd as they stumbled out of his way. He looked down at the builders, trying to maintain a steely expression that echoed Duke Francis's stern countenance, but Isaac saw the corner of Edward's mouth twist upward in a look of satisfaction that betrayed his true nature. He enjoyed intimidating people.

It was the master carpenter Joseph who took a brave step forward to challenge Sir Edward.

"Watch your horse, milord. The cardinal would be upset if any of his builders took injury from it."

Edward yanked his steed around to face Joseph. He purposefully avoided making eye contact, as if the carpenter was beneath his notice. When he spoke he addressed himself to the crowd at large.

"Do you have any thieves on this building site?"

There was a murmur of commotion as the site foreman came forward to stand beside Joseph. He was a short, bald man with a red face and a fierce temper, but even he looked nervous in Edward's presence. "No thieves here, milord," he said, "unless you've come to point them out to me."

Edward made another slow circuit of the area, eyeing the workers one at a time. Isaac stepped back behind the wall. Someone jostled his arm, and he looked around to see Sam standing beside him.

Calling over the crowd in a loud voice, Sir Edward proclaimed: "A farmer named Henry Shearer came to the sheriff yesterday insisting that two thieves had stolen wool from his sheep. He said his son recognised them as labourers from this building site."

Isaac's chest tightened. Henry Shearer's threats hadn't been toothless after all.

"I suppose old Henry does know the sheriff," Sam murmured. It seemed likely. Knights were rarely called upon to deal with simple instances of thievery outside their estates, but everyone knew Sir Edward was the sheriff's man, and he seemed to enjoy throwing his weight around in the name of upholding county law.

The foreman rubbed the back of his neck, following Edward's gaze. "Did Henry give you their names, milord?"

"No."

"If he could identify them in person—"

"Why do you let thieves work for you?" Edward interrupted him. "The sheriff already has enough trouble with outlaws as it is." The foreman tried to speak again, but Edward continued talking over him. "Aren't you paying them enough? Don't you know where your own men come from?"

It was an unfair question, a pedantic technicality Edward could have used to corner any foreman. Builders were only supposed to hire labourers who could be vouched for, but on remote building sites of this size that was not always practical. Tense silence answered each of the knight's questions. Isaac's worry grew, and not just for his own sake. He'd seen men of power in moods like this before. Sir Edward plainly had little interest in finding the men responsible for the crime. He'd come here to set an example.

Edward yanked on his reins and made another sweep of the building site. He rode through the work area next to the main house, scattering half a dozen carpenters as he went. There was a thud and a groan of pain as someone knocked over a bench in their haste to back away.

"Learn how to handle your damned horse!" a voice called out.

Isaac winced, hoping that whoever had spoken had the good sense to keep their head down.

Sir Edward rounded on the voice. "Who said that?"

No one answered. The carpenters were still righting their bench, helping up the man who had been caught under it when it fell.

"I'll have every last one of you flogged if I have to!" Edward shouted.

To Isaac's relief, the crowd began to disperse. No one wanted to catch Edward's eye now, and he was left glaring impotently after them as they turned their backs on him.

323

"Serves that pompous bastard right," Sam muttered. "If you ever feel bad about stealing from noble folk, remember you're stealing from men like him."

"Not all nobles are like that," Isaac whispered.

"Enough of them are. That one had me locked up in Rosepath Castle for months. Probably would've let me starve if Daisy hadn't brought me scraps."

Isaac didn't have time to ask who Daisy was, for a woman's shriek suddenly cut through the hubbub. Edward and his men had dismounted. The foreman was on the ground clutching a bloody nose, and his wife was struggling against the grip of one of the men-at-arms who had seized her.

"Stop this!" Joseph Carpenter shouted, but no one paid him any heed. Sir Edward drew his sword and pointed it at the foreman's chest. The man-at-arms threw his wife to the ground.

Instinctively, Isaac took a step forward.

Sam pulled him back behind the wall. "Stay still, you idiot. Don't get involved."

"But we are involved!" Isaac hissed. "What if someone gets hurt?"

"Better them than us."

Isaac shook his head incredulously, giving his friend a look of abject distaste. Sam slapped him, grabbed his shoulders, and shoved him against the chapel wall.

"You don't understand how it is, do you? If we show our faces, they'll hang us."

"Not for shearing some sheep!" Isaac retorted, his face stinging from the blow.

"The bastards'll do whatever they want. No one's going to stand up for folk like you and me."

Isaac tried to shove him away in anger. Sam pushed back, holding him in place. There was a wild look in his eyes that Isaac had never seen before. At first, he mistook it for aggression. He tried to twist himself free but stopped when he recognised the terror etched into Sam's face. It reminded him of the way he'd felt in the sheep pen two days prior. There was a vulnerability in that look, a raw helplessness that chilled Isaac to his core. It was the way hunted animals looked when they were cornered.

Could it really go so badly for them? What if Sir Edward decided not to bring him back to his father? Isaac's disappearance had allowed him to remain lord of Rosepath Castle. If he was recognised, what was to stop Edward from taking him into the forest and killing him in secret? It would be an easy way to ensure he kept hold of his new estate. Isaac knew Edward didn't like him very much. He hesitated, wondering just how many of the gruesome stories he'd heard about the knight were true.

"That's right," Sam said, relaxing his grip when the fight went out of Isaac. "Now just be quiet and let this happen however it's going to happen."

Isaac wanted to slink out of sight like the other workers, but a dreadful tug of guilt forced him to peer out from behind the wall and keep watching. Sir Edward had lost interest in the cowering foreman and his wife. His men were dragging someone else away from the work area now. It was one of the apprentices, an adolescent boy with a pimply face who Isaac remembered had a talent for winding people up.

Edward approached the lad. "Were you the one who called out?"

"You tell the man you weren't, Fred!" Joseph Carpenter shouted.

"Shut up." Edward pointed his sword at the carpenter without turning to look at him. "Or I'll have you and your woman up here to join him."

The tense atmosphere on the building site had turned fearful. Most people had gone inside, while a brave few were gathering in a group between Edward's men and the chapel. Yet no one tried to stop what was happening. The builders all had their own families to worry about.

"I didn't do anything!" Fred protested, his voice cracking with fear. It would have been better if he hadn't said anything. Even Isaac recognised his voice as the one that had insulted Sir Edward.

The knight stepped forward and punched the boy in the gut. The breath left his body in a wheezing gasp, and he began to vomit.

Isaac's stomach twisted at the needless display of cruelty. His face burned with shame. This was his fault.

"Tie him to that hitching post," Edward told his men. They dragged the whimpering youth to a horizontal beam bound between two posts at the side of the path. A groan of dismay sounded from the foreman's wife as Edward opened his saddlebag and withdrew the implement of Fred's punishment. Its cord-wrapped handle was about a foot long, nubbed near the base to prevent the hand from sliding off, with half a dozen leather thongs trailing from the tip. Each thong had been knotted several times so that it would catch and tear when it struck flesh. Edward handed the flogging whip to one of his men while the others held the squirming Fred still and tied his hands to the hitching post.

Joseph Carpenter stepped forward, fists clenched, but his wife grabbed his arm and pulled him back, hissing dire warnings under her breath. Isaac couldn't make out what she was saying, only the fear in her voice.

No one else tried to intervene after that. The foreman sat on the ground in his wife's arms, one hand pressed to his bloody nose as he stared mutely into the dirt.

A ripping sound split the air as one of Edward's men tore open the back of Fred's shirt.

"It would be cruel to force a man's punishment on a boy," Edward said, "so give him thirty lashes instead of sixty."

There were muted exclamations of shock from the workers. Thirty lashes was a horrendous punishment for such a minor slight. Most people would have suffered a day in the pillory at worst. Isaac could see Joseph Carpenter trembling with indignation.

"Come on," Sam said. "I've seen enough of this." He turned to leave, but Isaac stayed. Sam paused for a moment to wait for him, then muttered something under his breath and walked off. Isaac's guilt prevented him from turning away. What if the whipping killed the poor boy? Back in Cairnford people had been whipped regularly, but Isaac's father preferred most floggings to be light. He wanted the victims to live so that their experience served as a warning to others. Sir Edward didn't seem like a man of such restraint.

Without ceremony, the man-at-arms approached Fred's bare back and brought the whip down with a savage flick of his arm. The crack was audible all the way across the building site. So was the boy's scream. Isaac flinched. The man swung the whip again before Fred's first cry had ended, and the boy's voice trailed off in a breathless whimper of pain. There was no alternation of the lashes so they landed on opposite sides of his back. The knotted leather struck the same spot again and again, drawing screams, then welts, then blood.

Isaac felt wretched. He could do nothing but stand and stare, rooted to the spot by the terrible spectacle. He hated himself in that moment, but he hated Sir Edward even more. It was a curse for people to live under lords like him. Wealthy men like Henry Shearer might enjoy the sheriff's protection, but what chance did a carpenter's apprentice have of receiving justice?

Isaac wanted to look away when Fred started begging for the lashes to stop. A dark stain of urine had spread down the leg of his trousers. His back was sticky with blood, the skin trailing in ribbons from torn flesh that was becoming more ragged with each stroke. The flogging would leave him scarred for life. Some of the workers echoed Fred's desperate pleas, but Edward's men ignored them. Fred's body went limp with just three lashes left to go. As he tried to twist away from the whip one final time his knees folded, his posture slackened, and his head lolled sideways as he passed out.

"That's enough," Sir Edward called. He turned away from the boy's ruined back and addressed the remaining workers. "If you can't discipline your people, the sheriff will do it for you. I don't want to have to come back here." When no one said anything he went over to the foreman and kicked him in the leg. "Do you understand?"

"Yes, milord," the man mumbled through his broken nose.

"Good. You're lucky the sheriff won't be telling the cardinal about this. A man of God would never stand to have thieves working for him." Edward glared down at the foreman, turned his gaze upon his wife, then curled his lip and walked away. "Cut the boy down. And you can bring us some food before we go."

The foreman didn't seem to be in any state to give orders, so Joseph Carpenter took charge. "Fetch the nuns," he said gruffly to his wife, then to another man: "Get them some food so they'll leave."

Joseph and the other carpenters hurried forward to tend Fred. They cut the bindings and eased him down on the grass, making sure to lay him on his front. Isaac desperately wanted to help, but if he stepped into the middle of the building site Sir Edward would see him for sure. A few moments later, Joseph's wife returned with Sister Grace and another nun in tow. The three of them hurried to Fred's side and knelt around him. The boy still hadn't regained consciousness.

After a while Sir Edward came back with a venison-filled trencher in one hand, taking small bites of the meat as he stared at the aftermath of his bloody handiwork. "Will the boy live?" he asked a trace uncertainly.

The nun Isaac didn't recognise looked up. She was clearly frightened, but she spoke in a voice of authority, doing her best to conceal her distress. "He might, if there is no infection."

"It's up to God then, isn't it?"

328

"God did not move your hand to this wickedness."

Edward spat a piece of bone on the ground. "You worry over God's law, woman; I'll worry over the king's."

"You are a vile man and you will suffer in hell for this."

Edward's face coloured in anger. His free hand gripped the hilt of his sword, but he stopped short of drawing it. Even he wouldn't dare attack a nun in front of so many witnesses.

"What does a novice know," he said, then, after a pregnant pause, a smile touched his face. "A noble novice." The nun quickly looked away, but Edward kept on staring at her. He seemed to have forgotten about his food. His leather belt creaked as he approached the nun from behind, angling his sword hilt with his free hand so that the scabbard poked her in the back. "Where's your servant, milady?" he asked mockingly.

The nun whispered something Isaac couldn't hear. Edward snorted in amusement, leered over her a moment longer, then turned and walked away. He took a lazy stroll around the building site while he ate, oblivious to the hateful looks he was receiving. When he was finished with his trencher he tossed the last bit of bread to a dog and mounted up. The knight and his men spurred their horses away, disappearing down the wooded path. As if breathing a collective sigh of relief, the rest of the builders began trickling back to work.

Isaac hurried out from behind the chapel and went to see whether there was anything he could do for young Fred. The nuns, Joseph Carpenter, and Joseph's wife were all kneeling around him, shooing away anyone else who got in their way. In his haste, Isaac didn't see that he wasn't the only person running in their direction. As he hopped over the line of pegs marking the edge of the unbuilt stable, someone bumped into him and their arms tangled as they tried to brace themselves against each other simultaneously.

"Watch where you're going!" the woman shouted.

He stumbled back. Beneath a tangle of straw-coloured hair, he saw the flustered expression of the girl who'd sided with the farmer when they argued over lost horseshoes. A look of consternation crossed her face, then she swept past him to join the others at Fred's side. Isaac found himself excluded from the group, standing awkwardly to one side while the straw-haired girl conversed with the unfamiliar nun.

"Go inside, Liz," the nun whispered urgently. "He asked me about you. What if he comes back?"

"What about Fred?"

Sister Grace said: "I have some salves for cuts and scrapes, but nothing like this."

"The monks could treat him at their infirmary," said Joseph's wife. "We'll pay the fee."

Joseph Carpenter nodded. "Aye. The boy's parents won't have the money for it. Are you sure you can't do anything for him here, sisters?"

"I've not studied very much medicine," the younger nun said apologetically. She was very well-spoken, with an authoritative air about her that she seemed to suppress beneath a veil of timidity. She and Sister Grace had rinsed Fred's wounds and covered his back with a piece of clean linen, but it was already soaked through with blood.

"Then you'd best get him back to town as quick as you can," Joseph said. "You can have one of our carts. I'll pull it myself. Robin!" he called to one of the carpenters. "Fetch us a hand cart."

"You're needed here," the girl called Liz said.

That was when Isaac spoke up: "I can pull the cart."

The group turned to look at him. Joseph was about to say something when Liz shook her head.

"No, thank you. We can have Brother Daniel pull it."

"What if we run into trouble?" the young nun said.

"She's right," said Joseph. "You want that monk with his hands on his staff and his eyes on the road. Carts tell people you've got something worth robbing. Take the lad here. He looks strong enough for the job."

Liz gave Isaac an uncertain look. Had she been alone he suspected she would have put up more of an argument, but she didn't waste time debating the point any further.

"Poor Fred," she said, resting a hand on the boy's arm. "He didn't deserve this."

"I always told him his mouth would get him into trouble one of these days." Joseph shook his head bitterly. "That Sir Edward's a nasty piece of work. Must've had wire or stone in the knots of that whip for it to cut so deep." His gaze lingered on Elizabeth and the young nun for a moment, as if he expected them to add something to his observation, but Robin returned with the cart before they could discuss it any further. The cart was a simple hand-drawn thing with legs at right angles to the handles so that it could stand upright when unattended. The platform was a little too small for a person to lie on, so Joseph fetched his tools to remove the planks from the end.

"We need something soft to put under his head," Liz said. "He'll break his teeth bumping up and down on the road."

"I'll fetch my cloak," Isaac volunteered, hurrying off before the girl could find a reason to argue. She'd clearly taken a disliking to him, and the stubborn look on her face suggested that her opinion wasn't likely to change any time soon.

Isaac's cloak was still dirty with mud and droppings from the sheep pen, so he'd left it under a bush behind the building site with the intention of washing it after work. It wouldn't make for the most comfortable cushion, but it was better than nothing. When he arrived he found Sam eating a handful of blackberries in their usual spot.

"Have they gone?" Sam asked.

"Yes, but the boy's half dead. I'm going to help them take him to Tannersfield."

"Why? You might run into Sir Edward on the road."

"This happened because of us. The least we can do is try

to make amends."

Sam sighed and shook his head. "It's not like we're the ones who flogged him. We didn't hurt anyone."

"I'm going anyway. You can stay here if you want."

"If you disappear off the site again you'll be in trouble."

Isaac didn't particularly care about his livelihood at that moment. He gathered up his cloak and hurried back to the building site, leaving Sam to his berries. Liz wrinkled her nose at the state of his cloak, but she took it from him and bundled it up with another to make a cushion.

By now Joseph had pulled some of the nails out of the back of the cart with his pliers. Isaac lent him a hand tugging off the boards, doing so carefully so that they could be reattached later.

"You've got a steady hand on you," the carpenter said, clapping him on the arm once they were done. "Might want to try your hand at a proper craft someday. Come on, help me up with the boy."

They lifted Fred up carefully on another cloak Sister Grace had brought and eased him over into the cart. Liz put the cushion beneath his cheek.

"Go on now," Joseph said. "Best hurry if you want to get back before nightfall. Oh, and take this to pay the monks." He passed Liz a handful of coins and touched her cheek affectionately. Isaac assumed they were probably father and daughter, though they didn't look very much alike. Neither Joseph nor his dark-haired wife shared her colouring. Perhaps she was a niece or a child from another woman. There was a homely attractiveness about her that most men would have found appealing, but it reminded Isaac too much of the buxom serving wenches who got drunk with his father's men and laughed too loud at their bawdy stories. It didn't surprise him when she took charge of the group heading to Tannersfield. Along with the semi-conscious Fred, they were accompanied by a startlingly tall monk called Brother Daniel and the well-spoken young nun, whose name he learned was

"Elizabeth?" he said when they reached the main road, guessing at Liz's full name.

She turned around and raised her eyebrows. "What?"

"Can you walk behind the cart and hold Fred's legs? He's going to slide off if we're not careful."

Elizabeth frowned and nodded. Their pace was slow but steady. Six months ago, the hand cart would have exhausted Isaac, but labouring with Sam had toned his muscles and built up his stamina. The dull burn in his arms was a small price to pay to ease the boy's suffering. He pushed on doggedly without rest, trying to avoid the bumpy parts of the road where he could.

Brother Daniel walked ahead in silence while Elizabeth and Kaylein conversed quietly behind them. Isaac tried not to listen, for he got the impression they wanted their conversation to be private, but it was difficult to close his ears to the anger in Elizabeth's voice.

"I wish Sir Edward were dead."

"Don't say that," Sister Kaylein replied. "God will punish him when his time comes."

"That'll be too late to help Fred."

"You still shouldn't wish such things upon people."

"I wish he were gone, then. If only Francis's stupid son had married that woman like he was supposed to, Edward would be back in Cairnford by now."

The back of Isaac's neck prickled with heat. As uncomfortable as it made him, there was no hope of closing his ears to the conversation now.

"We must be patient," Sister Kaylein said. "Duke Francis is the lord of this county, and Sir Edward is his knight. Those aren't things that are easily changed."

"You'll change them someday," Elizabeth whispered.

"I don't know if I will." Kaylein sounded desperately uncertain. "But I shall try."

The tingle in Isaac's neck grew stronger. What did they

mean? It sounded like they were plotting treason against his father, but what could a carpenter's girl and a novice nun possibly do against a duke? His thoughts turned feverishly as they walked. It was none of his business, he told himself; he wanted as little to do with his father as possible. But what if there was some hidden plot against him? What if the same fate that had been visited upon Count Leo came back on Isaac's family one day? The thought was a harrowing one.

Something had been bothering him about Sister Kaylein that he'd been unable to put his finger on, but when he thought about Count Leo it finally slotted into place. Leo's missing daughter had been called Kaylein. This nun spoke with the formality of a lady, and Sir Edward had called her a "noble novice".

Unable to contain his curiosity, he turned his head to the side and called back: "Are you Lady Kaylein of Rosepath?"

After a moment of silence, the nun answered softly: "No longer. I am simply Sister Kaylein now."

"It's not your business," Elizabeth said.

"Forgive me, I was just curious. I'm sorry about what happened to your family."

"I'd rather not speak of it," Kaylein said.

Isaac returned his attention to the road. He was glad the exertion of pulling the cart was already making him sweat, for he could feel the uncomfortable weight of Elizabeth and Kaylein's eyes on his back. Perhaps he was worrying about nothing. They couldn't really be plotting against his father, could they? It was probably just fanciful talk between two poor souls who had suffered under Duke Francis's rule. Common folk complained about their lords all the time. Nuns and carpenters' daughters couldn't raise armies.

Yet Isaac had difficulty putting it out of his mind. He wanted to make amends for what had happened with Fred, and that would probably mean crossing paths with Elizabeth and Kaylein again. Maybe that would give him an opportunity to find out what they'd been talking about. He shot another glance over his shoulder and caught Elizabeth staring at him. He shifted his clammy palms to get a better grip on the cart handles.

The thought of spending more time in her company was not an inviting one.

CHAPTER 22

The old monk at the monastery gate was reluctant to let anyone into the infirmary so late in the day, but he relented when Elizabeth thrust her handful of coins at him. His hesitance rankled her. The church was supposed to render aid before requesting compensation. While the men took Fred inside Kaylein tried to explain that the infirmary could not be run on goodwill alone, yet Elizabeth's temper still simmered. It was one more unnecessary sting at the end of a terrible day. First she'd had to hide from Sir Edward as she listened to Fred's awful screams, then there had been the agonising journey back to Tannersfield. She'd been unable to offer him anything but comforting words as he drifted in and out of consciousness. The bumpy road had been torturous for the poor boy's wounds, yet they couldn't stop for fear of running out of daylight. At one point he'd insisted on trying to walk, so unbearable was the motion of the cart, managing less than two paces before he slumped into Elizabeth's arms. She'd seen him crying after that, though he tried his best to hide his face in the cloak. By the time they reached Tannersfield, there were teeth marks on his wrist where he'd bitten himself to fight through the pain. Elizabeth's heart ached for him. He always wound everybody up at the workshop, but it was never mean-spirited, and he only did it to make the others laugh. The flogging had been horrendously cruel. Fred was the last person who deserved such a punishment. Elizabeth wished she could have stayed with him, but no women were allowed inside the monastery. Tomorrow morning she would have to find his family and explain what had happened.

She leaned back against the monastery wall, wiping her brow with the back of a hand. The day had run her ragged. Anger flickered in her stomach like the coals of a dying fire, a fearful and impotent fury. Today had been a reminder of just how powerless she still was—and how easily men like Edward could take away the security she'd built for herself this past year.

One day I will have money. One day I will be a woman of standing.

Edward had picked on Fred because he was an easy target. He'd been afraid of punishing Kaylein because she had the power of the church behind her. No one caused a stir when poor commoners suffered at the hands of their lords, but people of importance could not be treated the same way. That was the only escape from injustice, Elizabeth thought bitterly: money and status. And even those didn't always help. They hadn't helped Kaylein's family.

Nothing would have relieved her more than to curl up on her mattress and try to forget about the day's events, but she had to wait outside the monastery for the men to come back. It was getting dark, and Kaylein always had Brother Daniel escort her back to the nunnery after nightfall.

Eventually, the gate swung open and their companions returned. Elizabeth bid Kaylein farewell and thanked Daniel. Much to her annoyance, the man who'd been pulling the cart accosted her before she could leave.

"I can't leave this here," he said, giving the cart handles a lift. "Have you got somewhere to store it?"

Elizabeth put a hand on her hip and rubbed her eyes. Of

course. The cart. "Yes. There's a shed at the workshop. Come on, I'll show you the way." She'd hoped she wouldn't have to spend any more time in the handsome young man's company. He had a perplexing combination of good looks and a polite attitude that always seemed to be masking some hidden guilt. It made her feel as if he was up to no good, like a wolf stalking among sheep. Though he didn't strike her as the dangerous type, she suspected some ulterior motive. "I'm not going to pay you, you know."

He looked hurt. "I didn't expect you to."

"Perhaps you expected something else?"

"If I could sleep in your shed, I'd be very grateful. Otherwise, I'll be in the hay with my horse. It doesn't look like I'll be getting back to the building site tonight."

"You and your horses," Elizabeth grumbled, motioning for him to follow her as she crossed the road. "Why are you working on a building site if you've got the money to own horses?"

"I've only got the one."

"What about the horses you were trying to swindle that farmer with?"

"I sold those on. They weren't very good for the work they were doing. And I wasn't trying to swindle him—I just needed the money."

Elizabeth studied him, trying to puzzle out why he seemed familiar to her. That was another of the man's aggravating qualities. "What's your name?"

"Isaac. Like that duke's son you were talking about."

"Are you from Tannersfield?"

He shook his head. "I've travelled a lot."

It didn't seem like he was lying, at least. She'd been wondering whether he was the son of one of the Rosepath merchants, given his proper way of speaking. He sounded educated, but it didn't make sense for an educated man to be working as a labourer. His hair reminded her of Duke Francis's. What an outlandish turn that would be, if he really

338

was the duke's missing son and he'd thrown away his wealth to toil on a building site. Even pampered nobles weren't that stupid.

"So, can I?" he asked.

"Can you what?"

"Sleep in your shed."

"Oh." Elizabeth had forgotten he'd asked. "No, I'm afraid not. I don't know you, and there are valuable tools in there."

"I won't steal anything."

"I'm sorry. It's Joseph's workshop, not mine." Elizabeth had learned that a good way of getting people to accept her decisions was to imply that they were out of her hands. Customers at the workshop had a habit of assuming they could pressure her into changing her mind because she was a woman. When she told them the decision was Joseph's, they often shut up and listened.

Isaac looked disappointed, but he didn't debate the point any further. They turned a corner and trundled the cart toward the tradesmen's street, slowing to negotiate their way around a preaching friar who had attracted an inebriated crowd outside one of the public houses. The man wasn't orating particularly well, probably due to the cup of wine clutched in his hand, but that seemed to be part of the spectacle. There was something devilishly taboo about a holy man making a fool of himself in public. Elizabeth might have stopped herself had she been in a better mood. The friar was ranting about a slew of the town's leading citizens–presumably those he liked least–detailing the crude and oddly erotic punishments they were due to suffer in hell.

Isaac must have been listening to the drunkard too, for he said: "Sister Kaylein was very bold to damn Sir Edward to hell like that."

"I didn't hear," Elizabeth said. "Was he angry?"

"Oh yes. People get very upset about things like that, don't they?"

She shot him a quizzical look. "Of course they do. No

one likes being damned by a person of the church."

"I don't think it would bother me."

She scoffed at him. She'd not taken Isaac for the boastful sort. "Aren't you afraid of going to hell?"

"Not very. Do you really think men like that friar know anything about it?"

"He's just drunk. Priests still understand the scriptures better than us."

Isaac shifted his grip on the cart handles impatiently. "I got sick of hearing about their scriptures. Men like him were always coming to my–" He hesitated. "My father's house. When I went travelling I met priests who didn't believe in God. Well, they did, but they thought He was a different kind of god. Then there were some who worshipped lots of gods, the same way the heathen druids revere old spirits."

Elizabeth frowned. "Where do people think things like that?"

"Siraba and Khoketan."

"You've been there?"

Isaac nodded. "I've been to all sorts of places."

Well, he was still a little boastful, but not in the way Elizabeth had thought. What a strange man he was. On a whim, she asked: "Is it true that the Sirabans have more than a hundred letters in their language? And castles made of–" She struggled to recall the word. "Jade?"

"I've never seen a castle made of jade, but there are palaces with pillars and statues carved from it. And yes, Siraban is an awful language to learn."

"Can you speak it?" Elizabeth was intrigued. The only things she knew about the world beyond the borders of their kingdom were Kaylein's second-hand stories from her books. She would never travel herself, but it was interesting to meet someone who had.

"I can speak a little," he said, "read a little less, and write almost none."

Elizabeth pursed her lips as they drew up to the workshop

340

yard. It seemed like everyone she knew had some craft, skill, or story to tell. They cast long and impressive shadows compared to her.

"I don't know why you'd want to travel, anyway," she said, reminding herself that there was still something suspicious about Isaac. Not dangerous, she didn't think, but untrustworthy all the same. "It's risky and expensive, and there's no work if you keep moving around. Come on, bring the cart through here." All of the carpenters had gone home for the day and Luther had locked up, but Elizabeth had two keys of her own: one for the shed and workshop, the other for Joseph's house. She led Isaac across the yard and opened the shed doors for him, feeling around in the darkness to make sure there was space for the cart. She'd have to pay someone to take it back to the building site tomorrow, but that could wait until she'd checked on Fred and spoken to his parents.

Isaac turned the cart around and pushed it carefully into the shed, then took his bundled cloak off the back and shook it out.

Realising that Isaac would be returning to the building site, Elizabeth asked: "Will you take the cart back tomorrow?"

"Of course. Is there anything else I can do?"

"No, thank you. I'm sure the builders need you on site." She didn't know why he seemed so eager to help. He wasn't a friend or relative of anyone she knew, and she'd made it clear she wasn't interested in paying him.

"They might not want me back," Isaac said. He rubbed his forehead with a sigh. "This is the second time I've disappeared from work this week."

"You didn't ask your foreman before you came with us?"

"I didn't think to."

Elizabeth shook her head in bemusement. She wasn't sure whether to be touched by his selflessness or reproach him for his naivety.

341

"Are there any jobs you need help with here?" he asked hopefully. "Or something I can do to help the boy's family if he can't work?"

"Fred's an apprentice. He doesn't get paid. And his family are poor farmers, so I doubt they'll be able to hire you. None of us are wealthy, you know."

"I didn't think you were. You and your father just seemed so worried about him."

Elizabeth was glad it was dark, for she flushed at Isaac's assumption. "I'm not Joseph's daughter, I just help at the workshop. You should go. It'll be pitch black soon."

Isaac looked down the street, dawdling as he shrugged on his cloak and clasped it about his neck. Why was he so reluctant to leave? Was he hoping for a kiss of thanks? Elizabeth's temper flared at the thought. Had Isaac been a simple, honest man like Joseph she might have found his efforts chivalrous, but instead they annoyed her. She neither wanted nor needed his attention.

As she watched his sandy hair fall across his face her annoyance turned back on itself when she realised how vain she was being. She wasn't pretty enough for a man like him, anyway. Normally that thought would have left her feeling glum, but for once she was glad she wasn't an elegant beauty like Kaylein.

"I'll come back for the cart tomorrow," he said.

Elizabeth nodded and waited for him to go. He left the yard awkwardly, casting a backwards glance at her and quickly looking away when he realised she was staring. She let out a relieved breath once he was gone. She locked up the shed and let herself into Joseph's house. It was too dark for her to find a candle and practice reading, so she went straight to bed. She was exhausted anyway. She always kept fresh tinder in the hearth in case she needed a flame, but she lacked the energy to fumble for the fire steel and strike a spark off the lump of chert they kept by the hearth. Joseph would have chided her for not keeping a fire going, but Elizabeth had grown so used to living without warmth that she didn't mind it. It saved money, and leaving the house locked up with the hearth burning was foolish. One of her greatest fears was that something would happen to the house while Joseph and Rose were away. She didn't want to fail them.

Elizabeth tried her best to forget about the day's events and go to sleep. The empty room felt very lonely that night, and she kept thinking about Fred's horrible screams. A shiver wracked her body. Despite not being cold, she reached for the cloak she kept beside her mattress and pulled it over her. It was the same one she'd stolen from the merchant on the road to Tannersfield a year ago. Bundling up an armful of the garment so that she had something to hug, she closed her eyes again and tried to think of a place where people like her might not have to live in fear of men like Sir Edward. Perhaps it was different in Siraba and Khoketan, where people did not know about God and built palaces of jade. Maybe they didn't have knights and dukes there. It was a peaceful thought, and Elizabeth allowed it to lull her to sleep. Yet when she slept, she dreamt she was fleeing Rosepath again with Sir Edward chasing her on his fierce white horse. He had a whip with a carpenter's awl tied into every knot, and when he swung it the metal points stabbed into her back and pulled her skin off. She awoke before dawn in a sweat beneath the warm cloak. She didn't want to go to sleep again after that.

Elizabeth got up to open the workshop early the next day. Tannersfield was still grey and blue, the wild birds making the streets their own as they hopped and pecked at the previous day's leavings before the slew of commerce chased them off. Elizabeth preferred rising earlier than later, for it afforded her a short time to prepare herself for the day to come. She washed her face in Joseph's water barrel and relieved herself in one of the buckets behind the house, then went to unlock the workshop. When she rounded the corner she was surprised to see Isaac leaning against the shed door, dishevelled and shivering beneath his muddy cloak.

"I suppose you're here for the cart?"

Isaac jumped at the sound of her voice, blinking the weariness from his eyes. "Yes! Yes, I'll take it back right away."

"Move out of the way, then." Elizabeth waved him aside and unlocked the shed door.

"Have you got any food or drink for the journey? I'll pay for it."

She looked up at him and saw bits of straw sticking to the shoulders of his cloak. He really had slept in a stable last night. Her first instinct was to say no, for she didn't want to make another trip to the market for her supper that evening, but Isaac looked such a mess that she took pity on him. She exchanged the stale bread and tepid beer she had in the house for a penny and sent him on his way. The hand cart creaked its way out of the yard just as the carpenters began arriving for the day's work. Elizabeth rubbed the weariness from her eyes and hurried on with her chores. There was so much to do. She wouldn't have time to organise the workshop if she wanted to visit the strip of land Fred's parents tended for the sheriff outside town. It aggrieved her to miss another day's work, for despite her best efforts to keep the carpenters in line things had a habit of listing back into chaos if she was absent for long. Once Luther arrived she told him what had happened and went to check on Fred. For all of her worries about work, she was more anxious to see how the boy was doing.

The monks took a long time to answer her knocking at the monastery gate. After a heated argument, she drove off the pale, soft-faced brother who refused to let her inside and managed to speak with the sub-prior. He told her they were allowing Fred's wounds to breathe and take in clean air so that no ill humours built up beneath the skin. He was awake, but in a great deal of pain, and would likely remain that way for a few days more. Elizabeth knew nothing of medicine, but it seemed like the monks knew what they were doing, so she thanked the brother and went on her way.

The walk to the farmland outside town was not a particularly long one, but the morning traffic at the gates slowed her down. A herd of irritable oxen were stamping up the mud, creating a packed knot of people behind them. A hand pulled at Elizabeth's dress in the commotion, either searching for her money pouch or a palmful of her breast. She yanked herself away with barely a thought. She'd become accustomed to such intrusions upon her person in dense crowds. The town gates were prime territory for casual thievery, and no amount of extra watchmen seemed to help. If only the sheriff would lease more land for houses to be built on the far side of the river then some of the thieves and vagrants would at least have other places to go. Maybe the building work would create more jobs? Something had to be done sooner or later, for Tannersfield's problems were only getting worse. Elizabeth wondered whether things were this bad elsewhere in the county. The jobless often moved from town to town until they found work. What if it was like this everywhere? Hungry-looking families left town every day, but more always came in to replace them.

The land north of town was broken up into strips farmed by the local peasants and serfs. Most of it was owned by the sheriff, the church, or Tannersfield's knights. Serfs were indentured servants who worked the fields for their lords in exchange for protection and a portion of what they produced, while free peasants typically rented the land in a similar arrangement. Only a lucky few, like Henry Shearer, owned everything for themselves.

Elizabeth negotiated her way between the walls and ditches separating the ripening fields of grain, letting the pleasant summer air take her mind off the stresses of the day. Most of the farm labourers were out in the meadows cutting hay this season, so she had to walk further than she'd expected to find Fred's father. He was beyond a stand of trees to the north of his usual plot, at the foot of a hill where the bishop of Tannersfield's palace stood. The leathery man was swinging a scythe in line with the other labourers while his wife and a young daughter stooped to collect the freshly cut hay behind him. Elizabeth's eyes were sensitive to the dry grass in the air, and they soon began watering. She didn't envy the labourers their exhausting work.

There was no time to take Fred's family aside to speak to them in private, so Elizabeth told them what had happened while they worked. His mother seemed dully acceptant of the news, as if she'd expected her son to wind up on the receiving end of a lord's wrath sooner or later. His father was furious. Upon learning that Fred was in the infirmary, he threw down his scythe and began cursing Sir Edward and all the nobles in the county. Fred was an apprentice, soon to be a respected craftsman, and he'd be damned if he was going to let a boy knight take away the son who was destined to drag their family out of poverty.

Elizabeth decided to hold her tongue and let the other labourers talk Fred's father down. He'd caused a spectacle among the workers, stirring resentful murmurings and heated condemnations of Sir Edward. Everyone knew there was nothing they could do about it, but they hated the injustice all the same. Eventually Fred's father went back to work, chopping the grass viciously to work out his frustration. His wife thanked Elizabeth for bringing them the news and said they would visit their son soon, but there was a bleakness in her tone that suggested she'd already accepted the possibility that Fred might die from his wounds. Many women her age had already lost at least one child.

The only thing Elizabeth could take solace in on her way back to town was that Edward's reputation had been further sullied by the incident. By the end of the week, the labourers would have spread the story across every public house in Tannersfield. Most common folk did not like Sir Edward, but the wealthier citizens regarded him favourably, and that was ultimately what mattered. Elizabeth wondered whether enough voices railing against him could threaten to unseat the lord of Rosepath. She liked to think so, but in her heart she feared it was an empty hope. The world simply didn't work that way.

After getting some food from the market she returned to the workshop and tried her best to catch up with the day's work. She made a quick circuit of the yard and workshop, sweeping and tidying, then brought Joseph's trestle table outside and sat sipping a cup of water while she tried to organise the jobs that had come in. She had Kaylein's page with the letters of the alphabet in her left hand and an old broken chisel in her right. She had scraped the first two letters of each carpenter's name on a piece of slate. Next to each name she put a little picture that represented what they were working on currently, and then another depicting what they would start next. It helped her concentrate in moments of weariness if she could lay things out visually. It was like Kaylein had said: committing your thoughts to writing made them real and firm. One day Elizabeth hoped she would be able to write full names and proper words, but for now she made do with initials and crude drawings. She sometimes forgot which letter was which and had to look at Kaylein's alphabet to remind herself. She could sing a children's rhyme about the alphabet in her head now, and if she moved down the list as she went it reminded her which symbol corresponded to which letter.

Even with the assistance of her scrawlings, it was slow going to straighten out the work schedule in her head. When someone came around the side of the shop and blocked her light she put down her chisel irritably. It was Isaac, breathing hard and perspiring, his hair even more unkempt than it had been that morning.

"I brought the cart back to Joseph," he said, smiling as he produced a coin from the pouch on his belt. "He gave me a silver penny for it."

"That was generous of him. I wish he gave me silver pennies for running chores." Even now, Elizabeth could not help but eye the dull grey coin enviously. Ever since Joseph went away to the building site he'd been paying her two copper shillings a week. That was a bit less than three pennies a day, if her sums were correct. It was less than a tradesman earned and less than Lady Eleanor had paid her, but still a respectable wage. It would have added up quickly had Elizabeth not reinvested most of it into buying candles, having her brooms re-bristled, and stocking up fuel for the fire. It was her own small way of replaying Joseph and Rose for their generosity.

"Why are you back here?" she asked Isaac. "Don't you have work on the building site?"

"It's as I feared. The master mason doesn't want workers who keep going missing. Joseph tried to put in a good word for me, but it didn't help much." He shrugged. "So I came back here."

"I don't have any work for you either, unless you want to pay to use the yard."

"I was hoping you might have more errands. You go to the building site once a week to meet Joseph, don't you? I could do that instead. I can be there and back on my horse in a few hours, any day of the week."

Elizabeth was tempted by his offer, but she quickly thought better of it. People like her could not afford mounted messengers. Besides, despite all the inconvenience it caused she liked having an excuse to see Kaylein, Joseph, Rose, and the other carpenters.

She shook her head. "No, I can't afford that."

Isaac's expression fell. He tucked the sliver penny back into his pouch protectively, as if it were the last money he expected to see in weeks.

Elizabeth frowned at him. "I don't know why you're so upset. If there's anyone who can find work these days, it's people like you. Why don't you go to the castle and ask the sheriff if he needs a courier?"

Isaac paled at the mention of the sheriff, and she realised this was the second time she'd seen him react that way. He'd been worried about the sheriff when she argued with him about his draught horses, too.

"I was just hoping I could help here," Isaac said. He clearly wasn't an experienced liar. He had some ulterior motive, though Elizabeth couldn't fathom what it might be. He didn't look at her the way men usually did when they had a crush. She shook her head and went back to her work. There was a dull throb in her temples now, and she had to squint at the letters as she mouthed her alphabet rhyme. Adam was working on an order of eighty wooden pegs; she recognised the AD of his initials because she'd written the number eighty next to it. That order would be finished by tomorrow. Adam was good at complex work, and he would have gotten bored making simple pegs, so she decided to give him a difficult job next. A commission had come in for a strange loom of Siraban design that had a wide frame and pedals underneath it. Luther hadn't told her who it was for, but a plan had been provided with detailed instructions, so it was likely a noble or a merchant's wife. Elizabeth sketched a little cross-lattice that resembled threads of woven cloth next to Adam's initials and moved on, consulting Kaylein's page again to double-check the next pair of letters on the list.

"What are you doing?" Isaac asked.

"I'm organising the work for tomorrow, and it would go much faster if you didn't keep talking to me."

"That's just a piece of parchment with the alphabet on it."

Elizabeth's cheeks warmed. "I'm learning how to read and write. It's easier if I have this."

"I can read and write. Why don't I be your scribe?"

"I can't afford a scribe, and once I learn this for myself I won't need one." Elizabeth took painstaking effort to enunciate each word, hoping Isaac would get the message.

She didn't want to have to throw him out.

"Is that how you know Sister Kaylein?" he asked. "Are the nuns tutoring you?"

"No, she–It doesn't matter. I'm learning by myself."

"I could teach you if you want."

Elizabeth almost repeated her refusal for a third time just so that he would go away. The ache in her head was getting worse by the moment. But this time he'd offered her something she actually needed: a teacher.

"I can't afford schooling," she said hesitantly.

"I'm hardly a schoolmaster, so I wouldn't expect you to pay me like one. What can you afford?"

Elizabeth did have some money saved up. She'd hoped it would go toward a house someday, but schooling was important, too. Houses could fall down, while literacy was a skill that would last a lifetime. She was tempted by Isaac's offer, yet as he'd said, he was no schoolmaster, and she recalled how unreliable he'd proven to be with his draught horses.

"Come back tomorrow," she said. "In the evening, about an hour before sundown. If you can teach me something new, I'll think about it."

"How much will you pay me?"

"I'll have to think about that, too."

"Alright," Isaac sighed. "If that's the best I can hope for." For as educated and worldly as he appeared to be, he wasn't particularly shrewd. In an odd way, he reminded Elizabeth of Kaylein. He was clearly of respectable birth, but a little witless when it came to negotiating business.

She tried to focus on her work again after he'd gone, but it was more difficult than ever. Along with her concerns about Fred, Sir Edward, and the workshop, she now had to worry about what else this strange man wanted from her besides a few pennies for reading lessons.

CHAPTER 23

The summer months proved to be especially taxing for Elizabeth. It was the first time in her life she'd had so many responsibilities. She was nineteen now, at the tail end of anything that could be considered her youth, and she was beginning to feel it. Many women were busy with husbands and babies by her age, but Elizabeth had her work instead. It absorbed every hour of her day, so much so that she barely had time to think of anything else. For two weeks she visited the infirmary asking for updates on Fred's condition every day. The healing was slow, but he mercifully managed to avoid the killing fever that sometimes came on when wounds festered. If there was one place the wicked miasmas of sickness struggled to enter, it was holy buildings. Prayer kept the air clean and the patients safe beneath God's protective hand. Elizabeth brought news to Fred's parents whenever she could, for they were working from dawn till dusk at this time of year and rarely had time to visit themselves.

Fred's spirits seemed none the worse for his ordeal, but it was painful to watch him walk when he was finally healthy enough to leave the monastery. He had a constant hunchbacked stoop to his posture, and he moved with a slow, shuffling gait, as if afraid that one wrong step would split his back open. The monks said it would pass in time, but it was still a disturbing reminder of what had happened to the poor boy. Fred wanted to return to the building site right away, but Joseph insisted that he stay at the workshop for the time being. He didn't want any more trouble if Sir Edward decided to pay another visit.

Between Elizabeth's trips around town, she quickly found work catching up with her. She sometimes had to finish tidying the workshop by candlelight, and more than once she fell asleep at the table studying Kaylein's pages over a half-eaten meal.

Then there was Isaac. True to his word, he was no schoolmaster, but he was as literate as Kaylein and Joseph, and that was more than anyone else Elizabeth had on hand to teach her. She agreed to pay him three pennies to come to the house two nights a week and tutor her after work. She often had to leave things until the next morning to make time for their lessons, but it was worth it to have someone around who could show her not just how to recognise letters and word sounds, but to explain concepts like punctuation and grammar. The latter two utterly baffled Elizabeth, for there was no similar equivalent in mathematical notation. Isaac was patient with her, but he didn't always know how to explain things in a way she could understand. He didn't even think to tell her what a full stop or an apostrophe was until she asked him about it. When Elizabeth pressed him about who his schoolmaster had been, he was evasive. Isaac didn't like talking about himself very much, especially when she asked him about his upbringing. He was a little like Sam in that regard. Her half-brother had never talked about where he'd picked up the braces of geese he brought home for dinner, or who had given him his latest black eye, or why there'd been a girl screaming at him outside a public house the night before.

In the end, she resigned herself to the mystery of Isaac's personal life and decided to treat him as a simple business partner. She wouldn't have had time to squeeze any more worries into her life had she learned he was an outlaw or a disgraced nobleman. Perhaps he really was Duke Francis's estranged son, though she still struggled to entertain that thought seriously. Isaac was a mild, inquisitive, whimsical sort; quite the opposite of the fearsome duke.

One upside of Isaac being so recalcitrant with the truth was that Elizabeth felt no obligation to share anything about herself, either, which made it easy to shrug off his repeated inquiries about Kaylein. After several weeks, she had come to the conclusion that it was not her he was interested in, but her friend. It made sense. Kaylein was a refined beauty of the sort educated men like Isaac found irresistible, and her nun's robes had apparently done nothing to curb his interest. Some men saw novice nuns as a challenge to be conquered, for there was something sinfully tempting about seducing a pious woman away from God. Elizabeth found the idea distasteful, even if Isaac did have an innocent charm about him that had probably made many girls lose themselves in his pretty eyes. She would not be one of those girls. When she married, it would be to a strong, simple, honest man; someone who had a craft of his own and the good sense to take care of his family. Someone like Joseph. Even though he was twice her age, she envied Rose sometimes. Those were impious thoughts she preferred not to indulge, but they still returned to distract her now and again. Sometimes she imagined what it would be like to have a large man lying beside her on her mattress, with thick, rough arms that held her body with the gentleness of a craftsman's touch.

If only Joseph had a son.

Still, she had no time to think of love and no time to entertain Isaac's interest in Kaylein. She had work to do, and a long, hot summer to endure. The sun beat down on the workshop yard for a full month without respite. Work slowed as the carpenters nursed sunburned arms and took increasingly long breaks to sip water in the shade. Tempers ran hot, the streets grew ripe, and flies buzzed in and out of the house constantly. Scarcely a week went by without a fire breaking out somewhere in town, though thankfully none came close to the workshop.

Along with the fires came more hangings in the marketplace, six of which happened on the same day. The good weather meant an early August harvest, which had led to a disorganised harvest celebration outside town. Elizabeth hadn't gone, using the excuse that she was too busy, for local lords usually appeared at such events and she feared Sir Edward might be there. Fred told her a fight had broken out during the festivities that almost escalated into a riot. The sheriff's men had been forced to intervene, leaving a local peasant and a town watchman dead. The six bodies that hung from the gallows the day after were purported to have been the main instigators of the brawl. A grim mood hung over Tannersfield in the days that followed. Even the most celebrated day of the year had been tarnished by the town's ill fortune.

The sheriff imposed a curfew not long afterwards, enforced by a new town watch comprised of thugs that liked to bother young women and fight with drunks. They reminded Elizabeth of the people she'd had to avoid on the north side of town. Despite the impression that law and order had been restored in Tannersfield, Elizabeth felt like the sheriff had simply put clubs in the hands of the troublemakers and given them a pardon to do as they wished. She tried her best to walk on the other side of the street whenever she saw a group of them coming. The carpenters seemed to think the sheriff was growing weary in his age, deferring his duties to knights like Sir Edward and the brutish wardens who organised the town watch.

Elizabeth looked forward to her trips to the building site more than ever, for the time spent away from Tannersfield was a breath of fresh air. She envied Isaac whenever she saw him riding down the road on his elegant chestnut-coloured horse, coming and going as he pleased. His well-made clothes were getting shabbier by the day, but he was making enough money to get by thanks to Elizabeth's three pennies a week and some courier work he'd found with the mason's guild.

At long last, September brought an end to the sweltering heat. By October, the pace of life had slowed to a comfortable crawl. Joseph would still be working with the masons until November unless the frosts came early. The main house on the building site was complete, but the chapel still needed to be finished before winter halted construction. Elizabeth was looking forward to having Joseph back at the workshop, for she missed him dearly. With work slowing down, she would be able to spend more time in the winter months practising her reading. She hoped she might have learned enough to call herself literate by this time next year. Kaylein brought her new pages every few weeks, and Isaac read them aloud to her before explaining what all the new words meant.

Along with the autumn came an increase in communication with the carpenters' guild. Old Luther shared Joseph's distrust of the organisation. He'd worked with the guild longer than anyone, and in his eyes, they were lax and ineffective. Elizabeth tried to take a more optimistic attitude. If their reputation was so weak, surely it was a good thing they were taking a proactive interest in the well-being of the trade? Yet apprehension accompanied her optimism, for Joseph had always worked on the fringes of the guild's tolerance. If they tightened up the rules, it might mean problems for the workshop.

She shared her concerns with Luther as they made their way to the guild hall one afternoon. It was her first time visiting, and despite her trepidations, she was excited. Only masters were commonly invited to guild meetings, but Joseph was not in town that day, and Luther had asked her to come along to help him recount the workshop's recent business.

"There's not much choice but for the guild to get itself

together," Luther said, rubbing his fingers through his white beard. "You've seen the amount of sloppy woodwork people sell at market these days. We didn't lose much business to it this year, God be praised, but I expect that's thanks to the way you've had us running things. Most of the carpenters in town are struggling. There's too much competition from folk who aren't real tradesmen. The guild's been sitting idle for too long, letting people think they can take our work from us. It's about time something was done about it."

"But what can we do?" Elizabeth asked.

"Well, most of that bad work still comes from the guild's own workshops. I know some of them lend out their tools to anyone who'll pay. Joseph makes sure he knows everyone who works in our yard, but some masters aren't that scrupulous. It's a master's duty to check the work of his carpenters and make sure they're reputable. I should think the guild plans on yanking the rug out from under a few slackers today. There'll be fines, maybe even some expulsions."

"More people without jobs," Elizabeth said despondently.

"That's just the way of it, lass. If you let anyone with a hammer and saw do what they want it'll drive the trade into the ground. Who'll hire us if we can't maintain standards? Better to suffer a little pain now that a lot more later. The guild's already stabbed itself in the foot by turning a blind eye as long as it has."

"It sounds like Joseph should be here."

Luther grimaced. "He should. I'm guessing that's why the guild called this meeting at such short notice. They must have known he wouldn't be in town today."

"They must be out for blood."

"That they must. Joseph's never had much patience for their politics, but he stands up to them when they're in the wrong. It wouldn't surprise me if we see Theobald and his friends try to squeeze fines out of everyone today."

Elizabeth had heard Theobald Carpenter's name before, and the things Joseph said about him were rarely flattering.

He was a master who took more pride in his authority than his work, currying favour with the sheriff to secure prestigious jobs rather than letting the quality of his carpentry speak for itself. When Joseph came back from guild meetings in a bad mood, it usually had something to do with Theobald.

The guild hall was on a tidy merchants' street near the marketplace. The carpenters shared it with several other trade guilds in town, most prominently the masons and the smiths. It was a long, single-roomed building made of wood, with sturdy posts and frames that supported a high vaulted ceiling and a wide floor space. A step at the door kept the elevated floor free of some of the muck in the street, but there were no boards or stones to cover up the beaten earth. Elizabeth offered Luther a hand up the step, but he didn't need it. Despite being old, his body was still in fine shape. It was only his memory that had started to fail him.

A group of men were already seated at the long table that dominated the centre of the hall, while others leant on the beams listening to them speak. Luther and Elizabeth took seats on a bench near the door, realising that the meeting had already begun. Elizabeth received a few curious looks from the carpenters, but no one said anything to her.

"The problem is that we have no one's word but your own," a man with closely-cut black hair and prominent cheekbones was saying. "It's a guild's duty to maintain a standard of craftsmanship. Will you object if I send my son to inspect your workshop tomorrow?"

"Yes, I'll object!" the red-faced carpenter he was arguing with answered. "A journeyman can't appraise a master's work."

"Then we'll send a master. Are there any volunteers?"

A few hands went up. The red-faced man blustered indignantly, argued back and forth, and eventually submitted to the guild's decision. Whatever he'd been accused of, it seemed like he would soon be facing the consequences.

"That's Theobald," Luther whispered in Elizabeth's ear,

pointing to the dark-haired man. "Enjoying being lord of this hall, as usual."

"Do you have something to say, Luther?" Theobald called across the table.

Luther folded his arms. "Not right now."

Theobald's eyes flicked toward Elizabeth. "Who's this?"

"That's Elizabeth. She helps at our workshop."

Theobald did not look impressed. "We've been meaning to discuss what Joseph thinks he's doing letting a girl run our name into the dirt."

Elizabeth felt suddenly uneasy. She wanted to say something, but she wasn't dealing with difficult customers at the workshop today. This felt like being back in the great hall at Rosepath Castle, where men of high standing discussed things far above her station. She held her tongue and averted her eyes meekly, letting Luther answer for her.

"Elizabeth's done nothing but good for our business. If the guild needs to know anything about the work we've been doing, she can answer better than I can."

Theobald shook his head sadly, acting as if Luther was a doddering old invalid who'd brought a grandchild to the meeting by accident. Elizabeth felt her ears burning when some of the other masters chuckled.

The meeting continued on. One by one, each master from Tannersfield and the surrounding area was prompted to give an account of how many people he had working under him and what work they'd been doing. When there was a discrepancy between what one man said and what the others believed, a vicious interrogation ensued. It was often one-sided. Only the most quick-witted carpenters were able to allay the suspicions of Theobald and the half dozen other men who seemed to be leading the meeting. Just as Elizabeth had suspected, they were out for blood. The whole process was unsettlingly reminiscent of Sir Edward's visit to the building site. The carpenters were angry at the state of their trade and eager to pin the blame on someone. A few turned

358

on each other in attempts to duck responsibility, while others begrudgingly confessed that they had been unscrupulously taking on helpers without following the proper traditions. The guild agreed on fines based on the severity of the offence or called for further investigation so that a punishment could be determined at a later date. It seemed that several masters had been using untrained young men as a source of cheap labour, treating them as apprentices in name only. An apprentice was supposed to provide a fee in exchange for becoming their master's ward, whereupon they were fed, clothed, and trained for several years before being admitted into the guild as carpenters. Most of these new apprentices had paid no such fee, nor were their masters properly providing for them. It was a fine recipe for shoddy work and customer dissatisfaction.

Several people came and went as the meeting dragged on. There was weak wine at the table, but no food, and hunger only worsened the unease festering in the pit of Elizabeth's stomach. The more she heard, the more she understood why the carpenters' guild was regarded as a weak institution. The men here were stubborn and argumentative, more interested in defending their pride than improving the state of the trade. Even with Theobald attempting to move things forward, it took an age for them to agree on anything.

A brief change of subject interrupted the tense meeting when a plump, well-dressed man stood up to say his piece. He wore dyed clothing that matched the colour of the wine they were drinking, and on his head sat an embroidered feather cap. It was Harald Redcloak, one of the merchants from Rosepath. He'd been a regular face at Count Leo's court. Elizabeth wondered what he was doing at a meeting of the carpenters' guild.

"I can see things are hard for the carpenters of this town," he began. "These are difficult times for all of us. New taxes go to the church, the roads are in disrepair, and no merchant can do safe business in Tannersfield without hiring bodyguards."

"Get on with it," a carpenter who had just been fined ten silver shillings grumbled. "What are you doing here, Redcloak?"

"He was here with the masons yesterday as well," another man said.

"I'm here with an offer of good work for skilled hands. Tannersfield is a poor place for a man to ply his trade these days. The shrewdest among us already know it, and more reach the same conclusion each passing day."

"We still have the biggest market in the county," Theobald said, "and plenty of folk looking to hire us."

"That's true, but markets can decline. Mark my words, by this time next year all the merchants will be taking their trade to Rambirch."

"That doesn't bother us," Theobald said. "Most of us don't trade at market."

"The market is a town's lifeblood. If it goes away, so will the rich men who hire you. The sheriff will have fewer goods to tax and less money to spend on building projects." A concerned murmur ran around the table. Harald had succeeded in getting their attention. "A good businessman goes where the business is, and soon it won't be in Tannersfield. Not a day's walk down the road to the south you'll find a village with a lord eager to provide opportunities for skilled craftsmen such as yourselves."

"You mean Rosepath," Theobald said.

The carpenter who had just been fined snorted in contempt. "And Sir Edward. I'm not taking any work from him."

"His holdings have grown this past year," Harald said. "He has money to spend and empty houses to fill. He will sell them cheaply to tradesmen. With his low market taxes, he'll soon have merchants looking to build houses all over the village. In a few years, it'll be a bustling town with no shortage of work for men like you."

"Nonsense," said Theobald. He sounded annoyed, but Elizabeth suspected he was secretly nervous about Harald's proposition. If master carpenters left Tannersfield, the guild–and thus Theobald's own standing–would be further weakened. "I've heard Rosepath market is taxed more highly than ours."

Harald shook his head. "You're mistaken. Sir Edward charges only a penny a day for a spot at his market. The sheriff asks a shilling a week."

Some of the carpenters began conversing with each other. They probably suspected the same thing Elizabeth did: that other, hidden costs would make the move to Rosepath less lucrative than Harald was making it sound. Sir Edward might charge additional fees for specific goods or increase the price of market trading later on. These things were supposed to operate at a rate fixed by the king's law across each county, but in practice, local lords were able to raise or lower their taxes as long as they could provide a reasonable excuse to the king's court. Elizabeth had heard Count Leo discussing the subject many times with men like Harald.

Luther's voice rose firmly in protest. "Sir Edward isn't a lord any tradesman should want to work under, no matter how many merchants he courts. He whipped Fred Fielder half to death over nothing, and everyone knows he made Paul Builder repair his drawbridge for bread and beer last year."

Harald turned to look at him, and for an unnerving moment, his eyes caught on Elizabeth. A flash of recognition crossed his face before his attention returned to Luther. "Sir Edward was only acting on the sheriff's orders. And he forced Paul Builder to do nothing. He was not a man of means at the time, so he struck as fair of a bargain as he could. Now that my lord has holdings of his own, he will pay full wages to anyone who works for him."

The carpenters went on to discuss Harald's offer at length, though Elizabeth sensed most of them were simply trying to waylay Theobald's inquisition. No one seemed willing to risk uprooting themselves to seek greener pastures in Rosepath, but a few did express interest in visiting the village so that they could see for themselves whether there was any merit to Harald's assertions. Like any cunning merchant, Harald avoided sounding desperate by pressing them too hard. He was calm and to the point with his answers, acting as if he was doing the guild a favour by bringing them this opportunity. Elizabeth wasn't convinced. She knew Harald's reputation. He was good at making money, but his fortune rarely extended to those around him. Count Leo had fined him numerous times for working with traders who used false weights on their scales, put too much water in their wine, and dodged market taxes. He was a swindler adept at ducking the full weight of the law by staying a hair's breadth on the right side of it.

In a particularly quick-witted move toward the end of the discussion, Harald mentioned offhandedly that a man could take his trade to Rosepath the very next day and find an empty house awaiting him. It was a clear appeal to those who stood to face imminent scrutiny by the guild. Theobald and the others would find it difficult to impose fines on anyone who packed up their business and took it to Rosepath.

"We can finish this discussion another time," Theobald interjected at last, his patience plainly at an end. "Rosepath will be there for us tomorrow, but the reputation of our guild may not. Master Eadric, please tell us the name of every man working in your yard and list the work they have been doing."

Harald Redcloak relinquished the floor to the carpenters, looking quietly pleased with himself. Elizabeth resolved to warn Joseph about his interference with the guild the next time they spoke.

Three more carpenters said their piece, none of whom accrued any punishment, then it was Luther's turn. Elizabeth chose not to stand up alongside him, for Theobald's earlier comment about her damaging their reputation was still fresh in her mind. It would be wise for her to stay quiet and speak only when spoken to, lest she give the vindictive guildsmen another target for their frustrations.

Luther listed the name of every man that had worked under Joseph during the past year, then asked Elizabeth to tell the guild about the work that was being finished on the building site. Before she could begin, Theobald interrupted.

"Is that everyone? Every last person working for Joseph?"

Luther regarded the other man stoically, his thumbs tucked into his belt and his brow lowered. "It is. Every carpenter and apprentice."

Theobald jerked his chin in Elizabeth's direction. "What about her?"

"Elizabeth isn't a carpenter."

"Yet you have her doing a carpenter's work. Don't try to pretend otherwise. I've seen her in your yard."

"The only tools Elizabeth handles are her broom and bucket."

"Joseph has her talking to priests and merchants as if she's a master," Theobald snapped. "Making plans and giving out jobs. It's an insult to our trade."

"She takes money for carpentry work, too," one of the others said.

When Luther hesitated to answer, Elizabeth stood up and put a hand on his arm. Nervous though she was, Theobald's pedantic attitude filled her with indignation. She couldn't sit quietly while the guild insulted Joseph's judgement behind his back.

"I don't take money for carpentry work," she explained, hearing her voice tremble. "All I do is collect rent from the carpenters while Joseph is away. That money is his, not mine."

"So you're handling Joseph's money? Why doesn't he leave this to Master Luther?"

"She has a better mind for it than me," Luther said. "The girl picked up her numbers quickly."

A man sitting next to Theobald asked: "Is she educated?"

Luther looked to Elizabeth.

"A little." She spoke hesitantly, not quite knowing the right answer. "I know my numbers well enough to handle money, and I'm learning to read."

Theobald shook his head. "She isn't even literate. Is it any wonder at the state of our trade when we have girls doing men's work?"

To Elizabeth's dismay, a rumbling of agreement spread around the table.

"But I'm not a carpenter!" she protested. "There's no rule against Joseph hiring servants and helpers."

"A servant doesn't take on jobs and give out work like she's a tradesman," Theobald said.

"What about Joseph's wife? She handles tools and takes work like everyone else, and the guild never had a problem with her. Why can she do a man's work and I can't?"

Luther gave her a warning look as if telling her she was digging herself into a hole, but Elizabeth's temper was up and she wanted Theobald to justify himself.

"That's different," one of the older men said. "It's normal for a wife to help with her husband's trade."

Another elder carpenter held up a hand and fixed Elizabeth with a serious look. "Are you related to Joseph?"

"No, Sir."

"But you sleep in his house?"

A voice behind her said: "More likely in his bed when Rose is looking the other way. Why else would he be letting her get away with this?"

Elizabeth's face flushed red with indignation. Her cheeks burned and her hands trembled. "That isn't true! Joseph would never do anything like that."

Luther glared at the man who had spoken. "If you want to insult Joseph's decency, you might at least do it to his face."

"Regardless," Theobald said loudly, quelling the chatter beginning to rise around the room. "It isn't appropriate for

364

him to have an unmarried young woman living under his roof, much less handling his business for him."

The ayes of agreement from the guildsmen were near-unanimous. Elizabeth's temper shrivelled up, giving way to a crushing feeling. They were looking at her with the judgement of lords ready to dismiss an impudent servant. They had come to this meeting looking for someone to blame, and she had provided them with an easy target.

"Sit yourself down," Luther whispered. "There's no arguing with them today." He turned to Theobald. "Let Joseph stand here and speak his piece. There's no rule in any guild charter against Elizabeth's employment."

"There doesn't have to be if the majority are in agreement." Theobald looked to the men seated around the table. "Now isn't the time for delays and exceptions. It's that kind of attitude that got us here in the first place. We have a duty as guildsmen to protect our reputation."

Elizabeth bit the inside of her cheek, wishing she could cite some precedent in the guild's history the way Kaylein picked out passages from the holy scriptures to support her arguments. It took another stern look from Luther before she forced herself to sit down. It was a begrudging, stiff-legged effort, and Elizabeth felt the weight of the guild's disapproval upon her shoulders every inch of the way. She couldn't remember the last time she'd felt so humiliated. Couldn't they see it was their pettiness and self-interest that was the problem? She wanted to scream at them.

"The guild will insist that Joseph stop allowing this woman to perform the work of trained carpenters," Theobald said.

"And a fine!"

Theobald looked around the room for the guild's approval. "A fine of twenty silver shillings. Are the majority in agreement?" A show of hands confirmed the judgement. At least two-thirds were in favour.

Elizabeth stared down at the table, blinking back tears and

swallowing the barbed words that roiled in the back of her throat. It was the fine that stung more than anything. Had the guild simply demanded that Joseph stop employing her, she could have focused her anger on them and not herself. But now Joseph would return home to find that he owed the guild a weighty sum of money. She felt like she'd failed him. None of her hard work mattered in the eyes of the guild, and she'd dragged Joseph's reputation into disrepute along with her own.

The rest of the meeting was a blur of noise around her ears. When Luther eventually tugged her up to leave, she went without a word. She had lost her job, and she would lose her home along with it.

What was she going to do now?

CHAPTER 24

Edward's horse stomped and huffed irritably as he drove it up the slope to one of the dale villages west of Rosepath. The beast was weary from a day of riding, and its mood reflected Edward's own. He'd been in frustratingly mixed spirits since coming into his new holdings. Cristiana's unexpected rejection had been the start of it. The slight of that evening still stung like a firebrand. Sometimes, he believed he'd been foolish. Perhaps drink or overconfidence had clouded his judgement and he'd offended her by doing something unbecoming of a lord. But most of the time he was angry at Cristiana's uppity attitude. She'd been unfairly cruel to him on his night of celebration. The only reasonable explanation was that she didn't think him worthy. She was the daughter of a duke, him a lowly knight, barely established as lord of his own land. She was afraid her father wouldn't approve.

The truth Edward was afraid to voice was that he feared she might be right. What if he wasn't worthy? He harboured a lingering guilt over his past failures, doubts, and dishonours, to say nothing of his common upbringing. If he could win the admiration of his betters–if he could prove himself worthy of a woman like Cristiana of Cairnford–then he

367

would have no reason to carry that guilt any longer. He kept thinking about how that night in his chamber might have gone differently. Perhaps if he hadn't been cowed into letting her go–if he'd shown her that he was a man with a firm spirit and an iron will like her father–then she would have knelt before him in subservience and spent the night pleasuring him with the soft touch of her hands and breasts and mouth. Despite not being the type of woman Edward typically lusted after, something about Cristiana's insufferable attitude had sparked a hopeless yearning within him that was equal parts devotion and fury. He longed to have her as his noble wife.

The mail shirt beneath his surcoat rattled as he rode, pressing down on his shoulders with distracting weight. There had been no particular reason for him to ride out in armour that day, but every time he left Rosepath he secretly hoped he would cross paths with Marquess Alistair's soldiers. The rogue marquesses Alistair and Larmond were thought to have ridden north from the mountainous border counties, which would put them somewhere west of Tannersfield. They might be weeks away, or heading to a completely different part of the kingdom, but Edward nurtured the hope that Duke Francis had been right and Alistair would seek vengeance for his daughter's jilting. War was where men forged reputations that lasted them a lifetime, and Edward needed a warrior's reputation if he wanted to prove himself worthy of Cristiana.

That day he had been conducting his monthly tour of the dales to collect rent from his new subjects. It was another one of the tiresome duties he had to perform as lord of the manor, but at least it kept him active, which was preferable to the weary courts he was now mandated to hold. While he did enjoy having people bow to him in the great hall and beseech his judgement in flattering tones, it seemed as if most of them wanted nothing more than to cause him a headache. Farmers whined about the yield of their crops, siblings bickered over inheritances, fathers accused in-laws of not having paid their bride prices, and it was all somehow Edward's responsibility to adjudicate. He liked dealing with the people of Rosepath the most, for it was easy to validate their claims with the help of Harald and the castle chaplain, Father Gregory. When you knew who had a reputation for being honest, who was a liar, who paid their rent on time, and who had been in the pillory last week, a decision could be made on the spot. But disputes that arose outside Rosepath often required investigation, and it was beneath Edward to spend his days riding around the countryside making sure peasants were keeping to their fields and milking their own goats. If his subjects were unable to bring convincing arguments to court, he would usually turn them away or simply rule in favour of whoever he thought sounded more agreeable in the moment. It was exasperating business, but it was the price paid for stewardship of an estate.

Despite the cloud that hung over his good fortune, Edward was a man of action. He had wrongs of his own to right that didn't involve bickering farmers. One particular slight had been lingering in the back of his mind for many weeks now, and he took advantage of the quiet ride between villages to discuss it with Father Gregory. He'd made the chaplain his treasurer, for men of God were easy to trust with money. A wooden coffer strapped to the back of Gregory's saddle jingled enticingly with each step. Edward's two most trusted men, Stephen and Alderic, rode on either side with swords at their hips.

"My lord?" Gregory inquired when Edward called him forward.

"What do you know about nuns, Gregory?"

The priest's mouth twitched. He had a bald head and a neat beard flecked with grey, a look that suited the rugged symmetry of his face. Many women considered him handsome, much to his chagrin. Any talk of the fairer sex always made Gregory uncomfortable.

"I know something of their monastic traditions, my lord.

They are a reflection of those observed by our brothers in the monastery."

"Were you ever a monk?"

"I was, for twelve years, and I observe my vows to this day."

"Good. Then if nuns are just like monks, how do you get one expelled from her convent?"

"Well, it would require a serious misdemeanour on the sister's part, or intervention by a senior member of the church." He then added: "Backed by compelling evidence of some wrongdoing, of course."

"So, I need to get on the bishop's good side." Edward rubbed his stubbly chin, feeling momentarily aggrieved that he struggled to grow a proper beard like Gregory's. "What about that cardinal? The one who's building a house for his bastard near Tannersfield?"

"Cardinal Tybalt. Forgive me, my lord, but why would you want a nun expelled from her order?"

Edward allowed the priest to speculate as their horses crested the rise at the end of the valley. Dry stone walls meandered across the landscape around a small village ahead of them. Freshly-harvested fields stood empty, tended only by birds pecking over the farmers' leavings. On the higher slopes, a few dozen sheep grazed in the meadows, fluffy spots of white against the fading green of the autumn landscape.

"Lady Kaylein is the only surviving member of Count Leo's family," Edward said. "My duke believes she has given herself to God."

"He is correct. Lady Kaylein has been a sister under Mother Jane in Tannersfield for a year now."

"She's only there to hide. She'll leave that convent as soon as it suits her. Then we'll have another enemy joining Alistair and Larmond—one who can rally Leo's former knights against us."

Gregory fell silent for a moment before saying: "Lady

370

Kaylein was always a conscientious young woman, of good breeding and good education. I instructed her in the scriptures myself. I do not believe she would seek to raise a rebellion against you, my lord."

"What does a priest know of rebellion? She's impertinent, and she'll marry the first knight who promises to give her back her birthright." Edward had not forgotten the way Lady Kaylein damned him to hell the day he visited the building site. That was the real reason he'd brought this up. If anyone else had dared speak to him like that, he would have had them flogged to the bone. But Kaylein's sacred black robes had shielded her from his wrath that day. It would have been an unforgivable sin to lay his hands upon a member of the church, so he had reined in his anger. Still, Kaylein's words had convinced him that she was not the pious and obedient nun everyone took her for. She would cause trouble for him in the future if she was not dealt with now. It was Edward's duty to protect Rosepath for his duke.

Father Gregory sighed, but he had learned to pick his arguments with Edward carefully. "I'm afraid there is little you can do to interfere with matters of the church. Even if you were to send a letter to Cardinal Tybalt, he would be under no obligation to honour your request. And I doubt you will have much luck with the bishop. He is good friends with Mother Jane."

"Duke Francis helped put Fendrel on the throne. Without him, the cardinals would still be begging scraps from the king's table. They owe him their gratitude."

"Then perhaps you should appeal to the duke."

Edward grimaced and tugged on his reins, prompting a snort of aggression from his white stallion. Appealing to Francis would do no good. The duke had already washed his hands clean of the business with Count Leo. The only thing Francis cared about these days was Alistair and Larmond's simmering rebellion. When he wasn't in Cairnford, he spent most of his time at the king's court trying to still the aftershocks of last year's shift in power.

"What about you, Father?" Edward asked. "You're a man of the church. The nuns will listen to you more readily than they will me."

A look of distaste crossed Gregory's face. "It wouldn't be appropriate for me to intervene on your behalf."

"You're my priest, and I'm telling you to do it." Edward spoke patiently but firmly. He was being more careful not to let his temper get the better of him these days, even when his subjects were being disrespectful to him. It wasn't dignified behaviour for a lord to lose his composure, and Father Gregory himself was particularly keen on lecturing him about the precept of humility.

"To what end, my lord?" the chaplain said, struggling to hold a diplomatic tone. "Surely if you want the lady Kaylein to stay out of your way it would be better for her to remain at the convent. Duke Francis certainly seems to think so."

And here was the canny priest's trap. It would be difficult for Edward to admit that he wanted Kaylein killed or thrown in the sheriff's jail. He cast about for an answer, and, finding none, was struck by a sudden pang of guilt. Was he making a mistake? Was this the temptation of sin beckoning him?

It could not be. He knew he was in the right. The moment Kaylein damned him, he'd been struck with the dreadful realisation that she wanted revenge. It could happen any day now. He felt it deep in his gut, an indignant fear that wouldn't be quenched until Kaylein was put in her place. But how could he explain that to Gregory?

They rode on in silence, Edward's brow furrowed as he stared at the path ahead. He was not used to deep or complex thinking. Eventually, he settled on an answer that he hoped would satisfy the priest.

"Lady Kaylein had a servant who attacked me in the forest a year ago. That woman must be punished for her crime, and Kaylein is the only one who may know her whereabouts. A nun who protects lawbreakers doesn't

372

deserve to wear her robes."

"Have you told the sheriff about this?"

Edward ignored the question. "The nuns are protecting her. They turned away the duke himself when he visited their convent. I want you to speak with the prioress and convince her to expel Kaylein." This time he glared at Gregory, making it clear that his appetite for discussion was over.

The priest bowed his head in deference. "I fear it will do little good, but if that is your wish then I shall obey."

"Good." Edward smiled. He'd see Kaylein punished for what she'd said to him. Her and Elizabeth. If Gregory failed then he would send a letter to the bishop. If that failed, the next letter would go to Cardinal Tybalt. Eventually he would find someone in the church with the wits to see through Kaylein's facade of piety.

Satisfied that he'd settled on a course of action, Edward led his horse into the village and cast his eyes over the sorry group of farmers coming out to meet him. They didn't look like they had much silver to spare, but he'd make sure his coffer was full by the time he left.

* * *

The news that Father Gregory had come to see her came as a pleasant surprise to Kaylein. She'd all but put Rosepath out of her mind this past year, relegating it to a series of hazy memories that almost felt like they'd happened to another person. She'd assumed Father Gregory had died that terrible night, but when she thought about it logically, she supposed that was a foolishly bleak way of thinking. Most people in Rosepath would still be living their lives as normal. Francis hadn't come there to slaughter the whole village. It was only those closest to her who'd been taken away.

She was sitting in the writing room copying scripture, enveloped in the rhythmic trance that always took her when she wrote. It had become so natural that she could sit at her desk for hours on end. Even the strain on her bent back felt strangely comfortable, as if her posture was a crook her body had slowly moulded itself into until the fit was perfect. She sometimes forgot to eat and drink while writing, and when she went downstairs to the chapter house she had to brace a hand against the wall as a wave of dizziness hit her. Mother Jane had expressed concern that Kaylein was becoming too lost in her work, but sub-prioress Joan extolled her to the other novices as a paragon of studiousness. The sub-prioress's praise had the effect of distancing her from the other nuns, for they saw her as a teacher's pet. The more ambitious sisters considered her a rival. One evening when she returned to the dormitory she found that someone had scooped one of the big frogs out of the water channel and left it in her bed. Another day, her porridge tasted funny, and the novices working in the kitchen giggled at her all afternoon. She never found out what they'd done to it.

The slights were childish and upsetting, but Kaylein could endure them as long as she was allowed to carry on writing. Writing was her passion, and she put her heart and soul into it. The strokes of the pen had become so ingrained into her muscles that she could copy almost without thinking. She had learned to see drips of ink forming and catch them before they fell. Her quill was so expertly trimmed that the tip never slipped or bent. As her fingers worked, her thoughts turned, writing her own scripture within her head while her pen recounted the verse of the saints.

She was engrossed in one such trance when Sister Isabel came to tell her that someone was waiting to see her. Kaylein did not look up from her work the first time Isabel spoke, and it took a hand on her shoulder to break her focus.

"Sister Kaylein. You have a visitor waiting downstairs."

Kaylein blinked, set down her quill, and eased herself off the stool. Her back protested at the sudden shift in posture, but the pain subsided by the time she was downstairs. She'd been expecting Elizabeth, for no one else ever came to see her, and when she walked into the guest parlour her face lit up at the sight of her old tutor. She resisted the impulse to step forward and embrace him. It would have been inappropriate behaviour for a nun, and Gregory had always been tetchy around women. She recalled her mother insisting that she wore a hood and a plain dress fastened all the way up to the neck when she took lessons with him. Thinking about her mother sparked a surge of melancholy.

"Father," Kaylein said, offering him a warm smile and a bow. "It has been such a long time."

"It has, Sister." Kaylein heard the hesitation in his voice when he stopped short of calling her 'milady'. "I am glad to see you have taken to life under God. You always were a natural student of the scriptures."

"Thank you, Father. Perhaps this was all in God's plan."

Gregory frowned and looked away, then began to pace the length of the room. "I must be plain with you, milady," he said, forgetting to correct himself this time, "and God forgive me for the disobedience I am showing to my lord by coming to you and not the prioress. But I do not believe it is in His will for me to serve Sir Edward blindly."

A nervous tingle ran through Kaylein's fingers at the mention of Edward. "Saint Goldin writes that the foolish sceptic sees only his own answers, while the wise sceptic questions God, that he might better understand His will."

"Do you believe me wise?" Gregory asked. He sounded more uncertain than Kaylein had ever heard him.

"I do, Father. What did Sir Edward send you here for?"

The priest took a deep breath. "He wanted me to ask Mother Jane to expel you from the convent. He believes you will leave the church and raise a rebellion against Duke Francis. There was also some mention of you protecting a lawbreaker, but it sounded like a concoction of his own making to me. There are few men more adept at justifying their whims than Sir Edward."

"I mean to do no such thing," Kaylein insisted, trying to

find the glow of God's light to still her rising anxiety. She was afraid of Sir Edward, both for herself and for Elizabeth.

"I believe you. I told him as such, but he is not a thinking man. When he has a fancy in his head, he seldom cares for anyone else's opinion. We must pray that he soon finds another distraction to occupy him."

"And if he does not?"

"Then you may wish to take this to the prioress. I believe Edward will approach other church officials with his request, and depending on how successful he is, Mother Jane may find herself compelled to expel you."

A pinch of fear drew a gasp from Kaylein's lips. The church had been her refuge ever since she lost her family. She'd not dared to consider what might become of her if she was cast out.

Seeing her distress, Father Gregory said: "But as I say, Edward is not a thinking man. He will find it difficult to persuade the church to expel you."

"There is still a chance, though."

Gregory compressed his lips and nodded. "It would be wise to err on the side of caution."

"Thank you, Father." Kaylein made to excuse herself. She was desperate to take the news to Mother Jane. She would know what to do. "God was gracious in sending you with this news."

"I pray He was." Gregory stopped pacing, finally meeting Kaylein's eye. "God be with you, Sister. If anyone is worthy of His mercy after all they have suffered, it is you."

Once again Kaylein felt the urge to embrace her old tutor. The emotion boiled within her, pushing her forward like an invisible hand. For an instant, she resented her vows and the shackles they had placed upon her—but that was only the temptation of sin needling at her in a moment of weakness. Sometimes the urge to behave impiously seemed good and natural, and perhaps occasionally it was, but small erosions of a nun's discipline led to greater ones over time. Kaylein saw it every day in the sisters who bickered with each other during chapter, or took extra portions of food from the kitchen, or leaned out of the upstairs windows to jest with people in the streets. She wanted to heed Saint Goldin's words and only question the church's teachings when it seemed prudent, not when driven by impulse.

Once she had said farewell to Father Gregory, she went to find Mother Jane. It was almost time for midday prayer in the chapel, so Kaylein had to wait to speak with her. She mumbled through her verses with the other nuns, then went straight to the prioress's room after.

"You must stop hurrying in here straight after prayer," Jane reproached her, for once again Kaylein had run ahead without waiting. Before allowing her to speak, Mother Jane made Kaylein recite a verse of prayer as penance, then she stood by her writing desk and listened as Kaylein recounted Father Gregory's news.

"The good father is right," Jane said. "I will not expel you from this convent on the whims of Sir Edward."

"But the bishop or a cardinal could compel you?"

"Yes," the prioress admitted. Her expression softened when she noticed Kaylein's distress. "I will not abandon you, Kaylein. There may be a way for you to remain in the church even should the worst happen."

"How?"

"If I were to send you to another cell outside Tannersfield, it would complicate matters indefinitely. If you went to a different diocese you would be subject to a different bishop's authority. Messages would need to be sent back and forth. The delay and hassle would quickly grow tiresome for all involved, especially if I were to take my time with it. Believe me, I have seen more pressing issues lost in the inefficiencies of the church before."

Kaylein was taken aback by the mother superior's candour. "You cannot defy the church for my sake."

"I would do no such thing." Mother Jane's tone was

gravely serious. "I have many duties that require my attention. It is my prerogative as Prioress to defer some of those duties, and I do not believe sending messages regarding your whereabouts would be an urgent use of my time. Nor would it serve God's will."

"But I don't want to leave the convent," Kaylein said. Mother Jane's solution seemed almost as bad as being expelled. She would have to go to some other convent full of people she didn't know, with no Mother Jane and no Elizabeth. She might not even be allowed to write.

"I believe you would do well in any convent, Kaylein. As much as I would like to oversee the remainder of your novitiate myself, you have a great deal of unfortunate history here in Tannersfield, as this incident demonstrates. There are many other cells that would benefit from a bright young scribe like yourself. If you are afraid of Sir Edward and Duke Francis's interference, it would be prudent for you to leave sooner rather than later."

"Please, Mother," Kaylein implored her, "I don't want to go." In that moment she realised that, for as much as she feared Sir Edward, she was more afraid of losing what she had here. She wanted to stay in Tannersfield despite the danger.

The prioress gave her a long, hard look. "If you believe this is where God needs you most."

"I do."

"Then let us hope we hear no more from Sir Edward. But as your prioress, it is my duty to watch over you. I will send letters to some of my sisters in the church and ask whether they would be willing to accept a promising young novice. If Sir Edward continues his meddling, it would be prudent for us to act sooner rather than later."

Kaylein swallowed her unease and nodded. "Thank you, Mother. You have been so very kind to me."

Mother Jane guided her to the door. "Go back to your writing and try to put this worry out of your mind."

Kaylein exited the chapel, but she didn't return to the writing room. Instead she went to find the sub-prioress, who was in the sacristy counting out pennies for the nuns who would be going to market that afternoon. Though Joan was a stickler for rules, Kaylein's studious attitude had earned her a measure of indulgence from the elder nun. After some convincing, she persuaded Joan to let her run a market errand in place of another novice.

A short while later, she hurried out of the convent and crossed the marketplace to the other side of town. Father Gregory had mentioned Sir Edward accusing her of protecting a lawbreaker, and that could only mean Elizabeth. She didn't know whether Edward had his heart set on bringing Elizabeth to justice, but after the incident at the building site she was afraid of what he might do. She made her way through the streets to the workshop, for once oblivious to the packed crowds that usually made her so uneasy.

Elizabeth was not there when she arrived. Luther, the old master who'd been running the workshop in Joseph's absence, explained the situation.

"She rode off with master Isaac first thing this morning. They had a talk last night after the guild meeting. I said she should wait till you came by tomorrow, but that girl can be impulsive sometimes. I expect they've gone to the building site."

"Did something happen at the meeting?"

"The guild told her she can't work for Joseph anymore. I'd not have thought anything could break a spirit like hers, but she was barely herself after we left."

Kaylein's heart went out to her friend. By some cruel twist, the fate she'd feared for herself had already befallen poor Liz. She thought back to how Elizabeth had taken care of her after they left Rosepath, keeping her alive through misery and destitution. If Liz was about to lose her livelihood, she would do all she could to repay that debt of kindness.

"I shall return tomorrow," Kaylein said. "If she isn't back by then, Brother Daniel and I will go looking for her."

CHAPTER 25

Elizabeth would have felt guilty about pressuring Isaac into taking her to the building site had she not been so overwrought. She needed to speak with Joseph about what had happened at the guild hall. Luther had tried to make her wait, thinking she was being hysterical, but she could not bear the thought of spending a day sitting around the workshop with nothing to do. When Isaac came by to help with her reading, she insisted he take her to the building site. They set out the next morning, Elizabeth holding the back of Isaac's saddle as Blackberry trotted them down the road.

She dreaded giving Joseph the bad news. She didn't know if she would be able to bear his disappointment. No matter how many times she told herself it was the guild's fault for being vindictive, she could not shake the feeling that the blame lay at her feet. It was an unusual and unsettling state of mind for Elizabeth. Rarely did her doubts run so deep. For women like her, life was a simple matter of doing what needed to be done, day by day, week by week. If she stumbled, she picked herself back up. When tragedy struck, she grit her teeth and suffered through it. Yet now she stood to lose something she had grown to truly love. Unlike the massacre at Rosepath, which had been so far beyond her power to stop that it might as well have been an act of God, this was something she felt personally responsible for. She'd been on the path to happiness and security. If she fell off it now, she would always lament what might have been.

"You know how to ride a horse," Isaac observed as they stopped to let a caravan of merchant carts pass by. Elizabeth didn't feel like chatting, but he was doing her a favour by taking her to the building site, so she let him draw her into his conversation. Perhaps it would help take her mind off the worry gnawing at her stomach.

"How can you tell?" she asked.

Isaac turned halfway around in the saddle, patting Blackberry's mane as she snorted. "You know to keep your legs forward and hold the back of my saddle. You've ridden behind someone before."

"I rode with my brother like this until he taught me how to handle the horse on my own. I was terrified the first time. I was a lot smaller than the horse back then."

"You're much bigger now. I hope Blackberry can manage both of us all the way to the building site."

Elizabeth wondered whether he was trying to make a joke. "I'm not plump."

"No, but you've got large bones."

"I'll walk if I have to."

Isaac shook his head with a smile, urging Blackberry back onto the road as the final cart passed. He seemed able to do it without even having to press his heels into the mare's sides. It was a stark contrast to the way Sir Edward had ridden his stallion around the building site, yanking and wrenching the beast about as if he'd been hefting a stubborn sack of wool. Isaac handled Blackberry with the grace of a sculptor tapping his chisel, using the lightest touch to produce the subtlest of results.

"I'd like to see you ride her if one of us has to get off," he said.

"Why?"

The question seemed to surprise him, as though the answer should have been obvious. "Because it's interesting. Everyone rides differently. Besides, I want to see what Blackberry thinks of you." The horse whinnied, and Isaac gave her another pat on the mane. "Is your brother a horseman, then?"

"No, he was a thief. He stole the horse from a knight, then he had to run away from the village when he got caught."

Isaac chuckled. "I have a friend like that. He stole Blackberry here the day I—" He stumbled mid-sentence, mixing the words 'ran' and 'arrived' at the same time.

"I'm not surprised you're friends with outlaws."

"I'm not usually," Isaac said.

"No, I'm sorry. You're just strange. Most things you say don't surprise me anymore."

Isaac went quiet, either flattered or offended by Elizabeth's words. Once the moment had settled enough for a change of topic, he said: "Do you think Joseph can persuade the guild to let you stay?"

"I don't know. He'll put up a fight, but a lot of those carpenters were against me."

"What if he defied them anyway? Surely a man like him can do what he wants with his own business."

"They might expel him from the guild," Elizabeth explained. "He wouldn't be able to work with any of the other masters in town again. They wouldn't help him or Rose if they ever needed money, and his reputation would fall into the dirt. No one would want to apprentice their sons to him, and most of the boys at the workshop would probably leave. It would ruin him."

"It isn't fair for them to say who he should and shouldn't work with." Isaac was a calm man, rarely prone to frustration, but this time he sounded genuinely annoyed. There was a naivety to him that sometimes made Elizabeth question how he had survived travelling halfway across the known world.

"That's just how things are. Kaylein would say that's the way God ordered it." Elizabeth smiled fondly. "Then she would talk about how God sometimes *doesn't* order it that way, because people get His teachings wrong, and she'd start some sort of argument with herself."

"She's very clever, isn't she?"

"Yes. Clever enough to know better than to break her vows." Elizabeth hoped her hint wouldn't go over Isaac's head. She still believed the main reason he was spending time with her was because he wanted Kaylein. His response, however, was not what she'd expected.

"So you don't think she'd ever try to take revenge on Duke Francis for what happened?"

"Of course not! She's no fool."

"That day Sir Edward whipped Fred; you said she'd change things someday. And she said she would try."

"Not by having men fight for her, if that's what you're thinking. You won't get to be her champion and take back her lands." Elizabeth lowered her voice as a passing pair of youths looked up at them. "We shouldn't even talk about this. I think it's treason."

Isaac said no more about it. Perhaps she'd misjudged him and there was another layer to his interest in Kaylein, but right now she didn't have the mind to dwell on it. She tucked the thought away for later.

The remainder of their talk revolved around horses and dogs. It was a welcome diversion from her other worries, though no amount of small talk could set them to rest entirely. Blackberry was getting weary by the time they reached the path to the building site. She'd done well to carry them both so far, which Isaac attributed to Elizabeth's good riding posture. Elizabeth hurried on ahead while Isaac led Blackberry behind.

Where once there had been foundation pits, wooden frames, and pegged-out boundaries, there now stood a complete homestead. A scaffold still encircled the stone chapel as builders assembled the roof, but the main house was finished. Mortar was drying in the wall that now encircled the manor, and most of the labourers had turned their efforts to building the stables. It looked like all the major work would be finished before the winter frosts came, just as Joseph had hoped.

Elizabeth left Isaac to tie Blackberry to the hitching post and made for the main work shed. Joseph was inside helping Rose and the others assemble the chairs, tables, and bedsteads that would furnish the main house. The master carpenter's features creased with concern when he saw her. She never arrived early unless something was wrong. Elizabeth had to swallow a terrible lump in her throat when it threatened to choke her words into tears.

She explained what had happened, the news spilling out in a rush despite her efforts to slow down. When the carpenters started to stare, Rose ushered Joseph and Elizabeth outside for some privacy. By the time Elizabeth finished speaking, her hands were trembling. Joseph hadn't said a word. His leathery skin had paled slightly, and he was staring off into the woods.

"You won't throw me out, will you?" Elizabeth pleaded. "I can still stay at the workshop, even if it's just to clean."

Rose answered for her husband. "That isn't the worry." Her voice held a deep weariness that worried Elizabeth more than anger. "We won't leave you to fend for yourself, no matter what the guild say. It's the fine that's the problem."

"I know. I'm sorry, I really am, but there's more than enough silver in the chest to pay it. You must have lots of money from the work you've been doing here, too."

"That money isn't ours to spend," Joseph said at last. "I've promised it to Paul Builder. We agreed to lend him the money to build a new workshop in Rosepath. He gets the money from me now, and a portion of the rent from that place comes to Rose and I for the rest of our lives. We don't

385

have children to provide for us when we're old. We'll need that money if there comes a day when we can't work anymore. You're the one who made me think about investing in something like that, the way you're always planning for the future."

Elizabeth's eyes warmed with tears. "I'm sorry," she said again. "How much do you owe him?"

"Near everything. I've already given him the money I had here. I was going to tell you to expect him at the workshop to collect the rest when you came by tomorrow. We would've had about twenty silver shillings left to see us through the winter."

"And now that's how much the guild wants," Rose said.

"We'll talk them down." Joseph began to pace, but there was a stumbling, uncertain rhythm to his steps. The news had left him reeling. "They won't leave us penniless."

"Then they'll make you get rid of Liz. You won't be able to ask for leniency if you're butting heads with Theobald over the fine."

"Hush, woman, let me think." Joseph dragged his face through his palms and looked up at the sky. "Of all the times... I'll just have to ask Paul for the money back."

"I'm sure he'd let you keep some of it," Elizabeth said. She knew Paul Builder from Rosepath, and he had a reputation as an honest man. "He can't need it all at once, and you'll make more over the winter to pay him back with soon."

Rose shook her head. "One of his conditions was that we pay the money up front. He's got no patience for people stringing him along."

"Then we'd better hope he's understanding," Joseph said. "Or we'll be living on horsebread and boiled water this winter."

"If you need to get rid of me, I'll go," Elizabeth said quietly. No matter how much she wanted to stay, she couldn't bear seeing Joseph so distraught, not after all he'd done for

386

her.

"Don't be an idiot, girl," Rose snapped. Then, to Elizabeth's shock, she yanked her into a fierce hug. "I've spent half a year in this pit full of men. A nice quiet winter with you and Joseph is all I've been looking forward to."

Joseph walked over and put his hand on Elizabeth's shoulder. "I'd not throw any of my boys out just because the guild said so, and you're no different. If we have to pay their fine, we'll pay it. We just have to work something out with Paul. Maybe we can borrow money from one of the lenders."

A twinge of hope pushed through Elizabeth's uncertainty. "There are always merchants lending at market. I can go and see them first thing tomorrow."

Joseph nodded distractedly. He didn't look very confident. Moneylending was a troublesome business. Even small loans could lead to large debts that harried men like Joseph for years. Yet if he was going to fight the guild for the right to employ Elizabeth, he couldn't expect them to waive his fine. If they didn't want to back out of their deal with Paul Builder, borrowing money was the only option. It was an unenviable solution, but it was better than nothing. At least now they had a plan. Elizabeth would scour Tannersfield for a reputable lender, and she would do everything she could to make sure Joseph didn't get swindled.

His understanding and Rose's embrace meant more to her than she could express in words. There was a forceful pressure in her chest that yearned to escape. They were truly good people, kind and giving. She thought about how the guildsmen had been so eager to blame one another at the meeting. Most of them would probably have thrown her out on the street had she gone to their workshops instead of Joseph's. She'd been blessed to find him.

Lacking the articulation to communicate her feelings, she did what she always did and threw herself into work. She helped the builders' wives prepare the midday meal at the cooking pits and brought trenchers of venison to all the carpenters. There was cleaning and washing to do afterwards, so she pitched in with that as well. Most of the women were just as weary of the building site as Rose, and they were happy to let a fresh-faced girl shoulder more than her share of the workload. Elizabeth didn't realise it was well into the afternoon until Isaac found her washing pots at the edge of the river.

"Are you ready to leave?" he asked. "We'll need to be going soon if we want to get back before curfew. The days are getting shorter now."

The guilt Elizabeth had staved off for imposing on Isaac's generosity suddenly caught up with her. She'd brought him all the way out here and promptly forgotten about him. She looked away and rubbed her eyes, not wanting him to think she was being overly emotional. The day had taken a toll on her spirits, and even the slightest things were getting to her.

"Of course," she said. "I'll just finish here."

"Will you let me sleep in your shed this time? I don't think I'll be making it back to the farms tonight."

"If you promise you won't steal anything."

"I've had enough of stealing. It's more trouble than it's worth."

So he was a thief, but Elizabeth didn't think he was a dangerous one. He was more like Sam—troublesome, but not wicked. It was strange how Elizabeth's thoughts sometimes played tricks on her, for no sooner had she begun thinking of her brother than she heard a voice that could almost have been his. So many years had passed that she only had vague memories of that voice. When she turned to look, the man she saw swinging his leg over the wall had the same messy brown hair and sharp features her brother had borne.

"Afternoon, Isaac," the newcomer called, reaching out to clap him on the shoulder. "Is this your lady?"

"The one I've been teaching, yes," Isaac said. "Elizabeth, this is Sam."

This time there was no stifling her emotions. Hearing his

name was the final tap that fit all the pieces together. His voice, his face, his hair; they all belonged to the Sam she remembered. He looked different, more gaunt and wiry, as if he'd spent years eating little and working a lot. But there was no mistaking the resemblance.

"Sam!" she choked out his name in a rush of breath. All the years of pain he'd put her through came to the surface, all the seasons spent wondering where he was, the struggle of supporting their mother on her own, the worry over whether he was alive or dead. But rising through those emotions was an overwhelming surge of relief. It was as if the fist that had been clutching her heart all day had finally slackened its grip. Despite everything else, her only known relative was alive and well.

She threw herself against his chest. Her fierce embrace took him by surprise, and he tried to push her away. For a moment Elizabeth was hurt by the rejection, then she realised he probably didn't recognise her. She'd barely been a teenager the last time they saw each other.

"It's me!" she exclaimed. "I'm your sister!" Isaac's anecdotes about his troublesome, unnamed friend made perfect sense now. Of course it was Sam. Still stealing horses, still getting his friends into trouble. She wanted to be furious at him for not having changed his ways, but there was no denying the joy that burst forth from her heart like a fountain. He was alive, and he was here. She whispered her thanks to God. After a day fraught with so much worry, this felt like a sign. Perhaps everything was going to be alright.

Sam frowned, pulling back so that he could get a good look at her. "By God, you are." A slow grin spread across his face, brightening his expression with the same playful charm Elizabeth remembered from their youth. That charm had won him the affection of more girls than a boy as plain as Sam had any right to attract. "I thought you might be dead."

"I thought you were! Why didn't you come home?"

"You know they'd have thrown me in the sheriff's jail, or

worse."

"You could have sent a message!"

Sam just shrugged, but his smile held Elizabeth's frustrations at bay. "Look at you," he said. "You're a woman. Are you married yet?"

"No. I've been living in Tannersfield working for a carpenter. What about you?" She knew the answer before Sam shook his head. He would never marry anyone unless a girl's father forced him to at swordpoint. A flurry of excitement absorbed them as they threw questions back and forth, demanding to hear everything that had happened during their years apart.

Poor Isaac, leaning wearily against the wall, finally interrupted them with a cough as he pointed across the river at the dipping sun. Once again Elizabeth had let time slip away from her.

"Oh no," she said, her heart sinking. They would never make it back to Tannersfield before curfew now.

"Come back to the farms with us," Sam said.

Isaac looked perplexed, but he relented when Elizabeth gave him an imploring look. "I suppose it's warm enough for me to watch Blackberry outside for one night."

Elizabeth took the pots she'd been washing back to the building site, and once Sam had collected his day's pay from the foreman the three of them set out down the road.

The settlement Sam and Isaac had been living in could not really be called a village. The dozen or so wattle and daub huts were nested in a sparse copse on the edge of a farm, presumably housing the labourers who worked the fields. Ironically, Elizabeth felt safer amongst those flimsy huts than she did on the streets of Tannersfield. Thieves and outlaws didn't bother with places like this, for the desperately poor had nothing worth stealing.

She sat by the fire outside the hut talking to Sam, while Isaac, wrapped up in his cloak, leaned against the tree he'd hitched Blackberry to. A mangy old dog came out of the darkness and draped itself over his lap, but he didn't seem to mind.

When Elizabeth described how she'd fled Rosepath, a flash of anger crossed Sam's face at the mention of Sir Edward. He interrupted her to tell his own tale about the knight ambushing him in the woods a year prior. He'd been living rough with a gang of outlaws at the time, half of whom had never broken the law in their lives. The rest were poachers, certainly no saints, but hardly devils either. Yet Edward's men had slaughtered them indiscriminately, sparing only Sam. When he described what they'd done to a teenage girl and her grandmother, Elizabeth's blood ran cold.

"I was lucky he lost his nerve after that," Sam said. "He dragged me back to Rosepath and locked me in the tower for weeks. I'd have starved or got sick from my own filth if it hadn't been for Daisy. She made sure to come by every day to make sure I was still alive."

Elizabeth was relieved to hear that Daisy had survived the massacre. She was a little older than Elizabeth and had teased her when she first started working for Lady Eleanor, but they'd grown friendly as the years passed.

"How did you get out?" Elizabeth asked.

"I heard someone coming into the tower one night, so I bundled up my cloak against the wall and hid behind the door. It was Edward, come to slip a knife in my back." Sam gave a wry grimace. "He didn't realise I'd had nothing to do but exercise for weeks. I knocked him down and made a run for it."

"You should've killed him."

"I didn't want to."

"Why not?"

Sam shrugged. His reasoning never extended further than the end of his nose. Perhaps that was a blessing. Despite everything he'd been through, he seemed no worse the wear for it. An intense worry for her brother suddenly took hold of

391

Elizabeth. By all rights, he should have been dead by now, either in the gallows or at the hands of outlaws. If he carried on this way, it was only a matter of time before his carelessness caught up with him.

"You mustn't go looking for trouble anymore," she insisted.

Sam laughed. "You just told me to kill a knight."

Elizabeth punched him hard in the arm. "You know what I mean. We aren't children anymore. Don't you ever learn? Tell me, and be honest, when was the last time you stole something?"

Sam shared a look with Isaac. He opened his mouth to speak, then bit his tongue.

Elizabeth glared at him. "Tell me."

"We stole wool from Henry Shearer. You should've heard him yelling. There were sheep and dogs all over the yard."

Isaac sat up stiffly, prompting a forlorn whine from the dog in his lap. "It was Sam's idea."

Elizabeth pressed her lips together until they thinned.

"You look like Mother," Sam said.

She hit him again. "Fred Fielder got flogged because of that! He could've died!" Remembering Joseph's tenuous financial situation, she added: "Joseph Carpenter paid for the monks to tend him out of his own pocket."

Sam scoffed as if she was laying blame with the wrong person, but Isaac looked deeply guilty.

"I told Sam we're not doing anything like that again."

"You'd better not. If you need money, then–" Elizabeth trailed off. What could Sam do? Come to her? Part of the reason their mother had died with only a few silver shillings to her name was because she'd been forced to pay fines for her wayward son many times over. Elizabeth could see the trap she was laying for herself if she made her charity an excuse for Sam to keep being irresponsible. She felt the strains of the day weighing on her. She couldn't worry about Sam, Joseph, and herself all at the same time. It would drive her mad.

"Isaac," she said at last, hoping she wasn't making a mistake by putting her trust in him. "Will you promise to keep him out of trouble?" Strange and flighty though he was, he at least had more sense than her brother.

"I've been trying my best."

"Sam's stupid. He's going to keep doing things like this unless someone stops him." She carried on talking over her brother's protests. "He'll need work over the winter. Real work. If you keep an eye on him, I'll let you talk to Kaylein again." It troubled her to make such a promise, but it was the only thing she could think of.

Sam forgot his grievances with his sister the instant she mentioned Kaylein's name. "Lady Kaylein?" His eyes lit up, and he gave Isaac a teasing look. "I hear she grew up to be a beauty."

Elizabeth ignored him. "Isaac? Please?"

He gave her a sheepish shrug. "I was going to keep an eye on him anyway."

"Don't waste your eyes on me," Sam said. "Save them for the lady. A lordling like you should know all the right things to say to a woman like her."

Elizabeth wished she could have indulged her brother's humour, but she'd lost the mood for it. Now that the initial excitement of their reunion had faded, she was worrying again. Weariness took hold, and she went into the hut to sleep on Sam's blanket.

They rose early the next morning. Isaac needed to head back to town to check in with the tradesmen he'd been couriering for, and Elizabeth was eager to visit the moneylenders at market. The remaining labourers on the building site were only needed for half a day now that most of the unskilled work had been completed, so Sam came with them too.

After everything that had happened, Elizabeth had

completely forgotten this was the day she normally visited the building site. Halfway back to Tannersfield, they ran into Kaylein and Brother Daniel coming the other way.

"Liz, you had me worried!" Kaylein exclaimed, hurrying forward to greet them.

Isaac, justifiably weary of having to wait for others, rode on ahead while the rest of them stopped to talk at the side of the road, leaving Elizabeth with a look that said he would hold her to the promise of getting to speak with Kaylein later.

She began explaining what had happened with the guild, but Kaylein had something more urgent to discuss.

"Sir Edward is still looking for you. I think he's trying to use what you did to him as an excuse to have me expelled from the convent. Mother Jane is taking care of it, but," she bit her lip anxiously, "you don't have anyone protecting you. Promise me you'll leave Tannersfield if he comes looking."

Elizabeth groaned. All her efforts with Joseph and the guild would be for nothing if she was forced to flee town because Sir Edward still held a grudge. He'd threatened her with the pillory the day they met at the convent, but after Sam's harrowing stories she wondered whether he might go even further.

Sam stepped in before she sank any deeper into her quagmire of worries. "Don't worry about Liz, milady. If she needs to leave town for a while, Isaac and I can take care of her."

Kaylein peered at him. "Are you... Sam?"

"I'm flattered you remember, milady."

"You were brought before my father's court more than once. And please do not call me that. I am Sister Kaylein now."

Sam bowed, which only made her more uncomfortable.

"I suppose he's right," Elizabeth said with a sigh. What else could be done about it? She was just going to have to keep her head down and hope for the best. At least she had her brother now, though which one of them would end up taking care of the other remained to be seen. It was always the fate of people like them to live in the shadow of their lords. They would just have to hope the shadow Sir Edward cast was a short one.

As much as Elizabeth would have liked to stay and talk with Kaylein, they had business in opposite directions, and the road was only getting busier. Promising they would speak again soon, they said their farewells and parted ways.

Sam stared over his shoulder at Kaylein for a long time. Elizabeth was about to ask why when another unwelcome realisation stole up on her. It wasn't Isaac who harboured a secret desire for Kaylein. He'd rode off with barely a glance at her, while Sam had been full of smiles and platitudes. When he finally turned around with a foolish grin on his face, Elizabeth's suspicions were confirmed. Her brother was smitten.

CHAPTER 26

There was something comfortable about being back in Tannersfield with Sam. The bustle of the streets no longer grated on Elizabeth's ears. The scowls of the surly hawkers and red-faced laundresses trying to elbow her aside came across as silly rather than intimidating. It reminded her of being young, when Sam had led her by the hand through this marketplace looking for fallen apples and pennies they could pick out of the dirt. Those had been careless days. Even Elizabeth's concern over her brother's infatuation with Kaylein dimmed when she caught him staring after every other girl who walked by—though none of them made him grin the way Kaylein had.

Having Sam with her would make striking a deal with a moneylender easier. They might dismiss her out of hand or press her into a bad deal if she approached on her own. Sam began wandering in the direction of a public house on the south side of the market, enticed over by a woman with rouged cheeks who blew him a kiss when she caught his eye.

Elizabeth grabbed his arm and yanked him back. "Come with me to the moneylenders. They'll take me more seriously if I arrive with a man."

"How do you know?"

"That's how it always is with business."

"You sound like you know all about business now. Are you going to be rich one day?"

Elizabeth refrained from giving him a hopeful answer. She didn't want him to get the idea that she'd always have money if he came begging. "Not if I can't help Joseph pay his fine. Come on, they're just up here."

They approached a long, open-fronted hall at the southeast corner of the marketplace. A line of empty carts created a buffer between the crowd and the half-dozen men standing guard. Some wore swords–likely the sheriff's men or mercenaries. The moneylenders had chests full of silver inside their hall and they spared no expense ensuring they were well guarded. Elizabeth's shoulders tensed as she approached. She'd never struck a deal like this before. Perhaps she should have waited for Joseph, but there was no point changing her mind now, so she pressed on. A man wearing a sword belt and a leather hat came forward to meet them. Behind him, Elizabeth could see about ten well-dressed men sitting beneath the eaves, their tables covered with parchment, scales, and counting abacuses. She'd wanted one of those abacuses for herself ever since she started learning numbers. Counting out a dozen pennies to a shilling would be so much quicker if she could slide beads along the rods of an abacus to denote each calculation rather than having to hold them in her head.

The armed man looked them up and down, then asked Sam: "Who are you?"

"Elizabeth and Sam Carpenter," Elizabeth said before her brother could speak. "We're here on behalf of our master, Joseph Carpenter. He runs a workshop on the east side of town." She realised that she was wringing her hands anxiously and forced them to be still.

The man gave a small nod. "I've heard of him. Go on in."

Smiling in relief, Elizabeth stepped through into the hall.

There were even more guards inside. Voices murmured, an abacus rattled, and coins tinkled into a purse as one of the merchants counted out a weighty loan for the nobleman sitting opposite him. Just like at the guild meeting, Elizabeth felt uncomfortably out of her depth. Would she be expected to write something down? Loans usually involved a contract. She could probably manage penning her name, but what if they needed Joseph's name as well? It probably started with a J or a G, but when she tried to imagine the rest of the word it became a blur in her mind's eye. Realising that she was standing there foolishly, she began to walk the length of the hall. It would help if she could find a merchant she recognised, but she hadn't seen many of these men in town before. The only one she knew by name was Harald Redcloak, probably looking to make a few shillings from loans while he waited to meet with more guildsmen. Elizabeth didn't want to go to him. She walked to the far end of the hall and back again, still uncertain. On their second pass, Harald noticed them.

"Sam!" he called. "By God, there's a face I never expected to see again."

Sam grinned sheepishly. "Morning, Harald."

Elizabeth groaned internally. Perhaps it was a sign. She didn't like the idea of being in debt to Harald Redcloak, but he might be kinder to them than an unfamiliar merchant. Sam had worked as a carter for Harald several times during their youth. Despite the merchant's reputation, it had been one of the few jobs that earned Sam an honest wage. Forcing a smile, Elizabeth followed Sam to Harald's table. He gave her a curious look she couldn't read.

"Elizabeth."

She nodded courteously. "Good morning."

"I'm sorry about your trouble with the guild the other day," Harald said. "Does your master need help paying his fine?"

"Yes," she admitted.

"Joseph has a good reputation. I'd be happy to lend him the money. My rate is six pennies paid back on top of every shilling I lend out. Silver only."

Elizabeth tried to do the calculation. Harald waited patiently as she counted off on her fingers, mouthing the numbers under her breath. Six pennies on top of every shilling meant Harald wanted a return of half as much money again. If he lent them twenty, he would get back thirty. Elizabeth was sure it was an unfair rate, but if work was steady Joseph might be able to pay it off by the end of the winter.

"It's a very fair rate for a loan to a tradesman," Harald said. "Better than you'll get from anyone else here."

"What will happen if Joseph can't pay the money on time?"

"He'll owe me two silver pennies for each week he's late. Shall we say, by winter solstice?"

Elizabeth shook her head. "That's too soon. It'll have to be by the end of winter at the earliest."

Harald puffed out his cheeks, his expression full of exaggerated scepticism. It was all for show. He was trying to press her into a foolish agreement. She might not have understood all the intricacies of moneylending, but she wasn't completely clueless.

"That's no time at all," she insisted. "Plenty of businesses need a whole year to make their money back. I know the wool merchants spend all year buying and only sell their fleeces in the summer." She was half-guessing based on conversations she'd had with Martha Tailor, but she suspected she was on the right track. It made sense that short-term loans like the one Harald was suggesting would be the exception rather than the rule, for many people's incomes were limited by annual events like harvests and trade fairs.

Harald held his vexed expression for a moment, then relented. Elizabeth was not the foolish bumpkin he'd taken her for.

"Fair enough. Till the end of the winter, then, but it'll be six pennies a week if it's overdue."

"That's not acceptable," Elizabeth said, feeling emboldened. "Joseph is a respected tradesman. You don't need to worry about him swindling you."

"Then why is it a problem if I charge him extra for being overdue?"

"If something goes wrong, a bad loan could ruin him."

"It could ruin me too if I don't make sure I'm properly compensated."

Elizabeth sincerely doubted the loss of twenty silver shillings would bring a man who could afford expensive wine-red clothing to his knees, but she refrained from voicing that thought. It occurred to her that the overdue charge on the loan was the part that mattered, not the lump sum. Being unable to keep up with escalating interest was a deadly spiral.

"What about thirty-five silver shillings in repayment, and only one penny a week if it's overdue?"

Harald chuckled, turning to address Sam. "Your little sister's shrewder than my own lord. But a penny a week is a fool's rate. I could be waiting years to get back what I'm owed." It seemed like they'd reached an impasse until Harald rubbed a finger beneath his chin and looked at Elizabeth again. "I've got another offer for you and your master. You heard what I had to say at the guild meeting. What if I offered to pay your fine in full—all out of my own pocket? I could even put in a good word with Theobald about letting Joseph keep you on."

Elizabeth's eyes narrowed. It was plainly too good to be true.

"What do you want in return?"

"Skilled tradesmen for Rosepath," Harald said. "Sir Edward wants the biggest market in the county. Like I said at the guild hall, the village will be growing soon, and Edward wants builders around to support it. If you can get your master to send some folk our way, let's say, a dozen skilled

400

carpenters over the course of the year, then I'll pay your fine. No penniless vagrants, either. Edward wants them living in his houses and paying him rent."

Elizabeth chewed her lip, thinking it over. Every few weeks they usually had at least one travelling journeyman visit the workshop looking for a place to settle. Joseph might be able to sway some of the undecided guildsmen into visiting Rosepath as well. The offer seemed reasonable enough, but there was bound to be a catch.

"What if we can't send enough carpenters?" she asked.

"I'm sure you will. This town's packed full of them, but they're all superstitious about coming to Rosepath." Harald sneered. "They think the place is cursed after what happened to Leo, but I expect they'll change their tune if a master craftsman tells them there's good money to be made there."

"But what if they don't?"

Harald stopped rubbing his chin and stared at her. "Then I'll just have to let Sir Edward know about our bargain, won't I?"

Elizabeth's blood ran cold. He knew. Of course he knew. If he had Sir Edward's ear, he would be privy to all the knight's whims. The unspoken threat behind Harald's words was plain enough. She would have to do as he asked. She couldn't try to negotiate a better deal with any of the other moneylenders. If she did, Harald would tell Edward where to find her. The odd looks he'd been giving her since the guild meeting all made sense now. Perhaps she should have been thankful he'd stopped short of outright blackmail.

"Very well," she said stiffly. "I'll take your offer to Joseph. I'm sure he'll accept."

Harald smiled. "I'm sure he will. You can keep your job, your master can keep his business, Sir Edward can have his market, and I can stay in his favour. We'll all be happy. Make sure anyone who comes to Rosepath says it was Joseph who sent them, that way I'll know you're keeping up your end of the bargain."

Elizabeth ran her tongue over the roof of her mouth, finding that it had gone dry. "That sounds very fair."

"Good. I'm sure we'll do more business again soon." Harald turned to Sam again. "How about you, Sam? Do you need any work?"

Elizabeth gave her brother an urgent look, but he missed its meaning.

"Liz says I do. I've been working on a building site, but the job's almost done now."

"I can always use good strong lads like you. There's some carting I need doing once a week. Don't worry, you won't have to visit Rosepath. I know you've had some trouble there."

Sam lowered his voice and leaned forward. "It shouldn't be here in town, either. Some of the sheriff's men might recognise me at market."

"The work you'll be doing for me is out in the forest."

"This sounds dangerous," Elizabeth said. Reputable merchant business was not conducted away from prying eyes in the forest.

"No more dangerous than anything Sam's done before," Harald said. "And he can rely on me never to mention his name at court. It's the king's business to enforce his laws, not mine."

That's a lie, Elizabeth thought. Harald let other people take the blame for him all the time. They got their hands dirty so that his stayed clean. He'd pinned his misdemeanours on a dozen unwitting lads like Sam when he faced judgement at Count Leo's court. It was a bad deal, but what choice did they have? Harald could turn them over to Sir Edward any time he wanted. Elizabeth's only consolation was that the merchant probably wouldn't throw them to the wolves unless he needed to save his own skin. He valued loyal workers too much to discard them out of hand. Despite his lack of scruples, he wasn't stupid. They would just have to hold up their end of the bargain and pray nothing went wrong.

Elizabeth left the hall with a weight in her stomach. The looming threat of the guild had lifted for the time being, but this new debt to Harald had taken its place. Once they were back among the market stalls she rounded on her brother.

"Why did you agree to that?"

Sam frowned. "I thought you wanted me to."

"No, I didn't. I told you last night not to get yourself mixed up in any more trouble."

"There's no trouble. I'm just doing some carting."

"Even you can't be that slow. Do you really think Harald's doing fair business out there in the forest? He's probably buying stolen goods from outlaws."

"It's not as if I'll be the one doing the stealing," Sam protested.

"You know what Harald's like."

"He's not that bad. Why are you worrying so much? You really have grown up to be like Mother."

Elizabeth was getting angry, but the majority of it was directed at herself. "If something goes wrong, you'll end up in the gallows this time."

"It'll be fine." He stopped and took her by the shoulders, leaning down so that their faces were level. A lump rose in Elizabeth's throat. She remembered him doing this when they were children. It was his way of talking to her when she was upset. "People like us have to take chances. No rich man's going to treat us fairly. You never did anything wrong, but now a knight's looking for you and the guild want you thrown out. God doesn't watch over everyone, Liz, no matter what the priests say. He didn't watch over Mother."

"Don't say that."

"It's true. Now stop worrying. I'm not going to get in any trouble."

"Is that what you told yourself before Edward locked you up?"

Sam sighed and took his hands off her shoulders. "I don't want to argue with you. We got what we came for, didn't we?

Let's celebrate."

"You can celebrate. I need to get back to work." She turned and walked off, her throat tight with frustration.

"Liz. Liz!" Sam called after her. "I'll be back at the farm!"

Her step faltered, but when she looked back Sam was already heading into the public house he'd been eyeing earlier. Why did he have to see the world in such a cynical light? Things had been difficult, yes, but she couldn't bring herself to believe that God was blind to her plight. Kaylein believed in God's mercy, and she was cleverer than anyone Elizabeth knew.

Yet there was an unpleasant truth behind Sam's words that stuck with her all the way back to the workshop. Any day now she might lose everything she'd spent the last year and a half working toward. All it would take was a word from Harald or the wrong person recognising her in the street and Sir Edward could break down the workshop door tomorrow. Perhaps people like her couldn't afford to play by the same rules as everyone else. She wouldn't have survived if she hadn't stolen that merchant's satchel the night she fled Rosepath. Was honesty ever truly enough to see a person like her through life's pitfalls?

She began seriously considering leaving Tannersfield. It would mean abandoning everything she knew, but perhaps that would be better in the long run. There was simply too much bad history here, both for Sam and herself. They couldn't live their whole lives looking over their shoulders. Isaac had travelled. Perhaps he could take them to another part of the kingdom, somewhere peaceful, far beyond the reach of Sir Edward and Duke Francis.

The tightness in Elizabeth's throat grew worse when she approached the workshop and saw Luther and Fred sawing posts in the yard. Fred had just made a joke, and Luther was struggling not to crack a smile. How could she leave this behind? She loved her work. She loved the smell of sawdust and the rasp of saws, the scrape of chisels and the thump of mallets. She loved Joseph, and she wanted to take care of him when he and Rose grew old.

Perhaps that was worth a life lived in fear.

Elizabeth explained Harald's deal when Joseph returned the next day. At first he was pleasantly surprised, but as the conversation went on his mood darkened.

"It's an easy enough bargain for us," he said, "but is there really work to be had in Rosepath? Nothing I've heard about Sir Edward says he's a good lord, and if this Harald has to pay folk to sing his praises I doubt he's doing much to entice tradesmen on his own. I've built an honest reputation for myself, girl, and you're asking me to send fine working men to a place that might be no good for them."

"I know," Elizabeth said, "but what choice do we have? Rosepath was never a bad place to live, and I'm sure it's better than Tannersfield these days."

"Aye, that's true enough." They were sitting inside the house while Joseph counted out purses of money for Paul Builder. The heavy money chest already looked miserably empty. "But we can always strike a bargain with one of the other moneylenders. I'd rather deal with an honest contract than this shady business of favours."

Elizabeth's nervous habit of chewing her lip returned. The edge of her mouth had grown chapped over the past few days. She needed Joseph to agree, or Harald would tell Edward where she lived.

The carpenter turned around when she began scratching the fabric of her dress. "What's got into you, girl? You look like you're sitting on an anthill."

"I'm just worried."

"Aye, and about more than this guild business. The last time I saw you this way you were barefoot on my doorstep trying to sell me stolen tools." He put down the purse he'd been filling and swivelled on his stool to face her. "I've never asked for more than you're willing to share, but I know

405

there's some trouble following you. That nun you always come to the building site with, she's Count Leo's daughter, isn't she? The day Sir Edward whipped Fred the pair of you were whispering like thieves."

Elizabeth let out a strained breath. She supposed there was no use hiding it any longer. One way or another, he was going to find out. She hated putting yet more of her burdens on him, but if anyone had earned her trust, it was Joseph.

She told him everything: who she was, what had happened the night Duke Francis attacked Rosepath, the confrontation with Sir Edward, and why Harald Redcloak had forced her into accepting his bargain.

To her relief, Joseph was not as shocked as she'd feared. He seemed to have been half-expecting it.

"I suppose we've no choice but to take this merchant's deal, then. By God, you're in more messes than a girl your age has any right to be in."

"I'm so sorry. I never wanted any of this to happen. I never wanted you to worry."

"If you'd told me this the day you arrived, I'd have turned you away. Now you're living in my house running my workshop better than it's been run in years." Joseph shook his head in bemusement. "Well, I suppose this is where we are now."

This time Elizabeth didn't ask whether he wanted her to leave. The warmth Joseph and Rose had shown her on the building site felt like a turning point in their relationship. There was a bond of kindred between them now that went beyond employer and employee. She might have wept, but she'd spent enough time making a mess of herself in front of Joseph lately.

On a whim, she asked: "Have you ever thought about leaving Tannersfield?"

He gave her a curious look. "Why?"

"I don't know if I can stay here forever, not with Harald and Sir Edward around. But I don't want to leave you behind." She knew she was asking a lot of him. She couldn't expect him to uproot his life for her sake.

"We'd hate to see you go, but Rose and I are settled here. It's a big town with good trade. We've built a lot for ourselves here."

Elizabeth nodded glumly. It was the answer she'd expected.

Joseph leaned forward and planted his hands on his knees. "Though I'd be a fool not to consider it. Thin Robin's been talking about heading out to Rambirch with Adam, maybe building a workshop of their own. They're family men, those two, and they're worried about raising their children in a town like this. I hear it's got no better while we've been away."

"It hasn't. And the curfew just means it's the town watch you have to look out for instead of the cutpurses after dark."

"Still," Joseph said, "leaving would be a hard choice. I'd only consider it if I could get some of the boys to come with me. We'd need to sell the workshop and find somewhere to set up in another town. Someplace with lots of work and a good guild who'd treat us right." He sighed. "I can't spend weeks searching the county for somewhere like that. Not unless Tannersfield gets so bad I don't feel safe in my own bed."

"What if you hired Isaac to go looking for you?" Elizabeth suggested. "He's always travelling on his horse. He can read and write, too. If you gave him instructions, he could find exactly what you're looking for."

Joseph smiled, though Elizabeth got the impression he was only humouring her. "There's still the question of money. We'd be without work for a while, and we'd need to build a new workshop or find somewhere to rent. There's no telling how long it would take for regular work to start coming in. I'd want to be sitting on a fat chest of silver beforehand, and right now ours is empty."

Elizabeth's hopes had risen when they began discussing the logistics of moving, but faced with the magnitude of the task, she realised it would not be happening any time soon.

"It was a silly idea," she said.

"It's a difficult idea. Not one we can think about right now, at any rate. Maybe things will get better around here. Maybe Sir Edward won't trouble you again. Either way, if I'm to accept Harald's help with the guild then we'll be here for a while upholding our end of the bargain." He held out a leathery palm to Elizabeth. She placed her smaller hand within his, and he squeezed it. "Ask me about this again the winter after next. Until then, you keep yourself out of Sir Edward's way. If he comes looking for you, go to the farms and stay with your brother, alright?"

Elizabeth nodded. Hearing Joseph say it made her feel like things might just get better after all. "And I can keep on working for you in the meantime?"

"You've taken better care of my house than anyone I've trusted it with in ten years. If Theobald thinks he can make me get rid of you, he's got another thing coming."

Elizabeth gripped his hand tight. She wanted him to embrace her the way Rose had, but Joseph was the sort of man who expressed his emotions in other ways. He'd not given her the answer she wanted, but he'd agreed to everything he reasonably could. It was far more than she felt she deserved. She hoped they would never have to revisit the idea of leaving Tannersfield. God willing, she would stay with Joseph the rest of her life.

CHAPTER 27

A thin layer of white cloud covered the sky all winter, casting the world in a pale, shadowless light. There was no snow that year, only an intermittent battering of hail and wind that drove the cold into every crack of every castle. Cairnford's keep was no different. Steam rose from Edward's cloak as he warmed himself by the fire pit in the centre of the famous octagonal great hall Duke Francis was so proud of. It had taken Edward almost a week to get there, so slowed had his entourage been by the muddy roads and lashing rain. He'd been late to answer the duke's summons, but so had everyone else, so the court meeting had been postponed until today. Normally Edward would have been in a miserable mood after such a dreary trek, but this meeting was different. King Fendrel himself was attending along with half the lords of Cairnford, Tannersfield, and the surrounding counties. As a mere knight, Edward had not been privy to the importance of the gathering, but everyone said it had something to do with Larmond and Alistair's rebellion. The king did not usually tour the country unless he needed to muster support from his noble subjects, and he would need support if a war was brewing.

Edward shivered as the doors opened behind him and a draft wafted through his damp hair. The great hall was filling up fast. All around the eight-sided stone chamber stood clusters of nobles and their retainers. Barons, knights, sheriffs, counts, bishops, and monks drank cups of warm wine and conversed in low tones, all waiting apprehensively for the king to arrive. Edward hoped young Fendrel would take his time. It was a long, winding path from Cairnford town to the keep atop the cairn-studded hill from whence the county took its name. The walls of the castle sprawled in an uneven square around the top of the hill, standing more than a hundred acres apart in some places. An entire army could have camped at Cairnford with room to spare, and the spartan lodgings of the keep reflected a similar focus on military pragmatism. It lacked the comfortable, if somewhat cramped warmth of Rosepath, so much so that the king had elected to lodge at the bishop's house at the bottom of the hill rather than staying with Duke Francis.

Comfortable or not, Cairnford Castle was an intimidating stone monument. Edward could tell many of the nobles were impressed by the seat of Duke Francis's power. He himself had grown accustomed to it during his years as a knight. Now that he was steward of his own castle, he felt a smug sense of satisfaction in his ability to affect indifference to a place more powerful men regarded with awe.

Realising that his cloak was not going to dry, he looked about for one of Duke Francis's servants to take it for him. His own retainers were not present that day. He'd brought Alderic and Stephen to Cairnford along with Gwayne, his master of horse, but it would have been presumptuous for a knight to invite servants to the king's court, so he'd left the two men-at-arms with enough money to enjoy a brothel while Gwayne saw to re-shoeing their horses.

As Edward headed for the hall's entrance he saw Cristiana hurrying between the pantry and the stairs. He stiffened, his heart beating faster at the sight of her. She'd not prepared herself for court yet, and her hair tumbled loose about her shoulders instead of sitting in its usual coiled braids. He wanted to call out to her, but the words stuck in his throat, and he was left standing awkwardly by the stairs as she went by without seeing him.

"Take this," he said irritably to the next servant that came out of the pantry, shoving his cloak into the man's hands. "Make sure it's dry for me before I leave."

The man bowed and scuttled back the way he'd come. Edward raked his damp hair out of his eyes and returned to the fire pit. Another pair of knights had stolen his place while he was away. Their heavy fur cloaks dripped water on the floor as they laughed over cups of wine. Edward bumped shoulders with one of the men as he squeezed past. The knight turned around, provoking a flinch from Edward when he recognised his hideously ugly features. It was Sir Roger of Kinedwyn, known as Roger Half-Face to his peers. He was a good deal older than Edward, red-haired and leathery, and the poorly-healed sword wound that had once cleaved open his skull glistened unsettlingly in the firelight. It had left a permanent split in his nose and caved in one of the cheekbones, making one of his eyes bulge with the uncanny impression that it sat slightly lower than the other. The man who had been talking to him was Alfred of Copperway, another knight in Duke Francis's service. Alfred had always mocked Edward for his low birth, and he hated him for it.

"You're not a noble, are you?" Sir Roger asked cautiously, clearly wondering whether he needed to apologise for jostling Edward.

"That's the sheriff's boy from Tannersfield," Alfred said with a smirk. Edward wanted to punch his smiling buck teeth out of his face.

Sir Roger grinned. It was a strange expression to see on such a deformed face. "Perhaps I should apologise anyway. I hear you're lord of more land than some of the barons here."

"Yes," Edward said, his anger succumbing to a swell of

411

pride. "Yes, I am, and steward of my own castle."

"A cursed castle no God-fearing man should want," Alfred said with unmistakable jealousy in his voice.

Emboldened by the other man's bitterness, Edward peered over Sir Roger's head and fixed Alfred with a stern look. "You'll call me Sir Edward of Tannersfield, not 'sheriff's boy'."

Scowling into his wine, Alfred turned and walked away, leaving Edward with enough space to continue warming himself by the fire. It would have been more pleasant without Sir Roger lurking at the periphery of his vision, but at least the ugly knight didn't insist on talking to him.

Alfred wasn't the only one of Duke Francis's knights that looked down on Edward. Few considered him their equal, for he had neither come from a noble family nor squired for one. They thought him a dullard; a glorified man-at-arms grown fat on the sheriff's patronage. Never mind that in tending to the sheriff's men as a youth Edward had learned almost everything a squire would, including how to fight better than most knights. He itched for the day a tournament would be held in Cairnford. Then he'd have his chance to humiliate Alfred and everyone else who looked down on him.

The rain in Edward's hair had just about dried when the doors opened to admit the king's entourage. He jostled to get a good look through the crowd. King Fendrel's party was not much to behold. His knights were damp and plainly dressed, and the boy himself was short even for his middling teenage years. He had small dark eyes that flitted about the room like a nervous rabbit. Short blonde hair that was almost the same colour as his circlet covered his brow. He tried to walk with his shoulders back and his chin up, but the effect was that of a child dressed in his father's clothing. Edward supposed that wasn't far from the truth. Cardinal Tybalt and the bishop of Cairnford walked behind Fendrel, the former dressed in vivid green robes that contrasted strikingly with the polished brass skull cap that denoted his status as a monarch of the church.

If Edward could muster the courage, he would have to speak with Tybalt about Lady Kaylein later. Father Gregory had proven useless in his endeavour to have her expelled, and the letters he'd been sending to the bishop of Tannersfield seemed to be going nowhere.

The crowd parted to make way for the king. Fendrel sat in Francis's chair on the opposite side of the fire pit while the duke made do with the seat to his left. Cardinal Tybalt remained standing behind Fendrel, no doubt choosing a position that would make it easy for him to whisper in the young king's ear.

Once everyone had settled down, the discussions began. Just as Edward had suspected, the purpose of the king's court was to discuss Alistair and Larmond's brewing rebellion. As Duke Francis explained the situation to the assembly, Roger Half-Face leaned over to murmur in Edward's ear.

"I hear the duke wanted this meeting to happen in Rosepath. Your castle's one of the closest to where Alistair and Larmond are supposed to be. But the king wouldn't have it. His priests want to forget all about what happened there. The least they could do is admit who they killed to help put Fendrel on the throne."

The man's impudence surprised Edward, but it made sense when he remembered that Roger was one of Count Leo's former knights. He'd heard from Gwayne that Roger's home town of Kinedwyn lay on a distant northern edge of Tannersfield county, bordering on inhospitable hills and woodland where it was said only outlaws and druids lived. Edward tried to ignore Roger and focused on what the others were saying.

Much to Duke Francis's growing consternation, Fendrel and the clergy seemed reluctant to do anything about Alistair and Larmond.

"There has been little in the way of actual rebellion," the bishop of Cairnford pointed out. "Larmond burned a handful of mountain farms at first, but he's been quiet for almost a year since then. Our biggest concern is that we do not know what he wants, and since he refuses to communicate with us we have no way of finding out."

"We could meet him with an army and bring him to the king's court to answer for his disobedience," the count of Farrenwold, a dark-bearded, portly young man, said.

"That would invite war," said Francis.

"War would put an end to this. Isn't that what you want? It wouldn't even take a real battle. Larmond and Alistair can't stand against a united royal army. They'd surrender at the sight of anything bigger than a peasant militia."

"But we don't yet know where they are or how many men they have rallied to their cause. We need to send scouting parties into the moors west of Tannersfield—trained ones this time. We must have accurate information before we decide how to act."

"They can't have an army with them," the count of Farrenwold said. "There aren't enough villages in that part of the kingdom to feed more than a few hundred men."

"Which means they're likely to be travelling light, probably rallying support from other lords before they try to muster an army," Francis argued. "They've had plenty of time to sow the seeds of rebellion. If we send an army to find them, who's to say Larmond won't retreat to the mountains and have his own force assembled by the time we reach him? We can't attack them at home in the marches, not unless we want to spend a year sieging the very castles we built to keep our borders safe."

Cardinal Tybalt leaned forward, and in a soft voice said: "War is not the way of God, nor is it the will of our king." He looked to Fendrel for confirmation, and the boy gave a grateful nod. "Every effort must be made to keep the kingdom from tearing itself apart. Internal division makes us weak to our foreign enemies. If wars are to be fought, let them happen beyond our borders. Larmond and Alistair's misdeeds can be forgiven if they can be persuaded to return

414

home and resume their duty as vassals of the crown."

"Then what does the king suggest we do?" Duke Francis asked. He spoke courteously, but Edward could see the strain on his face. Despite being in agreement with Francis about not rushing into a dangerous and costly civil war, Tybalt was offering no solutions of his own. The cardinal was a man of inaction, more interested in building churches than quelling rebellion. Edward wondered whether Francis had been wise in his choice of allies. The kingdom could easily go to ruin under men like Tybalt, so fearful of bloodshed that they'd been afraid to even meet at Rosepath Castle.

"Perhaps Duke Francis is right?" Fendrel said hesitantly. His voice was high and thin, not yet broken into manhood. "We could send scouts and gather more information."

Mildly, the bishop added: "If Duke Francis's son could be found then Marquess Alistair might be placated with a groom for his daughter at long last. Without his aid, Larmond's cause would be severely weakened."

Francis's steely eyes twitched in the firelight. Everyone could tell the discussion had grown tense. To Edward's relief, the king called for a recess so the court could eat and discuss their concerns before resuming that afternoon. As Edward listened to the nobles talk, he got the sense that most of them wanted to bargain with Alistair and Larmond by offering prestigious marriages and accompanying dowries to the marquesses' children. Edward thought that was a stupid idea. It hadn't worked with Isaac; why should it work now? The only thing he liked was the prevailing idea that a network of spies should be assembled to keep the king abreast of Alistair and Larmond's movements. So far they'd had to rely on weeks-old news from lesser lords, often coming second-hand from peasants who'd seen Larmond passing through their villages. Edward wanted to volunteer himself for the job. He fantasised about riding out into the wilderness, bringing back dire news of a mustering army, and leading his men to face them at the king's vanguard.

415

He voiced his thoughts to Francis over a platter of pork and honeyed plums.

"You can't leave Rosepath undefended," the duke said.

"Of course not, my lord, but you know my men are well suited to this task. We're in the right spot for it, and Stephen is the best tracker in the county."

Francis grunted and took another bite of his food. He seemed distracted. Edward followed his gaze across the room and realised why. Cristiana, now dressed properly, had just come downstairs leading her mother by the arm. The duchess Gwendolyn rarely attended her husband's court, but when she did she had a habit of making a scene. With wide eyes and too-prominent cheekbones, she had an eye-catching look that was the result of something other than womanly beauty. Her curly black hair had been as dark as her husband's was light before pale grey began to steal its colour.

"Damnable woman," Francis said under his breath. He'd probably told her to stay upstairs during the king's visit.

"Lady Cristiana will take care of her," Edward said.

"She'll try her best."

A nervous thought occurred to Edward as he gazed at the duke's daughter. "The nobles are talking about arranging marriages to make peace with Alistair and Larmond. You wouldn't offer them Cristiana, would you?"

"Larmond has at least one unwed son that I know of."

"But after what happened with Isaac—" Edward bit his tongue mid-sentence when Francis gave him a sharp look.

"I doubt Larmond would want Cristiana, anyway," Francis conceded. "Alistair certainly doesn't. I offered her to him before Isaac. She is a difficult daughter to find matches for."

"Why?" Edward asked, bemused. "She's beautiful."

"And wilful. She has inherited the best of me and the worst of her mother. That makes for an impetuous woman. So far she has made three promising matches change their minds at the last moment. She besieges suitors with questions

416

as if she means to take over their estates the moment she moves in. She makes no secret of the fact that she intends to wield all the power afforded to her as a nobleman's wife. I have tried ordering her to hold her tongue, but–" Francis trailed off. He looked troubled, perhaps even a little fearful. It was a mood that often came over him when he spoke of his children these days. Could it be that he feared driving Cristiana away like Isaac by forcing her into an inappropriate marriage? His reputation would be irreparably ruined if it happened again.

"Perhaps you will have to marry her to a lesser lord instead," Edward said hopefully.

"Perhaps so. I often wish my son had been more like her and she more like him. It does a woman no favours to possess a man's spirit."

Edward agreed, but only in part. He would have liked Cristiana to be demure with him that night in his chamber, but her defiance had lit a fire in him that he couldn't extinguish. It would be such a thrill to tame that spirit.

"Go and keep an eye on them, would you?" Francis said, motioning to his wife and daughter. "Let the duchess gossip to you so her voice doesn't offend anyone else's ears."

"Of course, my lord." Edward was excited for the chance to speak with Cristiana again. He crossed the hall and put himself in the duchess's path, bowing to her first and then Cristiana.

"Sir Edward," Cristiana said, offering him a polite yet maddeningly dispassionate curtsey. She looked at her mother and said a little louder: "Mother, this is Sir Edward. Do you recall?"

Duchess Gwendolyn stared down her nose at him and asked bluntly: "How old are you?"

"Twenty-one, milady."

"Knights shouldn't be so young. You were even younger when you came to serve my husband, weren't you?"

Edward cast a sideways smile at Cristiana. "The duke has

a fine eye for talent."

"Stop looking at her. What talents do you have?"

Edward tried not to let the duchess aggravate him. He reminded himself that this was his lord's wife and the mother of the woman whose affections he coveted. "I am the lord of Rosepath Castle. It was my sword that defeated the duke's enemies there."

Gwendolyn regarded him with sudden interest. "Were you present when Count Leo died?"

"Mother," Cristiana said, "are you sure you want to speak of such things in the king's presence?"

"The king is not listening to us." Fendrel was far out of earshot, separated from them by several layers of conversation. Most people were attempting to ignore Francis's wife, for they knew her troublesome reputation, but a few curious knights were listening in. "How did he die?" Gwendolyn asked. "Was my husband the one to do it?"

"He was, milady," Edward said. "He slew Leo before he could even draw his sword."

"Do you think it pleased him?"

"Milady?"

"I said do you think it pleased my husband to kill Count Leo."

Edward wondered whether she was trying to pull him into some trap by making him say the wrong thing. He didn't like it when women outsmarted him. Had she not been of noble birth, Gwendolyn's attitude might have earned her the reputation of a witch or a madwoman.

"I think it pleased him as much as it pleases any man to slay a hated enemy," Edward said carefully.

Gwendolyn laughed. It was a shrill, barking noise that forced a momentary lull in the surrounding conversations as heads turned. "I'd truly like to know. He'll not tell me himself, and all his men are just like you. I think he's afraid to admit it hasn't made him as happy as he hoped it would."

"You're being loud, Mother," Cristiana said, squeezing the

duchess's arm.

"Calling me Mother will not keep me any quieter, *Daughter.*"

Edward wished Francis had sent someone else to deal with his wife. The woman really was insufferable, and he wasn't getting a chance to speak with Cristiana at all. Why did Gwendolyn have the presumption to question her husband's decisions?

Mercifully, the duchess lowered her voice and leaned in closer to Edward. "He was like you when he was young: a bold and brash man eager to serve his lord. Him, Leo, Larmond, and all the others. They all received titles for putting King Ralf on the throne. You're too young to remember that war, aren't you?"

"Yes, but I would welcome another. Men like me are made for war."

"And only men like you would brag about such things. It's a wonder my husband is not disgusted by the company he keeps."

"That's enough," Cristiana said sharply.

Gwendolyn paid her no attention.

"You insult your lord's knights," Edward blurted out in anger. He immediately regretted it. Fear seized his muscles as Gwendolyn glowered at him. Visions flashed through his mind of the duchess having him flogged for speaking to her in such a manner. To his shame, Cristiana noticed his mortification and came to his rescue.

"Sir Edward is right. You've no place speaking of the honourable men of Cairnford this way."

Gwendolyn let out another shrill bark of laughter. Bizarrely, she seemed to be enjoying herself. She truly was a madwoman.

"You fresh summer flower," Gwendolyn said. "You might think differently of knights were a band of them to break down your bedroom door and deflower you. That was the fate of your father's first fiancée, you know, the night

419

Count Leo took her family's estate during war. Oh, how he has hated him ever since." She threw a mocking look in Edward's direction. "So, did my husband relish it when he finally put his sword through the man who spoilt his beloved; the woman he truly wanted before he was forced to settle for me? Did he ravish Leo's wife in front of him, just to remind him of it?"

Cristiana's cheeks had grown flushed. Even she seemed at a loss for words now. Edward cleared his throat and said: "The duke is an honourable man."

"Honourable men do wicked things all the time. You cannot tell me my husband's men left the people of Rosepath untouched when they swept through the village."

"That is the way of war. It's not something women would understand."

Gwendolyn laughed again, though more quietly this time. "No, I suppose we don't. I hope my husband took some satisfaction in his revenge, however fleeting it may have been. Certainly nothing else good has come of Rosepath."

Edward tried to force a placating smile, but all he could manage was a grimace. As eccentric as Duchess Gwendolyn was, he didn't doubt the truth of her words. He'd heard rumours about Francis being engaged to someone else in his youth, but never anything about what had happened to the woman. If she'd been abused by Count Leo's men it would explain the hatred Francis harboured toward him. Edward tried to imagine what it would feel like if someone did that to Cristiana. What if, rather than being punished for it, the culprit had been rewarded with land and titles? A familiar hatred writhed in his gut, twisting through him like a serpent. No wonder Francis had ordered such a brutal attack on Leo's family. Edward would have done the same. The duke had waited more than twenty years for his chance, and the brief power vacuum created by King Ralf's death had finally given it to him.

Edward's grimace gave way to a smile as he remembered

the people he'd killed that night. If only he'd known the truth of Leo's villainy he never would've suffered those awful dreams about what he'd done. There had been justice in it after all. A feeling of euphoria took hold of him, calling to mind the disturbing glee he'd taken the day he ordered Alderic to hold the outlaw girl's head in the fire. He'd been guilt-ridden after that, too, but now he realised there had been no reason for him to feel that way. The desire to hurt those people had come from a place of honour—from a desire to serve his lord and the king. There was no shame in that, just as there was no shame in Francis taking revenge on Leo. Anger could be a righteous thing.

Edward's animosity towards Gwendolyn evaporated. In her own strange way, she had revealed a comforting truth to him. He walked to the duchess's side and offered her his arm in place of Cristiana's.

"Would you like to hear all the details of what happened at Rosepath, milady?"

Gwendolyn stared at him with something akin to hunger in her eyes. He could tell she despised him, but there was an insatiable desire within the woman to reach out and touch the taboos that propped up her gentle noble life. Madness it might be, but even the mad occasionally turned out to be savants. Gwendolyn let go of her daughter's arm and accepted Edward's.

"We should leave the hall," he said. "Talk of bloodshed is not for the ears of bishops and cardinals."

Gwendolyn nodded. "The rain has stopped. We can walk outside until court resumes."

"Lady Cristiana, will you accompany us?" Edward asked. He felt certain now that he could endear himself to Cristiana. Even if she looked down on him for being a mere knight, she would be enthralled by his passion when he spoke of the justice he'd wrought upon Leo's household. He would be just like her father: firm, ruthless, and immovable in his convictions. The thought of it was almost erotic.

Cristiana took a step back and crossed her arms. "No, thank you. I am sure you will take fine care of my mother on your own, Sir Edward."

He was disappointed, but he tried not to let it show. There would be other opportunities for them to spend time together. If she was as difficult to find a match for as Duke Francis said, he would have plenty of time to prove himself worthy.

The sky above the keep was as dreary as ever, but the stone walls kept the wind off them while they made a slow circuit of the small compound. As Edward recounted everything he remembered about the battle of Rosepath, he began to wonder whether there was some wisdom in the lectures on patience and humility Father Gregory was so fond of boring him with. He had learned something about himself today through enduring Duchess Gwendolyn's company. Duke Francis would surely be pleased with him for keeping her away from the other nobles by satiating her lust for tales of the explicit and macabre.

Sure enough, when they returned to the keep Gwendolyn quickly tired of the king's court and went upstairs without causing any more trouble. Edward practically glowed with joy when Cristiana gave him a nod of thanks before following after her. He found it easy to sit through even the dullest parts of the meeting after that. The talk went on for what seemed like hours. Many of the other knights broke off and began talking amongst themselves in the corners, but Edward took pride in standing resolutely near the fire pit all afternoon.

Court had begun to adjourn when Francis beckoned him aside so that they could speak privately.

"What was my wife barking about earlier?" he asked. "She was turning half the heads in the room."

Edward decided it would be best not to touch his lord's temper by telling him the whole truth.

"Nothing important. She wanted to hear about battles and

bloodshed, so I thought it best to take her outside."

"You did well. You're a reliable man when you do as you're told." Francis paused for a moment, then said: "The king needs to be informed of Larmond and Alistair's movements each week. Every few days, if possible. If you still think your men are up to the task, the duty is yours."

"It would be my honour."

"Good. I'll send Sir Alfred to Rosepath with some of his men to assist you."

"The castle is already full up," Edward said. It was a lie; he could easily have found space for another dozen people in the keep alone, but he didn't want Sir Alfred feeling like he was his equal. "They'll have to find lodgings in the village."

Francis nodded. "It's your village. You can put them wherever you want."

Edward would make sure Alfred enjoyed his time in Rosepath next to the stink of a dyer's house or a pig pen.

He bowed graciously. "I will not fail the king."

"See that you don't."

There was one last thing Edward wanted to do before court adjourned for the day. Mustering his courage, he approached Cardinal Tybalt and caught the holy man's eye during a break in the conversation. Having slipped into the manner of conducting himself at court, Edward inquired courteously about how the cardinal's son was enjoying his new house in Tannersfield. During the pleasantries, he mentioned how there had been some trouble with the builders last summer, but through his timely intervention he had seen to it that the culprit was flogged and order restored.

"There was another disturbance, too," Edward said. "A nun tried to interfere with the sheriff's business. She was insolent to me, and despite my repeated inquiries her prioress refuses to expel her."

Tybalt listened as Edward explained the situation with Kaylein. He seemed a shrewd man, quickly deducing that he was being asked a favour. Placing a hand on Edward's wrist, he said: "Duke Francis wants you to inform us of Marquess Larmond's activities, is that right? The disciplining of novice nuns is not normally a cardinal's business, but if you are the man responsible for maintaining law and order on my son's estate then it appears I owe you a debt of gratitude." He looked Edward in the eye. "Bring us news of Larmond, and I may find time to send a letter to the bishop of Tannersfield on your behalf."

Edward bowed deeply. "You have my highest assurance, Father. For the glory of God, I will see it done."

CHAPTER 28

A tentative hope appeared to be brewing in Tannersfield for the coming spring. It was a weary feeling, perhaps born of simple exhaustion amongst the townspeople. They were tired of packed streets, dangerous roads, hard winters, and repeated curfews. Perhaps this year, things would change. There was an old saying that when a bucket hit the bottom of a well, it had nowhere else to go but up.

The town needed its hopes. Several waves of sickness had swept through Tannersfield over the past year, the most aggressive of which had arrived during the heart of winter. Isaac had been shocked when he returned to town after a week of riding to see bodies being dragged out of alleyways as carts heaped with dead travelled from door to door. He'd found Elizabeth shivering by Joseph's fire that day, but warm strew and thick blankets had been enough to help her fight off the illness. Tannersfield's old and infirm had not been so lucky, to say nothing of the homeless. The priests called the blight God's punishment for the town's many sins; it was a great scouring, justly earned and long overdue.

Isaac wasn't swayed by the preachers, and neither was Sister Kaylein. The pair of them had talked several times over the winter and found they shared a great deal in common. Kaylein did not believe the sickness was a punishment from God because it afflicted the wicked and the vulnerable indiscriminately. Those who were already weak suffered worst, and that was not the act of a kind and just god. She grew yet further convinced when Isaac told her how he'd encountered the same thing in other towns during his travels. The larger a settlement was, the more common it seemed for sickness to run rampant. The idea intrigued Kaylein, and they spent all afternoon discussing it at Joseph's workshop. If sickness did not come from God, perhaps it was spawned by evil deeds; a drifting miasma that rose from sites of concentrated sin like steam from boiling water. Or perhaps it was more like the weather, a cycle that came and went in tune with the seasons.

Kaylein was fascinated by the invisible workings of the world that could only be explained through religion or science. When she was not debating theology with Isaac, she talked about the books she'd read on medicine and surgery. Nuns often served as nurses, though they were not regarded as having the expertise of trained physicians or barber-surgeons. Academic though their discussions were, it was nice having another educated person he could talk to.

By the end of winter, Isaac concluded that Kaylein was not plotting any kind of rebellion against his father. She eventually confided in him that she hoped to write a book of her own someday, one that would denounce the relationship of the church with ruthless lords like Duke Francis. That seemed to be the extent of her ambitions, and Isaac did not think a book could do any real harm. It was a weight off his mind, for he liked Kaylein.

He'd planned on leaving Tannersfield once he put those worries to rest, but even with his doubts settled, something held him back. It had been over a year since he ran away from his wedding to Lady Emilia. Sam and Kaylein were no longer passing acquaintances, they were his friends. Even

Elizabeth's frosty attitude seemed to be thawing. Joseph Carpenter had never forgotten Isaac's help with young Fred, and he always greeted him with a smile and offered him supper when he visited the workshop.

Since losing his job at the building site, Isaac had cultivated a quiet reputation as a courier with a few of Tannersfield's merchants, though he was cautious not to advertise his services to anyone who might bring up his name at the sheriff's court. Merchants always had orders to place, inventories to gather, and letters to send to their partners across the kingdom. A man like Isaac could deliver their correspondence swiftly, reliably, and cheaply. The work helped satiate Isaac's lust for adventure and provided him with enough money to take care of himself and Blackberry. He got to spend long hours in the company of his beloved horse, and she adored the chance to stretch her legs after spending so much of the previous year stabled. He found himself wondering some days whether he could live like this forever. So long as he had his freedom, he didn't think he would mind it. Pangs of regret followed him when he thought about his mother and Cristiana, but aside from that, there was precious little he missed about his noble life. People like Elizabeth and Sam would have thought him mad for giving up stone walls, servants, and a well-stocked pantry to live in a draughty farm hut. Perhaps he was a little mad. People had always said he took after his mother. Yet it seemed to Isaac that the best way to live life was somewhere in the middle, neither as a noble nor a serf, but as a free man with a stable livelihood. No shackles and no obligations. That was where true freedom lay.

Everyone's spirits lightened when winter faded and the days grew longer. Isaac sat in a quiet public house on the east edge of Tannersfield sharing ale with Sam, Elizabeth, and Kaylein. Fred Fielder had come along too and was eyeing the dregs of a sleepy monk's cup, for he had failed to beg a spare penny for a drink of his own that evening.

427

It had been difficult to get Kaylein into a public house at first, for she took her vows very seriously. While there was no direct prohibition against nuns visiting taverns and alehouses, many such businesses had reputations as dens of sin. They'd had to find one with an owner who served weak ale and didn't allow gambling or whoring beneath his roof. It was hard for Kaylein to spend time with them, but every couple of weeks she managed to find some errand that necessitated her leaving the nunnery for a few hours. The prioress was lenient with her as long as she got her work done. She could spend her time in the public house writing up inventories of market prices on a slate or drafting letters that required input from Elizabeth and Isaac on local events.

"Do you think people will start selling property again soon?" Isaac asked offhandedly. A year of sickness and an increasingly dire reputation had stymied the problem of overpopulation in Tannersfield, which meant more empty houses and open plots of land.

"Nowhere nice," Elizabeth said from the bench opposite him. "You can find a hovel on the north side of town, but nothing better. You should've seen the grave carts coming out of there in the winter. It was awful."

Isaac didn't much like the sound of living in the northern part of town. "It was just a thought. It would be nice to live somewhere closer to the stables."

"You should find work with the sheriff," Kaylein insisted, looking up from her slate. "Have the merchants vouch for your services. The sheriff could see to it that you have a proper place to live, maybe even somewhere in the castle."

Sam chuckled. "Men like us don't work for the sheriff, Sister."

A look of perplexity crossed Kaylein's face. She was clever enough to have an inkling that Sam and Isaac were not always on the right side of the law, but there was an obliviousness to her that suggested she'd spent precious little time outside her father's castle before becoming a nun. That obliviousness extended to the looks Sam gave her. Everyone except Kaylein knew about his crush. Isaac couldn't blame him. Beneath her dark hood, Kaylein was beautiful. She had a noblewoman's delicateness to her that was exquisitely enticing. She was intelligent, passionate, and shadowed in tragedy. Minstrels wrote songs about women like her. Yet unlike Sam, Isaac was wise enough not to let himself become infatuated with a nun, no matter how pretty she was. It would only end in unrequited longing.

He exchanged a look with Elizabeth, who just shook her head wearily. She'd been fretting over Sam all winter. He was making a fair wage working for Harald Redcloak, who had proven true to his word and paid off Joseph's fine along with helping persuade the guild to overlook Elizabeth's continued employment. Yet the debt made her deeply uncomfortable, and she was worried the sheriff's men would catch her brother collecting Harald's illicit goods from the poachers he dealt with in the forest.

Of all Isaac's friends, the only one he still didn't know quite what to make of was Elizabeth. He admired her work ethic and her level head. She was quick, decisive, and forceful when she needed to be. According to Fred and the other apprentices, she had a mind for business that would have put many a merchant to shame. A degree of rashness and presumption followed her, however, manifesting in a thorny disposition that echoed something of Joseph's wife Rose. For someone born so common, she reminded Isaac of the young lords he'd often seen at his father's court–the ones who were new to authority and still growing into it. Elizabeth struck Isaac as a woman who had yet to explore her limits. Father had always warned him to be wary of such people. They could be bold and foolhardy, making unwanted enemies when they stepped over boundaries they had no business crossing. She'd already had one close run-in with the guild, to say nothing of Sir Edward.

"Even if you wanted to live in town," Elizabeth said,

"prices are still high. Everyone's afraid things will get worse again. And I had another purse stolen last week."

"Are you alright?" Kaylein said with concern.

"Yes. I keep all my real money in my belt." Elizabeth untied the strings of the purse she wore beneath her cloak and dumped its contents on the table. It was full of bent nails and wood chippings.

"Why do you have that in your purse?" Kaylein asked.

"So they'll grab something worthless instead of beating her up and going for her belt," Sam said.

"That's awful. You shouldn't have to wear false purses for thieves."

"I've never had anyone try to steal from me in town," Isaac said.

"That's because you're a man," Elizabeth said as she collected her nails and wood chips. "It probably helps that you've got a horse, too. You look like you could be someone's squire. People who rob men like you get hanged."

"Thieves want easy pickings," Sam said.

"You would know," Elizabeth replied.

The door banged open, throwing in a gust of wind from outside. The sleepy monk whose drink Fred had been eyeing jolted upright, splashing the last of his ale on the floor.

"Is Sam here? Is there a Sam in here?!" Harald Redcloak's breathless voice bellowed. The merchant staggered into the house, his cap clutched in one hand while the other wiped sweat from his brow. His roving eyes snapped to their table. "There you are. Come here."

Sam began to stand up, but Elizabeth caught his arm.

"What's this about?"

Harald waved Sam over impatiently. "I need your brother."

"What for?"

"Nothing you need worry about. Come on, Sam!"

"Just stay here," Sam said to Elizabeth.

"I'll keep an eye on him," Isaac said, rising to his feet.

430

Harald smiled. "Good. You can help, too. Hurry now, there's a silver penny in it for both of you!"

The promise of money lit a fire beneath Sam's heels. Isaac followed him outside. Dusk had begun to fall, and the street was quiet.

"Down here," Harald said, hurrying down the street at a jog. "There's some trouble with one of our carts."

"What sort of trouble?" Isaac asked. This sounded like exactly the sort of thing Elizabeth didn't want her brother getting involved in.

"Wool sellers. They think they can tell me what I can and can't bring into town. It's all because I'm taking business away from them at market. They can't handle the competition, so they're trying to strong-arm me."

"Don't you have a writ from the sheriff? They can't argue with the law."

"Of course I do," Harald blustered. His face had grown as red as his cap. "But I can't run back to Rosepath and get it right now, can I?"

Isaac wondered whether that was true. Harald should've gone to the sheriff's men instead of his hired hands if the problem could be solved legitimately. They followed the old town wall north until they were near the eastern gate. A group of men stood around a sack-laden cart that had been pulled into an empty yard. There were six of them, two of whom seemed to be guarding the cart while the others menaced them in a semicircle. A pair of town watchmen eyed them from across the road but made no attempt to intervene. Isaac wondered whether Harald or the wool merchants had slipped them a coin to turn a blind eye to whatever was happening. His trepidation grew when he recognised one of the men as Will Shearer, Henry Shearer's youngest son. They'd fled from him and his father the night they stole the wool. He nudged Sam's arm and nodded in Will's direction.

"I see him," Sam murmured.

"Let's hope he doesn't remember us."

431

"We've nothing to worry about," Harald panted. "Just look like you're ready for a fight. They'll back down."

Isaac hoped so. Will Shearer was big and broad-shouldered, with muscles like knotted rope. He looked like he could've upturned Harald's cart with his bare hands.

"Get out of here!" Harald called to the group. "We're taking our cart and leaving."

Will folded his arms and stepped in front of them. "No you're not."

"Are you going to stand in the way all night?" Sam asked.

Will frowned at him for a long moment. Isaac tensed. There was a glimmer of recognition in Will's eyes, but it seemed uncertain, as though he wasn't quite sure where he remembered Sam from. Harald's two carters came to stand with them. They outnumbered Will's group five to four now.

"We'll stand here till curfew." Will Shearer smiled. "Then you'll have to leave your cart where it is."

Harald shot an aggravated glance at the pair of town watchmen across the road. It would take more than a few pennies to keep his wool safe if he was forced to leave it out in the open. Sam tried to step past the men blocking their way, but Will grabbed him by the shoulder and shoved him back.

Isaac wanted to tell Harald to pay off the watchmen and leave his wool till tomorrow. Will Shearer clearly wasn't in the mood to back down, and butting heads with him would only escalate things. But the merchant was stubborn, and he didn't like being pushed around by his competitors. Isaac sensed a fight brewing. He heard footsteps on the road and looked back to see Elizabeth and Kaylein coming around the bend.

"How about we strike a bargain?" Isaac said, racing to think of something before the altercation turned violent. What did he know about merchant competition? Not much, but he'd dealt with the wool sellers a few times during his courier work. He wasn't particularly eager to help Harald out of his predicament, but Elizabeth would never forgive him if

432

he got her brother into a fight. Stalling for time, he asked Will Shearer: "You don't want Harald selling this wool in Tannersfield, is that right?"

"I don't mind honest competition," Will replied. "What I mind is Harald pushing his business where it doesn't belong."

"My lord will hear of this," Harald said.

Will glared at him. "Do you want to take this to the sheriff?"

Harald shut his mouth, trembling with anger.

Hoping the merchant wasn't too furious to catch on to his idea, Isaac motioned him aside and said under his breath: "I don't know why you want to sell in Tannersfield, anyway. Why not take your wool on to Rambirch?" He made sure he was speaking loudly enough for Will to hear.

"I'm not sending my carts another three days down the road when there's a better market right here!"

"Tannersfield market is bigger, but prices are better in Rambirch," Isaac explained. "I was there just last week. You can sell wool like yours for two shillings a yard."

Harald gave him a doubtful look, then his anger cleared as realisation dawned. "Really. I didn't know that."

He didn't know because it wasn't true. While the merchants in Rambirch did get away with higher wool prices than in Tannersfield, Isaac hadn't come across anyone who paid two shillings a yard. Harald made a show of considering what he'd said.

"Who's paying that much for wool?" Will Shearer asked. He'd taken the bait.

"Never you mind," Harald said. "Maybe the lad's right. I don't need to compete with you if I can get better prices elsewhere."

"Hold on." Will stepped in again. "How can people in Rambirch afford to pay that much? I already struggle to sell my mother's cloth here, and no seller in Tannersfield is that expensive."

Isaac raced to think of a good answer, then he

433

remembered what Elizabeth had said earlier about high prices in town. "It's probably because everything else here is so expensive right now. Not as many people are going to buy wool or visit tailors when they need to keep their families fed and their fires burning. Rambirch is better off, so the people there can afford to pay more for wool."

Will looked from Sam to Isaac. "Who's this merchant paying two shillings, then?"

"Don't you tell him!" Harald snapped, still playing along with Isaac's game.

"Will you let the cart past?" Isaac said.

"Tell me the name and we'll see."

Isaac made something up. "Alan Tailor."

"I've never heard of him."

"I don't know every merchant in the county, either."

Will Shearer snorted, then gestured for his friends to step aside. Isaac tried not to let his relief show. He hoped Harald wasn't planning on selling any more wool in Tannersfield, because the same trick wasn't likely to work on Will a second time.

Harald gave Sam an approving grin as the two carters began moving his goods out of the yard. "Clever friend you have there," he said under his breath. "They'd never have believed that coming from me. Here." He loosened his purse strings and gave them each a penny. They were copper, not the silver he'd promised. "I'll buy you both some ale if you want, and a pair of women. It's been a long day."

Isaac shook his head. "No, thank you."

Harald shrugged. "Sam will join me, won't you?" He looked over at Elizabeth and Kaylein, rubbing his lower lip back and forth hungrily. "And what about that sister of yours? She owes me a favour. Do you think she'd come with me for a silver penny?"

"I doubt it," Sam said. "She doesn't do that."

"Your mother did. What about two silver pennies?"

To Isaac's distaste, Sam actually turned around and went

to ask Elizabeth. Isaac didn't begrudge men whoring, but Harald throwing his money around to try and buy anyone he wanted seemed vile. He could see why Elizabeth didn't like her brother working for the man. Sam returned to tell Harald the bad news after his sister turned him away with a few choice words.

"That's a shame," the merchant said. "Do you think Lady Kaylein would come to my room instead if I promised to build her a church?" He gave a throaty chuckle. "I might even do it, just to imagine the look on her dead father's face. That bastard was always making life hard for me."

"I'm sure your new lord's much better," Isaac said drily.

"Much. As long as there's money coming to him, he's happy with anything. A man like that's a merchant's dream."

Isaac bit back a response. He wanted to ask Harald what he thought Sir Edward would do if he caught him trading with poachers in the forest. Everyone knew Edward had a brutal reputation when it came to dealing with outlaws.

Harald left with his cart and Sam made to follow, but Isaac caught him by the arm.

"What?" Sam said. "He promised me a drink and a woman."

"You've already got a drink waiting for you back at our bench, and wouldn't you rather sit with Kaylein a while longer?"

A stupid look came over Sam's face as he gazed at Kaylein. "You're right. It'll help me keep her in my dreams till we see each other again."

They headed back toward the women, but Isaac hesitated when he saw that Will Shearer was still standing at the side of the road. He'd been looking at them for a while. The pair of town watchmen had left. Will waited till Harald's cart had disappeared around the corner, then whistled in their direction and strode forward.

"What do you suppose he wants?" Isaac asked.

"Maybe to hear that merchant's name again?"

He did not. The second they were within reach, Will lunged. Sam tried to duck the punch, but it came too fast. The blow cracked the side of his temple so hard he staggered sideways, tripped, and hit the ground face-first. Isaac tried to catch him, but Sam's weight threw him off balance and Will grabbed him by the front of the shirt. He braced himself for a blow, expecting Will's fist to break his nose at any moment.

"Stop!" Kaylein's shrill voice called down the street. "In God's name, stop!"

Will hesitated. In an instant, Elizabeth was beside them, knife in hand. Will's confidence left him at the sight of the blade. He snarled in Isaac's face and shoved him away. "If I see the pair of you near the farm again, you're dead." He turned and ran, leaving Isaac to pick up his fallen friend.

"I suppose he recognised us after all," Isaac groaned.

Sam didn't answer. He was still stunned from Will's punch, sprawled on the road with his limbs tangled. Isaac put an arm beneath his shoulders and patted his face. His brow creased with worry. Sam's head was lolling on a limp neck, his eyes half-lidded and blank.

"Kaylein," he called. She was the only one who knew anything about healing.

"Don't let his head move like that," she said anxiously, hurrying to Sam's side. "He probably hit it again when he fell."

Isaac eased his friend down and stopped trying to wake him up. Elizabeth crouched beside them, her eyes wide with fear.

"Is he dead?"

Kaylein put a hand on Sam's chest and brought her ear to his lips. "No."

Elizabeth's shoulders sagged with relief. "I knew something like this would happen. I knew it wouldn't be long."

"We should take him inside," Isaac said.

"Yes," Kaylein agreed, "but don't pick him up in your

arms. We should have a carrying litter for him."

"Where will we get one of those?" Elizabeth asked, her voice tight with frustration.

"Perhaps the monastery?"

Isaac knew the monks wouldn't let them in at this time of day. They would all be reciting their evening hymns. They could take Sam to the infirmary, but Isaac didn't have enough money on him to pay for it, and he doubted Elizabeth did either.

"Couldn't we put him on a board from the workshop?" he suggested.

"Yes," Kaylein said. "I think that would do."

Isaac and Elizabeth hurried back down the street, calling Fred out of the public house on their way past. He went to keep an eye on Kaylein while they fetched the board. It wasn't far to the workshop, but finding a straight board big enough to carry someone proved difficult. Joseph asked what in the world they were doing as they hauled stacks of wood out of the storage shed. Isaac offered a breathless explanation as he hefted the broadest board he could find beneath his arm and followed Elizabeth back up the street.

Sam still hadn't regained consciousness when they returned. As delicately as they could, they lifted him so that his back rested along the length of the board. Elizabeth bundled her cloak beneath his head. Isaac and Kaylein lifted one end of the plank while Elizabeth and Fred took the other. A few onlookers had gathered in the doorways by then, but no one offered any help. They probably didn't want to get involved with whatever trouble Harald Redcloak and Will Shearer had started.

Not knowing where else to take him, they brought Sam to the workshop. Elizabeth looked ashamed when she met Joseph's eye, but most of her concern was centred on her brother. Isaac knew she felt perpetually guilty about all the trouble she kept bringing to her master's door. If Joseph was upset, he gave no sign of it, opening the door so they could bring Sam into his house. They put him down on Elizabeth's mattress near the fire. Rose began filling bowls of pottage for everyone, but no one seemed hungry. Elizabeth hadn't stopped fretting at her brother's side.

"What if he doesn't wake up?"

"I'm not sure," Kaylein said. "I don't know what to do for him besides keeping him still and praying. It's dangerous to bleed people for head wounds."

"We'll need to find a physician," Isaac said.

Kaylein agreed. "He should be in the monks' infirmary."

"If he doesn't wake up, we'll take him first thing in the morning," Elizabeth said. "I have some money saved." From the tone of her voice, Isaac suspected she'd be sacrificing a lot. The infirmary was not cheap, and Elizabeth treasured every penny she had. Depending on how long Sam had to stay, she might end up burning through months of savings. It didn't sit right with Isaac. Tomorrow he would go and dig up the money he kept buried in the forest. He hated the idea of being penniless again, but that would be a small price to pay if it meant saving Sam's life.

"What about if Harald puts up the money?" he suggested. "This wouldn't have happened if it wasn't for him."

"Or if you and Sam hadn't stolen from Will's father in the first place," Elizabeth said.

Kaylein gave them a concerned look before returning to wetting Sam's lips with a damp cloth. Elizabeth's scorn hurt Isaac. She should have been angry at Harald, not him.

"I'm going to go and speak with him," Isaac said. "He got Sam into this. He should be the one who makes it right."

"You won't have any luck," Elizabeth said bitterly. "Harald doesn't have a decent bone in his body."

Isaac suspected she was right, but he wasn't going to let his friend suffer while he stood around doing nothing. He felt sick when he looked at Sam's still body and lax expression. For better or worse, Sam was the one person who'd been with him since he left Rosepath. The thought of him dying or being rendered an invalid filled Isaac with a horrible uncertainty he hadn't felt since his ill-fated wedding. He wasn't going to dawdle and agonise this time. He needed to do something.

"Will you stay and pray for him?" Elizabeth asked Kaylein.

Isaac turned away to hide the look of misgiving on his face. He didn't have any faith in the healing power of prayer. He'd seen people pray to all sorts of gods, and it seemed to succeed and fail at random. Sick people needed physicians, not prayers.

Dusk was falling on the streets of Tannersfield when Isaac went outside. There wouldn't be much time for him to find Harald before the town watch started enforcing curfew. Rather than letting fear take hold of him, he focused on the sting of his indignation instead. Deep down he knew the fight had been just as much his and Sam's fault as it had Harald's, but in the moment it was easy to see Harald as the villain.

Most of Tannersfield's merchants kept their goods in the storehouses near the marketplace, so that was where Isaac went looking. He found Harald in an expensive tavern across the street with a cup of wine in one hand and a whore's breast in the other.

"You changed your mind," Harald said with a smile, raising his voice over the hubbub when he saw Isaac approaching.

"No, I didn't." Isaac placed his palms on Harald's table and leaned forward menacingly, but then the whore tried to drape her half-naked body over him and he jerked back upright, startled by her attention.

The merchant laughed. "You don't like women?"

"That's not what I'm here for." Isaac tried to marshal his composure. "Will Shearer attacked Sam after you left. He nearly broke his head off."

"That's a pity. I thought we did a good job outsmarting him, you and I."

439

"I was the one who outsmarted him. And you promised me more than a copper penny for helping you."

"I think it was just a penny."

"Well, Sam's hurt. We need to take him to the monks."

Harald took an aggravatingly casual swallow of his wine and waited to hear more.

"You need to pay their fee," Isaac demanded. "You owe Sam."

"I don't see how it's my responsibility."

"He was doing you a favour! You wouldn't have got your cart out off that street without us."

Harald's nostrils flared with indignation. "Do you think I can't handle my own business? I paid both of you for your help. Whatever happened afterwards has nothing to do with me."

"Come on, Redcloak. The monks' fee must be pennies to a man like you."

"Can his sister afford it?"

"Yes, but—"

"Then she'll pay it." Harald took another swig of wine and rubbed his lips together. "If she needs more money she can always join Gilia here in my bed." He slid his hand around the whore's waist and pulled her back to his side.

Isaac couldn't believe the man. Even Sam's misfortune was an opportunity for Harald to get his lecherous way.

"You're despicable."

"Watch your tongue, lad," Harald warned.

"What if Will Shearer finds out you don't have a writ to sell wool in Tannersfield? I expect he'd be far more eager to take your dispute to the sheriff then." Isaac smiled at the look of outrage on Harald's face before realising his mistake. Without warning, a hand seized him by the hair and yanked him away from Harald's table. It belonged to one of the carters from earlier.

"I don't want to see you begging work or favours from me again," Harald said. Isaac writhed in the man's grasp, but the second carter appeared and twisted his arm behind him. Harald gave them a nod. "Throw him out. Aim for that heap of horse shit by the door if you can."

They marched Isaac back through the tavern and pushed him over the doorstep. He twisted free and turned around, ready for a fight. One of the men hit him in the stomach. It wasn't as vicious as the blow Will Shearer had given Sam, but it was enough to drive the wind from Isaac's lungs and make him want to vomit. He pitched over in the street with the men's laughter ringing in his ears. Smelling dung, he put out a hand to brace himself before he rolled into the filth. His bowels knotted with pain. He tried to breathe deeply until the discomfort subsided. By the time he had the strength to stand, the men had gone back inside. He leaned against the wall, trying not to listen to the rumble of mocking voices coming from the tavern.

Elizabeth and her brother were right to hate people like Harald. Was this what it was like for them every day, always at the mercy of those with power and money? Not knowing what else to do, he limped back to the stables and slipped the owner a penny to let him sleep in the hay with Blackberry. Before he fell asleep, he offered up a quick prayer for Sam.

Not that he thought it would do any good.

CHAPTER 29

Sam would not open his eyes, Elizabeth would not stop worrying, and midnight had passed by the time Kaylein realised how late it was. Curfew or not, she couldn't leave now. She hoped none of the senior nuns would notice her absence, but none of her prayers were wasted on herself that night. Sam was the one who needed God's mercy. The only time he stirred was to splutter on some water Kaylein dripped between his lips, then he retched and vomited. Elizabeth had dozed off against the wall by then. Kaylein was glad she didn't wake up, for her brother's distress would only have upset her. She rolled Sam onto his side so he didn't choke and used her wet cloth to wipe the bile from his lips. She hoped it wasn't a sign of imbalanced humours. It was her understanding that injury, especially to the head, could upset the equilibrium of blood and bile within a person the same way sickness could. If Sam was not kept still and allowed to rest, he might wake up with some impediment to his wits or mobility.

Rose came through from the back room and knelt beside her. Kaylein pressed a finger to her lips, indicating Elizabeth's slumbering form.

"He's still asleep?" Rose whispered.

"He is."

"That's not good. A bang on the head should only put a man out for a moment or two."

"But his heart and breathing are strong."

Rose set a fresh pot of water above the hearth to boil and took away the bowl Kaylein had used to clean up Sam's vomit. "Do you care for him?"

"Of course I do. He is Elizabeth's half-brother."

"That isn't what I meant. I know you're a nun, but even nuns have blood in their veins."

Kaylein was confused. "I don't know what you mean."

"Haven't you seen the way he looks at you?" Rose studied her for a moment, then realisation dawned. "Oh, you've never been with a man."

Kaylein flushed. She quite liked Sam, but she'd never considered that he might be attracted to her. He just seemed interested in her company and the things she had to say. But now that she thought about it, it was different from the way Isaac behaved around her. Isaac liked to debate and exchange ideas. Sam was warmer and simpler. He'd sat listening to her read a page of scripture once, and when she finished he'd asked her to read it again. He said it was like listening to a song without a rhyme; a conversation without stops and starts. Something about that had flattered her.

Rose smiled. "Well, you're not a sworn nun yet. Maybe one day he'll change your mind."

Kaylein didn't say anything. She felt very uncomfortable with Rose kneeling beside her. Folding her hands in prayer, she closer her eyes and resumed her vigil. After reciting several pleas for Sam's health, she opened one eye and saw that Rose had gone back to bed. Breathing easy again, she stole a glance at Sam's face. It embarrassed her to watch him sleep after what Rose had said. It seemed inappropriate somehow. Even though she had no intention of breaking her vows, a flush of shame still warmed her cheeks when she

443

rested a damp rag across his brow. Her fingertips brushed his forehead momentarily, and she jerked back as if she'd touched a hot coal. She was being silly. Sam needed her prayers, not fears about the temptation of sin.

Perhaps it was not temptation. The source of her nervousness might have more to do with Sam's past. She remembered him being a troublemaker from her time in Rosepath, and earlier that evening Elizabeth had mentioned him stealing wool. Kaylein wasn't sure how to feel about that. It reminded her of when she'd learned Elizabeth's mother was a whore. She knew it had been wrong to judge Liz for her mother's sins, but at the time she'd reacted instinctively. A similar feeling had taken hold of her now, conjoined with another, far more confusing one.

Was it wrong to feel a hint of flattery from a thief's affections?

Whether Sam was a sinner or not, Kaylein was duty-bound to pray for his recovery; that part, at least, did not trouble her. It was the thought of being romantically admired by such a man that got under her skin. Sam seemed a decent enough person, if sometimes crude and improper the way commoners were wont to be. But if he was a criminal, what did it say about her that she attracted such men?

She tried not to dwell on those thoughts. They were selfish at a time when selflessness was needed. Perhaps her existential worries were a blessing in their own strange way, for they helped keep her awake as she maintained her vigil.

Shortly after dawn, Sam stirred. A desperate groan left his lips, and he raised a hand to cover his eyes. Kaylein put her hands on his shoulders to stop him getting up.

"You must not move," she whispered. "How do you feel?"

"It's too bright. I need to piss."

He probably needed water more than anything, if his cracked voice was anything to go by. Kaylein gently tipped a bowl against his lips, and he drank it empty. Each time Sam tried to move, waves of faintness came over him, reinforcing Kaylein's suspicion that his humours were unsettled. He was groggy and difficult to understand, and he kept complaining about the light. Kaylein couldn't fathom why it was bothering him so much. It was barely dawn, and the glow of the fire was soft and gentle, yet Sam found it agonising. She thought it would be unwise to move him away from the warmth, so she put the rag she'd been using for his head over his eyes instead. To her relief, that settled him down.

"Have you been awake all night?" Elizabeth asked when she awoke, roused by the sound of her brother's voice.

"I think he may be recovering," Kaylein said. Her own weariness was not worth worrying Elizabeth over. "But moving his head bothers him, and he can't stand the light. I don't think he can manage a trip to the infirmary."

Elizabeth leaned over and touched Sam's brow. Poor Liz. She'd been without family for years, and barely a few months after reuniting with her brother she'd almost lost him again.

"Did Isaac come back?"

Kaylein shook her head. "I don't suppose he had any luck with the merchant."

"I'm going to find a physician anyway. If we can't bring Sam to the monastery, someone will have to come to us."

"I'll stay with him while you're gone."

"Don't be silly. What about the convent? Rose can sit with him. You look exhausted."

"Joseph and Rose have to work. My only work is for God, and He needs someone to watch over Sam." In truth, Kaylein was weary and anxious to get back, but her duty here seemed more important now. She'd never helped another person like this before; it had always been others helping her. The nuns might not understand, but God would.

Despite her best efforts to stay awake, she dozed off several times that morning. The monk Elizabeth returned with proved to be of little help. He only told them what Kaylein had already deduced: that Sam should be kept still and allowed to rest. Sam began mumbling and complained that he needed to relieve himself again. Kaylein was too embarrassed to know what to do about that, so she stared into the corner while Elizabeth fetched a bucket and helped him go.

Sam was more lucid in the afternoon, but the light still bothered him. He complained of terrible pain and nausea, and he kept trying to get up despite Elizabeth and Kaylein's insistence that he had to rest. They tried talking to him, but he struggled to hold a conversation for long before losing its thread. The only thing that succeeded in soothing him was when Kaylein read scripture from the pages she'd been bringing Elizabeth. They'd accumulated quite a collection by now, many of them covered in Kaylein's own thoughts on the nature of God and the church. She read through every page, then started over again from the beginning. Eventually, Sam dozed off to the sound of her voice. Kaylein ate some of Rose's pottage and fell asleep by the hearth.

When she woke, it was nighttime again. Elizabeth had brought in some extra straw to lie on and looked like she was asleep. Someone had wrapped a blanket around Kaylein's shoulders and put one of Rose's feather cushions beneath her head. When she blinked the sleep from her eyes, she saw that Sam was awake and watching her. She startled slightly, and he grinned. He was looking more like his old self again.

"I thought you were an angel reading God's words to me."

Kaylein's skin warmed. "You've taken the rag off your eyes. Are you feeling better?"

"No. A little. The light isn't so bad anymore. Will you read to me again?"

"It's too dark."

"Liz has candles."

Kaylein pressed her lips together uncertainly. Sam didn't seem like he needed soothing with gentle words anymore, but he looked like a hopeful little dog with his wide eyes and winning smile. She hadn't the heart to refuse him. Lighting a candle from the fireplace, she crossed her legs and began reading in a whisper. Unlike the previous night, she no longer felt uncomfortable in Sam's presence. The reading had as much of a calming effect on her as it did him.

Kaylein woke up at noon the next day and realised she needed to return to the convent. Her lack of sleep must have dulled her wits, for she'd been gone almost two days. Her absence would certainly have been noted. They might even have sent the sheriff's men looking for her. What a fool she'd been, not sending a message. She'd grown uncomfortably sweaty beneath her robes during the night, and her legs had fallen asleep. Staggering upright in a daze, she realised that Sam was no longer lying on the mattress. She went outside and found him sitting at Joseph's trestle table with Isaac. He was clutching the seat as if he was worried he might fall off, but otherwise seemed much like his usual self. Relief blunted the edge of Kaylein's anxiety. He was on the mend.

After bidding the boys a hasty farewell, Kaylein went around the side of the workshop and found Elizabeth at work in the yard.

"Isaac paid for the monk yesterday," Elizabeth explained, "so I suppose we're no worse off for it. We're going to keep an eye on Sam till his headaches pass. I can't let him go back to work for Harald after this."

"I'm sure he's in good hands," Kaylein said. "I must return to the convent."

"Thank you." Elizabeth gave her a grateful look, then leaned forward to kiss her on the cheek. "I'm in your debt. Your prayers kept him strong."

Kaylein didn't think Elizabeth could ever be in her debt after all she'd done for her, but she wasn't about to stop and argue. Her attention was focused on what she was going to say when she got back to the convent. People might get the wrong idea when they learned she'd gone to a carpenter's

447

house to tend a young man for two nights in a row. Now that Sam was past the worst of his ailments, she spared a brief prayer for herself as she hurried back across town. She felt as if everyone in the marketplace was staring at her, curious as to why a dishevelled nun with straw on her robe was in such a rush.

Sister Grace opened the convent door when Kaylein arrived, and she slipped in with a sheepish dip of her head.

"Where have you been?" the red-haired nun whispered. "There's an emergency chapter in session about you right now. Mother Jane is trying to find out if anyone knows where you went."

Kaylein hurried through the cloisters. Her heart was in her mouth as she approached the door to the chapter house. It was worse than she'd thought. An emergency meeting meant most of the nuns would have been called away from their work. The entire convent had come to a halt because of her. As she reached up to open the door she noticed her hand was shaking. Everyone would be there to witness her shame. She tried to remember that she was the daughter of Count Leo and Lady Eleanor. Her father would want her to be brave and strong. Yet it wasn't enough. She lowered her hand, drawing a shrill breath. What if she just went to the dormitory and waited for the meeting to be over? Then she could go and find Mother Jane afterwards, avoiding a scene. But the thought of hiding made her feel awful, as if her heart was shrivelling up and receding into something fragile enough to break from the slightest touch. She'd been trying to escape that feeling for two years. She couldn't go back now.

Looking over her shoulder at the statue of Saint Caridwen, she took another deep breath and sought out the glow of God's light within her. She'd done something foolish, but for a good and selfless reason. God and the saints knew that. If she went into the chapter house with her head held high, the others would see it too.

She pushed open the door and went inside.

Mother Jane was standing at the centre of the bench circle with about two-thirds of the convent's sisters gathered around her. Several people were talking at once, indicating that the meeting was a hurried and informal one. The door knocked loudly against the stone wall. All eyes turned in Kaylein's direction. Relief flashed across the prioress's face when she saw her, followed immediately by a look of reproach.

"Sister Kaylein," she said loudly. "Where have you been?"

"Good," Sister Trea, an old, plump, and short-tempered nun said. "We've found her. Now we can get back to work."

"Chapter is still in session, Sister," the prioress said. "Remain seated. Sister Kaylein, come here and explain yourself to the convent."

Kaylein did as she was told. The stares of her sister threatened to steal her courage, but she managed to speak slowly and without faltering when she explained what had happened two days ago.

"What were you doing with these people in a public house?" Sub-Prioress Joan demanded. "You were supposed to be updating our list of market prices."

"I prefer to work indoors. I completed my survey beforehand, so I thought there would be no harm in sitting with them while I wrote."

"You should have returned to the convent."

"Have you stayed out with these friends of yours before?" Mother Jane asked.

"Yes," Kaylein admitted.

"I wouldn't have expected this of you," said Joan. "You have burdened us all with a great deal of worry, to say nothing of the disruption your absence has caused."

"All the more reason to get back to work," Sister Trea grumbled. "Give her penance and let's be done with it."

There was a murmur of assent from some of the older nuns, but the younger women seemed eager for Kaylein's interrogation to continue. Catching the infallible Lady

449

Kaylein in trouble was an unexpected drama that would no doubt provide a source of gossip in the dormitory for many days to come.

"I'm very sorry," Kaylein said. "I should have sent word."

"You should not have gone to a public house in the first place," Sister Joan said.

Mother Jane raised a hand to stay the growing murmur of voices. "There is no rule against nuns stepping into public houses. The town monks certainly spend enough time in them. I am sure Sister Kaylein believed she was acting charitably by offering to help this injured man, but, as she admits, it was gravely irresponsible of her not to inform the convent. A monk should have been called in her stead, and she should have returned home before dark."

"It was too late to fetch a monk," Kaylein explained, "and Elizabeth couldn't have afforded a physician to watch him all night."

"You were with him all night?" Sister Joan asked. "Alone?"

"No—well, for a time, yes, but only during the next day."

Some of the novices began to snigger. Kaylein knew her face was turning red. She wished the prioress would give her penance and get it over with.

"This is exactly why a monk should have been called," Mother Jane said. "It was deeply inappropriate for you to go into a man's house and stay with him overnight."

"Did he behave untowardly?" Sister Joan demanded. The curls of grey hair poking out from beneath her hood resembled a storm cloud around her tightly-drawn face. For all of her insistence on rules and discipline, Kaylein could tell that part of her hungered for an excuse to lay down the law. A disciplinarian held no power if everyone behaved.

"No!" Kaylein said. "He was injured and I was watching over him. It was nothing but an act of charity." She gave the prioress an imploring look. Surely there was no need to carry on with this? It was only going to make things sound worse than they were. "I am ready to accept my penance, Mother Superior."

Sister Joan glared at her. "The penance will be decided based on the severity of your transgression." It was the sub-prioress herself who had allowed Kaylein to run errands in town. Her pride had clearly been wounded by the realisation that her generosity had been taken advantage of. She would argue for a harsh punishment.

"I believe Sister Kaylein had been forthcoming with us," Mother Jane said. "That being said, discipline and obedience are important virtues for a nun to observe, a novice especially. Your responsibility to God and the convent must come before your own whims. We will discuss your penance now."

"A fortnight of solitary prayer would be fitting," Sister Joan said.

"A birching," Sister Trea suggested. "It'll be over with quicker, and she'll remember it for longer." A few of the novices voiced their agreement. Beating a sister with birch twigs was a far more dramatic punishment. Kaylein shuddered. It wasn't as bad as a flogging, but the principle was the same. The thought of being publicly humiliated before the convent was mortifying. She knew some of the novices thought her a spoilt noblewoman who shirked physical labour and got off lightly with her duties in the writing room. They would be lining up to swing their bundles of birch twigs at her back.

"Sister Kaylein has never flaunted our rules before," Mother Jane said. "I think her studiousness should be taken into consideration before we decide anything."

"Studiousness!" someone said derisively. "She's idle."

Mother Jane gave the woman a stern look, then allowed the other sisters to speak. Most of the senior nuns agreed that solitary prayer would be the most appropriate penance for a woman like Kaylein.

"I concur," the prioress said once everyone had had their

say. "Sister Kaylein is a thoughtful woman, and given time to dwell on her actions I am sure she will come to regret her wrongdoing."

Some of the younger nuns looked disappointed, but the votes were against them. Kaylein was relieved to have been spared the birch, but solitary prayer was a daunting punishment as well. It meant being locked in a cell by herself with no outside contact. She'd seen nuns return from extended periods of confinement looking pale and haunted. It was little different from being thrown in a dungeon.

"One week," Mother Jane said, "should suffice." She gave Kaylein a firm look, but there was a hint of sympathy beneath it. Had the choice been hers alone, Kaylein suspected she would have been lenient, but chapter was a time for communal decisions.

Kaylein lowered her head in deference. Chapter was concluded, and Sub-Prioress Joan led her through the cloisters into the cellar beneath the kitchen. There was one narrow window near the ceiling covered in horn panels that kept out the vermin but only let in a murky smudge of light. By the glow of a candle, Joan guided Kaylein through the barrels and hanging sacks until they came to a solid oak door at the end of the cellar. The room beyond was small and bare save for a bucket in one corner. Kaylein stood still, suddenly wishing she was back upstairs in the cloisters. The cellar had a dry, musty smell of old cheese and the sickly fragrance of fruit that had lain in barrels too long. Sister Joan stood aside and pointed into the empty room.

"You shall remain in prayer for one week. A sister will come to bring food and remove your excrement at dawn and dusk. You will not speak to her, or your penance will be extended."

Kaylein nodded dumbly. Pleading with Joan would only make things worse. She stood there for as long as she dared before forcing herself to walk forward. The sub-prioress closed the door behind her, sealing in the darkness. The air

452

was uncomfortably warm. The ovens in the kitchen must have been right above her. She took a step forward and extended her arm until her fingers brushed against rough stone. Kaylein's breathing quickened. The room was even smaller than she'd thought. There wasn't even space to walk around.

Realising that the warmth and confinement would make her panic if she didn't calm down, she knelt on the hard floor and tried to focus her thoughts on prayer. Her skin prickled. The darkness was horrible. It didn't matter whether her eyes were open or shut, for it made no difference to what she saw.

After what felt like an hour, she could no longer focus. She crawled to the wall and slumped against it, letting out a weary sob. Had it really been an hour, or just a few moments? How would she know when the week was up? The prospect of the endless, unknowable darkness made her panic rise, but then she remembered she could judge the passage of time when the sister came to bring her food twice a day. She would have fourteen visits. If she counted them down one by one, freedom would always feel one step closer.

Kaylein wondered what her friends might be doing. A nun was not supposed to have friends outside her convent. They were distractions from the holy purity of isolation. Was Liz having a good day at the workshop? Was Isaac happy to see Sam awake and lucid? Would Sam keep getting better, or would he relapse again? Kaylein tried not to dwell on what-ifs, but with nothing else to occupy her thoughts, she couldn't help herself. Her mind drifted back to memories of her family. She thought about gauging the passage of time, and how her mother had taught her the concept of hours using a sundial. She'd always kept that sundial in her window, though the light had only been able to catch it for a few hours each day. She wondered whether it was still there, or if one of Duke Francis's men had thrown it away or sold it.

As the intangible hours passed, Kaylein listed between hope, misery, and a breathless feeling of isolation. Prayer was something she could only focus on for so long. She began to understand why the other sisters always left solitary penance looking so disturbed. A birching would have been the more merciful of the two punishments. At some point that night, after a sister had brought her bread and the weakest, warmest beer, she discovered that only one thing could bring her solace in the dark.

She spoke aloud the lines of scripture she had copied out dozens of times in the writing room, and she imagined Sam was there listening to her.

CHAPTER 30

Kaylein's subsequent days in the cellar were every bit as enervating as the first. Isolation was an insidious thing, bringing with it all the devils of thought that were usually dispelled by conversation and hard work. After a time, Kaylein became unsure of whether she was in conflict with her own mind or phantom spirits sent to torment her with all the evils of hell. In those dire moments, even prayer could not bring her solace. As she counted down the number of meals she had left–nine, eight, seven–she tried to sleep as much as possible, for at least in her dreams she was free of her prison. She palmed crumbs of bread from her meals, rationing them out over the course of the day so that she could pretend she was eating something lavish and succulent. This crumb was a honeyed oatcake; that one a bite of juicy duck breast. Such mundane distractions quickly became her whole world. She learned how many stones there were in each wall, where there was a spot of loose mortar she could pick at to pass the time, where the floor was coolest, and where she could press her ear against the door to listen for the sound of people talking in the cellar.

Waking or sleeping, eventually everything felt like a

dream.

After an age of darkness, Sub-Prioress Joan came to let Kaylein out of her cell. The air had never tasted so fresh, the grass around Saint Caridwen's statue had never looked so green, and the overcast sky glowed with a light so pure it felt like God himself was reaching down to touch her.

Sister Joan allowed her to stand in the cloisters and savour her freedom for a few moments before hurrying her into the laundry room so she could wash and put on a clean robe. After that, she was taken into the chapel.

"You won't be returning to your duties," Joan said. "The prioress wishes to speak with you."

It would be nice to speak to another person, especially Mother Jane. Kaylein doubted she would be allowed to leave the convent again soon, but perhaps if she was humble she could persuade the mother superior to send someone to find out how Sam was doing. She'd thought about Sam many times during her penance, and some of those thoughts had been confusing ones.

Kaylein felt itchy and uncomfortable as she approached Mother Jane's chamber. She wanted to sit in the open light of the writing room again. Her week in the cellar had been one of the longest she could recall, and it had reminded her just how much she'd grown to value life in the convent. Perhaps that was the whole point of the punishment.

Mother Jane was sitting with a letter spread out in front of her. Kaylein could see a large wax seal on the corner, but the rest was obscured from view by the slanted writing desk. Joan closed the door and left them in private. Kaylein didn't say anything, waiting for the prioress to speak first. It seemed prudent to show humility at a time like this.

"I am sorry for the length of your punishment," Mother Jane said at last. "It could not have come at a more inopportune time. I can only conclude that this must be God's will." She sighed. "Perhaps it is my punishment for

456

planning to deceive my superiors in the church. This letter arrived three days ago. It bears Cardinal Tybalt's seal, and it calls for your immediate expulsion."

Kaylein's stomach dropped.

"The cardinal claims that it is inappropriate for the daughter of the former count to serve a convent in Tannersfield," Mother Jane continued. "The reasoning is nebulous, but the wording is very firm, the instruction very clear."

"But–" Kaylein stammered. "He can't! The church accepts nobles all the time!"

"I think we both know that the reasons are a farce. Perhaps Sir Edward struck some bargain with him. One way or another, he has compelled me to expel you, and unless we wish to make a plea to an ecclesiastical court–one which could be compelled just as easily–there is nothing to be done. We cannot argue with the word of a cardinal."

Kaylein felt dazed. She hadn't even had time to adjust to her freedom. It was as if she'd stumbled out of a bank of fog only to topple over the edge of a cliff.

"Then you'll have to transfer me to another convent."

Mother Jane gave her a pained look. "It is too late for that. If this letter had arrived today, perhaps I could have sent you away immediately, but too much time has passed. Sister Joan has seen the text, and several others know that an important letter was delivered by the cardinal's messenger. I cannot pretend that I decided to transfer you before it arrived, and if I had ended your penance early it would have been obvious what I was doing. I am left with no choice but to formally expel you."

"Please," Kaylein begged, desperation welling up inside her, "let me stay."

"I wish I could, Kaylein, but the timing is too unfortunate." Mother Jane stood and grasped both of Kaylein's hands. "All is not lost. You can still join another convent. It isn't likely the cardinal or Sir Edward would ever learn of it unless they went looking. But I cannot send a letter guaranteeing your acceptance as I had planned. Anything you do now must be done on your own."

"What if I asked for sanctuary here? Not as a nun, but as a noble?"

Mother Jane shook her head. "It would be an obvious act of defiance."

Kaylein crumpled against the wall and slid into a sitting position. Her lower lip trembled. "But I don't know what to do."

Mother Jane crouched beside her as if comforting a child. "I won't abandon you. God sent you to this convent for a reason, and I cannot believe He means for your talents to be wasted. You have the mind of a scholar and a heart filled with faith."

"I just wanted to stay here and write."

Mother Jane squeezed her hands again. "And write you shall, but not here. Have faith, Kaylein. I have written down the names of five convents that I know to be led by good and godly women. One of them is sure to accept you. They will see in you what I saw." She pressed a purse into Kaylein's hands that felt like it contained money and a piece of parchment. "Perhaps your friends from the workshop can help you travel. I cannot take much from the convent's coffers without Sister Helen noticing, but this will be enough to support you for a while."

Kaylein swallowed the stiffness in her throat, trying not to weep. The thought of travelling the kingdom alone terrified her. There would be vicious outlaws, sinister merchants, and opportunistic lords like Sir Edward who would take advantage of her if they found out who she was. Another family was being ripped away from her. She tried to summon up the warmth of God's light, but it was a dim speck that day. The week in darkness had drained too much of her strength.

Some time later, she left the convent clutching the purse

to her belly in a daze. She had a thick travelling cloak about her shoulders and a satchel under her arm containing a flask and some food. Mother Jane had said she could stay and collect her thoughts for a day or two, but Kaylein refused. She knew it would only make leaving harder. The convent no longer felt safe. The church had withdrawn its protection, and she was alone again. Until she found another nunnery that would take her in–a distant and daunting prospect–the only person Kaylein had to turn to was Elizabeth. Once again she would have to throw herself upon her friend's kindness and pray that everything would work out. She wondered whether she would always be running from her father's enemies, travelling from town to town, convent to convent, forever living in fear that her past would catch up with her. The thought filled her with such despair that she wanted to slump down in the street and cry. But crying would not help her now; it would only invite someone to snatch the purse from her hands and leave her even more helpless than she already was. No matter how awful she felt, she could not become the same feeble wreck she'd been after fleeing Rosepath.

When she walked into the workshop yard, Elizabeth greeted her with a look of surprise that quickly gave way to concern. She could tell something was deeply wrong. They went to sit at Joseph's trestle table behind the workshop so they could talk.

"Is Sam well?" Kaylein asked, realising her mouth was dry when the words came out in a croak. She'd forgotten to eat or drink anything all morning.

"Yes, he's been getting better. He and Isaac are back at the farm. What's happened to you? Wait, let me fetch something to drink first."

Over a cup of water that had been boiled with herbs for flavour, Kaylein explained in faltering tones what had happened. At first Elizabeth was disturbed by the description of solitary penance, then angry when she learned of the expulsion.

"That weasel Edward! I bet he knows the cardinal because of the building site."

Anger at Sir Edward could not have been further from Kaylein's mind. "What am I going to do, Liz?"

Elizabeth took her hand. "One thing at a time. Let's look at that list the mother superior gave you."

Kaylein put her purse on the table and opened it. Inside were about three shillings worth of copper pennies and a piece of parchment with the names of five convents on it, along with directions and the names of the prioresses who ran them. Elizabeth tried to sound out the words by herself, but she still had great difficulty reading and Kaylein had to help her.

"Would this money be enough to get me there?" Kaylein asked. "Perhaps Mother Jane can lend me more if it isn't."

"I wouldn't go back to the convent if I were you," Elizabeth said. "Edward might come looking. I bet he's been waiting for this for weeks." She counted the pennies and shook her head. "I don't think you could hire anyone to take you very far with this. Maybe to Rambirch, but I think some of these places are in other counties. Isaac would know how to reach them. We might have to wait till someone we know goes travelling. You can't walk there on your own."

Once again Kaylein felt drained by the scope of the task ahead of her. That morning she'd been thinking wistfully of the writing room. Now she was making plans to travel halfway across the kingdom. The journey might take months if she had to visit all five convents before finding one that would accept her.

"I don't want to leave," she confessed. "I don't want to start all over again. I feel like I've only just found my legs here."

"Both of us may have to go eventually." Elizabeth stared at the table in thought. "I've spoken to Joseph about leaving Tannersfield. Things were bad last year, and business is slowing down. We might move to Rambirch next winter if the sickness hits Tannersfield again."

Kaylein felt a twinkle of hope. One of the convents on Mother Jane's list, Saint Saina's Mill, was near Rambirch. If Liz came with her, she wouldn't feel like she was facing the world alone.

"That's still a long way off, though," Elizabeth said, trying to mitigate her friend's expectations. "It might not happen."

"I could wait and see."

"How? Where will you live in the meantime?"

"I could stay with Sam and Isaac."

The look on Elizabeth's face told Kaylein just how little she thought of that idea. "And what'll you do for money?"

Kaylein hadn't thought about that part. Her vow of poverty meant she knew no more about money now than she had as a noblewoman. That needed to change.

"I will find work on the farms."

"That's hard labour. You don't have the strength for it."

"I have to learn!"

"It isn't something you can just learn," Elizabeth tried to explain. "The women who work those farms have been doing it all their lives. They've been toughening up in the fields since they were children."

Kaylein didn't want to hear it. She couldn't have her hopes dashed again. "I don't have enough money to travel, so what else am I to do? Sam will know somewhere I can find work till the end of the year."

"You don't want the kind of work he knows about. You need a convent."

"And I will find one when I'm ready."

Elizabeth looked frustrated, but she didn't let it escalate into an argument. "Alright. If you need somewhere to stay for a few days, I'm sure my brother will be happy to take care of you. Just make sure he knows you're still a nun."

Kaylein's cheeks flushed at the implication. Even if Sam did behave inappropriately towards her, she would never reciprocate.

* * *

Edward had been eagerly awaiting the news of Kaylein's expulsion. After weeks searching the moors west of Rosepath for Marquess Larmond, he'd finally found an opportunity to remind Cardinal Tybalt of their conversation at the king's court. The cardinal had come to visit his son at his new manor in Tannersfield. As a prominent local lord, Edward was invited to join them for supper one evening. Tybalt's son was a man of action too, and he was more than happy to swap tales of hunts and fights with Edward over many cups of wine. After a little wine of his own, Tybalt had been persuaded by the pair of them that a woman like Kaylein could become dangerous in times of civil unrest. It would be better for all of them if the church released her from its protection. Then, Edward insinuated, he would be able to deal with the problem quietly. He was glad to see Cardinal Tybalt possessed the same coy ruthlessness about such things as Duke Francis. It was no wonder the pair of them were allies.

Some days later, after another scouting trip across the moors, Edward rode through Tannersfield's western gate with half a dozen of his men. The crowd scattered before the hooves of their horses as they clattered down the street. A whore spat a curse as Edward's steed kicked muddy water over her dress. He grinned at her, but he couldn't be bothered to stop. There were more important things on his mind than insolent whores these days.

The men with him were the king's newly appointed verderers—officers tasked with enforcing the law in forests and other uncultivated lands outside towns—all of whom Edward had put forward from his own garrison. His men were bored in Rosepath after months of inaction, and he could only send them out hunting for so long before they tired of it and started causing trouble in the village. At first he'd overlooked their behaviour, but as the complaints mounted and court sessions dragged on he'd accepted that his men's indiscretions were making his life difficult. Some of the townspeople had even threatened to take matters to the sheriff, and that was something Edward wanted to avoid. Thankfully, giving the worst offenders positions of responsibility over the king's land kept them busy. The verderers' status was largely ceremonial for now, but it might become official if Duke Francis or the king decided they wanted permanent eyes on the moors. Edward's men would have houses like the ones on the road between Rosepath and Tannersfield, lords of their own little pieces of wilderness. They wouldn't be able to cause any trouble out there. No trouble, at least, that would ever find its way to Edward's court.

Ever since the meeting at Cairnford, Edward had been scouring the vast western moors between Tannersfield County and neighbouring Farrenwold. No lord technically ruled that land, for there was no clear road or major river to delineate where Tannersfield ended and Farrenwold began. Desolate or mountainous parts of the kingdom were often the same. Lords only cared about which settlements, forests, and cultivable lands belonged to them, not who held the rights to the worthless wilderness in between. Thus borders tended to be defined by villages as opposed to landmarks. All of this meant that it had been easy for Marquess Larmond to camp a sizeable entourage on the moors without anyone keeping an eye on him.

Edward had learned that the rogue marquess was travelling with about a hundred men, half of them mounted, and about a hundred more peasant followers. They had caught sight of parts of his army when they camped, but had never able to get close. Larmond was cunning and kept dividing his forces, never remaining in one spot long enough to become vulnerable. He had his own scouts roaming the moors, and their bows had forced Edward and his men to turn back on more than one occasion.

Despite their difficulties, Edward's verderers had succeeded in carrying out the king's orders. They now knew roughly where Larmond was and the strength of his immediate forces. Furthermore, spies in other parts of the kingdom reported that Marquess Alistair was back in his home county on the southern border. Edward wanted to attack while their two enemies were divided, but Duke Francis and the church were still keen to avoid war. Edward didn't know how long they could possibly sit and wait while rogue lords held their lands to ransom. For all intents and purposes, Larmond and Alistair were lords of their own kingdom now: a rival kingdom that needed to be brought to heel.

But Edward could do nothing until his duke gave word, so he focused his attention on more personal enemies instead. He rode with his men to their usual public house, stabled his horse with the others, and paid the owner to take care of them for the night. It cost a lot of money to pay his men's upkeep, but between collecting taxes, scouting the western moors, and holding court in Rosepath, he was rarely idle these days. That suited Edward just fine.

Rather than joining his men for a celebratory drink, he went to find Harald Redcloak. Harald had been keeping him abreast of matters in Tannersfield, including the situation with Lady Kaylein. The merchant was probably somewhere in the town square, hopefully convincing more people to take their business to Rosepath. The village market had been doing well this past year thanks to Harald's efforts. Some of the empty houses had filled up with new tenants, but to Edward's annoyance people still seemed to be leaving as quickly as they arrived. Still, the market was the important thing, and the more business it did the more money Edward got. More money meant more men, horses, and prestige.

He found Harald in one of the guild halls used by the

moneylenders.

"Has Tybalt's letter arrived?" he asked. "Is she out on the streets?"

Harald tapped his fingers together nervously. "That is my understanding of it, my lord."

"It is your understanding?" Edward glared at him. Harald could be aggravatingly slippery when he didn't want to admit something. "I thought you said you'd keep an eye on her?"

"I can't have people watching the convent night and day."

"Why not? You're not lacking the money for it."

"She's been expelled, but I can't say for sure where she is right now."

"Aha," Edward said. "Finally, there's a real answer from you." The thought of Kaylein begging on the streets in a filthy nun's robe was immensely gratifying to him. "Then find her for me. She's got to be here somewhere."

"What do you want to do with her?"

Edward shrugged. "I don't know. Lock her up. Put her on trial. It's not as if she has anyone to defend her now. Maybe you'd like to marry her, Harald? You're a bit old not to have a wife."

The merchant gave him a thin smile. "I wondered if you might prefer her for yourself. That would make quite a name for you, if you married the former count's daughter. No one could dispute your claim to Rosepath after that."

Edward thought about it. He hadn't had the opportunity to look at Kaylein for long on the few occasions they'd met, but people said she was very beautiful. It might be a thrill to make her marry him.

He dismissed the thought. He'd rather see her humbled and humiliated, and besides, it was not Kaylein he wanted. Cristiana was the woman he pictured in his mind's eye every time he lay with a whore these days.

"I've no appetite for nuns," he said. "So, will you find her for me?"

Harald moistened his lips with the tip of his tongue, his

465

eyes flitting about the room. "I've been trying. She doesn't seem to be in town."

Edward's satisfaction disappeared beneath a flash of anger. He slammed the table with his fist. "Are you telling me she's slipped away? Again?!"

"Not necessarily," Harald said quickly. "I have a lad working for me who knows her. His sister, too." It looked like he was about to say more, but he stopped himself. Edward sensed there was something the merchant didn't want to tell him. Harald was cunning, but Edward had known him long enough to spot when he wasn't being entirely truthful.

"Who is this boy?"

"Just an old acquaintance from Rosepath. I've not seen him in a while, but he'll be back. There was some trouble with one of my carts recently. Someone beat him up and he's been recovering."

"Where can I find him?"

"I don't know. He'll be back, just be patient."

"Don't talk to me like I'm an old man, Harald!" Edward yelled. "Where is he? Where's this sister of his?"

Harald shut his mouth and set his face impassively. Edward was furious enough that he could have drawn his knife and driven it right through the merchant's pretty red tunic. He gripped the edge of the table and took a deep breath. Perhaps he would have Harald hanged one of these days. The merchant was certainly dishonest enough to justify it. But he was also indispensably useful, and worst of all, he knew it. It was a bitter truth to swallow, that a noble man like Edward had become reliant on a charlatan like him.

Edward hit the table hard to get out some of his anger. His knuckles began to throb, all except the one that had been pierced by Elizabeth's chisel two years ago. He'd long since accepted that the feeling would never return to his little finger, but it still aggravated him. It was part of the reason he struggled to use a bow properly and had thus failed to

466

impress Cristiana when she went hunting with him. Lady Kaylein and her servant were responsible for that indignity, too.

"When will you see this lad again?" Edward said once he'd calmed down.

"Soon."

"You'd better pray it's soon enough. If Lady Kaylein leaves Tannersfield, I'll tell the duke you let her go."

Harald gave him another blank look. What was going on in that crafty head of his? Was he laughing at him? Edward fantasised about plunging his knife through his chest again. He reminded himself that he was a lord: a man of the kingdom. Harald was nobody. It was beneath him to rise to a mere merchant's provocations.

"Go back to your work," Edward looked around the hall, "whatever it is you do in here." The other moneylenders pointedly avoided his gaze. Their tables were covered in documents Edward couldn't read and the frames of beaded rods people used for counting. He didn't understand how merchants could make money by giving it away. It seemed almost mystical to him, like the rituals performed by priests or the illustrations surgeons made of medical work. He supposed free men who were not brave or strong needed to make a living, too, so they ended up doing things like this. Edward pitied them, settling for such a strange and dour existence. Pity helped mask the jealousy he felt when he saw the stacks of silver coins on their tables.

Throwing his cloak over his shoulder, he turned around and left. There was nothing else for him to do that afternoon, so he decided to take a wander through the market. He'd need to send letters to Duke Francis and the king reporting on his latest scouting trip, but his page would write those for him tomorrow. For now, he could relax and enjoy the looks of admiration and fear people gave him as he walked by. Despite not having his splendid silk cloak on that day, he still cut a striking figure. The eye-catching red of his surcoat and the yellow hawk of Cairnford were not worn by many knights in Tannersfield. He was determined to make the yellow hawk the heraldry of Rosepath someday. It would impress Duke Francis to see banners bearing his own insignia hanging from the walls the next time he visited.

Allowing the thought to percolate, he walked to the stalls of the cloth merchants and began inquiring about how much they charged for Cairnford red. The prices were obscene. As he was haggling, he spotted Harald scurrying away from the guild hall with his head down and a smile on his face. What did he have to smile about after being yelled at? Curiosity bubbled up in Edward, dispelling his interest in cloth banners. Breaking off his conversation with the merchant, he pushed through the crowd and followed after Harald. He was up to something, and for once Edward felt like getting one step ahead of his crafty companion.

It was easy to follow the red feather bobbing atop Harald's cap. Despite not being a tall man, the merchant always cut the most distinctive figure in a crowd. Edward pulled his plain cloak over his surcoat and made his way to the edge of the marketplace, trying to look inconspicuous. He followed Harald down the main road past the monastery and into the tangled streets that made up the southeast quarter of town. Free from the throng of marketgoers, Edward had to keep his distance to avoid standing out. Thankfully, Harald wasn't bothering to look behind him. The merchant left the street he was on and disappeared into a gap between two houses. Edward hurried to catch up, but when he looked into the alleyway Harald was nowhere to be seen. He cursed and broke into a run, wishing he'd stayed closer. What was Harald up to, skulking into alleyways in this part of town? None of the merchants did business here. The cramped houses around him were part of a ramshackle tradesman's district used by people who lacked the money or prestige to work their trades on the main streets. Now that he was a knight, Edward had no reason to come here. He hadn't visited this part of town in years. He could hear the rasp of a saw somewhere nearby, and the air had exchanged the earthy odour of animal dung for the acrid fumes of a dyer's vat. He tried to listen for the sound of Harald's footsteps, but there were too many other noises distracting him. A sickly pig snorted in its small pen behind one of the houses. A woman hanging up her washing line gave him a nervous look as he passed by. Edward threaded his way between the buildings, turning his head back and forth to try and catch a glimpse of Harald's red clothing. The search proved fruitless. The merchant had lost himself in the messy warrens of Tannersfield.

Edward was about to turn back when he heard a pair of voices on the far side of a fence. They were trying to speak quietly, but the heated nature of their argument was getting the better of them. One of the voices was Harald's. Straining his ears, Edward crept to the edge of the fence and squatted to peer through the cracks. The boards were tight, but he found a knothole. Moving his head back and forth, he picked out Harald standing with a woman next to a trestle table. Another building blocked the view behind them, but Edward could hear the sound of a wood saw in the yard beyond. The woman's voice seemed familiar. When Edward placed it, his heart leapt with excitement. Chancing a look over the top of the fence, he recognised her head of straw-blonde hair immediately.

It was Elizabeth. She'd been in Tannersfield all this time.

CHAPTER 31

"I can keep your secret as long as you need," said Harald. "You and your brother can rely on me. We're good working folk, all of us."

"I don't know what you want," Elizabeth replied. She sounded desperate.

Edward savoured the fear in her voice, fingering the hilt of his sword as he listened. It felt underhanded to skulk and eavesdrop like this, but he couldn't deny that there was a thrill in it. Kaylein be damned, this was the real prize. Now that he'd found Elizabeth, he could arrest her for attacking him on the road two years ago, then he'd make her tell him where to find Kaylein. At last he would have justice for the bitter indignity they'd saddled him with in the wake of his glory at Rosepath. Both of them would regret making an enemy of him. He recalled how he'd offered Elizabeth the chance to give up the night he chased her through the forest. Well, she'd had her chance; he wasn't going to be merciful this time.

"Your master has money," Harald went on. "It's dangerous for me to lie to my lord, but I could do it for the right price."

"We need that money! Business is slow for everyone right now. Even if I could persuade him, it would hardly be anything to a man like you."

"Carpenters make good money."

"Please," Elizabeth begged, "don't tell him about me."

Edward was enjoying their exchange. It was fun listening to them agonise over a bargain that was destined to go nowhere.

"Maybe if you keep repaying my favour," Harald said. Through the hole in the fence, Edward saw him move closer to Elizabeth.

"We're still sending folk to Rosepath whenever we can."

"You can do better than that. I have to spend good money when I need a woman most nights. Sam says you don't do what your mother did, but maybe you've changed your mind. I'd never say a word about you or Lady Kaylein to Edward, I swear. We'd both be happy."

Edward wrinkled his nose at Harald's duplicity. He was as sly as they came, trying to play everyone off against each other for his own benefit. Threatening a woman into sleeping with him revealed another layer to his depravity. Part of Edward admired his gumption. Perhaps if he'd been this bold with Cristiana she wouldn't have rejected him.

The conversation fell momentarily quiet. Harald moved again, and Elizabeth stepped back.

"You'd just tell him anyway once you got bored of me," she spat.

"I never go back on my word."

"You're a liar, Harald Redcloak. God damn you and your lord to hell."

"Do you know what he'll do if he finds you?" Harald said impatiently. Edward strained to get a better view of what was happening. The merchant had her backed against the wall.

"Don't touch me!" Elizabeth said in a shrill voice. Harald recoiled in shock as a flash of steel appeared in her hand.

"You're as stupid as your brother!"

471

"Get off with you!" Elizabeth's voice was firm, but her knife trembled. A woman couldn't play at being a knight.

Edward listened to the sound of Harald's footsteps hurrying out of the yard before stealing another glance over the fence. Elizabeth had disappeared into one of the houses. Listening to her argument with Harald had got Edward's blood up. He wanted to vault the fence and drag her out into the street, but he forced himself to think before he acted. If he broke in through the back like a thief, someone might try and stop him. He couldn't risk letting Elizabeth slip through his fingers again. What if he gathered his men from the inn first? No, that would look cowardly. He didn't need half a dozen swords to deal with one servant girl. He was a knight. All he had to do was walk into that yard with authority, and no one would dare stop him.

Hurrying back between the houses, Edward found his way to the street on the opposite side of the yard. From there he could see it was part of a carpentry workshop. The house behind it must have belonged to the owner. His excitement mounting, he checked his sword and threw his cloak over his shoulder so it wouldn't get in the way. He strode into the yard and made straight for a group of carpenters dressing a pile of logs. He recognised some of them from the cardinal's building site. Their master, the one with the thick black hair and matching beard, approached him with a wary nod.

"Good day, Sir Edward. Do you need a carpenter?"

Edward smiled at him. He wondered if the man would try and lie to protect Elizabeth.

"Didn't I flog your apprentice last year?"

The carpenter looked at the ground. "That was Master Luther's apprentice."

"He works here too?" When the carpenter said nothing, Edward raised his voice. "I said does he work here too?"

"He does."

"And who else works here? Any women?" Edward was savouring every word. His blood hummed in his veins. This feeling of confidence, of absolute superiority, was what he lived for.

"Just my wife."

"What's her name?"

"Rose."

"Not Elizabeth? She's not a young, fat-bottomed thing with long yellow hair?"

"No."

Edward tired of the game and strode past him.

"This is my workshop!" the carpenter protested. Edward ignored him and went into the building. To his annoyance, Elizabeth was not inside. Several more men were working at benches along with a middle-aged woman at the far end of the room. Edward approached her and slapped the chisel she was using out of her hand, leaving a long scratch in the ornamental plate she'd been etching. She let out an exclamation of anger, then immediately shrank back when she realised who he was.

"Where is she?" Edward demanded. "Elizabeth the servant."

"Keep your hands off my wife," the master carpenter growled behind him.

"Don't, Joseph," the woman said sharply.

Edward looked back at the man with a sneer before pushing open the workshop's rear door. He emerged into the small yard he'd seen through the fence. The carpenter's house stood in front of him with its door half open. He barged through and squinted into the darkness. Elizabeth had to be in here. There was nowhere else she could've gone.

"You can't force your way into a man's house!" Joseph yelled.

Edward felt a heavy hand grip his shoulder. He drew his sword and turned around. Joseph let go and backed away, palms raised before him.

"Your door was open," Edward said. "I'm looking for a lawbreaker. Get in my way again, and I'll have you in the

473

pillory alongside her." He turned around and examined the room. There was an old mattress leaking straw next to the hearth, a chest, table, chairs, and several bags hanging from the ceiling; a common way of storing food beyond the reach of vermin. The back part of the house was dark, but it looked like there was another room screened off from the first by a hanging blanket. He heard a scuttling sound. Perhaps it was a rat, perhaps a person. Edward pushed the door fully open to let in more light, then pulled the blanket down. He edged forward into the rear room. There was a proper bed with a wooden frame and another chest against the far wall. A pile of clothing and rags sat on a chair next to it. Fingering the grip of his sword, Edward braced a hand on the end of the bed and bent down to look underneath. He couldn't see anything in the darkness. Resting his blade against the floor, he shoved it under the bed and swept it back and forth. Besides a few pieces of old straw, it found nothing.

Edward stood up and searched the house again, his temper mounting. She had to be here. There was nowhere else she could have gone. Had the girl jumped the fence while he was in the workshop?

"Where is she?" he yelled at the carpenter in the doorway.

"As you can see, there's no one here, milord," Joseph said. Edward fancied he heard a note of smugness in the man's voice. He must have some secret hiding place. He was hiding Elizabeth and laughing at him about it.

"Then who sleeps on that?" Edward pointed to the mattress by the hearth.

"An apprentice."

Clenching his teeth in anger, Edward kicked a stool into the wall. To his annoyance, it didn't break. Carpenters made things too well. Pushing past Joseph, he went back outside and threw the trestle table over, then stormed through the workshop.

"Where's that girl?!" he shouted again. If these carpenters wouldn't tell him willingly, he'd force them to. Seeing a collection of tools hanging from wall pegs, he picked up a mallet and hurled it across the room. A man yelled as it bounced off the wall next to his head. His companions were already on their feet. One of them came forward, but he backed away when Edward waved the tip of his sword in his face. "Come on. Tell me." His heart pounded with anger and excitement. He hoped one of the carpenters would come at him with a hammer. Once there was blood on the floor, someone would start talking. Edward grabbed a half-finished chair from the nearest bench and threw it down, shattering the thing to pieces.

"You can't ruin a man's livelihood like this!" Joseph yelled behind him. "I'll go to the sheriff!"

Edward was too angry to listen to him. *Put your hand on my shoulder again,* he thought, his sword hand itching. He put his foot through a delicate wooden frame one of the carpenters had been assembling on the floor, then marched into the front yard. An ox cart with a broken axle was up on its side. Edward swung his sword to drive away the men working on it, then shoved the cart as hard as he could. It toppled over with a crash, one of the side boards snapping in half as it went. People had started to gather in the street, watching in awe as Edward ransacked the yard. *Let them watch,* he thought. They'd all see what happened to people who defied him. Realising there was a storage shed he hadn't checked yet, he yanked on the door to try and open it, but it was locked.

"Open this up!" he demanded. None of the carpenters moved to obey. Too impatient to wait, Edward put his boot into the door until the lock tore itself free from the wood. Another wave of fury swept over him as he found the shed empty. Where was she? Where could the carpenters possibly be hiding her? He was sick of this. Stamping back outside, he saw the apprentice he'd flogged at the building site. He made a grab for him, but the boy ducked out of reach and ran back to the others. Joseph stepped forward to block Edward's way when he tried to give chase. The carpenter had a mallet in one hand and a heavy piece of wood in the other. Looking around, Edward noticed several of the other men had also armed themselves with tools. He felt a twinge of anxiety and brought up his sword.

"Get out of my way."

Joseph shook his head. There was fear in the man's eyes, but he held his ground. "If you take your sword to a single man here, you'll never step out of this yard."

Edward was incensed by his arrogance. "You wouldn't dare attack one of the duke's knights." He jabbed his sword threateningly. Joseph flinched and narrowed his eyes.

"You're the one breaking the law here. We've more than a dozen witnesses watching. No court would convict us for defending ourselves in our own workplace."

With a shiver of incredulity, Edward realised Joseph might be right. Unless he could find Elizabeth, he wouldn't be able to prove they'd been hiding a lawbreaker. Then he would be the one who ended up looking like a criminal. The very real possibility that these carpenters might kill him stole up on Edward like a sliver of ice at his back. He glanced around the yard again. Even Joseph's wife had a piece of wood in her hands. His grip on his sword faltered. He hadn't come here expecting anyone to stand up to him.

"If you don't bring her to me, I'll have all of you hanged! Every last person here!" The threat was Edward's last hope, and it sounded weak even to his ears. He edged toward the street, still keeping his sword up. None of the carpenters tried to stop him. "I'll be back. I'll make you sorry for this, Joseph Carpenter." Edward tried to move calmly so that the people watching didn't think he was afraid. The shame of it was maddening. What had he done wrong? He'd underestimated the carpenters, that was what. He hadn't expected they'd be willing to fight him. Perhaps he should have tried to get one of them on their own, then they would've talked.

Trying to salvage the remnants of his pride by admiring the carnage he'd wrought in Joseph's yard, he gave the carpenter one last scornful look before turning away into the street.

They were fools if they thought they'd won. He had half a dozen men waiting for him on the other side of town. It would take more than a few hammers and chisels to scare him off when he returned. Edward dropped his sword into the sheath and twisted his fingers around the crossguard.

He'd see every man in that yard dead or locked up by the day's end.

* * *

Elizabeth's arms and legs burned, but she didn't dare let go of the slats on the underside of Joseph's bed. She'd almost screamed when she heard the rasp of Edward's sword on the floor inches from her back. It had caught a lock of her falling hair, and for an instant she'd been certain he would find her. But the blade was sharp, and it had sliced through before it could catch and tug. The darkness at the back of the house and the wooden skirt covering the lower part of the bed frame were the only things that had saved her. She thanked God that Rose had made her husband build them such a sturdy bed.

When Edward left, the shouting and the crash of wood were almost as bad as the sword. She was terrified that a cry of pain would cut through the sounds of destruction at any moment. If Edward hurt anyone, it would be her fault. She thought about coming out and giving herself up to him, but to her shame she was too frightened. She could stand up to lechers like Harald, but not Edward. When she thought about confronting him, she remembered the swordsman outside Kaylein's room, the fear and helplessness, the blood on the hall floor, and the face of her dying mistress.

Eventually the commotion died down, but Elizabeth still clung to the bed. She was sure her arms were bruised from keeping them wedged between the slats and the mattress so long. The door creaked open, and she held her breath.

"Come on out, girl. Are you under the bed?"

Elizabeth sobbed with relief as she crawled out and threw herself into Joseph's arms. He squeezed her tight and kissed the top of her head.

"Don't fret now, don't fret. We saw him off. He didn't get you with his sword, did he?"

Elizabeth shook her head, struggling to find her tongue. Once the shock began to fade she let Joseph take her outside. She needed to breathe.

Rose hurried over and embraced her. It felt to Elizabeth like she was saying goodbye. She had to leave now. There could be no more waiting and hoping; no more fantasies about working with Joseph the rest of her life and praying Edward never found her. She didn't know if she could give up everything and start a new life again. It was all happening so fast.

"I have to go," she heard herself saying as she pulled away from Rose. "I'll go with Kaylein. We'll find one of her convents and– and I'll just be a nun with her."

"No, you won't," Joseph said firmly. The gentleness in his voice had gone. His face was drawn, his eyes glossy and twitching. Elizabeth didn't think she'd ever seen the kindly carpenter so furious.

"I have to," Elizabeth pleaded with him. She couldn't bear the thought of Edward taking his revenge on the people she loved. "You don't understand. He'll come back."

"Even knights aren't above the law. He forced his way into my home, threatened my wife, and vandalised our property. He's the one who should be afraid."

"You can't take a lord to a court of law," Rose said.

"Yes I can!" Joseph yelled. "Everyone here saw what he did, and half the street, too! I'll take the whole damned guild to the sheriff's castle if I have to."

Elizabeth remembered Joseph saying he didn't want her bringing trouble to his door. Perhaps this was why. When

478

Joseph had something to fight for, he was every bit as furious as a knight on the battlefield. His passion made her wonder whether there might be hope after all. If Edward could be tried and convicted under the king's law, he might be stripped of his title. Perhaps he'd lose his land and have to go back to Cairnford. She'd never have to worry about him again.

"First things first," Joseph said. He led them through to the work yard. "Fred! You've got young legs. Run to the castle as fast as you can. Fetch one of the watch constables—fetch the sheriff himself if he'll listen. Tell them what happened and get someone to come here right away."

"I'll go with him," Elizabeth said.

"You've had a shock. You stay here."

"They'll be more likely to listen if there's two of us." Elizabeth still felt guilty about hiding. She didn't want to sit idle while everyone else tried to salvage the disaster she'd caused.

"She does look like she's had a fright," Rose said. "They'll listen to a woman in distress."

Joseph didn't seem happy about it, but he let her go. Hitching up her dress, she ran down the street with Fred and turned left down the road toward the sheriff's castle. Her heart thumped in her chest. They might not have long. Edward could already be on his way back. Crossing the edge of the marketplace, they turned toward the castle and hurried up to the entrance. The main gate was open, but it was guarded by the sheriff's men-at-arms. One of them stepped into their path as they approached.

"What's happened?"

"We've come from Joseph Carpenter's workshop," Elizabeth said breathlessly.

Fred carried on while she gasped for air: "A man with a sword came in and threatened everyone. He smashed half the woodwork in the yard, and he says he's coming back."

Fred was probably wise not to mention Sir Edward's name. The sheriff's men might be less eager to help if they knew they were about to put themselves at odds with a knight.

They were led into the castle where a well-dressed man met them in the great hall. Elizabeth didn't have time to admire how much larger and more lavish the hall was than Rosepath's. She and Fred explained what had happened again. The official listened intently, their breathless panic seeming to convince him that the situation was serious. When they mentioned their attacker might be coming back, they were told to wait again. The official returned promptly with a sword at his hip and two men-at-arms beside him. He introduced himself as Simon Bailey, the sheriff's bailiff.

They hurried back across town. By now it was starting to get late. The main road heaved with traders leaving the marketplace, but they made way when they saw the sheriff's men coming.

"Was anyone hurt?" Simon Bailey asked.

"No, I don't think so," Elizabeth replied.

"And you didn't recognise who this man was?"

Fred answered ahead of Elizabeth: "Some lord."

"A man who should have known better, then." The bailiff had a shrewd, calculating look about him, as though he was already scribing a mental list of what needed to be done.

There was no sign of Sir Edward when they returned to the workshop, but Elizabeth's relief didn't last long. Simon Bailey had barely begun to examine the damage when one of the onlookers gossiping in the street cried out a warning. Edward and four armed men marched down the road toward them.

Elizabeth shrank back and felt Rose's arms close protectively around her. She tried to fight the nauseating twist of fear in her stomach. She wouldn't hide this time. She had to be brave. If it looked like Edward was going to start a fight, she would give herself up to him. Joseph and the others couldn't risk themselves for her again.

Simon Bailey turned and regarded Edward's men with a

cold stare as they approached. Would he be able to stop them? What if he sided with the knight instead of Joseph? Everyone knew Edward had strong ties with the sheriff of Tannersfield.

Edward's group came to a halt at the front of the yard. Simon Bailey and his men blocked their way. Edward was red-faced and breathless. He must have hurried to get back. When he saw Elizabeth standing with the others, he drew his sword and pointed it at her.

"I want that woman. Get out of my way, and there won't be any trouble."

"She's done nothing wrong," Joseph said.

"You and your men should accompany me to the sheriff's castle," Simon Bailey said to Edward.

Edward gave him a furious look. "Do you know who I am?"

"Yes, I know who you are, Sir Edward."

"Then you know I have the right to punish those who break the law!"

Simon stared him down, unfazed. "In Rosepath you do. Tannersfield is the sheriff's town, and knights don't dispense justice here without his say-so."

"This isn't some peasant squabble," Joseph said. "You've damaged the livelihood of a trade guild. It's for the courts to settle this now."

"Are you accusing *me?*" Edward asked incredulously. "You're the ones in the wrong!"

Simon raised his voice and called to the onlookers in the street. "Were all of you witness? Is this the man who ransacked Master Joseph's workshop?"

Elizabeth held her breath waiting for someone to answer. It was dangerous to speak out against a knight, but people hated Sir Edward. One by one, a few brave voices rose in confirmation.

"This is ridiculous!" Edward blustered. "They don't know a thing! Are you going to listen to them over me?" As angry as he was, Elizabeth could see he was getting nervous. He might think he could intimidate servants and tradesmen, but if he crossed swords with the sheriff's bailiff he'd be thrown in jail. Unlike their previous encounters, he wasn't acting on behalf of the duke or the sheriff this time.

"Master Joseph," Simon Bailey said, "are you making a formal accusation against Sir Edward?"

"I damned well am."

"I'd ask you not to blaspheme," the bailiff said curtly, then turned back to Edward. "Your men will have to leave. I suggest you come to the castle with me now."

Edward rubbed his neck uncomfortably, casting about as if in search of someone who might come to his aid. "Are you going to put me on trial?"

"We'll see. Master Joseph, you and Sir Edward will take your disagreement to the sheriff. As this is a guild matter, I expect he will agree to hear you tomorrow. You should bring any witnesses you deem necessary. Then the sheriff will decide whether this should go any further."

"What does that mean?" Elizabeth called out.

Simon turned to look at her. "This dispute involves a knight of the realm. It cannot be settled in a lower court. If Sir Edward is to be tried, it must be before one of the king's judges. Until the matter is resolved, I recommend neither you nor Sir Edward cause any more trouble for each other." He fixed his gaze back on Edward pointedly. "Is that understood?"

Edward looked like he was trying to twist the handle off his sword. "Yes," he said through gritted teeth.

"Good. Then you'll come to the castle with me. Master Joseph, you'll be sent for when the sheriff is ready to hear your plea."

"The sooner the better," Joseph said.

It took a nudge from one of the bailiff's men before Edward uprooted himself and turned to leave. Once they were gone, the onlookers in the street came over and erupted into excited gossip. By tomorrow this would be the talk of the town. Elizabeth didn't know whether to feel shocked or relieved. The law had protected them. Edward had made a fool of himself, and now he might stand to face serious punishment for what he'd done.

"How will we persuade the sheriff to hold a trial?" she asked Joseph. "Didn't Edward used to be one of his men?"

"Like I said, I'll bring the whole guild to the castle if I have to. Men from the other guilds, too. There's no shortage of folk in Tannersfield who've reason to hate Sir Edward."

"What if he accuses you of hiding me?" Elizabeth's fear returned as she imagined the hearing turning against them. What if they were the ones who ended up being punished? No one would believe the word of a servant girl over a knight if he made her out to be the villain. She wished she knew more about courts of law. Count Leo had dealt with village disputes back in Rosepath, but anything this serious had always been taken to the sheriff.

"I don't know," Joseph admitted, "but if you ever want to stop looking over your shoulder, this is your best chance. I don't want you leaving us."

Elizabeth chewed her lip anxiously. "Will you still make your plea to the sheriff, even if I go?"

"I will."

"Then I'll come with you." Elizabeth felt a weight lift from her shoulders as she made up her mind. She was afraid, but her fear had a certainty to it now. She was no longer hiding from Sir Edward. Soon she would confront him, and there was a chance she might win.

At noon the next day, they walked into the sheriff's castle with a group of two dozen respected carpenters and tradesmen at their back; a collection of guildsmen and witnesses from the night before. They jostled and bumped shoulders as they lined up on one side of the hall under the direction of Simon Bailey. Sir Edward stood on the other side with a mere two men-at-arms accompanying him. He shot a venomous glance at Elizabeth and Joseph when they entered, but his fury from the previous day seemed to have deserted him. He looked young and anxious now, the same way Elizabeth felt. It emboldened her to remember they were a similar age. Even though he was a lord, Edward probably didn't know much more about what was about to happen than she did.

Wallis Reeve, the sheriff of Tannersfield, sat in what would have been the lord's chair at the high table. He had a hunched back and lank, grey-black hair that Elizabeth thought made him look like an old raven bent over his table. Wrinkles creased the corners of his sunken eyes. Despite the tension humming in the room, he looked as though he was already weary of the day's work. People said the sheriff had grown lax since Count Leo's death. Seeing him in person, Elizabeth believed them. She hoped he would treat them fairly.

Behind her stood Theobald and three other masters from the carpenters' guild. Elizabeth hadn't been happy to see them after their last encounter, but Joseph had shouted up such a storm in the guild hall that morning that half the men present had been cowed into giving him their support. Despite opposition from Theobald, who was reluctant to butt heads with the sheriff, Joseph had argued that their guild would never be taken seriously if they allowed men like Sir Edward to treat them like common serfs. Given the sentiment of Theobald's recent rhetoric, it had been difficult for him to argue back. The guild had their reputation to consider, and this was their chance to put their foot down.

Joseph was asked to present his accusation to the sheriff first. He spoke simply but concisely, explaining exactly what had happened and presenting a written appraisal of the monetary damage Edward had caused. Along with Simon Bailey attesting to what he'd seen at the workshop, the sheer number of witnesses, and the official complaint of the carpenters' guild, they put forward a strong case for Edward's indictment.

Edward spoke next. He did not attempt to deny the accusations, but he argued that he'd been within his rights to search the workshop for Elizabeth. Several voices among Joseph's party rose in angry defiance of the assertion. Elizabeth didn't know whether the law was on Edward's side or not, but it was clear that everyone disagreed with him terrorising innocent carpenters. Edward's defence came across as weak and faltering following Joseph's argument.

"It's clear to me that Sir Edward has erred," the sheriff said at last. "He was not within his rights to damage your workshop. If he believed you were harbouring a lawbreaker, he should have come to me first."

Edward gave the sheriff a look of frustration. Perhaps he'd been hoping he would lie and pretend he'd given him the authority to search for Elizabeth beforehand. But even if they were friends, the sheriff at least seemed to have an even hand when it came to dispensing justice.

"I believe it would be best to settle this quickly," the sheriff continued. "If Sir Edward pays a fine in excess of the damage caused, I think that would satisfy everyone."

Joseph's group erupted in protest. A fine was not enough. Even-handed or not, the sheriff was clearly trying to spare Edward any lasting punishment.

"I won't accept a fine," Joseph said loudly.

The sheriff slid his weary gaze in Edward's direction. Elizabeth sensed that if Edward insisted on paying, the sheriff would force Joseph to accept his compensation and leave it at that. But the knight did not seem to realise that he stood to lose far more than a few shillings by refusing.

"They don't deserve my money!" he said, his face colouring with indignation. "I've done nothing wrong!"

"Are you certain of that, Sir Edward?"

"Of course I'm certain!"

The sheriff sighed. "Then this will have to be settled in

court. The king's judge next visits Tannersfield on the sixteenth of May. Given that one of our duke's trusted men stands accused, I will insist that a trial be held on that date."

The sheriff dismissed them, and they were led out to make way for the next set of petitioners. Edward stormed off ahead, leaving Elizabeth and the others with Simon Bailey outside the keep.

"Judges don't often find knights guilty," the bailiff told them.

"But we have so many witnesses, and the carpenters' guild is backing us," Elizabeth said.

"The guild can make the sheriff listen, but not a judge. He'll have no stake in the politics of this town. If all it took to bring down a knight was the word of a few commoners, half the villages in the kingdom would have deposed their lords."

Elizabeth had started feeling confident after Edward's misstep in refusing to pay the fine, but now she wasn't so sure. "Then what should we do?" Simon seemed like a just man with a strong sense of fairness. She hoped he was on their side.

"If I were you, I'd try my best to stop him justifying his actions. He insists you are a lawbreaker. If you're innocent, make sure you can prove it to the judge."

CHAPTER 32

Isaac heard about what had happened before he arrived at the workshop for Elizabeth's reading lesson. Sir Edward's trial was all the gaggle of carters and stable boys could talk about as he unsaddled Blackberry and got her settled. It wasn't just the stablers who were talking; as Isaac walked down the street he heard Sir Edward's name mentioned by a couple conversing loudly through an open door, then again at one of the market stalls where a group of town watchmen were chatting with a gossipy seamstress.

The news seemed to have stirred up a fervour of excitement in Tannersfield. Two years ago, the tales from Rosepath had seeded an undercurrent of resentment toward Duke Francis and the knights who'd brutalised the village. Edward had become a symbol of heavy-handed oppression since then, a reputation he seemed all too keen to indulge with his brutal treatment of outlaws and harsh taxation of his serfs. Every peasant who'd ever had to deal with a cruel landlord or a miserly tax collector was thrilled at the prospect of seeing a man like him hang. Isaac knew enough about courts of law to understand that Edward would never go to the noose for what he'd done, but the townspeople's gossip had already run away with them. His father had forced him to sit in on sessions of the king's court when it was held at Cairnford Castle, and charges against knights or lords usually ended poorly for the accusers. Even if Edward was found guilty, at best he might be fined or stripped of his title. Offences that left outlaws swinging from the gallows were viewed as silly dalliances when noblemen were involved.

The constant gossip set Isaac's nerves on edge. He already had Kaylein on his mind. She'd arrived unexpectedly at the farm a few days ago. He'd been unsure whether it was a good idea to let her stay with them, but of course Sam had leapt at the opportunity. He'd already spent a day and a half building Kaylein a wattle and daub hut next to theirs so she could sleep in privacy. He was besotted with her, and whenever Isaac asked what they were going to do for money Sam just waved him off and said they'd work something out. Isaac wouldn't have minded supporting Kaylein for a while, but she was hopeless with manual chores. A noble's daughter through and through, she'd been made for books and courts, not rough living. She couldn't help Sam fish or trap rabbits to feed herself, and no farmer was going to take her on as a labourer.

He tried to put it out of his mind as he turned down the street toward the workshop. He wasn't used to worrying. Regardless of what happened with Edward's trial, he expected he'd be leaving Tannersfield soon. He had enough money buried in the forest to take care of himself for a month or two. Kaylein would go looking for a new convent once she realised how difficult it was living rough, and Sam would probably follow her. Isaac could go with them. Perhaps if Elizabeth lost the trial against Sir Edward she'd come too, though her heart seemed to belong with Joseph and the carpenters. Despite the friendships he'd forged, Isaac still felt like he'd been treading water for the past year. He'd only meant for Tannersfield to be a temporary stopping point, but one thing had led to another and he'd kept putting off his departure. Like Elizabeth and Kaylein, he was anxious about crossing paths with Sir Edward or anyone else who might recognise him. He wanted to put that fear behind him and start afresh.

His year in Tannersfield had taught him what he truly wanted: the freedom to be his own man. The idea of having land and subjects and courts to attend made his shoulders stiffen and his stomach clench. More than anything, he didn't want to become a hard and bitter man like his father, one who only saw value in the things he could control. Isaac wanted to find a wife who would marry him for love, not duty, and have children who would be a joy to raise, not a burden to endure until they could be married off.

A whimsical mood took hold of him as he daydreamed about the future. His smile brought a sceptical look to Elizabeth's face when he arrived at the workshop. She wasn't much of a dreamer, Elizabeth. No—that wasn't quite true. She did dream, but of practical things like warm houses and cellars full of food, not adventures and romance. She was a simple woman in that regard. It made it difficult to see eye to eye with her at times, but there was something stimulating about their disagreements. She was very spirited, and she saw the world in a way Isaac never had. Part of him envied the hardiness of her character, but he felt sorry that it had been forced upon her by the cruelties of life. As they sat down for their lesson, Isaac was struck with a feeling of fondness as he imagined teaching Elizabeth to read in a comfortable hall with a real book. He pictured the look that might come over her the first time she managed to lose herself in the written word. Perhaps the subtle tension she held in her face would soften, the creases in her brow smoothing out as her eyes sparkled with joy. A book about carpentry or mercantile trade might be able to evoke the dreamer in Elizabeth.

"Why are you looking at me like that?" she asked.

Isaac pulled himself out of his inner thoughts. "I was just thinking I might want to be a schoolmaster someday," he half-lied. "I enjoy teaching people."

"I thought you wanted to run stables and kennels."

"I want lots of things. Don't you?"

"Right now I just want Sir Edward gone. I wish we didn't have to wait till the trial."

"He won't cause any more trouble for you in the meantime, will he?"

"Not unless he wants to wait in the sheriff's jail."

They tried to go through some of Kaylein's pages, but Elizabeth struggled even more than usual. Isaac corrected her mistakes patiently until she pushed the pages away with a sigh.

"It's no use. I can't remember anything today. Perhaps we should just stop these lessons until the trial's over. I'll still pay you for this week."

"You shouldn't fret so much," Isaac said.

"How can I not?"

"It's only worth fretting over things you can do something about."

Elizabeth sat back on her side of the trestle table and folded her arms huffily. "I *could* do something if only I knew more about the king's law. I'm sure Edward has Harald Redcloak and half a dozen other men telling him what to say to the judge."

The back of Isaac's neck itched at the mention of Harald. He hadn't forgotten the way he'd thrown him out into the street a couple of weeks ago. The idea of getting back at the merchant started his finger tapping against the table. "Maybe I can help."

Elizabeth raised an eyebrow. "Do you want to be a witness?"

Isaac knew he couldn't stand up in front of Edward and a royal judge. He'd be recognised immediately. "No, but perhaps I can do something else. I've seen what happens in courts like this before."

"Of course you have," Elizabeth said with a hint of

490

mockery. "You've seen everything."

"Do you think Edward will have people like Harald standing up for him?" The beginning of an idea was forming in Isaac's head.

"I don't know, but Harald was always good at getting himself out of trouble in Rosepath. I'm just worried Edward will convince the judge he was justified in searching the workshop because I attacked him before." She went on to recount the tale of what had happened the night she fled Rosepath. Isaac had tried not to listen the last time she'd told it at Sam's fire, for it made him uncomfortable to think about his father's involvement in the massacre. This time he paid attention.

"The problem is, it's my word against his," Elizabeth concluded.

"No it isn't. He can't use that argument against you at all."

Elizabeth frowned. "Why not?"

It seemed starkly obvious to Isaac given his knowledge of court witnesses. "Kaylein was with you that night. Edward might be a knight, but she's a count's daughter. If she says you acted in self-defence to protect her, you'll have a prestigious witness on your side. And believe me, no one wants what happened with Count Leo coming up in court. Edward would have Duke Francis breathing down his neck if he tried."

Elizabeth's expression lit up. "I never thought about that."

Isaac leaned forward excitedly. "He won't have any way of justifying himself. Defending yourself and your noble mistress was no crime."

"That night felt like war. I don't suppose the law matters during wars, does it?"

"No, it doesn't."

"But what if Edward tries to bring it up anyway? Kaylein isn't a noblewoman anymore. The judge might not listen to her."

Isaac thought about it. His father and the church had done everything they could to posthumously brand Count Leo a traitor. If the judge believed those stories, he might side against Kaylein. It would still be foolish for Edward to bring it up, but his reputation was not that of a level-headed man. They needed some way of ensuring he stayed quiet about it.

"I might be able to handle that," he said. "Where can I find Harald?"

Isaac rode Blackberry down a forest trail halfway between Tannersfield and Rosepath the next day. According to Elizabeth, this was where Harald brought his carts to the poachers. If his schedule hadn't changed since Sam stopped working for him, their paths should cross around noon. Isaac knew what he was doing was risky, but having Blackberry's swift legs beneath him gave him confidence. If Harald tried to set his men on him again, he'd be gone before they got close.

Birds twittered under the dappled sunlight, branches rustling all around Isaac in the springtime breeze. The greens were bright and the browns soft at this time of year. For all the striking landscapes he'd seen across the world, something about a bright forest trail still charmed Isaac to his core. Had he not been here with a purpose in mind, he could have meandered through the woods for hours.

Beneath Blackberry's hooves, he saw that someone had brushed leaves and loose loam over some cart tracks using a broom. It was a lazy way of hiding a trail, but it might fool someone who'd never hunted before. Isaac kept his eyes open and watched the swivelling of his horse's ears, knowing she would be able to pinpoint any strange sounds more accurately than him. After about an hour, Blackberry nickered and came to a halt. Isaac listened, tilting his head in the direction she was looking. Sure enough, he caught the sound of a cart trundling along in the distance. He turned Blackberry around and retraced his steps until he found a spot where the trail widened. He wasn't going to confront Harald recklessly this time. Once he was confident he had space to turn his horse and gallop away at a moment's notice, he stopped and waited.

Harald and four men appeared around the bend. The merchant was in plain clothes for the forest trek, but he still had his feathered cap on. Two of his men pulled hand carts stacked with what looked like cuts of smoked venison. The other two led horses on foot. Isaac noticed one of them had a sword.

"Harald!" he called out. "I'd like a word with you."

The merchant looked up with a start and motioned for his party to halt. When he saw Isaac on the path ahead, he smiled and strode forward with his thumbs tucked into his belt. "You again. Where's Sam? I've missed him these last few trips."

"I want to talk to you about Sir Edward's trial."

"You've picked a strange spot for it." Harald glanced around. "I've a feeling you're trying to catch me out."

"It's best we don't discuss this in town. I want to know what your lord plans on saying against Elizabeth at the trial."

"And why should I tell you that? I thought I said I wasn't interested in seeing you again." Harald looked back at his men. The one with the sword grinned at Isaac and touched his weapon.

"Because I know you've been selling wool in Tannersfield without a writ, and I know you're dealing with outlaws. Maybe you're even paying them to poach the duke's deer yourself."

Harald scowled at him. "So you're going to tell the sheriff, is that it?"

"No, but I could tell Will Shearer and a few of your other competitors. I expect they'll do a much better job causing trouble for you than I can."

Harald's dirty look held for a moment, then he laughed. "You're going to regret this, and so's that whore's daughter

493

Elizabeth. Edward'll have her pilloried and the skin flayed off her back."

Blackberry pawed the earth nervously. Isaac swallowed his fear and pressed on. "Edward's going to accuse her of attacking him in the forest, isn't he?" His confidence swelled as a flicker of unease crossed Harald's face.

"That's right. Her word against a knight's. She's got no chance of winning."

"You know that's not true."

Harald's unease gave way to a grimace of frustration. Isaac held back a smile. The merchant hadn't expected him to know anything about courts of law.

"What are you talking about?"

"Lady Kaylein was there, too. She'll turn it back on Edward and make him look like he's the one in the wrong." This was the part where Isaac had to be cunning. He'd managed to outwit Will Shearer one step ahead of Harald before, but this was a more delicate lie. He didn't want Harald to think he was doing this because he was afraid Elizabeth might lose. Men like Harald preyed upon such fears. Ruthless self-interest, on the other hand, was something the merchant could appreciate. "We both do business in this area. I don't think either of us want Sir Edward losing his knighthood when he lets men like us go about our business for the right price. Elizabeth and Kaylein are going to tear him apart at the trial if he brings up what happened with them. If you tell him to keep his mouth shut, I'll keep what you're doing here in the forest to myself."

Harald looked like he was seething at being caught out, but he wasn't stupid. He looked back at his men. Isaac squeezed Blackberry's bridle.

"Is that it, then?" Harald said.

Isaac shrugged. "You know it makes sense. I just want to make sure you're not going to let your lord do something stupid."

"Get out of here, and keep my business to yourself if you

494

know what's good for you."

Isaac sensed he'd gotten what he wanted. Harald had probably been doubting Edward's chances already, and now he had an extra incentive to make sure his lord kept quiet. Turning Blackberry around, Isaac clicked his tongue and urged her away at a trot.

A few moments later, he heard the sound of hoofbeats coming after him.

"Time to run," he whispered to Blackberry, nudging her sides and lifting himself up in the saddle. As his horse sped up to a canter, he glanced behind him and saw the man with the sword galloping down the trail. Isaac's heart raced as his pursuer gained ground, but he resisted the urge to drive Blackberry on any faster. Even though she could fly like the wind, it was dangerous on a rough trail like this. He kept just enough distance with the horseman to prevent him drawing level, then let Blackberry slow and dance around the roots of a twisted oak that marked a tight bend in the path. She moved with such grace that the horse behind them sounded like a lumbering ox by comparison. Its rider yelled and yanked back on the reins to slow down, realising too late how tight the bend was. The beast snorted and bucked, blundering off the path before coming to a full stop. By the time their pursuer negotiated his way around the bend, Isaac and Blackberry had an insurmountable lead. Two more twists of the path, and the horseman was out of sight.

Isaac leaned forward to rub his mare's mane when they emerged back onto the relative safety of the road to Tannersfield. "Why would a man need land and subjects when he has you, hm?" He blew Blackberry a kiss. She flapped her ears dismissively at him.

Isaac's chest was bursting with excitement on the ride back to town. He couldn't wait to tell Sam about his little adventure, to say nothing of the look he'd provoked on Harald's face. Most of all, he was eager to see Elizabeth's expression light up when he told her he'd succeeded. She deserved to stop worrying for a while.

* * *

Edward hadn't been in such a vile mood since the night Cristiana rejected him. He was having trouble sleeping again. Even his forays across the moors weren't enough to take his mind off the impending trial. He still couldn't understand how it had happened. One moment he'd been on the brink of his long-deserved revenge, the next he was shackled by the king's law. It was unjust. He'd had every right to do what he did, but Joseph Carpenter had whined and begged to the sheriff's bailiff, and Simon Bailey was a dour man who couldn't understand that a knight sometimes had to let his passions guide him.

It was two weeks until the trial, and Harald had delivered yet another blow to Edward's mood when he told him he could no longer defend himself using the argument he'd prepared. He sat at the high table in Rosepath Castle rolling a goblet between one hand and the other. Harald and Alfred of Copperway sat across from him while Father Gregory scribbled away at his vellum on the far end. Everyone else had been told to stay out.

"It's not fair," Edward muttered. "Lady Kaylein should be punished for what her servant did to me. Now you're saying I can't accuse either of them?"

Harald shook his head. "It isn't worth it." He sounded on edge, but Edward put that down to what had happened the day he ransacked the workshop. Harald knew he was on thin ice for having kept Elizabeth a secret from him

"You've really humped your own mare this time, Edward," Alfred said. His smugness was infuriating, but he was one of the few people in the castle who knew anything about law. Apparently his grandfather had been one of the foremost judges in the kingdom in his day.

"Stop talking muck and tell me what I can do!" Edward

496

said. "You're making it sound like I should just let them accuse me without fighting back."

Father Gregory looked up from his writing. "If the accusations are true then a humble man would submit himself to the justice of the law."

"Oh, shut up, Gregory," Edward said. He had no time for the priest's sermons.

"He may be right," Harald said. "If you try and accuse Elizabeth of anything she'll have Lady Kaylein stand as her witness and denounce you. Then the penalty could be even harsher."

"Only if the judge is a fool. Who is he, anyway?"

"Audley of Crownacre," Alfred said. "He's a royalist and an old friend of King Ralf's. I don't expect you'll get much sympathy from him if you say you were only running down a pair of teenage girls because Count Leo's murderer told you to."

Edward felt hopelessly trapped. If he hadn't been so frustrated at the unjustness of his situation, he would have been terrified. It seemed like there was no way out of it. He was damned no matter what.

"So if I can't defend myself, what should I do?" he asked Alfred.

The other knight cast a luxuriating glance around the hall, savouring Edward's discomfort before he answered. "Try and seem humble. Claim you acted passionately, then offer to pay the carpenter for the damage you caused. If you'd just done that when the sheriff gave you the chance you wouldn't be in this mess."

"I can't—"

"You don't have a choice. Grovel, beg, and plead with God for forgiveness. If you're lucky, the judge will let you off with a fine."

"And what am I supposed to pay my men with if the carpenters' guild empty my coffers?!"

"I don't know. Sell some of your horses. Get rid of a few

servants. I'll still be able to pay my men to carry out the duke's orders even if you can't."

Edward snatched up his goblet and threw it at Alfred in anger. He ducked, and the ceramic vessel shattered on the floor behind him. As if things weren't bad enough, now he had to endure his rival taunting him. Father Gregory gave them a tense look as if he expected the pair to begin brawling in the hall, but Edward reined in his temper. Harald had been unusually quiet for a while.

"What are you thinking about, Harald?" Edward asked in a huff, trying to ignore Alfred's gloating.

"If the judge is Audley of Crownacre then I might have an idea."

"Well go on then, spit it out."

"Audley has a son in Tannersfield. I met him a couple of years ago to see if he could introduce me to his father."

Edward perked up. "Do you think he could get the judge on our side?"

"I don't know. He doesn't have any of his father's connections, but I do know he wants to be a knight. He came here hoping to find a lord who would take him on as a squire. Somehow I suspect he's still looking."

"Is he a halfwit?"

"No, just a little useless. The sort who wants to succeed on his own merits. Doesn't want any help from his father to get him into a noble household. He was mopping up blood for one of the butchers last I saw him."

"So if he's a nobody and he doesn't have his father's ear, how is he going to help us?" Edward said.

"Perhaps you could be the herald of his good fortune? Take him on as your squire. If his father sent him out here to prove himself, I doubt he'll want to punish his son's new patron too harshly. It might just be enough to get you out of the courtroom without any lasting wounds."

Edward didn't want a squire. He enjoyed the practicality of doing things for himself, and he already had a page to run domestic errands at the castle. But if it spared him the judge's wrath, he was willing to give it a try.

"Well well, you're still useful after all." He gave Harald a smile. "Go and find him for me. Send him to Rosepath and I'll make him my squire right away."

"Don't you think that'll look suspicious?" Alfred said. "Judges are wise to tricks like that."

"Let him be suspicious. If he wants his son to succeed, he'll be lenient."

Father Gregory murmured something about underhandedness, but Edward ignored him.

"Sir Alfred is right," said Harald. "We should have Audley's son send him a letter before the trial. The sooner he learns about the arrangement, the less suspicious he'll be. I can date the letter a few weeks ago and pretend it was delayed. It'll look like you took his son on before this business with Joseph even happened."

Once again Edward's distaste for Harald's duplicity was outstripped only by his admiration for his usefulness. He'd never have thought to put a false date on a letter. Now that they had a plan, he was feeling confident again. He wouldn't have to suffer any lasting indignity over this. Of course he wouldn't! He was in the right, after all. So what if Elizabeth and her carpenter friends had managed to make him squirm for a bit? He'd be the one laughing in the end.

The boy came to Rosepath two days later, riding a lame pony that almost keeled over the moment Gwayne Stabler tugged it toward the stalls. Edward had just come back from a hunt. He appraised the judge's son as he stood before him in the courtyard. He was about the same age as him, perhaps a year or two younger, but that was already old for an aspiring squire.

"What's your name?" Edward asked.

"Oswald, my lord."

"And you want to be my squire, is that right?"

Oswald's face lit up. "More than anything. I must have spoken to every other knight in Tannersfield this past year, but none of them—"

"None of them want you," Edward finished for him. He could see why. Despite being tall, Oswald had a lanky, awkward look that told Edward he was probably clumsy. His arms were too long and his legs too short for his body. The rancid odour of offal wafting off his clothes made it clear he'd been working in a slaughterhouse.

"I know I'm old for it," Oswald said, "but I'm literate. I know how to fight and conduct myself at court. It won't be my first time in a manor house. I'll work as hard as you need me to."

"Good." Edward wondered whether Oswald had been dissuaded at all by the news of his impending trial. Everyone else in Tannersfield seemed to have heard about it. But either the judge's son was too desperate to care, or he didn't believe Edward would suffer any lasting consequences. "I'll take you on as my squire. You'll come to live here at the castle."

"Thank you, lord!" Oswald looked beside himself with joy. "I'll return to town immediately for my belongings. Thank you."

"Before you go, take a day to rest. It looks like your horse needs it. You can use the time to write some letters."

Oswald gave him a confused look.

"Letters to your family," Edward said impatiently. "Won't your father want to hear the good news?"

"Oh. Of course. Yes, I'm sure he'll be delighted."

Edward smiled. "Good. Go inside. My page will bring you pen and parchment."

If Oswald was suspicious, he showed no sign of it. He had the demeanour of a serf who'd stumbled upon a gold crown buried in the road and was too enamoured with his good fortune to question it. Maybe the fellow was a halfwit after all. Well, as long as he wrote his letter he could be as useless as he wanted for the next two weeks. Edward could always find a reason to get rid of him after the trial was over.

CHAPTER 33

A hum of nervous anticipation had enveloped Tannersfield. It was like a swarm of bees flitting through each street, turning heads and stilting conversations, interrupting chores and halting marketgoers in their tracks. It was the same exchange repeated over and over. "Have you heard? It's happening today. Yes, really. The whole guild! They say he's going to hang. Edward. Yes, Edward. Sir Edward."

Elizabeth had never heard a person's name spoken so often by so many people. Some whispered it under their breath, others spat it out scornfully. When she looked down the road past the nunnery, she saw a crowd already gathering outside the sheriff's new courthouse. Edward's trial had become a spectacle.

The tense excitement squirming in her gut wasn't exactly a feeling of hope, but she could almost taste it. Tonight might be the first night in years she put her head down without the fear of Edward in the back of her mind. It was like a pebble beneath her mattress, a pebble that had become a boulder ever since Edward ransacked the workshop. One way or another, this day would mark a turning point in her life. If the judge didn't find Edward guilty, she would have to leave

Tannersfield. Her few meagre belongings were already bundled up in her cloak on Joseph's table. The carpenters who had been thinking of moving to Rambirch, Adam and Thin Robin, had decided to put their families on a cart tomorrow, and they'd invited Elizabeth to join them. If they found reliable work and a good place to settle, Joseph and the others might consider following them in the seasons to come. After hearing about Harald's attempt at blackmail, Joseph didn't care about staying in Tannersfield to repay the merchant's favour. The mood of the carpenters had soured against their home town, and many of them seemed to have made up their minds that they would be moving on sooner or later.

Elizabeth's suppressed hopes lent a restless energy to her step as she went around the market filling a large basket with bread, fish, and eggs. The carpenters were going to share a meal at the guild hall before heading to the courthouse for the trial. Even Theobald, who Elizabeth still resented for causing her so much trouble last year, had helped rally the guild behind Joseph. Despite their internal squabbles, when someone outside the guild threatened one of their own, the carpenters banded together. There was nothing like a common enemy to forge unity. In a strange way, Theobald had been partially responsible for all of this, for if he'd never drawn attention to Elizabeth she might not have caught Harald's eye at the guild meeting. When Elizabeth thought about it that way, connecting all the steps that had drawn her into this situation, she wondered whether it was evidence of God's plan at work. It would be heartening to think so. Perhaps God wanted to punish Sir Edward, and this was how it was supposed to happen. Kaylein said God would be on their side that day. Elizabeth hoped she was right.

Sam, Isaac, and Kaylein were all waiting for her when she arrived at the guild hall. The carpenters were in boisterous spirits, invigorated by their righteous indignation. They slapped Joseph on the back with words of encouragement, promising him that today would be the day their guild made a name for itself in the king's court. If they could stand up to a knight like Sir Edward, no one would dare question their reputation again. Elizabeth put down her basket of food and went to join her friends.

"How are you feeling?" Kaylein asked. She looked tired and anxious, but she was trying to put on a confident face for Elizabeth's sake. The weeks on the farm had clearly been difficult for her. Her nun's robe was growing threadbare around the hem, its rich black fading to a bluish brown as the daily mud caked on and washed off. Seeing Edward punished would be as much a relief for her as it would Elizabeth.

"I'm ready for the judge," she said, trying to bolster Kaylein's confidence with a smile of her own. Both of them would be going to the courthouse as witnesses that day, though Kaylein would only need to speak if Edward brought up what had happened in the forest. Sam and Isaac would be staying behind to watch the workshop. A house of law wasn't the best place for either of them to make themselves conspicuous.

"Good luck," Isaac told her. "You stand a good chance of winning. Better than most people would against a knight."

She thanked him and gave Sam a hug. Isaac had grown on her since he'd accosted Harald in the forest. She wouldn't have expected such bravery from her brother's strange, half-noble friend. According to Isaac, the law in their kingdom relied heavily on witnesses. Since so many people were willing to speak out against Edward, they would have a heavy advantage on that front.

They sat and ate with the carpenters, though anxiety had displaced most of Elizabeth's appetite. Sam finished the last of her bread for her, and she drank water instead of ale so her head would stay clear.

Joseph rose to his feet afterwards.

"Alright, it's time. We'll make that judge believe us if we have to keep him in the courthouse till sundown." He led

Elizabeth outside with a hand on her shoulder, and the rest of the guild followed. They were met with calls of encouragement from the bystanders who'd gathered outside. As they crossed the marketplace, more people joined the procession. The crowd parted to let them through, the buzz of gossip growing to a thrum.

It was happening. Joseph Carpenter and his guild were on their way to challenge Sir Edward in court.

Never before had Elizabeth felt so many eyes on her at once. It was as emboldening as it was terrifying. Not everyone rallied against Sir Edward. Shouts of scorn occasionally joined the words of support. At one point she had to duck a rotten onion thrown by a woman who screamed at them from her doorway. Edward had been well-liked by the residents of Tannersfield before his reputation turned against him. A few townsfolk still saw him as a brave local boy who'd defied his humble origins to become a knight. The rich and powerful disliked any challenge to the established hierarchy, and those who looked up to them took them at their word.

Elizabeth gasped when the courthouse hove into view. The crowd had grown ten times over since she last saw it. It looked like half of Tannersfield was there. The town watch and several men-at-arms were shouting and waving their weapons to keep the road clear. A mounted knight with large front teeth smiled at them as they went by, calling for his men to clear a path to the courthouse doors. There was so much noise Elizabeth could no longer tell whether people were yelling encouragements or insults at her. She stayed close to Joseph's side, keeping her head down and her eyes on the road as boots stamped and voices roared all around her.

She breathed a little easier once they entered the cool, dim interior of the courthouse. It still had the woody smell of a new building, which reminded her of the workshop. Over a hundred people were packed into the long hall, but their talk was subdued in comparison to the thundering crowd outside.

Some might be waiting to have their own cases tried by the king's judge that day, but most were there for Edward.

The judge sat at a raised table at the end of the hall, much like the setup in a manorial court. He was a middle-aged, red-haired man whose stern demeanour appeared undaunted by the baying crowd. Once all the witnesses had assembled, he rang a handbell to call the court to order. Several men-at-arms corralled the attendees toward benches that lined the back of the room like church pews. There weren't enough seats for everyone, so most people remained standing.

"I know why most of you are here," the judge said once the hubbub had settled. "So I suggest we clear out this noise as swiftly as possible. Sir Edward of Tannersfield and Joseph Carpenter, please step forward."

Elizabeth drew a tense breath and moved to find Kaylein. The trial had begun.

A stirring of movement on the opposite side of the hall revealed Edward and his entourage. The knight was dressed splendidly, though he wore no sword in the sheath on his belt. The sheriff's men had probably taken it from him before he entered the courthouse. With him were Harald Redcloak, the toothy knight Elizabeth had seen outside, and a lanky young man she didn't recognise. Joseph and Edward drew level with one another as they came to stand before the judge's table. Simon Bailey and another armed bailiff rose to flank them, poised to settle any violent outbursts that might arise mid-trial. The far end of the hall seemed conspicuously empty to Elizabeth. Beside the judge's table, a row of unoccupied chairs lined one of the walls.

"I think those are for the jury," Kaylein said when Elizabeth asked about them. "They usually have one in big courts like this. It's how they determine whether a person is guilty or not. I don't know why there isn't one today."

The judge rang his bell once more and asked Joseph and Edward to state their grievances. Elizabeth hoped he would be just and fair. She'd heard a dozen tales over the past week about how judges could be bribed and intimidated by ruthless nobles. This one didn't look like the sort of man who was easily bullied, but the absence of a jury worried her.

"Have faith," Kaylein whispered, squeezing her hand tight.

To Elizabeth's surprise, Edward did not attempt to justify himself after Joseph finished laying out his accusations. The knight sounded tense and hesitant as he proclaimed his sincere regret for what had happened at the workshop. Elizabeth looked across the courthouse and saw Harald smiling. A nervous shiver ran down her spine. Edward wasn't behaving like his usual, bull-headed self. Someone had told him to act this way in front of the judge.

"So, you confess to the accusations made by Joseph Carpenter?" the judge asked Edward once he had finished.

"I do, but his accusations are not the whole story. I would like to plea for lenience, not exoneration."

Kaylein whispered: "That's why there's no jury. Edward must have agreed to confess his guilt beforehand."

"Very well," the judge said. "Then the witnesses here will paint us a fuller picture of exactly what happened, and how severely it deserves to be punished." He eyed the crowd of carpenters at the back of the room. "I hope you don't mean to have every single one of yours testify, Master Joseph."

"Theobald Carpenter will speak on behalf of the guild," Joseph answered.

Elizabeth was quickly losing the thread of the legal proceedings. Most of the disputes she'd seen in manorial courts had been grievances between villagers that were swiftly adjudicated by their lord or some other person of authority. They hadn't been all that different to some of the arguments she'd seen in public houses. Edward had confessed his guilt, but he still wanted to argue about something. Elizabeth didn't know what exoneration meant, so she turned to Kaylein again, who explained that Edward was trying to persuade the judge to treat him lightly by arguing that his crime was not as severe as Joseph made it out to be. Elizabeth's anxiety grew. She'd been expecting Edward to rail against the carpenters, an approach that would surely have backfired with so many witnesses to counter him. But now he was trying to soften the blow, which meant he might survive with his title and holdings intact. It would still be a victory for Elizabeth and Joseph, but there would always be that lingering fear that he might come after them again someday.

She shared her worries with Kaylein as Theobald stepped forward to voice the concerns of the carpenters' guild.

"Even if he's only fined," Kaylein whispered, "that could still ruin him. Knights are no good to their lords without money to pay for men and horses. That's why they're given land to tax."

"Can't Duke Francis just give him more land?"

Kaylein shook her head. "Lords don't want vassals who can't take care of themselves. They're supposed to be reliable, and Duke Francis has trusted Edward with a lot. Did you see that other knight with him?" She pointed at the man with the prominent front teeth. "I think he's called Sir Alfred. He's one of Francis's men, too. The duke might take away Edward's holdings and give them to someone like him instead."

Elizabeth began feeling confident again. Even if Edward didn't lose his knighthood, having him shamed and sent away to some lesser holding would achieve much the same result. But it was still early in the trial, and there was a lot that could happen to turn things against them. After Theobald had spoken–making a firm if somewhat passionless argument about the importance of trade guilds doing business without living in fear of upstart lords–Harald Redcloak came forward to speak on Edward's behalf.

"While my lord has done wrong," the merchant began, "I fear these tradesmen are trying to make a cruel example of an honest mistake in order to further their own ends. Master Theobald and his guild brothers will be able to tell you that

508

I've attended several of their meetings over the past year, and the subject of improving the guild's standing is never far from their lips. You need only look outside to see the spectacle they've drummed up with this trial. While I would never ask for my lord's crimes to be overlooked, I would appeal to the judge to take into consideration the self-interested motivations of the men accusing him."

There was an angry stir among the carpenters.

The judge rang his bell for quiet. "Master Theobald, is what he says true? Has this man been present at your meetings?"

"Yes," Theobald admitted.

"And do you often discuss means of improving your guild's standing?"

"Of course we do. Any guild would."

The judge nodded. It was hard to tell whether he was being swayed by Harald's argument.

Harald continued: "Joseph Carpenter himself is far from an honest man. I paid a fine on his behalf last year that he has yet to reimburse me for."

Joseph scowled at the merchant. "We agreed on a different form of repayment and you know it."

"I remember agreeing to waive the loan until you were able to pay me back." Harald kept his focus on the judge, maintaining his composure while Joseph grew heated. "It was an informal arrangement, of course, which is why I haven't taken it to court. I was a fool to give my silver away so freely, and I've suffered for it. Joseph Carpenter is not a trustworthy man."

"I agreed to send carpenters to Rosepath in exchange for that money!"

"Your own carpenters?" the judge interrupted.

"No, milord; journeymen who were coming through town."

"A very easy agreement for him to ignore," Harald said.

Elizabeth wished she could have told Joseph to calm

down. He wasn't doing himself any favours by raising his voice while Harald remained formal and polite. The judge went on to ask whether the nature of their agreement could be confirmed by any other witnesses. Naturally, Harald knew the carpenters' guild could attest to him having paid Joseph's fine, but there was no way of proving Joseph had held up his end of the bargain. The journeymen he'd sent to Rosepath had been asked informally, usually in private. Even the men at the workshop didn't know about most of them. It was a heavy blow against the carpenters. Now Joseph and the guild looked sloppy and self-interested, which lent credence to Harald's narrative about them wanting to humiliate Edward for their own gain. Elizabeth had also noticed that the judge kept looking over to Edward's side of the room—in particular at the lanky young man who'd arrived with them. There was something else going on here she wasn't privy to.

Harald continued making arguments that cast the carpenters in an unflattering light, citing things that had been said at guild meetings, their long-standing reputation for uselessness, and the frequent infighting that divided them. To Elizabeth's dismay, the judge's questions toward Joseph grew increasingly pointed and accusatory the longer he went on.

By the time Harald sat back down, she was feeling disheartened. The cunning merchant had come prepared with an approach they'd not expected. Instead of tackling the impossible task of proving Edward's innocence, he'd decided to drag everyone else down to his level.

The trial plodded on as they worked their way through the witnesses. Elizabeth's turn came soon after Harald's. Given that the focus had turned away from Edward's attempt to take revenge on her, she had relatively little to say. Isaac had advised her to speak with emotion about what had happened the evening Edward came to the workshop. If she could paint a harrowing picture of the knight's brutality, the judge would feel sympathetic towards her.

She described the events as best she could, but she was

not a gifted storyteller, and it was hard to make her tale sound both vivid and truthful. Isaac made it look easy when he told stories, but it was different speaking in front of such a large crowd. It didn't seem like the judge was very interested in what she had to say, so much so that he didn't even ring his bell for silence when people began talking behind her. She tried to speak with the authoritative voice she used in the workshop, only to realise it did a poor job of conveying the fear she'd felt hiding under the bed as Sir Edward's sword scraped the floor beneath her. In the end, her testimony came across as awkward and stumbling.

She caught Edward giving her a mocking look as she returned to the back of the room. Her first impulse was to avert her eyes in fear, but she was frustrated at herself for her weak performance in front of the judge. She pressed her lips together tightly and held Edward's gaze. Her defiance surprised him, and his brow furrowed in anger.

"You did well," Kaylein whispered when she returned to her spot.

"I don't think so. I sounded like a confused little girl."

"You told the truth, and that is what matters. If the judge is wise, he'll see that."

Despite Kaylein's encouragement, Elizabeth's unease had given way to a creeping sense of dread. The trial wasn't going well for them. Edward and his entourage looked confident, while the carpenters had started muttering furtively among themselves. They were saying the lanky man on Edward's side was the judge's son. The looks the judge had been giving him made sense now. Some underhanded bargain had been struck beforehand.

"I hate Edward," Elizabeth whispered to Kaylein. "How can the king let men like that serve him?" It was better to be angry than to despair. When Kaylein didn't respond, she looked over to see her friend's eyes closed and her hands clasped in silent prayer.

Sir Alfred of Copperway spoke on Edward's behalf next.

He struck Elizabeth as an articulate and educated man who knew his way around a court of law, but his argument did not seem to do Edward many favours. Despite reminding everyone that Edward was a knight of the realm, to be treated with dignity, respect, and deference, he soon fell into a lengthy diatribe about how reckless and hotblooded commoners could become when raised up to knighthood. His attempts to excuse Edward's actions were mired in thinly-veiled scorn. He was trying to argue that his companion hadn't realised what he'd been doing, but instead of making Edward sound youthful and inexperienced, he ended up portraying him as a bumpkin who barely knew how to manage an estate. In the end, it was hard to tell whether his contribution ended up helping Edward's case or hindering it.

Most of the important witnesses had spoken now. Elizabeth wondered whether Sir Alfred's weak performance had been enough to tip the judge's sympathies back in their favour. Regardless of whether some bargain had been struck, the judge still seemed like he was being swayed back and forth. Elizabeth prayed his sense of justice would win out over any personal motives.

The trial had already taken up a significant part of the morning, so the judge began to hurry through the remaining speakers. Almost all of them were prominent locals, guild representatives, and townspeople who had witnessed what happened at the workshop. One woman, the wife of the blacksmith who worked on their street, was fond of performing in the mummers' farces, and her theatrical account of Edward's brutality was exceptionally captivating. Several people gasped as she described how he had smashed a cart and drawn his sword on a young apprentice boy before the brave carpenters stood their ground and forced him to leave.

Elizabeth realised with mounting excitement that it was these impassioned accounts, not the dry testimonies of the key witnesses, that were swaying the mood of the courthouse in Joseph's favour. It would be difficult for the judge to ignore the sentiment of the crowd. Perhaps he might even think twice about allowing his son to squire for a man with such an abysmal reputation.

The assault against Edward's character refused to let up. As speaker after speaker stepped forward, Elizabeth realised that the knight's trick of making the trial about lenience rather than guilt had backfired. He hadn't expected so many people to speak out against him. He was sitting at his bench with his head down, hands clenched together in rage as he was forced to listen to the people of Tannersfield damn him again and again. A farmer who knew Fred Fielder's father spoke out about the unjust flogging that had taken place at the building site. The foreman whose nose Edward had broken attested to the same thing. Trappers who had the sheriff's permission to hunt in the forest described how they'd met harmless vagrants whose friends and family had been brutally slaughtered by Edward's men.

The mob was hungry for justice, not just against Edward, but as vindication for the hardships their town had suffered since Count Leo's death. It was just like what had happened at the guild hall when Theobald rallied the carpenters against Elizabeth. Tannersfield was suffering, and the people needed a show of action to prove that things could change. Whether it was justified or not, Edward had become a figurehead for their anger. That was why the courthouse had drawn such an enormous crowd that day. If Edward was stripped of his knighthood, it would be a sign that Tannersfield was on its way back to its former glory. The people needed this victory.

Even though it was working in her favour, the sheer strength of the town's furore unnerved Elizabeth. She prayed she would never be on the receiving end of such a mob. Folk who stood out attracted attention and blame. They became the scapegoats of problems and the villains of public gossip. After this was all over, she would be happy to keep her head down and remain inconspicuous for the rest of her life.

At noon the judge rang his bell and had Simon Bailey corral everyone to the back of the hall. Not every witness had been given the chance to speak, but it didn't seem to matter. More than enough criticism had been levelled at Edward to paint a repugnant picture of his character. The proceedings had left Elizabeth exhausted. She was thirsty and her legs ached from standing in one place so long. She just wanted it to be over and done with. There had been so many shifts back and forth between hope and anxiety that she didn't know what to expect anymore, but in her heart, she sensed they'd won. The judge could not possibly excuse Edward's crimes after hearing so many people speak out against him.

Joseph and Edward were called back to the front of the hall. The knight stepped forward with his shoulders hunched, his gait stiff and uncomfortable. Was he afraid? Elizabeth hoped so. After all the fear he'd put them through, he deserved a taste of his own medicine.

The crowd grew silent as the judge rose to speak. Even those who were not there for Edward's trial had become engrossed in the proceedings.

"We've heard enough for one day. I think the answer is clear to everyone in this room. Sir Edward has erred, and he must face punishment for his crime."

A roar of approval rose from the carpenters. Elizabeth stood up on the balls of her feet, pressing a hand to her mouth in excitement.

Once the judge had silenced the noise with his bell he continued: "However, nobody was harmed during the incident at Joseph Carpenter's workshop, and he has already refused to accept a fine in repayment for the damage. With that in mind, it is my verdict that Sir Edward will submit himself to spiritual penance, the nature of which shall be determined by the bishop of Tannersfield at his ecclesiastical court."

A moment of confused silence followed the judge's proclamation. Much like Elizabeth, most people in the room did not seem to know what spiritual penance meant. She turned to Kaylein, but before she could finish asking her words were drowned out by shouts of anger rising from the crowd.

"That's no punishment at all!"

"He's killed people!"

"He's a villain!"

The judge beat the air with his bell. "That is my judgement! Silence! Silence!"

Simon Bailey restrained Joseph with a hand on his arm as he tried to step around the judge's table. The courthouse seemed moments away from descending into chaos. Desperation took hold of Elizabeth as she cupped her hands to Kaylein's ear and said: "What does it mean?"

"It means the bishop will give him penance like he would a monk. It won't be a real punishment."

Elizabeth's heart dropped to the pit of her stomach. Had they lost after all? A monk's penance might humiliate Edward, but it wouldn't break him. It would only make him angrier at the people responsible.

Elizabeth suddenly felt lost in the baying crowd as a numbing veil descended over her. Sam was right. There was no justice for people like them. Even judges were subject to the whims of lords. She would never be free of Edward, not as long as she remained in Tannersfield.

The realisation of what she had to do was like someone snapping their fingers in her ear, dragging her back into the moment. That was it, then. There was no point despairing over it. She didn't have time.

"I need to leave. I'll go to Rambirch with Adam and Robin first thing in the morning." She didn't know whether Kaylein could hear her over the noise, but she nodded when their eyes met.

Simon Bailey finally managed to restore order when he tipped over one of the jurors' chairs. The heavy oak back slammed against the wooden floor with such a bang that it

515

opened up a moment of silence. The judge roared for everyone to sit down and for Joseph's group to leave. Anyone who disobeyed, he said, would find themselves in the sheriff's jail awaiting a trial of their own.

A modicum of composure returned to the courthouse as Elizabeth left. The same could not be said of the crowd she found waiting outside. A lot of people had grown tired of waiting to hear the verdict and gone home, but a busy knot of townsfolk still filled half the street. Elizabeth went out with Joseph and Kaylein at the back of the group. They said nothing to one another until the press of the crowd enveloped them. Word already seemed to have spread about the verdict. People were yelling and jostling. Elizabeth wished they would go away. Their anger wouldn't change anything. It never did.

"Stay close to me," Joseph said, putting his arm around her shoulder. "We'll get off the main road and head home another way."

Elizabeth's heart ached to hear him call the workshop home. It would be hers for just one more night, then she would be gone.

People tried to pull Joseph aside and talk to him about what had happened. He cursed and pushed past them until they were free of the crowd. Elizabeth could feel his hand trembling on her upper arm. The judge's verdict had hit him just as hard as it had her. They were about to head down a street on the opposite side of the road when a roar of noise erupted behind them. Turning to look, Elizabeth saw a stir of movement near the side of the courthouse. A few moments later, Sir Edward and Sir Alfred rose above the heads of the townspeople as they mounted their horses. Someone threw mud at Edward, and with a snarl he yanked his horse in the direction of the culprit. A woman screamed and the crowd drew back, the sudden crush of movement causing several people to fall over. The yells grew louder. A child began wailing.

"People are going to get hurt," Elizabeth said, realising with horror that the crowd was on the verge of rioting.

"All the more reason for us to get going," Joseph said, pulling her and Kaylein away.

"What about the others?"

Joseph gripped Elizabeth's arm tighter. None of the other carpenters were with them. "I'll fetch them, but you two hurry back to the workshop. Don't argue now!" He let go and waded back into the crowd.

People were still struggling to get out of Edward and Alfred's way as they drove their horses down the street. Elizabeth felt a stab of fear as Edward appeared to glance in her direction. She drew back behind the wall of the nearest house, but he didn't seem to have noticed her.

Kaylein tugged at her hand. "Come on," she said anxiously. "We must do as Joseph said."

Elizabeth allowed herself to be led away from the mob. The yelling followed them for a long time until they reached the marketplace, where the bustle of commerce finally drowned out the noise. If anything happened to the carpenters, she would never forgive herself. Joseph had taken Edward to court because of her, and it had ended in disaster. She still couldn't believe the judge had sided against them. It must have been because of his son. Edward and Harald had been busy scheming to get him on their side. Dwelling on it made her feel sick, but she couldn't help herself. It was the only way to keep her head above the flood that felt like it was sweeping away the life she'd built in Tannersfield.

They arrived back at the workshop and shared the bad news with Sam and Isaac. When Elizabeth saw her brother, she hugged him and didn't want to let go. She wanted him to take charge and tell her what to do like when they were young, back when his cocksure confidence had made the world feel safe and her troubles few.

"I'll come with you tomorrow," Kaylein said. "We'll go to Rambirch together."

"Me too," said Sam.

Their support was a spark of warmth in the midst of Elizabeth's despair. It would have been a miserable journey to face alone. At least now Kaylein and her brother would be there to share the burden.

Joseph and the others returned soon after. A few of the carpenters had bruises, but no one had been seriously injured in the commotion.

"We were lucky," Joseph huffed. "Edward and that other knight might as well have trampled half the crowd with their horses. I saw a little girl get stepped on by her own father in that mess."

"At least you're safe," Rose said, kissing her husband's cheek. Rose's hard attitude had softened considerably in the days since Edward came to the workshop. She'd drawn her flock close around her, turning her anger outward toward the people who threatened them.

"We should all stay indoors tonight," Joseph said. "There's going to be trouble. This is just the start of it. That mob's going to get angrier and angrier till the sheriff's men break it up."

"Did it get worse after we left?" Elizabeth asked.

Joseph nodded. "Everyone followed Edward to the market. He couldn't get his horse through the stalls, and the roads were blocked up so badly from the courthouse crowd no one could move their carts. Edward couldn't reach the south gate, so he went to the castle instead. By the time we left, the marketplace was a mess. Must've been a hundred people outside the castle gates chanting for Edward and the sheriff to be hanged."

"Lord have mercy," Rose said.

"Has anything like this happened before?" Elizabeth asked.

"Aye. You'd be too young to remember it, but it was near the end of the war, back when I was a lad." Joseph looked at Kaylein. "I'd come into town to see your father hang the old

518

count. That's the only time I've seen so many folk this angry. Half of them weren't even there for justice. They just wanted to let something out. Must've been three dozen houses burned and twice as many folk dead by the night's end."

Elizabeth shuddered. "The sheriff wouldn't let anything like that happen again, would he?"

"We'll see." Joseph turned to address the others. "Everyone, get back home. There'll be no work today. Keep your doors barred and your families close. If that mob comes anywhere near you, pick up your silver and come here. Luther, you still have that sword?"

The old carpenter nodded. "Behind my woodpile."

"Have one of your boys fetch it, just in case."

"Do you think Edward might come back?" Elizabeth asked.

Joseph shook his head. "It's not him I'm worried about, girl. It's the rest of the sinners in Tannersfield who'll have idle hands tonight."

CHAPTER 34

For a while there, Edward had been afraid. Everything in the courthouse was going against him. Harald's plan hadn't worked. The carpenters had managed to gather up too many witnesses, seemingly every person Edward had slighted since becoming lord of Rosepath. But his fears had been groundless. The judge was no fool. He knew how commoners got wild ideas into their heads, blaming their hardships on lords rather than their own moral failings. Edward had first-hand experience of such delusions, often having felt that way himself as a boy. But he had worked hard and deferred to his betters, dragging himself out of the squalor with grit and hard work. Now he harboured only pity for those who lacked the will do to the same for themselves. The witnesses in the courthouse had been jealous and resentful of him. He'd been half-disappointed when they settled down at the end, for it would've been gratifying to see the lot of them crammed into jail cells.

In the end, things had worked out for him, as he should've known they would. Perhaps the judge had realised Edward was a benevolent man for giving Oswald the same opportunity the sheriff had once given him. Edward had intended to dismiss his new squire after the trial, but that idea made him feel guilty now. If the judge had recognised he was a man of honour, perhaps it was his duty to prove him right by keeping Oswald on. It was something he'd have to think about later, for right now he had bigger worries. Thanks to the commotion stirred up by the mob, he and Sir Alfred had been forced to take refuge in the sheriff's castle. Harald and Oswald had been fortunate enough to slink away without being accosted.

Edward paced the length of the table in the great hall as Alfred, Simon Bailey, and the sheriff and his wife ate their supper. It was getting late, but the noise of the rabble was still audible outside. If anything it seemed to be growing louder.

"Will you sit, Edward?" the sheriff said irritably. "You're like a hen pecking at my floor."

Edward stopped pacing. "What are we going to do about this?" He gestured toward the noise rolling in through the high windows. "It's getting worse."

"It always does before it gets better. They can beat their fists against my gate till they tire themselves out. Tomorrow we'll find the ringleaders and make examples of them."

Simon Bailey cast a sceptical look toward the door. "The constables have been sent to gather up the watch, but that was some hours ago."

"The watch are useless," Edward said. "They're probably out there looting alongside the thieves."

As much as it clearly pained Simon to be on the same side as Edward, he nodded his head in agreement. "Something has to be done. If the watch aren't attending to their duties, there's a risk of fires starting, to say nothing of robberies."

The sheriff scowled into his wine. Edward had greatly respected the man once, but these days he was a shadow of his former self. He'd let his town go to ruin these past two years, and it had culminated in the carpenters putting Edward on trial. Had it not been for his deep sense of obligation to the sheriff, he would have suggested Duke Francis petition the king to replace him.

"Make sure we have people up on the walls," the sheriff said. "I don't see what more we can do with that mob blocking the gates."

"Pray it rains and the weather drives them all home," Alfred said.

Edward began to pace again, but the sheriff gave him a sharp look and he slumped into his chair in a sulk. The noise of the mob made him nervous. He didn't like sitting still at the best of times. Even the sheriff's good wine couldn't distract him that evening. Well, if the sheriff wanted to sit in his keep, so be it. If the town burned down around him, it would be a disaster of his own making.

Edward glared at his untouched plate of food, his brooding thoughts returning to the trial. The bishop of Tannersfield was a friend of Duke Francis, so he doubted his punishment at the ecclesiastical court would be too severe. Even so, he'd probably face some humiliation to prove he was repentant. He'd seen disobedient monks lashed to carts and forced to drag them through town like oxen before kneeling to kiss the bishop's feet. If he was forced to do something like that, the shame of it would follow him forever. He'd never be able to hold his head high in Tannersfield again. Damn that Joseph Carpenter and his bitch of a servant. It would be difficult to take revenge on them now. The trial had been a sobering reminder that he couldn't do as he pleased outside Rosepath, no matter how justified he felt in doing it. If he went to the workshop again there would be dozens more witnesses eager to speak out against him, and he doubted he would survive a second trial.

He managed to pass the time thinking about how else he might make Joseph and Elizabeth suffer. Maybe there was a way of ruining the carpenter's business? Harald might be able to help him with that. But no—the carpenters had a whole guild backing them up. A guild could be just as powerful as a lord and his estate. Perhaps he could have his verderers watch the roads around Tannersfield instead? Elizabeth might lose herself in the woods someday, and no questions would be asked if she appeared to have run afoul of a group of outlaws.

Thoughts of revenge helped him feel a little better about the verdict. The servants began lighting candles and building up hearths as dusk fell. The smell of smoke reached Edward's nostrils, stronger than usual. He realised that the dull roar of the mob, which had faded into the background of his awareness, was now punctuated with the occasional scream.

One of the sheriff's men hurried into the hall.

"There's fires, my lord. One at the north end of Parson's Street and another around the storehouses."

At long last, the sheriff looked worried. "Are the watch dealing with it?"

"We can't know without going out there."

The sheriff fingered his goblet with a frown. "Keep an eye on it. Hopefully it doesn't spread."

"Hopefully," Alfred said with a sardonic lilt in his voice.

Simon Bailey got up and accompanied the man outside. Edward watched the sheriff out of the corner of his eye, wondering whether he was finally going to take action. It wasn't long before Simon returned, his leather-soled boots slapping urgently against the stone floor.

"The fires are spreading," he said. "People seem to be fighting back the one at the storehouses, but there's another near the nunnery now. Our own stables nearly caught alight when someone threw a burning brand over the wall."

"They're trying to burn down your castle!" Edward said to the sheriff. "What if they build a bonfire against the gates next?"

The sheriff ran a hand through his long hair, engrossed in thought.

"Alfred and I have a dozen armed men with us," Edward pressed on. "You must have at least a dozen of your own here in the castle."

"And swords and shields for a few stout servants," Alfred

523

added.

The sheriff gave them a look of consternation. "Do you really think you can get the rabble under control?"

Despite the seriousness of the situation, Edward couldn't keep the bitter scorn out of his voice when he replied. "I don't know, my lord. The last time I drew my sword on your townspeople you sent me to court for it."

"You have my blessing," the sheriff snapped.

"Your blessing to do whatever needs doing?"

"As long as you break up this riot and put the fires out, you're acting under my authority."

Edward smiled. He pushed his chair back and rose to his feet.

He sat astride his horse in the courtyard half an hour later, his sword at his hip and a heavy mail shirt about his shoulders. Alfred and their best riding men sat astride seven good warhorses from the sheriff's stable. About thirty other men were on foot behind them armed with swords, spears, and square shields.

"Come out in a line behind the horses," Alfred yelled over the din coming from beyond the gates. He knew more about commanding men in large groups than Edward, so he would be the one giving the orders. Edward just wanted to fight. "Keep the shields together and push the crowd back. Knock them down if they won't move, and use your weapons if they fight back. No matter what happens, stay together."

Edward drew his sword as a group of servants prepared to lift the heavy bar from the castle gates. He didn't bother listening to the orders Alfred gave the horsemen. He was remembering the hateful faces he'd seen outside the courthouse. In a few moments, he'd be trampling those people beneath his hooves. If the dregs of Tannersfield were going to behave like animals, he'd treat them like animals. The familiar thrill of serpentine fury writhed within him. His heels itched to kick into his horse's flank.

When the bar fell and the gates swung inward, he

bellowed out his anger to the crowd of torchlit faces on the other side. Shocked by the line of horsemen charging toward them, the mob broke up and tried to flee. Edward drove his horse forward. Hoofbeats drowned out the screams of panic as those who didn't move fast enough were knocked to the ground and trampled. Edward's steed wobbled beneath him as it stepped on a hunched shape in the darkness. He was at the head of the group, spearheading the wedge that would split the crowd apart. Scattered fires lit the marketplace ahead of him, but their flames paled next to the roaring blaze that had consumed a house on the western side. A skyline that should have shone with pale moonlight was fringed orange by the embers of a dozen burning buildings.

Edward had never seen anything like it. He was so mesmerised by the hellish spectacle that his horse momentarily slowed and someone leapt up to grab his saddle. With a snarl, he swung his arm and hit the attacker with the pommel of his sword. Their grip loosened, but they didn't let go. Edward turned his blade on them and thrust down. He heard a man gasp as the point bore through clothing and cartilage. He twisted his sword free and dragged himself back upright, feeling the dead weight drop away. The burning town was a terrifying sight, but Edward's blood boiled as hot as the fires around him. The monks would have much to pray for in the morning, for this would be a night of death in Tannersfield.

* * *

By the time Isaac retrieved Blackberry from the stables, he could see Joseph's fears were well-founded. As dusk fell the tang of smoke grew sharp in the air. The fires that blazed in the marketplace were no longer the merry roasting pits of food vendors, but broken carts and shattered stalls piled up into bonfires. Groups of people roved through the smoke yelling their grievances to all who would listen, revelling in the chance to vent every blasphemous thought they'd bottled up. Unconstrained fury swept Tannersfield, the shattering of a patience bent long past breaking point. Those who wanted no part in the disorder barred their doors and barricaded their yards, knowing they could expect no help from the watch. The town hadn't descended into chaos yet, but any fool could see it was only a matter of time. The crowd outside the castle were worst of all. They called for Edward's head, splashing buckets of paint and filth against the gates as they hurled stones and other projectiles over the wall. Their protest had been the spark that ignited the fire, and now everyone was taking advantage of it.

Isaac knew he had to leave before things got any worse. Sam and the others would be safe at the workshop, but he couldn't keep Blackberry in town tonight. His heart would break if she was stolen or injured in the chaos. When he reached the east gate in the old town wall, he was dismayed to find it blocked. The traffic had slowed to a standstill earlier that day, and the sudden rush to pack up the marketplace had crushed the congestion into a complete blockage. Two wagons had overturned near the gate, forcing every other cart to turn back into the tide of foot traffic. He might be able to squeeze Blackberry through if he found an opening, but the crowd was two dozen heads deep between him and the wagons. When he saw a merchant fighting with someone who'd just snatched a sack off the back of his cart, he decided getting through here would be more trouble than it was worth.

He headed back toward the marketplace, hoping the south gate would be less congested. That was when he saw flames rising over the rooftops. These were no bonfires. Houses were burning down. He clutched Blackberry's reins and put a hand on her neck, calming himself with the touch as much as he hoped to soothe her. Rather than risk crossing the marketplace again, he turned around and rode back toward Joseph's workshop. It was no stable, but at least he could take

Blackberry out of sight around the back and keep an eye on her till morning. He was surprised by how easily he made the decision to stay. Isaac didn't like crowded towns at the best of times. Getting stuck in the middle of a riot was one of his worst fears. It was an oppressive, stifling sort of danger that pressed in from all sides. Out in the open, he could always run, but in the warrens of Tannersfield he was like a rabbit cornered by a huntsman's ferrets.

Sam, Kaylein, and Elizabeth were cornered too. He imagined what it would be like to leave Tannersfield only to look back and see the whole town ablaze behind him. He shivered in discomfort. There were some things he didn't want to run from, no matter how much they scared him.

When he got back to the workshop he found Joseph, Luther, Adam, Thin Robin, Sam, and a few other men guarding the yard. Sam was holding Luther's old sword across his lap, fiddling nervously with a piece of leather that had come loose from the hilt binding.

"Can I put Blackberry behind the workshop tonight?" Isaac asked Joseph as he rode up.

"Aye, go on. Leave her with the girls and get back out here."

Isaac dismounted and led Blackberry around the side of the workshop. Elizabeth, Rose, and Kaylein were in the back yard. He could see two other women minding three children through Joseph's open door. Elizabeth was the only one who knew how to handle a horse, so he passed off Blackberry's bridle to her. He felt safe trusting Elizabeth. If the way she'd leapt into action after Fred's flogging was anything to go by, she'd be reliable in a crisis.

"Take good care of her," he said, squeezing Elizabeth's hand as he pressed the reins into it.

Her face was wrought with worry, but she forced a smile. It was a simple moment of understanding that touched Isaac's heart. They'd been dubious of each other before, but in that moment he felt a spark of something else bridging the gap between them.

When he returned to the yard, Joseph took the sword from Sam and offered it to him.

"Sam says you're the only man who knows how to swing this properly."

Isaac hesitated. It had been a long time since he held a sword. He remembered his martial lessons well enough, but his muscle memory would be out of practice.

"If I swing that at someone, it's liable to kill them," he said. Swords were made with one purpose in mind, and he had no desire to become a murderer.

"Bugger the sheriff's law tonight. Everyone else will. Do you know how to use it or not?"

Isaac gave a reluctant nod and Joseph pushed the hilt into his hand. The blade was speckled with rust and poorly balanced, but it would do. He hoped he wouldn't have to use it.

Joseph clapped him on the shoulder. "Just hold it up at anyone who comes down the street and look frightening. The lot of us out here should be enough to scare off anyone who comes sniffing around."

The other men were armed with hammers, iron spikes, and pieces of wood that would serve as clubs. They made for a vicious-looking mob. On a night like this, it was reassuring to know they were on his side. Isaac heard what sounded like a scream from the direction of the marketplace and looked up to see more orange glows outlining the rooftops.

"Do you think the fires will spread here?" he asked.

"Can't say," old Luther muttered. "We've got buckets around back, but not much water."

"There wasn't time to fetch any," Joseph said.

A pair of unfamiliar figures came down the street, but whoever it was hurried past, giving the workshop a wide berth. Isaac sat on the low fence at the front of the yard, flipping the sword in his lap as his heel tapped against the ground. Evening gave way to dusk, then nighttime. Every now and again he would hear yells or screaming, but it always seemed to be a few streets away. The smell of smoke thickened until it was like fog, making his eyes itch and his throat tickle.

The others passed the time by talking quietly amongst themselves. Adam and Robin, whose wives and children were in the house with Rose, seemed most anxious. They said they'd thought about fetching their cart and leaving right away, but decided against it when they saw the rioters in the marketplace. Travelling the roads in darkness would be dangerous, especially on a night like this.

At what Isaac judged to be a couple of hours before midnight, a fire broke out nearby. The flicker of flames leapt up behind the roof of the blacksmith's house across the road, bringing with it a fresh tang of smoke.

"That looks like William Cooper's house two streets over," Joseph said. "Poor fellow."

People started coming out of the houses around them, anxious to see whether the fire looked like it was going to spread. The blacksmith's wife came across the road and asked whether they had a bucket to spare. Joseph offered her two, and one of Adam's sons went with her to help fight the fire. Everyone else stayed behind.

Not long after the people in Joseph's street had dispersed, a scream came from the end of the road. Isaac stepped out of the yard and tensed when he saw half a dozen figures silhouetted in flame. They carried burning brands, and a woman was trying to fight them off as they set light to her thatched roof. The pointlessness of it stung Isaac with anger. Accidental fires spread by stray embers were one thing, but purposefully burning a person's home was a wicked act.

"Hey!" he yelled, running forward with Luther's sword in front of him. One of the figures turned in his direction. Isaac saw a club in the man's hand and almost hesitated before remembering Joseph and the others were behind him. He led the charge, hastening his pace as the carpenters followed.

Their yells filled the air as they closed distance with the arsonists. When the group realised they were outnumbered, they fled back up the road and disappeared around the corner. Isaac and Sam followed them to the end of the street while Joseph picked up the woman they'd attacked. She'd been thrown to the ground and was bleeding from the head.

"We've got to stop the fire!" Joseph yelled. "It'll hop from one roof to the next if we don't!"

Tucking the sword beneath his arm, Isaac sprinted back down the road to help the others fetch buckets. The burning house had a well in the yard, but there was no room to fill more than one bucket at a time, so the carpenters began breaking up loose earth with their tools. Those who had no room to collect dirt scooped up filth from the latrine to throw on the fire instead.

"Why would they set fires?" Isaac asked breathlessly as he hauled a bucket up the well, trying to go as fast as possible without spilling it.

"Fires get people distracted," Sam said.

An uneasy feeling gripped Isaac. He thrust the bucket into Thin Robin's hands and ran back into the road. He looked left and right. At the opposite end of the street, the arsonists had reappeared. Now that everyone was busy with the burning house, there was no one to accost them.

"Joseph!" he yelled, gesturing wildly. "They're lighting fires to keep us busy while they go thieving!"

The master carpenter cursed. He looked like he didn't know what to do. They could either run back to protect the workshop, or stay and try to put out the fire. Looking up at the blazing thatch, Isaac realised it was a lost cause. They'd quenched the fire at the front of the roof, but it had just raced up higher to escape them. There wasn't enough water.

"Are we the only ones here?!" Joseph yelled.

"Everyone else went to help William Cooper," Adam called back.

Isaac looked down the road again and saw a man with an

armful of firebrands standing outside the blacksmith's house while one of his companions broke down the door with an axe. The tradesmen on this street were richer than most folk. There would be tools, goods, and silver inside all these houses.

Joseph called for everyone to abandon their firefighting efforts. The injured woman wailed and begged them to stay. Her pleas burned the back of Isaac's neck worse than the heat of the fire. While the others ran ahead, he turned back and put his arm around the woman, dragging her away from the blaze.

"We can't save it!" he told her. "Stay with us. At least you'll be safe."

She struggled a little, but her efforts were weak. Eventually she gave in to despair and allowed Isaac to half-carry her down the road. She'd probably just lost everything she had.

Isaac left her in the workshop yard and ran after the others. Joseph was bellowing his lungs out at the thieves. They'd managed to break open the blacksmith's door, but only the bottom part of it. The sturdy bar on the other side still held the top half shut. Realising they'd been caught again, the thieves turned and ran once more. A young girl peered out through the hole in the door to watch them go, her face pale with fear.

By the time Joseph had gathered up the blacksmith's family and taken them over to the workshop, the fire at the end of the street had grown out of control. The burning house was like a giant candle wicking its blaze up into the sky. The roof of the next building had already begun to catch. Isaac realised with horror that it was going to spread all the way down the street. If they hadn't been able to stop it then, they wouldn't stand a chance now.

"We can't stay at the workshop," he told Sam.

"Maybe it won't spread this far."

"If we try and fight it, those men will come back. We can't

531

deal with both problems at once!"

Sam looked around, licking his lips nervously. "We should leave. Get out of town with Kaylein and Liz."

He was probably right, but they couldn't just abandon Joseph and the others. They were in this together now.

"You won't get Liz to leave Joseph," Isaac said.

"Then let's convince him to leave too."

They found Joseph inside the workshop. He'd unlocked the door to make room for the blacksmith's family, and Rose had come in to console the children.

"Joseph," Isaac said. "What if those men keep coming back?"

"Then we'll scare them off again."

"While we fight the fire?"

Joseph cast a tense look through the linen-covered windows. Sweat glistened on his brow. He looked terribly weary. Everyone had been looking to him for guidance that night. Turning his back toward his wife, he put his head against the wall and closed his eyes. A tear ran down his cheek before disappearing into the dark tufts of his beard.

"God, don't put me in this place," he said under his breath. "Don't take it all away."

Isaac's heart went out to him. He gave Joseph a moment before stepping forward to rouse him. They didn't have time to waste. As soon as his foot creaked on the boards, the carpenter jerked upright and rubbed his eyes.

"We'll have to leave," Joseph said. "If we can't stop the fire, we'll just have to leave."

"What can we do to help?"

"Get the others on a bucket chain from the well. If there's no buckets left, start taking these tools down from the wall. We'll bury them under the shed so no one can take them if we have to leave."

Isaac gathered the others and dispensed Joseph's instructions. By now several people had returned from William Cooper's, realising their own houses were in danger.

Isaac handed over their buckets to the firefighters, but with such a limited water supply there was only so much they could do. Back at the workshop, Elizabeth organised the carpenters so they wouldn't get in each other's way, tasking Robin and Adam with collecting tools while one of Adam's sons broke up the earthen floor in the shed with an iron spike. Luther held a torch to give them light, and the wives watched the street in case the thieves returned. Everyone else did their best to dampen the wooden shingles on Joseph's roof.

"It won't be enough," Isaac heard Joseph say. He feared the carpenter was right. There just wasn't enough water to go around, and burning embers were raining down constantly from the houses that had already gone up in flames. It seemed inevitable that the fire would consume every building on the street. Only the stone walls of Joseph's house would be left by the end of it. But wood and shingles could be replaced. As long as Joseph buried his tools and money, he could still rebuild.

When the fire reached the house next door, the heat and smoke started to become unbearable. A disorganised crowd filled the road, some people sobbing in despair while others continued their desperate efforts to stop the blaze. There was still a chance the houses on the blacksmith's side might be saved, but most people had given up on Joseph's half of the street. Isaac saw a man and woman stumbling out of their burning house with a heavy chest held between them. He hoped the thieves wouldn't see them struggling away with their wealth. His eyes streamed from the smoke. All of Tannersfield had become a hell of fire and sparks and shouting. He no longer had any sense of how long it might be until morning. Blackberry began to whinny and stomp in the yard, and he ran to comfort her. She was usually so calm. She'd travelled half the world with him, always curious, never frantic. Even the commotion and the flames hadn't been enough to unnerve her, but now she was afraid. She sensed the mood of the people around her and knew Joseph's workshop was no longer safe.

Isaac led her into the front yard where the others finished burying Joseph's valuables. Elizabeth tried to count out how much money in the carpenter's chest belonged to her, but there was no time. Joseph scooped up a massive handful of silver pennies and poured them into her belt pouch. It looked like she was carrying everything she owned. She had her big cloak bundled up beneath one arm, a rolled sheaf of her treasured reading pages poking out between the folds.

Blackberry whinnied loudly and reared away when a burning piece of thatch landed on her nose. Isaac patted her neck soothingly until she calmed down. He couldn't keep her here much longer.

Thin Robin caught his eye and said: "Adam and I are going to fetch our cart before this gets any worse. We should've left hours ago."

Joseph overheard him as he stamped down the last of the earth inside the shed. "We'll come with you. It'll be safer crossing town in a group."

"What about the workshop?" Isaac said.

Joseph tried to hide the pain in his voice by coughing. "Nothing to be done about it now."

"We shouldn't go by the east gate. It was chaos earlier."

Thin Robin nodded. "Our cart's by the west gate, anyway. We'll be heading that way down the king's road to Rambirch. There's a priory you can stay at a little ways out of town until it's safe to come back."

Elizabeth rounded up the others. The blacksmith whose family Joseph had taken care of came across the road when he saw the carpenters gathering to leave.

"You can stay at mine, Joseph," the man said breathlessly. "Any family on this street would be glad to take you in."

"If the town's still standing tomorrow, I'll hold you to that." Joseph looked back at the flames licking up the side of his roof. The shingles were already burning. "I've got to get my lot away from this till it's over. Just watch my yard, would you? I've buried everything under the shed. If anyone comes sniffing around, scare them off for me."

The blacksmith nodded and squeezed Joseph's forearm firmly.

Elizabeth took Blackberry's bridle from Isaac. He couldn't remember where he'd left Luther's sword when he set it aside earlier, but it was in her hand now. She pressed the pommel into his palm.

"The streets won't be safe."

"I know."

"I'll look after Blackberry. You keep an eye out for anyone like those men from earlier."

Isaac swallowed hard, wishing he had a drink of water to soothe his aching throat. Crossing town in the midst of a riot would be dangerous, but right now seemed the lesser of two evils. Thin Robin had been right. If they'd known it was going to get this bad, they should've left hours ago. Perhaps it was a twisted blessing that Joseph's workshop lay in the path of the fire, for now they had a reason to leave town. Those who stayed behind to protect their property would be stuck in the heart of the chaos for hours, perhaps even days. Who knew how long it would be before the fires died and order returned to Tannersfield?

The group left the yard with Isaac and Sam in front. Elizabeth led Blackberry behind, shielding Kaylein and the children with the horse. Joseph was last to leave. He stood in the yard watching the fire spread across his roof, fingers clenched tight around the handle of his hammer. When Rose pulled him away, he made no attempt to hide the tears rolling down his cheeks.

CHAPTER 35

Isaac had never experienced anything like the fear that gripped Tannersfield that night. The light of the burning houses transformed the town into a hellish reflection of itself. People who might have been neighbours by day became furtive devils in the dark. Every silhouette was a danger, every shout a warning. Anxious crowds clustered in the yards of the larger houses while smaller groups struggled to fight fires leaping from rooftop to rooftop. Isaac saw three broken-in doors as they walked. The last one had a dark shape slumped outside. He tightened his clammy fingers around the sword handle, reminding himself that common thieves would find easier pickings than them that night. It disturbed him to think that the riot sparked by Edward's trial had devolved into an excuse for the denizens of Tannersfield to sack their own town. How could people be so thoughtless? The band of arsonists that set fire to Joseph's street might get away with a few sacks of plunder, but they'd destroyed the livelihoods of dozens in the process. It would be years before Tannersfield recovered.

The southeastern quarter of town was relatively quiet, but as soon as they crossed the market road the full scale of the riot gripped them. Where before the disturbances had been few and far between, now the chaos was everywhere. The heavy scent of smoke filled every breath. Half a dozen figures lay crumpled in the yard of a blazing house, some of their cloaks still smouldering. Shouts filled the air as people ran back and forth, calling for help that would not come. A row of men with shields blocked the road to the marketplace. It seemed like they'd managed to drive the mob away from the castle, but they were making no attempt to go any further.

They crossed the road quickly and hurried down another street, following the old wall around the edge of town. Each street they passed was one step closer to safety, but they still had to press through the heart of the danger to reach it. The fires were so bad in some places that they were forced to change direction, retracing their steps until they found a safe route down an alternate street.

Sam babbled nervously at Isaac's side, trying to joke about how much of a mess Edward had made and what a tale they'd have to tell when it was over. Isaac barely listened. He knew his friend was only trying to stave off his anxiety. He wished he could have done the same. Cristiana called him brave when he talked about his adventures, but he didn't feel particularly brave that night. Perhaps he was just an idiot who didn't recognise danger until it was nipping his heels. In truth, he wanted to run for his life. He wanted to break away from the group, mount up on Blackberry, and ride until the burning town was far behind him. Isaac was no fighter. The sword felt wrong in his hand. His clammy grip made the handle slip about uncomfortably, the weight of the blade never sitting quite right. But because he was young, tall, and strong, people looked to him as their protector. That was a man's duty, after all. He'd run away from his duty once before. What was stopping him now?

He motioned for the others to wait when he saw a group of people wielding tools halfway down the next street. He edged forward alone, heart pounding in his chest. It looked like they were trying to break into a building, but as he drew closer he realised they were hacking at the beams of a half-burnt house, trying to demolish it safely before it collapsed against a chapel next door. He called the others forward, and they hurried past.

This was a different kind of duty. A noble's duty was to oaths and obligations, things other people decided for him; vague concepts like honour and chivalry. Here and now, his only duty was to his friends. That was something Isaac found much easier to understand. He swallowed, wiped his sweaty hand on the side of his coat, and gripped the sword handle again. Sam was afraid, too. So were Elizabeth, Joseph, Blackberry, and the children behind him. When he thought about their fear, his own seemed to diminish. Perhaps if he led the way confidently they wouldn't feel so frightened.

They were almost at the storehouse that held Robin and Adam's cart when they heard the sound of horses galloping down the street behind them. A cry rent the air, and Isaac turned to see a trio of men-at-arms riding down a figure with a sack in his hand. The man was running for his life, his arms flailing wildly as the contents of his sack—perhaps coins, perhaps grain—spilt out in a glittering spray. The lead horseman gained on him, reversed his grip on his spear, and swung the pole like a club. The blow struck the man's back so hard he dropped face-first into the ground, rolling over once before falling still. The rider who had felled him circled back around, but the other two kept coming.

"Out of the road, quick!" Joseph called from the back of the group. They hurried into the shadow of the town wall moments before the horsemen tore past them.

"Those were the sheriff's men," Sam said.

"If we stay out of their way, they shouldn't bother us," said Isaac. "We're doing nothing wrong." He hoped he was right. Lords could be heavy-handed when it came to subduing a rabble.

They didn't see the horsemen again on their way to the

storehouse. Thin Robin banged on the doors for what felt like an age before someone finally opened them. The owner ushered them inside, guiding them through a dingy stable by candlelight. Half the building seemed to be livestock pens. Robin and Adam wheeled their cart out and the owner fixed two oxen to the yoke. The bed of the cart was piled high with the carpenters' belongings, including two heavy chests containing their money and tools. They threw a blanket over the valuables and had the children sit on top. They were tearful and exhausted from the frightening walk, but the most difficult part–getting through the gate–was yet to come.

"It won't be far," Adam's wife soothed them. "Soon we'll be out under the stars and you can have a nice sleep on the road. Pray with the good sister. She'll make sure God keeps us safe."

The children joined Kaylein in prayer, but they were too tired to stay focused. Despite having started to wheeze from the smoke, old Luther refused a spot on the cart. He found a torch to hold instead, insisting they would need someone to carry a light once they got out of town. The fires were so large and numerous that they'd been able to cross Tannersfield without getting lost, but on the open road they'd be in pitch darkness.

Joseph and Sam hauled open the heavy doors at the front of the building, and the storehouse owner hurried them out. The oxen moved quickly, perhaps spurred on by the smell of smoke and the distant shouting. The street curved, leading them onto the king's road that ran west out of Tannersfield.

Isaac's heart sank as the gate hove into view. The street was blocked with people trying to force their way through. It wasn't as congested as the east gate had been, but the chaos was almost as bad. People shoved and jostled to get to the front, concerned only with protecting themselves and their belongings. An old man riding a mule beat the people in front of him with a stick. A woman at the side of the road shrieked as someone tried to tear a haversack from her back.

"Everyone stay close to the cart!" Isaac called. "Don't get separated."

Staying together was easier said than done once the crowd closed around them. Another ox cart drew level with theirs, so close that Adam's sons had to climb on top to avoid getting pinned between the wheels. Elizabeth managed to stay behind the cart with Blackberry, but everyone else was forced to spread out in single file. Realising that he was going to be crushed by the oxen if he didn't get out of the way, Isaac clambered back over the yoke and got behind the cart with the others. The oxen would do a better job clearing the way than he could.

"Hold hands!" Joseph bellowed behind them. The carpenter said something else, but his voice was lost in the din. Every other person was calling to their loved ones, screaming for people to get out of the way, or fighting with the opportunists trying to steal bags in the melee.

"Clear this road!" a fierce voice yelled over the crowd. "Clear these carts and make way!"

Isaac looked up and saw a horseman riding toward the gate. His powerful warhorse scattered the stragglers at the back of the group, but the press of bodies was so dense that he had to slow as he came closer.

It was Sir Alfred, one of Father's knights. Isaac tensed, desperately wishing their cart would move faster. They were still at the rear of the group, and Alfred was almost upon them. If he saw Isaac's face, he'd recognise him for sure.

Elizabeth cried out in alarm. Isaac turned around and saw her staring past him, her eyes wide with fear. Following her gaze, he saw a second knight driving a white stallion through the crowd, scattering carts and foot traffic alike as his half-crazed courser snorted and bucked like a wild beast. The rider looked like he was going to fly from the saddle at any moment, but for the time being he still had control.

It was Sir Edward, and he was charging straight toward them.

* * *

It wasn't a battle, but in a way, Edward enjoyed this even more. It reminded him of the fight in Rosepath keep: a staccato of short, intense confrontations with opponents who were only half-ready for him. Every time he drove someone to the ground beneath his horse or felt his sword bite into flesh he felt a giddy thrill of vindication. This was his first proper fight in a long time. Chasing Larmond's men across the moors hadn't satisfied him. A knight didn't prove himself by managing his estate and spying; he did it by wetting his blade with the blood of his enemies. There was real danger in the air tonight, and it was intoxicating.

The sheriff's men had left at least a dozen people dead in the marketplace before the mob dispersed. Since then, they'd been riding through the streets clearing the way for the town watch to fight the fires. The houses belonging to the wealthiest townspeople had been saved first, and now they were turning their attention to the outlying streets. Alfred, who had set his mocking attitude aside for the night, was commanding the men like a born leader. Edward resented his natural authority, but he was too caught up in the rush to truly care. Caring was for tomorrow. He'd deal with the aches of his body, the bruises on his legs, and the temperament of his increasingly erratic steed in the morning. Right now he wanted to keep riding, keep driving the people of Tannersfield out of his way, keep swinging his sword at anyone who dared lay a hand on him.

They'd gone to the western gate to try and clear the way for a bucket line from the river. The local wells weren't enough to fight the fires properly, and the water barrels were quickly emptying. It would be a hopeless effort, Alfred said, unless they could clear out the knot of people blocking the west gate.

Alfred slowed and raised his voice as they rode up to the

541

crowd, giving the mob time to disperse before his horse ran them over. Edward had no such compunctions. They would never get the road clear if they dawdled. He yanked on his horse's reins, gripping tight with his knees to prevent the beast from bucking him off. It was neighing like a demon, whipping its mane back and forth in defiance as spittle frothed from its mouth. Edward kicked its sides hard and it lurched forward into the crowd. A woman groaned as a hoof kicked her in the leg. A man dropped his hand cart and dove out of the way. The crowd began to scatter in all directions, half of them leaving their belongings in the road.

Realising that his horse was out of control, Edward cursed and tried to dismount, wrenching the reins as hard as he could in an attempt to slow the beast long enough for him to swing his legs off. The horse faltered, but he was only halfway out of the saddle before it lurched and threw him sideways. A flash of terror blinded him as he imagined falling on his head and being dragged away by the stirrup. He yanked his leg as hard as he could and felt his foot come loose. The impact of the road jarred through his shoulder, driving the hard mail into his padded undershirt with a force he felt in his bones. He rolled over and got his feet beneath him, reeling with dizziness. Suddenly he was no longer riding above the chaos, but trapped in the midst of it. He swiped the air wildly with his sword, thankful that he hadn't dropped it when he fell. His left arm had gone slightly numb, but the pounding of his blood kept the pain at bay.

When his senses cleared, he saw his horse charging away through the crowd, rearing and bucking in its fervour to escape. Uncontrolled though it was, it was doing a good job of clearing the road. Even the oxen were trying to drag their carts away from the wild animal. The crowd had thinned enough that Edward could see through to the gate. A bearded man glanced back at him, and their eyes met.

It was Joseph Carpenter.

Edward hesitated. Something told him to ignore the man

and find Alfred. He was here to clear the road, not take revenge on the people who'd wronged him. But if not now, when? It looked like Joseph was trying to leave town. If he disappeared, Edward might never see him again. He looked around frantically for Alfred, but the other knight had vanished amidst the chaos. There was no one else standing in his way. Edward's anger surged, twisting and boiling beneath his skin. He remembered how humiliating it had been to walk away from the workshop with his tail between his legs. He remembered every insolent word he'd had to endure in the courthouse.

Flexing his bruised arm, he dove into the thinning crowd. Nobody tried to stop him. As soon as they saw his sword they shied away, fleeing and cowering. He pushed past one person, then another, and then the back of Joseph's black-haired head was in front of him. Edward thrust the tip of his sword forward. Joseph cried out as it pierced his shirt, but he managed to twist away before it went in deep. The carpenter rounded on him, wild-eyed. Edward relished the look of fear on the man's face as he realised what was about to happen. Joseph had a hammer in his hand, but it was no match for a sword. He swung out. Edward stepped back and brought up his blade in a reflexive guard. The keen edge sliced into Joseph's forearm, and the carpenter dropped his hammer with a groan. A woman screamed his name and ran to his side. It was his wife. She tried to get in Edward's way, putting herself between the sword and her husband.

With a snarl of frustration, Edward drove his blade into her chest. Her shocked gasp was lost in the noise of the crowd. Deep down, some small part of Edward's soul recoiled in horror as he felt the weight of her body dragging at his blade. The stupid woman had got in his way. Why had she done that?

Seeing the look of unbridled rage on Joseph's face, Edward stepped back and shoved the woman away from him, twisting his sword free before it got stuck. Joseph threw

543

himself forward with a cry of such terrible anguish that Edward recoiled in fear. The man was wild. As shocked as Edward was by Joseph's fury, he wasn't so dazed that he couldn't defend himself. He stepped to the side and swung his sword inexpertly, but the cut struck true. Joseph staggered past him with blood running from his stomach. It was a mortal wound. Seeing that he'd won, Edward's excitement returned. In the heat of the moment, all he wanted to hear was Joseph's cries of pain as he bled the last of his life away.

The carpenter stumbled and fell. Edward heard a woman shriek his name, but he paid them no mind. He put his foot on Joseph's back, amused at how easily the burly man had fallen. He lifted his sword and drove the tip down until he felt it grate against the stones in the road. The carpenter spasmed, tensed, then faltered as the ebb of death took hold. Edward wrenched his sword free and turned around.

A malevolent grin spread across his face when he saw who'd called Joseph's name. Elizabeth stood in the road, eyes wide with horror as she clutched her trembling fingers to her mouth. She screamed Joseph's name again. Edward strode toward her. She didn't seem to realise the danger she was in until a young man with messy brown hair grabbed her and pulled her back. He seemed vaguely familiar to Edward, but he couldn't be bothered to try and remember who he was. The crowd was giving him a wide berth now, repelled by the blood on his sword and the murderous act they'd just witnessed. He felt invincible. The people who'd tried to punish him were running in fear. The man responsible was dying in the dirt behind him. As soon as the press of the crowd halted her, Elizabeth would be next. There was nowhere left for her to go. He saw her fair hair flash in the light of an old man's torch. Lady Kaylein appeared beside her. Edward swiped the air with his blade, laughing as it made Kaylein shrink back in fear.

But before he could reach them, a man with a sword shoved past the old torchbearer and got in his way. Edward was so caught up in the moment that he barely broke his stride. No one could hurt him that night. Yet part of him reacted to the sword in the man's hand, and he drew his weapon up in a guard as it flashed toward him. The ring of steel on steel dispelled Edward's euphoria. Suddenly the danger was real again. The man facing him adopted a swordsman's stance, his body tilted sideways with his left arm clutched to his chest. Edward stepped back and raised his sword to parry another blow, realising this was a real fight. His opponent looked like the duke's son, Isaac, but it couldn't possibly be him. The resemblance distracted Edward, making his next guard rise too slowly. The swordsman's high cut caught him in the shoulder, stinging the bruise he'd taken when he fell from his horse. It was only a swipe, harmless against his mail, but it was a hit he shouldn't have taken. Gritting his teeth in anger, he stepped back to give himself space, then lunged in with a thrust of his own.

The man fighting him knew how to use a sword, but he didn't have a knight's experience. Within a few strikes, Edward knew he was going to win. His confidence surged, pressing him to be more aggressive. Swordplay was all about reflexes. A man could study every cut, thrust, and guard in the world, but unless his body could make those movements without thinking he was little more dangerous than a peasant with a stick. Edward stepped forward, turning each guard into a parry that forced his opponent back. He gave the other man no opening to advance. As soon as he ran out of space to retreat, he would be dead.

Sensing that his opponent's next backstep was about to falter, Edward turned his sword to the side and sliced down at his leg. The tip raked across the man's knee, tearing open his clothing, but it didn't fell him. In the moment it took Edward to withdraw from his overextended swing, the messy-haired man who'd grabbed Elizabeth appeared in the periphery of his vision. He turned to face his new attacker, but he couldn't get his sword up in time. The man had a heavy piece of wood in his hands, and he was swinging it as hard as he could. For the second time in a row, Edward took the hit in his bruised shoulder. He screamed in pain as numbness erupted into agony. Staggering sideways, he blundered into the remnants of the crowd. He tripped over the back of a cart and grabbed a woman's dress to keep himself from falling. Someone pushed him from behind. He wheeled around and came face to face with a man who, either in surprise or fear, punched him in the jaw.

Edward fell over, a flash of red crossing his vision as the back of his head struck the ground. His senses reeled. He didn't know where he was or who was around him, but enough of his wits remained to realise that he would be trampled if he lay there in the road. Getting a hand beneath him, he tried to push himself up and screamed as his shoulder flared with pain. He would need to use his sword arm to get up. Praying his attackers were no longer nearby, he let go of his sword and pushed himself up with his good hand. Somehow he'd fallen at the side of the road. People jostled all around him, still trying to push through the congested gate. He looked for his sword, but it seemed to have vanished in the darkness.

Edward's bloodlust deserted him. The man who looked like Isaac was gone, and now he was alone in the middle of the mob with no weapon to defend himself. He backed against the wall of the nearest house, clutching his aching arm to his side. Every pair of eyes around him seemed to leer with predatory intent. He felt like a child again, hurrying through these streets with a few ill-gotten pennies for his father, praying no one would kick him to the ground and beat him up before he got home.

"Get away from me!" Edward yelled, swiping out with his fist when a young man came close. He looked for Alfred, but he was nowhere to be seen. "Don't you dare touch me!" Overcome with fear, Edward turned away from the gate and ran.

Amidst the chaos, he was just one more figure fleeing from the bodies of the carpenter and his wife that lay crumpled in the middle of the road.

CHAPTER 36

Elizabeth pushed Isaac onto the back of the cart with the children. Kaylein clasped her hands over his gashed knee in an attempt to stem the bleeding. Sam was nowhere to be seen. A cold veil had descended around Elizabeth, cutting her off from the surrounding world. It was like hearing the courthouse verdict again, except this time the veil wouldn't lift. She wasn't herself anymore, only an observer to the terrible chaos filling the street. It was worse than the courthouse. It was the slaughter at Rosepath all over again. Had Lady Eleanor felt this way when she saw her husband and sons cut down in front of her?

She couldn't bring herself to look back at the spot where Joseph and Rose had fallen. If she did, she feared the strength would drain from her legs and she would collapse in grief. She'd seen violence before, but never like this. Never against people she loved. Never as she looked on in horror, helpless to stop what was happening as Edward's sword flashed, his bloodthirsty snarl turning upon Rose, then Joseph, and finally upon her.

"We're almost through," she heard Luther say. Her legs were still moving, carrying her forward with the momentum of the crowd. The press of bodies had closed up around them again. Edward was gone, but what if he came back? Hearing a clatter of metal, she looked down and saw Isaac's sword fall to the road. She snatched it up before anyone else could.

"Liz," Isaac said, looking past her urgently. She glanced over her shoulder and saw Blackberry falling behind. With nobody to hold her, she'd been squeezed back by the crowd. Elizabeth pushed her way to the horse's side and got a hand on her bridle. She was acting instinctively, without thought or reason. There were things that still needed doing, and she had to do them. Her mind had gone to a blank place where only the task in front of her mattered.

They were moving through the west gate now. The old stones enclosed them momentarily, then they were out among the hovels on the edge of town. The road broadened, but the crowd only seemed to grow denser. Elizabeth was pressed against Blackberry's side, the sword nicking her skin as she held it flat against her body. The traffic slewed over the bridge spanning the swampy floodwaters from the river, then they were out on the king's road. Tannersfield burned behind them, its firelight flashing eerie orange phantoms over the dark countryside.

"Get off me!" Elizabeth yelled as someone grabbed her shoulders. Blackberry whinnied angrily. She spun around. The person let go when they saw the sword in her hand.

Something was wrong. They were clear of the town, but the air was still full of screaming. Elizabeth squinted into the darkness. There were fires along the side of the road, some built from broken carts and empty sacks. She saw a group of men standing in the firelight, clubs and farming tools in their hands. One of them pointed to a cart being drawn by a lone man and his two daughters. Three figures ran forward. Two of them shoved the carter to the ground and began tearing through his belongings. The other hit one of the girls in the head with a club when she tried to stop them.

Despair overwhelmed Elizabeth in the face of such

cruelty. People were being robbed out in the open. The thieves weren't even attempting to hide what they were doing. They knew that few of the frightened folk leaving town were going to stand up to an armed mob, and the sheriff's men were all busy that night. The thieves behind Tannersfield's walls might have been rats scrabbling for plunder, but the ones outside were wolves selecting their targets with predatory precision.

Elizabeth had fallen behind the cart when she went to get Blackberry. The cart was veering to the side of the road closest to the fires. In a few moments, the thieves would see them. Adam and Thin Robin didn't seem to have noticed what was happening, preoccupied with leading the frightened oxen. With Isaac injured, they would be easy pickings.

Elizabeth's body wanted to give out. She felt like slumping to her knees and letting the lump of grief burst free from her chest. She didn't even know if she was terrified anymore. The way she felt seemed to have gone beyond that. Something had to give, and if it was not her will to survive then it had to be her sense of reason.

Elizabeth threw a hand over Blackberry's side and dragged herself up into the saddle. Remembering how Edward had driven the crowd away with his horse, she kicked Blackberry's sides until she whinnied and lurched forward.

"Get out of my way!" she screamed, gripping the sword so tight her fingers hurt. The people in front of her fled as Blackberry's hooves crashed toward them. She rode to the cart, circled around it, then came back again, shouting at the top of her lungs as the crowd scattered. The carts behind them slowed. Those in front drew away. Soon her companions were free from the traffic, but they had drawn level with the fires now, and the thieves had seen them. Elizabeth heard someone approaching through the darkness. They were hurrying, at least two or three of them, their shadows flashing in the firelight.

Elizabeth turned Blackberry around and put herself

between the shadowy figures and the cart. The torches carried by the other travellers were far away now, and Luther was on the other side of the road, leaving her blind to her immediate surroundings. Hearing a scuffle of feet somewhere to her left, Elizabeth swung the sword in that direction.

"Don't come near us!" she yelled. Her voice was so hoarse she barely recognised it. She swung the sword again. This time the tip clipped something firm. A voice wailed in pain. Elizabeth screamed a wordless sound of anguish back at them. The footsteps of her attackers withdrew into the darkness. She rode Blackberry around the cart in another circle. She could barely hold on to the saddle. Tears blurred her vision. She didn't care if she'd meant to kill the thieves or just scare them away. She didn't even care when she turned around and saw them moving on to rob the family behind them. She had no compassion left to give.

When the fires finally grew small behind them and the shouts began to fade, she stopped circling the cart. They were out in open grassland, the dark outline of the forest swallowing up the horizon ahead. Soon the road would take them into the trees. Cold wind twisted Elizabeth's hair into a tail behind her. Tears froze on her cheeks. Shaking, she dropped the sword on the road beside her.

Sam had found his way back to them at some point in the commotion. He stepped away from the cart and picked up the sword. They hadn't lost anyone except Joseph and Rose.

No one spoke. Even the children were silent. Luther strode on doggedly beside the oxen, his torch in one hand and a knife in the other. The darkness of the forest enveloped them, finally blocking Tannersfield from view.

When she realised they'd escaped, the dam within Elizabeth burst. She slumped forward and wept, sobbing into Blackberry's mane until Sam helped her down and put her on the cart with the others.

They spent the rest of the night at the priory Robin had

551

mentioned. The monks were kind and invited them into the church along with the other travellers who'd fled west. Elizabeth sat between Kaylein and Sam with her back against the wall, shivering in her cloak as she waited for sleep to take her. It was a dismally long time in coming. Isaac sat on Kaylein's opposite side. His wound wasn't bad, but it clearly pained him. He kept shifting throughout the night. Every time Elizabeth heard him move, her thoughts flashed back to what had happened, and her grief became so intense she wanted to vomit or bite her tongue or dig her fingernails into her palms until her mind turned away from the memory.

Joseph and Rose were dead. She would never sweep their workshop again. They would never count out wages together at the end of the week. She would never have the chance to take care of them when they grew old.

Even if she'd been forced to leave Tannersfield alone, at least she would have done so hopeful in the knowledge that she might see Joseph again someday. They could have sent letters to each other when she learned to read and write. She remembered Joseph teaching her to read numbers and felt sick again. All those fond memories were now needles in her heart. She almost wished Edward's sword had pierced her chest too. At least then she wouldn't have been left feeling like this. Half her world had burned away in Tannersfield.

She hadn't felt this miserable when her mother died. That had been a slow sadness. Day by day, week by week, it had grown worse, and by the time she realised her mother's sickness wasn't going to get better, she was prepared for it. This time the grief was swift and brutal, like the sudden loss of a limb. It ached with physical pain inside her, squeezing her chest until every breath hurt and her head throbbed.

She'd never quite dared to think of Joseph as her surrogate father. It had seemed presumptuous and improper. But now that he was gone, she could think of him as nothing but. He'd been the closest thing to a father she'd ever know.

At some point, she realised she was crying again. Kaylein's

hand touched her cheek. She let her friend guide her head into her lap, and she lay there until grief ran her dry and sleep took hold.

A few hours later, a grey, drizzling dawn brightened the church windows. Elizabeth wanted to lie there on the floor and never get up. The idea of staying in the church for the rest of her life was somehow comforting. She understood why Kaylein had wanted to become a nun. Was that to be her fate as well? She couldn't conceive of remaking her life in Rambirch with Adam and Robin. The effort of starting over again felt insurmountable. It would be easier to give herself to a convent, where all she had to worry about was praying and attending her chores. Perhaps she was destined for a life of humble service after all.

Kaylein made her sit up. They drank a little of the monks' watered-down beer and used the rest to soften some bowls of oats. Elizabeth was hungry, but the effort of swallowing made her nauseous.

"Can I come to a convent with you?" she croaked. Her throat felt swollen as if she was ill.

"Of course," Kaylein said gently. "One of the ones on Mother Jane's list was near Rambirch, wasn't it?"

"Yes," Isaac said. He was upright and walking on his injured leg. Despite his obvious discomfort, the linen bandage around his knee seemed to be holding him together. "I've ridden through that area a lot. I can help you find the way."

"You be careful on the road," Luther said.

Elizabeth looked up at the carpenters. "I'm sorry, but I can't come to Rambirch with you."

Adam gave her an understanding nod. "We'll be there, all the same."

"Good luck to all of you," Luther said. "I'm heading back to town as soon as it's safe. The others need to know what happened with the workshop." He avoided adding that he

553

would need to tell them about Joseph and Rose, too.

"What'll happen to the money you buried?" Sam asked.

"We'll use it to rebuild the workshop, or to move on to Rambirch if it's not worth staying."

"How much damage do you think the town suffered?" Kaylein asked. "Will the convents and church be safe?"

"I expect so. They're big stone buildings. Can't say the same for the rest of the town. Tannersfield might go back to being a castle and a few farms after this."

"It'll recover eventually," Thin Robin said. "They say market towns always do."

Luther grunted. "Maybe, but not in my lifetime."

The carpenters began gathering their families to leave. Sam was anxious to go, but Kaylein and Isaac could tell Elizabeth wasn't ready. She still hadn't stood up that morning.

"Thank you for keeping Blackberry safe," Isaac said.

She gave him a small nod.

Kaylein smiled at him. "Thank you for stopping Sir Edward. And you too, Sam. You were both so brave."

Isaac looked uncomfortable, as though he didn't feel deserving of such praise, but Sam smiled back. At least one of them could be happy that morning. Kaylein was putting on a brave face, but she was obviously shaken. It was only because Elizabeth was so helpless that she'd stepped up to take charge.

I am helpless, she thought dismally. She'd failed to outwit Edward at the trial. She'd been powerless to stop him at the gate. The only time she'd felt in control last night was when she threw caution to the wind and used Blackberry to scatter the crowd. She'd managed to protect her friends, but how many other people had fallen victim to the opportunists on the road?

She couldn't think about that. There was no space in her heart for any more grief. Perhaps this was just the way of things; the good had to be victims to the wicked, because to

554

be strong you had to be cruel. Kaylein would have told her something about their rewards awaiting them in heaven, but she didn't know if she could believe that.

Eventually, she got up. She didn't feel like eating, or travelling, or doing anything at all for that matter. But she knew she had to. More people were arriving from Tannersfield by the hour, and the church was getting crowded. If Sir Edward came searching for them, this was the first place he'd look. Elizabeth's fear of the knight motivated her to get moving. As awful as she felt, she didn't want to lie down and die.

They put up their hoods against the drizzle and said goodbye to Luther, then headed west. Isaac tried to keep their spirits up with stories as he rode beside them. His voice helped fill the cold quiet of the journey. He said the road they were on spanned the breadth of the kingdom, leading all the way from the capital on the northwest shore to the ports in the far east. An ancient monarch was said to have cleared it to make way for his people when God called up the sea to flood their coastal villages. That was why they called it the king's road.

Isaac was good at telling stories.

Elizabeth should have been warmer toward him, she realised. Despite their uneven beginnings, he'd been a good and true friend. Had she not been so shocked by the deaths of Joseph and Rose, she would've been in awe of his heroism when he defended them from Edward. It was the sort of thing she wished she could do, but women didn't learn to fight with swords.

They travelled with Adam and Robin for half a day before reaching a fork in the road. Isaac said they could keep following the king's road Rambirch, or take the left fork for a quicker path to Kaylein's convent by way of the nearby villages. Elizabeth felt nervous about staying on the main road, so she voted to part ways with the carpenters and take the quieter route. The others agreed with her. After saying their goodbyes over a brief meal by the roadside, they headed on, Adam and Robin's group staying on the king's road while Elizabeth's took the fork.

The new path was narrow, but the woodland wasn't dense, and a ditch on the side made it apparent that someone maintained this route regularly. They weren't likely to run into any outlaws on a path like this. The opportunists roaming the area would probably seek richer pickings on the king's road. All the same, Elizabeth kept her eyes on the trees. Sam walked close beside her with Luther's sword in his hand. The old carpenter had insisted they take it with them before he left.

The patter of drizzle on the back of Elizabeth's hood soothed her despite the cold. The king's road was probably a muddy mess by now, but the forest path remained firm underfoot. Isaac said that if they kept going they would reach a village called Duckley before nightfall. It had no church where they might find charitable shelter, but between the four of them they had plenty of money to purchase lodgings in someone's hall. After that, it would be a couple more days to Kaylein's convent.

The screen of shrubs beyond the ditch thinned as they went on, revealing the beginnings of the rugged moors that stretched between Tannersfield and Farrenwold south of the king's road. Elizabeth had never been this far west. Perhaps if she went far enough she'd be able to forget about what lay behind her.

The sound of hooves distracted her from the moors. She turned around, drawing close to Sam and Kaylein. They moved off the path to make room for the rider. It sounded like they were travelling fast. A horseman rounded the bend. He was wearing mail and had a sword at his hip. Elizabeth's heart beat faster as he came to a halt a dozen yards away.

"Hello," Sam called.

The rider said nothing. He stared for a moment, then turned his horse around and galloped back the way he'd come.

"Maybe he thought we were outlaws," Sam said, holding up Luther's sword with a grin. He was the only one who didn't seem at all troubled by their situation. That had always been Sam's way. He had a short memory for most things, especially if they made him feel bad. Elizabeth envied him that.

"I think I recognised that man," Isaac said in a troubled tone. "I saw him at Rosepath Castle."

Elizabeth frowned. "When?" She couldn't remember Isaac mentioning Rosepath before. He always said he didn't know anything about the place when it came up in conversation. Her unease deepened when Isaac didn't answer. He climbed off Blackberry and tested his wounded leg, then offered her the saddle.

"We should hurry on," he said. "I can walk for a little bit. Whoever's tired can take turns riding Blackberry."

Elizabeth declined the offer. They couldn't all ride without breaking a sweat like Isaac. Kaylein hadn't been on a horse in two years, and Elizabeth preferred walking, so Sam mounted up instead, passing off the sword to Isaac.

They quickened their pace down the path, Isaac limping doggedly along beside them. His wound didn't slow him down, but he had to walk awkwardly with his leg held stiff. Elizabeth suspected he would have to get back on Blackberry before long. The overcast sky started to darken. The drizzle became rain, pattering down into puddles that spread rivulets into the ditch. It was hard to tell if dusk was falling, or it was just the weather. There was still no sign of the village of Duckley. The flooded path softened beneath their feet, sucking at their boots as dirt became mud. They pushed on for about an hour before the sound of hooves returned behind them.

This time Elizabeth sensed the danger before she turned to look. A dreadful shiver prickled her spine as three horsemen rode around the bend. One was the man they'd

557

seen earlier. Sir Edward was beside him, dark hair plastered to his scalp by the rain. The horse he rode wasn't his usual white courser, but it looked large and fast.

"Ride, Sam!" Isaac said. He grabbed Elizabeth's hand and pulled her off the path. Sam kicked Blackberry's sides and galloped away. The rest of them fled into the trees. Elizabeth hitched up her dress and felt thin branches scratching her bare legs, fear making her oblivious to the pain. The sound of hooves pursued them into the undergrowth as Edward yelled for his men to follow. The trees would slow him down, but they weren't dense enough to stop a horse entirely.

Elizabeth's throat was so tight she struggled to breathe. Her lungs burned, numb terror stealing her strength as she ran. She wanted to look back, but if she did she might trip and fall. It sounded like their pursuers were inches behind them.

Isaac managed to stay ahead even with his wound, but Kaylein was flagging. Her breaths came shrill and ragged next to Elizabeth. It looked like she would fall at any moment. Elizabeth grabbed her arm and hauled her on, knowing that if they stopped they were dead. She didn't have the breath to say anything, she just kept running. The trees thinned ahead of them. Elizabeth glimpsed the side of a thatched roof in the distance. It was the village. If they could get to a house, perhaps someone would protect them.

The trees ended at the edge of a field. Elizabeth tried to run across, but the recently tilled soil had become swampy in the rain. Her foot sank in to the ankle before she staggered back and followed Isaac along the treeline where the ground was firmer. Her legs throbbed with the effort. If she slowed now, she knew she wouldn't be able to speed up again. On the far side of the field, she spotted a group of hooded figures speaking to a farmer. They looked like huntsmen returning from the forest. Several of them carried bows, and one was pointing in their direction.

"Help us!" Isaac called breathlessly. "We're being chased!"

One of the huntsmen stepped forward and touched his bow, but another held him back.

Elizabeth's skin crawled as Edward's voice burst from behind her: "Stop them! They're outlaws!"

Her muscles felt like they were about to snap as they closed the distance to the huntsmen. These people would be their salvation or their executioners. Kaylein staggered. Elizabeth hauled her back to her feet. One of the huntsmen lunged forward, grabbed Isaac, and knocked the sword from his hand.

Elizabeth's heart dropped to the bottom of her stomach, dragging her to the ground as it went. She fell to her knees in the dirt, and Kaylein slumped with her. All she could hear was her pulse pounding in her ears. They'd been so close. If only they'd been just a little faster, they might have reached the village before Edward.

Edward stomped up behind them, gasping his own exhausted breaths. He must have abandoned his horse somewhere in the woods. Elizabeth couldn't bring herself to look up. It was all over now.

Please let Sam have gotten away, she thought. *Please let him be safe.* She realised she was praying. Her lips formed the shapes of words her lungs could spare no breath on. She took Kaylein's arm and clung to her.

"Milord," one of the huntsmen said respectfully, recognising Edward as a man of status.

"Leave them to me," Edward said. "Go away, all of you. I'm here on the sheriff's business."

The huntsmen backed away to the edge of the field, talking quietly among themselves as they watched.

Edward's men approached with swords drawn and flanked them. To Elizabeth's surprise, Edward ignored her, walking to Isaac and pulling back his hood instead.

"I thought it was you," he said under his breath. "You and Lady Kaylein together. I wish I could tell your father."

Elizabeth didn't know what he was talking about. She

559

gave the huntsmen an imploring look, but beneath their heavy hoods it was impossible to tell whether they were even paying attention to her.

"Take me back to him, then," Isaac said bitterly, "but leave the women be."

Edward slapped him across the face.

"You cost me a good sword."

"I'll cost you more than that if I tell my father what you've done—" Isaac's words trailed off in a groan as Edward hit him again.

"You're not going to tell your father anything," Edward said in a breathy whisper. "You're a disgrace to him, and he'd be better off without you. I'm the one who's going to have your castle, and your sister, and everything else you threw away."

Elizabeth felt some vague, long-discarded suspicion beginning to piece itself back together in her mind, but she was too frightened to fully grasp what it was. It fled her thoughts when Edward stepped away from Isaac and wrenched her up by the hair. Kaylein wailed in anguish. Elizabeth tried not to react, but fear made her flinch when Edward drew close. There was a look of perplexity on his face, angry and disturbingly excited. She screwed her eyes shut to block it out.

"Why did you do it?" he asked. When Elizabeth said nothing, he shook her violently. She felt the tip of a knife prick her eyelid, forcing her to look at him. "I would've let you go!" He threw his knife into the field and held his left hand in front of her face. "You made a cripple of me. I can't use a bow properly. I can't feel a damned thing in this finger!"

Elizabeth could only blink in confusion. He shook her again. She heard a fearful whimper leave her lips. Edward threw her back to the ground.

"Kill the other two," he said. "Not her. I'm going to hang her in front of the castle next to her master's body."

Kaylein cried out. Isaac made a grab for his fallen sword,

560

but Edward stamped on his hand before he could reach it. There was a nasty cracking sound from his fingers. Isaac grit his teeth, stifling a scream of pain.

"Go on," Edward told the man beside him.

"He's the duke's son," the man-at-arms whispered.

"Do you serve him, or me?"

The other man touched his sword to Kaylein's neck.

"I'm the duke's son!" Isaac yelled at the huntsmen. "I'm Isaac of Cairnford!"

Elizabeth thought he'd gone mad. The vague recollection she'd been struggling with came back to her. His age, the way he spoke, his education, even the way he looked–they all made sense. She'd wondered whether he might be Isaac of Cairnford when they first met, but it had seemed so unlikely a possibility that she'd chased it from her mind. There was no time to consider how she felt about it now. He was doing the only thing that might save their lives.

"He's the duke's son!" she screamed. "Stop them!"

Would it work? Even if the huntsmen believed them, they might not want to defy a knight. Edward's men were still hesitating, unnerved by Isaac's sudden shout. Edward grabbed for one of their swords. Elizabeth shut her eyes, praying with all her heart.

"Is that true?" a deep voice called. One of the huntsmen stepped forward.

"This isn't anything to do with you!" Edward said.

"Put those swords away." The huntsman didn't sound like a commoner addressing a knight. There was a smooth confidence in his voice that held no fear.

Edward ignored him and wrested the blade from his man's hand.

"Shoot one of them," the huntsman said quickly. The words had barely left his lips before an arrow pierced the chest of the man standing over Kaylein. He staggered back with a choking sound and fell to one knee.

Edward froze, his eyes darting to the huntsman in

disbelief. "You'll hang for this."

"Leave," the huntsman said. "I'd rather not kill a knight."

"Who do you think you are?!" Edward yelled, an edge of shrillness in his voice as he brandished his borrowed sword.

"Shoot him."

A second arrow leapt from the archer's bow. Edward moved at the last second and the shaft struck him in the thigh. He fell to the ground with a groan. His remaining man-at-arms grabbed him beneath the shoulders and began dragging him away while the other rattled out the last of his breath in the mud.

"Wait!" Edward pleaded as the huntsmen advanced, his face wrought with terror.

Elizabeth dug her fingers into the earth, hot tears blinding her as she stared at Joseph's murderer.

"Kill him," she sobbed.

The archer already had another arrow notched to his bowstring.

The lead huntsman stepped past her. He spoke as nonchalantly as if he'd just felled a buck in the woods. "Let them go. He's no more fight in him. We don't want a dead knight on our hands if we can help it." He stood and watched as Edward struggled upright with the help of his companion and hopped away into the forest. Once they were gone, he turned to Isaac. "Let me look at you." He crouched down and drew back his hood. He had a head of thick brown hair, the foremost locks woven into rough braids that held back the rest of his mane in a knot behind his head. A long, narrow beard hung from his chin in a similar braid. His light complexion was not that of a peasant. "You *are* Isaac," he said with a smile, then turned his attention to Kaylein. The look of amusement on his face became one of serious contemplation. "And by God, unless my eyes deceive me, you are Count Leo's daughter."

Elizabeth didn't know whether to weep with relief or shy away from their rescuers. She was at the end of her tether. All of them were. Isaac nursed his broken hand. Kaylein shivered like a leaf in the wind.

"Who are you?" Elizabeth said.

The strange man had his followers help them up. They weren't hunters, Elizabeth could see that now. Beneath their cloaks, they wore padded gambeson jackets and sword belts.

"He's Larmond," Isaac said unsteadily. "The marquess of Saintsmarch."

"The rogue marquess, as they call me these days," Larmond said. "Though I believe I am truer to my kingdom than any other lord in this land. You wear a nun's robe, Lady Kaylein; you must see the Lord's hand in this as well." He smiled. "I came to this village seeking food for my men, and instead I find the children of two noble houses sprouting in the fields. Come to my camp. You shall have rest, shelter, and a physician to tend Master Isaac's hand."

"Are we to be your prisoners?" Kaylein asked, wiping the rain and tears from her eyes.

Larmond frowned. "Only if you try to run."

The Book of Roses continues in *A Heart in the Hills*. Read on for a preview.

With their lives in Tannersfield behind them, Elizabeth, Isaac, and Kaylein are forced to strike a difficult bargain with the cunning Marquess Larmond as he plots rebellion against the crown. The price of their freedom leads them to the remote hilltop village of Kinedwyn, where they hope to begin a new chapter of their lives. Isaac seeks to ingratiate himself with the lord of the manor, while Kaylein, torn between her heart and her vows, struggles to rebuild the local priory. Elizabeth pursues her dream of becoming lady of her own house, oblivious to an unexpected romance that creeps up on her as the years pass by.

But as the spectre of civil war stirs the kingdom to arms, Sir Edward has not forgotten his revenge. War is a time of advancement for knights. Seeking glory, vindication, and a prestigious marriage to a new bride, he bides his time waiting for the moment he and his old enemies cross paths again.

Hearts are wayward things, and neither Elizabeth, Isaac, nor Kaylein will escape unscathed from the follies of love as Edward's terrible revenge draws near.

Thank you for taking the time to read this book. I write because I hope to give others the same experience I get when I'm curled up with a good novel, lost in a story that grabs hold of me and doesn't let go. If I managed to give you that for even a few moments of your day, it makes it all worthwhile.

If you enjoyed your time in these pages, I'd humbly request that you consider leaving a review on the site you purchased the book from. As an independent author, I rely on word of mouth and community reviews to keep me afloat. It really would make my day!

For information on new releases, visit my website where you can find purchase links to all my books, follow my social media feeds, and subscribe to updates via email:

kellyriverbooks.com

Other novels by Kelly River:

The Book of Roses:
Elizabeth of Rosepath
A Heart in the Hills
The Embers of Daylight

Lavender's Wolf (Coming mid 2024)
Calia's Needle (Coming late 2024)

A HEART IN THE HILLS PREVIEW

CHAPTER 1

Kaylein had been trying to hold herself together ever since they left Tannersfield. She could feel a deep, dark terror within her struggling to reach the surface, the same terror that had crippled her the night she fled Rosepath. Kaylein had never believed herself to be good in a crisis. She liked quiet, surety, and order; for her, life was at its best when structured like the neat sentences of a book. To be thrown into the midst of such violent chaos made her feel like a wisp of hay caught in a fire's updraught. At any moment she feared she would shrivel in the flames, reverting to the same helpless girl she'd been in the weeks following her family's death.

But she didn't falter this time. Perhaps it was because Elizabeth was in no state to take care of her. Perhaps it was God's light shining through her fear. Or perhaps the last two years had changed her more than she realised.

She held Elizabeth up by the arm as they staggered along with Larmond's men. They were both filthy with mud, their legs quaking with exhaustion. They kept going as night fell over the moors, leaving the village of Duckley far behind them. Wherever they were headed, it was far from civilisation. Larmond was leading them into the wilderness between the counties. Kaylein didn't know what to expect when they arrived at his camp. She'd heard rumours about what the rogue marquess had been doing since the crown changed hands, and few of them were reassuring. He was said to have defied the new king, burned villages, and allied himself with Alistair of Henmarch after Isaac snubbed Lady Emilia. She looked over at Isaac, still not quite believing that the cordial, adventurous young man she'd befriended was Duke Francis's son. He was limping badly from his knee wound, dragging himself along with his broken hand clutched to his chest. Part of Kaylein, the part that still echoed the voice of her father, wanted to hate him for who he was. Duke Francis has slaughtered her family. Perhaps if she'd known who he was from the start, she'd never have been able to trust him. But Isaac had ingratiated himself with her under a veil of anonymity. Even though that veil had lifted, she couldn't pretend he'd become a different person overnight. He'd risked his life to defend them from Sir Edward, just like Sam. Kaylein felt a twinge in her heart when she thought of Sam. She hoped he was safe. He'd probably galloped Blackberry to Duckley and hidden there when Edward chased them, perhaps even watching from afar as Larmond's men marched them away.

They reached the marquess's camp a short time after nightfall. It was hidden in a narrow valley, home to about fifty fighting men and a few dozen camp followers; just one part of a larger army, if what she'd overheard was to be believed. The hastily erected shelters and picketed horses suggested the camp was a temporary one, though it was difficult to tell in the gloom. There wasn't much protection from the elements out on the moors besides the tall slopes of the valley. The rain had dried up enough for Larmond's men to light fires, though Kaylein couldn't imagine what they'd found to burn in this barren landscape.

Larmond took Isaac to have someone look at his hand while Kaylein was shown to a blanket held up by some sticks. She huddled down beneath it with Elizabeth, hoping the fire would dry her damp robes. To her relief, they'd been put with the camp followers, who were mostly women. She doubted she would've been able to sleep surrounded by Larmond's gruff-looking soldiers.

Elizabeth hadn't said a word all evening. Kaylein felt she should comfort her, but she'd never been good at handling complex feelings at times like this. She was afraid she'd say something insensitive or talk down to Elizabeth like a mistress to a servant. She'd learned to speak of sensitive matters with open, academic frankness in the company of the senior nuns, but the ability to converse with a commoner's easy tongue still eluded her.

She missed the convent terribly. Her heart was still there in the writing room, recalling lines of copied scripture in her dreams and composing verses when she was awake. She felt isolated and vulnerable without the convent's stone walls around her.

An older woman watched them curiously from across the fire, perhaps wondering who they were but hesitant to ask. Larmond might have told his people not to speak to them. Kaylein wondered what the marquess wanted with her. Her brothers would have known. They'd always been interested in the great wars of the kingdom when men like Larmond roved the land burning villages and taking hostages. She'd often played the role of the princess captured in the castle during their childhood games. Unlike her brothers, she had little interest in military history, preferring religion, science, and tales of far-off countries. The only applicable fact she remembered from her schooling was that captured nobles were often ransomed for hefty amounts of gold and silver. If Larmond was preparing for a rebellion, he would need money. Isaac would be valuable to him as a hostage, but she would not, for her noble house was dead and gone.

Afret with uncertainty, she fell asleep that night with the banter of Larmond's men and the howling wind in her ears. When she awoke the next morning, Elizabeth was fast asleep beside her. Kaylein touched her brow and found she had a fever. The exertion of travel and the cold rain must have taken their toll, to say nothing of her grief. They said grief could kill a person if it was strong enough, but if that were true Kaylein felt sure she would have died after losing her family. Elizabeth was hardier than her, so it was probably just a touch of sickness.

She got up and negotiated her way between the smoky campfires. The women who hadn't gone to the men's beds the night before were already preparing the morning food while the soldiers took down their shelters. Larmond himself had a small tent set up in the centre of the camp. One of his men rose to stop Kaylein when she approached. She swallowed the nervous lump in her throat. She'd never been in a military camp before, and the gazes some of the men gave her were unnerving.

"I would like to see your physician," she said. "My friend is ill."

The man pointed her toward a blanket shelter guarded by three of his companions. Walking around to the front, she found a short man wearing a faded priest's robe sitting with Isaac. She explained Elizabeth's fever to the man. He expressed his sympathies and went over to examine her, leaving Kaylein and Isaac under the eyes of the guardsmen.

Isaac was hesitant to meet her gaze. His hand and knee had been bound up in strips of cloth, and three of his fingers were supported with splints.

Unsure of what to say, Kaylein asked: "How is your hand?"

"Apparently two of my fingers are broken and one is badly sprained, but I should live." He grimaced as he stood up, struggling to put weight on his injured leg. Running on it yesterday must have made the gash worse. "You know who I am now."

"I do, yes."

"Do you despise me?"

Kaylein shook her head. "I've tried my best not to think about your father these past two years."

"You and me both. I would've been happy carrying on as Isaac of Nowhere forever."

"Then I suppose we both know what it is like to give up our noble names."

Isaac forced a grim smile. "Not that it's done us much good."

Kaylein glanced toward Larmond's tent and said under her breath: "What do you suppose he wants with us?"

"I don't know. Nobody's told me anything."

"Perhaps we can strike a bargain? He might let Liz go if she isn't of any use to him."

"What would we bargain with?"

Kaylein tried to think and came up wanting. "Ourselves?" she said dejectedly. "What more do we have?"

"Larmond might give me to his ally, Marquess Alistair. I was supposed to marry his daughter before I left Rosepath."

"Why didn't you?"

Isaac shrugged. It was a response he seemed to have inherited from Sam, but while Sam used it to shed worries like water from a duck's back, Isaac's shrug was that of a man taking pause to think.

"I was afraid of being bound to a woman I didn't love in a life that would've made me miserable. I know it sounds foolish. It probably was."

Kaylein didn't think so. People found joy and despair in a great diversity of things. That was another realisation she'd come to during her time as a nun. Once upon a time, the studious solitude of the convent would've seemed drab and depressing to her. Now, she missed it with all her heart. She thought about Isaac's engagement to Emilia and wondered what her life might have been like if her father forced her to marry someone like Sir Edward. The idea made her shudder.

"God says we should not regret the past if we believe we can atone for it."

"What does that mean?"

It disappointed Kaylein to hear the derision in Isaac's voice. He was the only educated man she'd met who seemed sceptical of God's word.

"It means you must do your duty to ensure no harm comes to Elizabeth because of us."

That, at least, seemed to resonate with him.

"Alright," he said, touching his bound fingers gingerly.

They were allowed to walk around the camp, but the watchful eyes of Larmond's men followed them everywhere. They couldn't have run far even if they tried. The moors were so open they would be seen long before they got out of the valley, and if by some miracle they did slip away, Larmond's horsemen would catch them before they got half a mile.

The older woman who'd shared their fire the night before brought them bowls of thick but tasteless stew. They ate while the priest mixed a concoction of herbs and seeds to help bring down Elizabeth's fever. It smelled vile. The mixture didn't remind Kaylein of any remedy she'd read about, but the priest had done a good job setting Isaac's hand, so she didn't question it.

Larmond came to find them when his men finished striking camp. "You'll both walk close to me today. As I said before, you'll only be treated as prisoners if you try to run. Tonight we'll rejoin the rest of my men, then we'll talk."

"Can we not talk now?" Kaylein asked. She hated the cloud of uncertainty hanging over them. The incessant fear in the back of her mind had become numbing. The sooner they knew what Larmond wanted, the sooner they could confront it.

"No," the marquess answered simply. He reminded Kaylein more of a woodsman than a high-ranking noble. His braided hair and beard echoed the wild druidic traditions of the mountain men whose ancestral home he hailed from. The heart of those traditions had long since been burned out of civilised society, but a few of their savage affectations still remained. Larmond had the look of a warrior about him, one who traded mirth with barbarism night by night. He was one of the most intimidating men Kaylein had ever met.

"Why not?" Isaac asked with more courage than Kaylein could muster.

"We must leave swiftly," Larmond replied. "We are very close to the villages of Tannersfield here, and the knight who pursued you may whisper his lord a tale of what happened yesterday." A smirk touched the marquess's lips. "Assuming he can stomach the shame of it. Besides, I have yet to decide what to do with you. The day's journey will give me time to think."

"My lord!" Kaylein called after him when he turned away. "Our friend is ill. Might she have a horse for the journey?"

Larmond looked back at them distractedly. "So that she can ride away? I think not. If she cannot walk, we will leave her here." He raised his eyebrows. "Unless she has some value?"

"She has value to us," Isaac said.

"You can't leave her alone on the moors with a fever," Kaylein pleaded.

Larmond thought it over, then nodded. "Very well. She can be carried. Remember this kindness." He gave them a pointed look. "Remember also that I am the man who saved your lives."

"For which we are grateful, my lord," Kaylein said. True though it was, gratitude to a man like Larmond seemed a heavy burden to bear. He didn't strike Kaylein as the sort who left his debts uncollected.

Elizabeth was wrapped in a large cloak that served as a carrying sling and lifted up between two burly men. Larmond's riders headed out to scout the surrounding area

574

while the rest of the group set off on foot. Horses with sleeping bundles, food, and cooking pots tied to their backs clattered along on Kaylein's left, while half a dozen archers marched on her right. Larmond strode a few paces ahead, as indistinct as the others beneath his hood. At the insistence of the priest, Isaac was eventually given a horse to spare his leg, though it was a small, feeble-looking beast, and its bridle was bound to a rope held by a man so tall he looked like he could've picked up the beast and carried it.

The bowmen were deadly shots, bringing down a handful of hares and small birds as they walked. They never broke their stride, leaving the women to collect the game behind them while they scanned the moors for new prey. Everything about the marquess's band seemed lean and efficient. At first Kaylein had assumed the women travelling with them were either wives or whores, but they seemed just as used to living wild as the men. She watched with fascination as the woman who'd shared their fire skinned and gutted a hare on the march, tossing its entrails over her shoulder before trussing the carcass to the end of a stick. Others wove bowstrings or repaired clothes as they walked, never wasting a moment. The atmosphere was one of subdued purpose. Every person in Larmond's entourage seemed to understand and accept their place with him. These were not sellswords marching for a day's wage, but loyal followers who would ride and die with their master.

Kaylein was weary from two restless nights in a row, but she kept pace with the march as they traversed slope after slope of the rolling moors. Larmond's people knew the land well. They took unexpected routes to circumvent difficult terrain, taking advantage of every bit of sparse foliage to conceal their movements as they foraged for wood and berries.

Midday came and went with only a brief rest, then the band pressed on south. By the time they joined up with the rest of Larmond's force late that evening, Kaylein was

575

exhausted. Their fires spread out around the base of a hill scarred with sheer protrusions of white rock, no doubt a good vantage point to keep watch over the surrounding heathland. It looked like the number of soldiers and followers totalled about two hundred in all. Kaylein stayed close to Elizabeth and the priest as they approached, intimidated by the raucous noise coming from the camp. The soldiers seemed like they'd been waiting for a while, and they were exuberant at their lord's return. As they walked to a large tent near one of the biggest outcroppings, Kaylein saw a pair of shirtless men wrestling in a square while others placed wagers on the victor. A few paces on, she almost tripped over a couple fornicating beneath a cloak. She looked away in embarrassment, her cheeks warming. Loyal or not, the marquess's band were truly a savage brood. She hadn't felt so out of her element since she lived in the slum on the north side of Tannersfield.

Larmond left them outside his tent with the priest, who seemed a congenial fellow despite bearing scars that suggested he'd once been a fighter. Kaylein began to fret over Elizabeth while they waited. She was awake and lucid, but very quiet. She ate slowly and answered questions in as few words as possible.

"What do you suppose is wrong with her?" Isaac whispered when his conversation with the priest dried up.

"It isn't the fever, it's grief," Kaylein explained, recalling the heavy memory of her own depression. It was a weight that never truly went away, though it did become easier to bear with time. It was like a phantom lurking in the corner of your eye, one that gradually lost its horror until it was just an uneasy part of the scenery. A casual glance often overlooked it, but every now and again it would catch you unawares, and the grief would return. "We must be patient with her. If you pray tonight, spare a few words for Elizabeth. God will bring her back to us eventually. He was able to do so for me."

Larmond came out of his tent and beckoned them over.

576

"It's time to talk. My tent is large and my men know how to close their ears. We'll be able to speak freely."

Kaylein helped Isaac up and held his arm as they went inside. She wondered why Larmond was so keen on secrecy. It seemed like no one besides the men who'd found them had any idea who they were.

The marquess hadn't burdened his followers by making them carry any furnishings for his tent, but he did have a fire pit and several furs heaped in piles for people to sit on. He sat down on the far side of the fire and bade Isaac and Kaylein sit opposite. He stared at each of them in turn, hands clasped beneath his chin, appraising them like a fisherman looking over his catch.

Kaylein broke the silence when the weight of his gaze became too uncomfortable. "What do you mean to do with us, my lord?"

"Isaac is the son of a man who stands to become one of my greatest enemies in the near future." Larmond paused for effect. "And you are the daughter of one of the few counts who might have taken my side against him."

"My father is long since dead," Kaylein said stiffly.

"Sadly so, but you could still make a claim to your birthright. Your voice in the king's court, weak though it might be, would help tip his sympathies in my favour."

"What is it you plan to do?" Isaac asked. "Kill my father and take his lands?"

Larmond gave a snort of amusement. "Even I would not relish another war. They sound like grand things until you fight in the front line against a hundred enemy spears." His expression darkened. "But I have been making myself ready for war all the same. Believe me when I say that I have not sat idle these past two years. I wish for the rightful steward to be returned to the throne and young King Fendrel extricated from the church's grip until he is old enough to see through their manipulations. Already many lords buckle under the weight of new taxes that feed the cardinals' coffers."

"The church uses those taxes for good and the glory of God," Kaylein said.

Larmond glared at her. "A man's wealth should be his own to do with as he pleases. God does not need gilded statues and palaces for his priests."

The passion in the marquess's voice told Kaylein that it would be unwise to continue this line of argument with him. She recalled that her father and many of his noble allies had been opposed to the church's influence over taxes. Her personal belief was that more good came of that money going to the church than it did from making men like Larmond and Francis richer. Lords built palaces and gilded statues too, often with far less concern for their immortal souls.

"So, you mean to threaten the king and church?" Isaac asked.

"I mean to make it clear that they should listen to my voice, and if they send an army to silence me, they will pay dearly for it."

Kaylein thought about the ease with which Larmond's men had crossed the moors. She'd listened fearfully to her servants telling stories about ghosts roaming these lands when she was little. This was an untamed and unfamiliar part of the kingdom. Despite not knowing much of war, even she could surmise that a rival army would struggle to meet Larmond on favourable terms here, especially if he'd been preparing. Perhaps he really could drag the kingdom into civil war. If that were true, it was her duty both as a nun and a noble to try and prevent it.

"Lady Kaylein," Larmond said, eyeing her filthy robe deliberately. "You would be a welcome ally to my cause. Accept my offer, and I will restore you to a life of comfort. One day you may even sit as lady of Rosepath Castle again."

Kaylein's heart skipped a beat. She'd never imagined returning to her old life. As strong as the temptation was, her excitement turned to gloom when she realised what the marquess would ask of her in return. It was the reason

Francis had wanted her dead in the first place.

"You would have me marry into your family," she said.

"I would. My son Peter is without a wife. He is strong and level-headed, and he will make a fine husband for you."

Kaylein shook her head. "But I am sworn to God."

"Have you taken your final vows?"

"No–"

"Then you can still marry."

Kaylein felt like she would choke if she tried to say anything else. She didn't want a husband. She wanted to be a nun. It had brought her peace and freedom from the terrible rivalries of the nobility. If she married Larmond's son, she would be able to live in comfort again, but she would brand herself an enemy of Duke Francis for life.

Noticing her reluctance, Larmond said: "I would settle for your betrothal for now. I need my son at my side for the time being anyway. He will have little time for a wife if war breaks out. But once the nobles agree to listen to me–once the kingdom is in a shape that is malleable for reformation–then I would welcome your bloodline to strengthen my own."

"He means that if he ends up killing my father, he'll use you to stake a claim to Tannersfield," Isaac said.

Larmond smiled. "The boy is blunt, but he is right. Offer my son your hand in marriage now, and he will accept it later, when the kingdom is at peace. You will be recognised as the legitimate heir to Tannersfield, and the county will be mine."

"And if I refuse?" Kaylein said in a thin voice.

Larmond's expression was impassive. "I am no savage. I will not force you." *Nor will I be kind to you,* his tone implied. "Think on it if you must. Speak with my son tomorrow. You will see that he is a worthy man."

To Kaylein's relief, Larmond spoke no further of the proposed marriage. She had a lot to think about, and it was difficult to speak confidently with so much weighing on her mind. What would the marquess do with her if she refused? Send her back to the church? He seemed to have a sense of

579

honour in his own wild way, so she doubted he would throw her to his men, but how could she be sure? If she said no, she would have to do so carefully. She couldn't afford to invoke Larmond's ire.

As they sat there talking, the realisation stole up on Kaylein that she was back in a nobleman's court. She might be sitting in a tent on a pile of furs, but this was still a negotiation between two lords and a lady. The thought strengthened her resolve. She knew how to conduct herself at court. Her mother had spent years preparing her for this. She tried to imagine she was sitting in a great hall as Larmond turned his attention to Isaac.

"You I am still not sure what to do with. You could be a thorn in my heel."

"I don't wish to be," Isaac said. He also seemed to be shifting back into the manner of a noble conducting himself at court. His curt way of speaking and guarded demeanour was that of a man who'd been schooled in the same lessons of etiquette as Kaylein. She felt foolish for not having realised the truth about him sooner. It was no wonder they'd become friends so quickly. He was the only person she knew who understood what it was like growing up in a count's household.

Larmond steepled his fingers beneath his chin. "Before I say anything more, tell me why you were a stranger to your own wedding last year."

Isaac sounded uncomfortable as he told Larmond the same thing he'd told Kaylein: that he was simply afraid of being bound to a fate that would make him miserable. Kaylein felt sorry for him. She'd faced her own shame when she struggled with giving up her family's honour to become a nun. It must be even more difficult for boys, who lived all their lives with the burden of their fathers' legacies on their shoulders. Isaac had never struck her as a man who believed in nepotistic interpretations of honour and duty.

Larmond's expression betrayed no scorn as he listened.

He remained in thought for a long time after Isaac finished speaking. Eventually, his chin dipped in a slow nod. "Yes, I think I believe it. There is something of the wandering minstrel about you. You'd be happier in an alehouse than at a lord's table."

"I'd be happier on the road with my horse," Isaac said with a hint of longing. While Kaylein had been fretting over Elizabeth, he'd probably spent his day worrying about Blackberry.

"So you have no desire to marry Marquess Alistair's daughter, nor to return to your father's side?" Larmond asked.

"No, my lord."

Larmond looked bemused, but pleased. "Then help me solve my problem. What am I to do with you? Marquess Alistair is a valuable ally to me, but he is a fickle man. If he learned that you had been found, I think he would insist you fulfil your promise to marry his daughter."

"That was my father's promise, not mine."

"Indeed it was. And it would bind Alistair to your father instead of me. If you married Lady Emilia, I doubt it would be long before Duke Francis coaxed Alistair into switching sides again. I cannot have that. Whatever else happens, you must remain a secret for now."

"If you let me go, I would happily disappear."

"I believe you might, but I would be a fool to toss a gold coin into the river for fear of my friend stealing it. If it comes to war, you will be a precious hostage."

"A hostage you can do nothing with," Kaylein said. She'd been paying careful attention to the marquess's words. He'd revealed a great weakness in his bargaining position by telling them about Alistair's tenuous loyalties. "If you try to ransom Isaac to his father then everyone in the kingdom will hear of it, Alistair included. He'll know you went behind his back. However much Duke Francis pays you will not be enough to make up for losing Alistair's support."

Larmond shot her an annoyed look. His smooth tongue and clever way of speaking were those of a man who assumed he was always one step ahead of everyone else, and Kaylein's ability to keep up had caught him off guard.

"Lady Kaylein is correct," he conceded tersely. "You are a gold coin I cannot spend."

"Then if I'm of no use to you, why not let me go?" Isaac said. "The longer I stay here, the more likely it is your men will start gossiping. The rumours will reach Alistair eventually."

"You need to be put away for safekeeping. You're of no use to me now, but you could be in the future. Neither you nor Lady Kaylein will be mistreated. Perhaps we can keep the pair of you together."

Kaylein's hopes dimmed again. They would not be mistreated, but they would be kept in an isolated location where no one could find them, prisoners in everything but name. They owed Larmond a debt for saving their lives, but he was asking for their freedom in return. It was a bleak prospect, especially if it ended in forced marriage for one or both of them. She could tell Isaac was as uncomfortable with the idea as she was. They needed time to think. Larmond wanted them to be compliant, and that was something they could use to bargain with.

"Will you give us time to consider your proposal?" Kaylein asked.

Larmond nodded. "Tomorrow I will leave again for three days. As Master Isaac says, rumours will spread if he remains here too long, so I expect an answer as soon as I return."

"Thank you, my lord." Kaylein breathed a sigh of relief. They had bought themselves a little time. Poor Isaac stood little chance of negotiating anything more than the comfort of his captivity, but she still had a choice before her. The prospect of choosing between marriage to a man she didn't know and the uncertainty of Larmond's wrath made her stomach squirm. She tried to think about what God would want of her. She'd believed that her purpose was to write for Him; to use her experiences to warn others of dangerous men who perpetrated evil under the protection of the church. If she remained a nun, she would be able to return to that path. It would take many years, but God would guide her there if that was her destiny.

Another conflicting thought occurred to her as she left Larmond's tent. If she became a noblewoman again, she wouldn't have to wait years before returning to her writing. She would have money to buy ink and parchment. She could hire scribes to copy her work and bind it into books, and illuminators to make the pages glow with colour. With a noblewoman's influence, she could even see to it that her writing was distributed to convents all over the kingdom.

The true magnitude of the choice Larmond had set before her finally struck Kaylein. Was this a chance to uphold the honour of her father's name while still remaining true to her commitment to God? Not as a nun, perhaps, but as a pious noble like her mother. If Larmond's attempt to defy the king succeeded, she could become the new countess of Tannersfield. If he failed, she might never have to marry his son at all. When she thought about it logically, the choice seemed obvious. She would be a fool to say no.

She wished her heart could be as logical as the stern voice inside her head, for no matter how sensible it seemed, the prospect of marriage dismayed her. She didn't want to break her vows of chastity. She didn't want to give up the peace and safety of a convent for the politics of court. That life was behind her, and it had taken all the willpower she had to move beyond it. She'd become a stronger person as a nun—a better person—and she wanted to carry on that way.

Too tired from the day's march to worry over it any further, she lay down next to Elizabeth and prayed for guidance. She would have three days to decide.

Perhaps when she met Larmond's son, her path would become clearer.

Printed in Dunstable, United Kingdom